I0613549

God's Warriors

Book One
The Eden Conflict

By Peter Way

The Eden Conflict: God's Warriors – Book 1

Published by Lulu 2009
ID: 5505687

In this work of fiction, names, characters, places and incidents are the product of the author's imagination or they are used fictitiously. Any resemblance to actual events, locales or persons, living or dead, is entirely coincidental.

Cover design by Expanded Graphics
www.expandedgraphics.com.au

Paperback Edition:
Edited by Ruth Kennedy
Published by Lulu 2009 - ID: 5505687
ISBN: 978-0-646-58258-0

Visit God's Warriors on Facebook and let me know what you think.
http://www.facebook.com/pages/Gods-Warriors/363572710343158

Follow the Author on Twitter @PeterWay5

Dedication & Thanks

I dedicate this book to God, who has used me as an instrument to tell this tale. To my wife, Trish, and my two daughters, thank you for your understanding and sacrifices, during the creation of this book. Finally, to those that have helped me with the proof reading, editing, theology, science and general feedback, thank you, your input has been invaluable.

Praise the lord, all his angels,
You mighty beings who carry out his orders
And are ready to obey his spoken orders.
Psalm 103:20

Put on all the armor that god supplies. In this way you can take a stand against the devil's strategies.
Ephes. 6:11

Then Elisha prayed, "LORD, please open his eyes so that he may see." The LORD opened the servant's eyes and let him see. The mountain around Elisha was full of fiery horses and chariots.
2 Kings 6:17

PROLOGUE ONE

Then there was war in Heaven. Michael and the Angels under his command fought the dragon and his Angels. And the dragon lost the battle and was forced out of Heaven.
Revelations 12:7-8

The tension was palpable. The traitor had been caught and all of his followers with him. Michael had his captain, Lucifer, in a tight grip with his sword held ready.

The Lamb stepped forward to stand beside the Lord and spoke to Him: "Lord, the Spirit is causing a change in the appearance of all the angels who have rebelled. They will be easily identifiable as demons within minutes."

"You will never stop me this way, only delay me," Lucifer hissed, as a shadow appeared to pass over him. It had, however, settled on him, making him appear to be the shadow itself. His light, the "glory" of God, no longer shone through. In every other aspect, he still looked the same. All, that is, except his weapon. That too had lost its glow, its inner light.

"SILENCE!" spoke the Lord. "Your treachery is unprecedented and deserves a punishment of the highest order. You deserve finality for your mutinous ways. But... for the greatness of your past deeds, I will allow some leniency. You are to be thrown down from on high, to the darkest depths of Sheol, where you will be with your own kind: the traitors, the defilers, the false gods, the blasphemers, the liars, the murderers, the adulterers and lustful, the greedy and hateful, and the thieves. You are no longer recognised as a friend of Heaven. You are allowed to enter the Earth. You may petition me from time to time, but you, and your servants, will not be welcome here. You will be known forever after as "the evil one" or Satan, the accuser. Those of your followers that have only been deceitful will have a chance for redemption if they request forgiveness now. If not, they too will be cast out and counted as the fallen ones, along with those who have been marked." The Lord turned to the deceitful ones and asked, "Do any of you seek forgiveness?"

Lucifer, the evil one, glared at his followers as if to dare any of them to turn traitor on him now. "Be warned," he said, "I am watching. Betray me and you will be first to feel my revenge."

Maybe it was the threat and maybe it wasn't; either way, no one sought forgiveness from the Lord.

Michael sadly looked at Lucifer's followers and then the angels, who held them in check. Nearly one-third of the Host of Heaven had turned. They were now in the custody of the Lord and the angels who had remained faithful. Many of his friends had been injured during the battle, while trying to subdue the deceivers. How had his captain come to believe that he could lead a rebellion against the Lord of all?

None of the followers had sought forgiveness, as deceit was in their hearts. None felt that they could trust the Lord to forgive, as they wouldn't have if they were He.

"So be it", the Lord said. "You will all share the fate of the evil one."

"We will fight you and turn your deeds against you, *Lord,*" Lucifer, now known as Satan, sneered as he said the last word, "wherever, and whenever, we can. You have started this war between us. One day, I will defeat you and sit on the throne and rule all. This is not over!"

"No," replied the Lord calmly, "you are wrong. It was *you* who started this war, Satan, with your lies and deceit. You will never win. You will never sit on the throne. However, you are right about one thing, we will be enemies until the final day is upon us. Now it is time that you left." He turned to Michael: "Cast them out, all of them."

This great dragon — the ancient serpent called the Devil, or Satan, the one deceiving the whole world — was thrown down to the Earth with all his Angels.

Revelations 12:9

Michael pushed Lucifer, the evil one, off the edge of Heaven at the Lord's command. The Host of Heaven then proceeded to thrust Lucifer's followers out of Heaven also. Once they were all cast out, the Host of Heaven was diminished by one-third of all the angels it had once held.

Michael looked first at Jesus, the Lamb of God, and then at the Lord of Lords, God Almighty. He could feel the Spirit moving freely through the throng of angels once more. "Lord?" he asked.

"Yes Michael? What troubles you?" the Lord replied.

"Who will lead the Heavenly Host? Do we dare appoint another leader? What if we make the wrong choice?" He paused for a moment. Then, very quietly he continued, "Who will be my captain now?"

The Lord looked out over the entire Host of Heaven, catching the eyes of several of the warriors, the guardians and the messengers. Then He looked back to Michael.

"You led the war against the evil one and your fellow angels followed without question. You shall lead the Host of Heaven now, Michael. You will be captain and I shall be your commander."

Michael's jaw dropped, "But Lord, I am not worthy of such a role and I do not seek it for myself."

"I know. That is why you are the best candidate. Your reluctance and humbleness shows you are the right choice. Your concern for another usurper taking the role shows that you are well suited. You will be a great captain!"

The angels cheered for their new captain and praised the Lord, for they knew that the Lord's judgement of Michael was just and that there was no better choice among them.

The Lord continued: "Your first task will always be to guard against the evil one for he will keep his promise to upset my plans, whenever he can. In this task you will require help. David, step forward please."

An angel stepped out of the multitude and moved to stand alongside Michael.

"David, your assistance to Michael during the recent troubles has not gone unnoticed. The two of you worked very well together," the Lord paused as He looked from David to Michael. "I appoint David as your second in command, your Watchtower. The two of you will pick twelve angels as Pillars, to watch over certain sections of the Earth. They are to report back any sightings or activity of the evil one and his servants," said the Lord to Michael.

"Yes Lord, let Your will be done," Michael and David replied.

They then bowed, first to the Lamb and then to the Lord of Lords.

The Lord noticed a puzzled expression on David's face and asked him about it: "Does something trouble you about this David?"

David looked up to the Lord and said, "Yes Lord. Why the Earth? It is desolate and flat, dark..." he paused for a moment, "and only water."

The Lord looked at the Lamb knowingly. He turned back to David and replied so all could hear, "Very soon you will all help me to mould the Earth, shape it and make something more of it. It will be a place of wonder and sorrow, beauty and ugliness. It will contain our greatest achievements and biggest disappointments. That is all that shall be said, for now."

The Lamb turned to the Lord and spoke loudly enough for all the angels to hear. He asked the Lord, "Was banishment to Earth enough for the evil one, my Lord?"

"Yes," replied the Lord, "for he still has his part to play in the world to come. He will be back and he will try to upset my plans," the Lord paused for a moment, "but only I know what they really are."

Prologue Two

"Are you sure he is the one?" the angel named Itzal asked.

Michael, the Captain of Heaven's armies, nodded his head. "Yes, the Lord told me Himself."

Itzal looked back towards the man. He was standing at the floor-to-ceiling windows in the building before them. They were hiding in the bushes, out of sight of any prying eyes.

"When will it happen?" Itzal asked, turning to face Michael.

Michael smiled in a knowing way, "You should know better than that. The Lord never reveals his timetable to us. He tells us only what we need to know and only when we need to know it."

Itzal smiled too. "I know. His plans are His plans and only He knows what they truly are."

"That's right," replied Michael.

Itzal turned back to look at the man. "What about them?" he asked, indicating the two little demons hovering around the man's head.

"They must not suspect a thing," Michael replied.

"They are to be left alone?" Itzal asked with amazement.

Michael sighed. "That was what He said. They must survive to be able to report back what they have seen."

Itzal raised an eyebrow as an idea came to him. "Both of them?"

Michael smiled, "Well... at least one of them."

Itzal thought for a moment. "That *will* make it harder."

"I know, but if any angel is up to it, you are," Michael said, putting one hand on Itzal's shoulder.

Itzal looked at the hand and then at Michael. "So my *special* skills are required here then?"

Michael smiled and looked back at the man.

Itzal followed his gaze.

"Yes, *your* skills are just what he will need," Michael stated, "your *special* skills."

ONE

Tuesday, May 8, 2001
Eden, New South Wales, Australia

The wind roared outside the Sunny Days Bed and Breakfast. It was only four in the afternoon in the coastal town of Eden and it was almost dark. The storm was approaching fast. The rain-heavy clouds were moving in and starting to blot out the sun's rays.

"Perfect," the man said, as he looked out the floor-to-ceiling windows at Twofold Bay. "I'd better start getting ready," he said to himself with a look of grim determination in his eyes.

He turned away as the rain started to beat against the windows and headed to his room. He flicked on the light switch as he entered the room, picking up his trusty travel bag and placing it on the end of the bed. He proceeded to pack the half-empty travel bag, not wishing to leave behind a mess for someone else to clean up.

When the task was completed he looked around the room to make sure he hadn't forgotten anything. His hand was shaking as he reached into his jacket pocket and pulled out an envelope. He stared at it for the longest time.

Lightning flashed through the windows, breaking him out of the spell. He looked around once more and then placed the envelope on top of his bag. With a determined and even stride, he walked out of the room, turning the light off and closing the door behind him. The thunder crashed as the door closed; the man raised his eyebrows in response. He looked thoughtful for a moment and then he fixed his features with a look of grim resolution and headed for the front door. He didn't look back once.

He smiled as he passed the elderly couple from Melbourne in the hall. He even said hello to the young family returning from their day of sightseeing. He held the front door open for them as they rushed inside to get out of the rain. Then he pulled his jacket tight, put on his Akubra hat and walked out the door, into the storm.

Two black shadows followed him.
"Do you think he will?" asked one.
"Why else go out in this storm?" replied the other.

****

An hour later, the man was standing on the beginning of one of the wharfs, holding onto a light pole while watching the dark, angry waves wash over the other end and carry on until crashing on the shore. The other three wharfs were in a little cove which was protected by a large breakwater; but not this one, not tonight. This was what he wanted.

He could hear the waves crashing on the nearby beach too but could not see it in the dark.

He had been standing in this position now for almost half an hour. Not moving, just watching. As if he were waiting for something...

His demonic companions were standing on his shoulders and getting restless because of the delay.

"Come on, you can do it. Just run and jump," whispered one in his left ear.

"You won't feel a thing!" hissed the other in his right ear.

"What have you got left? Nothing!" said the first one again.

"Do it, do it, do it", they started to chant, one in each ear.

The man watched the waves, trying to decide if he should give in to his despair, and he wondered if death really was the only option.

"Come on, you can do it," he repeated to himself, "just run and jump. You probably won't feel it. There's nothing left for you anyway... you already wrote the note. There is nothing else but to end it!"

He steadied himself against the wind and started to jog, gradually picking up speed until he was almost running. This wasn't easy with the wind blasting him in the side one moment and the face the next.

Then the wind lulled. The waves stopped crashing over the wharf for a moment and he hit full pace without the wind holding him back. And then he was there, at the end, with nowhere else to go and still running full steam. As he leapt off the wharf, there was a blinding flash of light.

Despair and Death kept up with the human easily. The wind and rain did not affect them in the same way that it did the man. But when the wind lulled and he took off suddenly, they looked first at each other and then back at the man.

"What is happening?" Despair asked, slowing down a bit.

"I... I'm not sure," Death replied, trying to catch up with the man. "We better keep up with him or he might change his mind."

Despair flapped his wings faster so he could get back alongside the man again.

Then the man jumped.

"Oh no," they both thought as the light flared and blinded them.

And then, with a small pop, like a balloon bursting, the light disappeared and it was dark and stormy once more.

Despair drew his sword as he stopped and looked around and listened. But there was nothing there, nothing to see or hear. All he could hear was the sound of the waves crashing on the nearby beach, the wind in his ears and the rain hitting the water all around him. A wave washed through him and kept going.

"Was that lightning? Please tell me that was lightning. Because if that wasn't and it was... what I think it was... then where are they?" Despair asked Death.

But there was no reply.

Despair looked all around but did not see Death or the man anywhere. He put his sword away as he didn't appear to need it and landed on the wharf. The waves were still washing over the wharf, causing Despair to vanish from sight whenever they did. He walked to the edge and leaned over. With his head under the water, Despair looked around.

Seeing nothing he stood back up, scratching his head.

Despair was confused. He didn't know what had happened or where they had gone. He stood there thinking for a moment and then had an idea. He flew to the beginning of the wharf, turned around and flew back as fast as he could to see if it might happen again.

But nothing happened.

He hovered there for a moment, undecided on what to do next. Wait or go back? Normally he would go back but this wasn't normal.

Despair shrugged his shoulders, deciding he'd better return to the room. Maybe Death would be there already.

****

Death was wishing he was anywhere but where he was. He looked at the sword pointing at his nose and then up at the hulking form in front of him.

"Where did you two come from?" the angelic being, a cherubim named Starr, asked.

"Does it matter?" Shamira, another cherubim, replied. She looked down at the human who was peering back at her with a look of disbelief on his face. "The demon is not allowed here and has breached the protocols. Send it into the Abyss."

"Goodbye little trouble maker," Starr said to the demon.

The man turned just in time to see Starr cut a hole in the air with his sword. Then there was a sound of rushing air, as if the wind was rushing to balance itself between the two locations. It reminded the man of a sound from his childhood. It was the sound the wind made when blowing through the pine trees on his sister's farm.

Then the cherubim hurled the demon into it.

"NOOOOOOOOoooooo," they heard the demon cry as it tumbled into the Abyss. Then Starr swiped his sword over the hole. It closed, cutting off all sight and sound. There was a slight pop as the air settled back down again.

"What was that thing?" the man asked timidly. "Better yet, who are you and where am I?" He looked around at his surroundings for the first time. "Am I dead? I thought drowning would be a little... wetter. Why am I in a forest when I jumped off a wharf into the sea? There was a flash of light... did I get hit by lightning?"

"You are full of questions young one," Shamira said.

"I must have been hit by lightning and this... this is all an hallucination brought on by it," the man said to himself.

"None of which I am going to answer," Shamira continued as if the man had not spoken. "Stand still please," she said, as she placed a hand on the man's head and closed her eyes.

"What are you doing?" he asked, looking up at the cherubim, who had to be at least eight feet tall.

Shamira stepped back from him and stooped down so she was at eye level with him. "You are free of your tormentor now. I believe he was a Death or Despair demon. Do not worry, he will not return to bother you. But there are others like him so do not return to the places you have visited. That is where they find you and latch on. I shall return you now."

"Wait, what places? Return me where?" he asked the cherubim anxiously. He stopped suddenly and just stared at the two Heavenly beings, "Did you say demon? That thing, that black... shadowy thing with the orange eyes and smelly yellow breath... was a demon?"

The two cherubim looked at each other.

"I don't think he believes you," Starr said to Shamira with a smirk on his face.

"If that was a demon, what does that make you?" the man thought out loud.

"I wouldn't either if I was he," Shamira replied to Starr. "I don't think you should return to Eden or anywhere else close to the water. I am sending you back to a place called Broken Hill," Shamira placed a hand on his head again. "May God bless you and keep you from harm."

"Angels?" the man asked and then looked up at Shamira as she drew her sword and held it high above her head.

Shamira said a quick prayer in a language the man did not understand. This didn't bother the man; in fact, he didn't even hear her. He was too busy watching the sword.

"What are you going to do with that?" he asked very quietly, pointing at the sword.

Shamira smiled and swung the blade, going from above her head down to her feet. A rift in time and space appeared where the blade had travelled and the noise of the wind started again.

The man was still watching the blade and didn't see Starr move behind him. Starr lifted him up and passed him gently through the rift, pushing him on his feet. Starr saw that another man was nearby, with an angel. He pinched a nerve in the first man's neck and then leaned back from the rift.

The last thing the man remembered was the blinding light again and then he was standing again. He looked around and then darkness surrounded him as he passed out.

****

Despair was just arriving back at the bed and breakfast. He entered the room and sat on the bed, trying to work out what had happened and waiting to see if Death would return. He was supposed to be there anyway – he had to make sure the letter was found. He stood up and flew over to the writing desk next to the window. Despair stood there, so he could watch the storm and try to catch a glimpse of Death.

Suddenly, light flared in the room behind him. Despair reached for his sword as he turned to face the portal.

Shamira quickly opened another rift after closing the last one. Reaching through the rift, she quickly retrieved the envelope from on top of the bag left in The Dawn Room of the Sunny Days Bed and Breakfast. She retreated and closed the rift behind her. She had not seen Despair watching from the writing desk.

Despair watched as an arm came through the rift, took something from the top of the bag, then disappeared back into the rift. The rift shimmered for a moment and then disappeared. There was no mistaking it. The arm had belonged to the enemy!

Despair stood there, rooted to the spot with his sword drawn, waiting to see what was going to happen next. The vapour seeping from his mouth was slowly creating a cloud around his head.

Then something clicked in his little brain and his orange eyes glowed brighter with disbelief, before narrowing, once again, into slits of orange light. He exclaimed loudly with anger, "They took *my* envelope!"

As the impact of that action sunk in, Despair started to feel like his chosen targets. His shoulders began to sag. He almost dropped his sword.

"I have failed," Despair said to the empty room.

Knowing that there was no point waiting there anymore, Despair sheathed his sword and took off through the window. He was headed for his Den in Sydney to report what he had seen. Even though it may be the last thing he ever did.

Two

Later that same night, Despair reached the Den, located in the heart of Sydney. It was in one of the tallest buildings to grace the skyline.

He was stopped at the entrance on the top floor by two sentry demons, one named Guard, the other Sentry.

"Why are you here?" asked Guard.

"What is your business?" Sentry asked at the same time.

"I am here because this is where my master is. I need to report to him about the interference of the enemy in my mission," Despair said. Then he asked quietly, "Is lord Avarice in a good mood?"

"Are you afraid of losing your head?" Sentry asked, and chuckled. Guard joined in laughing at Despair.

"Wait! That's horrible," Guard said, not laughing anymore.

"Why?" Sentry asked him, still chuckling.

"Because we will not see it!" said Guard, and he started to laugh even harder.

Despair stood there, trying to ignore their taunts while waiting for them to give him the all clear.

Eventually Sentry said, "You may pass little one."

Despair hurried on but as he neared the end of the corridor he could still hear their laughter.

On reaching the inner sanctum, he stopped and looked around at all the lieutenants, advisors and other self-important demons lining the path through to lord Avarice. There were at least a hundred in this room, each at least four times his size. Their number and size made the room appear a lot smaller than it was.

Despair gulped and tried to hold his head up as he walked amid the leaders and decision makers for the demon's empire in this part of the world. As he walked passed them, he noticed they would stop talking to look down on him. Some, he saw from the corner of his eye, elbowed one another, others sniggered. He tried to pay them no heed as he stumbled on, focusing his full attention on lord Avarice and those surrounding him at the far end of the room.

He was only ten feet from his lord when he was stopped by one of the surrounding advisors. "What do you want little one?" he was asked gruffly.

"Step aside, I have a message for lord Avarice concerning my mission," Despair said to the advisor boldly, hoping his fear was not showing through his bravado.

Lord Avarice chuckled as he waived the advisor aside. "You are lucky he did not remove your head for your insolence, little one. Who are you and what do you need to tell me so urgently that it could not go through the normal channels?"

"Forgive me, my lord, I am Despair. I thought that you should know of what happened to me today to cause the failure of my mission."

Lord Avarice's mood changed almost immediately. "What was your mission?" he asked in a low voice that made Despair tremble.

"Death and I were assigned to drive a human to take his own life. Another soul to add to our Master's service," Despair explained.

"And?" lord Avarice asked.

"I am not totally sure, my lord." Despair responded and then continued as quickly as he could. "It was going according to plan. He was all set to go through with it. Death had him. I mean he *really* had him. He took off running... Death followed... he jumped... and they both disappeared in a flash of...", he paused and looked up at lord Avarice trying to see what his reaction was so far.

Lord Avarice was leaning forward, waiting for the little demon to continue. "What? What happened? Was it the enemy? How did *you* get away?" lord Avarice asked, his voice trembling with more and more anger with every new question he asked.

"It wasn't like that lord," Despair responded, almost pleading.

"Then how was it?" lord Avarice asked, as he placed one of his hands on his sword and glanced over at one of his advisors.

"I... I... that is... what happened is... there was a flash of light as if the enemy was there... but I did not see them, if they were, and the man and Death... were gone. Then the light went out."

This caught their attention.

"Do you mean to say that the human and your counterpart both disappeared in a flash of Heavenly light?" lord Avarice asked, frowning, seeking clarification. Most of the surrounding demons winced at the mention of Heaven.

Despair nodded his head furiously, "Yes, yes, that is exactly what happened. I even checked all around, trying to find the body. But there was nothing!"

There was a pause as everyone looked from Despair to lord Avarice, trying to judge what his reaction would be. Lord Avarice stroked his chin with his other hand.

"What did you do next?" lord Avarice asked.

"I went on with my mission. I returned to the room where he was staying and had left the usual note. I was to then follow the letter and spread my talent on to the next person," Despair explained. "But..."

Lord Avarice's eyes narrowed. "But?"

Despair tried to swallow but found it very difficult all of a sudden. "There... they... that is...", he stammered. Despair managed to swallow and continued, "I... waited in the room... looking out the window... to see if Death would return." Despair paused to swallow again. "Behind me... bright light... I turned and saw... an arm... reaching. The letter... gone. They took... the letter", Despair said haltingly, trying to explain. Then with more conviction and a little bit of anger, "They stole my letter!"

There was silence for a moment. Lord Avarice waited to see if Despair would continue and Despair waited to see if lord Avarice would draw his sword.

"I think it is safe to say that Death will not be rejoining you. But, again, why did *you* survive? Why did they let *you* go?" lord Avarice asked Despair again, as he sank back in his chair.

"They did not see me, lord. I only saw an arm but it was enough to know that it was the enemy," Despair explained quickly.

Lord Avarice nodded. He spoke again and as he did, the advisor he glanced at earlier silently drew his sword. "Tell me, where did all this take place? Where did this angel steal your letter?"

"The town's name had something", as Despair answered the advisor moved behind him, "to do with", the advisor drew his sword back, "Eden, but not... angel... cherubim."

Swish, the advisor swung the sword and removed Despair's head from his shoulders.

A cheer went up as both the head and the body of Despair started to dissolve and get sucked into the rift, linking them to the Abyss. The rift had appeared as the sword connected with Despair's neck. As it dissolved, what had once been Despair's body was being pulled into the rift, swirling around, just as if it was in a whirlpool. Even though he was one of their kind, the demons enjoyed the execution. The only time they didn't was when it was their own execution.

Two of the demons were not cheering. They were the advisor and lord Avarice. The advisor was revelling in the cheers, as if they were for him, while lord Avarice was sitting back and rubbing his chin, deep in thought.

"Eden. Flash of light but no Warriors of God. Only an arm. Eden. Cherubim? Could it be?" lord Avarice had a suspicion that he had just made a mistake in having Despair despatched.

Three

Sunday, May 13, 2001
Broken Hill, New South Wales, Australia

The minister had just arrived to start opening up the church. He had his key in the lock when he heard a noise behind him. Turning towards the noise, he saw a young man looking around as if he didn't know where he was. Then the man passed out and collapsed.

The minister quickly went to the young man and checked his pulse. He then went back, opened the door and went inside. He returned a short while later with a cup of cold water. He bent down alongside the man and tipped the cup to his lips.

The young man drank a little but most of it went down his chin and neck. The coldness of it was enough to bring him round.

The man blinked up at the minister. "Who are you?" he asked.

"My name is Tony. I am the minister of this church. This is my wife, Isabel," he replied, indicating a woman nearby. "How are you feeling?" the minister asked. Are you able to get up?"

"I think so. I..., he stopped as he sat up and tried to remember what had just happened to him. He remembered being in a storm and being wet. There was something else too. He couldn't quite remember it clearly. It was something about a forest? He looked around and then down at his jacket. He could see it was still wet. He saw his hat nearby and that looked damp too. He reached over and picked it up.

Tony watched his visitor, wondering what he was looking at. Then he noticed that he was wet as if he had been in the rain.

The man looked at Tony, then at the ground and then at the sky.

"Tell him to take his jacket off," Isabel said to Tony.

"I think you should take that jacket off and hang it out to dry" Tony suggested.

The man looked at Isabel and then Tony. "This may sound strange, but can you tell me where I am?"

Tony sat back, eyeing the stranger off again. His appearance did not match his surroundings at all. He was dressed for rain. He even looked as if he had been in the rain. But here he was, in an outback town very close to the desert. A town that, even when it was cold, didn't see much rain.

"You're in Broken Hill," Tony replied. "Do you know where that is?"

"Broken Hill," the man paused as he suddenly remembered everything that had happened. Then he continued as if nothing had happened, "but that's got to be over a thousand kilometres away from Eden!" he said, mostly to himself.

"Eden?" Isabel asked.

"Eden?" Tony asked. "Is that where you're from?"

"Oh. Uh. No. Not exactly," the man stammered, "I am sorry if I have upset you or wasted your time," he said, as he stood up and took off his jacket.

"Not at all," Tony replied as he stood too, "why don't you come in and rest a moment. The service doesn't start for another hour. I always get here early, to set up and make sure everything is in order. Even after all these years, I still get nervous before preaching."

"I'm sorry if I have bothered you. I shouldn't keep you from your preparations."

"He shouldn't be going anywhere, insist that he stays. Maybe he could help you?" Isabel suggested to Tony.

"Nonsense! Anyway, I insist. Besides, you could help me setup, if you don't mind. I'm not as young as I once was," Tony said with a wink. "While we are at it, maybe you'd like to tell me what happened to you?"

The man looked at Isabel and then Tony again. "I don't think you would want to hear it," the man said. He looked back at Isabel for her reaction.

"Don't take no for an answer. He came here for a reason and you need to find out what it is," Isabel said to Tony again, eyeing the man curiously.

"Forgive an old man's curiosity, but I am not going to take no for an answer. Besides, I think someone dropped you on my doorstep on purpose," Tony insisted. "Come on, we can hang your jacket and hat just in here, they'll be perfectly safe, and we can talk as we work."

"You're not going to take no for an answer, are you?" the man asked, more to Isabel than Tony.

"No, you're not," Isabel told Tony.

"No, I'm not," Tony replied. "Come on, there's a coat hook just in here, behind the door."

The man just watched Tony as he started to walk towards the door to the church. Isabel was still standing where she had been, she was watching him.

"Wait," Isabel called out to Tony.

Tony stopped walking and turned around to see him still standing there. "Come on," he said with a disarming smile. The man sighed and started to follow the minister towards the church. Isabel turned and walked alongside him.

Tony waited for him to catch up the few extra steps and then put a hand on the man's shoulder to help guide him towards the door and stop him from changing his mind. With Tony on one side and Isabel on the other, they walked towards the church.

As they entered through the door, Tony asked the man one question. "What's your name?"

The man looked at the elderly minister and thought that just maybe he would understand. He might even be able to help him make sense of what had just happened. "Call me Jack," there was short pause while he considered what to say next, "Jack Daniels."

Over the next half hour, Jack told all that he could remember to Tony and Isabel, including his suicide attempt.

His description of the demon, the angels and the jungle was of special interest to Tony and even more so was what they said.

"Let me think and pray about what you have told me. I should be able to give you some sort of explanation later on. However, I do not think that we should repeat what happened to too many people," Tony told Jack.

Tony promised to help Jack get his bag back, if possible, but only if Jack stayed with him until it arrived. Jack agreed and stayed for the service. Afterwards, Tony introduced him to a few of the locals.

It wasn't until later that afternoon, when they rang the Sunny Days Bed and Breakfast that they discovered it had been five days since Jack had disappeared from Eden.

FOUR

Friday, March 22, 2002
Daintree Rainforest, north of Port Douglas, along the coast of Northern Queensland

Glen Niman stopped the four-wheel drive that he had hired. He left the power running so that he could still have the air-conditioning and music on. He had brought his own CDs with him from Sydney and he was listening to one of his favourite Michael W. Smith songs. It was nearly over so he took the opportunity to look around while he listened. When the song finished, he turned the keys and removed them from the ignition. He stepped out of the air-conditioned four-wheel drive and into the tropical heat of the rainforest. Straight away he felt uneasy and unhappy. But it wasn't the heat that bothered Glen, not that he liked the closed-in, sticky feel to the air. It wasn't the sudden deluge of noises from the dripping of water, to the pounding of the waves in the distance; in fact that was kind of calming. Even though the lack of trees in certain spots and the darkness ahead concerned him, this wasn't what was really making him feel uneasy. It was the fence and the guard that blocked the road ahead of him that was making him feel this way.

"Dear God, what is this world coming too?" Glen prayed under his breath to himself, as he walked towards the guard.

What Glen couldn't see was that four big, ugly, warty, filthy demons and one little demon were perched on the fence next to the guard. But Glen's guardian angel, Kyle, could see them and they could see him. Kyle had been sitting on the roof of the four-wheel drive since they left their apartment in Cairns. As Glen approached the guard, Kyle stayed where he was so that he could be as non-threatening as possible. He was, however, watching the demons very closely, with his hand resting on his sword, just in case. The presence of the demons was a bit of a surprise to Kyle but it didn't worry him. He had faced demons bigger than this before. Beyond the fence and further up the road, Kyle could see a huge black mass moving which could only be hundreds of demons. He wondered why there were so many. "Is one of The Seven here?" he thought to himself.

As he approached the guard, Glen looked beyond the fence and saw darkness, as if the sun was blocked out by something. He then looked straight up and he saw clear sky overhead. Not a cloud anywhere. He checked his watch. It was nearly 1 p.m. "Why is it so dark ahead?" he thought.

"Hello. Nice day, isn't it?" Glen said to the guard as he came closer to him. "Dear Lord, please send your angels to watch over me, to guide me and protect me," he prayed, as he got nearer.

Kyle got down and came over to walk next to Glen, with his hands away from the sword at his side, and stopped next to Glen when he stopped.

The demons looked at each other and the little one came forward, landing on the guard's shoulders and placing its hands on the guard's head. "Stop, you're not permitted any further," the demon spoke to Kyle.

"Stop, you're not permitted any further," the guard said to Glen in a broad outback accent.

"Can you direct me to the site manager please? I have an appointment. My name is Glen Niman and I am a reporter from *The Gazette*. He is expecting me."

"And I go where he goes," Kyle said to the demon.

"No angels allowed!" came the brusque reply from the demon.

"No reporters allowed!" came the brusque reply from the guard.

"Listen ah... sorry I didn't get your name?" Glen asked.

"I didn't give it to you," another brusque reply from the guard.

There was a slight pause as Glen stopped and looked at the guard. "There is no need to be rude," he said, as he looked at the guard. "Lord, please give me strength," he prayed silently.

"STOP THAT, NO PRAYING!" the demon shouted as he grew physically agitated.

In a flash of light Kyle had drawn his sword and pointed it at the demon, the tip inches from his throat. The demons reached for their weapons in response but the one in front waved them down.

"You are called *Persuasion*, are you not?" Kyle asked the demon.

"I am," Persuasion replied, a little shakily.

"Release his mind and allow him to talk for himself, *please*," Kyle emphasised his request by poking Persuasion with the tip of the sword.

"Look, as I said, reporters are not welcome here and I'm not giving you my name. You're not going to blame me in some crummy article where you bad mouth us because I won't let you in." The guard sounded like he was trying to give an excuse, not an explanation.

"That's better," Kyle said, lowering the sword enough that Persuasion leaned backwards and got off the guard, only to hover slightly behind him, while looking at Kyle with daggers in his eyes.

"You have no authority here, I could have you killed for that," Persuasion warned Kyle icily. He then turned and joined the other demons.

Glen was getting curious now. "Okay, I understand, but I do have an appointment. I organised it with Mr Guzman before I left Sydney. Here is the letter he sent me, advising me of the time and place of our meeting. It even includes directions on how to get here," Glen explained, as he took the letter from his pocket and held it out towards the guard. He didn't mention that Henry Guzman was a friend from high school who had invited him up to talk about strange things that had happened in and around the site.

"Pass the letter to him," Kyle encouraged Glen. To himself he said, "I hope the Holy Spirit is sending for more protection to help Glen in this situation." He shuddered at the thought of entering the darkness ahead. Persuasion was right: he didn't have authority here in the enemy's territory and it was only the two of them. It wasn't the first time that they had been in enemy territory, only there had never been so many demons and just one angel.

"Such a congestion of evil spirits must indicate a leader. It must be one of The Seven, but which one? It doesn't really matter I suppose. How can I protect Glen if we enter in there? I do not know if we could survive an encounter alone with a 'leader', especially if it *is* one of The Seven, not to mention all of these foul servants of his with him. But, if it is the Lord's will that we enter such a place, then we shall do it," he thought to himself. "Surely we have to survive long enough to pass on this information to the Captain? Michael must know of this den and its location."

"You've been had mister," the guard said looking at the letter in Glen's hand, not even bothering to reach for it. "Mr Guzman is not even here! He was called back to Sydney for some reason. He left early yesterday."

"Oh, um, okay. Well, thanks for your time," Glen said, feeling a little disappointed. He started to turn but had another idea. "Would there be anyone else I could talk too? A public relations consultant perhaps?"

"All PR is run out of Sydney. Occasionally one comes up to Cairns but we never see them out here."

"Would you know when Mr Guzman is due back?"
"Don't even know if he will be back, if you know what I mean."

Kyle watched while Persuasion came forward. Persuasion rested a hand on the guard's head again. Realising that this was the end of it, he returned his sword to its sheath but did not remove his hand from it.

"Now go away! I'm done letting him talk to you!" Persuasion spat, as he placed his hand on his weapon too.

"Now clear off! I'm done talkin' to ya now!" The guard spat, as he put his hand on the butt of his gun.

Glen got the feeling that the guard's gun was the only thing that would talk from here on if he asked any more questions. "Thanks again for all your help."

"He thinks I helped 'im," the guard laughed, as Glen turned and headed back to the car.

"Lord, thank you for your protection, but can I ask why you got me this far, only to have the door shut in my face?" Glen prayed as he walked. "Surely you have a greater purpose in my being here? Will you open my eyes and show me, please Lord? Let your will be done, Amen."

Kyle walked beside Glen, listening to his prayer and added an Amen of his own. He whispered words of encouragement to Glen and prayed for understanding too. The further the two of them got from the fence, and the demons, the better they both felt. "The Spirit is moving," Kyle thought. He looked back over his shoulder at the darkness and the leering faces of Persuasion and his fellow demons at the fence. Kyle, getting a sudden impulse, spoke to Glen. "Quick, turn around and look at what God would like you to see."

Glen, used to receiving these sudden, strange urges, stopped and turned around to stare at the fence, the gate and beyond. He looked up to the sky again, to try to see why it was so dark over there.

In the distance, high above the building site, both Glen and Kyle could see a glow in the sky. It was getting bigger and brighter, as if it were coming closer. It was moving so fast, that Glen thought it must be a meteorite. His brain was telling him to run but his spirit was telling him to watch.

Kyle recognised the glow and his keen eyes could see the shape of an angel, sword drawn, diving alone, down towards the enemy.

The demons had also spotted it now. They too, recognised the glow of an angel, descending full speed towards them. A few of them scattered and hid. The rest stayed and drew their swords ready for a fight.

Glen heard the collective swords being drawn but did not know what had made the noise. He looked back at the building site to see if he could pick out what made it. He noticed the dull red colour of the swords glinting through the darkness but he couldn't comprehend what he was seeing. He couldn't make out any shapes. Glen looked up again. The light was drawing nearer. He looked back down. It looked as if the darkness was waiting to swallow it up. He looked up once again — the glow was nearer. It was getting closer and closer all the time. He was becoming hypnotised; he could not take his eyes off it. Then, with only metres to spare, there was a loud sound, like a clap of thunder and the light turned sharply and shot off out to sea.

And the darkness followed it.

Five

Michael felt the stirring of the Spirit and knew that something big was about to occur. He looked out across the paths of Heaven and spotted David heading his way.

When David was close enough, Michael spoke to him, "Did you feel it too?"

"Yes. In fact every member of the Host that is here has felt it. Something big must be happening for the Spirit to rouse so many of us," David replied.

"The evil one is on the move again. He must be after another Earthly kingdom. I wonder which one this time?"

"Will the Saints be ready? Will we have enough prayer cover? Where is the location of...?"

"Enough, David," Michael tried to calm his edgy counterpart, "the Spirit is moving and that is all we need to know for now. The Lord's plans are in motion and if the Spirit knows of something, then we will too, as soon as we are required."

Suddenly Daniel, possibly the bravest of the warriors, shot passed them. He continued on, straight over the edge of Heaven, towards the Earth. He was a blur of rushing wings and glowing as bright as any angel appears when glorified.

Michael and David looked at each other.

"It has started," Michael said, as he looked back at Daniel's quickly receding glow. He turned to David, "Make sure the Warriors of God are ready to go: they may be needed at a moment's notice. For the Glory of the Lord and His Kingdom!"

"For the Glory of the Lord and His Kingdom!" David responded to the call to arms and rushed off to find the warriors, to warn them to be prepared.

Michael looked around for a messenger. He saw Nicole nearby so he called her over. "Nicole, we need to send word to the Pillars to see if we can find out where the enemy is congregating. Can you organize enough messengers to visit one each, straight away? Ask them to get their Saints praying too."

"It will be done right away," Nicole said. She turned on her heel and ran off looking for other messengers to help.

Michael stared for a moment at the edge where Daniel went over on his way to the Earth. Then he turned and headed for the Throne. As he walked, he could see the movement he had started. Angels were rushing here and there in preparation. He noticed a group already headed for the edge and onwards to deliver his messages. He was worried about the upcoming trouble and what it may involve. He felt blind and out of control, as he knew nothing yet about his enemies' objectives and couldn't put anything formally together to fight it. "I will inform the Lord as to what I have set in motion. He will know what is going on, as the Spirit will have told Him. I will ask Him what He would like me to do and for the Spirit's guidance in this matter," Michael said to himself as he walked.

As Michael approached the Throne, Gabriel intercepted him and asked, "May I have a moment Captain?"

Michael stopped and looked from Gabriel to the Throne and back to Gabriel. "Only a moment old friend. I have urgent matters to discuss with the Lord. If it is about sending your messengers off without consulting you, I am sorry."

"That is quite alright. I didn't know you had, but even so, you are within your right to assign them without my counsel. I may be the chief messenger but you are still my Captain. As you said you are in a hurry, I will be brief. I have been given a special assignment from the Lamb. I would like your help with it."

"From the Lamb? I would be honoured. Name it Gabriel and if I can do it I will."

"I need to check on the security of Eden and I may need to increase the quantity of guards. Can you spare some warriors? Or guardians if no warriors are available?"

"I do not know, but if Eden is under threat, it will be done regardless. How many do you think you will need? I may be able to pull some cherubim from other stations if you prefer."

"Until I survey the threat, I will not know for sure. Can I start with five and request more if I feel the need?"

Michael thought for a moment. Coming to a decision he said, "You shall have seven warriors now and I will reserve word with seven more, that they may be required. Two messengers will be with them and will alert me if you activate the warriors. I will then prepare seven more warriors and another messenger, in case you need them too. Would you prefer cherubim instead of warriors? It will take some time to gather them but it could be done. I could insert warriors to relieve some cherubim of current duties, on a two to one ratio. This will allow them to be posted to you. How does that sound my friend?"

"Wonderful. I pray that I will not need any of them. The warriors would be adequate. I already have the cherubims stationed there and I shouldn't require more. Can you send the first seven warriors to meet me in the Hall of the Lamb when you have them ready?"

"I will see to it as soon as I have spoken with the Lord."

"Thank you, Captain. For the Glory of the Lord and his Kingdom!"

"For the Glory of the Lord and his Kingdom!"

Gabriel left Michael and headed for the Hall of the Spirit. Michael watched him for a moment. He did not believe in coincidences. If there was a threat to Eden, then that could be what the Spirit was preparing them for. Or was that another front from which this new threat could be coming? Or are there two different threats? He definitely wanted to counsel with the Lord now. He turned to move off again, when he noticed that Saint Peter was approaching him.

"Are you alright Michael?" Saint Peter asked as he came near. "You look troubled?"

"I am headed for the Throne. Will you walk with me please? I do not want to be rude but I feel that I have little time. I must seek the Lord's counsel on events that are unfolding while we stand here."

"Of course I will walk with you," Saint Peter replied, and they started to walk. "I do not wish to hold you up though, so if you are that burdened, I shall only walk a short way with you. What is it that has you feeling so?"

"I fear the evil one has a new scheme afoot and I do not know anything about it as yet. I am headed to the Throne to seek the Lord's counsel in the matter. I also need the Lord's counsel about a possible threat to Eden that Gabriel has just requested my assistance with."

"Eden?" Saint Peter stopped and looked at Michael.

Michael noticed the look on Saint Peter's face and stopped too.

"What is it?" Michael asked.

"Well, it is strange that you mention Eden. I have sought you out to ask you to tell me about Creation and the Garden of Eden, from your experience. Quite a coincidence, wouldn't you say?"

"I do not believe in coincidence, sir. It is from the Spirit that you have felt compelled to hear that tale and I will gladly tell it to you, after I have spoken with my Lord, organised the help that Gabriel requested and laid some plans for the encounter ahead. Will you come with me? It seems that I may need your help and counsel too, since the Spirit has sent you my way."

Six

Glen couldn't understand what he had seen. It didn't make sense to him. How could a meteorite turn a ninety-degree angle and keep moving at the same pace? And why did the darkness turn red just before the meteorite arrived and then follow it?

Kyle on the other hand knew exactly what was going on. Kyle watched a good three-quarters of the demons chase the brave angel. He was heading out to sea so fast that it was surprising that they could still see him, let alone think they could catch him.

The building site was quite easy to see as, now that the demons were gone, the darkness had lifted — as if they had been the cause of the darkness.

The first thing that caught Kyle's attention was the destruction of the natural surroundings that the development had caused. It didn't appear that the builders had any concern for the state of the rainforest or the surrounding coastline. If anything it was a thorn in their side, as they needed to remove it to build their resort. All that cost of tearing it down and removing it, just so they could replace it with cement and glass and all the other tourist distractions they wanted to have. There was no attempt to hide the fact that they were not even trying to keep any of the natural surroundings incorporated in their designs or even to recycle what they were removing.

Glen could see it all too. He thought he knew what the construction was all about but was still surprised at what he saw. When his friend contacted him, he immediately started to research all about this new tourist resort. It was to be one of the largest hotels on the north coast of Queensland with several shops, a golf course, swimming pools, nightclubs and even a cinema — every distraction that was found in a normal hotel and every other distraction you would find in a holiday attraction area. There was still bidding going on to see if they could attract a theme park of some sort. There would be no need to leave the resort for anything until the holiday was over. The only thing that he didn't see signed off on in his research, something that he would have expected, was a casino. Now that he was standing in front of the chosen location, he could see several signposts that indicated a casino was included.

"Interesting," he thought, "either they have started to build it before getting their licence or the agreement has been buried, probably so they do not scare the locals or welfare groups by its presence here.

Speaking of groups, the blatant destruction of the environment has not been noticed either, otherwise there would be protestors here too."

Wanting a closer look, Glen dove in the car for his binoculars.

While he was getting them, he heard a loud and clear noise. It sounded like another clap of thunder. When he came back out with them, he noticed it had started to get darker again. Assuming a thunderstorm was coming, he raised the binoculars to his eyes and looked around as quick as possible. He took in as much detail as he could, while wishing he had a camera to record what he saw.

Click

Glen thought he heard the open-shut noise of a camera shutter. "I must need some sleep," he thought, "one minute wishing for a camera and then hearing one, I must be tired."

Click, click, click, click. He heard it again, several times.

Glen lowered the binoculars and looked around for the source of the noise. He heard the thunder-type noise once more and almost turned back. Then he saw a woman behind him, not far from the edge of the rainforest, holding an SLR-style camera and taking photos like crazy.

Click, click, click.

Glen looked back to the guard, sure that he was going to react to the presence of another unwanted person, especially one who was taking photographs. The guard's eyes looked glazed, as he was looking off in the direction that the "meteorite" went, as if he wasn't really aware or was in a trance.

Glen noticed that the dark was coming back so he didn't bother with the binoculars again. Instead, he decided to try to speak to the woman. As he started to turn back to her, the guard came back to life and looked around suddenly.

"HEY!" the guard yelled as he caught sight of the woman. "I THOUGHT I TOLD YA: NO PHOTOS! GIMME THAT CAMERA NOW!"

As Glen looked around, the woman turned and ran. He looked back to the guard in time to see him pull out his radio and start to speak into it. "The crazy broad with the camera's back," he heard him say.

As the guard listened to the reply, he started to unclip his pistol.

Glen decided that now was a good time to leave so he jumped in the car and started it in one quick motion. He was grinning to himself as he moved forward slightly, stopped and then put it in reverse. His attempt to turn around was also helping the escaping woman. He managed to block the guard's view of her as he moved the car back and forth. It took Glen eight moves, back and forward, to get the car pointed in the right direction. With no good reason to stay there any longer, he planted his foot hard on the accelerator, throwing up dirt in the guard's face and creating a small dust cloud.

The guard cursed and swore at Glen. He lowered the gun as he raised the two-way radio.

Glen tore off up the track, looking for the woman or another vehicle. Not far up, he saw her running along the road, not looking back. Suddenly, she turned and disappeared into the undergrowth. Glen checked his rear-view mirror and saw that the security gate was opening behind him. He slammed on the brakes where he thought the woman disappeared. He leaned over and opened the passenger door and called out to her, "Quick, jump in, they're coming! Lady, if you can hear me, you had better hurry!"

Unseen to Glen, Amy, another angel, looked up out of the rainforest at him and then at Kyle, perched on the roof. Kyle motioned for them to hurry. Amy bent down and spoke in the woman's ear, "You will be safe with him, quickly now! They are coming and those pictures must be seen by others!"

One little black demon was also there. He was yelling out to the other demons, "Quick, over here, she's getting away!"

Amy watched as the woman stood up and ran to the car, jumping into the passenger seat, closing the door as Glen took off again, as fast as he could. The demon did not want to be left behind so he quickly grabbed hold of the bumper bar, just as the car accelerated away. The woman ducked down onto the floor, so she wouldn't be seen from the outside.

As Amy waited for the car to get around the next bend and out of sight, she started to study the trees around her, until she had chosen the right one. She then drew her sword in a dazzling display of brilliant light and with one slash, she cut through the tree, separating it at just the right angle. It fell across the road and blocked it totally. As soon as she was happy with where it lay, she returned to the remaining trunk. Amy put her hand on the trunk and prayed. Within seconds a new shoot appeared from it. Happy that she had caused no lasting impact, she took off after the four-wheel drive.

Glen kept one eye on the road and the other on his mirrors as he drove, sure that any minute he would see their pursuers. The woman just sat on the floor, with her head down. Kyle was now in the back seat, reaching forward to comfort the woman and give strength to Glen at the same time. Occasionally, he looked back at the demon, still hanging on to the bumper. Amy caught up to them within minutes and alighted on the roof. She spread her wings so they covered the whole car and then prayed. Her wings slowly changed colour. From above, the four-wheel drive completely disappeared. It was as if it was invisible.

Three pursuing vehicles and scores of demons left the building site and entered the forest's canopy, not more than ten minutes behind Glen. They knew these roads better so they expected to catch up very quickly. When they reached the fallen tree and saw how big it was, they knew they would not catch up and cursed their bad luck.

Five of the biggest demons, that hadn't gone off after the crazy angel that buzzed the den, kept after the car and its passengers by following the road. Five against one sounded okay to them. They caught up to the car without even knowing it and kept going.

The rest of the demons searched the forest and found the woman's car. The demons led their humans to the car. After searching it, the humans hotwired it and drove it back to the construction site.

****

Glen drove as fast as he thought he safely could for the next two hours. Apart from the ferry crossing, which had been agonisingly slow but was not stopped, Glen only slowed down to go through towns and when they reached the outer suburbs of Cairns. Once there, he headed straight to the apartment where he was staying. He had kept watch in the rear-view mirrors for any pursuit but saw none the whole time, which he thought was very strange.

When he had pulled up in his assigned car park, he stopped and prayed a quick prayer of thanks and then turned to the woman. Not a word had been spoken between them during the whole trip.

"Hi, I'm Glen," he said, breaking the silence. "We are at an apartment that I have rented for a few days, I hope that is okay. I think we should be safe here as I used a different name when I booked in. They can't trace us here."

The woman looked up, her eyes were red and swollen and her face was still wet from the tears she had cried.

"Are you hurt?" Glen asked, concerned.

"No, I..." she started to reply and then passed out.

SEVEN

Daniel was chuckling to himself as he landed on the roof of the apartment building in Cairns. He had led the demons on a fast-paced chase over the water, through the rainforests of several islands off the coast and back again. They eventually gave up the chase and returned to their den.

"Glory to the living God," Daniel said.

"And to the risen Lamb," Kyle responded, as he stepped from the shadows. This specific "Call and Response" is used as an identifier because it is impossible for a demon to acknowledge Jesus in such a way. The demons have been known to alter their appearance to try to infiltrate angelic meetings or to give misinformation. This method has stopped such infiltrations from happening.

"My name is Kyle."

"I am Daniel."

"Thank you for the distraction, Daniel," Kyle said. "Did they catch you?"

Daniel chuckled again. "No, the snakes were too slow." He paused for a moment. "A distraction, you say? You are a guardian, are you not Kyle? Did you get your charge away okay?"

"Yes, we had a bit of a chase but through the actions of Amy, another guardian, we got away cleanly."

"Another guardian? Are there more or only the two of you?" Daniel asked.

"There are five of us all together, our two charges, a minor demon and the two of us guardians." Kyle paused. "Did you see much of the Den? You drew at least one hundred demons away and we all saw it quite clearly!" he said excitedly.

"I was moving too fast to see much of the Den," replied Daniel. "At least one hundred guards on the outside? They never have that many guards unless... it must be one of the Seven!" he said, almost to himself.

"That's what we thought too. We have requested a messenger to alert the Captain of our suspicions," Kyle said.

"I think I should tell Michael too," said Daniel.

"Are you heading back so soon?" asked Kyle

"Not until I know you are all okay. This sounds bigger than anything we have seen since the New York incident, and that ended in one of the biggest battles that we have ever had." He paused for a moment and then turned to Kyle, with a look of seriousness that made Kyle think they had been seen. "What about this minor demon you mentioned. Is it one of the usual small harassers?"

"Yes," replied Kyle, "a spirit of pride I believe."

"Hmmm," thought Daniel, "he may be a problem later on. He might try to give them away. Are you keeping a close eye on him?"

"Absolutely: Amy isn't letting him out of her sight."

"Good, but all the same, your charges are probably still in danger from the occupants of the den that they discovered. What room are they in?"

"606. Shall we go down?"

"Be patient, Kyle. I need you to stay here and keep an eye out for the enemy. I'll go down alone, if the messenger arrives, send them down too," Daniel said and turned to go but Kyle put a hand on his shoulder to stop him.

"Do you really think they are still looking for us?" Kyle asked.

"Wouldn't you be if they stumbled on your secret hideout?" Daniel replied over his shoulder to Kyle.

"Why are we waiting then? We should leave as soon as we can!" Kyle said, as he released Daniel's shoulder.

Daniel turned back to face Kyle. "They are hoping, if not expecting, that we will do exactly that. We will lay low for now and head out by road via the least suspicious route, once we have made our plans and passed on what we know," Daniel explained.

Kyle nodded as he pondered what Daniel had said.

Daniel patted Kyle on the shoulder, then turned and started to move towards the stairway door. He had only taken two steps when Kyle asked, "Why by car?"

Daniel stopped and turned back to face Kyle again. "What do you mean?" he asked.

"We can take almost any boat and go in almost any direction," Kyle suggested.

With a smile starting to spread across his face, Daniel replied. "That is a very good suggestion Kyle, sneaky too. I think I will enjoy working with you. You think like I do!"

Daniel turned and walked away, towards the stairway, once more. He passed through the door, proceeded down the stairs to the sixth floor and then on to room 606. He quickly looked around and then walked through the door into the room.

"Glory to the living God," he said, as he entered the small room. He quickly surveyed it from the entrance. It was a typical apartment-style room, with a side passage off to the bedrooms and separate bathroom, while the main passage led to the living and kitchen areas. He spotted them all in the living area, the female charge was lying on the couch and the male was bent over her holding a cloth to her head. Amy, the guardian angel, was sitting on the kitchen bench top, watching them. The little demon was sitting in the corner, furthest from the windows, arms crossed and pouting.

Amy looked up surprised, "And to the risen Lamb! Daniel?"

"Hello Amy, everything okay here?" Daniel asked while indicating the humans and then the demon.

"Yes," replied Amy. "Kerri fainted after we pulled up to the hotel. Glen carried her up here and we are waiting for her to come to. He," she indicated the demon, "is behaving himself too. Was that you who drew the demons away?"

"It was I. It is good to see you again, Amy. I have not seen you since the Battle of New York," Daniel said, as he walked over to the humans. "I thought I would check on you all before I report back to the Captain."

"Not another feather head!" said the demon, loud enough to be heard.

Daniel ignored him as Amy spoke. "Please Daniel, I don't like to be reminded of our failures," she said looking down.

"From what Kyle told me, you did a wonderful job of getting your charges out. Why do you consider that a failure?" Daniel asked looking up at her.

"Oh, not that, I meant New York," she replied.

"Oh, New York. Yes, well, that would depend on how you look at it, wouldn't it. I don't call New York a failure — I think of it more as a defeat. We may have lost that battle but the war does go on, and we win in the end! Never forget that!" Daniel said, with a gleam in his eye.

"I know," she said out loud, "it is foretold. But it doesn't take the sting of defeat away."

Daniel looked Amy over, studying her quickly. It was all starting to make sense now. When Daniel had last seen Amy, she had been a warrior, fierce in battle and a great strength for the Lord. Something must have happened to her, something that had taken away her spark and reduced her confidence. He was sure she hadn't been among those injured so she hadn't dropped back to being a guardian to rebuild her strength. She must have been demoted, probably because of the defeat. Although angels knew they were fighting a battle against the evil one that they would eventually win, it didn't stop them from experiencing normal emotions about such things as defeats. Look at the fallen ones, they had been greedy and over-ambitious to think they could take the Kingdom from the Lord of all. That is why they were thrown out of Heaven in the first place. Although Amy's allegiance hadn't faltered, her confidence in battle must have.

The demon listened and saw another chance to increase Amy's pain, "Yes, that's right, you lost. We took several souls that day and it was..."

"Enough or I shall gag you with your own ears," Daniel interrupted, while turning to face the demon. Placing his hands on his hips he asked, "What is your designation?"

"Pride," replied the demon boastfully, but holding his large ears down by his head, trying to hide them.

"Well, Pride, the shed blood of Jesus has already defeated you and you know it. You are only here because of one of them," Daniel pointed at the humans, "and it will be easy enough to get them to pray or cast you aside."

"They have been trying. She will not give me up easily. I have been here a very long time."

"And yet, you are still one of the smallest Pride's I have ever seen," Daniel said, trying to provoke Pride into a fight. "You can continue to do what you must to the woman but you will not throw your poisonous words at us, or I will..."

"You'll what?" interrupted Pride. "You cannot do anything until she gives you leave."

Daniel walked over to Pride and bent down. His clear blue eyes were only centimetres away from the demons fiery orange orbs. "I will take it as a personal attack and respond with an attack of my own," Daniel said, patting his sword as he spoke the last words.

"Who do you think you are?" the demon responded, putting as much hatred into his voice as he could.

"I am Daniel," Daniel said, as he stood back up. "You may know me as Daniel the Lion Tamer or Daniel the Brave."

Pride just stared for a moment. "You! I..." he started to speak again and then closed his mouth. Pride's eyes narrowed to slits as he said, "I will do as you wish, for now, but I will remember you. When the time comes, I will change my name to Destroyer of Daniel."

Daniel stepped back and studied Pride for a moment. "My, you are an ambitious one. I will be ready and waiting for the day that you try to earn that name."

With that, he turned his back on Pride and walked over to stand before Amy. He took her hand and led her away from Pride so he could not overhear their conversation.

"Amy, we can't win every battle, otherwise we may become complacent and allow the enemy", Daniel indicated Pride behind him, "to win where they should not. And although the taste of defeat is bitter, it is a teacher that allows us to study the enemy's tactics. There are now more prayer warriors in place to prevent a disaster of that magnitude from happening again. We may not like the immediate results but the overall outcome has been positive for the Lord's Kingdom."

"So, the end justified the means?" Amy asked, looking at Daniel, a questioning look on her face.

"No, I don't believe so. The Lord simply turned the defeat, the disaster, into a rallying point and used it to increase the Kingdom," Daniel explained.

"Did the Lord allow it to happen then?" Amy asked.

Daniel thought for a moment before he replied. "Were you fighting to stop the enemy or did you pretend to fight to allow them to win?" he asked.

"I was fighting to stop the enemy!" Amy replied almost indignantly.

"And were you prepared to be struck down for the Lord that day?"

"Yes, and I still am!" Amy was starting to stand straighter and her hand was inching towards her sword, as if getting ready to draw it and fight. "Do you doubt my loyalty?" she asked, not really feeling sure where Daniel was going with this.

"No, I do not," Daniel reassured her. "None who fought that day expected to lose. Plenty were struck down for the Lord and some are still recuperating today. If I had known the enemy's plans, I would have done *everything* to prevent the first plane's takeover. By the time we were aware of their intentions, the first plane had already struck, the second was on its way and a veritable wall of demons surrounded it. We managed to get the third down earlier than they wanted. As a result, their target wasn't as damaged as it could have been. We almost had control of the fourth plane. The humans were overcoming the terrorists when they crashed it anyway. A fifth plane, in LA, and the sixth and seventh planes, in the UK, never even left the ground. You are probably unaware that we had every plane covered with at least two cherubim for at least six months afterwards. They were around all the airports in the Americas and the UK."

"I did not know that. Wow, cherubim? Really? I didn't think they came to Earth anymore? Who was left to guard Eden? Or the Throne?"

"The Lord knew what was required and he ordered it. The Captain was not happy but he obeyed the Lord's orders without a question of doubt. But you could see it in his face. The Lord himself reassured the Captain. After all, he still had him, the rest of the archangels and the seraphim. Besides, it was evident that the evil one was still very busy, too busy to try a direct attack. As for Eden, it has been well hidden since the fall of man. Even so, it was still guarded by the cherubim — just not as many of them there."

Amy settled back down but had a different look about her now.

"Don't you let that little demon's words pull you down. You know he has no power over you so do not listen to him. How long have you been around him?"

"He was with Kerri before I was. I am still not really sure why I was assigned to her," Amy admitted. "I have been with her for only a few months now and she is not a believer."

Daniel looked over at the woman. "All of God's children are precious and He would have all of us assigned to them if they all believed. They have to start somewhere and I am sure that if you were assigned to her, either she needs it or He is going to use her for the growth of His Kingdom. Or maybe even both. What you need to do is focus in on the Spirit and let Him refresh you."

"Thank you, Daniel, I will pray on that," Amy said.

It appeared that what Daniel had said had gotten through to her, now the Spirit would help reassure her and rebuild her courage and zest for the Lord. Daniel felt sure that he would see her back in the ranks of the warriors again.

Daniel turned back to look at the humans. "Unfortunately, I am not here to discuss old times. Can you tell me what is happening to these two?"

"Did Kyle not inform you already?"

"He mentioned a Den and around one hundred of the guards chasing after me."

"The Den is in a construction site for a new holiday resort, with all the usual distractions and a few more. It is well guarded against humans and angels," Amy explained. "Kyle's charge, Glen, is a reporter from Sydney. He had a friend working at the site who had become suspicious or uneasy about something. He invited Glen to visit him so he could show Glen what it was. But when Glen arrived, his friend had left, or that is what they told him. Kerri also had a friend..."

It was at this moment, while Amy was starting to explain to Daniel what this appeared to be about, that Kerri started to wake up.

EIGHT

"WHAT DO YOU MEAN YOU CAN'T FIND THEM?" he yelled down the phone.

"That's what I am trying to say, they just disappeared!" George Murphy replied, trying not to get yelled at and not succeeding at that either. Mr Jenkins, the CEO of snomeD Australia Inc, was on the line from Sydney and he was not happy. "I can't explain it, they were there and then this big tree was blocking the road. They couldn't have gotten passed it but... somehow they must have."

"Let me see if I can get this right, George. I send you to oversee what is possibly the biggest gamble this company has ever taken and you let some photographer and reporter snoop about?! Then, before you can stop them, they disappear into the rainforest?! Is that it George? Or did I leave something out?" Mr Jenkins asked, condescendingly.

"When you put it like that, sir, it sounds a lot worse. If you give me another chance, I will find them. I won't let you down, I promise!" George pleaded.

"Can you put Kane on the phone, George? Or do you need help with that too?" Mr Jenkins asked.

"Yes, sir, I mean no, sir, I mean... here he is, sir," said George, feeling flustered.

There was a slight delay as George handed the phone over to Kane.

"Kane here, sir."

"What are you doing about it, Kane?" Mr Jenkins asked.

"I have my people going over the photographer's car right now. So far, we have only found empty film packets. I have a contact at Registrations and Licensing running the number plate to see who owns the car. I think it is a rental," Kane said

"Are these contacts trustworthy?" asked Mr Jenkins

"Yes, sir, they don't know why and they never ask either," Kane explained.

"Good. And the reporter?" asked Mr Jenkins.

"The guard got his name. We are checking all the hotels to see where he is staying. He headed south so we are checking everywhere from here to Cairns. His vehicle had a rental agency sticker in the back window. We have someone looking into that too."

"Very good, Kane. As head of security, it is your responsibility to take care that whatever they find out does not get out, if you know what I mean." The line went quiet for a moment and then he asked, "How much do you think they saw?"

"We are unsure, sir, but somehow it got very bright and clear suddenly. I think they saw right into the compound, including *all* the sign posts." Kane said. "Our visitor was outside too..."

There was silence from the other end for a moment. "Damn. First, I am going to have to have a word with the construction boss about putting the signs up too early. George should have known better than to allow it too. He seems to have outlasted his usefulness there, Kane. What would you suggest we do with him, hmm?" asked Mr Jenkins.

"Me, sir? I don't know." Kane felt a little put on the spot, as he had never been asked such a question by Mr Jenkins before. "We can't let him leave the company just yet. He has seen and knows too much. Maybe a job that keeps him too busy to be able to do anything else? Somewhere far from here, so that even if he did talk, no one would listen or care."

"That is a good suggestion, Kane. Do you have a task in mind or a location?" asked Mr Jenkins.

"What about the Kings Canyon project?" replied Kane.

"Kings Canyon, Kings Canyon, Kings Canyon", Mr Jenkins stroked his chin thoughtfully as he repeated it to himself, pondering the possibilities and weighing up the pros and cons. "Yes, I think that would be perfect. Another good idea, Kane." Mr Jenkins paused for a moment, and then continued, "Now, Kane, until I can get a new overseer there, you will have to fill that role too. Do you think you can you handle that?"

"Yes, sir," Kane responded. "How long do you think it will be for, sir?"

"I will send Mr Fisk up as soon as I have briefed him on the situation," replied Mr Jenkins.

"I will have someone meet him at the airport when he arrives," advised Kane.

"Good. About our special guest, why was he outside? Was he unsettled by what happened?" Mr Jenkins asked.

"As far as I am aware, he doesn't even know about it, sir," Kane replied.

"Very good, keep it that way but remind him he must stay inside."

"I will suggest it... carefully, sir," Kane said.

"Yes, carefully, but, if necessary, tell him that I insist upon it. Now Kane, what was that about it getting bright and clear?" Mr Jenkins asked.

"I don't know how else to explain it sir: it was dark and gloomy and then suddenly bright and clear," Kane explained.

"Changes in the cloud cover, perhaps?"

"No sir, there hasn't been a cloud in the sky all day."

"None?"

"No, sir."

"Kane, you better send someone to check on the psychics. Do you understand what I am asking you?" Mr Jenkins asked.

"I think so, sir. I didn't consider that earlier but will check on it right away."

"Top priority Kane. If our opponent has found our newest location, they will surely try to infiltrate it. We can't allow that now, we are too close to completion and they may find out our true goal. Put George back on now."

"Yes, sir, top priority!" Kane said into the phone. He put his hand over the receiver and he called out, "He would like to speak to you again George."

George came back over, looking a little green as if he may be sick any moment. Taking the phone, he said, "George here, sir, at your service."

"I am going to give you another chance, George, even though I don't think you deserve it. I need you to go to Kings Canyon and prepare the way for the arrival of the CEOs. This is vitally important, as we have not all met together for some time. Do not draw too much attention to yourself by having too many security guards, or the media may guess our intentions and have a welcoming committee. Do you understand your task?"

"Yes, sir. You are most gracious, sir. Thank you, sir, for the-"

"Stop grovelling!" Mr Jenkins interrupted, "I hate it. The only reason you are alive is that I do not waste my resources lightly. But if you mess up again it may be a different story! Understand?"

"Yes, sir."

At the same time that this conversation was going on another was taking place that the humans could not see or hear. Although their human hosts were on the phone the demons could speak to each other through it just as well as the humans could, but only while the humans used it. This is what was said..."

"WHAT DO YOU MEAN YOU CAN'T FIND THEM?" he hissed in the phone.

"We searched the entire forest from the air and we couldn't find a trace of them. They must have had help getting away," the demon named Grom replied. Grom was not much to look at, not terribly imposing, as you would expect from someone of his rank. He was, however, very slimy, which may give an idea as to how he achieved it.

"Grom, I have groomed you for this opportunity and you have let me down. You are not deserving of a name anymore, you will have to go back to your previous title if you cannot do these simple little things I set you," Porva, the demon lord of Avarice spoke.

"Please lord, not that. Give me another chance. It is this host – he is not very smart but I can train him!" Grom pleaded.

"That's enough grovelling you worm, now put Cain on."

Cain, hideously grotesque, thin as a rake but full of malice (that was his name before he reached his current rank), stepped up to the phone.

"Yes, my lord?"

"Find them, Cain, however you need to do it. I will make sure it is cleared with the local covens," Porva advised.

"I have already contacted some of the locals to get their help," Cain said. "I promised nothing, but said you would be very grateful to the one who finds them."

"Very inspiring. Will it work?" asked Porva.

"I believe so, lord, they didn't ask any questions," Cain explained.

"Well done, Cain. Were the humans alone?" asked Porva.

"No, sir, an acolyte by the name of Persuasion reported an encounter with a guardian whilst speaking to the reporter. He never saw if there was another guardian with the female," Cain replied.

"That is not good news, Cain." Porva paused in thought and then asked, "How much do you think they saw?"

"Too much, lord," Cain said, and explained why he thought that. "There was another angel seen. He streaked straight out of the sky, towards the Den and then turned and headed out to sea at a tremendous speed. It lured a lot of guards after it and our cover was weakened somewhat, allowing a lot of light in. That allowed the humans a good view of the compound, including all the signposts. Our guest was outside too..."

"Arrrgh," a throaty rumble came down the line. "We can't allow these stupid mistakes to happen. Grom will need to be reassigned. Do you have any suggestions for me?" Porva asked.

"Cast him out to the Abyss!" Cain suggested. "Or if you think he still has a use, put him on the other project. He shouldn't be able to cause too many problems out there." Cain felt proud that he had been asked to contribute by the lord Avarice. It showed the trust he was now earning.

"I don't know which suggestion I like more," Porva said.

"He could help get the new site secured, ready for my arrival, once I am no longer required here. Then I can prepare it for your arrival, lord, and for the rest of The Seven." Cain was testing the water here, as he knew the other project was more important than this one and he wanted to be in on it.

"That has merit, Cain. Yes, I think that is a perfect choice." There was a pause on the line while Porva thought for a moment. Then he spoke again. "Now, Cain, until I can get a new overseer there, you will have to fill that role too. Do you think you can handle that?"

"Yes, lord," Cain responded. "How long do you think it will be for, lord?"

"I will send Lucas up as soon as his host is ready," replied Porva.

"I will have a detachment of guards waiting to meet him at the airport when he arrives," advised Cain.

"Good. What was our guest doing outside?" Porva asked.

"I'm not sure, I only just found out. He came inside in a hurry though."

"Remind him that he could jeopardise everything, if he is seen."

"Yes, lord, I will tell him of your orders."

"Good. Now, Cain, about this other angel... could it have been a decoy?" Porva asked.

"A decoy? To draw away some of the guards and allow the light in for the humans to see?" asked Cain.

"Exactly. Did this angel get caught?"

"No, sir. No guard could catch it and all returned."

"All?'

"Yes."

There was a pause. Porva was thinking and Cain knew not to interrupt.

"The Spirit is aware! Check on the psychics. Do you understand the consequences of this?" Porva asked.

"Absolutely, sir, I was in Babylon when it fell. I didn't consider that earlier but I will check on it right away."

"Top priority, Cain. If our enemy has found our newest den, they will surely try to infiltrate it. We can't allow that now, we are too close to completion and they may find out our true goal, if the Spirit hasn't already worked it out. Now put Grom back on."

"Yes, sir, top priority!" Cain said into the phone, and then he turned to Grom: "He would like to speak to you again."

"Grom here, lord. At your service."

"I am going to give you another chance, Grom, even though I don't think you deserve it. I need you to go to Kings Canyon and prepare the way for the arrival of The Seven. This is vitally important, as we have not all met for some time. Do not assign too much security or The Host of Heaven may guess our intention and have a welcoming committee. Do you understand your task?"

"Yes, lord, you are most gracious, lord. Thank you, lord, for the..."

"Stop grovelling!" Porva interrupted, "I hate it. The only reason you are not going to the Abyss, is that I do not waste my resources lightly... But if you mess up again, I will dispatch you myself! Understand?"

"Yes, lord."

NINE

Saint Peter followed Michael quietly as he left the Throne, not wanting to intrude on his thoughts. The audience with the Lord had gone well, he thought, although he did not understand what was going on. The Lord had referred to places that Saint Peter had never seen when he was on the Earth and devices that had not been around. He knew that Michael now had to formulate some sort of strategy to combat this new threat. Saint Peter did not want to bother Michael but he was feeling a strong need to hear this tale of Creation right now. Or at least a part of it.

"Michael?" Saint Peter tried to get his attention.

Michael stopped and looked at Saint Peter. "Sorry my friend, my mind is elsewhere right now. Can we do this later?"

"I do not believe that we can," said Saint Peter. "The Spirit is giving me a great sense of urgency in hearing of *your* experiences, and *only from you.*"

"And I feel a need to tell it too," Michael admitted. "However, I did promise Gabriel that I would organise some reserves for him. Can I tell you as we walk to the Hall of the Archangels?"

"Absolutely," replied Saint Peter, and they started to walk again.

"I am sure you know how the passage starts..." Michael began:

In the beginning God created Heaven and Earth.

The Earth was formless and empty, and darkness covered the deep water. The Spirit of God was hovering over the water.

Then God said, "Let there be light!" So there was light. God saw the light was good. So God separated the light from the darkness. God named the light day, and the darkness he named night. There was evening, then morning — the first day.

Genesis 1:1-5

"Long before the rise of the evil one and the subsequent Battle for the Throne, the Lord God created various planes of existence including the Earth, and helpers, which are, of course, me and my fellow angels. Of the planes of existences, He chose two to mould and shape. The first was Heaven. I can remember watching as His thoughts became reality. He described to us what He was trying to achieve; a place of beauty and peace, a place to rest and enjoy all His creations, a place to share, to laugh and sing and to praise Him above all others. You only have to look around to see what He made, for it has not changed since the day it was created. Sure, some parts got destroyed in the Battle but they were rebuilt just the same. What you see is what we saw."

"Really?" Saint Peter asked.

"Yes. However, the second plane, the Earth, was very different. As the Bible says, when the Earth was first created by God, it was nothing but a formless and empty place, and totally dark. Have you ever seen a human child make mud pies? The Earth was much the same — it was a great big ball of mud. There was no separate piece of land or water. They were all mixed together.

"This was because there was no movement to the Earth; it sat still in the vastness of space. Without the spin or rotation of the Earth, the mass was so low, that there was almost no gravity and without that gravity the soil within the water just sat there. It did not sink or rise, it just sat there.

"Let me explain a little better for you. Mass is the measure of the matter an object contains. (This shouldn't be confused with weight, which is the measure of how your mass is affected by gravity.) Mass itself can be affected by gravity and inertia; and inertia is measured by how much effort is required to move an object.

"Now, the Lord, the Lamb and the Spirit visited the Earth and kind of swam around it as we watched. We didn't understand the significance of what was happening, but the Lord was creating little bits of energy and infusing it, along with parts of Himself, into the Earth. Their movement around it caused the Earth to start spinning. It moved slowly at first, gradually increasing until they were happy with the speed of the rotation and then they came back to the edge of Heaven.

"Once this movement was applied to the Earth, its inertia was increased. That, coupled with the energy, started a reaction; the Earth's mass started to increase and as the mass increased the gravity also increased.

"The result of this was that the mud started to separate and land masses and bodies of water started to appear.

"The Lord then said, 'Let there be light!' and there was light. We were amazed: with but a word the Lord had created a ball of light! 'The Sun', he called it. He was happy with the Sun and was happy that we were happy with the Sun (and to this day he still likes to just sit and bask in its rays whenever he has an opportunity).

"Now we had two balls in the dark: one gave off light and the other didn't. The Sun was so bright that the light reached the Earth. Now, because they are both balls, only one side of the Earth could see the Sun at any one time. This caused a separation on the Earth. One portion would always be in the dark while the other would be in the light. The Lord named the light side Day, and the dark side Night. As we watched the Earth spinning, we noticed that no one point on the outside of the Earth would forever remain in the Dark or Night side. As we watched, He explained that if we stood in one spot on the Earth that we would see the

Sun rise on one side of us and set on the other side. He called the rising of the Sun morning and the setting of the Sun evening. The Lord then told us that one whole revolution of the Earth, from one rising of the Sun to the next, would be called one Day. As we watched from our vantage points in Heaven, we could see the Earth spinning and we saw that all this had been done in one day. The Earth had experienced its first Day cycle."

As Michael finished, he and Saint Peter arrived at the Hall of the Archangels. Saint Peter was not surprised that Michael had timed it so well.

"Do you mind waiting here while I organise the reserves for Gabriel?" Michael asked Saint Peter.

"Of course not, I think I shall need a little time to take in 'the first day' anyway. Please, go ahead. I shall wait right here for you," Saint Peter replied.

With that, Michael went in to the Hall of the Archangels and left Saint Peter standing there.

It never failed to amaze Saint Peter how the Lord's creations were so simple for Him to make and yet were such complex things. Over the years, since he had come to walk Heaven's paths, he had studied some of the Lord's handiwork, including the Sun. What a complex series of things made up the Sun! And yet it is such a simple device, a self-sustaining energy source that also gives off light. But for it to produce even the tiniest amount of energy, it needs to consume so much, and in that process it creates more of itself to burn later, a cycle that goes around and around and around. And all He did... was say, "Let there be light!"

Ten

Kerri looked around as she sat up. She saw that she was in a hotel room and that the only other occupant was Glen.

"Not so fast, you will probably make yourself dizzy. How are you feeling?" Glen asked, concerned.

"Okay, I guess," Kerri replied. "Where am I?" she asked, backing away slightly from him.

"We are at my apartment," said Glen.

"Who are you?" Kerri asked again.

"My name is Glen, Glen Nimon. I am a reporter from Sydney. Would you like a drink or some food?"

"Water please," Kerri said, as she looked around again. "What sort of reporter? What were you doing there? Are you writing about the construction? Why did-"

"Whoa, slow down. How about I answer your questions one at a time and then I will ask you some of my own?" Glen asked, as he got up and went to get Kerri a drink of water.

"Umm... look, sorry, I don't want to be ungrateful to you, but I don't know you and I don't want to be a story you plaster all over the TV or papers or whatever you report for... or to." Kerri paused for a moment, "Or maybe you work for 'them' and have pretended to be nice to me while really waiting to turn me over to them. So, forgive me when I say, I'm not telling you anything!"

"Fair enough, I wouldn't want to talk to a stranger either. I don't know why, but *I* think *I* can trust *you*. I think God has brought us together for a reason. You have a choice to make... trust me or don't. But let me say this, if I was working for them, I would have turned you straight over when you jumped in my car. What reason would I have for continuing to run away from them? Why bring you to a hotel in Cairns, instead of turning around and going back to the site?" Glen asked as he poured water into a glass.

"I don't know, maybe to trick me into feeling comfortable. Then you could learn all I know and then turn me over?" Kerri suggested, as she watched him.

"I see your point. Well, I don't know how else I can prove myself to you. But, if it helps, I will answer all your questions and more. You can use the phone to check my credentials if you like or if you trust me to drive you somewhere, I can take you wherever you like," Glen offered, as he walked back over to stand in front of her. "You are not a prisoner here. If you want to leave, you can. How's that for a start?"

"Um, okay, I guess," said Kerri, feeling a little taken aback by his offer and a little guilty of her suspicious attitude. "Sorry if I was out of line but you understand what I mean don't you?"

"Yes, I do, I wouldn't want to be giving away too much myself if I didn't think I could trust the other person," Glen responded. "Here is your water."

"Thank you," she said, as she took it and had a sip. She looked at him, almost studying him. He was taller than her, possibly six foot, with short blond hair and blue eyes that looked very caring; he had a neatly trimmed goatee, and nothing pierced, not that she could see anyway. He was watching her as she looked at him, his movements were fluid, almost graceful, and his voice sounded very sincere. She made up her mind to trust him, but not fully. "He has to earn that sort of trust," she thought. "I can't tell him what I've done. He wouldn't trust me at all. But if he is a reporter, he could ruin all their plans. Should I tell him? Not yet, but if he is sent by God (after all I did pray for help), then maybe I can start by telling him my name."

"You can call me Kerri," she said finally.

"Hi Kerri, it's nice to meet you," Glen said, as he held out his hand to shake hers.

Amy, Daniel and Pride watched the humans as they started to talk to each other. They listened as Kerri voiced her objection and as Glen approached her with the water, Amy moved to stand behind Kerri and whispered words of encouragement in her ear. She also told Kerri that she could trust Glen.

Pride also moved to stand near Kerri, but he was not whispering. Pride was practically shouting, "You can't trust him! What if he finds out what you did! You're lost! No one cares about you! He doesn't care who *you* are!"

Amy shot Pride a distasteful glare but felt the Spirit holding her back. Daniel was watching Pride and listening to the taunts too. He was hoping that the Spirit would let him act soon. Amy smiled in a sneaky way and whispered into Kerri's ear.

"Why did you mention God before?" Kerri asked. "You said you think God has brought us together. What do you mean by that?"

"DON'T ASK THAT!" Pride screamed at her.

"Simply that I am a Christian and I believe that God does things like that. I have often been put in situations where I recognise God's hand at work. This situation feels like that to me now. I don't know what you believe so if I have offended you or scared you, then please excuse me. That was not my intention. However, I have found that if I do not voice my beliefs and if those involved don't know that my actions come from His guidance and not my own, then the situation can get out of hand," Glen explained.

"Okay, thanks for your honesty. No, it doesn't scare or offend me. I have some Christian friends who sometimes talk God around me. It's not that I don't believe, it's more that I have never made that choice to only believe, if you know what I mean," Kerri said.

Pride slumped, giving up for the moment. He started to walk towards the windows.

"Stop there. Your place is by the wall," Daniel said pointing to where Pride had been sitting before.

"You can't dictate my actions to me!" Pride said to Daniel.

Daniel started to withdraw his sword slowly. Pride watched for a moment and then stopped him.

"You made your point. I will do as you wish, for now. But know this," Pride said, his eyes burning with hatred as he looked at the Heavenly warrior, "your time will come."

"I understand, I think most of us go through that. Some without even realising it and they never change from it, unfortunately. You are lucky that you can admit it to yourself in that way. It means that when the time comes for you to make the decision, you will recognise the moment and not let it pass by. I'm sure I speak for your friends too when I say that I pray you choose to believe when the moment comes," Glen replied. "For now, though, let's start with your questions. I am a writer for *The Gazette*, a paper that comes from Sydney."

"I have read it a few times," Kerri interjected, "when I have been in Sydney. Why were you at the site?" she asked, bringing the subject back.

"I was invited. A friend works, or should that be 'worked' there. He noticed some strange things going on and called me. I came running, not so much for the story but mostly for my friend. He sounded worried, almost scared. But that was almost three days ago now," Glen explained.

"What happened to your friend?" Kerri asked.

"I don't know. When I asked the guard if I could see him, that I had an appointment, he said Henry had left for Sydney yesterday. I pray that he is safe and well."

"I hope so, although, if I know that place, I'm afraid he probably isn't," Kerri said.

"What do you mean by that?" Glen asked.

"They are not very nice people, the owners or whatever they are. I knew someone that was working there too and they disappeared also, just over two weeks ago now. Not so much as a 'see you later'. When I started to ask questions, they said they hadn't even heard of him. I spoke to the police and they asked a few questions. They told me that he had been moved to another project of the owners, somewhere in Central Australia," Kerri explained.

"But you think something's wrong with that?" Glen asked.

"Alan would have told me if he was leaving, we were pretty close. When I told the police that, they tried to infer that he might have been trying to get away from me. I don't believe that; I know Alan would have told me. We've known each other since high school. We weren't lovers, so he wouldn't have been trying to get away from that. We are mates, like brother and sister. You know what I mean? Really good mates; we told each other everything. It doesn't make sense to me that he would just up and leave and not tell me where he was going." Kerri's eyes started to mist up as if she would cry again.

Daniel and Amy watched as Kerri started to open up and explain about her friend Alan. They were impressed by Glen's composure and compassion.

"I believe you," Glen said. "I know what you mean about that sort of friendship. I have lots of friends like that. Henry is one of them. I came running because I owe it to him. A number of years ago I got into some trouble and he helped bail me out. He's the sort of person that I would trust with my life. When he called me... I knew I had to help him, no matter what."

Glen had a faraway look on his face that Kerri didn't really want to interrupt. Besides, the more he spoke, the less she had to tell him about herself. He shook his head as if coming out of a dream.

"Friends can be very handy at times. In fact, I may be able to track yours down if he has gone interstate. I have some friends that might be able to help. Do you know where exactly they said he has gone? Central Australia is pretty wide open."

"No, the police didn't say. I did try to search on the internet under the company name that I found but I didn't get very far. Maybe it's not the same construction crew, assuming it is another building site," Kerri said.

"Give me the name of the company you searched for. I will make a few calls and see what I can find out," Glen suggested. "But before I do that, I think you need to tell me why are 'they' after you? Is it just for the photos that you were taking? Or something else?"

Kerri paused and then asked, "You saw me taking photos?"

"Yes, quite a few from the sound of it. I heard you first right after the thunder clap," Glen replied.

"Thunder clap?" Kerri thought for a moment. "I heard a loud noise too but wasn't sure what it was. I thought it came from the construction site so I started taking as many photos as I could. I think that is what they were after but I am not sure what the photos are of. I couldn't see clearly. We should get the photos developed and find out what is on the film," Kerri said, in her most convincing way.

Glen thought for a moment but he wasn't fooled.

"The guard seemed to know you. I think there is something you haven't told me."

Kerri slumped slightly.

"You're right. But I don't think I should tell you about that, not yet anyway. It's kind of... personal."

As Kerri paused, Amy leaned forward and whispered words of encouragement in her ear, things such as, "you can trust him" and "he can help you if you let him".

Pride looked on and was about to speak but decided to wait and see what happened first.

"Kerri, if you don't want to tell me, that's fine. But please understand that I am not here to judge you. That's not up to me. But if we are going to work together, to find our friends, then we need to be honest with each other. There are different types of 'after someone', and it doesn't seem that they want to have a chat with you. I saw the guard draw his gun! If you are in mortal danger, it could change how we act, how we move about, who we can talk to and be seen with. Do you understand what I mean?"

Pride stood up, his orange eyes wide open. "NO! Don't trust him! He will turn you over to the cops! He *will* judge you and leave you, like everyone else!"

Daniel turned to Pride and asked, "Are you sure you are Pride and not Despair?" Daniel smiled at Pride's unease.

Pride glared back at Daniel, his anger was building. "Your time will come," he said to himself.

Kerri looked away, weighing up what she should do or say, or how much she should reveal. She stood and walked over to the floor to ceiling windows and looked out at the ocean.

Finally she spoke: "I understand. I am not proud of what I did but I am not sorry either," Kerri started to explain. "When I didn't get the answers I wanted, from any of them, including the police, although they got more answers than what I already had, I decided to take matters into my own hands. I know it is wrong but I started to investigate them. I took photos. I followed them if they came to town. I even broke into the office here in Cairns to see if there was anything on file."

Pride looked on with great interest. Amy bowed her head waiting to see if Kerri would reveal all that had happened that night.

"I did find some information and took it," Kerri continued, "that is why they are after me. What I found, if it gets out to the right people, it could not only close the construction site down but could put them out of business permanently. The only problem is... it looks like it is only half of the information. There are no names or dates, only references."

Pride laughed.

Daniel shot Amy a questioning glance, as if to say "what's that about?".

"That's not all that happened," Amy replied to Daniel's unspoken question. "Hopefully the Spirit will convict her and she will reveal her secret."

"Did you understand any of it?" Glen asked.

"Not really. There were references to other projects all over the world. The word 'Eden' was written several times. Sometimes it was crossed out, sometimes circled. I don't understand what that means. There were some references to other people and businesses but I think they were coded. There were maps, too, of the locations of some of the projects – nothing on Central Australia though. I have it all in a safe place. We can get it if you want to have a look?" Kerri offered, glad that she hadn't slipped and told him everything.

Daniel looked at Amy, startled by what he had heard. He turned back to listen to Glen.

"I think we should set the search for the other site in motion first and then get out of here. We can pick it up on the way. The construction site was for the Asheron Group of resorts, so we can try that. Was the company name you searched for the same one or something different?" Glen asked.

"The one I was searching for was the Nirvana Group," Kerri replied.

"Okay, I'll make the call to my friends and let's see where it gets us," Glen said, as he moved over to the telephone.

Daniel was even more shocked to hear the company names. He had faced both of them before and even thought the Nirvana Group was no more. He turned to Amy and asked quietly, "Did you get a look at the documents?"

"No," she replied, moving closer so that Pride couldn't hear, "I was too busy distracting the guards. Do you think they are referring to the Lord's Garden?"

"I do not know Amy, but it wouldn't surprise me. The evil one has been looking for it for centuries. I don't see the connection though. It doesn't make sense to me. Maybe the Captain will understand it."

"I have faced Nirvana before," Daniel continued. "Their king is Sloth, one of the Seven. I have also faced Asheron, but I do not know which of the Seven is their king. If we are facing two of The Seven, two of the evil one's Generals at the same time, we are going to need help. We need to get a messenger sent off straight away!"

Eleven

The Same Day
The Road between Port Lincoln and Ceduna, South Australia

They came out of nowhere, or at least they appeared to. It felt like only minutes and not about an hour since Phillip had left Port Lincoln on his motorbike.

He loved to ride – to feel the wind on his face and the freedom of the open spaces. It was a peaceful time for him and he often used the time to reflect on things. He was due to preach Sunday morning in Ceduna and he had hoped to prepare the sermon while riding. Phillip hoped he could get in a day of rest and maybe some fishing before he was due to deliver it.

He had been going over the sermon in his head when a biker gang suddenly materialised around him. He reprimanded himself for not paying attention, as he hadn't seen them coming up from behind him.

Normally, he didn't have a problem with bikers, but for some reason he was feeling uncomfortable now.

His unseen companions, a guardian angel named Dmitri and a messenger angel named Troy, shared his feeling of unease. The reason was obvious to them. Along with the sixty-three motorbike riders, were sixty-three demons, ranging in size and shape. The bikers closed in around Phillip and the demons closed in around the angels.

Phillip was praying for help or deliverance but it was like waving a red flag to a bull (which is kind of what the lead demon looked like). Before he knew what hit him, he was lying on the side of the road, unconscious.

Dmitri and Troy fared better but fell eventually too, though not without taking some of the demons with them. Nine demons were sent to the Abyss, before the angels were knocked unconscious.

Then something strange happened. Phillip's unconscious form was lifted and put into a sidecar, while Dmitri was bound up and carried by four demons.

Troy, however, was left lying on the side of the road, alongside the damaged motorbike.

With a note slipped under his belt.

TWELVE

The Same Day
Somewhere in Central Australia

Henry knew, exhausted or not, he had to keep moving.

"Should... have... reached the... river... by... now," he gasped out as he stumbled onwards.

Henry had been walking for almost eight hours and hadn't seen one person or tree the whole time. He had escaped through an exhaust tunnel and had started walking before the sun had risen. When he saw the sun start to rise behind him an hour later, he knew he had gone the wrong way. He immediately turned left and headed south.

After being out in the sun for almost seven hours without shade or water, he was not only parched and very sunburnt but also starting to feel the effects of heat stroke. He had been hallucinating for the last hour and things were just not making any sense at all.

"Where have... all... the trees... gone?" he said. He thought he was talking to one of his workmates.

He tripped on one of the desert plants and fell to his hands and knees. He stayed there for a moment, just looking at the backs of his hands. Still staring at his hands, he managed to get himself up on his feet again.

"Hey mate, you... got any... sunscreen... left?" he panted.

He waited for a response.

"Mate?" he said, as he looked around.

"Doug?" he called out, still looking for his friend.

"Where'd he go? Bet he... took all... the water too!"

Henry's legs gave way and he fell to the ground again. As he lay there, he lifted his left hand to try to block out the sun. Having very little success at that, he decided to try to sit up.

"Where am I?" he said, still using his hand to shade his eyes, as he sat and looked all around. "This doesn't look... like the rainforest?"

"Come on Henry, you can do it. You are in the desert now, don't you remember? You're escaping from the people who brought you here," Gage spoke quietly to Henry, trying to get him back into the right frame of mind. He had appeared alongside Henry, as his friend Doug, to try to help him along. It was causing the hallucinations to get worse so he was back to being himself now. The added bonus of that, was that he had his wings stretched up to try and block some of the sun's rays.

Gage suddenly turned and looked back the way they had come. His ears had picked up the sound of something approaching.

Henry could hear something coming from behind him so he turned and stared until he spotted it. A helicopter was coming his way.

Gage's eyes could pick out the helicopter quite clearly, even from this distance. He could also see six demons flying around the helicopter. He looked back down at his charge and then around them. There was nowhere to go. Nowhere to hide.

"It's them Henry. They are coming. I don't know if they have seen you yet but it is only a matter of..."

"Oh God, they've found me!" Henry said, and suddenly got up, turned and tried to run.

"Wait! If you don't move they might not see you..." Gage tried to warn Henry. "They will see you for sure now," he said to himself, just watching Henry try to run in a straight line.

"God, help me! I..." Henry called out as he half ran and half stumbled over, around and through the small bushes that lined this part of the county. "Oof," he cried as the wind was knocked out of him, from yet another fall.

Gage stopped very still and listened to the Spirit's instructions. He turned, drew his sword and waited for the helicopter to get overhead. He took off, straight at the nearest demon.

The demons were flying in ranks. Gage picked the angle that would give him the best chance. Before they knew he was there, two of the demons were dissolving in mid-air and being sucked into the Abyss. The third one saw him coming and managed to dodge, just in time. Gage doubled back on him, before he could draw his sword completely out of its sheath. Deciding it was better to run than stay there struggling with the sword, the demon dropped like a rock, with Gage right behind him.

Too panicked to make a coherent sound, the demon concentrated on dodging the attacking angel's sword and the larger bushes along the ground. The other three demons had only just seen Gage chasing down their comrade. They immediately noticed that Gage was gradually catching him up.

"Let's get him!" one shouted.

The three of them dove straight for Gage. They managed to do what their comrade couldn't and drew their swords ready. Gage saw that he had drawn all three into the chase and smiled to himself. He looked around quickly to see where Henry was, then turned and headed in the opposite direction.

Now that the angel was no longer chasing it, the first demon stopped in mid-air and managed to get his sword drawn. Then he saw some movement out of the corner of his eye. It was a human. He watched the human for a little while. He was running, stumbling, falling and then trying to get up and run some more. The demon dove down towards the human. As he got closer, he saw that it was the one they were looking for. The demon rushed back to the helicopter and pointed the human out to the pilot.

"There!" one of the searchers said pointing. The pilot turned the helicopter into a nose dive, straight at Henry.

Gage saw that the helicopter had turned and was now headed for Henry. His look of disappointment quickly changed to one of determination, as he turned around. He was headed, as fast as he could fly, straight back at the demons.

As he passed the three chasing him, he managed to flick his sword and remove a wing from one, but got nicked in the arm by one of the other two. The injured demon spiralled out of control and crashed into the ground in a big puff of red smoke. The other two turned to follow Gage.

Gage spotted his previous target. He raised his sword and went through the demon, as it emerged out of the helicopter. Gage then turned and headed for Henry. As he landed near his charge, he quickly checked him out visually, noticing that Henry was not looking too good.

The Spirit stirred in Gage.

"It's okay, Henry," Gage said, "I will make sure they do not hurt you. Stop and rest. We cannot escape them now anyway. Save your strength for your recovery."

Henry stopped and looked at the helicopter that was now circling, trying to find a flat spot to land. Even though there were very few trees, there were still plenty of small desert plants which could make a landing tricky.

"I don't think I can outrun them Doug. I might just sit here. Save my energy," Henry puffed to his imaginary companion. Then he collapsed where he was. He tried to sit up and watch the helicopter land.

While they waited, Gage stood over Henry with his Sword still drawn but not looking overly confident. The Spirit was telling Gage to provide a convincing surrender. If Henry had stayed in the sun for much longer, he would not have had the energy to keep walking. Then his exposure to the heat would be made a lot worse and he would have died right there. This way, their pursuers should be convinced that they had won.

The remaining demons approached haughtily, looking from Gage to Henry. One spoke to Gage mockingly, "Do you think you should keep fighting little angel? Even if you defeat us, he doesn't look like he could survive another hour out here. And then you would be out of a job."

Gage glanced at Henry and then back to the demons. "Will you look after him? Get him healthy again?"

The demon laughed. "They will. They need all the healthy men they can get," he said, indicating towards the humans that were now approaching across the red sand and salt bushes.

Gage lowered his sword in surrender. The demons approached him cautiously and took it from him. They all watched as the humans loaded Henry on a stretcher and started off towards the helicopter with him. The demons then gave Gage a push, to follow them.

Thirteen

The Same Day
Asheron Building Site, North Queensland

Kane moved through the building like a whirlwind. When he reached the sub-basement, he knocked on the door marked 'Private'. When no one responded, he opened the door and walked in cautiously. The room was dark, with candles providing the only illumination. He stopped just inside the door and closed it again. He waited for his eyes to become accustomed to the gloom. Once they had, he looked around the room, studying it. There were thirteen people in here, in various states of meditation and consciousness. Kane approached the one he knew to be the 'leader'. As he did, Hildegard opened her eyes and gradually focused on him.

"Why do you interrupt us?" Hildegard asked with a German accent.

"I needed to see you," Kane replied.

"Why? Is it about the disturbance earlier?"

"Yes, it is," Kane replied. "What can you tell me about it?"

"There was a 'Bright One'. The Masters were displeased and some chased it away. It did not come back. They were happy again," Hildegard explained.

"What about in here? Was anyone hurt? Or sleeping? Did you sense anything different? Is everyone still active?" Kane pressed.

"Nothing happened here. It was out there," Hildegard said while pointing up. "Nothing changed here. Some were resting before," she said indicating the other psychics around her, "but when the 'Bright One' was spotted, the alert was given and we were all on guard."

"Do you think we were infiltrated during this diversion?" Kane asked.

"No one entered the protected areas," Hildegard assured him.

"Thank you for answering my questions, I will leave you to your work now," Kane said and he started to leave.

Eleven of the thirteen psychics looked relieved. The other two looked uncomfortable, one was the leader, Hildegard, and the other was Umar, one of the most experienced of the group. Umar looked at the leader and the leader nodded.

"Wait!" Umar said. "There is something else we need to tell you."

"Shut up, fool!" one of the other psychics called out.

"You cannot be sure," another said.

"You doom yourself for speaking out!" said yet another.

"SILENCE!" Hildegard yelled. "You users are not yet experienced enough to recognise the danger, but he is. Tell him what you know Umar."

"Yes," Kane said, feeling a little uneasy but turning to the one who spoke anyway, "what else?"

"There were *others*," Umar said, with a Middle Eastern accent.

"Others? Other 'Bright Ones'?" Kane asked.

"No, maybe. We are not sure. It was hard to tell. They were not 'lit up' but they were not like the masters. There were five of them altogether. If I were to guess, I would say it was two like us but not dark, one like the masters and two like the 'Bright One' but not 'Lit Up'," Umar tried to explain.

The room was silent, waiting for Kane's reply.

"I see," Kane said eventually, although he didn't really. He started to wander around the room as he considered this. "Five? The guard at the gate only saw two people. If there was one like the masters, then that is not out of the ordinary. There are agents everywhere," he vocalised his thoughts as he tried to work out what Umar was telling him. "There were two more you say?" he asked Umar, as he turned back to face him. But before Umar could reply, Kane asked another question. "Are you trying to tell me there were two more... presences, that were... smoking or something?"

"No, sir." Umar replied. "You will understand if you think about it a bit more. I cannot explain it any better."

Kane stood there considering the psychics and noticed that the 'inexperienced' ones had moved away from Umar, as if expecting him to be struck by Kane. But Umar was not scared. In fact he looked confident. "What is Umar trying to tell me?" Kane thought. "Not the humans but with them..."

"No!" Kane said suddenly, "Impossible!"

"Is it, sir?" Umar replied quietly.

"Do you agree?" Kane asked Hildegard.

"I do," Hildegard replied.

"If you felt their presence, then the Master's enemies may be onto us!"

Cain had come too, with his host, and he had a slightly different conversation with the psychic's demonic counterparts. He got a better understanding of the situation as they explained it differently...

"Why do you interrupt us?" Seer asked Cain as he entered, dodging the fast-moving messengers.

"I needed to see you," Cain replied, ducking his head as another messenger sped from the room.

"If you stand still, they will go around you," Seer advised. Then getting back to Cain's reason for being there, she asked, "Why? Is it about the disturbance earlier?"

"It is," Cain replied, trying his best not to flinch as the messengers continued to buzz about the room. "Was there another guardian with the female human?"

"There was. His presence was noticed as soon as he arrived. As we raised the alarm, the other one shot out of the sky. We were too late to warn everyone to hold their positions," Seer explained.

"What about in here? Was anyone hurt? Or sleeping? Did the messengers see anything else? Are they all still active?" Cain pressed.

"Nothing happened here. It was all out there," Seer said while pointing up. "No messengers were lost. Some were resting before, along with their masters," Seer indicated the other "psychic" demons around. "When the first guardian was spotted, the alert was given and we were all on guard."

The demons are not really psychic. They use smaller and faster demons as messengers. These messengers bring them information and also deliver instructions. Instructions about the "vision" that was "seen" by the human "psychic" – really something that the demon "psychic" suggested. Then the demons try to reproduce it for the human. This process has been perfected over the centuries.

"Do you think we were infiltrated during this diversion?" Cain asked.

"No one entered the protected area," Seer assured him.

"You did well," Cain said praising them. "Next time, try to get the warning off earlier."

Eleven of the thirteen "psychic" demons looked pleased with themselves. The other two looked uncomfortable, one was Seer and the other was also of rank enough to have a name. Esper had thought his name was clever when he picked it. Now though, it was a warning to most that he seemed to know what was going to happen before it did. His 'pets' (as he called his messengers) were well trained. Esper looked at Seer and Seer nodded.

"Your praise is unwarranted, leader Cain," Esper said. "For there is more to tell you."

"Shut up, fool!" one of the other eleven called out.

"You cannot be sure," another said.

"You doom yourself for speaking out!" said yet another.

"SILENCE!" Seer yelled. "Sorry leader, the inexperienced worms do not recognise the danger, but Esper does. Tell him Esper."

"Yes, Esper," Cain said, "tell me about the danger?"

"My pets tell me that we were *seen*!" Esper said.

"You were seen? By the guardians?" Cain asked in disbelief.

"Not *us*, my leader. By us, I mean the troops... up there," Esper tried to explain.

The room was silent, waiting for Cain's reply.

"I see," Cain said, although he didn't really. He waited, expecting more of an explanation to come out. When it wasn't forthcoming, he said, "I know we were seen by the angels. Why do you repeat what I already know and speak as if it is more dangerous? Do you want me to strike you? I know you earned your name from cunning and strength and not stupidity!"

Esper didn't move. He didn't cower, he didn't flinch, he didn't reach for his sword. He simply stared at Cain and waited.

The others, except for Seer, had moved away expecting a fight to break out between them at any moment. Their messengers also started to give Cain a wider berth, not wanting to be hit by accident.

"You know I am not stupid Cain," Esper said quietly. "Do you need me to explain it to you? I didn't think I would need to."

Cain stood there considering Esper and studied his pose. Esper was giving off an air of quiet confidence. Cain did in fact know Esper. They had worked around each other for centuries. As Malice, Cain had to learn to read others' attitudes so that he could work his 'talent' on them. Esper, who was simply a psychic back then, had always had an air of confidence and his messengers were the same ones back then as they are now. That sort of continued loyalty from them meant that they were very attuned to Esper and gave him reliable information. Cain knew that part of the reason Esper chose his name was because he seemed to know things before others did (which was because of his messengers). "So what does Esper know, that I do not? He is not afraid of me, which means he is not talking about the angels," Cain thought to himself. "So who..." then a thought struck Cain.

"No!" Cain said out loud. "Impossible!"

"That is what they think too," Esper said, indicating the other demons behind him. "But Seer and I agree. Somehow, they both saw us. I don't think they understand what they saw, but it occurred when the woman was taking photos."

"You don't think..." Cain left the question hanging.

"It is possible that if they could see us, then they could take photos of us too," Esper suggested.

Cain turned to Seer, "And you agree?"

"Yes," Seer replied. "As the angel dove out of the sky, their confusion was at its highest. Why would they be confused if they couldn't see anything?"

"Why indeed?" Cain said thoughtfully, "All the more reason to find them. If what you suspect is correct, then we need to get that camera too."

FOURTEEN

Michael entered the "Hall of the Archangels" and went straight over to Jasper. He had to walk between several groups of warriors who were practising various fighting techniques, some with weapons and some without. They stopped and acknowledged their Captain with a slight nod of the head, saying, "Captain", as he passed.

This often made Michael uncomfortable, as he was afraid that the recognition may appear as praise to some and he knew that the angels should praise only God. Michael had mentioned this to the Lord once. The Lord told Michael they were showing him respect: respect for his position, respect for his character and respect for his dedicated service to Him, the Lord of All. In any case, if any angel did do the wrong thing, then the Holy Spirit would instantly mark the offending angel for all to see, as had been done since the Battle for the Throne.

"Hello, Captain," Jasper said when Michael reached him. Jasper was currently assigned to oversee the Hall of the Archangels. "As you can see," Jasper said, while indicating all of the training angels, "training is progressing well. All of the fencing trainees are in their final session and will achieve their new skill level once it is completed."

"Let me know when that is and I will perform the presentations," replied Michael. "However, that is not why I am here."

"I didn't think so," Jasper said. "The truth is, I have been expecting you. Who do you need and how many?"

"You know why I am here?" asked Michael.

"I felt the Spirit move, then Daniel took off like a rocket. It took me nearly an hour to clean up and have everyone back training again," explained Jasper.

"Clean up? Did he leave a mess?" asked Michael.

"No, he didn't. He was moving so fast, that some of the equipment and papers, got sucked up in his wake."

"He was in here when he got 'called' to Earth?" asked Michael.

"Yes, he was instructing at the time. Then David came shortly after to tell everyone to be ready, though he couldn't say what for. But I am sure you did not come here to check on Daniel and David. What do you need, my Captain?" asked Jasper.

"I need several warriors for special assignments," Michael stated.

"Special assignments?" asked Jasper.

"Yes," replied Michael, "some for security and others in reserve, if required. This is a high priority so I need the best in several areas of expertise, including speed, agility, swordplay, watchfulness, stamina and stealth. And they need to be free thinkers too."

"Free thinkers?" Jasper asked.

"Able to make decisions on their own and act on them without authority," Michael explained.

"May I ask what needs the security detail?" Jasper enquired. "It may help with the selection process."

Michael looked around to see if anyone was watching them. He leaned forward and spoke quietly to Jasper. "I understand your need to know," Michael reached forward for a pad and pen as he was speaking, "so I will tell you... but you need to keep it to yourself. We do not need to tell anyone who is not involved. The reserves will be told when called upon and not before. Do you understand?"

As he spoke Michael wrote "Eden" on the pad. He showed this now to Jasper, who looked down and read it and quickly looked back up with a questioning look on his face.

"I will go myself!" he said to Michael, in the same hushed tones.

"No," replied Michael, "I cannot allow that. I need you here to direct the training and send reserves as required. That way, we will not attract too much suspicion from the other angels."

"But Captain, if there is a risk to..." Jasper pointed at the pad as he paused, "then the entire Host of Heaven will want to help."

"I know, and they would all go. But who would be left here?" Michael spoke, still in hushed tones.

Jasper looked at Michael, understanding creeping into his eyes. "Yes, I see your point," he said at normal volume.

"Good," Michael said, as he tore the page off the pad and screwed it up. "I will explain the details to the warriors in the Hall of the Lamb. I also need to include some messengers. Please allow a little time for me to go to the Hall of the Word and organise them. What I need you to do, my friend, is to send the first seven over to wait for their assignment from me. After I have told them, I will send a messenger over for the next seven, the reserves. I will need you to pick another seven, in case they are needed too. Every time I send for more, you need to pick the next seven so there will be no delays between each group, if possible. Do you understand?"

"Yes, my Captain," Jasper responded.

"Good. I also need a staging area or room. Can you give me any suggestions? It will need to be near the Hall of the Lamb and its purpose is not related to the other matter, as far as I know."

Jasper thought for a moment. "What about the Hall of the Saints? You would be halfway between everything. I would think the Saints would be happy to relocate to the Hall of the Chronicles or the Hall of Worship for a while. They hardly leave those Halls anyway."

"Thank you Jasper, that's a marvellous idea. I have Saint Peter outside, waiting for me. He can help me organise the Saints," said

Michael. "I must go now to see to the messengers I require. Can you send the first seven within the next fifteen minutes?"

"Absolutely!" replied Jasper, "I already have three in mind."

"Excellent," said Michael. "For the Glory of the Lord and His Kingdom!"

"For the Glory of the Lord and His Kingdom!" replied Jasper.

Michael turned and walked back out of the Hall. He found Saint Peter waiting exactly where he had left him.

FIFTEEN

Same Day
Palm Valley, West of Alice Springs

Jack Daniels stepped out of the four-wheel-drive tour bus and into the dry mid-day heat of Central Australia. He moved away from the tour group to look at the ghost gums and rock formations.

"We will set up camp just over there," a tour guide called out to everyone. "For those of you who can't wait to see the pre-historic palms, meet me by that ghost gum in ten minutes. Make sure you have on your hiking boots. The terrain is a bit difficult in a few spots. You will also need to bring water, as we will be gone for a couple of hours. Those not wishing to walk just yet can help set up the camp site."

Jack watched the guide step down from the door of the bus and go talk with the driver, who was opening the luggage doors on the side of the bus. Seeing the luggage reminded Jack to check his backpack. He had taken it on the bus with him because one of his water bottles had leaked earlier. He was glad to see that it hadn't done so again. He placed it back in the pack with the other two bottles.

"Eager to go on this walk, aren't you?"

Jack looked up and smiled at Tony and Isabel.

"Sure am. Are you coming too?" Jack asked as he closed the backpack.

"Just try and stop us!" Tony replied as Isabel nodded her agreement.

Jack's smile became wider. "I'm glad." He sobered up a little as he stood and added, "You know you didn't have to bring me with you."

"That's enough of that, Jack," Isabel interrupted him.

"Since you've been with us, you have been the spark that has lit the fire for God within me again. My ministry has been better than it has ever been and I can't thank you enough for that. I know you don't believe us but you are like family now, like the son we never had," Tony added. "It wouldn't have felt right if you weren't here."

"Besides, you had to keep an eye on me anyway," Jack added with a smile.

"I told you already Jack, that is not the case at all," Tony replied seriously. "Since that day you appeared outside the church and told me how you got there, you have not shown one sign of wanting to try to... you know."

"End it again?" Jack prompted.

"My counselling training tells me that is a great sign," Tony explained. "You have shown yourself to be very willing and eager to listen to what I have said and taught you. You have responded well to our sessions. On a personal note, even though you haven't missed a church service, you still haven't become a Christian. I know that the Lord is waiting to welcome you into His family, just as we are."

"You've always been straight with us Jack," Isabel said, with a twinkle in her eye. "We believe that God sent you to us for a reason."

"I can never thank you enough for what you have done already. I only hope that I can repay you someday," Jack said, trying to keep the tears out of his eyes. He wondered where this emotion was coming from lately. "As for God... well I am still not sure he would want someone like me," he said.

Isabel laid a hand on Jack's shoulder and looked into his eyes. "Do not doubt that, Jack. God loves and accepts everyone as they are."

Tony stepped closer so he could add to what Isabel had said. "He does, Jack, he really does," he said, "and one day you will see that for yourself."

"Okay," Jack said. "I guess I will just have to wait and see. Anyway, I am glad you found me and welcomed me into your lives. It's only been a short while but you are both like how I always thought family should be, even if my own family can't treat me that way."

The three of them just stood there for a moment in the uncomfortable silence that had fallen after Jack's comment on his family. Then Tony broke the silence.

"We better join the rest of them, if we are going too," he said, indicating the gathering group at the tree the guide mentioned previously.

Jack bent over and picked his pack up. The three of them walked over to the gum tree, joining the rest of the group who were going on the hike.

As they stood there waiting, Tony struck up a conversation with the American couple who had been sitting a few rows behind them on the bus. Jack was looking around and watching the guides to see if they were coming, he was really looking forward to this hike. Mick, the guide who spoke earlier, was nearby, checking his pack. In the distance, Jack heard something in the bus, over the CB. He couldn't hear it clearly from where he was so he turned to see what was going on. He saw the driver climb back in and speak on the radio for a moment. Jack watched him listen to the radio, reply and then put down the microphone.

"Hang on, Mick," the driver called out to the guide as he climbed out of the bus.

Mick looked up, turned and nodded to the driver. When he finished checking his pack, he got up and walked back towards the driver, who was walking towards them.

Jack was close enough that he overheard the driver tell the guide that there were going to be some more passengers joining them for the rest of the tour. They would be arriving in the morning, before the bus was scheduled to leave for the next stop. More passengers joining in the middle of a tour – this sounded odd to Jack.

Jack's musings were interrupted as the guide joined them again and announced it was time to go. As the guide started off towards the sight they were there to see, Jack shouldered his pack and followed, still pondering why someone would join a tour already in progress.

Sixteen

Later the Same Day
Cairns

The angel alighted silently on the roof of the building. Not seeing anyone, she checked the name again. She was in the right place. She looked around, trying to spot the contact she was told to meet here. The sun had set about ten minutes ago and the shadows were still deepening. Maybe the contact was hiding in case of trouble. She had felt that she needed to be as inconspicuous as possible, as if this was a secret meeting.

"Is anyone here?" she asked quietly, but got no response. She walked silently over to a corner of the building, trying to stay near the shadows but also visible enough for someone close by to see.

"I know you are here," she whispered to nobody in particular, "I can feel your eyes on me."

"Then you also know I will not reveal myself in case you are the enemy," a disembodied voice spoke quietly from somewhere nearby.

"Of course, forgive me. I should have identified myself," she said, "Glory to the living God."

"And to the risen Lamb," Kyle responded quietly. "You were followed," he warned her.

"I did not see anyone!" she exclaimed.

"Calm yourself, you will give me away," Kyle said in almost a whisper.

"Where are they then?" she asked.

"You will not see them, they are very clever. I know they are there because I have been watching. Watching long enough to know that there is a difference to what I am seeing. For example, a demon is trying to blend into the shadows under the water tower, on the roof of the third building over on the west side. The shadows there are now thicker than they were. Plus, I can sense its movement, as if it is unsure about waiting," Kyle explained quietly. "Do not try to spot it or it will know it has been seen. We will need to leave here very shortly. When I appear you will need to act like we haven't spoken yet, okay?"

"Yes. What is your plan?" she asked, still looking around as if she was alone still.

"Do you know the 'Jonah Bluff'?" Kyle asked.

"Yes, I am familiar with it," she acknowledged.

"Much the same, except no whale, and we are Jonah," Kyle explained. "We will need a replacement for the whale, any suggestions?"

"I would imagine something we can get lost in, like a crowd, maybe a bus or train," she suggested, still looking like she was waiting for someone.

"Excellent. Give me a few more minutes and I will join you," Kyle said.

"Okay but don't be too long. I can feel them trying to get closer now," she warned.

"I feel it too. See you shortly," Kyle said and then he sank through the roof and was gone.

Kyle dropped right down through the basement and took off east under the ground. Once he had gone a little way offshore, he turned upwards and came out of the water. Then he turned back to shore and the messenger waiting for him, moving slower now so that he could be seen.

Pretty soon, Kyle was landing on the roof again. He looked about as if he was looking for someone watching him.

Meanwhile, the female messenger had moved slightly into the shadows. She was still visible if you looked for her but not if you just glanced around.

Kyle hadn't seen her when he landed and felt a little apprehensive. "Glory to the living God," he said aloud.

"And to the risen Lamb," replied the messenger as she stepped out of the shadows.

A wave of relief washed over Kyle when he saw her. "Welcome, I am Kyle," he said to her.

"Thank you, I am Ruth," the messenger replied. "What is your message and who is it for?"

Kyle looked around again, acting as if he was trying to spot the enemy. This also helped him confirm that the demons he spotted earlier hadn't moved positions.

"Not here," he said, "I am afraid we may be seen or overheard and what I have to pass on is way too important."

"Where then?" asked Ruth, knowing that it was pointless to press for the information.

"Follow me," Kyle said, "you need to hear it from my charge and his friend."

"Okay, lead the way," Ruth replied.

Kyle looked around once more. He stopped at the water tank and stared. The demon there had to know he had been seen.

Ruth noticed he was looking at something. She followed his gaze to the water tank. "What is it?" she asked. "Can you see something?"

"Quick," Kyle said, "they know we are here!" and he took off, straight up and fast.

Ruth took off and followed Kyle. Kyle looked down to check Ruth was with him and then checked for the demons. Three had appeared and were giving chase. Kyle knew there were more so he changed direction suddenly, hoping to lure them out. They were now heading back east, the way he had come from. Ruth followed the movement with ease because she was expecting it. Four more demons appeared from directly below them, as if they had been waiting for them. The angels were moving too fast for the demons to cut them off and block them in. Kyle and Ruth got passed but with only metres to spare.

"There are at least ten more back there now!" Ruth was almost shouting to be heard over the rushing wind.

Kyle looked back in shock. He hadn't seen that many follow Ruth in. That made seventeen chasing them, which would make them harder to lose. "We need to go faster and try to lose some through speed," Kyle said to Ruth.

"Okay, lead the way, I'll keep up," Ruth replied.

Kyle sped up and Ruth followed as he dove down into the tangle of streets and buildings. They weaved in and out, around buildings and traffic, gradually leaving their pursuers behind.

Two of the demons separated from the rest. They headed above the buildings to try to observe the angels from up high. However, the angels were moving so fast that they found it difficult to follow them.

The angels disappeared into a building and lost the demons altogether.

Kyle and Ruth dove down after they entered the building. They kept going down through the building until they were below street level. Then they turned and angled back up so that they came up across the street, inside another building. They flew up the elevator shaft until they reached the elevator car. As they entered the ascending elevator, they checked for any other occupants. There was no one inside.

Kyle and Ruth entered the elevator and landed on the floor, just as it stopped. The doors opened to reveal a man and woman, holding hands, waiting for the elevator. A minor demon was waiting with them and eyed the angels suspiciously.

The couple entered the elevator and turned to face the doors. The demon followed but did not turn around. The man reached forward and pressed the button for the ground floor and stood back to wait. As the doors closed the man started to put their room's key card in his back pocket.

In the blink of an eye, Kyle drew his sword and flicked his wrist. The sword knocked the key card out of the man's hand and out through the closing doors.

This action caused several things to happen at once. The man dove for the door. The woman dove for the buttons. The demon started to draw his sword. Ruth, who had reached for her sword as soon as Kyle's cleared his sheath, had the blade of her sword resting across the demons neck, before it had its sword fully drawn. Kyle turned with his sword to face the demon. Kyle's sword was at right angles to Ruth's, resting just above the demons left shoulder.

The doors reopened and the man and woman rushed back out to find the key card.

"Go," Kyle said to the demon and nodded in the direction of the open doors.

The demon didn't need to be told twice. It edged away from the swords slowly. Once he was just beyond the point of Kyle's sword, he rushed out after his humans.

Kyle leaned forward and pushed the button to close the doors with the tip of his sword. As the doors closed, there was a flash of light from inside.

Several minutes passed as the elevator descended. When the doors opened at the ground floor, the two angels exited, now unrecognisable. They now appeared to be the two humans.

Kyle was wearing faded jeans and a denim shirt, while Ruth was wearing a pair of slacks and a silk, short-sleeved shirt. They were even holding hands, just as the couple had been when they entered the elevator.

Ruth and Kyle walked out into the street in their disguises. They walked around the humans they saw and looked for a taxi. Not seeing one, they walked to a taxi stand and talked while they waited. They did not mention anything that could have given them away. They could see the demons flying around, still trying to spot them within the building opposite.

"Do you know Daniel?" Kyle asked.

"I have never met him but know of him from his reputation," Ruth replied.

"Well, you will meet him soon. He is helping with the project now too."

"Really?" Ruth asked.

"Yes, it's quite amazing to be working with someone of his calibre but then, it also underlines how important this project is."

Kyle then spotted a taxi and waved it over. "Here we go," he said. When it stopped, he leaned down so his head was at the open window of the passenger side. He asked the driver if he could take them to the apartment building.

"Sure thing mate," replied the driver.

As soon as they were seated the driver pulled out and drove off. They made small talk with the driver as he drove them to the hotel.

When they arrived, Kyle pulled the exact amount of money out of his pocket and put it in the driver's hand.

Ruth watched Kyle, admiring the way he seemed to know what to do. How he covered even the littlest of details. She wouldn't have appeared to the cab driver. She would have suggested to him that he needed to drive there. This way they appeared human to everyone, demons especially.

Once Kyle was finished with the taxi, he turned and looked all around the sky and then at Ruth.

"What a beautiful night," he said.

"Yes," Ruth replied, continuing the ruse they were playing. She also had a quick look around at the skyline and then back at Kyle, "I think we may be in for a change though."

"It must be time to go in and prepare for the presentation then," Kyle said, as he took her hand again and led her into the hotel.

As they entered, they became invisible to the human eye once more. The desk clerk looked up as the door opened but was surprised to see no one there. He scratched his head, shrugged and went back to the crossword puzzle he had hidden under the desk. Kyle and Ruth headed straight to the elevators. Once one arrived, they rode it up to the correct floor. They exited the elevator and walked down the passage to the correct door. Ruth looked around as Kyle pretended to search for the key card in his pockets.

"We're clear," Ruth said quietly.

"Okay, after you then," Kyle said indicating the door.

Kyle watched as Ruth walked through the door and then he followed.

SEVENTEEN

Same Time
Somewhere in Central Australia

"That was very foolish," said the warden in his South African accent. "Are we not looking after you enough? You have food and drink, good medical care, a roof over your heads and comfortable beds to sleep in. Why do you want to run away?"

Henry did not answer. He was nearly asleep from the medication that he had been given for his very bad sunburn. The pain had to be quite intense as the sunburn covered nearly eighty per cent of his body.

Alan Bryan had been called to the medical centre to attend to the man, as he was one of the few that had first-aid training. While he was attending to the sunburnt runaway, the warden, Mr Kepler, had come to inspect the runaway's injuries.

"Besides, it is at least a four-day hike through the desert to the nearest town," Mr Kepler said, trying to taunt the injured man.

"I don't think he can hear you, sir," Alan said quietly. "He appears to have fallen asleep."

"How long will it be before he is well enough to go back to work?" Mr Kepler asked.

"A few days at least, sir, maybe a week," Alan replied.

"Maybe a week!" Mr Kepler exclaimed.

"I should monitor him overnight," Alan continued, "to make sure his fluid intake is good. He is very dehydrated and the first twenty-four hours are the most critical. He will need to have the bandages changed and inspected regularly, and he needs to be kept in a sterile environment until the scabbing stops. I am afraid the dust in the tunnels could cause infections if it got into the bandages and then in the wounds. If that happened, he would be unable to work until the infection cleared and that could take another week or even two."

"Two weeks?!?" Mr Kepler said in shock. He looked at the patient and the bandages covering his face, neck and other normally exposed areas. "He does look a mess and quite... thin. Make sure he is well fed too. I will need him at full strength when he returns to work. A week is better than two," he said begrudgingly. "What do you need so that you can stay up here too?" he asked next.

Alan was surprised. He didn't think Mr Kepler would let him stay with the patient. He thought for a moment and then answered, "I will need a few personal things from my... room. Some additional medical supplies, just in case there is an emergency with him in the middle of the night."

"Okay, tell Rasheed what you need," he said indicating one of the guards, "and he will collect it from the medical supply room. Bob will accompany you to your room to collect what you need and then escort you back here." Mr Kepler turned to Rasheed and Bob and explained to them what they needed to do.

Alan looked at the patient and then back to Mr Kepler, "How long was he gone, sir?"

Mr Kepler looked at Alan, surprised that he asked the question. He weighed up whether he should answer and, if he did answer, whether he should tell the truth. He decided on the truth: "About thirteen hours, if you include the time taken to load him into the helicopter and the ride back here. Rasheed and Bob will be guarding outside these doors so do not try to do anything stupid."

Alan looked Mr Kepler in the eye and said, "What makes you think I want to look like that this time tomorrow? This is the third patient I have treated for these symptoms since I arrived two weeks ago. It is obvious to me what would happen if I tried to get away too, so don't worry, I will not be trying to escape tonight."

Mr Kepler took in what Alan said and then turned to Rasheed and asked, "Do you think I should make the rest of them see him like this? Would that change their minds about trying the same thing?"

Alan hesitated. He thought about it for a moment. Then he decided to take the chance and he interjected, "Excuse me, sir, if I may..."

Mr Kepler turned to Alan and sized him up, "Go ahead."

"I don't think it would," Alan said. "They either don't think it would happen to them, or don't care if it does. I think differently because of the medical training I have had, even though it isn't much."

Mr Kepler looked at Alan and decided he was telling the truth. He started to leave but was stopped at the door when Alan asked another question.

"Can I ask a question about him, sir?" he said indicating the patient.

"Ask and I will decide if I should answer," Mr Kepler replied, still facing away from Alan.

"What is his name?" Alan asked. "He may respond better to me if I use his name."

Mr Kepler turned back to look at Alan and then looked at Rasheed and nodded. Rasheed lifted a clipboard he was holding and read it, "Henry," he said.

"Anything else you feel you need to know?" Mr Kepler asked Alan.

"When did he arrive here, sir?" Alan asked feeling a little bolder since his questions were getting answered.

"Is it important to know this?" Mr Kepler asked.

Alan looked down at the ground and said quietly, “No, sir,” afraid now that he had overstepped the mark.

“HA!” Mr Kepler barked out a short laugh. “I like you, medical man, you are not afraid to ask tough questions, questions you don’t really need to know answers to.” He turned to leave again and paused, “One warning though: you may ask the wrong question one day and then I will not like you anymore.” He paused again and then continued, “Two days he has been here now.” Then he left the room, his footsteps echoing as he went down the passage.

Alan looked down at Henry and then turned to Rasheed. He started to list off what he would need and Rasheed started to scribble it down.

Once the list was completed, Rasheed left to get what he could from the supply room. Alan turned once again to Henry and checked his vitals one more time.

“Well Henry,” he said, “I guess it is just you and me tonight. I will be right back with some of my things. Don’t go anywhere, will you.”

Alan and Bob left the room, with Bob locking it behind them. “Two days,” Alan thought, “and almost one of those was spent trying to get away. *He* didn’t waste any time.”

EIGHTEEN

Later the Same Day
Palm Valley, West of Alice Springs

The tourist group had just finished the dishes and clean-up from dinner. Most of the people were now making a hot chocolate, a cup of tea or a coffee and settling around one of the campfires. The group Jack, Tony and Isabel were with were discussing the hike and what they had seen.

Jack was sitting, listening intently and thinking about what he had learned, remembering back to the day he had jumped into that forest. He was trying to compare mentally between the two. The Valley of the Cycads was pretty impressive, especially the Red Cabbage Palm, which was estimated at over five thousand years old, virtually pre-historic. But none of it compared with what he had seen that fateful day. It wasn't just the plants themselves but also the feeling, the emotion, the serenity.

The valley today was peaceful, Jack thought; quiet, except for our presence and the other tourists. There were, of course, animal noises, frogs, insects and birds and none of the other intrusions like traffic. But it wasn't the same. There was no stirring inside... no soul-stirring emotions. Not like when he was in the other place.

Jack looked over at Tony and saw that he was talking to Isabel.

Tony noticed that Jack was looking his way and that he looked thoughtful.

"What is it Jack?" Tony asked.

Isabel turned to look at Jack too.

"What did you feel today, standing in that valley?" Jack asked.

Tony and Isabel looked back at Jack in a way that told him that they thought it was a strange question.

"Well?" Jack prompted them after giving them a moment to think about it.

"Calm, yet amazed and awestruck, all at the same time," Tony replied. "Why?" he asked.

"What about you Isabel?" Jack asked, turning to her and ignoring Tony's question for the moment.

"Much the same as Tony but I also felt at peace," Isabel replied to Jack.

"Why Jack?" Tony tried to ask again.

"Do you remember the day you found me and where I told you I had been?" Jack asked.

Suddenly it clicked for Tony and he knew it was time to explain what he thought to Jack. "You are trying to compare today's experience with the one you had that day, aren't you Jack?"

Isabel looked down at the fire and just listened, knowing what Tony was about to tell Jack. They had discussed it a few times themselves.

"Yes. I am and I'm unsure what to think. When I saw we were coming here, I thought that it would feel very similar."

"But it didn't," Tony stated.

"No." Jack couldn't hide the feeling of disappointment he felt about it.

"I think I know why that is. Do you want me to tell you Jack?"

Jack looked at the fire for a moment and then back at Tony, not quite sure if he did want to know. He was suddenly afraid of what he was going to find out.

"Do you remember me telling you that I had an idea about what you had seen and I would explain it to you one day?" Tony asked Jack.

"Yes, but you never did," Jack said, sounding curious now, "I always wondered why you didn't tell me then. I thought that you had forgotten that by now."

"I never forgot Jack. I was waiting for the right time."

"And you think it is now?"

"Yes. But are you ready to hear what I have to say?"

Jack thought about that for a moment. "I have waited for this moment and now I am not sure..."

There was such a long pause that Isabel turned and looked at Jack. Isabel reached out and put her hand on Jack's and let it rest there. Jack looked down at it and then up at Isabel.

"Whether you think you are ready or not, God is telling us that you are. Listen carefully to what Tony has to tell you. You have waited a long time to hear this and hear this you must," Isabel told Jack.

Isabel turned back to Tony. "Don't rush it, tell it exactly how you told me but don't get excited. You will lose your flow if you do."

Tony looked at Isabel and nodded, "Thank you, dear. I will do exactly that."

Isabel turned back to Jack and watched him closely as Tony began to speak.

"It was not hard for me to realise where you had come from, especially when you told me right from the start. Then as you told me the complete story, I knew my suspicions were correct. You described it to me as a forest and later to Isabel, too, but I think the correct term for the place that you had been is 'garden'.

"All my life I have been a Christian, I have studied the Bible and other theological works. When I was young, I longed to be visited by an angel or to hear God speak to me. As I got older, I started to just 'live'. You see it had all become routine. But the day you fell on my doorstep, that all changed. I knew that it was time to get really serious *about* God and *for* God. Your story, if it was true, inspired me and later, when we rang about your bags, I knew that what you had experienced was true. What you had told me was an answer to my own prayers.

"I had you share your story with select people. Because you were there, it was more believable than if I tried to repeat it for them myself. I spoke with all those people in private later. We discussed what we thought about it and we all agreed about who you saw, what you saw and where you were.

"The reason you did not feel the same today is, in part, because of where you were but mostly because of whom you were with."

Tony paused for dramatic effect, unintentional, of course, as it was something that he had picked up from speaking every week from the pulpit of the church. It was a way of seeing how many people were really listening to him.

Jack sat still, looking at the fire and listening to Tony. It was as if they were the only two people there.

"You were feeling completely calm, relaxed, as if you were somewhere you were meant to be. The 'garden' was not forbidding or dark but totally welcoming, peaceful and serene. Something like what the 'valley' was today but a lot more intense. The 'valley' was like a very poor reflection, like you could just see the outline and some details but not enough to really know what it was. Is that correct?" Tony asked.

Jack thought for a moment, "Spot on," he answered.

"Now you are wondering how I know this. That is the description given by many who have died and spent some time in Heaven, before coming back to tell about it. That is also the description given by those who have been visited by angels."

Jack looked up at Tony. "You think I was in Heaven with angels?"

"Not exactly... let me explain it a bit more. When you first were talking to me, you mentioned that you were a long way from Eden, meaning the town. Later, you told me that was the name of the town where you had been before the 'garden'. With such a story following your initial statement, it was easy to lean towards Eden being the name of the forest and to think that you had been in the Garden of Eden. What you said the angels told you matched up perfectly with the little we know of the story of 'the Lord's Garden'. I did pray about it after and that led me to do some reading about near-death experiences and angelic encounters. I was more convinced after that but I still wanted someone else's opinion. That's when I asked you to tell the other people. You know what they thought? They agreed with me. In fact, some even told me that before I had a chance to ask them about it.

"I believe that you landed in the Garden of Eden and you were speaking with angels. The demon that had been following you and harassing you was sent into the Abyss, where it belongs. That, above all else, is why I think you are cured and will not try to end it again. You had a religious experience, a specific one that is very hard to duplicate.

"So, yes, I think you were with angels but not in Heaven itself. In a place created by God, for His and others' enjoyment: the Garden of Eden."

Jack stared at Tony for what felt like the longest time.

Eventually, he looked to Isabel but before he could ask her, Isabel put a hand up to his mouth to keep him quiet.

"Before you say anything, before you ask if I agree, which I do, just think about it and let it sink in. Only *you* know how you felt. Close your eyes and picture it again; try to relive the moment."

Jack did as Isabel suggested. He looked as if he was praying or meditating to anyone else who looked at him, but Isabel and Tony knew he was back there, reliving it in his mind. Suddenly, his eyes snapped open with a look of amazement in them and his mouth slowly opened but no sound escaped.

Isabel smiled and Tony nodded his head.

Jack looked at them and spoke, slowly and quietly at first, but getting faster as he became more excited with each realisation. "It's true. I was in *the* Garden of Eden. If I was there, then it really exists. If that exists... then they had to be the angels who guard it. If they were angels... then there has to be a God! And if there is a God —"

"Then the story of Jesus is true," said Tony, finishing Jack's running thought where he had stopped.

"I need some time to think about this and... take in what I have just learnt. Will you excuse me?" Jack said, standing up. He turned and walked away before anyone could answer.

NINETEEN

"All done?" Saint Peter asked, as Michael came out of the Hall of the Archangels.

"Here, yes, but not overall, I still need to organise some messengers and the Saints," replied Michael.

"The Saints?" asked Saint Peter. "Anything I can help with?"

"Yes, my friend, but I will tell you more about it in a moment. How about we continue on with Creation as we walk to the Hall of the Word?"

"Will we fit it all in? We do not have far to go?" Saint Peter observed.

"I think so," said Michael. "Day two is recorded like this in the Bible..."

Then God said, "Let there be a horizon in the middle of the water in order to separate the water." So God made the horizon and separated the water above and below the horizon. And so it was. God named what was above the horizon "sky". There was evening, then morning — a second day.

Genesis 1:6-8

"We, the angels, experienced it much the same, but I will tell it to you in my own words." Michael paused for a moment as they walked, and then continued. "The Lord was standing at the edge of Heaven and looking down at the Earth, so we came and stood beside him and looked down too. The Lord then spoke again and He explained to us what He was creating as it was created. He said, 'There will be a separation in the midst of the waters so that it divides them from each other,' and the separation was evident to us. The firmament that took shape, in the separation, had a horizon below it and the firmament was between the waters. It was in place where the liquid water had met the airless water. The firmament is what the humans call the sky or atmosphere and it separated the waters below, the oceans, from the waters above, the vastness of space.

"The Lord told us what was above the horizon would be called the 'sky' and that some humans would call it 'Heaven' as it is above the Earth. He explained to us later that it was important for the place we lived to be called 'Heaven' also, so that when Man asked where we came from, he would find it easier to understand. I should mention that Man had not been created at this stage, so that gives you an idea how much later He explained that.

"When the Lord had finished explaining this to us, He looked back down to the Earth. So we looked back down too. We saw that all this had occurred during another day period on the Earth; the second day was finishing.

"I know it doesn't sound like much was done but when you consider what the 'separator' is and what it does, you will see that more was done and went into it than what I have described. What it is made up of, how it filters the light, how it stores and layers all the gases – every one of these separate 'tasks' required its own period of time to form. In other words, the process wasn't as quick as it sounds. We had noticed that the change had started to occur when we first looked down but it was not completed until the Lord told us that it was created."

As Michael finished the tale they arrived at the Hall of the Word. Saint Peter looked up and then at Michael.

"Once more, I shall wait for you while you do what you must," Saint Peter said.

"Thank you," Michael said, and continued into the building alone.

Saint Peter sat down on the steps and considered what Michael had said. He thought about what he knew of the Earth's atmosphere from what he had studied in the Hall of the Scribes.

Gases, layers, wind currents, dust particles to filter light and radiation... the list of what it did and contained was large. And it was all secured by a thin, outer layer, held in place by the speed of the rotation of the planet. It was kind of like a balloon, but spinning, he thought; lots and lots of wondrous things, little miracles, so to speak. He was no longer surprised that it took all day, and realised that Michael was right to say that it shouldn't be passed over as something quick, just because the Bible does not give the full description. The Bible only mentions the "Main Project" and not all the little ones that had to be done to complete it. Similar to building a house and not mentioning the walls, doors, roof, windows etc., he thought.

"Amazing," Saint Peter said aloud, "truly amazing."

TWENTY

As they moved down the passage to the humans, Kyle and Ruth changed their appearances back to normal. Amy looked up as they entered the living area.

"Glory to the living God," Kyle and Ruth said together.

"And to the risen Lamb!" Amy said in response, as she stood up to greet them. "Welcome, I am Amy," she said to Ruth.

"Thank you. I am Ruth, the messenger you requested."

"Are you the only one?" Amy asked Ruth.

"Yes, I am. Why? Did you ask for more?" Ruth asked.

"No, I just thought the Spirit would send more," said Amy, slightly disappointed. She turned to Kyle, "I am glad to see you have returned Kyle. Glen is getting nowhere with his friends in the search for the company names in tracing the location of the Central Australian compound. I am hoping you can help him by thinking of someone he hasn't tried yet. Pride is sulking somewhere in the kitchen. Would you please watch him while I go get Daniel off the roof?"

"No need," said Daniel, as he entered, "I am already here." He stopped and turned to Kyle and Ruth, "And to the risen Lamb!" he said, giving the response also.

A quick look of relief passed over the others' faces.

"I saw you arrive and came down straight away," Daniel continued. "Nice piece of subterfuge you used to get away from the enemy. Was that a variation of my 'Jonah Bluff'?"

"*Your* bluff?" Kyle said, looking bewildered at Daniel.

"Yes, my bluff. I was one of the angels that were assigned to Jonah. It was almost a complete disaster. I thought we were going to lose him. He was quite rebellious," Daniel explained. "That was until the demons had him thrown overboard. They would have drowned Jonah if I hadn't got that fish to swallow him. Luckily, we had the snakes distracted at the right moment and they never knew where he went."

Amy, Ruth and Kyle looked at Daniel with a renewed sense of respect. Not only was he brave but also clever and resourceful. None of them took what he had said as bragging; they knew he was only telling them so that they knew more about him and his abilities. Especially considering Kyle had just used that very same style of bluff.

Daniel continued, "It was the Spirit's guidance, of course, that influenced me to try that. Yes, I called it my bluff as I used it and it worked, but it was the Spirit that led me to try it."

"Praise the Lord!" Ruth said.

And they did. When they were finished, Kyle introduced Ruth to Daniel and then indicated the humans who were in the room too.

Ruth looked at the two of them. Glen was pacing and Kerri was watching him.

"So what is the situation? What is the message and who do I take it to?" Ruth asked.

"We think we have found one of The Seven and part of a plot, possibly against Eden," Daniel explained.

"It seems that at least another one of The Seven is involved too," said Kyle.

"That makes the situation all the worse. Have you heard of the companies called 'Nirvana' or 'Asheron'?" asked Amy.

Ruth looked from one to the next as they spoke, stopping at Amy with a look of concern on her face.

"Now I understand the secrecy of this meeting. 'Nirvana' is Sloth's kingdom, isn't it? And I think 'Asheron' is Envy's. If you suspect the two of them are working together, then that could mean more of them are involved, especially if they are after Eden!" Ruth said, processing the information as she went. "I assume, therefore, that the message is for the Captain. Quickly, tell me what else I need to know, for I sense there is more that you haven't told me yet."

Kyle turned to Amy and Daniel, "You start to tell her while I help Glen. Let me know when you need me to tell our part." With that, Kyle went over to where Glen was standing, looking out the window. Amy started to tell what she knew, starting with Kerri's friend Alan and his strange disappearance.

Twenty One

As Alan checked over Henry's vitals again, he started to reflect on what had happened to him. He checked the doors behind him and could see the silhouettes of Bob and Rasheed outside. Sitting down on a stool alongside Henry's bed, he started to tell Henry how he got there and what had happened since then, even though Henry was asleep.

"It's almost three weeks since I arrived here. I don't know *how* I got here or *where* here is exactly.

"I had been working on a construction site in North Queensland and sleeping in one of the supplied trailers. It was easier than travelling from Cairns every day. Plus, it was free. The company was paying for it, I think. Doesn't matter now I guess. I thought everything was going quite well. I had been telling my friend Kerri about it over the phone on the last night I was there. She asked me all sorts of strange questions about the rainforest and the ecological impact and so on, but I didn't think too much about it at the time. I went to bed when I hung up from her.

"But when I woke up... he shuddered at the memory. "I was locked in a room with no windows. The walls were dirt and the door was steel and cold. The air was different too, sort of dry and still, as if I was underground. It reminded me of Coober Pedy – a place in South Australia I stayed at once. The whole town is built into the side of hills or under the ground. It's an interesting place to visit.

"Anyway, I soon found out it was the case when they let me out of the room for 'orientation'. Everywhere they took me was underground, all the tunnels and even the rooms. The guards came and opened the door and indicated I should come out. I didn't argue as they were carrying guns. One had a rifle and another had what looked like a small machine gun. They took me to a communal dining area (a huge underground room) and told me that I was in group twelve. When asked if I had any special talents, e.g. medical, drilling etc., I told them that I had first-aid training. I soon ended up spending more time here than down in the tunnels digging. Better that way really.

"Most of the other inmates end up in here with breathing issues. Sometimes other injuries occur because of the tools that are being used and occasionally someone like you. Most escapees end up back here, sunburnt and dehydrated. Some don't recover, especially if they aren't picked up within forty-eight hours."

Alan stopped for a moment, thinking of the unfortunates who had lost their lives because of a failed escape attempt, wondering if they were better off now or if they should not have tried to escape in the first place.

"How many?" a low voice said, startling Alan.

Alan looked at Henry and saw two clear eyes looking back at him through the bandages on his face.

"I thought you were asleep. You should be resting you know," Alan said, as he got up and started to check Henry's vitals again.

"Can't sleep... too much... pain... all over," Henry replied slowly.

Alan looked at Henry, knowing it was the pain that was causing him to pause every few words. "Okay, but try not to talk too much, you might split open one of the sores on your face and that will hurt more. I can't give you any more painkillers yet as it's only been a few hours since I gave you the last dose."

"It's... not too bad," Henry lied. He paused for a moment. "Are you going... to... answer my... question?"

Gage looked at the door again to see if anyone was listening, but no one was. He had been surprised that they didn't keep one of the Guard demons inside with them. They must really be confident that no one was going to try to escape from in here.

Gage looked back down at his charge, Henry, and noticed that he was recovering quickly. He didn't understand why the other human, Alan, had wrapped more bandages around Henry than was necessary but he also felt the Spirit tell him not to question it. Alan had wrapped Henry with bandages in places where there was little to no sunburn. He had especially covered Henry around his face and head.

When he and Henry were captured they had moved to hurt Gage, but he had grabbed his sword back from the demons and told them that he would allow them to do what they must to Henry but he would defend himself if necessary. Grudgingly, they left him alone and, as he is linked to Henry, he was allowed to come back too. They had watched him like a hawk so he had done nothing to provoke them.

Once they arrived back here, they pushed him along after Henry, as if they were in control of where he went. Gage had silently laughed to himself at that. As if they could physically remove him from Henry's side.

The bond between a human and his guardian angel is stronger than anything they can throw at it. The only way that link would be broken is if the human renounced God, died or the angel suffered a significant injury that required he return to Heaven for healing. If they renounced God, the angel would be gradually pushed away until there was no link left at all because of the distance between the human and God. But if they ever came back to God, they would be assigned a new guardian straight away. The old guardian would have been reassigned by that time anyway.

"Sorry, what question was that?

"How many? Escapees..."

"I know of, and have treated, three, including you. I lost one of the other two to dehydration. The organs had been too badly damaged by the lack of liquid in his system and there is no medical equipment here to deal with that sort of condition. After all, this is not a hospital. The other one died too but I don't know why, probably from too much exposure to the sun."

"That's... too bad, Doc," Henry paused and took another breath before continuing, "Am I going to live?"

"Yes, and I am not a doctor. Only the most qualified person here. You were only gone thirteen hours so you are not too bad. You have shown good signs with your fluid intake. Your sunburn may leave some scarring, unless we can get you to a hospital but I know they will not allow it."

"That's okay. What do I call you then?"

"My name is Alan."

"Henry."

"How much did you hear?"

"From about 'Cairns'. I came... from there too."

"What does it look like up there?" Alan asked, knowing the answer would cause Henry more pain to speak it but noticing the pauses were getting further apart. "Above ground? Are we in the middle of the desert?"

"No, but it looks like we're... on the edge of one. There... are cliffs to the north... a yellowish haze to the... west and an endless heat... haze and saltbush... I think... to the east and south. I headed south, hoping... to see some sign of... the coast. Didn't get far... as you probably would guess... I wasn't expecting it to be so... hot out there. Sapped most... of my energy within... four hours."

"You would not have found the coast, even if you were still out there now," Alan said.

"Why not?" asked Henry.

"Well, just after you fell asleep earlier, Mr Kepler said it was at least a four-day hike through the desert to the nearest town."

Henry looked at Alan. He blinked before commenting. "I wish I knew that... beforehand."

Alan smiled, "Don't worry," he said, as he leaned in and looked around conspiringly, "we will be better prepared next time."

Gage checked the door again. He then looked back at Alan and Henry. Did he hear correctly? Was Alan planning to escape and wanted to take Henry too?

Gage went to Henry and spoke quietly in his ear, "find out what he is talking about".

Henry looked at Alan again, trying to work out if he had heard correctly. "Next time?" he asked, "We? What are you talking about?"

"Even though I have seen what it does to be out there too long, I have also seen what it does to those who stay here too long," Alan explained. "I travelled a fair bit when I was younger, almost a modern-day drover or swagman you might say. I know a little bit about desert survival and what equipment you need. Thankfully, my duties here as the medical man allow me access to some things that others can't get. I have been steadily storing things and requesting things that I can use. And I think that you need to come with me."

"Why me?" Henry asked, trying to raise himself up to look at Alan better.

"A number of reasons," Alan started and paused. "One, they will punish you by sending you back to work earlier than you should." Alan started to indicate the numbers with his fingers as he spoke. "Two, you need better medical treatment if you don't want scars from your sunburns. Three, you've already been out there once and know a bit more of what to expect and where to go. Four and most importantly," Alan smiled, "it will take two people to carry all the stuff I have been stashing."

Twenty Two

"That's what I am trying to tell you! They just disappeared," the demon warrior spoke. He was thin and black, little spikes stuck out of his spine and his posture indicated someone who was sure of themselves but also grovelling.

"HOW?" shouted Cain. "It was a simple plan, what could go wrong? Even Grom understood it." He started to pace the room, causing the rest of the assembly to move away, in case his rage spilled out. "You follow the messenger and intercept it when it meets with the guardians and humans. Then hold the humans, while we send our humans to get them."

"Yes, sir, that's what we tried to do."

Cain stopped and faced the speaker, "What is your title?" Cain asked.

"Anger, sir."

"Well, Anger, it would appear you were seen," Cain said.

"Impossible, sir, we stuck to the shadows. We followed the messenger and she didn't even know we were there," Anger said defiantly.

"Then the guardian was watching for you before you arrived," Cain said, looking for the only possible explanation.

"But he wasn't there when the messenger arrived. He came a little later, from the direction of the water," Anger explained.

"What happened after he arrived?" Cain asked.

"They spoke quietly and then looked at one of us and took off —"

"Which one of you?" Cain interrupted and looked around.

Anger looked around too and pointed at a larger, slimier looking demon. "It was Misdirection," he said.

Cain walked slowly over to Misdirection, placing his clawed hand on the hilt of his sword as he went. "You were seen?" he asked.

"N-n-no. Th-that is, I don't th-think so," Misdirection stammered, looking from the sword to Cain's face worriedly.

"Why not?" Cain asked. "If the enemy looked at you, what makes you think they didn't see you?"

"I-I don't know. He couldn't have seen me. I was in the deepest shadows."

"To hide your larger bulk?" Cain sneered.

"No," said Misdirection quickly. "It was what you told us to do," he blurted out, clearly afraid. "I picked the shadows of a water tower. They looked deeper and..."

Cain struck quickly. He had drawn his sword in the blink of an eye and cut Misdirection in two from the hip to the opposite shoulder.

Misdirection's large body, both parts, slowly dissolved and disappeared from sight.

Cain looked around at the squad he had sent on this mission. There were fourteen standing in front of him and all except Anger were shaking. Two of their number had been left behind to continue to search. "It appears to me that they had a plan in case we sprung that trap. After all, it is not the first time we have tried it."

Cain turned away and looked to the rest of his advisors and hangers-on. "Our opponent appears to be more cunning than usual, possibly my old *friend* Daniel is involved. It smells of his tricks." He paused for a moment in thought and then continued: "Bull, I need you to go and warn Grom. He should almost be at The Kings Resort. You may even beat him there if you hurry. Warn him and Commander Wraith that our opponent is cunning and may have some leads that tie them to us, particularly the humans we sent there recently. Wraith will know what to do."

"Yes, sir," Bull said, as he stood, unfurled his black leathery wings and took off through the roof.

Cain waited for Bull to leave. Once he had, he continued, "Deceit, take over the search. Use all the tricks you must." He then turned back to the squad, "Deceit is now your leader. You must do what he says. I don't think I need to tell you what will happen if you do not. Now go, all of you."

There was a chorus of, "Yes, sir", as they left through the roof. Deceit waited to see if there was more and Cain noticed this and smiled to himself. "Here is one who knows his place and anticipates my actions." To Deceit he said, "They are holed up somewhere and the messenger is now with them. She will leave soon, probably for Heaven, to pass on what she knows to the Captain. Do not let her reach Heaven. The information she carries could bring the Host of Heaven down on us and we do not want that yet. If possible try to catch her alive so we can find out what they know and where they are."

Deceit waited for more but there wasn't any more. "Yes, sir," he said and took off after his troops.

As before, Cain waited for his departure before continuing. "Do you all understand what we are up against?" he said to those remaining. "If our part of the operation is at risk, the whole operation is at risk," Cain stopped to allow that to sink in. "Pandora, prepare a group to meet Lucas and Mr Fisk. Make it appropriate for them. Go."

"It will be done," said Pandora, and left through the wall.

That only left five other demons with Cain. He looked at them. "You two go and check on the security," he pointed at Luthor and Goliath. "Bliss, go and check on the psychics and warn Seer of the new arrivals coming. And you, Highrise and Hammer, go back to the construction site and keep them working; we need this completed as soon as possible. Then we will not need to sneak around. Plus, I need to get to the next project before Grom messes that up too."

They rose and left, without a word, through the walls and roof, heading directly to their appointed tasks.

Cain paced for a moment, reflecting on what he knew so far. There was more than one angel present at the building site. What did they see? What did they photograph? Then they were expecting an ambush when the messenger arrived. How did they know?

"I'd better see what Tarvyn was doing outside. I will need to visit him and ask. As for the messenger, Porva will want to know about it," he thought, "but I am not ready to contact him yet. I will pass it on to Lucas when he arrives, along with the humans. He can deal with Porva. Then Porva will send me on to the main project. Any other issues will be out of my hands and in Lucas's. If I delay visiting Tarvyn too...," Cain smiled conspiringly.

Twenty Three

Kyle spoke quietly to Glen, "Tell me what has happened with your contacts, and repeat it out loud so that I may help you. You may have missed someone."

Glen didn't hear Kyle in a physical sense but more of a spiritual one. "Maybe I should run through it all again," he said to himself, feeling his frustrations lessen slightly.

Kerri had been watching Glen all afternoon and decided it was time to do something else. "Before you do," she said, "I was wondering something?"

Glen turned to Kerri, who was seated on the couch, "What?" he asked.

"Well, I am starting to feel a little anxious and tired. It's been a long day. I'd like to have a shower and lie down for a while. Maybe have a sleep. Does this hotel room have only one bed?" she asked, feeling a little awkward.

Glen felt embarrassed not having spoken about this earlier. "I'm sorry Kerri. I haven't been a very good host. There are two bedrooms, back up the passage and on the right. You will also pass the bathroom down the passage to the bedrooms. There are clean towels in there and a lock on the door. I have put my stuff in the first bedroom on the right but if you want it, just say so and I will move into the other one. Would you prefer me to show you around quickly?"

"It's okay, thanks. I'm sure I can find it on my own but if I get lost, I'll call out," Kerri said, as she stood up.

"Would you like me to order something from room service?" Glen asked.

"Not for me but you go ahead if you like. I will have a soak first and see how I feel after that," Kerri said over her shoulder, as she headed off down the passage.

The angels had watched the interaction. Amy suddenly felt a need to follow Kerri so she turned to Daniel, "Can you continue with Ruth until Glen is ready? I think Kerri needs me to guide her to 'The Path'. I only hope the Gideons have left their usual deposit in the rooms."

"You go if you feel the Spirit's urging. I can handle it until Kyle is ready," Daniel said, as Amy moved off after Kerri.

Kyle turned back to Glen, "Please Glen, who did you call and what have you said."

Once Kerri had disappeared from sight, Glen turned and looked at the phone as if trying to replay in his head what had happened earlier.

"Let's see," Glen said out loud, "I tried Jimmy at the office. He's trying to find out about the two companies and also to see if he can find Henry, if he has returned there. I called Pastor Williams to see if he knows the companies, since he once worked as a Corporate Counsellor. He told me it was with the transport industry and not big businesses, but he knows some people who may know. He will try them and call back if he uncovers anything. Phil, I mean Pastor Hunter, was travelling and therefore, not contactable for probably forty-eight hours. I left a message for him to call me back. I even called a few people from the prayer chain to get them praying for us and our missing friends."

"Excellent. What about Max?" Kyle suggested.

"I haven't tried my brother Max!" Glen said, surprised at himself for forgetting him. "I should call him too. He has some good contacts in the real estate and building industries." He suddenly felt a fresh surge of hope from the idea. Max wasn't really his brother but a really close friend with whom he had grown up. In fact, they were so close, that they called each other brother and each other's family was like their own. He walked over to the phone, picked it up and dialled.

Kyle, happy that he was able to suggest someone else, turned back to Ruth and Daniel but kept his ear out for what Glen was saying too. Daniel was just telling Ruth of his chase with the demons and meeting Kyle and Amy here.

Ruth stopped him and turned to Kyle. "When Daniel appeared, that is when you first saw Kerri and Amy?" she asked.

"Yes," Kyle said, as he approached them again. "We heard the camera, turned around and there they were."

"Camera?" Ruth and Daniel asked together.

TWENTY FOUR

Grom glided in and landed quietly beside what was to be the main entrance to the "New Kings Resort". There was not much to see as yet; the approvals for construction in the middle of the national park had taken a while. All those bribes, tricks and lies take time to organise and get to the right people. The Watarrka National Park is not as big as some, not considered as important as others nearby, but it is the only one with a patch of land called the 'Garden of Eden'. This alone was the reason for their presence here.

It was dark but Grom could see clearly with his demon eyes. He felt pretty important as he stood there looking at what was now part of his assignment. Lord Avarice had sent him here personally. The fact that it was because of a failure on the last assignment meant nothing, as this was a much more important assignment. "Prepare the way for the arrival of The Seven," he had said.

A guard appeared out of nowhere. "What do you want here little worm?" it asked Grom, interrupting his thoughts.

"Little worm? I could have your head for that!" he spat back, turning to look at who had spoken to him. He was staring up at a huge demon with a rather scary appearance. But then all guards look similar to this, he thought: long, clawed fingers; tall, imposing body; large wings partly unfurled to help add to the imposing height by adding width; muscular arms holding a large curved sword; and an ugly horned head. "I am Grom," he said out loud, "go tell your master that I have arrived."

"Who? I have not heard of you. You do not look important enough to have a name, little worm. I think you should come with me to the interrogation rooms until we have found out who you really are and what you are doing here," the guard said, as he poked Grom with his sword.

Grom glared at the guard and then at the point of the sword. "YOU WILL LOWER YOUR WEAPEN AND BOW YOUR HEAD TO ME!" Grom roared at the guard, his eyes starting to bulge out of his head as he continued. "LORD AVARICE HAS SENT ME HERE PERSONALLY AND IF YOU DO NOT TREAT ME CORRECTLY, I WILL HAVE YOUR HEAD ON A STICK, MOUNTED ON THIS VERY SPOT, AS A REMINDER TO ANYONE WHO QUESTIONS MY AUTHORITY!"

The shouts drew more attention and more guards started to appear. Grom was impressed with the security, as he had not seen a single one until now, not even the one harassing him. His shouts had caused the desired effect. His guard was now looking a little unsure of himself but hadn't lowered the sword. Grom knew the guard was committed to his duty and knew that if he wavered it could mean reassignment.

"You *will* lower your voice, before you attract the wrong kind of attention," another demon spoke as he approached.

"And who are you to advise me, Grom, what I should and shouldn't do?" Grom said a little bit more sedately.

"I am Security, the overseer of the guards here. Why are you here, Grom, and what right do you have to threaten my guard?"

"I am here by order of the lord Avarice. I am to start the preparations for his, and the rest of The Seven's, arrival. Surely you were notified of my coming?"

"We were advised of someone coming but we expected someone... bigger... and with a human host," Security replied. "What proof do you have of who you are? And why did you not use the required passwords?"

Grom looked at Security and all the guards present. "King George. My human will arrive tomorrow."

"Password accepted," Security replied.

"Well done, Security, and well done to this guard," Grom said. "Considering what my role here will involve, I wanted to make sure that your security was up to scratch. It is. In fact, it is even better than I expected. You have done well, Security. I did not spot even one of these guards until I started shouting. I would suggest though, that only one or two additional guards appear and not all of them."

Security started to chuckle. He then turned and whistled, it was a very high-pitched whistle. Suddenly, the air was filled with demon guards; there were at least a hundred. Grom's jaw dropped in amazement. Security whistled again and they disappeared, all except the one who had originally approached him.

"That was quite a risk you took, Grom. If it was me you spoke to like that, I would have removed your head before you finished shouting. In future, I suggest you use the password earlier and request a demonstration of security afterwards," Security commented.

Another guard appeared by Security's side. "Another one approaches, sir," he said to Security.

"Back into your positions," he said to the two guards as he grabbed Grom's shoulder. "Follow me Grom, very quickly and quietly. You will see again our security precautions but from the other side this time."

"Very well," said Grom, as if he was being given a choice.

Security led Grom quickly into an underground shelter, which had small openings to see out through. It reminded Grom of what the humans built in their last World War, a bunker of sorts. The holes were not visible from the outside, as they had been covered by scrub and underbrush.

As Grom watched, he saw a largish demon descend rather quickly and land a bit further to the left of where he had landed himself. It was puffing as if it had flown as quickly as it could to get here. It looked around as if surprised it hadn't seen any guards and then it said to itself quietly, "What good is knowing a password if there is no one to give it too." The still desert air carried the words clearly to them as if the demon had whispered it in their ears.

A guard appeared suddenly beside the demon. So suddenly, in fact, that the first demon, sensing a presence close by, reached for his sword and started to draw it, in case he was under attack. He stopped before it was fully drawn from its sheath. He recognised that the demon was a guard.

The guard had its sword drawn already and watched as the newcomer relaxed a little and put its own sword back in its sheath.

"Why are you here?" the guard asked.

"King George," the newcomer said. "I am here to see Grom and Commander Wraith at Cain's request. Has he arrived here yet?"

"Who are you?" the guard asked.

Inside the bunker, Security looked at Grom. "Shall we?" he asked.

Grom nodded, wondering why Cain had sent someone to him already.

Security and Grom rose up and went over to the newcomer.

"I am Bull," the newcomer said to the guard, not having noticed Security and Grom approaching him from behind.

"What is your message?" Security asked as they came near.

Bull turned and recognised Grom at once. "Sir," he said, "Is it safe to speak?" he asked indicating Security.

"Bull, this is Security," Grom said, as a way of introduction. He turned to Security, "Bull here was one of my best advisors at my previous assignment."

"Cain has sent me with a warning for you and Commander Wraith," Bull said, as Grom turned back to him.

Grom looked back at Security and said, "We should go inside now and speak with Commander Wraith."

TWENTY FIVE

As Michael walked through the Hall of the Word, he had to dodge many of the messengers as they ran or flew passed him on their way out of the hall. It appeared to be a little busier than usual to him but he didn't really know, he didn't visit here often. He trusted Gabriel to do what he had to do, without his interference with the messengers. After all, Gabriel had been head messenger for longer than Michael had been the Captain.

There was no sight of Gabriel in the Hall but Michael did spot Zagzagel instead. Michael made a beeline for Zagzagel.

"Welcome, my Captain!" Zagzagel greeted Michael.

"Thank you, Zagzagel. May I ask what brings you to the home of the messengers?" Michael asked, wondering if some other threat was occurring of which he hadn't heard of yet.

"I ran into Gabriel and he asked for my help. It seems he is on a task for the Lamb and needs to be away for a short period, so I agreed," replied Zagzagel.

"I am aware of his task and that is why I am here. I am organising help for him and will need to have three messengers assigned to me, to help in his task. I also ask for you to keep another one here, on standby, as a replacement." Michael didn't feel the need to explain any further. If Zagzagel was asked to help, he may already know what the task was. "If one of them is called away, I will send another back here for the replacement. As soon as the replacement is called, please pick another and place them on standby. They will need to be ready to go at a moment's notice."

"How soon would you like the first three? They can be ready immediately if you need," Zagzagel offered.

"Thank you," replied Michael, "please send them over to the Hall of the Lamb in ten minutes' time."

"It will be done, my Captain."

As Michael turned to go, Nicole walked in, having just returned from Earth where she had been delivering Michael's message to one of the Pillars herself.

"Captain," she said as she approached them, "I have just returned from the Russias, where I passed on your message to Anya, that area's Pillar. Her response was that there is no news on enemy activity. Their saints will be praying for the enemy to be uncovered, wherever they may be."

"Excellent. Thank you, Nicole," Michael said in response to her message.

"That is both good and bad news," Zagzagel spoke, "is it not, my Captain?"

"That is correct Zagzagel," replied Michael. "Good that there is nothing to report and bad, as it means we still do not know where the threat is."

Twenty Six

"Yes, camera. Why?" Kyle asked.

"We'll need that film developed," Daniel said.

"What do you think is in it?" Ruth asked.

"Amy said earlier that when I appeared, Glen was walking back to his car. He then stopped, looked up and reacted as if he could see something."

"I told him to," Kyle interrupted Daniel, "the Spirit compelled me to do it."

"Right, then Kerri started to take photos like crazy," Daniel continued, feeling that he was onto something, "and kept taking them until I was out of sight, with the demons following me."

"Which was when the guard yelled at her and we all ran, Kerri and Amy into the forest and Glen and I to the car. What are you thinking Daniel?" Kyle asked.

With a look in his eye and his voice sounding excited, "They could see..." Daniel replied quietly, almost as if he was thinking out loud, "they could see... something. What could they see? What was there? I was there. Me? They could see... me?" Turning to Kyle he said it again. "They could see me. *They* saw me."

"They *saw* you?" Kyle asked.

"Yes, they saw *me*!" he said louder, excitement now clearly in his voice.

Ruth and Kyle looked at each other both thinking Daniel had lost his mind.

Daniel looked from one to the other, seeing the looks on their faces. "Don't you see it? You said it yourself, Kyle — the Spirit compelled you to tell Glen to look and when I left with the demons following, it was clearer, as if a light was turned on where it had been dark before. For us, that is explainable. The demons' departure! But what about them? Why could they see clearly?" Daniel was really getting excited now. "They could see some of what we see! And if they did..." he quieted down some and then continued a lot more subdued, "then maybe the camera did too."

There was a silence between the angels as Ruth and Kyle took in what Daniel was implying. The only sound was Glen in the background, still talking on the phone.

Ruth looked sceptical. "You mean that they may have photos of you and the demons on the camera?"

Kyle was getting excited now too. "Yes, that's what the Lord wanted him to see. Glen prayed to be shown what the Lord wanted him to see, I told him to look and he saw it all! I don't think he understood it. I don't think Kerri did either because they haven't spoken of it."

Ruth still looked unconvinced. She asked, "Will it change what I need to pass on to the Captain?"

Daniel and Kyle looked at each other questioningly. Kyle looked over at Glen and Daniel turned back to Ruth, "Possibly," he said.

"It may mean we do not need to be so hidden from Glen and Kerri," Kyle said.

"And that they may get a better understanding of what is really at stake," Daniel added.

"Okay, I get it. But do we have time for me to wait for confirmation of this or do I need to get the rest of the information to the Captain as soon as possible?" Ruth asked.

Daniel and Kyle thought about that for a moment.

"Ruth's right," Kyle said to Daniel. "We can't wait that long. They can't go out yet and if the enemy knows of the camera, they may be waiting for the film to be dropped in for processing."

"Not if it's digital," Daniel said. "Does Glen carry a laptop with him?"

"Yes, but he wouldn't have the cables to connect it," Kyle replied.

"Maybe Kerri carries them with her?" Ruth suggested. "Who needs to continue telling me what happened? The other one can go check with Amy, while you continue the message for the Captain."

"How much between seeing Kerri and when you meet me on the roof is there to tell?" Daniel asked.

"Glen picked up Kerri, a little way into the forest and we drove here. We avoided the pursuit with Amy's help. When we arrived, I knew someone was coming to meet us so I went up to the roof to wait. Then you arrived," Kyle recounted.

"Well, I can continue from there to now, which isn't much either. You go and check with Amy. We *need* to see what is on the camera, as soon as we can!" he said, as if this was the most important thing in the world.

Twenty Seven

Troy awoke with a splitting headache and a pain in his chest. He opened his eyes and thought they were damaged, as he couldn't see very well. Then he realised it wasn't his eyes but that night had fallen. After a moment, his eyes adjusted and he could see as clear as if it was day again.

"What happened?" he thought as he looked around himself. When his eyes fell on the pile of motorbike parts alongside him, it all came back in a rush.

"Phillip!" he said as he jumped up, and almost collapsed again.

"I must be hurt worse than I thought," he said, as he tried to stand again. He looked around carefully and didn't see any sign of Phillip or Dmitri. "They wouldn't have left me here alone? So where are they?" he thought.

He took a closer look at the mess that once was a motorbike. He wondered why they left it in such a state or if maybe someone else came along and destroyed it. He searched through the wreckage, to see if he could find any evidence of where they may have gone. He found nothing.

He looked around the surrounding area where they were attacked. Still he found nothing.

"I need to check to see if maybe they did get away and left me, to draw away the enemy," he said to himself. He looked up the road the way they were travelling and then took off as fast as he could.

TWENTY EIGHT

Saint Peter looked up as Michael came out of the hall. "Where to now Captain?" he asked.

"The preparations are in progress," Michael replied. "Everyone will meet us in the Hall of the Lamb, where we will also catch up with Gabriel. We have ten minutes, why don't we continue with Creation while we wait. Let's go to the edge first and then we will head to the hall."

"Okay, Captain," said Saint Peter.

They started walking and Michael continued with his recollections.

Then God said, "Let the water under the sky come together in one area, and let the dry land appear." And so it was. God named the dry land "earth". The water which came together he named "sea". God saw that it was good. Then God said, "Let the earth produce vegetation: plants bearing seeds, each according to its own type, and fruit trees bearing fruit with seeds, each according to its own type." And so it was. The earth produced vegetation: plants bearing seeds, each according to its own type, and trees bearing fruit with seeds, each according to its own type. God saw that they were good. There was evening, then morning — a third day.

Genesis 1:9-13

"The morning had come, which told us a new day was dawning. We waited to see if the Lord would create more or if it was time to investigate this new world. The Lord stepped off the edge and went down to the Earth. He turned back to look at us and motioned for us to come down too, instead of watching from the edge of Heaven.

"When we were all with him again, He said, 'Let the waters meet in places and separate in others, and let the land dry up so that it is the separator.'

"The whole Earth shook and we saw the waters recede to leave dry land visible. There were still large groups of water, some of them in the middle of the land, but the biggest groups separated the lands from each other. Some were small separations and some were vast; and some of the blocks of land were small and some very big too. The Lord then told us that the largest of the groups of waters was called 'the sea' and he showed us how it was all connected. And we saw Him smile.

"Later, we learnt that most of this was a result of work that was started on the previous day. Gravity had been increasing still and the result was that the waters were compressed down towards the centre of the planet. This allowed the landmasses to appear.

"Then the Lord looked around at the Heavenly Host and I saw a knowing look come into His eyes. He indicated towards the other angels, so I looked over to see some of them turning to leave. It seems they had thought that the Lord was finished for the day and had turned to head back to Heaven.

"Then He spoke again, 'Let the lands have plants and herbs and trees. Let them bear seed and fruit with seeds, and each type of seed will then produce the same kind of plant or tree as to what it came from.'

"Yet again, as we watched, it occurred: the particular landmass we were closest to started to change colour. The ground went from brown to green and these things started to come up out of it. At first we were concerned, but one look at the Lord and His smile reassured us. This is what he wanted to happen.

"Pretty soon, there was a forest beneath us. Then we felt the wind. We knew of the air from the day before, but now it was moving of its own accord. As if it was alive. We could see how it caused the sea and the trees to wave.

"We could see the mangroves and water plants, as well as the larger trees inland, well away from the sea. As we watched, the sky over the sea changed slightly and what was blue, now had small white patches. As the patches moved inland, pushed by the wind, they became larger and changed colour to grey. Then water fell out of them and they disappeared. Somehow, the sea had touched them even though they were so far away. We realised later that the patches were clouds and the water was rain, and we learned what was the purpose of that wind/rain cycle, but at that moment... we were in awe of the beauty of it all.

"It was quite impressive to have seen all this occur and then, as we watched, to see them interact. Over time it became apparent how much they all interacted but, at first, it was just the fact that they touched each other and could move each other.

"Then the sky turned red and started to go dark; we didn't know what was happening. We wondered if more water was going to fall from the sky. I looked around and saw that the Host of Heaven was all around me. They were also looking around to try to see what was going to happen."

"Then David, who was on my right side, pointed at the horizon and I looked where he was indicating. I saw that the sun was disappearing over the horizon. I turned to the Lord to see his reaction. I was sure it was Satan's doing, for he had vowed vengeance and, as yet, he had not shown his face. But the Lord was smiling again, even more than before.

"I said to Him, 'My Lord God, creator of Earth and everything on it, what is happening? I feel worried because the light is going but your smile reassures me. Should I be afraid or happy too, Lord?'

"The Lord turned to me and smiled. 'Feel how you want to feel, Michael. You are experiencing something new to you and it has been so long since you have experienced anything new that it frightens you. Yes, it does, I can see it on your face. You do not need to be frightened. It is only the sun setting. You have seen it before, but not from this angle, only from Heaven's edge. You see, Michael, what I have done here today has finished and now, so does the day itself. The Earth has to have rest periods too, away from the light. However, during the night there will be other plants, plants that don't like the light and prefer the darkness. It is now time for them to grow and flourish.'

"We waited and we watched. Just as the Lord had told us, new plants started to grow. We had trouble seeing them at first, as it was totally dark now, but of course our eyes are different to that of men, so we could still see quite well. We have the glow of Heaven to aid our vision.

"As we watched, we could see it getting lighter again. We knew that the third day was over and the fourth about to begin."

They had reached the edge and stopped there, in the middle of Michael's recollections. Saint Peter had been an avid listener, not looking away from Michael the whole time. Now that Michael had stopped talking, they both looked down at the Earth and could see the oceans and seas and the foliage of the various continents.

Saint Peter looked at Michael's face and saw that he was still lost in his memory. He looked back at the Earth and thought about what he knew of life on it. For life to survive, it had to have specific requirements met. Food, water and air were the three most important, if not the only, real requirements for survival. All of this was created in one day and in such a way as to allow for its continual supply. These things, the plants, the waters and the air, all worked together to continue that cycle. The plants helped to refine the air into the required elements needed to breathe and to clean the water to remove the unclean or waste elements. In the case of the rivers and lakes, it made it clean to drink and in the case of the seas it was okay for the seaweed to live in. The air, in turn, spread the seeds and pollen required for the plants to multiply. The water helped to clean the air when it rained and it also helped the plants grow. If you took one away, the others would become polluted and life would, eventually, not be able to sustain itself.

Saint Peter could already see the steps that were being taken to prepare the world for the habitation of humans. Each day another step was taken.

TWENTY NINE

Amy had followed Kerri into the second bedroom, after they had confirmed which one Glen was using. Kerri sat down on the bed and began thinking about everything that had happened.

Amy looked at Kerri and felt a surge of excitement. The Spirit was here and was working in Kerri's heart. Amy went over to the cabinet alongside the bed and put her head inside it, looking in each drawer, from top to bottom and then the cabinet underneath.

Amy stood up with a smile on her face. Just like almost every hotel, motel or bed and breakfast in the world, the Gideon Society had left something in the cabinet.

Amy spoke to Kerri, "Look in the cabinet: you will find something in there to help explain what is happening to you."

Kerri looked at the bedside cabinet. She reached over and opened the top drawer. It was empty. Kerri opened the second drawer and found that it was also empty. Not knowing what she was expecting to find, she then opened the bottom cabinet. In it she found a book. Picking it up, she saw that it was a Bible. Remembering what Glen said earlier about God she opened it, not really knowing what to expect, but she knew that this book was about God.

As Kerri opened the front cover of the Bible, Amy slipped her sword out of its sheath and slipped the tip in between the pages, like a bookmark.

Kerri flipped the pages until it felt like the right place to stop.

Amy's sword was revealed where Kerri had stopped. Amy bent over putting the sword aside and covered the pages with her hands, so that only one verse was visible.

Kerri scanned the page, not knowing what she was looking for. As she did, one verse stood out to her:

If we say, "We have never sinned," we turn God into a liar and his Word is not in us.
1 John 1:10

Amy watched Kerri as she felt the Spirit start to teach Kerri what the verse meant to her.

Kerri stared at the verse trying to understand it. "It would appear that if anyone is to believe in God and what this book says, then they need to admit that they have sinned," she said out loud. "Well that's easy so far, I know that I am not perfect. Therefore God is not a liar. What else does it say," she said, as she started to flip the pages again.

Amy slipped her sword into the next spot and waited for Kerri to find it. Once she did, Amy put her hands over the page again to show Kerri the next verse in 'The Path'.

Kerri looked over the page and another verse seemed to leap off the page at her:

God does not play favourites.
Here's the reason: Whoever sins without having laws from God will still be condemned to destruction. And whoever has laws from God and sins will still be judged by them.
Romans 2:11-12

"So," Kerri said, thinking out loud again, "God treats everyone the same. It doesn't matter if we know God's laws or not. If we sin, we will be punished or 'condemned to destruction' as it says. That's a bit scary. But sounds like normal laws too. Whether you know the law or not, and you are caught breaking the law, you could be fined, imprisoned or both depending on the law you broke. Ignorance is no excuse they say.

"If God is real, then it doesn't matter if I believe or not, he will still punish me if I sin. He treats everyone the same. And from the first bit I read, I *have* sinned, otherwise God is a liar. So, according to this book then, I have sinned and will be punished. There must be more to it than that, otherwise why would people follow this. Who wants to be punished? I'm sure that I have heard that God is love, but it doesn't sound that way yet. What else is in here..." and she started to flick the pages again.

The payment for sin is death, but the gift that God freely gives is everlasting life found in Christ Jesus our Lord.
Romans 6:23

"Okay, that's pretty clear. Because I have sinned, I am condemned to Death. But through Jesus, I can get everlasting life."

Amy was getting close to tears — she was so happy that Kerri was doing this and paying attention to it. Amy prepared the next verse for Kerri to read.

"Here we go," Kerri said, continuing to vocalise her thoughts. "Something about God's love..."

God loved the world this way: He gave His only Son so that everyone who believes in Him will not die but will have eternal life.
John 3:16

"If we believe in God, we will not die. Let's see, I have sinned and will be punished, but if I believe in God, then I will not die but live forever, because of His Son. That's Jesus isn't it? That more or less repeats the last verse I read, but says that it is because of God's Love that Jesus came to us. What did Jesus do that is so important?

"My Christian friends once told me that Jesus died for my sins. Is that what they mean by 'gave His only Son'? Did God want Jesus to die?"

Kerri started to flick pages again and Amy prepared the way...

Not one person can have God's approval by following Moses' Teachings. Moses' Teachings show what sin is.

Now, the way to receive God's approval has been made plain in a way other than Moses' Teachings. Moses' Teachings and the Prophets tell us this. Everyone who believes has God's approval through faith in Jesus Christ.

There is no difference between people. Because all people have sinned, they have fallen short of God's glory.
Romans 3:20-23

Kerri continued to talk to herself, feeling that this was helping her understand what she was reading. "Moses' teachings? That's the Ten Commandments isn't it? Moses' showed us what sin is, through the commandments, but that isn't the way to gain God's approval, it is through something else. Moses and the Prophets tell us that something else is the way to God's approval. Back up the point by making it twice, okay, and I'm guessing they're referring to the eternal life thing as God's approval. But who are these Prophets? I guess that's not the important part here.

"God's approval can be gained by believing and having faith in Jesus. And again it mentions that it is 'all people'. So everyone is treated the same, therefore, everyone needs Jesus and God.

"What have I learned so far? I have sinned, I deserve punishment, that punishment is death, but because God gave his Son as a gift, and if I believe and have faith in Jesus, then I will receive his approval and eternal life.

"That all sounds pretty easy and straightforward. There must be more to it than that though..." Kerri said, as she kept looking.

Jesus, our Lord, was handed over to death because of our failures and was brought back to life so that we could receive God's approval.
Romans 4:25

"Okay, so that is what Jesus did and it was in the plan from the start, by the looks of it. Wow. God sent His Son to live, die and to take on our sins. Then he was brought back to life so that we could receive God's approval and then, eternal life.

"Having faith in Jesus must mean that we have to believe in His resurrection. And Glen believes all this. I'll have to think about it some more. Looks like there is more to it than I thought before," Kerri said, as she closed the Bible and put it on the bedside cabinet. She then got up and started to prepare to have a shower.

Amy was overflowing with joy at seeing Kerri come so far, so quickly. Was it enough though? Would this get her through the trials that were coming? Amy knew it would be tough.

Kyle walked in and saw Kerri and Amy and then the Bible. He knew instantly what was happening. He raised his eyebrows at Amy in a look that said, "Well, did she?"

"Not yet, but she is getting close," Amy said, unable to stop smiling.

"That's good; she is going to need Him very soon. If she doesn't have Him with her by then, she may not make it through..." Kyle didn't finish what he was saying because he didn't want to think of the alternative.

"I know, everyone does, but we can only lead them to the information. It is up to the Spirit to convict her from here. I will be ready when the Spirit indicates it is time for her to see more."

"It's all we can do," Kyle agreed. "However, I didn't come in here because of that. I need to ask you about the camera..."

Thirty

Deceit was looking at his gathered troops. He had a mixed bunch of demons — some big and muscular, others small and quick. They had gathered on the very rooftop they had staked out earlier.

"This is the place?" he asked.

"Yes," replied one of the demons.

"Hmmmm," Deceit said, thinking to himself. He looked again and quickly counted his numbers. He had twenty-three demons with him now. A few more had joined with him when he asked for volunteers before leaving the building site. "Okay, this is how we will start off. We need to do a quick search, to make sure we haven't missed anything. They may have been in this building all along and we just didn't know it. Go in pairs, through this building and the surrounding ones. If you spot anything suspicious, come back here and get me. Anger, I want you to stay here with me."

"Yes, sir," replied two demons.

Deceit looked around at these two demons, both called "Anger". Thousands of years we have been at this and we haven't come up with a better naming system than this, he said to himself. "Which of you spoke with Cain about Misdirection's failure?" he asked.

"I did," replied one of them.

"Okay, you," Deceit turned to him, "will stay here with me and," he paused for a moment, "I am changing your name to Rage. Do you accept this?"

Anger thought for a moment and then nodded as he spoke, "Yes, I accept my new name, 'Rage'."

"Good, you are now my second in command. And you," he turned to the other Anger, "will go with the others." He looked around at all of them again, "Do not try to engage them yourselves — there are at least three of them together now. Understand? Then go."

All except Rage did as Deceit told them and left to search the buildings.

Deceit turned to Rage and noticed that his appearance had already started to change: he was beginning to look fiercer and as if he was in a permanent bad mood, to match his new title, "When they get back, we will set up a surveillance grid to watch for a departing angel. It cannot fly without revealing itself to us and when it does, we will attack and bring it down out of the sky."

THIRTY ONE

Kyle quickly brought Amy up to speed on the camera and the possibility of what was on the film.

"It's a normal film model. Kerri can't afford a digital version yet," Amy told Kyle. "I think it is still in the car too."

"Okay. We will need to get it processed at the next town then. We think the enemy will have the photo labs watched if they think of it," Kyle explained. "We have practically told Ruth everything so she will be off to the Captain soon and then we need to make our plans for leaving too. I will tell the others about the camera and film. Can you get Kerri to have some rest? I think it may be a long day tomorrow and she will need it."

They both looked at Kerri who had just returned from her shower and was sitting down on the bed drying her hair and thinking about what she had read earlier.

"I will do what I can," Amy said.

Kyle nodded and left, he headed back down the passage and turned towards the living area, where everyone else was waiting. He told Ruth and Daniel about the camera and about Kerri's first steps down 'The Path'. They were all excited about Kerri, as they could feel she was going to face a test somewhere ahead and, without God, they did not know if she would pass it.

"Well, if that is it, I guess I should get going," Ruth said.

"Yes," Kyle replied, "but first I think you are going to need some help. I will organise some prayer cover for you."

Kyle went over to Glen who was still on the phone with Max.

"We need you to pray Glen, and ask Max to pray with you. We need help getting Ruth safely to Heaven and that her message gets to the Captain. Pray also for Kerri. She is starting to come to Jesus. Pray that your influence will have a positive effect on her life. And, of course, pray for your missing friends."

While Glen and Max were speaking on the phone, Max was also surfing the internet looking up the information that Glen was asking about.

"Max," Glen interrupted, "I feel the need to pray, right now. Will you pray with me?"

"Sure," Max said, "I'll just turn the monitor off and turn away from the computer or I might get distracted. Okay, I'm ready."

"Dear Heavenly Father," Glen started, "You, who are above all others, mighty and powerful, yet loving and merciful. We come before you now to ask for your help. Please send your angels to guide us and lead us on this mystery that is before us. May they light our way and lead us not into temptation or harm, if it is not necessary for our growth. Please protect us and fill us with your Holy Spirit, so that we can face the enemy with the confidence and the knowledge that you are with us. Guide your flock home safely so that the message they bring can be passed on to those who need to hear it."

Glen paused long enough to allow Max to take over. "Gracious Father, we lift up our friends in this time of need, Alan and Henry. We ask that you send your angels to guide us to them, that they will be found safe and sound. Wherever they are, Lord, I ask you to be with them and let them know that you are there. We also pray for Kerri, Lord. Open her eyes, Lord, and send your Spirit to teach her and lead her into Jesus's loving embrace. I ask you to be with Glen and keep him safe. Send your angels to guide him and protect him and bring him home safe again. May his time with Kerri help her to see you, Lord, through his actions and words." Max went silent to indicate to Glen that he was finished and for him to continue.

After a moment of silence, Glen continued, "Loving Father, we do not know what we are getting ourselves into but with you by our sides we know that we can face anything. Just as the Bible teaches us, 'We can do all things through Christ, our Lord.' Please, also be with and guide Max and the other people who are helping us. Guide them to the information that we require to help our missing friends and to thwart the plans of the evil one and his minions. Thank you, Lord, for the new friend I have made today; be with her and guide her and love her, Lord. Thank you also for the experiences of the day and what is to come tomorrow. Please forgive us for any wrong doings and sins we have committed. In Jesus's name,"

"Amen," they said in unison.

The angels could feel the Spirit moving and felt renewed and strengthened by the prayers they heard.

"I had forgotten how good that feels, to stand in the presence of a saint as he prays," Ruth said.

"Before you go, Ruth, I have one more piece of information for the Captain. Can you tell him that I feel the Spirit's urging to stay and help protect these humans?" Daniel asked. "I would have reported back myself, except for the urgings of the Spirit."

"I will do that for you," Ruth replied.

"It is almost time you left, Ruth. I can feel something building," Kyle said, as he walked over to the window and looked out.

Thirty Two

Michael looked up so suddenly that Saint Peter stepped back and almost fell over the edge.

"What is it?" Saint Peter asked.

"The Spirit is calling for action," Michael replied and turned around to look back at Heaven.

Saint Peter followed his gaze and caught his breath. Several of the Halls were alight from within. As they watched, the angels who were glorified started flying out of the Halls and headed in their direction. They were headed for the edge of Heaven."

"Quick, give me your hands," Michael said, reaching for Saint Peter and extending his wings behind him as if he were about to take flight. Saint Peter reached out and Michael took his hands in a firm grip. Michael's wings came down so fast that the two of them left the ground instantly. The action caused Michael to move backwards, away from the edge, and Saint Peter to be lifted off the ground and into the air with him. They hovered there, several metres from where they had been.

"Thank you, Captain," Saint Peter said, as Michael landed gently.

The angels also called their thanks as they flew passed them, rather than over them.

Saint Peter and Michael watched as dozens of angels flew passed them and over the edge, down to the Earth. Saint Peter noticed that it looked like they were all messengers.

****

The demons looked up as the angels approached. It looked to them like it was raining angels. All they could see was what appeared to be comets and their trail. Somehow, they knew what they were before they could see the angels themselves.

Deceit looked around at them. There must have been at least fifty. His rage was building at the sight of it. He knew that someone must have been praying somewhere — this would make it very hard to spot the messenger as it returned to Heaven. His plan was virtually in ruins. He looked around at his ranks of demons, only to see most of them trying to hide.

"Cowards!" Deceit shouted at them. "They are not attacking! None of them even have weapons drawn. Stand your ground! They will not interfere. You," he pointed at one of the smaller of his ranks, "go to Cain and tell him what is happening. Tell him I request more soldiers to bolster our ranks and help if we are attacked."

"Yes, sir," the demon replied and sped off.

"Look sir!" Rage called out from his post.

Deceit looked at Rage and saw where he was pointing. A trail of light was going up, not down. Deceit smiled. It appeared the enemy's plan had failed. This was the only angel going up.

"Look sir!" another demon called out from behind him.

****

"Look!" Kyle called out from the window. Daniel and Ruth hurried over and looked out too.

They could see the angels raining down on Cairns and then they felt it, the Spirit was telling them it was time.

"Farewell and good luck!" Ruth said to them. "For the glory of the Lord and His Kingdom!

"For the glory of the Lord and His Kingdom!" Daniel and Kyle replied in unison.

Then Ruth was gone, straight out the window and up, as bright as all the other angels they could see.

****

Deceit looked around quickly and saw the demon pointing at another rising trail of light. His smile was wiped from his face and he felt his anger returning. He looked around and saw more trails going up. There was no way to tell which ones had just come down and which of them was the one they were really looking for. For a moment he considered attacking every one of them so that none of them would reach Heaven. He quickly discarded that plan, as he knew that it would cost too many troops. After this, they would be needed to add to the security of the building site. It would have been a waste of time, for if even one angel had made it through, it would have been for nothing. Better to prepare the defences for the inevitable attack that would come to the site. Meantime, he could still try to find the humans.

"Rage," Deceit called his second in command over, "it would appear we need a new plan. Send half the bigger ones back for added security to the site. Send one with a message for Cain about what has happened and that we do not need the extra soldiers after all. Have him also tell the one I just sent to come back. We are going to need the smaller, faster demons here."

"At once, sir," Rage acknowledged, and left to carry out his tasks.

Deceit watched a bit longer and then turned away. He needed to make a new plan — a plan that couldn't fail, that couldn't be interfered with. Meanwhile, he would station the smaller demons at every bus and train station, the airport, the car-rental agencies, every road in and out of town and even the jetties and wharves. They would have to turn up somewhere, eventually.

There was a tap on Deceit's shoulder.

Deceit turned around to see one of his regiment with another demon. A demon who he had not seen before.

"What do you want?" he asked his soldier.

"Sir, Pride here claims to know where we need to go," the soldier replied.

Slowly, a sinister smile spread across Deceit's face. He had his new plan.

Thirty Three

Gabriel's plan was slowly taking shape. All he could do now was wait for the warriors he requested and then start to put it into motion. He looked over at David to see how he was going with his task.

He had bumped into David just after he had been to see Zagzagel. David had been reluctant to help, as the Captain had already given him a task to do. So Gabriel asked him to come when he had finished his task, and he had. David wasn't sure what he was doing, as Gabriel hadn't explained everything to him. All he knew was that Gabriel needed a list of all the places on Earth with Eden in the name. It was turning out to be a very long list. Every now and then Gabriel would come over, look at the list and cross off some of the Eden's. He had explained that some of the places couldn't be the one he was looking for as it was in the 'wrong' place. David didn't understand this but kept looking for more anyway.

It was at this moment that Michael and Saint Peter walked in talking together about a recent departure of messengers.

Gabriel and David stopped what they were doing and looked up.

"When did that happen?" David asked.

"Just now," Michael replied. "We had to get out of the way as we were standing at the edge when they started streaming out of the Halls."

"How many left?" Gabriel asked.

"I would say about fifty," Saint Peter replied.

"Are you ready Gabriel?" Michael asked, changing the subject.

"Yes and no. I am ready to start sending out the first lot but will need more time for the rest. I have come up with another thought on how to approach this and asked David for his help."

"We are looking for all places on Earth with Eden in it," David added.

"We are continually refining the list, as it is not a short one. It appears to me that man has as much interest in Eden now as he did just after The Fall," Gabriel commented.

"So what is your plan now?" Michael asked.

"Well, I thought we would —" Gabriel started to explain but was interrupted by the arrival of the first lot of warriors and three messengers. "Right on time," Gabriel said to the new arrivals.

"We are reporting as requested," said Nashira, one of the warriors.

"As are we," said Antares, one of the messengers. Michael noticed that Nicole was one of the other messengers with them.

"Very good," Michael said. "Gather round please, this won't take long."

Everyone formed a semi-circle facing Michael and Gabriel, including David and Saint Peter, both of whom didn't really know what was going on.

"You have been called here for a special mission," Michael started to explain. "No one else knows of it except the Holy Trinity and Jasper. It is at the request of the Lamb that Gabriel has requested you for this mission. You are to tell nobody what you are about to be told." Michael turned to Gabriel and indicated for him to continue.

"The Lamb has advised me that there is a very real threat to Eden. Satan and his generals, The Seven, have once again started to search for a way in and we need to cover them all and be prepared to defend them, if necessary."

"Why us?" asked Nashira. "I mean, isn't guarding Eden normally the job of the cherubim?"

"Yes, it is. However, they are restricted to guarding from within and not from the outside, apart from the two who guard the old Earth entrance. You, however, are able to do both – guard inside and out," Gabriel explained. "You are the first team. As such, you will be situated outside the primary Earth entrance, the one that has been hidden since The Fall of Man, along with the two cherubim that are currently stationed there. I don't think I need to explain to you how to be a guard or what is required as a Guard of Eden, do I?"

The warriors shook their heads. "That is not necessary. We understand what we are required to do," Nashira replied for all of them.

Michael took over at this point, to address the messengers, "Antares, you will go with the guards. If you come under attack or require more guards, then you will come back to this hall. Once here, you will find another team waiting to be activated. You will then return to your team in Eden."

Turning to face the messengers, Michael continued, "Nicole and Micah, you will be waiting here with the next team."

Michael faced Nicole and addressed her directly, "Nicole, if Antares comes, you will need to go to Jasper in the Hall of the Archangels and request the next team, he knows what to do. Then you will need to go to Zagzagel and request another messenger; he also knows what to do. After that, you will find me, to tell me that another team has been sent. You will then come back here and wait to see if the next team is activated. If they are, you start all over again."

Then facing Micah, Michael gave him his instructions: "Micah, you will go to Eden with the next team to do the same as Antares is doing with his team."

"If Antares is unable to return to Eden for some reason," Michael said, now addressing all the messengers, "Nicole will come to me first and then go to Eden in Antares's place. The same would apply for Micah and any other messenger if additional teams get called into action. If that occurs, then I will go to Jasper and Zagzagel instead. I will also organise a replacement for Nicole. Then the whole process can start again, with both Antares and Micah able to call on reinforcements, if required. This process could be repeated over and over again. I will be explaining what is happening to each new group." He paused to let the messengers take in what he had told them, "Do you each understand your duties?" He looked from one to the next and each nodded as he looked at them. "Very good," said Michael, and he turned back to Gabriel, "how does that sound to you?"

"Excellent," Gabriel replied and then he turned and spoke to them all. "We do not need to impress upon you the importance of this mission, as it is not the first time we have defended Eden from the enemy. However, they appear to be closer than ever to finding an alternative way into Eden. It doesn't appear to be the main entrance that they are searching for. As such, I do not expect you to actually be under threat, but the main entrance may be attacked as a diversionary tactic. So be vigilant. David and I will remain here, trying to discern where other entrances may be. I will then send teams to check them out and guard them if required."

There was a pause as everyone took in what was happening and what he or she was going to be doing.

Michael added. "In the between time, I will be organising the Hall of the Saints with Saint Peter's help, so it can be used as a staging area for another issue. If you can't find me here, look there. If we move this operation in there, I will advise you through another messenger."

"Is everyone clear on what they have to do?" Gabriel looked around and everyone nodded. "Good, let's get to it then. First team over here and I will tell you exactly where I want you," the seven warriors, Antares and David followed Gabriel over to a map.

"Nicole," Michael said turning to her, "go to Jasper and ask for the next seven warriors please?"

"Yes, my Captain," Nicole replied and headed back out the door.

"Micah, please wait over there, for the rest of your party to arrive," Michael said indicating a seat against a wall.

"Yes, Captain," Micah replied.

Almost as soon as the words were out of his mouth, the doors were flung open and Ruth hurried in and looked around. She spotted Michael and hurried over to him. "Thank the Lord that I have found you, Captain. I have an urgent message for you!"

THIRTY FOUR

Troy landed in front of the little church in Ceduna a little after midnight. The seven angels who called this church home immediately confronted him.

"What do you want here so late?" one asked.

"Who are you?" another asked.

"Why are you here?" asked another.

"Stop," Troy said forcefully, "I know this tactic and I do not have time for it. I will tell you whatever you want to know after you answer a question for me."

"Glory to the living God!" a heavyset angel said, as he put his hands on the shoulders of two of the others in front of him and they parted to let him through. He looked Troy over quickly noticing his appearance.

"And to the risen Lamb! I am Troy," he replied.

"I am Abram, be at peace brother. You appear to have been in battle, would you like your injuries attended first."

Troy relaxed slightly, "Thank you, Abram, but I am more concerned for my comrade and our charge. Have they arrived here yet?"

Abram's eyes closed slightly as he took in what Troy said. "I am sorry brother, but I do not know who you are talking about," he replied.

"What?"

Abram closed his eyes and bowed his head. "No one has arrived but nor is anyone expected to." He paused for a moment and opened his eyes to look at Troy again. "Judging from your appearance, you were attacked. And by your question, I assume you were separated from whomever you are searching for."

"Yes, *we* were attacked. During the fight, I was rendered unconscious. I awoke on my own, alongside what is left of his motorbike," Troy paused for a moment and then continued. "Let me get this straight, you are telling me not only that they have not arrived – not even Dmitri, his guardian? – but that you weren't expecting us?"

The other six angels were standing around them, listening to the conversation intently. They all looked at each other as Troy asked about Dmitri and then back at Abram.

"It was a trap?" Troy said to himself. "Why?"

There was an uneasy silence as the possibility of what had happened started to sink in.

"Are you also carrying a message?" one of the other angels asked.

Troy looked at the angel strangely, "No, I am not. Why do you ask such a question?"

The angel pointed at a piece of paper that was sticking out from behind Troy's belt, "You have some paper tucked in your belt. I thought messengers memorised what they passed on and did not rely on the written message unless absolutely necessary?"

"What are you talking..." Troy started to say, as he looked down at his belt, where the angel was pointing, "...about?" he finished absently. He removed the piece of paper. "I do not know where this came from," he said, as he looked up at Abram and the others. "I do not carry paper unless it is given to me."

"Quickly," Abram said, "read it out loud to all of us."

Troy unfolded it nervously and read it out as requested...

Messenger,

We have taken your charge and your companion. You do not need to know why. You will not see them again. Do not try to find them. It will be a waste of your time if you do. Instead you should prepare for visitors!

Satan's Thorns

Troy looked up at the others as he finished it. They could see that his hands were trembling. He noticed that they were all as shocked as he was by this news.

"May I?" Abram asked as he reached for the note.

Troy handed it over.

Abram read it over again.

They were all dumbfounded. Never had an angel been captured by the enemy. Not even in battle! When seriously injured, the angels become immaterial and are transported instantly to Heaven for healing. They are, therefore, unable to be taken hostage.

THIRTY FIVE

Michael listened intently to Ruth's message. He didn't interrupt her once. He waited until she finished before calling Saint Peter, Gabriel and David over to hear it too.

When Ruth finished it for the second time, Michael spoke, "Things are starting to become clearer, thank you, Ruth. Do you feel up to taking a message back?"

"Yes, my Captain," Ruth replied.

"I thank you again. I will need to confer with my council on this matter first. Then I will need you to carry my message back," Michael said. "Can you fetch the other archangels for me please? Then please go and have a quick rest. Be back here in about two hours."

"It will be done, Captain," Ruth turned and left.

Michael turned around to the others with him. "What is your response to this news?" he asked. "Gabriel?"

"It does appear that the two troubles are related. It should make it a bit easier for us. I think it is important that David and I finish finding the entry points and have them checked out as quickly as we can."

"Of course. David?"

"I agree with Gabriel. The locations mentioned should also be checked out and be the priority right now. We would need to get more saints praying, especially for these humans who are being chased and the ones that are missing. It might also be worth sending some extra protection for them."

"Good idea. Saint Peter?"

There was a pause as everyone turned to Saint Peter. He stood there looking a little bewildered. "Me? Why do you ask me?"

"You have been brought into this from above. It appears to me that the Spirit wants you to be involved," replied Michael.

"I hadn't thought of that. I'd better consider myself part of this too, shouldn't I?"

"Yes, you should, because you are," Gabriel said putting his hand on Saint Peter's shoulder. "I know that if the Spirit has called on you, then you are supposed to be involved."

"Thank you, Gabriel," Saint Peter said solemnly. "Well then, knowing what we already knew and adding what we do now, thanks to Ruth's message from Daniel's party, it appears to me that we need to help the humans first. At least send more protection, as David suggested. They could go with Ruth, when she delivers your reply. We also need to help find the missing people. However, I think that in helping Daniel's party, it will lead to this being resolved. From what they have found out, it would appear that Eden is under threat from multiple points at once.

So it is vitally important that we find those possible entrances and close them off, hide them better or add more protection. But possibly the most important one, I think, is that the Captain finishes his retelling of Creation to me. The Spirit has impressed that upon me, so I believe I will find something in your recollections that we can use. The sooner you finish it, the sooner we may know how to repel the attack that is coming. If two of the Seven are involved, then the others can't be far behind. They don't like working together but when it happens, it usually involves all of them."

There was a stunned silence. The three angels were regarding Saint Peter with disbelief.

"What?" Saint Peter asked, looking at how they were all regarding him.

Then a smile started spreading across Michael's face.

"What?" Saint Peter asked, again looking at Michael's smile.

"Once a leader, always a leader," Michael said

David and Gabriel gave a quick laugh.

"Seriously though," Michael continued, "you appear to have a better grasp on what is going on than you may realise. Well done to you, sir."

Saint Peter appeared to blush slightly at the high praise from Michael. "I am sorry if I took over from you, Captain," he apologised.

"You do not need to apologise to me. We are, as always, at your service. Your counsel is quite correct, especially about the Seven. They don't like to work together. If they are, then it can only be because they have been ordered to. I doubt the evil one would order only two to work together." Michael turned to each one in turn as he spoke: "David, continue with your search. Gabriel, send the first group to reinforce the current guards and then continue to sift out the possibilities with David. Do not send anyone else out to investigate yet. The second group of warriors will arrive shortly, as will the other archangels. Saint Peter and I are going to discuss more of Creation, so I do not want to be disturbed. Get them all to wait and when we are ready, I will inform and instruct everyone on what is going on. Then we can mesh out some solid plans."

Gabriel and David nodded and headed off to continue with what Michael had instructed them to do.

Michael looked around and pointed to a relatively quiet and unoccupied corner. "We shall continue over there," he said and then led Saint Peter away.

As Saint Peter followed, Michael started to tell of the fourth day...

Then God said, "Let there be lights in the sky to separate the day from the night. They will be signs and will mark religious festivals, days, and years. They will be lights in the sky to shine on the Earth." And so it was. God made the two bright lights: the larger light to rule the day and the smaller light to rule the night. He also made the stars. God put them in the sky to give light to the Earth, to dominate the day and the night, and to separate the light from the darkness. God saw that it was good. There was evening, then morning — a fourth day.

Genesis 1:14-19

"The fourth day was beginning and we were still between Earth and Heaven. The Lord had seen us struggling to see the plants in the dark. So he spoke with authority, in what I call His 'creating voice', for as you know He has authority over everything, including that which has not been created yet.

"He said, 'Let there be lights in the sky', and millions of little lights appeared, some easier to see than others; some were really bright but with the Sun rising they were becoming difficult to see. The Lord explained what he had done: 'These stars and other celestial bodies will be hard to see by day but will help to light the night. Their presence will help to indicate a separation between the day and night. They will be used for signs and to mark religious festivals. They will appear to move through the sky and will change position in relation to the viewpoint from the Earth. Over time, they will return to the same positions. This "movement" will help to measure time. We already have a measure for days but this will help with seasons and years. Especially this one', and one of the lights got bigger and bigger, as if it was coming towards us (which it was), and it continued to increase in size and brightness until it was where the Lord wanted it to be. Then the Earth's gravity caught it and the Moon settled into orbit. It has been there ever since.

"'This is the Moon,' He explained to us. "It will do many things, including influencing the water levels in different parts of the Earth, depending on which part it is over. Most importantly, it will provide light at night. It does not do this by itself but by reflecting light from the sun. But when the Earth is between them or the moon between the Sun and the Earth, it will cause a temporary darkness. This will be called an eclipse. Remember this, for it is something you can use later on, for many things are afraid of the dark.'

"As always, we hung on to the Lord's every word and we could see in our minds eye exactly what He was talking about, although we didn't understand it fully. The Lord then turned back to His Creations and admired them. We too watched the Earth, the waters and the land, the movement of the wind through the trees and grasses and now the sun, moon and stars also.

"All this fascinated us, as we had never before experienced anything like it. I do not know how long we had existed before all this, because nothing had changed. The only event I can really recall, before Creation, was the Battle for the Throne, which culminated in Lucifer being thrown out of Heaven. When I think of it now, it is like it was just mere moments after that when the Lord, the Lamb and the Spirit started to mould the Earth into what it became."

Saint Peter had listened very closely and was starting to see something in what Michael was telling him. Every now and then, Michael was recalling his feelings and observations on what he was reminded of, whilst telling the Creation story. Some parts stood out more than others.

Saint Peter was still amazed at the Lord's authority, as Michael put it, and at His knowledge. Saint Peter had watched human inventors create things; often, they managed them only after many efforts or by complete accident. But the Lord knew exactly what He wanted to create: He vocalised it first and then it came into being, exactly as He said it would be.

Saint Peter looked around and noticed that some of the others had started to arrive. He looked at Michael and saw that he had noticed too.

Michael looked at Saint Peter, "It is time we got some plans laid."

Thirty Six

Abram immediately took control of the situation. He turned to his companions and started the search and rescue operation. "Chris and Tracey, go wake up the church congregation and send them and their angels here. Rundle, wake the Pastor and get him praying; then bring him here too. Clare, you are the fastest of us: find out from Troy where exactly this all happened and go and inspect it. Report back your findings as quick as possible. Bruce, wake the police chief and get him over to the Pastor's place. Stan, you will help me prepare a message for the Captain." He stopped and looked at all of them. "If our suspicions are correct, then time is of the essence. Be as quick as you can. For the glory of the Lord and His Kingdom!"

"For the glory of the Lord and His Kingdom," they all replied in unison. Then they were gone. Streaks of light were all that was visible as they headed out to call the rest of their companions and their saints to action.

Clare quickly found out where the attack occurred and took off so fast that she was only a flash of light and then a quickly diminishing glow on the horizon.

Stan and Abram watched and waited until Clare was on her way before they approached Troy once again. "If an angel has been taken, as well as the minister, then we need to let the Captain know. Is there anything else you can tell us before we send the message?" Abram asked.

Troy looked at them both. "Maybe I'd better tell you everything that happened from when we were approached in Port Lincoln."

"Before you start, would you like your injuries attended to as you tell your tale?" Stan offered.

"Yes, thank you," Troy replied, and then he went on to tell of the reason they were in Port Lincoln — how Phillip was guest speaking at a church, how they were approached afterwards and asked to come to Ceduna to speak also, then the uneventful departure, the bikers and the demons, the sudden fight and waking up on the side of the road. He had to pause occasionally, because of the healing process. He repeated some details when they asked him to.

"Was there anything significant about the man who approached you?" Abram asked.

"Not that I can remember," Troy replied.

"What about the bikers' appearances?" Abram questioned. "Were there any similar markings or logos on their clothes?"

Troy thought for a moment before replying. "Now that you mention it, they did have a of logo on the backs of their jackets. A picture of some sort of demon, with something stuck in its back and the words...

the same as the signature on the note, Satan's Thorns!" He looked at Abram intently and then went on, "The picture would indicate that they consider themselves a pain in the demon's back."

"I agree," Abram said.

"If the demon is supposed to be Satan, as their name says, then they would be saying they are against him," Stan suggested.

"Then why would they have demons with them?" Troy asked.

"Good question," Abram said. "Maybe they are a splinter cell of demons who don't want to answer to Satan anymore."

"Another one?" Stan asked. "I thought the Host of Heaven had crushed the last one?"

"It did," Abram replied, "but it doesn't mean the demons don't want to try again. Without true leadership or organisation, they will always fail. But they do continually try to find a way to take over from him."

Troy tuned out for a moment, going over the day's events in his head again. Was there anything he had missed and hadn't mentioned?

Meanwhile, Abram started giving Stan instructions. They stopped talking when they saw Troy sink to the ground, lost in thought.

"Troy?" Abram asked.

Troy looked up at the two angels.

"Are you alright? You look lost?" Stan asked.

"I... I don't know," Troy replied.

"I think he's in shock," Abram said to Stan.

"I will go alert the Captain," Stan said.

"Yes, go with all haste Stan," Abram replied. "For the glory of the Lord and His Kingdom."

"For the glory of the Lord and His Kingdom," Stan repeated and then took off, straight up.

Abram and Troy watched him disappear from sight. Once he had gone, Abram looked back at Troy. "You will need to rest, before everyone else arrives. Then you will need to tell of your day's experiences again. Come, I know of just the place for you to rest," Abram helped Troy to his feet and led him into the church.

THIRTY SEVEN

Saint Peter watched as Michael called everyone present together, including Ruth, who had returned after resting. He thought to himself, what a collection – the seven archangels, known as the Council of the Host, together with seven warriors, three messengers and one of the "Chosen Twelve".

Michael looked around at his audience and, when he felt sure they had all waited long enough, he started. "Thank you for coming at such short notice. This is going to be a bit unusual for a Council meeting because of the presence of warriors, messengers and Saint Peter. You are all here because all of you need to know what is happening. I am sure, when the time is right, more of the Host of Heaven will become involved. Right now, I need to ask you all to keep what I am about to tell you to yourselves."

The warriors looked stunned, as did Uriel, the archangel who oversees all of the warriors.

"Before you ask Uriel, it is that important," Michael said before Uriel could question him. "If any of you do not think you can handle such an important secret, you need to say so right now." This was directed at the warriors more than anyone else, but still Raphael raised his hand. "No, that doesn't apply to you to Raphael."

Raphael, known for his humour, lowered his hand smiling, while some around him chuckled. Noticing that Michael, who normally appreciated some humour, didn't even smile, told most of them how serious the situation really was. "Forgive me, Captain, but you did not smile. Is it that serious a threat? If so, why do we have such a small force assembled to combat it?" Raphael asked.

"Please, forgive my lack of humour Raphael, but there is so much going on, that I cannot allow myself to be humoured right now," Michael explained. "The threat we are facing is coming from many fronts at once and is mostly directed at the Lord's Garden. It may involve all of the Seven."

Several of the warriors and Raphael inhaled in shock.

"Eden is under threat? From the Seven?" Raphael asked.

"Yes, but not a direct attack this time," Michael continued, "It appears our old adversaries think there are hidden entrances they can get through. Allow me to explain what we have learned so far."

Michael went on to give details about Gabriel's warning from the Lamb and Daniel's diversion, the missing humans and their worried friends, the information that Kerri had uncovered about Eden-related sites all over the globe and the two companies involved. He then explained what the warriors were to do, what Micah and Nicole were there for, that Ruth was there because she had brought the message from Daniel and would be taking one back and how Saint Peter had come to him seeking the Creation story, as he felt the Spirit leading him to do so, and that by now they were up to the fifth day.

"Now you know as much as we do. David, Gabriel, Saint Peter and I have devised some simple plans but I feel that we need to all agree on them or make other plans, before we carry anything out. If you have any ideas, please share them now — and that includes you non-council members too. You are playing a role here and I would rather you suggest something now, rather than say, 'We should have...' later." Michael looked around at each of them.

The council turned to Zagzagel: known as the wisest of them, it usually falls to him to start everyone's thoughts going. As usual, he already had some suggestions. "The obvious thing would be to send some help back with Ruth, to the humans. Get them out of harm's way while searching for the missing friends. Meanwhile, continue looking for possible entry points and, when we find them, shut them or guard them. You, Captain, must finish your chat with Saint Peter. Is that what you came up with so far?"

"Yes, Zagzagel, it is," Michael replied. "Do you have anything else?"

"As a matter of fact I do," Zagzagel answered. "The rest of us can help in particular areas. I will help with the entry points, by being the inspector, with this team of warriors and Micah. That will allow Gabriel to concentrate on the list with David. I will get someone else to pick messengers for your squads. Uriel can start preparing the warriors for the upcoming battles. Raphael can go with Ruth. He can prepare some guardians to go with them, to support and help Daniel, Kyle, Amy and the humans in any way they can. Israfel can get the Pillar's saints praying. As for the Seven, we will have to wait until we know more before we decide how to handle them this time."

There was silence for a moment as they all pondered on what Zagzagel had suggested.

Nathaniel, one of the warriors, cleared his throat and then spoke, "I have a suggestion."

"Yes, Nathaniel," Michael said as he turned to him, "go ahead."

"Well, instead of waiting for the enemy to find a way in and then defend it, why don't we lead them into believing that a particular entry is real, when it isn't, and have a trap waiting on the other side?"

Uriel smiled a big grin, proud of this warrior Nathaniel for coming up with such a bold plan.

"Opinions?" Michael asked.

"Great idea, if we can pull off the fake defence first without taking too many injuries," Raphael said.

"Too risky," Israfel said, "there would be a high risk of danger to the humans when we spring it."

"That would depend on where it was," David said. Then he turned and walked over to the desk he had been using and started to consult the lists he had already made. He had a gleam of excitement in his eyes as he walked away. Gabriel noticed his excitement so he followed him.

Saint Peter simply said, "I like it. It is fairly plain and simple."

"So do I," added Uriel and Zagzagel in unison.

Gabriel and David were muttering to each other, while flipping pages at the desk. Everyone else kept glancing over at them, wondering what they had in mind.

"Appears they have something to add, or perhaps somewhere?" Zagzagel said, indicating Gabriel and David.

"Yes, we have," Gabriel said, as they started to walk back.

"The perfect place," David added, "and I would bet they are nearby, if not already on top of it." He handed a map to Michael with the location circled.

"Yes. How could they not try there? And judging from the location, it might shed some light on other avenues too," Michael said, handing the map around. "Zagzagel's suggestions are on the money but need rearranging with Nathaniel's suggestion too. Zagzagel, you keep up your appearance in the Hall of the Word or else the rest of the angels might start asking questions. That will also allow you to send out some more messengers to the Pillars, for more prayer cover. Israfel, you are the stealthiest of us, so you go with the warriors and Micah to check out this location. Assess the area, search for the presence of our enemy and the risk to any humans that are around. Micah, please report back what you find. Uriel, prepare a line of defence as Zagzagel suggested and the trap as Nathaniel suggested. Have a backup plan, in case they have a large battalion already in place. Raphael, go with Ruth. The rest of us will continue to do what we were already doing. Do we agree on this course of action?"

There was a chorus of, "yes", "okay" and "sounds fine to me".

"If no one has any questions, then let's get to it," Michael said.

"I have one!" a voice called from the doorway.

THIRTY EIGHT

"First, I checked with the admin team of demons and humans to see when Mr Fisk and his party would arrive. From there I went to see Security and Luthor at the Security Centre. I asked them to provide enough guards to accompany me to Cairns Airport to greet our new overseer, to ensure the safety of his arrival and journey from the airport to the building site," Pandora explained to Cain.

"From there, I went on to the partially completed hotel and spoke with Concierge, the demon in charge of it, and made sure that a suitable room was being prepared for Mr Fisk. They couldn't use the same room as George, as he hasn't left yet and there would not be enough time to make the necessary changes.

"Overall, I am happy with all the arrangements and everything will be ready when they arrive," Pandora said, as she finished her report.

"Very good, Pandora," Cain said, "and what about you, Bliss? How did you go with Seer?" Cain asked.

"Well," Bliss replied, "the psychicsss are prepared for the new arrivalsss and the departure of Grom'sss group went well. George will be leaving in the morning and a sssmall group of demonsss are ready to accompany himmm."

"Good. The sooner we see the rear of them the better. What about the Security of the building site?"

Luthor stepped forward as he spoke, "The site is secure and well prepared for the arrival tomorrow. One legion will accompany Pandora. We have plenty more staying behind. We will not be compromised during their time away."

As Luthor stepped back Goliath stepped forward. "The rest of the den is also secure. Most of the guards have taken up hidden posts so as not to give away our numbers again. They have all been advised that if more of the enemy appear, they are not to reveal themselves but to leave it to those that are already visible."

"Good thinking Goliath, well done to both of you," Cain said. "Hammer, what have you to report?"

Hammer stood, "The construction is continuing on pace. The humans have noticed the new disappearance. A rumour was started about him leaking some information to the press in regards to the secret designs. They appear scared and will keep their mouths shut for now."

"For now?" Cain asked.

"Yes, sir," Hammer answered. "When they start to get restless again we can beat up the dissident and if that doesn't work we can make him disappear too."

"We will face that when it happens and see what is necessary. As long as they continue working, that is all that matters to me right now. What about Highrise? Where is he?" Cain asked Hammer.

"He will be here shortly. He wanted to check on the temple's progress first," Hammer explained.

"Very well, I will speak with him —" Cain started to speak but was interrupted by the entrance of Deceit and Pride. Cain and his advisors all reached for their swords, not sure why anyone would interrupt an advisory session without following protocol.

"I must speak with you at once, Master Cain," Deceit burst out as he entered.

The advisors all looked to Cain for their next move. Cain nodded at Bliss, who was closest to the door. Bliss smiled as he drew his sword slowly, to let Deceit see what was in store for him.

"Wait, Master, I have someone who you should meet and I could not allow any delays," Deceit said, watching Bliss advance towards him.

Cain waited for a moment before responding. "Hold!" was all he said and Bliss stopped moving forward and waited, not taking his eyes off Deceit. "You know the correct protocol for a meeting. Why would you ignore it? Tell me quickly or Bliss will remove your head."

"Master, this is Pride," Deceit said, indicating the small demon hiding behind him. "He belongs to one of the humans and can take us to where they are hiding!"

There was silence while Cain just stood there.

"Pride," Cain spoke finally, "if that is your name, why are you here?"

"Master," Pride said, stepping around Deceit and bowing slightly, looking anxiously at the curved blade that Bliss was holding and then at Cain. "I am Pride, assigned to the Human who likes to take photos of your building site. I can take you to her and tell you where she has hidden the information that she has stolen from you."

"What sort of information?" Cain asked testing Pride.

"Maps from all over the world, with writing on them about building sites. The word 'Eden' appears several times," Pride answered.

"Bliss, sheath your sword," Cain instructed and Bliss turned and nodded while lowering his sword. "Deceit, you will follow proper protocol next time or Bliss will complete what he started today. You can wait outside for now. I will call you back when you are required."

Deceit backed out of the room, looking relieved, and ran straight into Highrise as he was entering.

"Finally," Cain said to Highrise, who was staring daggers at Deceit.

"Sorry, master, there was a small complication with —" Highrise started to voice his excuse.

"Later," Cain interrupted, "we have a special guest here who is about to help us. Now Pride, how many of the enemy is there and do you know their names and purpose?

Thirty Nine

The angels and archangels all turned towards the voice, only to see a messenger standing just inside the door.

"Who will organise the search-and-rescue party?" the messenger asked.

They all turned and looked at Michael. Michael looked at Gabriel questioningly.

Gabriel turned back to the messenger and asked, "What do we need a search-and-rescue party for Stan?" Gabriel knows the names of all his messengers so no one was surprised when he called the newcomer by name. "Who has gone missing?"

"Sorry for interrupting your meeting, but something has transpired that, to my knowledge, has never happened before," Stan explained, while he walked closer. "A guardian has disappeared, along with his charge, a minister of God."

There was a stunned silence at these words. A few of the archangels looked sceptically at Stan.

Michael spoke up, "You are correct that this has never happened before. What makes you so sure that it has now?"

"Forgive me. I am coming at this from the reverse end. I have a message from Abram and Troy, in Ceduna, for the Captain."

"Very well," said Michael, "what is the message?"

"The messenger, Troy, along with the guardian, Dmitri, were attacked by demons while escorting their charge, Pastor Hunter of Melbourne, to Ceduna, where they thought he was due to preach. The Pastor was also attacked. A motorbike gang and their demonic counterparts were the perpetrators. We know this because Troy was left unconscious on the side of the road. When he awoke, Pastor Hunter and Dmitri were not with him. A little while later, he found a message from the demons that had attacked them. We think it was a trap," Stan paused, allowing the full impact of what he had just said to be absorbed.

"A trap?" Michael asked.

"Yes, he was not expected in Ceduna, contrary to what they thought," replied Stan.

"We have faced traps before. What bothers me is the message from the attackers. Can we see it?" Raphael asked.

"Yes. I have it here and would like you to see it for yourselves," he said, holding out a piece of paper for them all to see.

Michael indicated to Israfel to take it and pass it over, as he was closest.

Israfel reached over and took the note from Stan. It was then passed from angel to angel until Michael had it in his hand. Michael read it to himself and then looked up at Stan. "Has this all been verified?" he asked.

"Abram has set that in motion. First, he sent someone to check the site of the attack and then he called for the town's saints to gather and pray. Then he questioned Troy about the details again and sent me here to pass on what we learnt. He also suggested that I get you to test the paper, the ink etc., for he knows that there are better resources here," Stan explained.

The other angels watched Michael as he looked back down at the note in his hand. There was a murmur between the warriors. Uriel looked at them with a piercing glare. Settling on one of the females he said, "You will be silent and respectful, Kella."

"Sorry Uriel," Kella said, "I did not mean to be rude or intrusive. Forgive me, Captain."

"That's okay, Kella. Uriel, do not be too upset. I am sure Kella is saying what the rest of you are thinking: '*What does it say*?' Let me put your minds at rest. I shall read it out."

The room was silent as Michael read out the note. He gave them a moment to think on it before asking what was on everyone's mind. "Do we know this demon group? It isn't familiar to me."

No one answered. As Michael looked around, they each shook their head or said, "No, Captain."

"If I may, Captain," Stan said, stepping forward, "we, that is Abram and those of us who read the note earlier, believe it may be a splinter group. Troy described the emblem of the Biker gang as being the usual emblem of the Devil but with thorns sticking into the body, as if they were stabbing it."

"With that sort of emblem, it is hard to argue against that conclusion," Zagzagel said, "but it could be a ruse."

"We can't take anything for granted," Michael said. "I will take this note to the Lord for testing and then, if it is authentic, seek His guidance. Does anyone have anything to add before I go to the Throne?"

"It could be connected," Nicole ventured.

"To the Eden threat?" Gabriel asked.

"Yes," Nicole continued, "the comment about visitors strikes me as too coincidental. Maybe they have some thought of using Dmitri as a key or gateway?"

"Or maybe they are warning us in order to distract us from searching for them?" Saint Peter argued.

"We can debate what it means endlessly. I don't believe in coincidence so I guess they either know of the Eden threat or are part of it. Either way, it is additional evidence that we must move with our plans straight away. I will go now to the Throne and speak with the Lord. Stan, you must stay here and await my return. What you have just heard about Eden you must keep to yourself, for now. All will be revealed when the time is right."

"As you wish, Captain," Stan replied.

"The rest of you," Michael continued, "go on with your missions and if I require your assistance further, I will let you know. Thank you all for your counsel."

Those that were not already standing, stood up. They all raised their weapons with their right hands and said in unison, "For the Glory of the Lord and His Kingdom!" Then they went their separate ways to carry out the missions they had each been given.

"What shall I do until your return?" Saint Peter asked Michael.

"You will come with me so we can continue our part too," Michael replied. Michael looked around to see that everyone was on their way and then turned and walked towards the door, with Saint Peter alongside him.

FORTY

One of an angel's favourite parts of the day is dawn: something about watching the sunrise gives them a fresh surge of hope for the new day. For Daniel, it was a constant reminder of the day the Lord made the Earth and the first sunrise that he saw. Admittedly, that was from Heaven's edge but it is pretty much the same from on Earth.

Through all the thousands of years, the sunrise itself has never changed. The place from which he has seen it has, many times, and this was his first time in Cairns.

Daniel was standing on the balcony of the hotel, looking straight at the sun, rising over the water and what little there was of the city between him and the beach. He wasn't afraid of being seen or challenged, as he was not the only angel outside, watching the dawn. From where he stood, he only had to look around to see other angels doing the same thing. Some on other balconies, some on rooftops and some were just hovering in the air, wherever they could see it. His companions were also watching: Kyle had gone up to the roof and Amy had gone over the road, to a neighbouring rooftop.

Daniel had the sudden urge to sing, so he did, in a clear tenor voice. He sang what some call a child's song but he felt it was fitting for right now.

"This is the day,
This is the day that the Lord has made,
That the Lord has made,
We will rejoice,
We will rejoice and be glad in it,
And be glad in it.
This is the day that the Lord has made,
We will rejoice and be glad in it!
This is the day,
This is the day that the Lord has made."

He took a deep breath of the clear morning air and smiled. He felt refreshed, renewed and, more importantly, ready to tackle whatever was to come his way.

Then he realised he hadn't seen Pride since before Ruth had arrived.

Forty One

Michael and Saint Peter left the Hall of the Lamb and headed for the throne. Saint Peter could see the tension in Michael and recognised it for what it was. Michael was worried about the humans.

"We'd better talk while we are walking," Michael said to Saint Peter.

"We won't finish in time, will we?" Saint Peter asked.

"Probably not, but we can continue on the way back," Michael responded. "Day Five started like this..."

Then God said, "Let the water swarm with swimming creatures, and let birds fly through the sky over the Earth." So God created the large sea creatures, every type of creature that swims around in the water and every type of flying bird. God saw that they were good. God blessed them and said, "Be fertile, increase in number, fill the sea, and let there be many birds on the Earth." There was evening, then morning — a fifth day.

Genesis 1:20-23

"The sun had started to rise around us, indicating a new day was beginning. I wondered what the Lord would do next or if this was it. I could not have imagined the things the Lord had created so far let alone conceive of what would come next.

"I think the Lord knew what I had been thinking because, at that moment, He turned and looked at me, smiling. Then He looked back at the Earth, spread his arms wide and spoke, 'Let the waters be filled with creatures, swimming and breathing within the water.'

"Hearing what the Lord had said, we all looked at the waters and moved closer so we could see what was happening more clearly. Where the water had been quite clear and we could see the water plants on the bottom before, now we couldn't. What we saw instead was really amazing. I know some of the other angels felt the same, by the looks on their faces. I could see streaks of light flashing passed, under the water. Sometimes it was a large patch and it would turn and move as one, other times, there were but a few creatures. In some places, I only saw one.

"I looked at the Lord, seeking His permission. Knowing what I intended to do, His smile grew wider and He simply nodded once, almost imperceptible. I smiled back at Him, turned and dove down into the water."

"I looked around and saw my first fish. Then I realised that what I had seen earlier was many silver-scaled fish and the light reflecting back off them as they moved through the sunlit areas. Now that I was closer to them and in the water too, I could see hundreds of types of fish. As I looked closer I started to see other types of sea creatures: there were crabs, squid, an octopus and others too.

"I was amazed by the variety of colours and shapes that I could see. I started to swim and follow one and then another, and I noticed I was heading out to sea, to deeper water. I saw larger and larger creatures – seals first, then dolphins and sharks, and then I saw some whales.

"I was in awe and I could have followed these creatures for days. I suddenly felt there was to be more, so I surfaced and returned to the Lord's side."

At that moment, they arrived at The Throne. Michael indicated to one of the angels on the door that they needed to see the Lord. The angel instructed them to wait and went in to see if they could go in.

While they waited, Saint Peter said, "Why don't you continue while we wait?"

So Michael continued with the tale.

"The Lord looked at me, as if looking for my reaction to what I had seen. I smiled. My eyes must have been reflecting my amazement and my excitement because He smiled and nodded in understanding.

"He then held up His right hand with his forefinger extended. I knew He was telling me to wait. Then He indicated the sky with a wave of his left arm, as if revealing something else to me. I looked where He indicated and didn't see anything.

"I turned back to Him in confusion and just as I was about to ask about it, He spoke again: 'Let the skies be filled with birds and flying creatures, all over the Earth.' And it was so.

"I looked again and coming up out of the trees were birds of all sorts of shapes and colours. I looked back at the Lord again and He was smiling, almost laughing in pleasure. I remember that I laughed and it was a nice feeling. I understood what had happened: the Lord had indicated to me that there was more to come, for there was an empty place in the world. Then He filled it.

"When I looked back at Him I noticed He was watching me again. He gestured for me to go with the birds as I had with the fish. So I flew off to follow these amazing things. I could list to you all the types I saw but it would take quite a while. Again, I thought they were all the same, but with different colours, and then I noticed the differences in shape, size, length of leg and the shapes of the bills. I followed one and then another. A thought suddenly hit me – another change had occurred. The fish had been silent but the birds... what a noise! Some were very loud and others quiet; it was something I hadn't picked up on at first, I don't know why, but it indicated something to me. These birds were talking to each other. I wondered if the fish did it too. I couldn't hear it from in the sky so I dove back into the water and listened.

"There was noise there too, but it was hard to tell where it came from. I tried to follow it and eventually found the whales again. Then I heard other types of noises, like clicks and pops, and I followed these too. I found that it was coming from crabs and other bottom dwellers.

"I resurfaced and flew off to the trees again. I sat in the branches, listening to the birds and picking up the different types of noises. There were squawks, whistles and hoots. I watched one as it made the noises and then at another as it reacted to the noise. They were definitely communicating with each other but I had no idea exactly what they were saying.

"I went back to the Lord. 'Lord, I have been studying the new creatures, the fish and the birds, and I noticed that they have their own languages. Different birds speak differently and different fish speak differently. Can they understand each other? Or are they just different pitches, like the difference between my voice and yours?'

"He simply smiled at me knowingly and said one thing, 'Why don't you find out and come back and tell me?' I was a little taken aback by this answer. I had so many questions to ask Him about these fish and birds and He knew it too. I asked another question, one that I hadn't originally intended to ask but, because of His question, I felt that I had too.

"'Would I not be doing something against you, Lord, by studying these creatures for myself?'

"'Why would I tell you to do something that is against me? I am not testing you, I have no need to, I know you,' the Lord replied.

"'Forgive me, Lord, I did not mean to question your intentions. However, these are your creatures and you know all about them. Wouldn't it be easier for you to tell me?' I asked.

"'Michael,' the Lord said to me, 'with life there are no easy answers. I can tell you all you want to know and you will walk away thinking you understand. Then you will think of more questions and come back again. There is nothing wrong with that, except you are learning from someone else and not experiencing it yourself. I can tell you what a Kookaburra sounds like but unless you hear it yourself, you will not know how that is different from a Hyena. If you go and study these things for yourself, then what you learn will stay with you for eternity because it is your experience. When you pass on the knowledge, gained by the experience, you can say that you have first-hand knowledge of it, rather than second-hand knowledge. Besides, I am not creating these things to then just tell you about them – I could do that without creating them. Rather, these creations are for all of us to enjoy. You see, life can be unpredictable.

Even though I have created them using a set of guidelines, I have also allowed them some freedom of thought and action. Therefore, I cannot tell you everything about them; they could behave differently if their situation changes.'

"'I see,' I replied. 'So, it is your will that we learn about these things first hand.'

"'Yes, Michael, it is,' replied the Lord.

"'One more question Lord... what is a hyena?'

"The Lord laughed to himself and then said to me, 'That is part of the next step. It hasn't been created yet but will be soon. Then, you will understand why I picked that animal to compare with a kookaburra.'

"'I look forward to doing just that, Lord,' I said. I was about to turn and go back to study these new creatures, when the Lord turned and raised His arms above His head.'

"I watched as the Earth grew silent. All the creatures stopped and silently turned to face the Lord. They appeared to bow their heads to Him.

"Once all were acknowledging Him, He spoke to them, giving His blessing and instruction. This is what He said, "Be fertile and reproduce, until you fill the waters and the air." Then He lowered His arms and the creatures went back to what they had been doing. The Lord was smiling and nodding His head – it was almost unnoticeable, but I was close enough to see it.

"I looked back to the Earth and could see that many birds had spent a great deal of the day preparing a place to rest and they were now returning from a last-minute feed. The sun was setting and they were settling in for the night.

"As it got dark other birds started to come out – the nocturnal birds. There were owls, snipes, rails, soras, nighthawks and loons, to name a few. Again, there was something to see and study. It didn't stop just because it was dark. Rather than everything disappearing and sleeping, some creatures acted just the opposite: they slept during the day and were active at night. Admittedly, there were not as many, but still, there was activity throughout all of the day cycle.

"It has made it very interesting to study these creatures. Even though I was never restricted to only daylight or only darkness, I still haven't got all the creatures covered. I have seen them all, even the ones yet to be discovered by man. Even so, I do not have all the time in the world to study every single one. But whenever I feel like a little break, I leave for a while and go study another creature. I try to see some new trait or behaviour, something that I have not seen before. My favourite-"

At that moment, the angel returned from the Lord. Interrupting Michael, he said, “He will see you now, Captain. Saint Peter is to accompany you.”

Forty Two

Glen looked up as Kerri came into the living area. "Good morning. Have a good sleep?" he asked her.

"Not too bad, thanks," Kerri replied. "Bed was a little uncomfortable, but I always find that when I sleep in a different bed than my own. How about you?"

"Much the same, once I went to bed. Hungry?"

"Starving! What's for breakfast?" Kerri asked.

"I thought we'd order room service, when you were ready," Glen replied. "How's that sound?"

"Great. Where's the menu?"

"Over by the phone."

Kerri turned to go and noticed Glen had some books on the table in front of him. "What are you doing?" she asked, as she went over to the phone and picked up the menu.

"My morning devotion," Glen answered.

"Your morning what?" Kerri asked, a little perplexed.

"Devotion. Some call it a Bible Study but it's really more than that," Glen explained.

"Oh, in what way?" Kerri asked thinking of her little excursion through the Bible the night before.

"You really want to know?" Glen asked.

Kerri thought for a moment as she sat down, opposite Glen. "Yes, I do."

"Okay. Well, the difference is rather simple," Glen explained. "A Bible Study is exactly what it sounds like. You read a passage or passages of the Bible, you contemplate what you have read and think about what it means to you. A 'Devotion', is more personal. As the name suggests, you are actually devoting time to spend with God, while reading and studying His Word and trying to see how that is relevant to your own life. Quite often people use a specific guidebook to direct their thoughts, there are several available and they can cover specific topics or books of the Bible. One of the more common is *Every Day With Jesus*. That's the one I prefer. I have used a few others and sometimes I use more than one — one for morning and one for night. That way I can focus my thoughts and actions on God through the day and when I sleep too."

Kerri just sat there, taking in what Glen had just said. She wondered if she should tell him about last night. She had some questions and wanted to ask Glen about them, but something was holding her back. She could sense her walls of pride were gradually being chipped away.

"I see the difference, thanks for explaining it. Sorry I interrupted you. I'll let you finish," Kerri said, as she stood up again.

"You don't need to leave, I was nearly finished anyway," Glen said, as Kerri went to walk away. "Why don't you pick out what you want for breakfast and I'll order it when I have finished here?"

"You don't need me to leave?"

"No," Glen said smiling, "I just need a little quiet to pray and then I'm done."

Kerri smiled too and sat back down. "Okay," she said and then lifted the menu back up and began to look over it. After reading the first line, she looked over the top to see what Glen was doing. He had his eyes closed and his head bowed slightly. Kerri couldn't help but stare at Glen: his openness surprised her but also encouraged her. She felt she should tell him about last night and ask the burning questions she had now.

When Glen finished, he looked up and caught Kerri watching him. Kerri quickly looked down again, raising the menu slightly, as if she was hiding behind it now too.

"Don't be embarrassed. I'm not upset at you watching me," Glen said, to comfort Kerri a little.

"Sorry, I shouldn't have been watching," Kerri apologised.

"No need to apologise," Glen said, "it's quite alright. In fact, I'm kind of used to it."

Kerri looked at Glen strangely. "Used to it?" she asked. "How can you be used to it?"

"I sometimes teach Sunday school at my church and the kids always watch you when you pray. It gives them an idea of what to do, until they are comfortable enough to do it themselves," Glen explained. "Now, have you picked anything out?"

"Oh, um no, not yet," Kerri replied, looking back down at the menu. "Do you know what you want?"

"Yes, the big breakfast," Glen replied.

"That sounds good, just make it two."

Glen got up and went over to the phone and dialled for room service.

"Can I ask you a question?" Kerri asked.

"I think you just did, but go and ask another one anyway."

Kerri was caught off guard at Glen's reply and it showed on her face. She wasn't sure what he was talking about.

"Sorry," Glen said seeing her confused look, "my strange sense of humour. What did you want to ask? Sorry, hold that thought." The room service people had answered; Glen gave them the order.

Kerri sat in thought for a moment, wondering what she should ask and where she should start.

Glen hung up and came back over to the table and sat down again. "Sorry, you had a question for me?"

"Yes. Why do you believe in God?" Kerri asked.

Glen sat there for a moment, surprised at the question. "Wow, I didn't expect that one. Most people start with, 'Do you really believe in Jesus?' or 'What church do you go to?'. Well, to be totally honest with you, it's not really something I have thought too much about. I just do."

Glen looked at Kerri and she seemed a bit disappointed with his answer. "Let me elaborate for you. If I told you how I came to believe, then I might answer it more appropriately."

"Okay," Kerri said, looking as if she was all excited to hear his story.

"Don't look so excited — it's nothing amazing really. I grew up in a religious family. We went to church every week. I was involved in different kids' and youth activities within the Church as I grew up, including playing different sports. My parents were a big influence and I kind of always believed. It wasn't until I was in my teens that I made the decision to dedicate myself to God.

"My youth group leader, Michael, was a huge influence there. Both he and his wife were friendly and loving. They showed me that being a Christian was more than going to church. It was something that you were, not just for one or two hours a week, but all day, every day. From their leadership, I learnt that I had to make a decision about whether I believed or not. Failure to do that was really a decision not to believe.

"You see, a core belief is that not only did Jesus live and die but that He will come back again. If you haven't made the decision to follow Him by then, it will be too late as you will never get the chance afterwards. And nobody knows when He will return. It may be years away or it could be today.

"With that in mind, I thought about it and thought about it, and I tried to think of something else but couldn't. I began to wonder if I would ever think about anything else again. Then one day, I just knew that I needed to decide right then and there. So I did.

"I went back to Michael the next day and told him and his wife. They were so happy for me. Not long after that, I got baptised and I haven't looked back since."

"Baptised? I've heard that term before. Isn't that when a baby gets its head wet in church?" Kerri asked.

"In some churches they call it that but in others it means a different thing," Glen explained.

"They have different names for that in different churches? If it's the same thing, why give it a different name?" Kerri asked.

"Quite simple really: it's because either they believe different things or they would like to demonstrate things in different ways," Glen started to explain. "You see, over the course of time, when a person, or group of people, didn't agree with the teaching of a particular church or how it was taught, they went off and started a new church. That's really a bit of a simplification of things but it is the essence of all the separate groups. The most commonly known one is the Church of England. One of the kings of England, Henry the Eighth, wanted to get divorced. At the time, the Church of England was a branch of the Catholic Church, so basically under the Pope's rule. One of the Catholic Church's rules was that you were not allowed to get divorced without the Pope's approval. Well, the Pope wouldn't allow King Henry to get his marriage to Catherine of Aragon annulled. That, combined with the underlying belief of the population of England that only the King should have authority over the Church, caused the King to 'reform' the Church of England. This basically means he went and started his own church, based on almost exactly the same practices and teachings, except that they would allow divorces and annulments."

"That doesn't sound right. Just because he wanted to get divorced and the Pope disagreed, the Church of England was reformed?" Kerri said in disbelief.

"It's true as far as I am aware. I saw it in a documentary about Henry the Eighth. That Church itself goes way back in time before that, but that is when they started to achieve a separate identity from the Pope and the Catholic Church. Anyway, it's not the only time something like that has happened. You can go back through the history of the churches and find out all sorts of reasons for splits within a church group. Pretty soon after the split, another denomination starts," Glen said.

"Denomination? What does that mean?" Kerri asked.

"Basically a different church group," Glen explained. "Baptist, Lutheran, Church of Christ, Uniting — these are all different types of denominations and there are many more. They all believe the same basic principles but their rituals differ. That brings us back to your earlier question. Baptism is one of the rituals which have been practiced differently by the denominations.

"In the church I grew up in, which was a Church of Christ, Baptism was performed on a person when they chose to follow Jesus and wanted to make it known publicly that they were choosing to live a Christ-like life," Glen explained. "You see, in the Bible, when Jesus chose to start his ministry, he was baptised by John the Baptist. It is described as 'a full body immersion' in water. That is how my church did it and how I experienced it.

"Some churches do it differently, in that they only sprinkle the water on the person. Some, as you said, do it to babies. In other churches, including my own, that is called Christening. I was taught that Baptism was when you chose it for yourself and Christening was the parent's choice, to show that this was how they choose to bring up their child."

"Okay, I think I understand that. Do most people go through baptism when they start believing?" Kerri asked.

"Most do, but some choose not to. Some are private affairs and done with a small gathering, away from the rest of the church," Glen answered. "Can I ask you, why the sudden interest in all this?"

"Um, well," Kerri stalled for time, as she felt a little embarrassed and didn't really want to answer Glen's question. "I guess it's because we have some time and I wanted to get a better understanding of you. You are not like my friends – they are a little secretive about this sort of thing and if you ask a question they full on go for the 'save', instead of just answering the question. I know they mean well but sometimes they need to back off and realise that I may not want to be pounced on when I mention the subject."

"I am sure they are just excited. I was like that to start with, too, until a friend of mine pointed out that it can scare someone new away."

"Exactly! Why are you so different? Is it because you have grown up around it?"

"How do you mean?"

"Well, you seem so... confident in yourself and in God."

Glen thought for a moment and then answered Kerri's question: "Faith mostly and a little bit of experience. But it doesn't stop there, just because I choose to believe. As you saw before, I continue to study the Word of God. I do that so that I can be more confident in every situation. By continuing to study the Bible, you start to remember verses. After a while, the relevant verse pops into your head just when you need it the most. To start with, I learnt one verse and it is one of the most important versus I have ever read: '*If God is for me, who can stand against me?*' Just knowing that one verse, I can walk into any situation and know that I will be alright, because God is *for* me. That tells me He will look after me and even if I don't come out too well in the end, I know that if I had done it without God, it would have ended a lot worse."

There was a silence in the room as Kerri took in what Glen had said.

"Do you think God could be for me too?" Kerri asked in a very quiet voice.

Glen smiled in the same way that a proud parent does at their child. "Of course He is. Another important verse that I learnt goes like this: '*For God so loved the world, that He sent His* only Son, so that whoever believes in Him will not *perish but have eternal life.*' That passage basically means that if we believe in Him, He will save us. Why? Because he loves us. To show us how much He loves us, He sent His only Son to live among us, to teach us and then to die for our sins, so that we do not have to."

"That sounds familiar," Kerri said excitedly, "I think I read that last night, only it sounds different."

Glen looked at Kerri with a new understanding. "You read it last night?"

"Yeah, I found it in the Bible that was in the cabinet..." Kerri said, slowing down at the end, just like someone caught in the act of revealing something they didn't want to.

"By your bed," Glen finished for her. "Thank God for the Gideon Society."

Kerri looked at Glen like an animal that had been caught in the headlights of a car. Glen smiled again. "Don't look so scared. So, you read the Bible last night? Learn anything new?"

"I'm sorry, I didn't know if I should tell you or not. I expected you would react like one of my friends that I mentioned before and go on and on about how great it is. Then they would ask if I wanted to pray to God with them and so on."

"You don't need to justify yourself to me, Kerri. You hardly know me and did not know how I would react. Well, in a way you're right — I do think it is great and if you have any other questions, I will answer them to the best of my ability, but that's all I will say. As for praying, well that can be a very personal thing at first and I am surprised that your friends haven't realised that."

Just then, there was a knock at the door.

"That will be our breakfast," Glen said, and he stood up and went to the door to get it.

FORTY THREE

Unseen by the humans and unknown by the demons, the angels Ruth, Raphael and two other guardians snuck back into Cairns. They had left Heaven and come down to an area inland of northern Queensland. Once there they waited along the flight path from Darwin to Cairns. They didn't wait long before a plane from Darwin approached. They boarded it mid-air, passing through the walls as it went by. Once aboard they changed their appearance to be human. Now if a demon saw them they wouldn't know any different.

After another twenty minutes in the air, they arrived at the Cairns International Airport. They alighted with the rest of the passengers and walked out of the Domestic Terminal towards the bus stops. They waited at the bus stops and boarded the first bus that was heading in their direction. They got off the bus about three blocks from the hotel and walked the rest of the way.

Ruth led the group into the hotel, up the elevator to the sixth floor and to the door of room 606. They looked around to make sure there was no one watching and then walked through the door.

"Glory to the living God," they said, as they turned the corner into the living area.

"And to the risen Lamb," replied Amy, Daniel and Kyle.

"Welcome back, Ruth," Daniel said as he stood, "I didn't expect you back so soon, or with company either. To what honour do we owe your visit, Raphael? Or is the situation that bad?"

Amy and Kyle had both stood as soon as they saw the archangel, both feeling nervous at his presence, for they were simply angels. The archangels are classed as the highest rank of the Heavenly Host. Those who achieve this rank are usually classed as leaders among the rest and held in high regard. It is the seraphim who are closest to the Lord: they are the ones in whom the Lord confides and to whom he speaks often; but the archangels are the Lord's generals and personal messengers.

"That it is, Daniel. You must be Amy," Raphael said to Kyle and turning to Amy, "and you must be Kyle."

Daniel, Ruth and the other two guardians both laughed at Raphael's ice breaker. Amy and Kyle weren't sure if they should correct him or not. They soon laughed, too, when they saw Raphael's big smile.

"I'm sorry, you looked so nervous I couldn't resist," Raphael apologised. "I am pleased to meet you both. You have done such an excellent job of caring for your charges. There are not many who could have gotten away from a den like that and then continued to keep them hidden for so long. Tricking the demons with your version of the 'Jonah Bluff' was superb Kyle. Amy, your use of camouflage with your wings was ingenious. Oh, don't look so surprised — Ruth told us what has transpired as we travelled together."

Daniel watched Raphael with interest. Raphael really knew how to relax others and diffuse the tension in the air that can surround someone of his stature. Daniel was impressed.

"By the way, this is Jade and Pia," Raphael introduced the guardians. "They are here to help us. Is that them?" he asked, indicating the humans who were sitting at the table.

"Yes," Kyle replied, "it is. They have been up for a while and although we are not pushing it, Kerri has been opening up to Glen and asking questions about God."

"We think she is close," Amy added, "she started down 'The Path' last night and now she has some questions."

"And Glen is answering them okay?" Raphael asked.

"Yes," Kyle said, "he knows his stuff."

"He's not getting any assistance?" Raphael asked again.

"Not from us," Amy replied.

"I knew it as soon as I walked in — the Spirit is at work on her. Praise the Lord," said Raphael.

"Praise the Lord," the others said together.

They watched and listened for a little while and then Ruth said, "I hate to interrupt such a beautiful sight but I have a reply from the Captain."

They all turned back to face Ruth.

"Right," said Daniel.

"Of course," said Amy.

"What did he say?" asked Kyle.

"It wasn't just the Captain. It was the whole Council and some others too," Ruth explained. "I have never seen such a gathering for something like this. I gave him your message and explained some of the parts in a bit more detail. They then told me of other things that are happening that appear to be connected."

Raphael watched her with interest here — the Captain had told her not to mention the threat to Eden that Gabriel was working on.

"All I can say is that you seem to have stumbled onto something very big. The Captain advises to get the humans to safety." Ruth had their undivided attention now. "In regards to the missing friends, possibly in Central Australia, he thinks they have a lead already. He has organised someone to check on it. The saints are being rallied too. There should be plenty of prayer cover. He sent Jade and Pia to help support you, and he sent Raphael to get a better idea of what we are all up against."

"What do you intend to do?" Raphael asked.

"We need to get out of here for a start, there is too much demon activity for us to stay hidden for too long," Daniel explained. "And our little demonic counterpart has disappeared too."

"You never mentioned a demon being present, Ruth," Raphael said, as he turned to her.

"I never saw one here," Ruth replied.

"If he's been gone that long, then we'd better move quicker. He could have already reported where we are," Daniel said, looking at Kyle and Amy.

"Our preliminary plans are to get out by boat but it's still risky," Amy started to explain to the new arrivals.

"May I make a suggestion? Do you have any brochures for tourist activities?" Pia asked.

"Yes," Kyle answered, "Glen grabbed some from the lobby when we arrived. I didn't know why, he wasn't planning on going on any. I think they are in his room."

"What's your idea?" Daniel asked.

"I know this area is very popular with tourists. I had a charge here once, he ran a tourist charter boat business," Pia replied starting to explain her idea. "I would suggest we go with the boat idea but meet up with another one offshore. Then head south to one of the other towns or islands. From there you can change back to air or land, depending on where you want to go."

"Sounds good. Let's look at them and see if we can make a plan with a workable timetable," Raphael suggested.

Forty Four

David was still making the list of all the possible places with connections to the Garden of Eden when Gabriel walked back into the room. Gabriel had been organising the next team and had seen them off.

"How goes the search?" Gabriel asked, as he walked over to David.

"I think the only real possibility is the one we gave to the others, which Israfel is checking out," David replied. "This means that what I am doing is not only pointless but also unnecessary."

"I agree… *if* Israfel is successful," Gabriel said. "If he isn't, then we will need another location immediately for him to check out. If we wait now, we could make it harder for ourselves later. On the other hand, if we search now, we may be wasting time too but not as much." Gabriel smiled at David, "Do not be discouraged, David. We will find them and stop them from entering the Lord's Garden before it is too late."

"Don't get me wrong, I know we will stop them. It's just that I feel my time could be used better looking for Dmitri and the minister instead," David replied.

Gabriel stared at David for a moment. He was considering what David said when he noticed some movement out of the corner of his eye. He turned his head to see Stan, still waiting for Michael's return. Turning back to David he said, "I, too, think it is something that we should be doing, but Michael is right: we need the Lord's guidance first. Besides, I am sure that Dmitri and the minister are okay. You just remember who Dmitri has looked after before. He kept him alive until the Lord called Saint Paul home."

"I remember well," David said. "I don't know anyone more courageous or privileged. To be Saint Paul's guardian would have been a fantastic experience. Rarely has there been any saint so in tune with his guardian or open to the Spirit. The things they did to help Saint Paul – creating an earthquake to get him out of prison, protecting him when they tried to stone him to death – these are but a couple of instances. I know he wasn't the only guardian with Saint Paul but, all the same, they went through a lot. There are not many who would be a better companion for the minister in this predicament."

"I agree, it was an exciting time for the believers. The demons didn't know what to do about the Good News and how quickly it was spreading. Only months before, the evil one thought he'd won when the Lamb was crucified, but he didn't know what the Lord's plan was." Gabriel paused as he remembered and then continued, "Exciting times, but not without peril. Don't forget that the demons got desperate and did some really nasty things. There were close calls and sometimes we didn't make it. I haven't forgotten that all of the Chosen Twelve, except Saint

John, were martyred. At times, it seemed like their guardians didn't stand a chance against the number of demons they threw at them. However, in every instance, their sacrifice has been recognised and they are all with the Lord now."

"Some guardians are still recovering from those events. They refuse to give up being messengers and take other guardian roles, from what I've heard. Yes, some exciting and also dangerous times back then. Now it's more psychological, don't you agree?" David asked Gabriel.

Gabriel thought about that for a moment and he realised that David was right. "Satan has been playing a very cunning game," he said, "on several fronts at once. He has been convincing people that he is not real for decades, convincing people that witchcraft is okay, having cute devil pictures and toys to soften his image and even creating religions with angel worship and spirit guides. And these things are only the tip of the iceberg, as the humans would say. The humans themselves are becoming so hard to get through to; they have so many choices that they don't recognise the ones that are dangerous to their eternal soul. Even *not* choosing is dangerous, as it says in the Bible...

Jesus answered him, "I am the way, the truth, and the life. No one goes to the Father except through me."
John 14:6

"By not choosing Jesus, they are not choosing God," Gabriel continued. "What they are choosing, by not making a conscious decision, is eternal destruction. An eternity spent in the fires that have been prepared for Satan and his followers. Whether you call it Hell, Sheol, Hades, Gehenna or Tartarus, it is the same location, with the same torment in store for all of them."

"And there's another misconception," David added, "Hell is not the place that Satan rules and uses to torment the sinners. Sure, he controls it now and uses it for that purpose, but that's not what it was created for. Hell is actually under the care of God, for its primary use, eventually, will be for Satan's punishment. But any who follow him will go there too, even if they don't know that they are following him."

"It's like that old saying, 'If you are not for me, then you are against me', and God takes that personally," Gabriel said.

"He sure does," David replied.

Gabriel realised that he had gotten sidetracked. "I'd never really thought about it like that before. You are quite right to call it more psychological these days. Anyway, enough of that. I think that we had better get back to the task at hand. What have you found for me?"

David looked back down at the list in front of him. He had almost two pages of 'Eden'-related locations for Gabriel to double check and he hadn't finished going through the America's yet. "I have found a number of other possibilities but I reckon I can cross most of them off straight away. However, there are a few that I think are good possibilities, although nowhere as great as the one Israfel is checking on."

David passed the first page of the list to Gabriel and he looked over it quickly. "I agree, there are many here that are nothing more than suburbs, small towns or tourist attractions," Gabriel said, as he looked down the list, removing the places as he went. "Nothing there worth checking out," he said, as he handed the now blank page back to David and took the second page from him.

"Edenhope, Edenville, Eden, New Eden, Garden of Eden... Gabriel read out the names as he went down the page and then he stopped. Halfway down the page he found one that caught his attention. "Where is this one?" he asked David, pointing to the name he stopped at.

"Let me check," David said, as he read the co-ordinates he had written after the name and cross-referenced them with his source books. He pulled out a map and pointed to the location, "Here."

"Hmmmm," Gabriel said, as he looked at the map. "I think that one will need checking out too. Not a strong candidate but more than a mere coincidence. I'll just mark that spot," he said, as he pointed at the map and then the page of names. On both pages, the location started to blink.

"Who are you going to send?" David asked.

"No one yet," Gabriel answered. "I think we should continue with the search and then one or both of us should go check them all out. How many more do you think there are?"

"I haven't checked the other eleven kingdoms yet, only North America. I don't think the Europes or Russias will have as many — the place names tended to be more specific back then — and the Asia regions weren't named for this sort of thing. Australia, New Zealand and their surrounding islands are younger, so may have a few locations each."

"Let's keep going then," Gabriel said, as he lifted the list back up. He started to read down from the blinking one. "It sounds like we could be here for quite a while."

Forty Five

"Okay, it's settled then. Pia, go to Tim, wait for the phone call and then get him out to the island. Jade, go to Max and get him started on the arrangements. Daniel, go to the railway and organise the feint. Ruth, update the Captain on our plans. I will organise some prayer cover," Raphael said to the angels around him.

"What about us?" Kyle asked, referring to Amy too.

"Continue to do what you are doing — look after your charges, okay?" Raphael replied. "Once you have settled on when and where, then get out of here and find somewhere else to hide. Make the call to Tim and Pia and we will meet you at the boat or on the island."

Kyle looked crestfallen. He had been looking forward to getting out and seeing some action. Daniel read Kyle's look and knew exactly what he was feeling.

"Kyle," Daniel said, "do not feel left out. Your mission is the most important of all, for without your charge, or Amy's for that matter, we would know nothing of this threat. As a result, the demon's are hopping mad and doing everything they can to find Glen and Kerri."

Kyle had looked up and was about to speak but Daniel continued before he could. "I know you want to see some action. I know you want to show the Lord that you are loyal, brave, strong and ready to move up in rank. I know because I can remember feeling like that too. Trust me when I say that you *will* have an opportunity to display all these traits and more before this is over."

Kyle looked around and smiled. The other angels were watching him and nodding or smiling. "Thank you, Daniel," he said.

"Let's get to it!" Raphael said.

"For the Glory of the Lord and His Kingdom!" they all said together and then all but Daniel, Kyle and Amy turned for the door.

Daniel felt reassured now that they had some plans in place, but was still a little concerned that Kyle may do something that would reveal them. "Kyle, are you satisfied? Or are you planning something of your own?" Daniel asked.

Kyle looked at Daniel and noted the concern on his face. "Do not fear, Daniel: I am satisfied. I am not planning anything nor do I intend to plan anything that does not include the rest of you or that would put Glen in danger."

Kyle was sure the plan would work but there were at least two reasons why it could go wrong: Kerri and Glen. The humans' free will was something they could never account for. When placed under extraordinary situations, humans could do almost anything. Kyle was fairly sure he knew what Glen would do, but Kerri was another matter.

As Kyle bent over Glen and explained that he should get ready to leave, he thought back to a few hours earlier. It had been fairly easy to get Glen to look at the brochures as he is tuned in to Kyle's urgings.

Kyle had suggested that Glen should start to think about how they would leave Cairns and that the brochures he picked up may give him an idea.

Glen had been trying to eat something. He was feeling anxious about his missing friend and also Kerri and her interest in God. He was praying silently about Kerri but was having trouble concentrating. His thoughts were not staying on the track he wanted. All he could think about was how were they going to leave Cairns and where to go from here. Suddenly, he remembered that he had picked up some tourist brochures when he arrived. He didn't know why he had done it but felt it was the right thing to do at the time. Maybe once he had spoken to Henry he would see some sights.

Glen stood up, leaving his half-eaten breakfast, and went into his room to get the brochures.

Kerri looked up as he stood. She watched him walk off down the passage and could hear him moving things in his room. Then he walked back out holding something in his hand. "What's that?" she asked, afraid he had gone to get some Christian handouts to push on her.

Since the breakfast had arrived, they had eaten in peace and quiet. The only time the silence was broken was when she asked for the salt and pepper, and when Glen had poured the coffee and had asked how she had it.

"Some brochures on different tourist things," Glen said. "I was just thinking that when we left, if we pretended to be tourists, we would be harder to spot. I had also thought that we should leave by either train or boat." He spread the brochures out on the table for Kerri to see them too.

Kerri reached over, picked one up and started to look over it.

The angels were gathered behind Glen and Kerri, looking over their shoulders at the different destinations or attractions. There were really only a few that would be suitable for what they had in mind. Kerri was holding one for Green Island and Glen was looking at the Kuranda Railway. Kyle was alongside Glen, ready to help influence his decision-making process, just as Amy was beside Kerri, ready to do the same. The others were behind either Glen or Amy, looking over their shoulders or at what was left on the table.

"Let's forget the railway for now and concentrate on the boats," Kyle suggested to Glen.

"I think maybe we should concentrate on the boats for now," Glen said to Kerri, as he put his brochure down and reached for another one.

"Why?" Kerri asked. "I mean, do we really want to limit ourselves that way?"

Daniel jumped in and spoke quickly in Glen's other ear, "There are limited places to hide in a train station. There is only one building and several platforms. But there are lots of places where you can get on a boat!"

"There's only one train station where we can catch these trains, but there are several places to get boats," Glen replied to Kerri. "Besides, I don't think they will look at the tourist boats at all, whereas the train station covers both tourists and passengers. Same goes with the car rental agencies and airport."

"Good point, we will stick to the boats then," Kerri said, agreeing with Glen's logic. "Where exactly do you think we should go?"

"It's not about where, but when. If we could go to one that will then allow us to connect with a different boat, we could return somewhere else — maybe somewhere south of here, like Mission Beach or Townsville. That would be more suitable," Kyle said to Glen.

"Wherever we can catch a different boat from, a boat that will take us somewhere south of here. Like Mission Beach or even Townsville," Glen replied.

"Why not just get one that will take us straight there?" Kerri asked.

"Because that may be more of a passenger trip and not a tourist cruise," Glen replied. "They might be watched too."

"So could the tourist boats. I don't know if we should be wasting time like this. I think we should go straight to the police and let them take care of us," Kerri suggested.

Glen lowered his head in thought for a moment and then looked back up at Kerri. "I have a strong feeling that we need to get out of here first and then contact the authorities. Did you notice the signs in the construction site? The ones mentioning the Casino?"

"Yes, I even have photos on my camera of them," Kerri replied. "But what does that have to do with anything?"

"Well, before I left to come up here I did some checking on what was being built. There was a big write-up in the papers a while back, when it was first announced. They mentioned in it what facilities were included and a casino was not amongst it."

"So what?" Kerri replied. "They probably changed their mind or were approached by someone else who convinced them to build one."

"I don't think so. You see, I also checked into what licences they had applied for or had already been granted. There were, of course, the usual ones that this sort of resort would have, but not the sort of gambling licence that is required for a casino."

Glen paused to allow Kerri to think about what he just said and then continued on, "I don't think they have a licence for that casino. If they do, it has been buried so deep that the usual concern groups cannot find it."

"That might be why they didn't like me taking photos of the site. If even one mention of the casino gets out, they may have to stop construction, until they get that licence. If they didn't... they may lose all the other licences and have to stop construction altogether," Kerri surmised.

"Exactly," Glen said, "which is probably why they are after you. They want the contents of your camera. But think about it a bit more. It would be pretty hard to keep this a secret. So... I think they would have to have help of some sort."

"Help? From who?" Kerri asked.

"Some sort of authority figure, or figures, who could keep this quiet," Glen replied.

"Someone like the police?" Kerri asked.

"Possibly, but if not, then from the local council, and they may have influence over the police," answered Glen. "I also think they may have the photo processing places under observation. That would be difficult: there could be a hundred or more outlets around a place like this that will process photos."

"I hadn't even thought of my camera since we left there. Where is it?"

"Over there", Glen indicated the counter top where a shopping bag was sitting on the counter. "I went and got it last night after you went to bed. I put it in the bag so as not to draw attention to it. Is it a film or one of the new digital types?"

"Normal film," Kerri answered Glen, as she got up and went over to the bag to get the camera. "I wanted to wait a little while before upgrading to a digital. So far the image quality is not there, unless you're willing to pay an absolute bundle for it. Which, I'm not."

Kerri, meanwhile, had been checking the camera and making sure it wasn't damaged in any way. She had been so preoccupied that she hadn't been listening to Glen's ramblings on technological advances. She lined the camera up on Glen and snapped off a quick photo. Satisfied that it was working, she checked the photo counter and started to pack it back up.

"I have another ten or so pictures left before this roll is full," Kerri said, as she put the bag back on the counter top.

"That's good, it will help you look like a tourist on the boat if you are snapping shots every now and then," Glen replied. "So which Island adventure looks the most suitable to you? Green Island or Fitzroy Island?" He asked holding up two brochures.

Kerri took one from him and looked over it. "I don't know. Neither appears suitable. They don't mention any other tourist boats going there," Kerri replied, as she handed the brochure of Green Island back to Glen.

Glen looked at the brochure and compared it to the Fitzroy Island one he was holding. He turned them over to see the tour information on the backs. "Of course not," he said, suddenly realising the heart of the matter, "these are for specific tours, from specific tour agencies. They wouldn't advertise a competitor going to the same location. We need to see if we have more brochures, for the same locations, from different agencies."

They both started looking through the pile of brochures but the only other one they found was from a charter company.

Pia smiled as they picked up the brochure and started to look over it. "That's the company that Tim ran. I wonder if it is still his?"

"Why did you leave him?" Raphael asked.

Pia looked at them all as she started to tell her story: "I was Tim's guardian. One day we got caught at sea in a major storm. It was caused by a small group of demons that had seen me and wanted to try to test his faith. I think they hoped to scare him into blaspheming or cursing or something, but he didn't. He held on steadfastly to his faith and prayed the whole time he sailed through the storm, checking the ropes, the charts and the sails with my help.

"This only angered them further and they physically attacked the boat and me. I don't remember telling him to concentrate on praying but he did — he stopped and knelt behind the wheel and prayed. He started to call out to the demons, telling them to leave. It was quite a sight.

"Then three warriors arrived and chased them off. I managed to get back on the boat, with one of the warriors' help. Then the seas started to calm down and the storm gradually subsided.

"When the other two warriors returned from their chase, they decided I needed to be healed properly. One stayed as the other two took me back to Heaven, for full healing. I was reassigned to be a messenger while I healed fully. I heard later that another guardian was assigned to Tim."

They all looked at her for a moment and then Raphael spoke, "Well done to Tim. Your wounds appear to have healed well. Are you ready for more action?"

"Absolutely," Pia replied, smiling.

"Good," Raphael said. "Here is what I think we should do... and he explained his plan.

FORTY SIX

All over the world, the messengers who had been visiting the Pillars were now leaving and returning to Heaven. The Pillars were sending for their own messengers. They needed to get the word out — get the saints praying so that the Host of Heaven would be ready to face the enemy, who has a major offensive on the way. Any information found regarding this was to be passed back to The Captain.

****

In Alice Springs, two groups of tourists accidentally slept in, not hearing their alarm clocks when they went off. The groups had met the night before in one of the local pubs. They all had a great time, comparing notes on where they had been and where they were going. Both groups were supposed to be leaving on tours that morning. One group was booked on a bus to go to see Kings Canyon. The other group was booked to take a helicopter, to go join a tour already in progress in Palm Valley. Unfortunately, both groups would miss their appointed pick up times.

****

In Sydney, at the offices of *The Gazette*, editor James 'Jimmy' McMillan, was getting off the phone from one of his insiders. This one was from a local building contractor company. He shook his head as he read over his notes.

There was no trace of Henry in Sydney. His family had not heard from him and assumed he was still in Cairns. As for the companies... he didn't like what he had found out.

"What has Glen got himself into this time?" he asked himself. "If he lives through this, it will make one hell of a story. I'd better try to confirm this through someone else before calling him back and scaring him."

Jimmy picked up the phone again and started to dial a source in the police department.

****

Max did not like what he was hearing either.

"Can you repeat that bit again? Did you say they are suspected to be linked to organised crime? As in the Mob?"

He listened for a moment as his friend, an owner of a building hardware supply shop, repeated what he had said. “No one knows for sure, but every now and then, they win contracts that they had no chance of winning. Everyone else suddenly revises their original estimates or just asks for them back and doesn’t resubmit them. On top of that, a few of the local builders, just small-time contractors, suddenly disappeared and no one wants to talk about it.”

“But this is all just rumours you have heard. Is there any evidence to back any of it up?” Max asked.

“If there was evidence, then I am sure the cops would have done something about it,” came the reply.

Forty Seven

Israfel's group was nearly ready to leave. He had gathered the team together at the edge of Heaven – seven warriors including Nathaniel and the messenger, Micah. He looked from one to the next as he spoke, "This is primarily a reconnaissance mission: we sneak in, check it out and sneak out again. First, check for the presence of the enemy and a rough idea of numbers if possible. Second, check for any evidence of a link to 'Eden'. Third, as long as it does not jeopardise the primary mission, search for the missing humans or any evidence that they have been there. And, finally, is it a good start point for the trap. Do you understand?"

"YES, SIR!" they all replied in military-type unison, while standing as if at a military parade. A few were struggling to suppress a smile.

Israfel raised one of his eyebrows. After studying them for a moment, he asked, "What are you doing?"

"Raphael suggested it, SIR," Nathaniel replied. "He said you have been studying the different human militaries, SIR, and that this is the correct stance when the ranking officer gives orders, SIR."

Israfel shook his head while chuckling. "I will have words with him when this is all finished. Okay, the joke's over. Let's get back to the mission. Are you ready to go?" They all nodded in response, relaxing their stance and smiling freely now.

"Follow me," Israfel said, as he jumped over the edge. As he fell to Earth he opened his wings to allow a slight measure of control. One by one, the warriors and Micah all did the same. By doing it this way, not a single one of them was glorified or actually flying. Instead, they were doing a combination of falling and gliding.

It didn't take long for them to come down out of the clouds and towards the ground. They allowed themselves to glide down towards Alice Springs in Central Australia. From there they split up: three landed in Alice Springs, while the other six headed west south west, towards Palm Valley.

Nathaniel was one of the three in Alice Springs, who, after landing, walked to the pickup point for Outback Tours. They changed their appearance as they walked. They now looked like tourists that were about to go sightseeing. They also made themselves tangible. This meant that others could see them and even feel them if they bumped into them. They replaced three people, who had overslept that morning and missed their pickup.

The six, including Israfel, continued gliding for a short while longer. When they were nearing Palm Valley, they split up again. Three landed at the camp for the MacDonnell Ranges Tours group. Israfel, and the other two with him, turned south west, towards Uluru.

The three in Palm Valley, including Micah, changed their appearances and made themselves tangible. They were also replacing a group who had slept in. They joined a group that was already on tour and getting ready to leave for the next leg of their six-day experience.

A short while later, Israfel's group landed in Yulara, where they changed their appearance to fit in with the humans around them. They became solid, too. They did not join a tour group like the rest of their team mates. Instead, they approached the concierge of the hotel in Yulara and asked to know where they could hire a minivan for a day trip. The concierge directed them to the Budget desk at the airport and called the shuttle bus to take them there.

Half an hour later, they found the car-rental agency at the airport. The hiring process didn't take them long. They had all the necessary licences to hand over when asked.

Once they had their vehicle, they were on their way to Kings Canyon. All three groups were to meet up in the Lost City before splitting up once more to check out the many tourist attractions including, specifically, a place called the 'Garden of Eden'.

Forty Eight

Henry awoke the next morning feeling a lot better. He opened his eyes and looked around the room. Alan was asleep on the only other bed in the room, which resembled a camp stretcher. It had six legs, a thick material stretched over the wooden frame and a thin foam mattress.

Henry sat up gingerly so he could take in his surroundings better. The bed he was in was more like a hospital bed than he thought it would be. It had wheels, retractable sides and a firm but comfortable mattress. The rest of the room was fairly sparse: a few medical-looking items on a cabinet nearby and a table with some paper and a pen.

As he was looking around, Alan rolled over and looked at him.

"You're awake. How do you feel?" Alan asked.

"Not too bad, actually," Henry replied.

"Good," Alan said, as he sat up and swung out of his bed. He stood up and went over to the cabinet, picked up a thermometer and an ancient-looking sphygmomanometer, used for measuring blood pressure. "Let's see if your body agrees." Alan slipped the thermometer in Henry's mouth and then he attached the sphygmomanometer around his arm and started pumping it up. He watched the gauge as the air escaped slowly, then set it to release the air and he removed it again. "That's good," he said and reached out for Henry's wrist.

After counting and watching his watch for fifteen seconds, he released Henry's wrist and reached for the thermometer to check that too.

"All good," Alan said to Henry, who was sitting there waiting expectantly. "If you will lay back down for me, I will check your bandages."

Henry lay back down slowly. Alan removed the bandages from his right arm and checked out the sunburn. He reapplied some ointment and wrapped new bandages on the arm. He repeated this process with the other arm and then both legs. Then he put some ointment on Henry's face, ears and neck. After washing his hands, he got some painkillers and helped Henry up so he could drink and take the tablets.

"Well?" Henry asked as he lay back down again.

"Apart from your sunburn, you're practically normal. I don't have a way of testing your dehydration level but the drip you have is a saline solution and it has been in all night. That will have rehydrated you as well as resupplied your body with necessary electrolytes. I changed it twice while you slept, so you have received a top up of about five litres overall."

"If I have had that much, how come I don't feel the need to go to the toilet?"

"Your body has been absorbing it and very little waste has resulted. That is good but I am going to turn it off soon and start you on food and water again."

"You're not going to take it out?" Henry asked.

"No, I want to give the impression that you still need it. We can't wait for you to be one hundred percent healthy before we go. If we did, it is more likely that they would take us back into the tunnels and we would find it much harder to sneak out. We also wouldn't have the things I have been putting aside. Do you think you can manage another escape attempt?"

"Apart from some discomfort from the sunburn, I don't feel too bad. Yeah, I think I can manage it."

"Good," Alan said smiling. "You will need to pretend to be worse than you are though. At some point during the afternoon you will need to pretend to have a fit or seizure. This will draw the guards in, allowing us to disable them and prevent them from raising the alarm. We will then go up and look for transport or a hiding place until the sun sets. Then we leave."

"Sounds simple enough," Henry said. "You have spent some time working this out haven't you?"

"Weeks. Now rest up a bit. I will fill you in on the details while I reapply your bandages."

FORTY NINE

Michael and Saint Peter stepped out of the 'Throne' after their visit with the Lord, God of all Creation. As always, Saint Peter had found it hard to concentrate in the Lord's presence. He always felt so relaxed and the singing of the Seraphim had such a calming effect on him. Even with the background noise of song and praise, Michael had spoken of the issues that had arisen. Jesus, the Lamb of God, had inspected the note and assured Michael that it was authentic. The Lord had turned to his son, Jesus, and nodded. He then turned back to Michael. Jesus had responded, advising Michael of what he should do to pursue those who had taken Dmitri and the Man of God. All care should be given to the minister. As for the Eden situation, they thanked him for the update and reassured him that they trusted his judgement in how to handle the situation.

Saint Peter looked at Michael and saw that he was reflecting on the visit too. "Do you think they will be okay?" he asked Michael.

Michael turned to Saint Peter and replied, "Of course. And if not, then the Lord has His reason for the delay. If the Lord only wants one of us to go, then so be it. It will be the best action in the long run, you will see. I do not doubt the Lord's wisdom and neither should you."

"Of course you are right, Captain. I do not doubt the Lord's wisdom or his counsel. I only meant to ask if they will be okay *until* we can get there."

"And my answer is the same."

They stood there for a moment, as if waiting for some silent signal that would tell them to move off. Then, as one, they started to walk, heading back to the Hall of the Lamb.

They walked in silence for a while. Saint Peter eventually broke the silence by asking, "Who will you send?"

Michael was deep in thought and didn't answer straight away. Thinking he hadn't heard, Saint Peter opened his mouth to ask again but Michael stopped walking. Saint Peter closed his mouth and stopped too, turning back to look at Michael. Michael had been walking with his head down. Now that he had stopped, he raised his head and looked at Saint Peter. "I think I need to tell you about the Sixth Day of Creation," he said.

Saint Peter watched Michael for a moment and then replied, "Okay."

As they started to walk again, Michael continued with his tale:

Then God said, "Let the Earth produce every type of living creature: every type of domestic animal, crawling animal, and wild animal." And so it was. God made every type of wild animal, every type of domestic animal, and every type of creature that crawls on the ground. God saw that they were good.

Then God said, "Let us make humans in our image, in our likeness. Let them rule the fish in the sea, the birds in the sky, the domestic animals all over the Earth, and all the animals that crawl on the Earth."

So God created humans in his image.
In the image of God he created them.
He created them male and female.

God blessed them and said, "Be fertile, increase in number, fill the Earth, and be its master. Rule the fish in the sea, the birds in the sky, and all the animals that crawl on the Earth."

God said, "I have given you every plant with seeds on the face of the Earth and every tree that has fruit with seeds. This will be your food. I have given all green plants as food to every land animal, every bird in the sky, and every animal that crawls on the Earth — every living, breathing animal." And so it was.

And God saw everything that he had made and that it was very good. There was evening, then morning — the sixth day.

Genesis 1:24-31

"Almost as soon as the sun came up over the horizon, the Lord was there. We were there too, right behind him, not wanting to miss out on anything.

"'Today,' He said, facing us, 'is the one that will be remembered the most. These other creations are wonderful, but today I will create something truly unique amongst all creation.'

"We wondered what it could be that would be so much more than all the rest. What would be so significant that it would be remembered for all time? What would make it unique? There were already birds that were unique and fish too. Was the Narwhal not unique? Or the Cassowary?

"As we watched, the Lord turned away to face the Earth. I saw Him smile as He looked upon it. Then He raised His arms, His smile disappeared and was replaced with one of the most serious expressions I have ever seen. The Lord was concentrating.

"The Lord spoke, loud and clear and with authority, 'Let every type of living creature come forth, the crawling, the domestic and the wild animal.'

"We watched and saw animals form and start to move on the land. We immediately flew down to have a closer look, just like with the fish and birds, and wherever we went, they were there. There were all sorts and the most noticeable thing about them was the differences. They were like nothing we had ever seen before. Large animals such as elephants and rhinoceroses, beasts of burden such as camels and yaks, domestic animals such as cows and sheep, crawling animals such as iguanas, snakes and crocodiles, small animals such as mice and smaller still, the caterpillars and ants and the fierce creatures, such as lions and jaguars. Everywhere we looked, there were different types and they were suited to their environments, be it alpine or meadow, hot or cold, wet or dry.

"I began to wonder if this was what the Lord had been talking about. The difference, the uniqueness of each animal. And then I saw similar creatures — horses and zebras, then emus and ostriches, and then the many types of large cats. So I started to look for only those that were unique. I found the platypus, the kiwi and also the echidna. Although they certainly were different, for various reasons, they were all still similar in other areas.

"I rushed back to the Lord to ask Him about this and which one He meant. When I found Him, he was walking through a particularly lovely part of the Earth and He was smiling again, enjoying all that He had created, including the new creatures.

"I opened my mouth to speak but He spoke first.

"'This day is not over and I am not finished with it yet,' was all He said, and then He walked passed me. I had to turn to follow Him for I now wanted to be by His side and see what else He had planned.

"We walked around in this paradise He had created in silence. He was looking around at the plants and all the creatures that were there. I shared His enjoyment of this place. I noticed that other angels were coming back to the Lord. They too showed their pleasure at the surroundings as we moved about.

"After a time, I noticed that we were back to where the Lord was, when I came back to Him. We had walked full circle, so to speak, although the path we followed was more elliptical in shape.

"Suddenly, a hedge rose up out of the ground. It was where we had walked. I looked at the hedge, then at the Lord and then back to the hedge. There were gaps in the hedge every now and then. They appeared to be evenly spaced. I turned to the Lord again and I must have had a questioning look on my face, as He spoke before I could.

"'It is a barrier of sorts,' He said. 'It is to keep certain animals out and certain ones in. It also allows others to pass between and go in and out, if they desire.'

Michael paused here for a moment.

After a short while, Michael looked up at Saint Peter and locked eyes with him. "It was then that the Lord spoke the words that I will never forget.

"The Lord said, 'It is time. Now I will create Man. He will look like us, in image and shape. He will rule over the fish, the birds, the domestic and the crawling animals.'

"As we watched He scooped up some earth and began to form something with it. It wasn't long before He was finished and we all noticed the shape of the new creation. Before I could comment on this, He bent down near to where the mouth appeared and He breathed on it. I thought I saw something pass from the Lord and into the form on the ground, but it happened so quick I wasn't sure. Then He said, 'I give you life, rise up!' His spoken word once again became reality and Man was created.

"As we watched the shape on the ground, it changed colour and texture. We saw the slight movement of the chest and then the eyelids fluttered and opened. We were amazed more than ever about this new creation. He was like us but also not like us.

"A short time later, the Lord created another human, this one was slightly different again — a female. I studied them both and soon realised that it was really only in appearance that they resembled us, for they were made of flesh, which we are not.

"But here was a creation of the Lord's that does have all those things and more. When compared with the rest of His creations, from over the past couple of days, here was one that could do things we do. It could talk like we do and think like we do. Not only that, but it could also do things that we couldn't, such as reproduce.

"Then the Lord spoke again and He told the Man and Woman to reproduce and increase in number, to fill the Earth and master it. He gave them dominion over the other creatures and then He explained to them about food. That the seeds and fruit of the plants and trees would sustain them and that the creatures would also eat the same food.

"After watching them for a while, I noticed a bit of a murmur rising in the background. I remember thinking that the angels were unsure of this new creation and everything that the Lord was giving to them. I could hear various questions and this troubled me. I looked to the Lord and saw that He was happy with this new creation and appeared not to be paying any attention to us angels. I watched Him and saw His pleasure as He spoke with the humans and how they loved and adored Him. They listened attentively, totally rapt in His presence.

"I turned to the angels and spoke loudly. Not only could they all hear me but also the humans and the Lord. 'Do not question the Lord! Everything He has done has been done according to His plan. What do you or I know of this plan? If He sees fit to put man in charge of these things and gives him authority to rule it all, then what right do you have to question Him? You are no better than the rebels! May the Spirit mark you and cast you out too if you continue in your rebellious ways!' I said angrily to them."

"'Michael, the Lord called to me quietly.

"I turned and looked at the Lord and bowed, 'Yes, Lord,' I replied to Him.

"'Rise up, Michael,' He said, and I did as the Lord asked. 'Do not be angry Michael. I thank you for your faithfulness, even though I know you want to ask the same questions.' I bowed my head in shame. 'Do not be ashamed Michael, or any of you, my Host of Angels. Michael, do not be harsh on your fellow angels but instead rise up on wing and look around.' The Lord then turned back to the humans, who we later learned were named Adam and Eve.

"I looked around from where I stood and saw the rest of the Host of Heaven looking around also. This confused me temporarily: I expected them all to be looking at me with looks of indignation, but instead they were also looking around at each other. I realised, as I looked around, that I could still hear the murmurs. But it appeared that no one was actually speaking.

"Then I did what the Lord told me to do: I spread my wings and, with one flap, I rose straight up into the air. About twenty feet up, I stopped and hovered in place and looked around at the Host of Heaven below me. I then started to try to search out where the sound was coming from. David and some of the others started to rise up too. I realised that if they did, I would not be able to see who was talking.

"'Please,' I called out to them, 'stay on the ground so that I can see who is speaking.'

"David and the few others who had taken flight glided back down and landed again. As they did, I looked at a few of them and something caught my eye.

"Why I hadn't considered this before, I did not know. What I saw, not only convinced me without a doubt as to who was speaking but also enraged me at their audacity.

"As I was watching, I saw movement behind David and I shifted my focus to that movement. The Rebels had come to Earth and were watching from behind the hedge."

"As I drew my sword, I called out a warning. David and the others in close proximity heard the sound of my sword leaving the scabbard and it caused them to stop and draw their swords too. All this had been done before my warning had left my lips, for such was our instinctive reaction since the rebellion. We had learnt during that time, that if we heard a sword being drawn, we needed to draw ours too, either in support or defence.

"'The rebels have come, Host of Heaven, arm yourselves!' I called out at the top of my voice."

"The rebels looked up and without even a fight, they turned and fled. I started to give chase but the Lord called out, 'STOP!' and we did. The Host of Heaven turned to wait for further orders. I turned to the Lord.

"'You want us to just let them go, Lord?' I asked.

"'Yes, just let them go,' the Lord replied.

"'May I ask why, Lord?'

"'All of you come here and put away your swords,' the Lord called out to the Host of Heaven. We did what He asked.

"'You may not like it, but they have as much right to be here as you do,' He started to explain to us. 'For this creation, this Earth and all the creatures and plants that are on and in it, are not here just for my enjoyment or yours, but for the sake of being themselves. They will have choices to make and if they only had us to influence those choices, then they would always make the same choice. Having the evil one and his minions around will make their choices harder and more complex. If they still make the choice we would have them make, then we know that they have matured spiritually.'

"'But what if they make the other choice?' David asked.

"'Then we know that they still have some growing to do,' the Lord answered. 'The good thing about choice is that they can always make another one, even after they have already made one. You may not understand this now but you will in time. You see, you and the rebels are made of the same things and you have only one choice — to follow me, your Lord, or not follow me. The rebels have chosen not to and I will not allow them to change their mind.

"'But with this creation, it is different. They have that same choice to make but they can make it over and over and over again. Once they make the choice to follow me, they will always be welcome in my presence. But if they continually choose not to, then they will never be welcome in Heaven.'

"There was silence as we listened to the Lord. After He had finished, we just stood there, accepting His explanation.

"'Come,' the Lord said, breaking the silence, 'it is time to return to Heaven and leave Adam and Eve in this garden for the night.'

"I looked around and noticed that it was starting to get darker. The Lord rose up first and, one by one, then in groups of twos, threes and more, the rest of us took flight too.

"The sixth day was over."

FIFTY

The telephone rang, making both Glen and Kerri jump. They looked at each other for a moment. Then Glen stood, walked over to the phone and picked it up.

"Hello?" Glen said into the phone.

"Hi! Can you talk?"

"Yes, you scared us!" Glen replied, and then to Kerri he said, "It's Max."

"Sorry," Max said.

"That's okay, what's up?" Glen asked.

"I think I have a plan for your escape," Max said straight out.

"So do we. What's yours?"

"I did some thinking, checking and praying. I think your best bet would be by boat. The trains and planes could be easily watched for boarders and the roads can be too. But anyone can go out in a boat and in any direction," Max explained.

"That's what we came up with too. From there, we thought it best to go out with a tour to one of the islands and then swap to a boat returning somewhere else," Glen advised Max.

The line went quiet.

"Max?"

"What is it?" Kerri asked, seeing and hearing the worry in Glen's voice and body language. Glen looked at Kerri and held up a hand to tell her to wait a moment.

"I'm still here," Max said.

"What's wrong?" Glen asked.

"Nothing. Nothing at all," Max said.

"What is it?" Glen asked. "You're scaring me again."

"You remember when we were younger and we would get that feeling that everything will be okay? Kind of like we are being looked after from above?" Max asked in return.

"Yes," Glen replied immediately.

"I'm getting it now," Max answered.

"Cool," Glen said, smiling and starting to relax a bit. "Why?"

"Our plans are identical by the sounds of it," Max explained.

Glen's smile grew larger. "Freaky," he said to Max. "What's next then?"

"I think it would be better if I booked all your tickets, to help you stay inconspicuous," Max suggested.

"Now I am getting that feeling too," Glen proclaimed.

"What feeling?" Kerri asked.

Glen put his hand over the mouthpiece and spoke to Kerri, "I'll explain in a minute."

"I have a better idea for the next part. I've heard of someone who does charters in his yacht. If I can get him to pick you up from Green Island, he can take you wherever you want to go from there."

"That sounds perfect!" Glen said. "What time do we go?"

"How does… hang on, I can't find where I wrote it down." Glen could hear Max shuffling papers on the other end of the phone. "Here it is," Max said, coming back to the phone, "How does four o'clock this afternoon sound? I'll have to get onto the charter guy and let you know if it's okay with him, but I reckon we can work from there."

"Sounds good! Four o'clock to Green Island, say about six o'clock pick up by the charter?"

"That sounds workable."

"I'd say we have a plan. Thanks Max."

"Anytime, bro'. Besides, you still owe me twenty dollars from our last poker night."

Glen gave a quick chuckle out loud. "I'll make sure I have it for you when I see you next."

"I'll bet you another twenty dollars, right now, that you won't," Max challenged.

"You're on," Glen agreed, chuckling into the phone.

"Okay." There was a slight pause, "Glen?"

"Yeah Max?"

"I have some info on who you're dealing with but I want some more confirmations before I pass anything on. All I will say for now is stay safe and get ready to get out of there."

"Now you really are starting to scare me."

"Good. Maybe it will keep you jumping at shadows. I will make the final arrangements and call you back shortly to confirm the bookings. Remember, stay safe and God bless."

"Thanks, and God bless to you too," it was Glen's turn to pause, "Max?"

"Yeah?"

"Thanks."

"Anytime."

Hanging up, Glen turned back to Kerri.

"Well?" she asked, as he came and sat back down opposite her at the table.

"Max is going to organise everything," Glen said. "Meanwhile, we need to start packing. Leave anything that you don't absolutely need."

Fifty One

George stepped lightly off the private plane. It was mid-morning at the Connellan Air Strip, just north of the Yulara Resort and Uluru. He had enjoyed the spectacular views of the great monolith in air-conditioned comfort as they flew over it. Now, however, he was standing on the airstrip itself and he found the heat and the flies almost unbearable.

"This way, sir," he was directed by his assistant to a waiting helicopter.

"What is this?" he said, as he stopped and looked at it. "If there's further to fly, why did we land?"

"The airstrip at the resort is not able to handle a plane the size of ours," the assistant explained. "It was either land here and swap to the helicopter for a short flight, or swap to a car for another three- to four-hour drive. This is the quickest option, sir."

"Very well," George said, not entirely convinced. Wanting to get out of the heat as soon as possible, he followed his assistant to the helicopter. He stood back and waited while his assistant opened the door for him.

George and his assistant climbed into the rear of the helicopter and sat down. They did up their seatbelts and waited. The co-pilot was already in his seat, performing the pre-flight check. He was checking things off a list when the pilot opened his door and climbed in.

The pilot turned to the men in the back, "G'day, how ya goin'? Hope it's not too hot out there for ya today?" he asked and without waiting for a response he continued on. "We've got a relatively short flight up t' the Canyon. Weather's pretty good for flying but still quite warm so I'll have the aircon on the whole way. There's a headset in the consoles on your right, bung 'em on ya scone if you want t' hear us, t' chat with us or just t' cut out the noise. Are ya strapped in?"

"Ah —" was all George got to say before the pilot was talking again.

"Great! What do ya say, let's get this show on the road, ay? Beauty!" With that the pilot turned, put on his headset and proceeded to start the engine.

George looked at his assistant, wondering what he had gotten them into. The assistant smiled meekly and shrugged. He pulled on his headset and handed another one to George.

Minutes later the helicopter was in the air, heading north and slightly east. The pilot launched into a tourist spiel about the surroundings and the views as they passed different points of interest.

George thought that he was in his own personal hell.

Fifty Two

Israfel's group was travelling along quite nicely. They only had another ten or so minutes until they would arrive at the resort, when a helicopter flew over them. It circled up ahead and then descended.

As it did, they saw a group of demons move up to meet it.

The three angels looked at each other.

"I don't think we really need to go any further do you?" one of the warriors asked, as he turned to Israfel who was driving.

The other warrior was looking at Israfel too. They waited for a response. Israfel kept them waiting while he looked ahead at the cloud of demons.

Finally he said, "If we were to turn around now, we would only draw attention to ourselves. We must act the tourist and continue on. As we pass the airstrip, try to see who is on the helicopter that requires such a welcoming committee."

The other two acknowledged the request and turned back to look at the descending helicopter. As they passed it, they thought they saw a largish demon join with one of the humans that stepped out. Then, as they watched, more demons started to appear. Their view was eventually blocked by the group of demons that had risen to greet the helicopter and were now descending with it. The warriors did their best not to actually look at any of the demons, as that would give them away. If they appeared threatened by the presence of the demons they did not show it, as that would also have revealed them to their ancient foes. They tried to keep their eyes straight ahead as they passed row after row of demon guard. It was as if the new arrival was someone of importance and they had all come out to see who it was.

As they passed the construction for the new resort, they noticed that it appeared to be the demons' den. They could see approximately twenty guards around and over it, spaced fairly evenly.

As they moved passed and on to the tourism offices, the number of demons started to thin out again. By the time they reached the offices, there were hardly any about. They knew they were still there, however: they could feel their presence. They would have to be very careful.

Nathaniel's group was not far behind Israfel's group. The road they travelled on had joined the same one that Israfel had taken from Uluru. They were only twenty minutes behind Israfel and his team.

They had seen the helicopter fly passed and circle in the distance before disappearing behind a black haze. As they got closer, they could see the cause of the haze. The demons were still near the helicopter. Not wanting to appear too interested in the demons or the helicopter, Nathaniel raised his hand to get the tour guide's attention.

Once the guide saw his hand up, Nathaniel asked about the small airfield. The tour guide launched into a tourist spiel about when it was first used and why. Nathaniel pretended to listen while he looked out the window with the rest of the tour group.

"Well done," one of the other warriors whispered in his ear.

"Thanks," Nathaniel whispered back. "We are going to have to be very careful," he said, more to himself than anyone else.

They watched as a small group of people walked from the helicopter, to a waiting four-wheel drive, accompanied by their demon counterparts. Then they were passed them.

The rest of the passengers on the bus were turning back to face the tour guide so they did too. The guide was now talking about a resort, 'The New Kings Resort', which was being built up ahead. They would pass it shortly. The resort would help draw lots more international tourists to this location. It was to be a sprawling complex that would accommodate just about every whim and desire its guests could have.

The angels noticed what the earlier group had seen: the demon guards surrounding the partially built building.

Nathaniel turned to the other two, "We are going to need a diversion of some sort. Then one of us can have a look around inside that building. Start thinking of what we can do and when we meet with the others, we can tell them of our plan."

The other two angels nodded their agreement.

Then they noticed the bus starting to slow down as if it were coming to a stop. They all looked up to see that they had arrived.

"Okay everyone, here we are. You can go inside and have a look around before we start the tour of the Canyon. Meet outside the kiosk in twenty minutes if you want to go," the guide said, as the bus continued to slow.

Micah's group was almost there too, but they had come from the other direction with the four-wheel-drive tour. The journey from Palm Valley had been enjoyable.

They were another ten minutes from the tourist offices and they had not seen any of the demons the others had.

Micah was just starting to think that this was not the right location when they spotted a small group of demons, only ten or so, around what appeared to be an exhaust tube coming up out of the ground.

Micah whispered into the ear of the passenger sitting in front of him. The passenger looked at the tube and called out to the driver who was also the guide.

"What's that out there on the right?"

The driver then explained about the new resort being built and that they were not fully sure what that was, except that it had not been there before the construction started. "I think it is used for natural ventilation – for the resort's air conditioning," the driver suggested. He then went on to explain that out here in the harsh outback environment most air conditioners are built into rooms underground. This helps to keep them protected from the searing heat of the sun and the sand and dust storms that spring up from nowhere.

The angels looked at each other.

"We need to have a closer look at that," Micah said to the other two.

"Look ahead," one of the other two said.

They all turned to look ahead and saw some of the demons over the resort in the distance. "I hope the others got through," Micah whispered.

Fifty Three

As the helicopter began its descent, George was looking at the tourist buses lined up in the car park for the National Park. Pretty soon the sight was gone and all that could be seen was the small airstrip that passed for the airport. His welcoming committee was waiting off to the side in the shade. They were trying not to get covered in the red dust that the downwash from the helicopter's rotor was kicking up.

George smiled to himself when he imagined the corporate heads arriving here in the same conditions. "What a sight that will be," he thought, "all those big important people covered in sweat and red dust."

The door opened, snapping George back to reality. As he stepped out from the air-conditioned comfort of the helicopter, the heat hit him like a wall and temporarily sucked the air out of his lungs. Sweat immediately appeared on his brow. He knew it wouldn't be long before it appeared on his shirt too.

Grom had watched the helicopter land and as soon as he saw his human step from it, he went forward and entered him, taking control of him once more.

"Welcome," Mr Kepler said, as he stepped forward to shake George's hand.

"Thank you," George replied, suddenly feeling a lot more comfortable, despite the heat. In fact, he hadn't felt this comfortable since late the previous afternoon, when he was 'requested' to stay in his room, pack and then wait for the trip to the airport.

"I am Ward Kepler, the 'Caretaker' of this facility."

"Pleased to meet you. I am George Murphy. I'm sure you are aware of why I am here?"

"Yes, to oversee the security preparations for the Chief Executive Officer's gathering. You will be working with our head of security, Isam," Mr Kepler indicated another man, standing about four feet behind him.

George looked around Mr Kepler at Isam and said, "I am sure we will be able to work together to incorporate the requirements I have with your existing security precautions."

"It is time we moved on. If you would please head towards the cars so that we can get back to the hotel," Isam said, not agreeing or disagreeing with George.

George noticed the attitude of Isam and thought to himself that he'd better keep an eye on him. George knew about the 'added personnel' they had here. He guessed that part of the reason that they had never had a successful escape was because of Isam's security measures;

measures that were so tough, they required replacements to that 'personnel' regularly. Such a man would be totally in control of everything that happened here and any changes to that would not be easily accepted, if at all. If Isam saw him as a threat, then his life could be in danger. If not his life, maybe his freedom. George wasn't sure which one would be worse.

Grom watched as Security motioned for them to get a move on. Wraith immediately moved off with his human, Mr Kepler, for the cars. Grom followed, thinking back to their first meeting the night before.

Bull's warning about the meddling humans in Cairns who are looking for their friends was not taken well. Both Wraith and Security had turned on Grom for letting them get this close to start with. The anger in the room flared and swords were drawn. It wasn't until after Bull had left, to return to Cairns, that Wraith had calmed down a little and put his huge curved sword down. After a few choice curses, Security also left. He went to check on the captives, the angel and the security precautions surrounding them.

Wraith had spoken briefly about what Grom would and wouldn't be allowed to do and then dismissed him. It wasn't until they had come out here to meet his human that he had seen either of them again. Grom thought he'd better watch his back around Security, especially as he appeared quite cunning and very in control of his troops.

George followed his companions to the waiting cars. They were then taken back to the hotel complex and the nearby building site, where an additional wing of rooms was being built. Mr Kepler left them and went back to his office. Isam offered to take him on a quick tour of his new surroundings.

The building site, as George already knew, was just a cover for the real construction, which was taking place underneath the earth. Additional to the normal underground tunnels, that connected both buildings and the air-conditioning systems was a temple, antechambers and meditation rooms. Very similar to what he had just left in Cairns.

George thought for a moment about the reason for the temple and these added rooms. "The CEOs believe that there is some sort of 'gateway' nearby. The link would lead them to an ancient power, one that would grant them wisdom and eternal life," he thought to himself.

"The plan was nicknamed "Eden", in reference to the mythical Garden of Eden mentioned in the Bible. It was rumoured to have contained two special fruit trees: the fruit of the first tree could supply the eater with wisdom; the other was supposed to add years to the eater's life, possibly even eternal life if you continued to eat the fruit regularly."

George shook his head in disbelief. He didn't much care for that ancient, mythical, mumbo jumbo. He just did what his boss told him, especially if he wanted to get paid the large sum they had offered him.

Grom also thought about the reason for this site. "The masters believe there is some sort of 'gateway' nearby. It will link up with the enemy's realm, where we originally lived long ago. The 'Garden' should be on the other side. This is especially sought after by Lucifer himself. Ever since his triumph there, he has been banished from entering it again. Therefore, all he wants to do is get back in. What a surprise that would be to the Lord!"

"Once we have control of the 'Garden', we can use it as a stepping stone to enter 'Heaven'. Then Lucifer can remove the Lord from his Throne, once and for all."

George's reverie was interrupted by Isam, who had been talking about the different rooms and the construction's progress.

"Sorry, what was that again?" George asked

"I said, the construction is ahead of schedule and will be ready before any of the CEOs arrive. That should make your plans a little easier," Isam repeated.

"That is good to hear. Should we go somewhere secure, to talk about them now?" George asked.

"As you wish," Isam replied with a short bow of the head. "Follow me."

George followed Isam into the tunnels, towards the meeting room that he had chosen earlier, for their discussions.

Fifty Four

Raphael stood quietly to the side, waiting patiently to see Sarah, the 'Pillar' for the Australasia region. Sarah was busy conferring with several messengers and Raphael could overhear some of what was being said. As a result, he felt he needed to interrupt the discussion.

"Excuse me," Raphael said, "may I interrupt for a moment?"

Sarah and the messengers looked up at Raphael. Her expression soon changed from one of displeasure, to one of welcome.

"Raphael?" Sarah asked. "I did not know you were here. Please, go ahead and speak."

"I've only just arrived here from Cairns, where I am serving the Lord by assisting in a most delicate and important mission. I think it involves the very thing you were just discussing," Raphael said.

"Really? Well maybe you can help enlighten me then," Sarah replied.

"May I ask what you know and what you have discovered first?" Raphael inquired.

"A messenger arrived yesterday," Sarah replied, "asking if I knew of a threat involving our enemy and, if I did, where they might be gathering. In response, I sent out my fastest scouts, all messengers, asking them to see what the local saints knew. I was unaware of any extra enemy activity in this region. At the same time, they were to get the saints praying for insight into the threat the Captain is concerned about. They have all only just returned and we were discussing the findings."

"Can you share them with me too, please?" Raphael requested.

Sarah looked at him momentarily before answering, "There seems to be some extra activity in various locations, all with one thing in common."

"Would that be construction sites?" Raphael asked before Sarah could say it.

Sarah was taken aback by the fact that Raphael seemed to know this already. "Yes, construction sites. We have a number of locations but two in particular have unusually high numbers of guards surrounding them. Both locations gave the scouts cause to question if maybe one of the Seven Princes of Darkness were present at it. I then checked on the Den in Sydney that we suspect is the home of the local Prince. That had an even larger number of guards, at least twice as many. We then rechecked both the earlier locations but found only minimal guards this time. I was about to send a reply to the Captain, advising him of my findings. Should I delay this message?"

"Only slightly, for once I have told you what I know of this I am sure you will understand more of what is at stake. With that in mind, you may wish to change your message," Raphael answered. "Are these all of the scouts that you sent out? What I have to say is not common knowledge but they are already a part of it. They need to know what it is they have become involved in. I am sure that in time more will need to know, but I need to press upon all involved the necessity for secrecy, for the time being."

Sarah looked at the messengers that were present. Everyone that she had sent had returned and was gathered with her. "We are all here," she replied.

"The mission I am involved in relates to the welfare of several humans, believers and friends of the believers. It appears that our old adversary is seeking a new entrance into the Lord's Garden. They believe that there is somewhere on this planet that will grant them access through some kind of back door. We are not fully aware of what the construction has to do with it, but we think that it may be for them to cover the real intent of their being in that location. We know of a building site north of Cairns, in the Daintree area. Is this one of the sites you found?"

"Yes. The other is in a place called Kings Canyon," Sarah advised.

"In Central Australia?" Raphael asked.

"Yes. Part of the location has a tropical rainforest, which the humans call the 'Garden of Eden'," Sarah told Raphael. "Do you think that is the connection?"

"Yes. Israfel is on his way there to investigate it but he doesn't know of the Den there," Raphael replied. "We can't worry about that right now. That is in the Lord's hands."

"What about the reduction of guards? Do you think that means they have abandoned that site?" Sarah asked.

Raphael thought for a moment before answering. "I think they may be expecting us. They know we have seen the Daintree site and suspect something there. Maybe they are trying to hide their presence now?" Raphael suggested.

"With all of this going on, I have come here to ask for prayer cover for the humans who are involved in this. We have a plan to get them out of Cairns and I know we are going to need prayer cover for it. Who can you recommend in Cairns that can get the saints praying for this?"

"One of the Churches there is very faithful to God. Their guardian is Sarosh and he leads the minister to prayer constantly. They should be your first visit," suggested Sarah.

She supplied Raphael with the names of several Saints and churches throughout Cairns and the surrounding areas, all of whom she felt he should speak with regarding the prayer cover. Once he had all the names, he left to get the prayers started.

FIFTY FIVE

Jade had been with Max as he made his previous phone call, listening to what he was discovering about the people who run the construction company. She was waiting for the appointed time to set her part of the plan in motion. Earlier, Max's guardian Ishmerai watched Max while listening to Jade explain what Glen had gotten himself into and what they had planned.

The Spirit moved. It was time.

Tim was looking over his books and planning out his next week as his phone rang.

"Tim's Yacht Charters, Tim speaking," he said into the phone after picking it up.

"Hello Tim, my name is Max. I was wondering if I could charter a yacht tomorrow. I know it is short notice but it is kind of an emergency."

"Tomorrow?" Tim responded, checking the calendar in front of him. "Would you require a pilot?"

"I think so. It would be to take one person out to Green Island, pick at least two people up and take them all to Townsville."

"Sorry, I don't work on Sundays. It's against my religion," Tim replied.

In the background Pia looked at Amna, who had replaced her as Tim's guardian. "We need to get him to do it this time. How can we convince him?"

"I'm not sure. Since that run-in with the demons out at sea, he hasn't gone out on Sundays," Amna explained.

Through the phone they could hear Jade, "As a fellow believer in Christ..."

Max asked, "Are you a Christian, Tim?"

"Yes, I am," Tim replied, while also thinking to himself, here we go, another plea to a fellow Christian.

"As a fellow believer in Christ, I need to press upon you the importance of this charter. I have a friend currently in Cairns and I believe he is being hassled by some demonic forces. If he leaves the city by any other means, they will find and follow him. Then they would probably lead some very nasty people to him as well."

There was silence on the other end of the line as Tim took in exactly what Max had just said. Max waited, knowing that Tim had heard him and was still there.

Pia knelt alongside Tim and Amna did the same on the other side of him.

"The Lord would like your help in this Tim. He will not forsake you for doing His work on a Sunday," Pia said quietly into one ear.

"Seek the Lord and be assured," Amna spoke in the other ear.

"Listen, Max was it? I need to pray on this for a moment. If you are truly a brother in Christ, you will understand. Should I call you back?"

Max thought for a moment and then responded, "I understand. I also know that you will not be long in getting your reassurance. I will wait, if that is okay with you?"

"Okay," Tim replied and he put the handset down on his desk. He turned the chair and dropped to his knees in prayer.

Pia and Amna stood over Tim with their wings raised high, enjoying the feeling of a saint at prayer, kneeling before the throne of God, seeking His guidance.

"Go and be blessed," the Lord of all spoke to Tim's heart.

"Amen," Tim said and raised his head up. Climbing back into his chair, he picked the phone up. "You still there?"

"Yep," Max replied.

"Okay, but I am going to need some more details."

Fifty Six

Raphael arrived at the church in Cairns that Sarah had directed him to. He felt the need to get the prayer cover started as soon as possible. As he entered the church, he saw a large angel straight away and made his way towards him, hoping that this was Sarosh.

Sarosh bowed as soon as he saw Raphael, as a sign of respect. "What brings you, Raphael, to our humble little church?" he asked.

"Are you Sarosh?" Raphael asked.

"Yes, do you seek me? For what purpose may I assist you?" Sarosh asked.

"I need to get some saints praying as soon as possible. It is a matter most urgent."

"Please, follow me. The minister and the elders are meeting right now. They have been quite responsive in the past in these matters."

Sarosh led Raphael into the church and then out an adjoining door, through to the offices. They found the leaders of the church gathered together in the meeting room.

"What are we praying for?" Sarosh asked Raphael.

"Deliverance from the evil one and his minions. For the actions that they are pursuing, in and around this city, to be bound in Jesus's name. For the safety of His saints who are in connection with this matter and for the Lord's will to be done," replied Raphael.

Sarosh turned to the minister and found that the man of God had already dropped to his knees. He and the Elders were so in tune with the Holy Spirit that they were already responding to the prayer request they had heard in their hearts.

Raphael, Sarosh and the other angels felt the presence of the Lord as these saints petitioned Him before His throne. Raphael started to sing praises to the Lord. Soon the other angels had joined him in worship of the Lord of all.

****

At the same time in Sydney, Pastor Williams was visiting with some of the parishioners from the church that he was associated with, the same church that Glen attended. There was a group of them and they were currently holding the weekly meeting of the Friendship club. They were discussing what event they should hold next.

One of the elderly gentlemen, Lance, was mid-sentence when Pastor Williams suddenly felt an urge to pray for Glen's safety and interrupted him.

"Forgive me, Lance, but I feel such a strong urge to pray for one of our friends right now that I don't think it will wait. Will you all join me in prayer?" Pastor Williams asked.

Claire, a younger member of the group, had also felt the stirring of the Holy Spirit. "Would you be referring to Glen? Who rang last night and set the prayer chain in action? I feel an urge to pray for him too."

Several of the others were also on the prayer chain and said they, too, felt the need to pray for Glen.

"Then let us pray for him," Pastor Williams said.

They all bowed their heads and joined together to petition the Lord to help Glen and keep him safe.

****

Henry was asleep in his bed when he awoke suddenly and looked around. Alan noticed his movements and looked over at him. Catching the look in his eyes, he came over to check on him.

"What is it?" Alan asked his new friend.

Henry looked up at him, "Do you believe in God, Alan?"

A little surprised by the bluntness with which Henry asked him such a personal question, Alan could only stare at him for a moment. Then he gathered his wits and replied, "I guess I believe in God but I am not sure about most of that. I have friends who have tried to convince me about Jesus, but I never really believed what they said about him. Why do you ask?"

Henry lowered his eyes for a moment as he searched for the right words. "I don't think you would really understand but I have just had a really strong feeling that a friend needs help right now and that I should pray for him. I didn't want to do it alone." He looked up to see Alan's reaction.

Alan just looked at him and then replied, "This feeling, what is it like? Because I suddenly can't get one of my friends out of my mind and I think that maybe she is in trouble too."

A smile slowly spread across Henry's face. "That's exactly the sort of feeling."

Now Alan looked down at the floor, "I was afraid you might say that. Do you think it is a coincidence that I felt that way at the same time you did?" he said looking back up at Henry.

"No. I think it happened on purpose. Will you pray with me about our friends?" Henry asked.

Alan looked uneasy. "I haven't done that before... I am not sure how to," he admitted.

"Don't worry, it's easy. We just bow our heads and speak what is in our hearts. I will start off... but first I need to tell you that my friend's name is Glen. What's your friend's name?"

"Kerri."

"Okay, here we go," Henry said, and then he closed his eyes and bowed his head. Alan watched for a moment and then bowed his head too. Every now and then, he opened his eyes to check on what Henry was doing as he spoke his prayer out loud.

FIFTY SEVEN

Daniel had arrived at the train station in Cairns. He had snuck in and was now waiting patiently for the appointed time to set the plan in motion. While he waited, he searched for a couple of demons who he could parade in front of.

Meanwhile, Kyle watched as Kerri paced the room and Glen sat before his laptop. Glen was working on putting some of this into a story for his newspaper but was finding Kerri's pacing to be distracting. Kyle could feel Kerri's frustration building. He turned to Amy and asked, "She doesn't like to wait for things does she?"

"Not really. I haven't known her very long but in that time she has been a woman on a mission. She hasn't even stopped to 'smell the roses', so to speak," Amy replied.

"It will not be much longer anyway. Max should be calling back any minute..."

As if on cue, the phone rang, interrupting Kyle. Kyle and Amy both turned to watch and listen. Glen stood and went over to answer the phone. Kerri followed him.

"Hello," Glen said picking up the phone.

"Glen, its Max."

"How'd —" Glen tried to ask but was cut off by Max.

"No time! Listen carefully. I will only say this once!"

"Can I get a pen and some paper?"

"No time for that. Are you ready?"

"Not really, but go ahead."

"The two of you are booked on a four p.m. boat to Green Island from pier twenty seven. I have organised a hotel room for you there, the bridal suite. Everything is in the name of Hughes. No first names given. The charter will pick you up tomorrow at ten a.m. The boat is named 'Asher'. Did you get all that?" Max asked.

"Four pm, pier twenty seven, Hughes, bridal suite, ten a.m., 'Asher'," Glen repeated. "Was that it?"

"Yes, now pack and get out of there. Go to a shopping mall or something. Just don't stay there. Get somewhere where there is a lot of people and it is hard to be seen," Max said.

"What? Max, what have you found out?" Glen asked.

"Glen, I can't tell you now. It would take too long and you need to get out of there as soon as you can! Call me from a payphone, from wherever you go," Max instructed Glen. "I'll tell you more then."

"Why can't you tell me now?" Glen asked.

"These people are obviously upset with you. They will not rest until they find you. They are probably on their way there right now. Glen, trust me on this, okay?"

There was a slight pause as Glen thought for a moment. "Okay," he said at last. "I'll call your home as soon as I can."

"Good. God be with you!" Max replied

"Thanks. Talk soon." Glen said.

"You'd better." With that Max hung up and Glen was left standing there looking at the phone and wondering what that was all about.

"Well?" Kerri asked.

"Let's pack and get out of here," Glen instructed as he replaced the receiver and turned to look at Kerri. "Leave behind anything you don't need. We have to be out of here as soon as possible."

"I only have what I am wearing and my camera bag. So I'm already packed. Would you like me to call a Taxi or are we going in your car?" Kerri asked.

"Call reception and tell them we are checking out and will be down shortly to fix up the bill. Ask them to have a taxi out the front for us in fifteen minutes," Glen said, as he packed up the laptop. "And see if they can return the hire car for me too."

Daniel had been watching two demons that were with a man near the payphones for fifteen minutes before deciding to use them as his assistants in his ruse. While he watched, the man had picked the pocket of a woman who was using one of the phones. He had decided just in time. He felt the Spirit prompting him into action.

Daniel ducked into the nearby toilets and into one of the stalls. He instantly changed his appearance so that he appeared to be Glen. He then became solid, stepped out of the cubicle and walked out of the toilets.

Daniel walked slowly towards the phones, looking all around as if he was looking for someone that might be following him. He made sure he walked into the man so that he and the demons got a good close look at him. This also doubled as a chance to pick his pocket and take some cash out of it. After apologising, he walked off quickly and made his way to the counter to buy a ticket. Daniel didn't feel bad about what he had done as he was sure the man had gotten all the money illegally.

Daniel looked around again. He noticed that the man had followed at a distance and was watching him. Daniel asked for a ticket for Atherton and paid for it with the cash he had just taken from the man. He then proceeded towards the platform that the train would be leaving from.

Daniel looked around again. He noticed that the man only had one demon with him now and was heading back to the payphones.

Daniel smiled to himself and turned behind a corner so that he was out of view and changed back to his normal appearance. Hopefully that would be enough to lead the enemy astray so that Kyle and Amy could get away easier. All he could do now was watch and wait. In the meantime, he would look for the woman and try to return the rest of the money to her.

FIFTY EIGHT

Abram and Troy had watched through the night as the angels returned and the church gathered to pray. The angels of the saints had listened to all the different groups and what they had found out so far. It was not much and had not given them any new information.

Rundle had been the first to return and Bruce was right behind him. Along with them had arrived Roger the Pastor, and Charlie the Police Chief. Roger had tried to convince Charlie that he had to send someone to check out the road between Coffin Bay and Elliston. When Charlie had asked why, Roger had admitted that he didn't know. It had come to him in a dream. The same dream that had woken him.

Charlie agreed. He had been woken by a dream too. In his dream, he had been told to speak to Roger about someone who had gone missing. He explained that it was a three-hour drive from Ceduna to that area but only an hour from Port Lincoln. He would call and ask them to check it out. Abram smiled as Charlie walked away, shaking his head and telling himself that this was not going to be easy to explain. Roger then went to the altar and knelt in prayer.

Pretty soon, he was joined by his parishioners. As they arrived, they took seats in the chapel and prayed too. They waited for their minister to explain why they were there, knowing only that they felt they needed to be there. Chris and Tracey arrived with the last of them.

Abram had then sent Chris and Rundle to search the hospitals and hotels for any sign of the minister or his kidnappers.

That had happened very early in the morning. It was now midday and they were all returning again from their searches.

"No sign of them anywhere," Chris said, as he and Rundle returned.

"Thank you for your efforts, none the less," replied Abram.

They all looked into the chapel to watch the congregation. They had gathered together to petition the Lord, for the safety and well-being of the missing minister. The other angels, Troy, Tracey and Bruce, were in the chapel too. They were helping to lead the humans in their prayers and joining them in their petitions before the throne of God.

"Go and join the others. If I have need of you, I will call. We can do nothing but wait until the return of both Clare and Stan.

****

It was another half hour before Clare arrived back. When she did, Abram called them all together for her report.

"I found the location easy enough and searched it pretty thoroughly. I found nothing further other than what Troy mentioned. I then waited for the police so that I could show them where the damage was and what was left of the motorbike," Clare explained.

"Did they find anything?" Troy asked eagerly.

"Nothing new, only what you already told us," Clare replied.

"Thank you, Clare," Abram said. "It's in the Lord's hands now. We must wait now to see what Stan says on his return and follow the Spirit's prompting until then."

They all turned and rejoined the congregation of the church in the chapel.

FIFTY NINE

Glen and Kerri were waiting downstairs at the apartment building, just inside the doors, for a taxi to arrive.

Kyle was just outside the doors, watching for any sign of the enemy, when he saw something that would have turned his blood cold if he had any. He slipped quickly but quietly back inside the foyer.

"Change of plans – Pride is back," he said as he entered, "and he has brought some friends with him!"

"What?" Amy exclaimed, "Where? Did they see you?"

"No, they are up there, flying straight to the room," Kyle replied.

"How many of them did you see?" Amy asked.

"Quite a few, which means their humans won't be far behind. What should we do?"

"What about a diversion? Just like Daniel is doing at the train station and you did earlier with Ruth and the taxi. You could use the hire car instead?" Amy suggested.

"Good idea. I'll do that and keep them occupied for a while. You will need to get Glen and Kerri to go somewhere public. Somewhere that has payphones," Kyle said.

"Okay, but where? The shopping mall they mentioned earlier?" Amy asked.

"That's a possibility," Kyle thought for a moment. "What about a pub or hotel that has pokies? They usually draw a crowd with some of the wrong sort of element. They wouldn't think to look for us in their own backyard, so to speak."

Amy nodded her agreement and then exclaimed, "I know, what about the Casino! With them out looking for us, it will be less guarded and there are usually a lot of people in their pokies room. That would give us a crowd to hide in too."

Kyle nodded his agreement, "Very well, I will see you there or on the boat. For the Glory of the Lord and His Kingdom!"

"For the Glory of the Lord and His Kingdom!" repeated Amy.

Kyle turned and headed for the rear entrance and the car park.

Amy didn't watch him but turned straight to Glen and said, "Time's up Glen, we can't wait anymore. If Max is right, then we have waited too long as it is. We need to leave now and walk if necessary."

Glen's patience had worn thin. He had been watching out the window for what felt like hours, but was really only ten minutes. He was considering taking Kerri over to the bar to wait, when he decided that they couldn't wait there any longer. He stood up, leaning over to Kerri as he picked up his bag and said, "If Max is right, we shouldn't be sitting here waiting for a taxi. We need to leave now. Even if we have to walk..."

A loud screeching of tyres broke through the silence of the hotel foyer.

"...there," Glen said, completing his sentence while turning his head, with everyone else in the vicinity, to look towards the street to see who was driving like a maniac. What he saw made him do a double take.

The hire car, *his* hire car, was shooting down the road away from the apartment block, with someone that looked at lot like him driving it. There was another small screech as the car and a taxi both quickly swerved to avoid a collision.

Glen looked at Kerri who was now standing alongside him. "Did you see that?" he asked her.

"It looked like you," Kerri said amazed.

"And that's our taxi, finally," Glen said, pointing to the taxi that was pulling up in front of the building. "Quick, while everyone else is distracted, let's sneak out."

Kerri helped Glen with his luggage. They slipped quietly out the front door. The occupants of the front bar were still looking out the front window, but at the quickly receding hire car and not them.

"That's it," Amy said, as she helped Kerri pass a particularly heavy case to the driver. She looked up to see a small contingent of demons, including Pride, quickly follow the hire car. One split off from the group and headed down to a small procession of cars which were now approaching the apartment building. Each car had at least two larger demons riding on the roof. There was some quick gesturing by the demons. Then the two cars quickly turned around and chased after the hire car.

Amy smiled, said a quick prayer of thanks and then one for safekeeping for Kyle, who could now be danger.

"Where to?" the taxi driver asked, as he loaded the last bag. "The airport?"

"The bus depot and then the Casino," Amy said.

"The bus depot and then the Casino please," Kerri replied.

Glen looked at her with a puzzled expression.

"We can't carry the luggage with us everywhere and I need to collect something," Kerri said, explaining her suggested destinations.

The driver raised an eyebrow at Glen, as if to ask if that was where he wanted to go too.

"Of course," Glen replied, "great idea, Mrs Hughes." He winked at Kerri as he said the last part. "Wouldn't be much of a honeymoon if I dragged my work gear around too, now would it." Glen turned to the taxi driver. "How do you like that? Not even married a week and she is already bossing me around," he said jokingly.

Kerri put on a look of mock seriousness and then laughed a short laugh that said, 'I know that was a joke but it was too close to the line'.

"Sorry sweetheart, just having a joke with the nice man," Glen said, as he took Kerri's hands in his.

Kerri smiled. Out of the corner of her eye she caught the driver roll his eyes, as if to say, 'not another couple of newlyweds'. She gave Glen a quick wink to let him know that their little ruse was working.

They slipped into the back seat of the taxi, holding hands and speaking quietly to each other. The driver pulled the taxi away from the curb and into the traffic.

SIXTY

Saint Peter and Michael entered the Hall of the Lamb and were met by several more angels than they expected.

Gabriel could be heard above all the other voices: "I am sure the Captain will be right back, he has gone to the Throne and cannot be interrupted right now." Gabriel sensed rather than heard the entrance of more angels and turned towards the door. "Here he is now, but let me speak first, please."

The twelve messengers to whom Gabriel was speaking turned as one to see Michael and Saint Peter standing just inside the door.

Michael was surprised to see so many messengers. Then he remembered: he was expecting to receive reports from the remaining eleven that he had sent to the pillars. He noticed that Ruth was the twelfth.

Gabriel indicated David at the end of the hall, still sitting at the table that had been set up for their research into the possible locations of gateways. Michael, Saint Peter and Gabriel all headed for David.

"You have returned just in time," Gabriel spoke as they reached David. "The messengers you sent earlier have all returned. They started arriving just a short while ago. Ruth has also returned with an update for you and Stan is waiting for your instructions. David and I are not having much luck, although, we have come up with a few more locations to check out."

"Thank you for the update. I think I will speak with the messengers first and then decide on the next course of action. Let us all hear what they have to say." Michael turned away from his little group. He called out to everyone else present, "Your attention please. Can I have everyone over here please? Thank you."

All the messengers and the warriors in the Hall, including those that were awaiting activation, moved over to where Michael was.

"We are all here for the same reasons. I think everyone needs to hear your reports," Michael said to the messengers. "Please, one by one, tell us what you have to pass on. You can start, Apostolos."

"I visited the Pillar of Europe, Konrad. He had nothing to report but will keep a look out. They have started their saints praying," Apostolos reported.

"Good," Michael said and turned to the next messenger, "Ryder?"

"Abidan of the Canadas reports the same. No activity noticed and saints praying as requested," replied Ryder.

"Okay, Nunzio?"

"I visited Nehemiah, the Pillar of the Southern and South Pacific Oceans and Antarctica. He asked me to pass on the same information – no activity detected and the saints are praying."

"Thank you. Driscoll?"

"Erik, the Pillar of the Scandinavian region, has noticed a build up on the Aland Islands, near a place called Eden," Driscoll paused for a moment as Michael shot a glance to Gabriel, who in turn looked at David, who had already started to look at his notes. Driscoll continued, "He has also passed on the prayer request to the saints in the area."

"Interesting. David do you have that town noted already?" Michael asked.

"No, but I have added it, with a note to check it out as soon as possible," David answered.

"Good. Who is next?" Michael asked. Not waiting for an answer, he picked out one of the messengers, "Rasul?"

"Yes, sir, I was sent to the North American Pillar, Susannah. She said she would try to spot any increases in activity and would send out the prayer request but had nothing to report as yet."

"Thank you, Rasul. Vesna?"

"Rutendo, the African Pillar advised that he will proceed with your prayer request at once. He did wish to advise you of a larger than normal congregation of demons at a town called 'Eden' in South Africa."

Michael looked at David with raised eyebrows.

"I already had that one down but I will highlight it," David said, without looking up.

"Good. There appears to be a pattern forming, which I am not surprised about. Does anyone else have an Eden to tell me about? Agathangelos? Did your Pillar have anything?"

"No, Captain," replied Agathangelos, "but Pascale, from South America, did say she would keep a watchful eye out."

"Malachi?"

"James, from the UK, had nothing to pass on," replied Malachi.

"Evangelos?"

"Sarah, from the Australasia region, was visited by Raphael while I was there," Evangelos advised. "He informed Sarah and her scouts of the issue at hand. Sarah confirmed the location of two gatherings, one in Daintree, north of Cairns, and the other in Kings Canyon, in Central Australia. This, he advised, is where Israfel is headed. Raphael then pointed out that both gatherings are centred on construction sites. A town called 'Eden' was also mentioned. They told me that there was evidence to show that the enemy had been active there, but whatever they had been doing appeared to be concluded. There is no activity there now."

Michael looked thoughtful for a moment before replying, "Thank you, Evangelos. That was quite comprehensive. David, add that Eden to your list, if you don't already have it. Please mark it as important. I would like it checked out, to make sure it is all okay. There may still be some remnants of the enemy that may require removing."

"I did have that one already," David replied, "I will mark if for a closer inspection."

"What about Melchior of Asia? Which of you went there?" Michael asked the remaining messengers, Sherah and Levi.

"I did," Sherah answered, "and he had nothing to advise."

"Okay. That would mean you went to see Bethel in the Middle East, is that right Levi?" asked Michael.

"Yes. It is a difficult area to pick up increased activity in. With all the wars and fighting still in the area, there is always lots of enemy activity. They chose instead to look for anything that appeared to be out of the ordinary for the enemy. What was noticed was that in the general area where the 'four rivers' are said to meet was a construction site with demon activity surrounding it. The location is in Iran, not far from the Persian Gulf. As for the saints, they have been roused and are praying for illumination as we speak."

"Thank you, Levi. Do you think you can show David where exactly in Iran that is?" Michael asked.

"Of course," Levi replied.

Michael turned to Gabriel and asked, "Did we think of checking there?"

"No, we hadn't. We were concentrating on the Eden connection," Gabriel answered. "But we will definitely check on that one now."

"Alright then," Michael continued, "Ruth, what have you got to tell us?"

"Raphael and company have been busy putting a plan together to get the humans out of Cairns and to somewhere safe. If all has gone according to their plan, they should be leaving right now," Ruth informed them.

"Can you give me a quick outline of the plan?" Michael asked.

Ruth nodded as she replied, "Yes, I can. They are going to try to leave on a tourist boat, meet a charter boat offshore and return to a different city down the coast." Michael looked like he wanted more information than that so she continued: "Daniel is organising a distraction at the train station, Raphael was organising prayer cover and the others were to visit the humans who would help organise things so that the plan worked seamlessly."

Michael listened carefully to what Ruth told him and then just stood there for a moment, quietly, with his eyes closed. The others looked on, wondering what he was up to — except Gabriel and David, who knew him best. Gabriel indicated to the rest that they should just wait quietly for Michael.

Finally, Michael opened his eyes. He looked at Gabriel and then Saint Peter. Then to all he said, "Thank you all for your reports. By now you should realise that this has something to do with Eden and more specifically the Lord's Garden. For some reason, the evil one thinks that he can sneak into the Garden from some back door on Earth. We do not know if it is possible, so we need to try to find out first, before we receive unwanted visitors. Gabriel has been attempting to check the locations that the enemy may try to enter from, before they get there. This hasn't always been possible as the enemy is ahead of us on this. What we are going to do is make sure that Eden is well protected. Then we are going to set a trap for the enemy.

"At the same time," Michael continued, "two humans have become involved because some of their friends have disappeared. We are trying to help them locate their friends before it is too late. Meanwhile, the enemy is aware of them too and is trying to find them. We need to help keep them safe, hence the escape plan that Ruth mentioned. That is where we are at right now."

Michael paused for a moment. His tone was a lot more serious when he continued, "I need you all to keep this to yourselves. The entire Host of Heaven will be advised when the time is right. I am afraid that if we told them now it could cause some to rush off to protect the Garden and leave Heaven open for a direct assault. Do you all understand?"

They nodded their agreement.

Michael started to pace as he outlined his plans: "On to the next step then. Here is what I would like you all to do. Ruth, you need to return again to the humans. I will send some additional warriors back with you, as the Spirit has told me that all is not as you left it. You will need to meet them out at sea on the boat. The rest of you messengers will need to see Gabriel for your next task. Warriors, we need to know exactly where this Den is in Daintree. Locate it but do so with extreme caution. See, but do not be seen. Gabriel, we need to check out all the locations mentioned as soon as we can. You will need to send some of the messengers to Jasper for more groups of warriors. Send a group to the location in Iran first. I would like you to go with a group to the Eden in Australia.

"David, I need you to attend to the other issue that we found out about. I will to talk to you and Stan about that in a moment.

"Do the rest of you understand your tasks as I have set them out?"

"Yes, Captain!" they all answered.

"Very well, off you go then. For the Glory of the Lord and His Kingdom!"

"For the Glory of the Lord and His Kingdom!" they all replied.

Michael turned and spoke again, "Stan, David and Saint Peter, please come over here with me."

The messengers and warriors moved off with Gabriel for him to assign their tasks. Ruth left to get some warriors to go with her. Stan, David and Saint Peter followed Michael over to a corner, where they could speak alone.

"Stan, you must not tell anyone about Eden. Not even Abram. I would like you to concentrate on finding the minister. He is of prime importance to you, although, I suspect he is just an excuse to try to keep us away. David, you will be going back with Stan to help in any way you can. I expect you, Stan, to be the only messenger I see in regards to this. Do not allow any other messenger to become involved. You stay with David and only you report back to me. Understand?"

"Yes Captain," Stan replied.

"What exactly do you want me to do?" David asked Michael.

"Lead the investigation, be my eyes and ears as I am stuck here," Michael answered. "The Holy Spirit is telling me that we need to do something to help the minister straight away and you are the one to send. The Eden issue is where I need to be right now. You need to follow where the Spirit leads and most importantly, find them."

"I will Captain. For the Glory of the Lord and His Kingdom!"

"For the Glory of the Lord and His Kingdom!" responded Michael and Saint Peter.

Stan and David turned and headed for the door.

"What are we going to do now?" Saint Peter asked Michael. "Are we going to see the rest of the Saints?"

"I don't think that's going to be necessary. I thought this Eden issue was a separate matter to the Spirit's initial warning. I was going to utilize the Hall of the Saints for our use and leave Gabriel alone in here. But now that I know it isn't separate, we will not need it. It would be better to operate from right here, as we already are," Michael replied, answering the second question first. He turned and looked back across the room to the maps of Earth that David had hung behind his desk. "We will prepare more warriors to check out every Eden that was mentioned and others that David and Gabriel are suspicious about. Then I will tell you about Day Seven of Creation."

Sixty One

Jack stepped off the bus and moved away from the door to stretch his legs. At a little over six feet tall, he often found travelling to be uncomfortable if he had to sit for long periods of time.

Jack looked at the other passengers as they got off the bus, paying special attention to the three new passengers that had joined them at their last stop, Palm Valley. So far they had stayed to themselves and not mingled with the other passengers. That was unusual for tour groups but not unheard of, especially if you joined later.

Jack thought that maybe he should make some extra effort to make them feel part of the group. He watched the three of them as they walked a short distance away. They were talking amongst themselves while looking at the new construction site.

"Please check in at the hotel before you go wandering off to look at the sights. We have a dedicated tour guide joining us at eleven and again at two p.m. She will take us through the areas that you cannot visit on your own anymore," the driver called from the door.

Jack looked over at the three newcomers. They didn't appear to hear the message. Jack thought it was the perfect excuse to approach them and introduce himself. He started to walk towards them.

Just as Jack reached them, he said, "Excuse me," and they turned to look at him, "Hi. Just thought you should know the driver advised us to check in first. The tours will be at eleven and two, if you want to see all of the attractions with the guide from here."

"Thank you," Micah replied. "We will do that shortly."

Jack stopped and just stared for a moment at Micah, his mouth open, as if his jaw had dropped.

Micah looked at his companions and back at Jack. "Are you okay?" he asked.

"You... remind me of someone I met," Jack replied. "Have you ever been to the Garden of Eden?"

Micah and his companions looked shocked for a moment and shared a look of concern. "I'm sorry. Did you say the Garden of Eden?" Micah asked Jack.

Jack noticed the shock and the look they shared. "Yes, the Garden of Eden. I have been told that it can be quite warm in the middle of the day. The sun comes down, into the valley from above and there is not much shade at that time. But later in the afternoon, it cools down nicely as the sun is out of sight behind the walls."

Recognition dawned across Micah's face. "That is one of the sights here isn't it?"

"Yes. Why? What did you think I was talking about?" Jack asked in reply.

"I had no idea," replied Micah trying to relax.

"By the way, I'm Jack," Jack said, introducing himself and he held out his hand.

"Micah," Micah replied shaking Jack's hand and then indicated his companions, "this is Ivor and Duncan."

"Nice to meet you," they said, as they shook Jack's hand too.

"Would you like to join me and my friends for some coffee, after you've checked in?" Jack asked.

"That would be nice but we have to meet someone else shortly," Micah replied.

Duncan had an idea and spoke to Jack, "We were just looking at the construction work first. I am interested in architecture and we were discussing whether this new building was going to suit the natural surroundings or not. What do you think?"

Both Ivor and Micah shot a glance at Duncan.

Jack turned to look at the construction site. "Hard to say at this stage. Without any outer walls, they could still do almost anything. However, it does appear to be a bit dark. As if it is in shadow. What do you think the flashing red lights are for? Or are they orange? Would they be lasers for levelling purposes or something else entirely?"

Ivor stared at Jack, Micah's eyes went wide and Duncan scratched his chin and looked at the site too.

"They could be laser levels or other tools with laser sights. Whatever type they are, I'm sure they would have to be something to do with the construction," Duncan said, as if what Jack had seen was nothing out of the ordinary. "As for the shade, they most likely have something rigged up for the workers, to help keep them cool."

"You're probably right," Jack said turning back to his new friends. "Well, if you have to meet someone else then I'd better not keep you. The offer of coffee is still there if you get back in time. Or maybe we could meet for lunch?"

"Thanks," Micah replied, "we will see how we go with the time. I think lunch might be a better idea."

"It was nice meeting you all," Jack said, as he shook hands with them again and then walked away to find Tony.

The angels just stood there and watched him walk away. Then they turned and walked off towards the entrance to the national park and their pre-arranged rendezvous.

Ivor couldn't contain himself any longer, "Did he say he could see their eyes?"

"That's what I thought he was talking about too," replied Micah. "How did you know to ask him about that and what he might see?" Micah asked Duncan.

"Simple really," Duncan replied, "he could see us."

Micah and Ivor both stopped walking and Duncan took another step before realising that they had stopped. Duncan turned back to look at them.

"What do you mean he could see us?" Ivor asked.

Duncan couldn't believe he asked that question. He bent over, picked up a stick and walked back to stand in front of Ivor. Then he poked it through him. They all looked at the stick, half in Ivor and half out of him.

Duncan spoke, "As soon as everyone else left the bus, we all became immaterial. Nobody could see us, remember? But somehow, he could still see us. I thought, if he could see us then maybe he could see the enemy too. Besides that, I noticed he had some sort of residue on him. A type of glow about him, which tells me that he has had encounters with other angels recently."

"Do you think he knows what we are?" Micah asked.

"I think he suspects it, yes. If that is the case, then we might need to get out of here as soon as we can," Duncan replied.

"Then we'd better find Israfel and the others quickly," Micah said.

SIXTY TWO

Luthor shuffled his feet as he waited on the roof of the airport – not an easy thing to achieve with his large, black, scaly hide. Pandora stood nearby, watching the sky for the plane that was bringing their new overseer in. She could hear the noise he was making with his feet.

"Relax," Pandora said to Luthor, not taking her eyes from the sky, "he can't be that bad. Grom was a nothing and unpredictable; Cain is totally the opposite and can be seriously scary. All the same, I would rather have him than Grom. Why would Lucas be much different to Cain?"

"From what I have heard about him, Lucas is really nasty. If you don't do what he asks right away... Luthor ran a finger across his throat to indicate what he meant. "No second chances."

"Since when have you not carried out an order straight away?" Pandora asked. "Respond to him the way you do with Cain and you will be okay. What were you before you were named? Afraid? Paranoid? Fear? What?"

Luthor bowed his head and said very quietly, "Panic."

"Well, that is not who you are now and not what you do. Snap out of it! You are one of the Named now. You have earned that right and if you continue to act this way, then you will not have to worry about Lucas but me instead!"

Luthor looked at Pandora, "Is that a threat?" he snarled.

Pandora took her eyes from the sky and looked at Luthor, "That sounds better."

"Was that a threat?" Luthor asked again, angrier this time.

"It was. And it got its desired effect. Just in time, I might add, as here they come," replied Pandora.

Luthor's orange eyes were mere slits as he watched Pandora turn back towards the gradually growing speck in the sky. His hand had strayed to his sword and he was unsure whether or not he should draw it.

"If you are going to do it, then do it now. We are almost out of time," Pandora said without turning around.

"Why did you provoke me?" Luthor asked, still angry but not as much as before.

"Simple," replied Pandora, "if you continued the way you were, you might have gotten us both killed. This way, you are more aware of what is happening around you. Now go and alert the troops. They are almost here."

Luthor just stood there regarding Pandora for a moment and then sank through the roof. Pandora turned to see the top of his head disappear. Then she took to the air and glided down to the tarmac to wait for the plane to land.

Unlike Luthor, Pandora was not overly large but was not exactly slim either. Where Luthor looked like a large sumo wrestler, she looked more like a body builder but moved with the grace of a dancer. From a distance, the guards that accompanied Lucas could have mistaken her for a human standing on the runway and not a demon like themselves. As the plane got nearer, they would see that she had features that no human had, like wings for a start. Then they would be able to make out the orange eyes and gradually, her other features would become more distinct, such as her horns, talons and the sword at her side.

As the plane landed and started to slow down, one of the guards spread his wings and let go of the plane. He allowed the momentum to carry him forward, away from the plane. He stopped and hovered just above Pandora. "Who are you and what do you want here?" he asked.

"I am Pandora. I have been sent to greet Lucas and escort him to our den, north of here," Pandora said, without moving or taking her eyes off the guard.

"We are expecting a larger force. Where are they?" the guard asked.

"They are waiting inside the terminal. We did not want to alert the enemy to your arrival. They have been more active recently," Pandora replied. "Would you like your escort to reveal itself now or meet them inside the plane?"

The guard looked up at the connecting tube that was being attached to the front door of the plane. This allowed the passengers to disembark through to the terminal.

"Let's go meet them inside."

The guard entered the plane and Pandora followed him. They both bowed before Lucas once they were within the plane.

"Everything has been prepared for you and your human as requested, lord Lucas," Pandora said, while still bowed.

"Good, let us depart this steel bird and be on our way," Lucas replied.

Twenty minutes later, they were on the road heading north towards the building site in the Daintree rainforest. A limousine carried Mr Fisk along with his demon counterpart Lucas. The humans, who guarded him, were either with him or in the other vehicles in front of or behind the limo. Pandora and Luthor flew just above the limo. Their demon guards were in the air surrounding them.

They arrived at the building site without any altercations with the angelic forces. In fact they never even saw them.

But the angels were watching them. From the moment they left the airport, a group of warriors, recently sent from Heaven by Michael, kept tabs on exactly where they went. One flew so high that he could not be seen easily, while the others were all on the ground, along the route to the Daintree building site. They were disguised as road workers, policemen and even the ferry-boat operator.

Sixty Three

Alan looked at the guards out of the corner of his eye. There were four of them now, two inside the room and two outside the door. A little after lunch the two new guards had just simply arrived without saying a word. He had tried to keep busy since then. He checked Henry's vitals every half hour. He shook his head as he wrote the results on a chart that he had made up. The results were made up too. Alan had tried to ask what the new guards wanted but they never replied. Not even in acknowledgement of being spoken to.

It wasn't until around an hour later, when Mr Kepler came in to check on the patient, that he found out why they were there.

Mr Kepler walked in and looked down at the sleeping form on the bed. He walked around the bed and back again. Turning to where Alan was sitting, watching him, he asked, "When will he be back at work?"

"His recovery is progressing slower than I had hoped," replied Alan. "If I had access to an x-ray machine or even a sonagram, I could do some checks on why. As it is, I can only give my best guess as to which organs need extra attention."

"Then you will have to continue to guess," Mr Kepler said flatly.

"The best thing for him is rest, but he is not getting it with these extra guards in here. Why are there extra guards now?" Alan asked.

"I felt that the added security was necessary," Mr Kepler replied.

"Why? Look at him, he is too sick to go anywhere," Alan pointed out.

"He has escaped once already. I do not want to take a chance on a repeat attempt," Mr Kepler explained.

"A commendable idea. If he was healthy I would agree, but he is not and their presence is not helping his recovery," Alan was trying to convince Mr Kepler that the guards were not needed. "It could cause some mental anguish or even some sort of panic attack if he thinks they are trying to take him before he is well again."

Mr Kepler stared at Alan and then at the sleeping Henry.

While he was looking at Henry, Alan stood up. He knocked a bed pan off of the desk in the process. Mr Kepler turned at the sudden sound. He watched as Alan bent over to pick the pan up and put it back on the desk. As he did, one of the new guards started babbling something that Alan did not understand.

Mr Kepler did, however, and turned to look at what the guard was talking about. "Disgusting!" Mr Kepler said moving as far away as he could from the bed.

Alan looked around and saw that Henry was shaking, having some sort of attack. While they watched foam starting to come out of Henry's mouth.

Alan moved over to Henry as quick as he could. He quickly looked in Henry's eyes and turned and picked up a syringe. He then turned back to Henry and tried to turn Henry on his side but had difficulties.

"You," Alan said pointing to one of the guards with the needle, "I need you to help me."

The guard looked panicked and then, putting his hand to his mouth, turned and fled the room.

Alan looked at Mr Kepler, "Sir, please?"

Mr Kepler turned a light shade of green. He turned to the other guard in the room and pointed at Henry. He shouted something at him in the same language that the guard had spoken earlier.

Alan turned back to Henry, "We need to get him on his side so I can inject this sedative into his buttocks."

The guard hesitated and Mr Kepler yelled at him again, looking a bit more threatening this time.

The guard moved forward as quickly as possible. Without looking, he helped Alan roll Henry on his side.

Alan leaned into Henry to hold him there. He then removed the cover from the needle and inserted it into Henry's exposed buttocks. He emptied the contents of the syringe into Henry.

There was a thump as the guard that had helped Alan hit the floor. He had passed out. Henry's body also stopped moving and slumped, as if he was asleep again. Alan moved away slowly, allowing Henry to roll onto his back once more.

Alan then stepped over the guard to stand before Mr Kepler. "Please," he asked, "remove the guards. I do not know if he will survive another attack like that and as you can see, he is not going anywhere."

Mr Kepler, standing as far from the bed as he could and looking slightly green still, contemplated the request. The guard on the floor stirred. Alan bent down and rolled him on his back. Alan then checked his pulse and even tried to listen to his heart.

"Is he okay?" Mr Kepler asked, not looking at either of them but at Henry still.

"He will be, but he should probably lie down for a little while. I have no more beds here so he will have to do it in his own bunk," Alan replied.

"Not him, I meant him," Mr Kepler said indicating Henry.

"He should be, if he can get the rest he needs. That was a panic attack. I gave him a sedative to help him sleep," explained Alan, as he stood back up.

They both stood there for a moment, Mr Kepler staring at Henry and Alan watching Mr Kepler, waiting for some sort of response from him. "Okay," Mr Kepler conceded finally, "he shall have his rest. You," Mr Kepler called to Rasheed, one of the guards outside the door, "put Oni in his room. And you," he pointed at Alan, "will go with them to make sure Oni is okay. Then you can come back here. There will be no more guards in this room as you request but if he has another attack... I will be forced to re-evaluate your effectiveness in his recovery."

"Yes, sir. Please allow me a minute to make sure my patient is comfortable." Alan turned back to Henry without waiting for a response and heard Mr Kepler move for the door to leave.

"I will check back later," Mr Kepler said from the doorway and then he turned and walked away, hurrying but trying not to look like it.

Rasheed came in the room and helped Oni stand. Oni was wobbling slightly so Rasheed put Oni's arm over his shoulders and around his neck. They walked slowly like this out of the room.

"I'll be right behind you," Alan said, as they reached the door. He turned back to look at Henry and asked very quietly, "You okay?"

Henry cracked open one eye so that he could see through the tiniest of slits. From a distance no one would have seen the movement but Alan, who was right next to Henry, saw it.

"Don't move yet, they are just outside the door and moving away slowly," Alan said, just as quietly as before.

"I'm fine, did they fall for it?" Henry asked just as quietly.

"Hook, line and sinker," replied Alan smiling. "That Alka-Seltzer tablet worked wonderfully. Did it create much foam?"

"Just in time to, I thought I was going to swallow it if I had to hide it in my mouth much longer," said Henry. "And what did you inject me with? I don't remember you mentioning an injection in your plan?"

"Sorry, it was a spur of the moment thing," replied Alan. "It was only a saline solution. Helps dehydrated patients like you. It's what's been in your drip so a little more won't hurt. Rest there a little longer, I have to go with the guards for a moment."

"Okay, but don't forget the door pass or we won't get far at all," reminded Henry.

Gage smiled as he watched Alan leave with the extra guards. He was impressed with Alan's resourcefulness and medical knowledge. He looked down at Henry and spoke quietly to him, "Rest up as it will not be long before we are out and on the run again."

SIXTY FOUR

Israfel and his companions were at the meeting place, looking around and pretending to be interested in the natural rock formations of the Lost City. Due to centuries of erosion, a group of dome-shaped rocks had been formed. They were in such close proximity to each other that, from a distance, they could be mistaken for a village of primitive huts. Hence the title the tourist guides used for the rocks.

Due to the extra erosion caused by too many visitors and abuse from those that did not appreciate the natural beauty, this area was not available to the average tourist but only to tour groups.

This detail was lost on the demons that were in the area. It was not close enough to their den to warrant too much attention. Besides, they were much more interested in one of the other attractions. So much so, that they pretty well ignored the others. Israfel, therefore, did not feel a need to be hidden from them. If one happened to pass by, they just acted like the many tourists that were around.

When they heard footsteps coming, they tried not to look up to see who approached. Instead, Israfel moved around the dome that he was pretending to be interested in so that he could see down the path.

As Nathaniel came into view, he indicated to Israfel that they were alone.

"Glory to the living God," Israfel spoke, as Nathaniel and his companions approached.

"And to the risen Lamb!" replied the three angels in unison.

All six angels paused. They waited for a moment to see if there were any demons lurking about who could have heard their greeting and response. There were no sounds or movement. They relaxed again.

"How many —" Nathaniel started to ask Israfel but Israfel held a hand up to stop his question.

"We shall wait for the remaining three. That way we do not repeat ourselves. Is that acceptable?" Israfel asked the new arrivals.

Nathaniel looked to his companions who nodded their agreement. Nathaniel looked back at Israfel and said, "We will wait."

"Why don't you keep watch for them on the path," Israfel suggested to the new arrivals, "position yourselves so that you cannot be seen by them as they approach. We will take up positions around here."

They turned and had taken only a few steps when they heard someone else approaching. They scattered in the blink of an eye, disappearing behind the domes of rock or behind what little foliage there was. They were not hidden for long before the other three angels appeared.

"Glory to the living God," they said, as they stood at the entrance to the rock city.

"And to the risen Lamb!" the other six replied as they slipped back into sight.

After another slight pause, Israfel indicated they should move away from the rocks. That way, if a tourist group did come through, they would not be seen or interrupted.

Israfel led them towards a lone ghost gum, about fifty metres away, perpendicular to the path that led to The Lost City. Once they reached the tree, they all sat in a circle on the ground.

"Initial impressions please," Israfel asked once they were all seated.

One by one they went around the circle — "Obviously a den", "We seem to be in the right place" and "Must have been a special guest to warrant that sort of greeting", were the initial statements.

"If we could organise a diversion, we could try to enter the building and have a better look around. See if we can determine who is here or why there are so many guards, if it is not to protect one of the Seven," Nathaniel suggested.

"We saw what appeared to be an exhaust port on our approach. There were a couple of guards around it too," Micah mentioned.

"That could be useful for a backdoor entry or even exit," Duncan suggested.

"We need to have a look at the Garden of Eden also, to see if it is a secret entrance," Israfel reminded them all. "Anything else?"

Micah, Duncan and Ivor looked at each other before Ivor spoke up, "We think we were seen by a human."

"We *were* seen," Duncan said, exasperated.

"We have discussed this, you two," Micah jumped in, looking hard at his companions. "We waited," he said, turning back to the others, "until everyone was off the bus and then we became intangible. We left the bus and walked off towards the construction site, trying to see if we could see anything out of the ordinary, when a human approached and spoke to us."

"Spoke to you? As if you were not intangible?" Nathaniel asked.

"Exactly," Duncan said.

"What did you do?" Israfel asked.

"We talked with him for a little while. He had noticed that we had kept ourselves apart and asked us to join him for coffee or lunch," Micah said.

"Then something else out of the ordinary occurred," Duncan said. "I asked him what he saw at the construction site. He said he could see the 'darkness' and lots of orange lights. I told him it was probably shade set up for the workers and laser sights for tools. I think he believed me, but if he works out who we are, then he may rethink that too."

They all sat there for a moment, taking in what Duncan had said.

"It wouldn't be the first time", Nathaniel pointed out, "that a human knew what we were without us having to tell him."

"That's not what has me concerned," Micah spoke. "If he has the glow of a Heavenly encounter —"

"What glow?" asked Israfel, interrupting.

"Didn't we mention that?" asked Duncan.

"No," Israfel replied.

"Duncan pointed out that he had a glow about him, as if he had spoken to other angels recently," Micah explained.

"Hmmmm," Israfel said thoughtfully. "Did he have a guardian?"

"No, he didn't," replied Micah.

Israfel sat there thoughtfully for a moment before speaking again: "Other angels wouldn't leave that sort of residue unless it was the Lord himself and He hasn't left Heaven recently. Not that I know of anyway. It's more likely that the human has been in one of the Heavenly realms. How did he look health-wise? Could he have had a near-death experience recently?"

"He looked very healthy for his age. He appeared young for a human adult. About thirty five human years, maybe a little more," Micah answered.

"Probably not that then," Israfel said. "I'm sure that if we need to know why, then we will learn. I think it is no accident that the Spirit has led this man here at this time. Perhaps he is to help us find out what the demons purpose is here. I think we should take him up on his offer, but we also have other things to check out here too. Let's split up again and try to cover all that we were sent here for and the other things that we have noticed."

After a slight pause, Israfel continued to outline his plan. "I think the same three groups are the best way to go. Micah, take Nathaniel and his group to meet this human. He may have a better chance at getting inside to look around for us. Then go back and try to look at the exhaust you saw. Mention it to the human first, as he may be able to check that out while he is inside."

"This is not the time to be seen, so let's keep with our disguises and not draw attention to ourselves," Israfel cautioned everyone. "Take note of your surrounds. Uriel will want to know everything so that he can use it in his plan. Meet back here once you have completed your assignments."

SIXTY FIVE

Kerri practically dragged Glen through the busy bus station to the area where the lockers were kept. They had just finished arranging for all of their bags, except for one overnight bag, to be sent to a hotel in Townsville. Now Kerri wanted to collect something. As they reached the lockers, Kerri moved quickly to her appointed number and then reached inside her shirt and lifted out a key. The key was on a chain around her neck.

Glen stopped and looked at her with one eyebrow raised.

"What?" Kerri asked.

"A bus station locker? A key around your neck? Could you be any more cliché?" Glen asked.

"I know, I know. I was in a hurry and at the time all I could think of were those old movies. So I did the same thing," Kerri explained.

"Fair enough. What are we collecting?" Glen asked, smiling.

"All the papers I told you about earlier, you know the plans and stuff that I stole," Kerri replied as she opened the locker and started to remove two bags from it. One was a rolled document carrier and the other was rectangular.

"Well, let's have a look then?" Glen prompted, as he leaned forward, reaching to take them from her.

"Not here!" Kerri exclaimed quietly. "Some of this is very sensitive material. We'll look at it once we reach the next town. Until then, we have to keep them safe."

"Of course. Let's get out of here then," Glen said. "The taxi's waiting for us anyway."

Glen took the rolled carrier and slipped its shoulder strap over his shoulder while Kerri carried the other one. As they walked back towards the entrance, Glen spotted the payphones and noticed that one was free.

Amy was walking with them, trying to look like she belonged here but she was gradually attracting the wrong sort of attention. When Glen suddenly detoured towards the payphones, Amy got worried.

"We don't have time for this," she said to Kerri and Glen.

"We don't have time for this," Kerri said to Glen.

"Just one quick call to Jimmy, to let him know we left the hotel," Glen said trying to reason with her. "It won't take long, and besides, he might have some info for us."

"I don't feel comfortable about this Glen."

"It's okay, I'll be off the phone before you know it," Glen said, as he reached the free phone and picked up the receiver.

Amy reached over and held the button down so that a connection couldn't be made. "Look, that's why the phone wasn't being used, it's not working, now let's go," Amy said, "it's not safe here."

"There's no signal," Glen said, taking the receiver away from his ear. "Maybe that's why it wasn't being used." Glen started to put the receiver back, when he noticed the button was stuck down. "It looks like this is the problem," he said, as he tried to pry it loose.

"Just forget it, okay. I don't feel safe here," Kerri said, grabbing on to Glen's shoulder and gently trying to pull him away from the phones.

Unseen to Glen and Kerri, a smallish demon was slowly approaching them. Other demons had seen them too and were urging the smaller one on.

Amy glared at it and put her free hand on the handle of her sword, while making sure she was still holding the receiver down with the other hand.

Glen looked at Kerri, "I think you're right. We need to get out of here before someone takes notice of us," he said quietly, so that the people on the phones around him couldn't hear him. "Let's go."

They turned and started to walk, a bit too quickly, out of there. This was not overly noticeable as many others were in a hurry too. Except that their walk was more of someone escaping something and not someone in a hurry to get to a taxi before everyone else.

Gradually, various pairs of eyes were turning and looking in their direction.

"A little too late for that, I think," Amy said, noticing more demons advancing towards them as they headed for the doors.

The smallish demon suddenly yelled, "IT *IS* THEM!"

At the same time two demons flew into the building from opposite directions. One called out, "We have them on the run! They're driving and heading south... and then the other called out, "We just chased one of them out of the railway station!"

They all stopped and started arguing over who was right and who was wrong. The smallish one had been distracted enough so that when he looked back down all he saw was the doors closing. He scratched his head, wondering if he, or any of the others, had really seen them.

Sixty Six

Jack found Tony and Isabel sitting with one of the other older couples, Peggy and Ray, who were on the same tour with them. They were in the cafeteria of the older hotel, which they were staying in, enjoying the cool air and drinking iced coffees.

"There you are," said Tony as he approached. "We wondered when you were going to join us."

"I was looking at the new hotel that's being built," Jack replied.

"I heard something about that," Ray said, "some concerns about it not matching into the environment. Or was it that it was not environmentally friendly?"

"I did see you head off that way. Well, what do you think of it? Will it match the surrounds as well as this one does?" Tony asked.

"Funny you ask that," Jack replied, "it's practically the same thing that the others I was with just asked me. As I told them, it's a bit early to tell – there are no external walls up yet. They can do almost anything with externals these days."

Tony looked at Jack confused. "What others? I didn't see you with anyone."

Jack was taken aback for a moment. "The three men that joined the tour this morning, before we left Palm Valley," he said, as if he shouldn't need to explain himself. "I thought they might like some company. I noticed they kept to themselves after they joined us, even during the bus ride. I saw them walk over to look at the construction site so I went over and talked to them. I invited them to join us for some coffee or even lunch, if they didn't have any plans already. Is that okay with you?"

Peggy reached over for Ray's hand, feeling a sudden chill go down her spine. "I saw him go over there. It looked like he did some sort of exercise. I thought it was a bit odd that he only used his right arm," she said quietly to her husband. "There was no one there though."

Tony could hear Peggy and looked at Isabel for her reaction but she just sat there quietly. He then looked up at Jack who was looking confused now.

"What?" Jack asked.

Tony turned to Peggy and Ray, "Will you please excuse me," he said as he stood up, "I think I better take Jack to our room and get him to lie down for a while. I think the heat is getting to him."

"By all means, go right ahead," they replied, sounding a little relieved.

Tony walked over to Jack and looked in his eyes. He winked with his left eye so that no one else except Jack could see the movement. "Did you have your tablets this morning?" he asked.

"My... Jack started to reply but Tony winked again so he caught on that Tony wanted to talk to him in private, "tablets?"

"You know... the little white ones?" Tony asked again.

"I don't remember," Jack replied looking down at his feet, like a naughty child who had been caught.

"Come on then, they're up in the room," Tony said, taking Jack by the arm and leading him away. Isabel got up and followed them.

Once they were out of earshot, Jack turned to Tony, "What is it? What's wrong?" he asked as they got into the elevator.

"Peggy said that she never saw anyone with you. She also said it looked like you did something with your right arm, something like stretches but not with your left," Tony answered him. "What would you have been doing with your right arm Jack?"

Jack thought for a moment. "I shook their hands as they introduced themselves. How could she see that and not..."

Tony smiled to himself as if he knew what had happened. Isabel just stood in the background, looking at her feet so that she did not intrude on this conversation.

The elevator arrived at their floor. They walked out of it and Tony led them in silence to their room. It had two separate bedrooms to allow them all some privacy, even if only for one night.

Once inside, Tony led them to the lounge area. Jack was lost in thought and was following Tony on auto pilot. He would have tripped on the coffee table if Tony hadn't grabbed him and guided him around it, to sit on the lounge. Tony tested his weight on the coffee table and then sat on the edge of it, right in front of Jack. Isabel stood off to the side, still not wanting to intrude.

"Jack?" Tony asked.

Jack looked up at Tony.

"Tell me about the three men," Tony prompted.

"They all appeared similar — tall, dark complexioned, blond hair, eyes that sparkled as if there was a fire burning inside them. Also quiet, yet confident. Although, they did appear surprised when I spoke to them."

"Did they remind you of anyone?"

"Yes they did," Jack said, remembering and starting to get a bit excited.

"Who Jack? Who did they remind you of?" Tony said getting excited too.

"You'll think it's silly," Jack said settling down a bit.

"After everything else you've told me? I don't think so. Who did they remind you of?"

"The angels," Jack said quietly. "But they weren't as tall."

Tony sat back a bit on the table. "I knew it!"

Jack looked startled, "You knew it?"

"Sure Jack," Tony said sitting forward again. "You saw them and no one else did. You shook hands with them and Peggy thought you were exercising."

Jack suddenly sat up on the chair. "No," he said, "couldn't be." Tony just watched Jack, with that smile back on his face. "But if they were, then that could mean that..."

Jack suddenly got up and went to the window. Not seeing what he was looking for, he moved across the room to another window.

"What is it Jack?" Tony asked, watching Jack from where he sat.

"Do any of the windows face the construction site?" asked Jack.

Tony thought for a moment. "No, we got the view of the National Park. Why?" Tony asked and suddenly he caught on, "What else did you see? What were the angels looking at?"

Jack came back over and stood in front of Tony, looking down at him. "They were very interested in the construction site. One of them asked me what I could see of it. I told him it was dark as if in shadow and that there were lots of orange lights, like laser sights on tools. But I couldn't see any workers and it bothered me that they would leave the lights on when they were not using them. It seemed irresponsible for someone who would be a qualified tradesperson."

"What was the description you once gave me of the demon you saw?"

There was a pause as Jack stood there, thinking of the consequences of the answer to that question. "You don't think..." Jack asked.

"Why not? If you could see the good guys, why wouldn't you be able to see the bad guys too?" Tony replied.

Jack sat back down, trying to take in what they had just said. "This is too much," Jack said. "I haven't really accepted what you told me last night and today... I saw them again."

"I think God is trying to get your attention," Tony said.

"Trying? He has it," Jack replied. "In all the sermons I have heard in the last six months, you never once said that He can be as subtle as a sledgehammer."

Tony smiled at Jack's description. "When He wants you and your attention, then, sometimes, there is no escape. You can still choose to ignore it, but I think it may be too late for that."

"How come?"

"You've already invited His angels to lunch." Isabel looked up and smiled.

SIXTY SEVEN

Saint Peter watched Michael as he spoke to another group of angels. There were seven warriors, just as there had been previously, but instead of the one messenger there were two. Gabriel was by his side as before. They were instructing them on what to look for – specifically, what the messengers should pay special attention to and report back about.

This was the sixth group to depart and they were going to check out the Aland Islands. Driscoll was one of the messengers with them as it is where he went earlier.

The first group went to the Garden of Eden to reinforce the existing guards. The second was Israfel's team at Kings Canyon. The rest had all come from the places mentioned by the messengers who had visited the Pillars. Those same messengers were returning to the locations they mentioned. Vesna was sent back to Africa with a group of warriors, Levi returned to the Middle East with a group of warriors and Evangelos returned to Australia, to the Daintree location. An extra messenger was sent with the three of them, bringing to nine the total number of angels in their group. The current group would be the same. The extra messenger would be James in this case.

Nicole had just left to get the seventh group. That would be the group that Gabriel was going with, to the town called Eden in Australia. Because Gabriel was going, they would actually have ten in their group.

"Remember, stealth is the key. You are all only trying to determine if that location has a link to the real Eden," Michael said in closing.

"You can appreciate the seriousness of this so do not speak to anyone on your way out," Gabriel continued. "You are the sixth group to find this out and leaving for a location that may be very heavily guarded by the enemy. There are only two reasons for them to have so many guards: because they are getting ready to launch an attack or they are guarding one of the seven. Either way, your mission is more dangerous and also more important than most. May the Lord bless you and keep you safe."

"For the Glory of the Lord and His Kingdom!" Michael and Gabriel said together.

"For the Glory of the Lord and His Kingdom!" the group responded. Then they turned and headed for the door and on towards Earth and their mission.

Michael came over and sat next to Saint Peter for a moment.

"All going well?" Saint Peter asked.

"Yes, it is. This next group, including Gabriel, will check the Australian town of Eden out. They will be looking for leftover forces but also to see if the demons found anything there. It seems pointless to do the latter because you would assume that if they did, they wouldn't leave but build up their forces instead," Michael explained. "However, it could be there and they missed it."

"How much time do you think we have until the next group is ready?" Saint Peter asked.

"Not that long. Jasper and Zagzagel should have them ready to go," replied Michael. "I know we haven't finished the Creation story and there is more to tell you of Eden and The Fall of Man too. Where were we up to?"

"Day seven," Saint Peter reminded him.

"Day seven..."

Heaven and earth and everything in them were finished. By the seventh day God had finished the work he had been doing. On the seventh day he stopped the work he had been doing. Then God blessed the seventh day and set it apart as holy, because on that day he stopped all his work of creation.

Genesis 2:1-3

"What can I tell you about day seven?" Michael said, as he thought back to that day.

"It started like all the rest, the sun rose and we were watching for what the Lord would do next. But the Lord wasn't with us. We looked around for Him and we found Him in The Garden. He was resting. Enjoying what he had created. I approached Him and asked what He was creating today.

"'It is finished,' the Lord replied, 'and I am relaxing.'

"'It is finished!' I called out to the host of Heaven. We all shouted out for joy!

"The Lord smiled at our expression of joy and then He was standing amongst us once more.

"'This day, this seventh day of creation, is a blessed day, for I have completed the work I set out to do and today, I stopped. Let the seventh day be forever set apart as a holy day,' the Lord proclaimed.

"The Host of Heaven burst into a song of praise for the Lord.

"Adam, who had been still asleep, was awakened by our song. He looked up. It was still fairly dark so he couldn't see us clearly but could hear us easily. He shook Eve awake and pointed up at us, floating in the sky singing."

"'Look,' Adam said, 'even the morning stars sing together in praise of the Creator.'

"The Lord went back to the Garden and relaxed for the whole of the day, in the company of Adam and Eve. Many angels visited there that day," Michael said finishing off his tale of Creation.

"That would have been some sight, all the Host of Heaven singing praises to the Lord in the pre-dawn light," Saint Peter commented.

"It was," Gabriel said. He had wandered over during the story and had listened to the end of it. "I can remember that day as clearly as if it was yesterday. It was before sin entered the world. One of the best days the Earth ever saw."

Saint Peter was looking up at Gabriel when he caught sight of other angels entering. "Looks like your next group is arriving," he pointed out to Michael and Gabriel.

"Gabriel," Michael said, "I have something to tell you. It may be connected to all of this or... it may have nothing to do with it at all."

Gabriel was intrigued by what Michael was about to tell him.

"Where you are going... I was there six months ago."

Sixty Eight

Isam was getting a bit hot under the collar. "Can you explain this to me again? You recalled *my* guards because...?" he asked Mr Kepler.

Ward Kepler was quickly losing his patience too. "I am the boss here and if I decide that their presence with the prisoner was unwarranted, then you will agree and do my bidding. Do I make myself clear?"

Isam just stood there, shooting arrows with his eyes. "You have trusted my security precautions for years. He arrives," Isam pointed at George, "and suddenly you are doing everything differently. Do you not trust me or my judgement anymore?"

George was still sitting at the table in the boardroom, doing his best to look innocent. Inwardly, he was really enjoying this.

Mr Kepler sat back down again and indicated that Isam should too. "I do trust your judgement. You have been my most loyal advisor for longer than anyone. But here, I don't think you are being objective enough. We need the workers but it appears you would prefer to work them as hard as you could, until they drop dead on us."

"Is that what this is really about?" Isam replied. "I told you that I took care of that. It was one isolated incident and the rest of the workers were inspired enough that their output increased. I think it is not a bad thing that one or two of them are pushed harder, every now and then."

"It is, when we have a limited supply coming in. Besides, two weeks later, their output was almost halved when most of them were dropping from exhaustion," replied Mr Kepler. "This is not like the operations we previously worked. We don't have a government under our control, let alone the police force. I have been advised by one of our infiltrators that their investigations are increasing. We will not be getting anymore workers for the time being. We must make do with what we have and we can't do that if you keep killing them."

"So you are going to baby them?" Isam asked. "Will you move them all above ground, to stay in the hotel?"

"Don't be absurd!" Mr Kepler replied.

"I still don't know what the problem is? Those guards were wasted there anyway. I need them to be up on the surface, covering the building site so that the tourists stop trying to have a closer look," George said, trying to get the argument going again.

"You stay out of this!" Isam said, jumping up and pointing at George. "I am quite capable of handling the tourists AND all preparations for the upcoming CEO summit." Isam turned back to Mr Kepler, "Let me kill him. I will make it look like an accident. I can drop him off one of the cliffs. Everyone will think he leaned too far and fell."

George looked worried for a moment, until he saw the smile on Mr Kepler's face.

"Calm down, Isam," Mr Kepler said. "I will speak with the Master again and try to convince him that we can handle this conference."

George was not worried about this, he had been sent here for a reason. If they could handle it, he wouldn't be here now. Obviously, they couldn't handle it. What he forgot was that he had been sent here because of the mistakes he had made at his previous work site. Mr Kepler and Isam both knew the real reason for his presence here and George did not know this. Most of the argument he had just witnessed was staged for him, to make him think he was causing friction.

SIXTY NINE

Jack was dumbfounded at his discovery and Tony's revelation about it. The two of them, with Isabel in tow, returned to the cafeteria to see if the angels had accepted Jack's offer.

The other couple had left but they sat at the same table anyway.

Once they were all seated, Isabel looked Jack in the eye and asked him straight out, "Do you believe in God now, Jack?"

Jack, even after all the time he had been living with them, was taken aback by Isabel's forward demeanour. He laughed slightly, trying to cover his uneasiness. "You don't dance around the issues do you?" he asked Isabel.

"No, and don't try to change the subject again. Well?"

Jack turned his head away for a moment. Then he looked down at his lap and feet and finally back up at Isabel and Tony.

"With all these occurrences, it is hard to deny the evidence. I never wanted to admit that it was even a possibility. But now..." Jack looked away, his eyes lost focus for a moment, "how can I not? It's like this: if I was in the real..." he looked around and lowered his voice so he was whispering, "Eden," and then he raised his voice back to normal again, "and saw and spoke with angels, then it is hard to argue against that part of the Bible. And if you can't argue against that part, then how can you argue against the rest of it. If you then believe the Bible, then God is... not only real, but *very* real."

Tony and Isabel were watching him carefully. Their smiles were almost wider than their faces and their eyes were starting to well up as if they might cry from the joy they were feeling.

"So... to answer your question," Jack continued, "yes, I do believe in God."

There was silence for a moment. They all let what he had just said sit there and be taken in by everyone that was present.

Tony leaned forward in his chair and put his hand on Jack's knee. "You know what comes next, don't you?" he asked.

Jack looked at the hand on his knee and then back up at Tony. "Jesus?"

"Yes, Jesus. If you believe in the Bible and God, then you believe that Jesus died on the cross for you. Do you believe that?" Tony asked.

"Yes, that is the next step isn't it," Jack said. "In answer to your question, yes, I do believe that he died for me," Jack replied, starting to choke up a bit.

"And your sins?" asked Tony.

"And my sins," replied Jack.

Isabel had tears streaming down her face.

Tony sat back, still smiling as he wiped at his eyes too.

Isabel spoke directly to him again, "Now we need to pray and you need to ask Jesus to come into your life!"

Jack smiled again at her directness but all he could manage was to nod his head in approval. His emotions about this were a bit of a surprise, but not as embarrassing as he thought it might be.

Tony took hold of Jack's right hand with his left and said, "Let us pray." They all bowed their heads and closed their eyes. "Great God in Heaven, hallowed by your name. We thank you for your mercies. Thank you for this moment, for Jack and his time with us. We ask that you would come into his life now and make a home in his heart." Tony squeezed Jack's hand. "Repeat after me, Jack: dear Jesus, forgive me for I am a sinner."

Jack did as he was told and repeated the words that Tony spoke. Then Tony continued on, with Jack repeating what he said as he finished each sentence. "I see now that you are the Son of God and that you died for my sins. You are my Lord and Saviour, please come into my life and make me one of your children. Amen."

"Amen," said Jack.

"Amen," repeated eight voices, including Tony and Isabel.

They opened their eyes and saw that they were not alone anymore. Six men stood around them. They were all smiling and had tears in their eyes or running down their faces.

Jack looked up and recognised three of them and immediately fell to the ground on his knees. Tony saw his reaction and realised who they were too. As he started to slip off his chair, one of the angels, Nathaniel, reached forward and put his hands on Tony's shoulders.

"Peace be with you," Nathaniel said. "Do not be afraid. Please, stay in your seats and be comfortable. Besides, you are not the only ones who can see us and we do not wish to attract any attention."

Tony slid back in his chair with a look of awe on his face.

"Hello again, Jack. Let me help you," Micah said, as he reached out and helped Jack back into his chair.

"Is that invitation for lunch still standing?" Ivor asked Jack.

"Absolutely! Please have a seat and join us," Jack replied.

Seventy

"Where are they?" Lucas asked, as he entered Cain's chosen meeting room, the boardroom of the partially built hotel.

"Welcome —" Cain started to reply when Lucas cut him off.

"Answer my question first, little worm!" Lucas said, as he stopped right in front of Cain, puffing out his chest and unfurling his wings slightly, to add to his already impressive bulk.

Cain had to look up as Lucas was at least three feet taller than him. However, he was not intimidated by Lucas or his attempt to bully him. "Our last report indicated that they were in a hotel room, in Cairns. I have sent two squads along with their humans to collect them and bring them back here."

Lucas turned his back on Cain and moved around the room, looking at the rest of the gathered demons. He stopped, turned and drew his sword. He pointed it at Cain's head. The tip was only inches from his nose. The move was so quick, that all Cain had managed in response was to get his hand on the hilt of his sword. "Why did it take so long to find them? They would have spoken to a messenger by now. That means the whole plan is jeopardised, laid bare for the enemy to organise some resistance. Did you think of that?"

"Of course, we set up an ambush, to allow us to capture the messenger," replied Cain, staring daggers over the sword.

Lucas looked at Cain and thought that he was trying not to show his fear at having a sword pointing at his nose. "And?" he asked, leering and looking away from Cain.

"The enemy anticipated us and managed to disappear from sight long enough to get away," explained Cain, as he slowly stepped away from the sword while Lucas's attention was not on him.

"What about stopping the messenger from returning to give its report?" Lucas asked, still not looking at Cain.

"They anticipated us again", Cain replied, as he took another step away from the sword, "and 'rained' messengers on Cairns for over half an hour. Then they all started to return and we could not determine which one we needed to stop. We did not have enough troops to stop them all and besides, if we had tried, they would have responded with several legions of their best warriors and the plan would be undone already."

Lucas looked back at Cain and decided to lower his sword. It was no longer pointing at Cain. He glared at Cain but stayed where he was, thinking for a moment. "Good judgement. What else do you have to report?"

Right at that moment, a thin demon dropped through the roof and stopped in front of Cain. "I have an urgent message for you, sir!"

"I'll take it," Lucas said from behind the messenger.

The messenger turned and saw Lucas. He immediately bowed before him. "Sorry, lord, I did not know that you had arrived."

"The message, quickly, before I remove your head!" Lucas said to the messenger, trying to regain some authority through more bullying.

The messenger stood and spoke, "Our forces watching the train station have seen the man that we were told to watch for. He was seen purchasing tickets for an afternoon train. When I left, a small contingent was following him."

Lucas looked over the messenger at Cain. "What do you have to say about that?"

"They are preparing to leave and we have discovered the means they have chosen. We do not have need of this information. We will catch them before they leave their —" Cain was interrupted by the arrival of another demon.

This one stopped mid-air when he saw Lucas and appeared confused. He did not know who he should report to.

"What do you want?" Lucas asked him.

"I have a message for Cain, sir," replied the newcomer.

"Whatever it is, it is now for lord Lucas," Cain advised.

"Very well," the demon replied and then landed before Lucas, alongside the other messenger. "We arrived at the hotel too late. They were seen leaving in the same car that was seen here. We followed it immediately. I was sent to report as the chase began."

"Interesting," Lucas said, looking again at Cain.

Another messenger arrived and before anyone could say anything, it blurted out, "We've seen 'em! We've seen 'em!"

"Where now?" Lucas asked.

"At the bussss..." the demon started to reply but stopped when he turned and saw Lucas. He immediately bowed as low as he could get. "Sorry, me lord, I did not know ye were 'ere."

Lucas looked like he might lose his temper. He spoke fairly quietly, "Get up and tell me where."

"S-sorry, me lord," the newest messenger stammered, as he stood but remained bowing, "The bus depot, me lord."

"What happened?" Lucas asked.

"As we approached 'em, others of our kind arrived, telling us they had seen 'em in other locations. But I knew they were wrong. I saw 'em with me own eyes."

Lucas looked at Cain. "What did he just say?"

"Irish said that he saw them too. That other demons told them of the other sightings but he knew they were wrong as he had seen them with his own eyes," Cain replied, translating what Lucas could not understand. "That's right?" he asked Irish.

"Aye," Irish said.

"How can he be so sure?" Lucas asked Cain.

Cain turned back to Irish as he started to reply, "It was both of 'em, 'n' there was a feather 'ead with 'em."

"He said it was the two humans and one of the enemy was with them," Cain translated again.

Lucas regarded the three newest arrivals. "It would appear that they are trying to mislead us," he said. "We need to —"

"Cain, where are you Cain?" said a voice from outside the room.

Cain looked around and started to move to the doors, when Lucas yelled at him, "STAY WHERE YOU ARE! I will *not* have any more of these interruptions!" Lucas moved towards the door, waving his sword again with such a look of rage on his face that everyone moved as quickly as they could out of his way.

"Uh, I wouldn't —" Cain started to warn Lucas.

But Lucas turned and shouted at Cain again, "STOP RIGHT THERE! YOU WILL NOT TELL ME —"

"I would have let him finish if I was you," the voice said again, as the demon came into the room, passing through the door and wall.

Lucas turned with his sword held ready to strike, "YOU WILL NOT... ooooh." Lucas fell to the ground when he realised who he was addressing. It was one of the biggest and foulest-looking demons that he had ever seen. "I am sorry, lord, I was not expecting to see you here," Lucas said in a very submissive way.

As Tarvyn, the demon lord of Sloth, had entered the room, the rest of the demons present had all gone down on one knee, with their heads bowed. Lucas was almost prostrate on the floor before him. Tarvyn looked at Cain, "Rise Cain, and introduce me to this impudent little fool."

Cain tried not to smile as he rose and approached Tarvyn and Lucas. "This, lord Tarvyn, is Lucas. Lord Porva has sent him to replace Grom, who has gone on to the meeting site to prepare it appropriately."

"Lucas. I have heard of you. Lord Porva has mentioned you to me," Tarvyn said.

Lucas remained on the floor as he replied, "Thank you, lord."

"Don't flatter yourself. You have yet to show yourself to be worthy of your new post," Tarvyn said, as he leant over Lucas. "It would do you well to listen to those who are your advisors, before you find *yourself* missing a head."

"Yes, lord. It's just that —" Lucas replied, trying to explain but got interrupted.

“I don’t want excuses. I want results. Cain has been getting them. I don’t see why we need you here but this is not my kingdom. Count yourself lucky, for now,” Tarvyn warned Lucas.

Lucas waited before answering, “Yes, lord.”

“Cain, when you have a moment, I would like to discuss something with you,” Tarvyn spoke to Cain, now ignoring Lucas completely, “in my room.”

“Yes, lord Tarvyn. Allow me another half hour and I shall be there,” Cain replied.

“No rush, but as soon as you are finished here.” Tarvyn looked down at Lucas, who was still face down on the floor. “Don’t keep him longer than needed.” He turned and disappeared back through the door, his long tail flicking Lucas in the head at the last moment. Then he was gone.

As Lucas slowly got to his feet, Cain watched him, waiting to see how he would respond to how he had been treated. The others also stood back up and looked over at Lucas and Cain.

Lucas wiped at the cut on his cheek, caused by Tarvyn’s tail, before looking at Cain. Cain bowed his head slightly and spoke, “Would you like me to take care of this while you have your cut attended to?”

Lucas, seeing a way out and still remaining respected by his underlings, nodded, “Yes, show me how *you* would handle this. If I agree, we will set it in motion.”

Cain bowed his head again and then turned and started to issue orders. “Hammer, get a healer to attend to lord Lucas.”

Hammer bowed and left.

“Pandora, what is your take on what these three have told us?” Cain asked, indicating towards Irish and the other two messengers.

Pandora stepped forward and spoke: “Sir, it appears that at least one of these is a real sighting and the others are fakes. Either way, the enemy suspects that we are up to something important or else they wouldn’t go to such lengths to try to distract us.”

As Pandora finished and stepped back, Hammer returned. He stood back where he had been earlier. A small, thin and almost bent double demon also entered and approached Lucas. He bowed and spoke quietly, “I am Malpractice, a healer amongst other things. Can I be of assistance?”

“Do what you must, but do it quietly,” Lucas replied.

Cain, having waited until Lucas was paying attention again, turned back to his advisors. “Do you all agree with Pandora’s assessment?”

They all nodded.

“Suggestions?” Cain asked.

Highrise stepped forward, “I have a question for Irish first.”

"Go ahead," Cain replied.

"Did you see where they went or is someone following them?"

Irish shook his head, "No, the others distracted us just as they were leavin'. By the time I looked 'round again, they were gone. I raced out to try 'n' spot 'em, but there was nothin' to be seen."

Highrise spoke again, "I would agree with Irish — that he saw the real targets — but that is still an assumption. We can't discount the others until we know for sure. We must run down every sighting to see which ones are real or not. I would suggest continuing the surveillance of the two current sightings and at least a score more, scouring the streets, to try to locate the third, and possibly the only, real targets."

Highrise stepped back.

Cain looked around at his advisers. "Anyone else?" he asked.

There was no response. Cain turned back to Lucas. "What do you say, my lord?"

Lucas nodded, "It's not much, but it is all we've got. I don't think that they will return to either the bus or train stations any time soon. Those groups are to join the search, while the others continue their existing surveillance."

Cain turned back to the three minor demons, "You have heard what lord Lucas has instructed. Go and carry out your tasks, passing on to your groups their instructions as well. Irish, Pandora will join you with a score of hunters," he looked at Pandora and she nodded. He looked back at the other three and said, "Dismissed."

"Yes, sir", and "Right away", were the responses. Then the three demons, plus Pandora, took to the air. They left the way they entered, through the roof.

"Now, if there are no more interruptions, perhaps lord Lucas would like to meet his remaining advisors?" Cain suggested.

Seventy One

Saint Peter watched as Gabriel and his group filed out the door, headed for the 'Edge' and on to Earth. Michael was following them to the door discussing with Gabriel any last-minute things they could think of. Michael stopped at the door and watched them go. Then he turned back to Saint Peter, who was still sitting down at the other end of the hall, where he would not be in the way. The only other occupant in the Hall was Nicole, who was at the opposite end, sitting with her eyes closed in prayer.

Michael went over to Nicole, who looked up at his approach. He spoke to her, too quietly for Saint Peter to hear. When he finished, Nicole stood and headed for the door too. Michael turned to Saint Peter once more and started towards him.

Once he reached him, Michael sat down beside the Saint. They regarded each other silently for a moment before Saint Peter broke the silence.

"With everyone else gone, what is the next step?"

"Nicole is gathering the next group, the first of the back-ups. I will need to instruct them once they arrive, but, until then, we should continue to talk about Eden and The Fall," Michael replied.

"So far I have told you of the Creation Story, and the way in which I have told you is kind of an overview. It is what I saw and experienced but it is not the fine detail, the full story so to speak. As I mentioned earlier, there is a lot more that went into the creation. Some of it is very complex and scientific, and other parts are just terribly hard to explain in detail.

"I can tell you about Eden itself and Adam and Eve in more detail. Many people get confused by the Biblical account, partly because it backtracks to something already mentioned, but also because some of the verses appear to contradict what has already been revealed."

"The Bible's account is like this..."

This is the account of Heaven and earth when they were created, at the time when the Lord God made earth and Heaven.

Wild bushes and plants were not on the earth yet because the Lord God hadn't sent rain on the earth. Also, there was no one to farm the land. Instead, underground water would come up from the earth and water the entire surface of the ground.

Then the Lord God formed the man from the dust of the earth and blew the breath of life into his nostrils. The man became a living being.

The Lord God planted a garden in Eden, in the east. That's where he put the man whom he had formed. The Lord God made all the trees grow out of the ground. These trees were nice to look at, and their fruit was good to eat. The tree of life and the tree of the knowledge of good and evil grew in the middle of the garden.

A river flowed from Eden to water the garden. Outside the garden it divided into four rivers. The name of the first river is Pishon. This is the one that winds throughout Havilah, where there is gold. (The gold of that land is pure. Bdellium and onyx are also found there.) The name of the second river is Gihon. This is the one that winds throughout Sudan. The name of the third river is Tigris. This is the one that flows east of Assyria. The fourth river is the Euphrates.

Then the Lord God took the man and put him in the Garden of Eden to farm the land and to take care of it. The Lord God commanded the man. He said, "You are free to eat from any tree in the garden. But you must never eat from the tree of the knowledge of good and evil because when you eat from it, you will certainly die."

Then the Lord God said, "It is not good for the man to be alone. I will make a helper who is right for him."

The Lord God had formed all the wild animals and all the birds out of the ground. Then he brought them to the man to see what he would call them. Whatever the man called each creature became its name. So the man named all the domestic animals, all the birds and all the wild animals.

But the man found no helper who was right for him. So the Lord God caused him to fall into a deep sleep. While the man was sleeping, the Lord God took out one of the man's ribs and closed up the flesh at that place. Then the Lord God formed a woman from the rib that he had taken from the man. He brought her to the man.

The man said,

"This is now bone of my bones and flesh of my flesh.
She will be named woman
because she was taken from man."

That is why a man will leave his father and mother and will be united with his wife, and they will become one flesh. The man and his wife were both naked, but they weren't ashamed of it.

Genesis 2:4-25

"This all takes place on the sixth day. From what has been told already, it gets confusing for most who read it. Remember I told you that on the third day the Lord created the plants?

"Not all the plants were created at once, or should I say were visible at once. The fruit- and seed-bearing plants, the Lord knew, would be needed by man straight away so He created them in a mature form.

That way, after a few more days, the fruit and seeds would be ready for consumption by man. The other plants, the wild bushes and trees, He planted and left as seeds in the ground, waiting for the first waters to help them germinate. The same went for what is now called crops, as farming had not been taught to man. The crop types of plants, wheat, rye, barley etc., were all included with the wild plants, waiting for proper germination before growing.

"While some parts of the Earth had started to experience evaporation and clouds were forming, only a little rain had fallen. None of which, had reached the ground to feed the plants. It would still take years for the clouds to be common enough that when they reached a land mass and went through the release cycle, the moisture would fall in a large enough quantity to not evaporate before reaching the ground.

"Instead, the natural flood tables were full to overflowing. Every now and then, the water table would rise and soak the ground, allowing the plants to be fed. This also started the germination processes of the seeds.

"This was still happening when the Lord said, 'Now I will create Man.' All I mentioned earlier was that the Lord spoke and it happened. Here is what He did, in more detail, to make that happen.

"The Lord was standing within the hedge that he had made earlier and He took a handful of dirt, or earth as some call it. He moulded the earth into the shape of a man. It started like children making snowmen and ended like a sculptor forming the fine features of the sculpture. I have seen the statue of David and, in all reality, what the Lord created looked very similar, with some very major differences internally.

"The Lord was not only sculpting the outside but the inside too, the organs, the interrelation of the systems and parts, and the complexity of the brain.

"Once the form was completed, He breathed on it and we saw something pass from the Lord into the form. It was not just breath but also spirit. The Lord had just put life, not just physical life, but also spiritual life, into this creation.

"The man took a breath, opened his eyes and moved. He was alive. I was totally amazed. This was a being that was like me but not like me. I am, that is we angels are, more spiritual beings than physical ones. We can become solid and interact with the physical universe, but our place is more in the spiritual realm. Here was a being that, while part spiritual, was more in the physical realm.

"Then the Lord named him Adam, which, as you know, is very similar to the Hebrew word *adamah,* which means earth. The Lord then indicated the hedge that surrounded us and spoke to Adam, 'This is Eden and this area within the hedge is the garden. Have a look around the garden. You are going to live here.'

"Adam looked around at his surroundings. We did too and as we watched, the Lord moved around the garden, admiring the plants and trees. There were the beautiful plants, flowers like roses and lilies, the fruit and seed plants like apples and bean stalks, and the trees, like fig trees and maple trees.

"Then the Lord moved to a clearing and we noticed that He had some sort of seeds in His hands. He bent over and made two holes and dropped the seeds into them. He retreated a few paces and the two seeds started to sprout and grow. It soon became evident that these were trees that were growing. They were a type that we had not seen on Earth previously. They were the Tree of Life and the Tree of the Knowledge of Good and Evil. These two trees grew in the exact middle of the garden.

"Just when we thought that there was nothing else to add, the Lord commanded a river to flow through the garden, to provide water for the plants, animals and Adam.

"Some of the angels, who were still flying above us, were pointing at a spot beyond the hedge where I could not see. I took off and flew above the hedge, to see what they were looking at. I must say, that I expected to see the enemy again but was surprised to see the river had separated into more rivers. There were four in total. The Lord spoke from where he was standing, which was now just outside the hedge, looking at the rivers.

"'The first river is named Pishon,' He said, indicating the one that meandered off, 'and that land will be called Havilah. It is where you can find some of the purest gold. Other products of that land are Bdellium and Onyx.'

"'The second river is Gihon,' the Lord continued, 'and the land that it winds through will be known as Sudan. The third river is the Tigris and it flows east of Assyria and the fourth river is the Euphrates.'

"'What is the importance of knowing these names?' I asked the Lord, as I landed alongside him again.

"The Lord smiled at me and turned to re-enter Eden. Adam and I followed on either side of Him. 'Everything needs a name,' He said, 'so that you can talk about it. A place, a river, a landmark once named can help you to know where you are, where you need to go or to indicate where you are going. Animals, birds and fish need names so that you know what you are talking about. Man needs names so that you know who you are talking to or who you are talking about. Without names, how would you know if it is the right person you are talking too? Or if you wanted to eat a particular fruit, how would you ask someone else to get you an apple if they didn't know its name? They might give you a pear or lemon instead! Does that make sense to you Michael? And you Adam?'

"I nodded to indicate my understanding and Adam said, 'Yes, Lord.'

"We were now near the middle of the garden again, when the Lord indicated the different fruits and trees to Adam. 'These plants are for you to eat from. The land is for you to farm and take care of,' He said to Adam. 'I will teach you what you need to know about farming. The only thing you must never do is eat from that tree there, the Tree of the Knowledge of Good and Evil, because if you do you will certainly die.'

"The Lord and Adam went off walking around the garden, with the Lord showing Adam the different trees and flowers. After a while, the Lord noticed that Adam appeared to be becoming overwhelmed with all the instructions and knowledge that He was imparting to him.

"The Lord God stopped and said in a loud voice, 'Man should not be alone and he needs help looking after this garden. Who is right for him?'

"One by one, the animals and birds came. They passed before the Lord and Adam. Adam named them as they passed, as the Lord had instructed him to do. But Adam did not think that any of them was suitable to help him, as the Lord had suggested.

"Adam suddenly appeared very tired and the Lord indicated a place for Adam to lie down, and he did. Once he was in a very deep sleep, the Lord opened Adam up and removed a piece of one of his ribs. The Lord then repaired the damaged rib that was inside of Adam and closed up the flesh so that there was no evidence of the removed rib.

"The Lord then took the piece He had removed. He started to duplicate it and the whole skeletal structure of Adam, with some differences. From that, He then went on to build the other systems of the body, just like He had earlier with Adam — the muscles and nervous system, the circulatory system and then the rest of the organs. Finally, He added the skin and hair. Once that was done, He breathed life into her, just as He had with Adam.

"After she had opened her eyes and looked around, the Lord took her by the hand and brought her to Adam. Adam awoke at once. He looked up at the new human and saw that she was the same as him.

"Adam looked at the Lord and asked, 'Where did she come from?', so the Lord quickly explained that He had formed her from one of his ribs.

"Adam then looked at her and spoke, 'Here is the helper that I was looking for. She is bone of my bone and flesh of my flesh. She shall be called *woman* as she was taken from man.'

"Then the Lord spoke, 'So shall it be. In each generation, the man will leave his parents and be joined with his wife.'

"The Lord then took both of them around the garden and continued to teach them about the different plants. He also repeated to the woman the warning about the forbidden fruit.

"At that time, they were both naked, just like all the animals. Neither of them felt any shame about it, for they had no knowledge of anything different.

"We all marvelled at how like us Adam and Eve were and yet how different. Where we seemed to instinctively know certain things, they did not and they had to be taught. They also had choices to make about certain things. But enough about that now or I will start to tell you about 'The Fall' and their banishment.

"Besides, Nicole has returned, and I must give this group their instructions," Michael said, indicating that the narrative was over for the moment.

Saint Peter watched the Captain stand and walk over to the other angels. He started to brief them on their roles just as he had done with the previous groups. Saint Peter then closed his eyes and reflected on what Michael had told him. What would that have been like, he thought, to live in harmony with the Lord and the land? To speak with Him, to walk with Him or simply to be near Him — what an incredible experience it would have been. He sat quietly, eyes still closed, imagining being Adam.

Slowly, his face changed until his eyes snapped open. "But what of that is relevant to now?"

Seventy Two

The Garden of Eden, located in Watarrka National Park, is a small tropical valley. It has a little tributary, Kings Creek, running through it. Kings Creek eventually opens up into a rock pool, which runs out at the other end as a small waterfall at the mouth of Kings Canyon. The canyon is a one-kilometre stretch of one-hundred-metre-high sheer cliff walls. The moist microclimate of the Garden supports a large portion of the six hundred species of plants found within the National Park. This is the highest plant diversity within Australia's arid zone, which also includes prehistoric cycads.

Israfel, however, was not paying enough attention to his surroundings to notice any of this. He was more concerned about the contingent of demons that were visible around the natural rock pool at the end of the valley. Their presence was enough to confirm what he had been told. They were here looking for some sort of connection to the other dimensional realm bearing the same name.

Israfel indicated to his companions to spread out and start to try and find any sort of ripple or tear in the dimensional barrier. This would indicate a link to the Lord's Garden. Most importantly, if there was a link here, had the enemy found it yet?

The hours passed as they searched the valley from top to bottom. Eventually, they regrouped back near the wooden steps, which were at the entrance to the valley. They found nothing to indicate evidence of any link between the dimensions.

Seventy Three

After dropping their bags at the tourist office for their boat ride, Glen and Kerri asked to be taken to the Casino. The taxi let them out across the road from the main entrance. After Glen had paid the driver, he joined Kerri and they just stood there, looking across the road at the large building.

"You sure this is the right place to hide?" Kerri asked apprehensively.

"No, but it sounded like a good idea at the time," Glen replied. "We better get across and in there before we draw too much attention by just standing here."

"Okay, lead on," Kerri said, as she took his hand again, to try to keep up the appearance of being honeymooners.

They crossed the road and entered the Casino. They were both surprised by the number of people they could see inside it. Especially around the electronic gambling devices, otherwise known as pokies. They wandered around for awhile, just eyeing off different machines, as if they were looking for just the right one. At the other end of the room they found a complimentary coffee service. They helped themselves to one cup of coffee each.

Nearby, they noticed some chairs around tables, all facing televisions with the Keno games playing on them. They picked a table that was a bit further away, in a darkened corner and sat down. Glen picked up a Keno sheet and a pencil and pretended to read it over. He was actually looking over the top of it, from time to time, to see if anyone was paying them too much attention. So far, no one had given them a second glance.

They both started to relax and enjoy their coffees and some small talk. Then Glen spotted some payphones on a wall nearby. One of the payphones was free.

Amy was trying to blend in with Kerri and Glen. She was sitting in a chair at the same table, holding a cup and pretending to drink from it too. She wasn't feeling relaxed. The number of demons in this building was amazing but so far she hadn't been spotted.

"I am going to try to make those calls again. Is that okay with you?" Glen asked.

Kerri looked around and saw the phones. "Sure, I'll come with you, after we've finished the coffees."

Glen looked at his cup, then lifted it to his mouth and drank the rest down in one go. He looked back across at Kerri and said, “I’m ready, how about you?”

Kerri laughed and replied, “Has anyone ever told you that you’re silly?”

“Not for the last couple of days,” Glen said with a smile. “Now are you coming or not?” he said as he stood.

Kerri lifted her cup and drained it too. She reached over and put it on the table and stood up. “Let’s do it.”

The two of them walked over to the phones. Luckily, the one that was free was also a bit further away from all the background noise. Glen pulled out his wallet and searched through it for his calling card. When he found it, he lifted the receiver and put his card in the slot, and proceeded to dial Jimmy. He sat on the stool provided and waited.

Amy walked with them, after putting her cup on the table too. She stood on the other side of Glen, so she could try to hear what was said on the phone.

Above her, sat a small group of demons, all Eavesdroppers she was sure. Somehow, she had to stop them from hearing this conversation, without giving herself away.

After a few rings, it was picked up by Jimmy’s receptionist. She immediately transferred the call through to Jimmy.

“Where have you been? You’re harder to find than a needle in a haystack,” Jimmy exclaimed.

“Sorry Jimmy, I’m here now so... what did you find out?” Glen asked.

“Tell me where you are first,” Jimmy insisted.

“If you must know, we had to leave the hotel. We are in the casino, trying to blend in with the crowds. Now what did you find out?” Glen asked again.

“The Casino? Oh Glen. Has anyone seen you? Are there any cameras pointing at you? Surveillance cameras?” Jimmy asked.

Glen looked around quickly, “There are some around but none are pointing at us at the moment.”

One of the demons, the only one not already listening into a conversation, lent closer to try to hear but Amy moved and blocked it. It tried again but Amy moved again. The other Eavesdroppers were watching and laughed at it, so he tried harder. It pulled out it’s little sword. It was so small that if compared with Amy’s, it would have been described as more of a dagger but to this little demon it was almost as long as his arm. He stabbed forward, to try to cause Amy to have a sudden headache but she moved again and he missed.

Unfortunately for Amy, his momentum carried him forward enough for him to hear a part of the conversation.

"I can make the cameras point at you!" he said, taking off for the nearest camera.

Kerri looked up too. She noticed the cameras and guessed that was what they were talking about. As she watched it, the camera twisted around and was now pointing at them.

Eavesdropper then disappeared up into the ceiling. "Don't want to be seen, huh?" he said to himself as he flew to the security office. "I will make sure you are then!"

"Listen carefully," Jimmy said, as he closed his office door and went back to sit at his desk. "I've spoken with a few different sources and they all say the same thing. These people are dangerous. One suggested links with organised crime, as in the mob, but the next one said that was wrong. Even the mob is scared of them. Listen to this. Your friend's disappearance? He's not the first but no one has ever been able to prove they were involved. They have some very good lawyers on their side. My advice to you — get out. Don't wait. I don't care how but get out of there now. *Especially* the casino, *they own it*!"

"Well, aren't you just full of good news," Glen said sarcastically. "We've got a plan on how to do that but we have an hour or so to waste first. We thought this would be a good place to hide as they wouldn't expect to see us here."

"Sounds okay in theory but I wouldn't want to try it. Just get out of there and wait somewhere else." Jimmy paused for a moment before continuing, "Glen, if you have any proof to pin anything on these guys, then you have to get back here alive."

"We have something but we need to go over it first, to check to see if any of it can be linked to them," Glen replied. "I'm hearing what you're saying but I have a couple more calls to make so I'd better go and get on with it. I'll check in when we're somewhere safer."

"You do that, and do it soon. Stay safe!" Jimmy said as his farewell.

"Will do. Talk to you soon," and Glen hung up.

The phone flashed a message at him, advising him that if he wanted to make another call on the same card, then all he had to do was pick the phone back up and dial now. So he did. It rang a few times before it was picked up.

"Hello?" said the voice at the other end.

In the security office, Eavesdropper arrived and quickly pointed to the monitor that had the phone booth with Glen and Kerri on it. He explained what he had heard to the demon on duty, a large skinny thing called Watcher. He then looked on as Watcher whispered to the only human in the room and brought his attention to the relevant monitor.

The human looked closely and then turned to a pin-up board. He looked at all the faces on it, searching for a match, and found Kerri's.

Eavesdropper was looking at the monitor again, trying to see the other one, the one that had blocked him. She wasn't there anymore.

The human picked up a radio and put out an alert to the guards.

Eavesdropper left them and smiled as he returned to his phone booth.

"Hi Pastor Williams, its Glen here. How are you?"

"Hi Glen. Thanks for calling back. I'm sorry, but I couldn't find out anything for you. Nobody I know has ever worked for any of those companies you asked me to check into," Pastor Williams advised Glen, getting straight into it.

"That's a bit strange isn't it?" Glen asked.

"That's what I thought too. Normally if no one I know has been the Chaplin in that industry, then someone else would know them. I do know a few Chaplins in their industry but no one that has ever had any contact with those businesses specifically," Pastor Williams explained.

"Thanks for trying for me, I really appreciate it. I'd better go now, but if you could pray for us that would be wonderful. Thanks again. See you soon," Glen said, as he started to hang up.

"You're welcome. We will keep praying for you. God bless!" Pastor Williams said, as he hung up.

When the phone asked if he wanted to make another call he picked it up a third time and dialled Max.

It rang and rang at the other end but there was no answer.

Amy was suddenly very alert. It was time to go. She wondered what had happened. Then she heard the camera and saw the demon drop back through the roof.

Glen hung up the phone after trying a second time. He scratched his head and then turned to Kerri. "Jimmy says we shouldn't wait here any longer. He thinks this was a bad idea."

Amy spoke to Kerri, "That camera is zooming in on you, they know you're here. You need to leave now!"

Kerri could see over Glen's shoulder. The camera was still pointing at them and she thought she could see the lens twisting, as if it was zooming in on something. Then she realised it was them it was zooming in on.

"I think they know we're here. That camera you looked at before just zoomed in on us," Kerri said quite calmly.

Glen stood up and took her by the hand and led her away. He stopped directly under the camera. Like most casinos the walls had mirrors or other reflective types of surfaces. Glen watched their reflection on a wall. The camera turned again as if trying to find them. As it moved passed the aisle that he wanted to go down, he gestured to Kerri to start walking again.

Amy followed behind them, waiting.

As they turned down another aisle, Kerri saw two men in suits go down the aisle towards the payphones, where they had just been. She turned suddenly and pushed Glen down a different aisle, while pointing out the men to him.

"Please God, send your angels to watch over us and guide us out of here safely. Amen," Glen quickly prayed.

That was it — just what Amy had been waiting for. She moved ahead of them and cast an illusion before their eyes.

The two of them started to walk faster but saw that there were too many people ahead. They would be forced to stop if they stayed in that aisle. At the next junction, they stopped and looked both ways, trying to decide which one to use.

A person stepped forward and waved at Amy as he passed her. He then moved down one of the aisles and repeated the same illusion that Amy had just performed. Amy recognised the other angel, even though he appeared to be a tourist too.

The aisle to Glen and Kerri's right, was similarly full so they turned left.

More angels appeared and waved to Amy, helping her create the illusions that kept Glen and Kerri on the right path, away from the security guards that were searching for them.

This happened to Glen and Kerri five times, they would reach a junction and see that there were lots of people in one or two aisles but the third aisle would be empty. It was as if they were being herded through the maze of pokie machines. They were just starting to think they should try to force their way through one of these groups when, quite by accident, they found themselves at the doors again.

They stepped outside calmly and immediately turned and walked down the road, crossing it as soon as it was safe, and turned down a side street. They found a taxi just sitting there. As they approached it, a man got out and the sign on top changed from engaged to available. The man walked passed them, heading for the casino. (He waved at Amy as he went passed.) Glen ran a few steps and tapped on the boot as the taxi started to pull away. It stopped at once.

Glen grabbed the door and held it as Kerri practically dove in the back seat. Glen slid in beside her.

"I am sorry. I did not see you there. Where would you like to be travelling?" the driver asked in an Indian accent.

"How about a little tour of the city?" Glen asked. "We have a tour boat to get on at four. If you could have us at the wharves at say... three forty five? We would appreciate it. I think fifteen minutes early should be enough. Until then, just drive around and I will give you a hundred dollars, okay?"

"It would be being my pleasure," the driver said, thinking this would be the easiest money he had made all week.

"And don't worry about the casino, we've seen too much of that already," Kerri added.

Seventy Four

David was standing in the little chapel in Ceduna, surveying the organised chaos that was around him, when Abram approached. Another angel was with Abram, someone that he hadn't been introduced to yet.

"David, this is Bruce, he has been assisting the Police Chief in his efforts," Abram said, as he stopped before David with the other angel.

"Glory to the living God," David said as a greeting.

"And to the risen lamb," replied Bruce.

"How goes the efforts of the local constabulary?" David asked Bruce.

"A bit frustrating. A police patrol has just returned from the site of the attack. They were able to confirm that some sort of accident occurred there, possibly involving several motorbikes," Bruce explained. "But they were unable to determine the cause of the accident or the whereabouts of the riders of the bikes involved. They can tell, however, the direction in which they travelled."

David stared at him for a moment and then thanked Bruce for his information. He then turned and went to stare at one of the stained-glass windows. It was a replication of the empty tomb and the risen Lord. It was quite good and gave him a certain sense of peace and purpose.

As David stared at it, he got his inspiration for what to do next.

"Abram," David called, as he turned back to face the centre of the chapel. A mix of angels and humans were there, trying to help with the search for the missing minister.

It only took a moment for Abram to cross the room and be back with David. Some of the other angels that were present drifted over too.

David addressed Abram directly, "I am leaving you in charge of this part of the search, the guidance and motivation for the humans. I am going to try to track the bikes myself. If the humans can find evidence of which direction the bikes were headed, then I should be able to find more than that. I will need two of your fastest flock to accompany me and two of your most observant. Who would you suggest?"

There was a slight pause as Abram looked out at the surrounding angels. "Clare is our fastest messenger; Stan is quick too; Rundle spotted the message in Troy's belt when no one else did and Chris —"

"You're not going without me!" an angel called out, as he stepped forward to stand before Abram and David. He turned to David, "I am Troy, the messenger of the missing minister."

David stared at him for a moment and then replied, "Of course, I would expect nothing less." David turned back to Abram, "I have no need of three messengers and I suspect that you will need one yourself. Clare will stay here and Troy will come with me in her place."

"Very well," Abram replied. "I will tell them all to meet you outside as soon as they can."

"Troy," David said, as everyone started to leave, "wait with me please."

Troy stepped back to stand with David. Once everyone had moved away from them, David turned around and indicated to Troy to do the same. He stared once more at the same window. Troy looked at it too.

"What emotions does this invoke in you?" David asked.

Troy studied the scene within the window before answering. "I am not sure what you want me to say. It reminds me of the Lord's sacrifice. That was not one of the best days I ever witnessed upon this earth."

"You do understand the importance of that day though, don't you?" David asked.

"Yes," replied Troy.

"And you understand what that means to the humans?"

Troy paused to think before answering, "Once they understand the victory that was won on that day, they look at the resurrection with a sense of awe."

"Some do, others see it as a scene of hope and inspiration. For me, it gives me a feeling of peace and purpose," David said.

Troy stared at it some more. Eventually he spoke again: "I understand why you would feel that way but right now, all I feel is sadness."

David turned and looked Troy in the eye. "Troy, you are still overwhelmed by what you have gone through. Are you sure you can be of help with the search?"

Troy looked back at the window and then at David. "I am terribly worried by what has happened and I am scared for my charge. I guess that is foremost in my mind and therefore my other perceptions are biased by it. I will try not to let it impose upon my judgement during the search."

"That is all I can ask. Now, let's go see if everyone else is ready to go."

SEVENTY FIVE

It was the most incredible and memorable lunch that Jack and Tony would ever have. The angels, even though they had no need for the nourishment, also ate, so as to appear to fit in with everyone else there. As lunch had started, Nathaniel had excused himself and walked away. The conversations were full of small talk, which was quite incredible as small talk with angels is not the same. For a start, angels do not gossip or lie and they have no need to discuss the weather. The small talk seemed to be centred on where they were: the beauty of the surrounding landscape, the buildings and the construction site nearby were the topics of conversation.

As their lunch dishes were taken away, their discussions were suddenly interrupted by a disturbance outside. From where they sat, they could not see what was going on. The dining area was enclosed by thick glass doors, with drapes that were used to help keep out the heat. Their view of outside was restricted to a small patch of garden, which was full of hardy native plants that could survive on the minimal amount of water they received each day. However, from where they sat, they could see that even though it was the middle of the day and the sun was high in the sky, the day suddenly became brighter and brighter and then the glow faded away, until the day was back to normal.

Micah looked at Jack, Tony and the others at the table seriously: "Please, we must now appear to be talking normally and not looking outside. What we just saw will be explained in a moment but, until then, we need to ignore it and appear to be chatting over coffee."

Jack looked at Tony. Tony nodded and was about to speak when he noticed someone standing beside him. He looked up to see a waitress.

"Would you like some coffee?" she asked.

"We were just discussing that, yes please," Tony answered her. "I'll have a flat white please and a cappuccino for you, dear?"

Isabel smiled and said, "Yes please."

"I'll have one too please," Jack added.

"What about you, sir?" the waitress asked looking at Ivor.

"Not for me thanks," he replied.

The waitress went around all the angels, one by one, and they all politely replied, "No thank you."

As the waitress started to turn away she was stopped by Nathaniel, "Excuse me," he said, as he walked back up to the table.

The waitress turned back to see two more men approaching.

"What can I get for you?" she asked.

"I'll have an espresso please," Nathaniel requested. "How about you?" he asked his companion.

"Can I have a cold glass of milk please?" the newcomer asked the waitress.

"Sure," she replied, as she wrote the additional orders on her note pad and walked away to fulfil her customers' requests.

As Nathaniel and the newcomer pulled up some more chairs, Nathaniel spoke, "I have briefed Elisha on the situation he is entering into but not why we are all here."

"It is a surprise to see all of you here. I was not expecting a welcoming committee when I was summoned," Elisha replied.

"We're not here for the same reasons but it seems we have a common link," Micah said indicating Jack.

"Interesting," Elisha said, as he focused on Jack for the first time. "Hello Jack. My name is Elisha."

"Hi," Jack replied, "are you... like them?"

"Yes," Elisha answered, "and at the moment all the people around here can see me."

"Are you *the* Elisha?" Tony asked, unable to stop himself.

"No," Elisha said smiling, as he turned to look at Tony. "I was his guardian. I was chosen to be with him before he was born. That is how he got his name — I told his parents my name and they gave it to him. It was how it was done back then and occasionally still is today."

Jack smiled at the look on Tony's face. "I'd close your mouth if I were you before you catch a fly." They all chuckled at his joke.

"Why are all of you here?" Jack asked.

"Jack!" Tony jumped in, "You can't ask them that. Please, forgive my friend. He is new to all of this."

"That is quite alright," answered Micah. "In truth it is not such a bad thing for him to ask, as we are here for specific reasons that are not all the same. I think that Elisha should go first."

"Of course," Elisha replied. "Jack, this is a unique situation that we are in, you and I. You see, I am *your* guardian angel. A moment ago you became a part of our family, the family of God. As such, the Lord has sent me to help look after you and guide you in your walk with Him."

Micah jumped in, "The flash of light we saw was Elisha arriving."

Jack sat there dumbfounded. He looked over at Tony and Isabel, then at the other angels present and then back at Elisha. "This is all happening so fast," he said.

"I understand," Elisha said in response. "Often when one is visited by an angel it can be... unsettling, to say the least. You, however, have been visited by eight today so it must be overwhelming to you."

"You can say that again," replied Jack.

"Why would I do that?" Elisha asked, feeling a little confused by Jack's statement.

"That's just a saying, you don't really have to say it again," Micah tried to explain to Elisha. Being a messenger, Micah was required to be familiar with current sayings, slang and the like. Then to Jack he said, "You will have to watch what you say now, not only with your 'colourful' language, but also with your sayings, slang and any abbreviations. You are considered holy now and need to reflect that. Besides, it has been a long time since Elisha was someone's guardian."

Elisha smiled, "I had begun to think I had been put away," he said.

It was Jack and Tony's turn to look confused.

"He means retired, not put away," Micah explained. "They haven't used that phrase for two millennia," he said to Elisha.

Elisha smiled and spoke to Jack again, "Looks like we may have some fun understanding the differences in the language we speak."

"So what does a guardian do?" Jack asked Elisha.

"Usually, we just follow you around and try to guide you through the experiences in your life's journey," Elisha explained. "We lead you to the information you need to grow as a Christian and try to protect you from demonic encounters. As one of the Lord's children, you are under His protection, but that doesn't mean that you will not encounter any demons. As one of the Lord's children they cannot harm you if you do not let them. However, we will have a slightly different situation."

"Why is that?" Jack asked.

"Because you can see me and them," replied Elisha. "Can I ask *you* a question?"

Jack looked at Tony and saw that he was looking a bit confused about something. Feeling a little distracted by that he answered Elisha, while trying to watch Tony out the corner of his eye. "Sure."

"Why is it, that you can see us?" Elisha asked. The other angels all leaned forward to hear the answer to this too.

Jack shrugged, "I don't know, honestly."

The others sat back again a bit disappointed.

"How long have you been able to see us? When did it all start?" Micah asked.

Jack turned to the other angels, "I don't know, just today I think."

"Not just today," Isabel spoke up, "it has been happening for longer than that."

Jack looked at Isabel, "How do you know?"

Tony looked at Isabel too. The look on his face was something that Jack had never seen before. It was a mixture of confusion, denial and sadness.

Isabel didn't answer Jack. Instead, she looked back at Nathaniel and asked a question of him, "So what is *your* purpose here?"

Nathaniel indicated his companions, "We are here on a mission for Michael and Gabriel. I can't give you all the details, obviously, but it has something to do with the construction site. There appears to be a large number of demons over there, so we can't get near it. Jack can see them as well as us, so he would be able to go where we cannot. They will not suspect..."

Jack sat there only half listening. He had been thinking about what both Elisha and Isabel had been saying. "Hang on," Jack said interrupting Nathaniel, "a moment ago you said that I had been visited by eight angels today. But I only see seven of you. Also, if I have a guardian angel, why doesn't Tony? He has been a Christian for a lot longer than me. Does that mean that he isn't really a believer? Or do guardians go away after a while?"

"I know the answer to that too," Isabel said quietly.

Tony stood suddenly, almost knocking over his chair. "I need to... that is I left... my... I need to be... I can't..." Tony said, as he started to back away from the table. "I don't want to know," he finished off quietly. With that, Tony turned and walked away, quickly at first but he slowed as he reached the elevators. Jack watched all this, stunned. He turned towards Isabel to ask her what was going on.

"I'll go," Elisha said standing up to follow Tony. "I think he has some questions for me about my namesake."

They all watched as Elisha got up and quickly chased after Tony so that he would not leave his sight.

Once he had left, they all turned to face Isabel.

Seventy Six

"Well?" Tarvyn asked Cain.

Cain stood there with an expression of deep thought on his face. Tarvyn was not used to being made to wait and started to tap one of his scaly, clawed feet in impatience. Cain, hearing the thumping noise of Tarvyn's foot, looked up and spoke, "My Lord, I do not know what to say. Your offer is... *very* generous, but..."

"It is generous, a little too generous, but I think you are worth it," Tarvyn said interrupting Cain. "Even though you have tried to keep me in the dark about the visitors you had and your search for them, I have still heard about it and been watching how you handle it. You have impressed me. I need someone like that at *my* side, to be *my* most trusted aid, *my* advisor."

Cain was flattered by the compliment, which was exactly Tarvyn's intention. All the same, Cain was not one to make any decision lightly. That is why he had gotten to where he was and had stayed there for so long.

"I hope you understand, lord, that I cannot make such a decision this quickly. I need some time to think about it," Cain said. "I will give you an answer in twenty-four hours. If that is not acceptable, then my answer is no."

Cain watched Tarvyn's face get angrier and angrier. He thought that if Tarvyn didn't do something to release that anger, he would explode. Unfortunately, he was the only one in the room with Tarvyn. He would be the focus of that release. Cain wondered if he could get out of the room quick enough, when he noticed a change come over Tarvyn's features.

"Very well," Tarvyn said. "I will allow you twenty-four hours but no longer. If you were anyone else, you would not be still here. The fact that you asked for the time to think is but one more reason that I would consider you an asset on my team."

"Thank you, lord," Cain responded, bowing from the hip. "Will that be all?" he asked while still bowing but looking up at Tarvyn.

Tarvyn looked at Cain for a short moment, then turned his back on him and wandered away slowly. After a couple of steps he spoke over his shoulder, "That will be all. See yourself out. Report back to me before the deadline tomorrow."

Cain turned and left the room at once. "That was a surprise," he said to himself out loud, as he walked down the passageway. "How can I use this to the best advantage?" He continued to walk and think on this. After a while he found himself standing outside in front of one of the signs announcing the Casino. Then he smiled a very cunning smile.

Seventy Seven

"I'm Tony's guardian," Isabel said, looking Jack in the eye.

"What?" Jack asked, feeling dumbfounded.

The rest of the angels just watched as the truth of the matter slowly sunk in.

"Why then do you pretend to be his wife?" Jack asked.

"I don't," Isabel replied. "It just appears that way to you. Nobody else can see me usually."

If Jack's jaw could have dropped any lower it would have hit the floor. "I don't understand," he said, "he talks to you and you talk back to him."

"Let's go back over what you have seen since you have been with Tony." Isabel started to explain how Jack could see the truth, but hadn't wanted to admit it to himself. "Right from the first moment that you appeared in front of the church, you could see me. Didn't you think it was strange that I didn't talk to you but only to Tony? Telling him what to do? What to say to you?"

Jack thought back to that first encounter. "Now that you mention it, I thought it was strange that someone who was strong enough to be a minister, a leader in a community, was also a henpecked husband. Come to think of it, at that time, I noticed that he didn't acknowledge you at all, either."

"Now you understand why," Isabel said in reply. "He didn't see me that morning. I have always thought it strange that on the days that he preaches, he doesn't see me. I think his mind is at its strongest when he is closest to God."

"But there have been other times when he does talk to you. Haven't there?" Jack asked.

"There are times when he sees me. I don't make it happen and I am not exactly sure why it does happen. Did you notice at all that before we came on this holiday, a lot of people were asking him if it was a wise thing to do?" Isabel asked.

Thinking back, Jack remembered quite a few people, especially the elders of the church, asking him to look after Tony. "I remember being asked to look after him while we were away. I thought it was strange that they were asking me and not you. I assumed they asked you too."

"No, they think his mental health is slipping and the only reason a lot of them let him come on this trip was because of you," Isabel answered. "They have noticed that since you have been around he has been better. I think it is because you can see me. You have never treated him as if he is crazy and I always try to be as discreet as possible when you are both around others."

"Why does he think you are his wife?" Jack asked.

"I used to be her, that is Isabel's, guardian. I first met Tony when he met Isabel. I have been around him from that moment. When they got married, his guardian, Rhys, and I worked together to watch after both of them." Isabel paused for a moment before continuing. When she did she looked away. "Then one night changed everything. They had been out at their small group meeting. On the way home, we were attacked. Spiritually, Rhys and I were assaulted by thirteen demons and physically, it affected them both. They tried to pray while Tony drove but the battle was a distraction for him. He never even saw the drunk driver that hit them. Neither did we until it was too late."

Isabel turned back to Jack. "Then it was over, they flew away laughing. They had struck at the minister and succeeded. Isabel was killed almost instantly and Tony was hospitalised with a few broken bones and some scratches. Rhys had been injured too so he returned to Heaven for healing. As there was no need for two of us any more, he never returned. I have been Tony's guardian ever since that day. I think the reason he can see me is because of the crash and the death of his wife. Essentially, I am a part of her that has not gone away. As such, there are times when his spirit can feel me near. It is at those times that he thinks I am she and that she is still alive.

"It is hard for me to understand at times, as I do not look like her, act like her or speak like her. There is no other reason for him to think I am his dead wife."

Jack sat there stunned. "I didn't know," he said.

"Why would you?" Isabel asked. "He doesn't talk about it and if anyone else starts to, he acts as he just did. He appears confused and runs away. He hasn't finished mourning her, he hasn't let her go."

Jack looked at the other angels. "You knew?"

Nathaniel answered for them, "Not all of that. We knew Isabel was an angel and that was enough for us. As much as we are saddened by the loss that Tony has endured and his inability to accept it, that is not why we are here."

Micah jumped in before Jack could reply, "Nathaniel doesn't mean to sound cold. You see death is not something that we experience like you do and we know that the soul continues. All that Tony is doing is grieving for his own loss."

Isabel smiled, "I know that his wife's soul has moved on, to be with her Lord."

"Have you tried to tell that to Tony?" Jack asked.

Isabel nodded, "Several times. But it is not my place to teach him about such things. The Spirit will do that when Tony is ready and listening."

Jack sat there. What a day he was having. It was almost too much for anyone to take in. "Can I help?" he asked.

The question was directed more at Isabel about Tony, but Nathaniel took it as if it was directed at him.

"That is why we are here. We thought that since you can see the demons at the construction site, you could go in there and see what you could find out for us," Nathaniel told Jack.

"Sorry, what?" Jack asked Nathaniel. "I was actually asking Isabel if I could help with Tony. But *that* is why you're here? To get *my* help?"

"Yes," Nathaniel replied.

"Do you remember the orange lights you saw in the construction site?" Micah asked. "You said you thought they were the level lights of power tools or something like that?"

"Yes, I do," Jack replied.

"They are actually eyes, Jack. The eyes of our ancient enemies," Micah explained.

"Demons?" Jack asked. "I kind of worked that out. So, I can see demons too."

"It would appear that way," Micah answered. "We have been sent here to investigate this location and try to discover why the demons are here. But we cannot go in there. They would know who we were instantly. From a distance, we are safe, but any closer and they would penetrate our disguises."

"When you spoke with us earlier," Ivor continued, "we were trying to deduce a way to enter the site and look around. We fear that one of their leaders may be here, which would be why there are so many of them guarding this place."

"Since you can see them, you can go in there and see things of a spiritual nature too. You could be our eyes and they would never suspect you, if you didn't give yourself away." Nathaniel concluded with the inevitable question: "Will you do it? Will you help us?"

All eyes turned to Jack as they waited for his reply. Jack turned to Isabel with a look in his eyes that silently asked for advice.

"I am not your guardian so I cannot help you," Isabel said quietly. "But if I was, I would tell you that it is very rare for an angel to ask for help from anyone other than another angel."

Jack's eyes took on a faraway look for a moment, and then they hardened with determination, as did his jaw. He turned to Isabel and spoke, "I guess Tony will have to wait for now." Jack then turned back to Nathaniel, "What exactly am I looking for?"

Seventy Eight

"Can somebody help me in here?" Alan called out.

Rasheed and Bob, the same two guards, looked at each other. Rasheed slowly opened the door enough to see through to see what was going on.

"That's it," Alan called to them, "in here. One of you, please. I need you to help me roll him over again."

Rasheed stepped back so Bob could see. Alan was leaning over Henry again, while Henry was having another attack. They could see the froth just starting on his lips.

Bob also stepped back and gestured to Rasheed that he should go.

Rasheed indicated that he wasn't going and Bob needed to.

Bob shook his head and after a quick pause, he lifted his right hand up with his fist clenched.

Rasheed was taken aback by Bob's fist at first. Then he realised what Bob was doing. He raised his right hand, with his fist clenched too.

By silent agreement, they both started at the same time.

One...

Two...

Three...

Rasheed won. He smiled.

Rock beats Scissors.

Bob slumped in defeat. He looked at the still slightly open door.

"Come on, quickly now! I need one of you to help me," Alan called again.

Slowly the door opened and Bob entered the room.

"About time," Alan thought as the door opened and Bob entered.

"I need you to help hold him right here," Alan said, as Bob started to turn green. "Don't think about it, don't even look if you don't want to, just come over here and hold him, while I give him another sedative. You can look back out the door at your friend if you need to."

Rasheed stuck his head in through the door, watching Bob and silently laughing to himself.

Bob moved as if in a daze. He reached out and held onto Henry as Alan pushed and tipped him up, almost on his side. He turned away slightly.

'Clink'

"Argghhh," Alan said in frustration.

Bob turned back to see the syringe lying on the ground.

"Quick, you need to hold more of his weight while I pick it up," Alan said to Bob.

Bob almost passed out at the thought. He swallowed and tried not to look where he was putting his hands. He reached over some more. He was leaning almost completely over Henry and holding him up. Alan swung Henry's arms over so that they were behind Bob. Bob was thankful that Henry had stopped shaking. It was easier to hold him when he didn't shake.

"Good, hold him there for a moment longer," Alan said, as he bent over, with one hand still holding Henry up and stretching for the syringe with the other.

But it was just out of his reach.

Bob was watching Alan stretch to his limits. He could feel Henry's arms still moving about and tried not to think about it. If he had chanced a look, he would have seen Henry remove the cover off of the syringe he had just pulled out of his sleeve.

Gage was watching all this, as well as the demon that had entered the room with Bob. The demon was currently watching Alan also.

Gage slowly reached forward and while it was sufficiently distracted he grabbed for its sword, withdrew it and swung as quickly as he could.

The demon ducked... right into Gage's knee.

As it staggered back from the blow, Gage stabbed forward and pierced it through the centre of its being. As the Abyss opened and sucked the dissolving demon in, Gage turned to see the second demon charging him.

Rasheed was also watching Alan and saw that it would be easier if he helped.

Alan saw Rasheed watching. He changed his position slightly so that it appeared that he had more of Henry's weight. In truth, Henry was completely in Bob's hands. "Can you help? Can you pick that up and pass it to me, please?"

Rasheed came into the room and as he bent over for the syringe, he felt a small prick in his bottom. He looked up to see Alan standing back up, with another syringe in his hand. Rasheed was stunned. Then he saw Bob slump over the legs of Henry, who was sitting up with a syringe in his hand too.

Then his vision started to cloud over. The blackness started to creep in from the edges of his vision. He heard his head hit the ground when he collapsed but he didn't feel a thing. Then the whole room started to echo and spin around him. "That should have hurt," he thought, as his last grasp of consciousness escaped from him, like sand running out of a funnel.

Gage twisted and swung the demon's sword at the demon as it passed him in mid-air. The demon dodged the move at the last moment but his momentum carried him forward and straight into Gage's sword.

Earlier, Gage had planned his part of the escape, after hearing Alan's plan. He had wedged his sword between two books on the shelf so that it pointed straight into the room. The angle of it made it almost invisible from the doorway. From then, he had made sure that Alan had not wandered over to this side of the room and into it.

The demon looked down in disbelief at the sword sticking into him from the book case. Another opening to the Abyss appeared from the centre of his wound and the whirlpool effect started. To anyone that did not know what was going on, it would appear that the demon was being sucked into itself.

Moments later, Gage and the humans were all that were left in the room. Gage dropped the demon's sword and retrieved his own. Then he moved over and stood in the doorway, watching for anymore guards.

Alan looked down at Rasheed. "For a moment, I didn't think I had used enough."

Henry looked at the prone form on the ground. "Give him more if you think he needs it."

"I think his head hit the ground hard enough to take care of that for me," Alan replied.

"Good, can I get some help here?" Henry asked.

"Sure," Alan turned back around and held Bob up while Henry slid out.

Together they undressed Bob and Rasheed and put a hospital gown on both. Next, they lifted Bob up into Henry's bed and slid Rasheed under it, with the sheets untucked. They hung down so far that you couldn't see Rasheed, unless you lifted one side up. If someone walked passed and glanced in, they wouldn't see anything out of the ordinary at all.

Then Alan removed Henry's unnecessary bandages and both of them put on the clothes that they had taken off their guards. They were not perfect fits but it would be enough to get passed anyone that didn't look too closely.

They collected a couple of backpacks and the equipment that Alan had packed into them from within his storage cabinet.

"How do you feel?" Alan asked Henry. "Are you ready to lead us out of here?"

"You bet," came the reply.

"Then lead on," Alan said, indicating the door.

Henry stuck his head out the room and into the passage. After looking one way and then the other, he withdrew back into the room. “Only one problem,” he said, looking back at Alan. “I don’t know where we are.”

Seventy Nine

Gabriel was standing on top of a church, casting his gaze across the many buildings of the small coastal town of Eden, in New South Wales, Australia. There was no unusual activity from the enemy that he could see. But there was something hanging in the air, as if the demons were there, hiding, waiting for some unseen signal to announce their presence.

He looked towards the open water. There was something out that way which kept catching his attention.

"Have there been any indications?" Gabriel asked.

Another angel stepped forward. He had been standing in the shadows and had not been clearly visible. Gabriel thought it was strange for an angel to like to stand in the shadows but Itzal was often found there.

"No," was all the reply Itzal gave. This frustrated Gabriel slightly. He was used to other angels being slightly intimidated by his presence and therefore eager to give more information than was necessary to try to impress him.

Gabriel turned to Itzal and noticed he was also looking where Gabriel had been. He was so still that he could have been easily mistaken for a statue. The only thing that would give him away was his choice of clothing and stance. The majority of angels prefer to dress similar in style – a loose white tunic hitched at the waist with a golden belt, which held their scabbard and sword, and simple sandals tied almost to the knees (reminiscent of Roman times).

Itzal was not like most angels. He chose to dress in a more human fashion. Currently, he was dressed in close-fitting long pants and a long-sleeved shirt. To coincide with his desire to keep to the shadows, he tended to wear black. If he put on a mask, he could almost pass for the Spanish Californian hero Zorro. Itzal's physical appearance added to this, as his black hair and darker skin tone gave him a European appearance.

Apart from his appearance, he moved and stood in a more determined and confident style. This was not too different from others of his kind but that was not how the human imagination has mostly captured them. The majority of statues, paintings and other artwork usually portray them as gentle, meek and soft. They can appear that way but that is not how they appear in the spiritual realm.

Itzal's stance told Gabriel much, but it also had him concerned for this angel's ongoing allegiances.

Itzal turned to Gabriel and spoke, "I worry you, don't I?"

Gabriel turned away while formulating his reply. When he did speak, he had turned to face Itzal again. “In some ways yes, but also no. I know of your exploits and I am glad that you are on our side. However, it doesn’t stop me from worrying that you may one day slip away. Your... tastes are not well received and if you appeared more often in front of the Throne...”

Itzal smiled to himself and looked back out to Twofold Bay. “An argument I have heard many times. I spend time with the Lord and he enjoys my... uniqueness. I agree I should visit more often but it tends to attract too much attention. I enjoy Earth and the people here. I go where the Lord wills me and I seek Him when He calls. Others of our kind do not like my presence. They think that I have fallen or I wouldn’t choose to live like this or stay away so long.”

Gabriel nodded in understanding. “Do you feel judged by your fellow angels?”

Itzal thought before answering. “No. The Lord is the only judge. If they did that, they would endanger themselves. They are only concerned, like you are. They are also slightly afraid of me. They are too afraid to speak to me about their concerns, as you have.”

Gabriel smiled. “So, tell me again what has been happening here.”

Itzal’s gaze tightened as he remembered and started to retell the events of the past months. “About four months back, we felt them arrive. The town has not recovered yet. Their presence still permeates the air.

“The first week, they roamed wherever they could,” Itzal continued, “up and down the streets leaving confusion and lawlessness in their wake. I followed some of the bigger ones and realised they were looking for something.

“The second week was a bit easier, as we confronted them and asked why they were here. They would not tell us anything but tried to pick a fight. We defended ourselves and retreated to here. I snuck back out and followed them again, but I could not determine what they were doing. It was clear, however, that they couldn’t find whatever it was that they were here for.

“It took another week for us to get a better understanding. We were confused by the fact that they were not looking at anything of a material nature. They never entered any of the museums or tourist attractions. They stayed close to the water and their numbers started to thin out.

“Except for one night, during a storm. That night they came out in vast quantities and raced around and around the town. The saints realised they were experiencing a spiritual storm, as well as a physical one. They started to brave the weather; they gathered here to pray for each other and then the town.”

Itzal smiled. "They didn't like that. Quite a lot of them left suddenly, with a little help from us. Finally, we were receiving the signal from the Spirit, that it was time to kick them out. So we did."

Itzal grew serious again. "But not all of them left. That is the presence you can feel in the air. Somehow they managed to stamp their presence here and I am sure that they are not very far away. I think they are waiting for some sort of signal and then they will all be back. Apart from that, there have been no indications of activity at all."

"Has there been any major construction start within that time?" Gabriel asked.

Itzal turned to study Gabriel for a moment. "Is that why you are here?"

"It has something to do with it," Gabriel replied.

"No, there hasn't been," Itzal answered the previous question and watched Gabriel's reaction.

Gabriel scowled and looked away. He had been hoping that there had been. That would make it a bit easier to check out possible locations here.

"Not from lack of trying though," Itzal added.

Gabriel's head shot back so fast, that he almost lost his balance. "Would you care to explain what that means?"

"A request to modify some of the structures around town has suddenly appeared but the historical society has fought it tooth and nail. So far, no approvals have been given. Why is that important?"

Gabriel thought for a moment and realised that out of every other angel in all of God's creations, Itzal was the only one who would not rush off and tell everyone else what this was all about. He decided to trust him.

He explained briefly about the other sites and the possible links to the Garden of Eden. He then asked Itzal if that sounded like a good enough reason for the interest in construction.

Itzal simply nodded and looked back out at the bay.

After a while he raised his arm and pointed at one of the stone wharves in the bay. "There. That is where we need to check."

Gabriel was a bit dumbfounded by Itzal's suggestion. "How can you be so sure? Is that the location that they are trying to build on the most?"

Itzal faced Gabriel again. "No. They haven't shown any interest in it at all. But I can't stop looking at it. And something strange happened out there... about six months ago."

"Six months ago?" Gabriel asked.

"I didn't see it myself," Itzal said.

"What happened?" Gabriel asked.

"It was a stormy night," Itzal continued. "We have found it useful to put two or three sentries up here during storms. It helps to prevent excessive damage by having an early warning system, of sorts."

Gabriel nodded in understanding, not wanting to interrupt.

"One of the sentries reported seeing some strange activity down there. A man, followed by two demons, tried to commit suicide. As he watched, he saw a flash, as if an angel was down there and glorified for a split second. Then only one demon remained. The sentry raised the alarm and raced off to try to help the man. The sentry did not find the man, the other demon or the cause of the flash of light. They simply disappeared. Another angel started to follow the remaining demon. It went to a room in a bed and breakfast before heading to Sydney. Once it entered their den there, the angel came back and reported to me where he had gone."

Gabriel looked back at the wharf. It was not much to look at and didn't appear to have much purpose these days. Not like it would have been a hundred years ago. That is often the way it is. The old, and often overlooked, places are still the ones with the most importance.

"My eyes kept getting drawn to it earlier," Gabriel admitted. "I think that we need to go and have a closer look, but without attracting any attention if possible."

"That should be easy enough," Itzal replied.

"But first, Itzal, Michael told me of his visit with you. It was about six months ago..." Gabriel said, turning back to face Itzal.

Itzal frowned for a moment. "He gave me a special assignment," Itzal eventually admitted. "A secret assignment."

"I know," Gabriel replied. "He told me about it. I need you to tell me what happened."

"I was to watch a man. A man who was to be the next warrior," Itzal replied. "He was being followed by two harassing demons. They were leading him to commit suicide. I opened a portal to keep him from it."

"Let me guess," Gabriel said, "down there." Gabriel pointed at the wharf.

Itzal nodded in agreement.

EIGHTY

Luthor looked out at the quantity of remaining guards and shook his head. "It's not right," he said to Security. "How can they expect me to properly guard our location and Lord Tarvyn, if they keep stealing my guards for other duties?"

"That is exactly why I thought you should be made aware of this," Security replied.

"I will take it up with Cain immediately. Return to your post and continue to keep me informed," Luthor advised.

Security nodded, turned and left.

Luthor also turned and went to find Cain.

****

"You will find Pandora on top of the apartment building they recently vacated. She will tell you what she wants you to do once you arrive," Lucas advised the guard detail that was standing before him. "Dismissed."

The guards bowed, then took to the air and disappeared through the roof.

Once they were gone Lucas turned to Cain, "Will they be enough? I hate to deplete our security by so much. If what you say is correct, though, then we do need to find them and recover that film at all costs."

"I agree, lord Lucas. If we don't try to recover it, then we can expect the enemy to attack. If we do retrieve it, then they will not know our full purpose here," Cain replied.

There was a knock on the door, following which one of Lucas's personal guards entered the room.

"What is it?" Lucas asked.

"Luthor is wishing to speak with Cain," the guard answered.

Cain looked at Lucas and Lucas nodded.

"Thank you, lord," Cain said, as he bowed and followed the guard out of the room, with a scowl on his face.

Once he was out and into the hallway, he looked at Luthor and noticed that he was angry about something. Cain took the offensive first.

"What is the meaning of this interruption?" Cain said, with his right hand on the hilt of his sword.

Luthor looked at Cain and his body language. He then noticed where his right hand was. He swallowed, thinking that maybe this wasn't a good idea.

Cain noticed that Luthor appeared a bit more apprehensive.

"I did not mean to interrupt Cain but I —" Luthor started to explain why he was there but Cain cut him off.

"Let me guess," Cain said, "it's about Lord Lucas reassigning your guards."

Luthor nodded slowly, "Yes, sir."

"Come with me," Cain said. He turned and re-entered Lucas's meeting room. He didn't look to see if Luthor was following; he knew that Luthor wouldn't dare disobey him right now.

Lucas looked up as they entered.

"It is as we thought lord: Luthor would like an explanation of why you have reassigned his guards without *his* approval," Cain told Lucas.

"Front and centre, Luthor," Lucas said sharply.

Luthor swallowed but stepped forward as told to.

"Are you questioning my authority?" Lucas asked.

Luthor immediately fell to one knee. "Oh no, lord Lucas, I would never do that. I was simply searching for a reason as to why my..."

Lucas raised his eyebrows.

"...guards were reassigned," Luthor finished, quite sure now that this was a bad idea.

Lucas was silent for a moment, which was making Luthor feel more and more unsure. Finally Lucas spoke, "A reason? I need to give you a reason for reassigning *my* guard force? But you *aren't* questioning my authority? It sounds like you are. Cain?"

Cain drew his sword slowly.

Luthor looked at it and panic flashed in his eyes.

"Forgive me, lord, but that was not my thinking. I am only concerned with your safety and the security of this building site," Luthor said quickly.

Lucas held up a hand and Cain stopped. He waited for Lucas's signal.

"It is as you thought Cain," Lucas said. "Please explain it to Luthor on your way out."

"As you wish, lord," Cain said, as he sheathed his sword again. "Come with me Luthor."

Luthor followed Cain, feeling a little confused.

"Well done, Luthor — you just passed the test," Cain said.

Luthor's head turned to look at Cain as they walked away from Lucas. "Test?" he asked.

"Yes," replied Cain, "Lord Lucas believes it is necessary to make sure that his advisors are trustworthy. That they are prepared to stand up and speak their piece if they feel that it is necessary."

Luthor scowled. He didn't like being treated like that. But it still didn't answer his question. "But what about..."

"The guards?" Cain finished for him.

"Yes."

"If they do not recover the camera, they will be back before the enemy attacks. If they recover the camera, then the enemy may not ever attack. Either way, they should return before we have need of them," Cain explained.

"Is that what they are doing?" Luthor asked.

"Yes," Cain answered, "It is not a permanent reassignment. Did you think it was?"

"I was not sure," Luthor replied.

"Is there anything else," Cain asked.

"No."

"Then get back to your post," Cain commanded.

Luthor walked away thinking he was lucky to still be here.

Cain watched him go, wondering how Lucas would have responded if he had removed Luthor's head. He smiled at the thought.

Then his smile faded and a predatory look spread across his face instead. "Stage two complete," Cain said to himself.

Eighty One

George stormed through the building, yelling at everyone he passed. He was in a very foul mood and most of it was because of one person. Isam.

After several minutes of storming through the corridors, he finally reached Isam's office. He barged straight in and found Isam sitting behind his desk.

Isam jumped to his feet at once. "What is the meaning of this?"

George threw a bundle of papers on the desk in front of Isam. "You tell me."

Isam looked down at them and recognised his own hand writing. He smiled and sat back down, picking one up with his right hand while his left pressed a hidden button under his desk. "Where did you get these?"

"Never mind where I got them. What are you doing issuing these orders? You have no right to undermine me. Especially this way," George said, indicating the papers.

Isam leaned back in his chair, making himself more comfortable and letting George rant for a while.

But George did not rant. He stopped, crossed his arms and just stood there waiting for an answer.

"You did not seriously think that I would turn over my security to you, did you? I have spent years training my guards and security officers. I will not have all that work undone by one incompetent upstart," Isam replied.

George became so angry that he changed three different colours of red before he answered.

Grom and Security were also arguing about the same situation.

"Lord Porva sent me here. Are you denying me the chance to do my job?" Grom asked.

"Your job? It is *my* job!" Security replied. "I have spent centuries training these guards. I will not have all that work ruined by you!"

Grom grew physically agitated by this. Apart from the fury showing on his face, his body started to shake. Any minute, his fury would boil over.

George was almost at boiling point too. His fists were clenched and teeth gritted. "You *will* acknowledge the fact that I am in charge of the security for the conference! You will send out a memo that reflects this."

"Ha!" Isam gave a short laugh. "I will not change what I have already sent out." Then he became very serious. He stood up, his hands on the desk with his body leaning forward, to emphasise his point. "I will not change what I have already written. You are *not* going to make me look like a fool in front of *my* troops! You do not have ANY authority here WHAT... SO... EVER!"

George didn't think about what he was doing, he just launched himself at Isam over the desk. Isam was not expecting George to do that, otherwise he might have tried to move out the way before George could get there.

The two of them crashed into Isam's chair and then onto the floor.

"You will not undermine my authority!" Grom said through clenched teeth. "But you will acknowledge me and before everyone."

"I will not and you can't make me! Besides, how would I look if I did that? Everyone would laugh at me," replied Security, sounding very much like a little child. "Anyway, everyone knows you are only here because you messed up. How could I let you do it? You would only mess it up again. That's because you're... ooof." Security never finished his sentence because Grom had tackled him to the floor.

Security and Grom rolled around and around, punching, kicking and biting each other. Security was larger and stronger than Grom. He would win if he could just get in one good punch. Grom was smaller and faster, as long as he stayed close to Security, he could inflict lots of pain. Security was trying to push Grom away, far enough so that he could throw a good punch. Grom was hanging on, so that he could stay in close.

Security's superior strength, turned out to be the determining factor. He managed to pry Grom loose and threw him across the room.

George was quick and strong but Isam was trained in the martial arts — he was more than able to fight and defend himself. They struggled and rolled around the floor, each trying to get a better hold on the other. George was going for a head lock but Isam kept slipping out of it.

Isam jabbed George in the abdomen with the tips of his fingers. This caused George to lose his breath and he stumbled backwards. When he recovered, he headed for Isam again, fists clenched and ready to punch him. But he never landed a blow.

George started to swing but Isam's foot caught him in the stomach. Isam quickly followed that up with a roundhouse kick to the head and George was flying across the room. He collided with the wall and slid to the floor.

George was disorientated for a moment. He slowly rose to his feet.

Isam stood in the typical karate pose, one foot forward, one foot back and arms at the ready. He watched George, trying to guess his opponent's next move.

George did something unexpected and pulled out a knife.

Isam's eyes narrowed. "I would think seriously about what you intend to do with that. I promise it will not turn out well for you if you don't put it away," Isam warned.

George didn't listen and started to advance slowly.

Grom got up and started to move in on Security, but didn't get far. Security's greater reach meant that he landed a quick right, which sent Grom staggering back against the wall again. Grom shook his head clear and growled at Security.

Security waited to see what Grom would do next.

Grom slowly drew his sword and waved it around in front of him.

Security nodded, "Okay, if that's the way you want it," and drew his own sword.

Grom swung and Security parried.

Grom swung again.

Security parried.

Grom stabbed.

Security parried and smiled.

Grom was getting frustrated already but kept swinging and Security kept blocking.

George swung and Isam jumped back, dodging out of the way.

George swung again and Isam dodged again.

George stabbed.

Isam dodged to the left and smiled.

George was getting tired already, each swing and stab was a little slower than the last one. Isam was finding it easier to dodge the knife.

Grom swung from the right and Security blocked him, but Grom was expecting it. He quickly changed and spun, now swinging from the left.

Security stepped back and Grom swung right through, ending up off balance.

Security stepped forward quickly and stabbed. He only just caught Grom in the side.

George moved forward, stabbing slower again. Isam dodged to the right, but George had anticipated it and swung quickly at him.

Isam was surprised but not unprepared. He grabbed George's arm and kicked out with his left foot, catching George in the side.

George stumbled back and almost fell. Isam was still holding his arm, which helped him stay on his feet.

Isam, however, took full advantage of George's stumble and forced George's arm down. This caused George to stab himself in the leg.

George screamed and fell to the ground. He removed the knife and dropped it. He held his wound, to try to stop the bleeding.

Grom cried out in rage at being struck first. Even though it was not very deep, it still caused a small puff of red smoke to escape. While he tried to inspect his wound, Security stabbed again.

This time Security got Grom in the leg, causing him to fall to the ground.

Grom dropped his sword and grabbed for his wound, trying to stop the red mist escaping. If he lost too much, the Abyss would open and take him.

"Damn you to the Abyss," Grom cursed.

Security smiled as he held his sword on Grom and kicked Grom's sword away.

Wraith entered the room at that moment and stopped just inside the door. "I came as soon as I could and it looks like I am just in time."

Grom smiled too. "Look what he has done to me," Grom said accusingly.

Wraith came over, picked up Grom's sword and then looked down at him. "Yes, I can see that you are not in a good way. Maybe you should pick someone who is more of your calibre of fighter next time. If there is a next time."

Grom's smile faded.

There was a knock on the door and Mr Kepler walked in. He stopped just inside the door and took in the scene before him.

George spoke first, "Look what he did to me."

Mr Kepler looked at the fallen knife and bent over to pick it up. "I have worked with Isam for many years. If there is one thing I have learnt over all that time, it is that you do not pull a weapon on him, unless he is already dead. Even though he never carries one, he is very proficient with all types. Guns, swords, knives, it makes no difference. I even saw him kill a man with a pen once."

George swallowed. It suddenly dawned on him that he never had a chance of taking Isam's position. His mission here was a lie. He wasn't needed at all. "There's been a misunderstanding," he said, trying to find a way out of this alive.

"Yes there has," Mr Kepler replied. "But it was all on your side. I have kept Isam with me because of his competence on all matters of security. No one, not even someone who the bosses send to me, will ever take over that position. Especially not someone who messed up his last assignment," Mr Kepler said, as he handed the knife to Isam.

George looked away. "Okay, I get the picture. I only came here because I was sent here." He looked back up, "I will leave and not come back. I won't tell anyone what happens here. Just get the doc to patch me up first and then I'll be on my way."

Wraith indicated the humans, "Did you really think that we were not prepared for you?"

Grom's jaw dropped. "What are you talking about?"

"It was a setup, right from the start," Security said.

"Lord Porva was not happy about your last mistake, at all. Even now, they are still trying to fix it up. It could be very costly. But that is not something you are going to have to worry about," Wraith said.

Security lifted the sword.

"Wait!" Grom said, holding up one arm to try to stall them. All he managed to do was to allow more red mist to escape his wounds. "I'll leave. I'll go far away and never tell of what is happening here."

Security swung and Grom's head came free of his body.

Both Security and Wraith stepped away so that the swirling mass didn't suck them in too.

Isam walked away from the limp form on the ground with the knife sticking out of it.

"I liked the idea of dropping him off the cliff," Mr Kepler said, referring to an earlier conversation.

Isam smiled. "I did too, but I don't think that will hide the stab wounds. I will get him dropped in the desert, in the usual spot."

"Very well," Mr Kepler replied. "I will leave it to you then. I must go and report in about the completion of our assignment."

EIGHTY TWO

Daniel was sitting in one of the seats in the waiting area when Kyle walked in. The first thing Daniel noticed was that Kyle was alone. Daniel waved at Kyle and smiled as though welcoming a friend that he would be travelling with. Kyle waved back and indicated that he would get a ticket and then join him.

Daniel continued pretending to read while watching the door.

There was only one other person in the area at present and she was sitting at the other end of the room. Daniel had been checking her out every now and then as he thought she looked familiar. But she hadn't done anything except read a magazine since she arrived.

Once Kyle had finished pretending to buy a ticket, he joined Daniel in the waiting area.

"Where are the others?" Daniel asked.

"We had to split up. Pride returned with company as we were all waiting for the taxi. We decided we needed another diversion so I took the rental car for a spin. I abandoned it in the Casino's car park," Kyle explained.

"You left them?" Daniel asked in amazement and anger.

"Amy and I discussed it first and both agreed on the plan," Kyle said. "The number of them that were converging on our location didn't give us much time to plan a joint escape. I drew them away and gave our friends the chance to slip away without being seen at all."

Daniel nodded slowly, "Maybe. How long ago did you leave them?"

Kyle looked at the clock on the wall. "About three hours ago."

Daniel's eyes widened. "Three hours? They have been wandering around this city for three hours without you?"

"Amy's there. She'll look after them," Kyle answered.

Daniel looked at the clock. "We should know soon. They've got twenty minutes until the boat leaves."

They both sat there quietly, waiting for Glen and Kerri, checking every person that walked through the doors to see if it was them.

Only eight minutes had passed but it felt like hours to the angels. Another twelve people had entered the building, purchased tickets and joined them in the waiting room. Then they arrived.

Kyle was visibly relieved when he saw the three of them walk through the door alone. Amy saw them but stayed with her charges until they had collected their tickets and bags. Once they entered the waiting area, Daniel and Kyle joined them.

Amy was relieved too. It had been quite an afternoon for her, Glen and Kerri. Amy quickly filled both Kyle and Daniel in on what had happened after they had left the hotel.

When she was finished, Daniel turned to Kyle. "That is precisely why you shouldn't have left your charge, even if it was with another angel. What would you have done if they didn't show up?"

Kyle never got to answer. At that moment, an announcement was made over the loudspeaker system, calling for the passengers to start boarding the boat that was to take them to Green Island.

They walked together as a group. Kyle took the lead, Kerri and Glen just behind him, with Amy and Daniel bringing up the rear.

Once onboard, they continued with their conversation.

"Don't be so hard on him," Amy said in Kyle's defence. "He did what we both agreed on. If he hadn't, then we may not have got away at all."

"Alright," Daniel conceded. "You did what you had to do. It was a chance, a very risky one, and it paid off. Next time, I think it would be better if you stayed with your charge and worked out another way."

Kyle just nodded, accepting the criticism.

Glen and Kerri, unaware of the conversation that had happened around them, just sat there looking out at the open water. They glanced occasionally at the other people and the pier, checking to see if anyone else was coming.

The angels settled into a guarded silence, keeping very alert eyes out for any sign of trouble.

Ten minutes passed before it was announced that they were preparing to launch. Five minutes later, they were leaving the bay and heading for the open sea.

Daniel counted another twenty three passengers onboard the boat. He relaxed slightly and tried to enjoy the gentle rocking sensation of a boat on open water. Little did he know that this was not to last very long.

Eighty Three

Elisha looked Jack in the eyes. "I can't follow you in there. This is a very dangerous time for you."

Jack smiled at Elisha. "Thanks for your concern. I know you are supposed to help me and protect me, but I think I can manage this one on my own."

"I'm coming with you," a quiet voice said.

"What?" Isabel said from behind them. "No, Tony. You can't."

"I can and I will," Tony replied. "I have to. Jack has helped me... and he may need me. But you can't come dear. You will need to stay out here and call for help if we do not come back."

Elisha had spent a fair bit of time with Tony. He had calmed him down so much. It was as if the conversation he walked out on only an hour before had not even happened.

Tony was looking in Isabel's eyes, waiting for a response. Isabel nodded her acceptance. Tony turned straight back to the others. "What are we looking for again?"

"Jack will be looking for anything that can indicate what the enemy is doing here. If you are going, you will need to watch Jack and make sure he doesn't stare at any one spot for too long," Nathaniel answered Tony.

"Why would he do that?" Tony asked.

"Some of the demons are rather... grotesque, which could be frightening to you humans," Amos (one of the other angels in Nathaniel's group) answered. "You will not be able to see them, but he will. If he is staring at one, it may appear to you as though he is staring at nothing. You will need to make sure he stops doing it or he will give himself away."

Tony looked at Jack. "Do you understand all of that?"

"Yep," Jack answered.

"Do you have all that you will require?" Elisha asked.

"I hope so," Jack replied, as he checked his bag once more.

"Then what are we waiting for? Let's go." Tony said.

Nathaniel indicated some trees across from the entrance of the partly constructed resort. "We will hide there and observe what we can. If you need us, try to set off the signal we agreed on and we will do what we can to help get you out of there."

"May the Lord of all creation, bless and keep you," Elisha said. All the other angels present said, "Amen."

EIGHTY FOUR

Micah and his team were only a hundred meters from the exhaust port they spotted earlier, hidden amongst the only trees they could find.

They were correct to think that this was something of importance. While they had been watching, a changing of the guard occurred. Thirty demons came up out of the exhaust and waited a moment. The ten that had been flying or standing in various places around the opening in the ground were suddenly joined by at least twenty previously unseen demons. They had just appeared, coming from their hidden posts as if out of nowhere. The two groups acknowledged each other and some words were exchanged between them. Then the new arrivals took the guards' places and the original guards went into the exhaust, disappearing from view again. This all took about three minutes to complete.

"Scratch that idea," Duncan said. "It was a long shot anyway."

"The classic 'distract the guards' at the change of guard is an oldie. So much so, that it is probably the first thing they train against," Ivor commented.

"I don't think we are getting in that way. But it may be possible that someone could get out that way," Micah suggested.

"Not a bad idea," Duncan replied. "Why don't you rush back and tell Jack before he goes in?"

Micah looked up at the sky and how high the sun was. "I wouldn't make it. He should be going in about now."

"All we can do then is hope that the Holy Spirit can lead him to it, if he needs it," Ivor said.

"One of us should go and update Israfel on what is happening," Duncan said.

"I'll go and do that," Micah answered. "You keep watch, just in case they do try to come out this way."

Duncan nodded and Ivor replied, "Okay."

Micah slowly moved on his stomach, back the way they had come, to not bring any attention to his companions or himself. Once he was far enough away, he stood and walked back towards the meeting place.

****

Israfel and his companions had been sitting and waiting for only a short while before Micah appeared. Micah informed them of what was happening and the possible escape route. Israfel sent Micah back to Duncan and Ivor and then he, and his team, headed off to join Nathaniel and his team.

EIGHTY FIVE

Gabriel and Itzal were standing at the beginning of the wharf.

"This is the one," Itzal told Gabriel.

"Tell me again what happened?" Gabriel asked.

"The man ran and jumped off the end," Itzal replied. "Then I opened the portal and he disappeared into it, with one of his companions."

"Where did the portal go?" Gabriel asked.

"Somewhere safe, I don't know exactly," replied Itzal.

Gabriel looked sideways at Itzal, a puzzled expression on his face.

"I didn't have time to plan it. Once I realised why he was running down this wharf, I had to race him from where I was hiding, to beat him here. Once here, I quickly opened the portal and then raced off. I do remember thinking that I wanted him to be safe. I did it all while still on the move. It all happened so quickly, that I don't remember if I closed it properly or just hid it."

Gabriel nodded his head in understanding and proceeded to walk to the end of the wharf. "Let's find out," Gabriel said as he walked.

Itzal followed him. "You know we are being watched, don't you?" Itzal asked.

Gabriel nodded. "It can't be helped right now. I need to check this out. In fact, I hope they are watching all of us."

Gabriel indicated the other two wharfs and one of the jetties. On them were the other angels of his team and they were doing exactly the same thing he was, walking down them in groups of two. That left three of his team unaccounted for.

Pretty soon, they were all standing at the ends of their respective wharves and jetty. As one, they drew their swords. Gabriel, his counterparts in each group, all lifted their swords, holding them straight out at arm's length and pointing away from the city behind them. Then they all waved their swords in ever increasing circles until... flash, flash, flash, flash. Then came the sound of rushing air. It wasn't very distinct, as it was very similar to the sound of the waves, crashing on the beach behind them.

A portal opened in front of every one of them. For three of them, it came as no surprise, the other three members of their team were creating them and waiting on the other side but for Gabriel, it was different. He had reopened Itzal's rift, which had been created six months ago. It went to somewhere else. Somewhere where Gabriel did not have a team mate on the other side, waiting for him.

All four groups stood looking at their portal. The 'opener' of each portal stepped forward and through it. The remaining angels turned and waited, guarding the entrances with their swords drawn.

Gabriel had stepped straight into the Garden of Eden and was met by three cherubim. They looked up surprised by the sudden arrival of an archangel.

"Glory to the living God! Gabriel?" Shadrach asked.

"And to the Lamb that was slain. Yes," replied Gabriel, "it is I."

"What brings you to the Lord's Garden?" Meshach asked.

"Thank you for confirming my location," Gabriel answered. "It is where I thought I would go but I was not sure. I need you all to carry out some tasks for me immediately."

The three looked at each other and Abednego answered. "What is it you wish us to do?"

Gabriel quickly gave his instructions to each of them and then stepped back through the portal.

Itzal looked at him questioningly, when he was fully back and standing beside him.

"Not now," Gabriel said, in answer to the look.

Gabriel glanced quickly at the other wharves and the jetty and noticed that the others were coming back too. Then he closed the portal and tried to put a seal on it. There was a popping sound as if a balloon had been burst but it didn't sound correct to him.

Gabriel heard three more 'pops' and looked at the others again. He saw that they had closed their portals too.

They all walked back to the beginnings of their wharves and met as a group on the grass overlooking the beach, between the three wharves. They talked in animated fashions, pointing and waving their arms about and then headed down the beach, away from the main wharf. They did not actually discuss what had been discovered. Instead, they pretended that it had been unsuccessful. They were now going to try again, in different locations.

Further down the beach they split up into the different groups once more and went through the whole process over again, some on the remaining wharves and the others on the beach itself. All, that is, except Gabriel and Itzal. Another two angels arrived to take their place. They made it look like they had delivered an urgent message so that Gabriel could leave. The two 'messengers' then took Gabriel and Itzal's place.

In all the groups, one would create the portal and the other would guard them. Then they would return and close it again. They continued doing this, all over the town, for the next three hours. Any demons watching, they hoped, would only assume they were unsuccessful at finding whatever it is they were looking for.

Gabriel, meanwhile, went back to the church. He organised for one of his messengers to go immediately to Michael and report what he had found. Gabriel would wait for confirmation that the portal was completely sealed before he left.

Itzal accompanied Gabriel back to the church. He then set about organising his warriors to defend that one wharf if the enemy tried to approach it.

EIGHTY SIX

Gage was leading them through the maze of passages to get them back to somewhere Henry might recognise. Alan and Henry couldn't see him, of course, but every time they came to a junction or new passage, they would stand there for a moment, until it felt right to move down one or the other.

Gage was scouting ahead, and was surprised that they were not encountering anyone at all. No other humans or demons… so far anyway. Surely the Lord was looking after them.

Alan was a bit worried about the same thing. He knew roughly where he was going but every other time he had gone between the upper and lower levels he had always been directed by a guard. "Tell me again why we need to go down, to get back up and out?"

"The escape route I used before was from where I was, which is down here. To find it again, I think I need to start at the beginning," Henry answered.

"If you told me where it was, then maybe I could get you there from here," suggested Alan.

"I am not quite sure of it. I was following my instinct. Which is what I am doing now and it just feels… right. Do you know what I mean?" Henry asked.

"I think so. Just like it felt kind of right for me to ask you to come with me," replied Alan.

Gage heard something ahead. He quickly retreated to Henry and whispered to him, "Someone is up ahead. Try to hide so that you are not discovered."

Henry stopped so suddenly that Alan almost walked into him.

"What is it?" asked Alan.

"I think someone is coming this way. We need to hide somewhere," replied Henry.

They looked around quickly and Alan remembered a doorway a short way back. He suggested they retreat to it and see if they could hide in there.

Henry agreed. They both turned and walked, as quickly and quietly as they could, back down the passage.

Gage preceded them down the hallway. When he found the door, he stuck his face through it first to see if it was empty. It was, so he passed through it and unlocked it. Then he went back out to the passage and waited for Henry and Alan, who were almost there.

They found the door. Alan tried it and found it was unlocked. They went in and left the light off. Henry closed the door and then thought twice about it. He reopened it enough to allow him to see out of it. He bent down low and watched through the crack. Alan was next to him listening.

It wasn't long before they heard approaching footsteps. Henry watched as a group of guards went by carrying a stretcher with someone on it. There was a sheet over the head and he thought he saw blood on the sheet.

The guards were grumbling about having to take the body of George out to the desert. Then they laughed about how he had come here, thinking he was some sort of big shot, and how their commander had proved him wrong.

Henry and Alan looked at each other. Then Henry went back to watching out the opening. It wasn't long before they were so far down the corridor that they couldn't hear footsteps anymore.

Gage had watched too and had seen many demons passing with the humans. They were laughing and sometimes complaining too. Once they were a fair distance away he moved out into the passage, to check it out again. When he was sure it was safe, he told Henry to come out.

"I think it is safe now," Henry said quietly to Alan.

They stood and slowly opened the door and re-entered the passage.

"Did they say that was George? That he had recently arrived and thought he was a big shot?" Alan asked.

"That's what I heard. Seems too much of a coincidence, doesn't it," Henry replied, as he started walking back the way they had been going.

Alan nodded his agreement as he walked alongside. "If it was the same George that was our site boss, even though I never liked him, I would never have wished that upon him."

Eighty Seven

Tony and Jack were walking very cautiously through the passages, not knowing exactly where they were going or what they were looking for. They had been inside now for almost twenty minutes. Their entry appeared to be unnoticed to Tony but Jack knew otherwise.

Jack had seen a number of demons shoot off down different passages when they entered and there were at least two following them. He couldn't be one hundred per cent sure as he didn't want to look directly at them. Their shadowy forms were not distinct enough to tell where one began and one ended. He had tried to count the eyes from the corner of his own but hadn't been able to see them all at the same time. The demons did not simply follow them but instead were trying to harass them. They were swooping, laughing and trying to scare them.

Jack had picked up that the demons appeared to be trying to steer them when they came to cross passages and other intersections. As a result, Jack was doing his best to try to go where they didn't want him too.

Jack was also getting concerned about Tony, as he was reacting to the presence of the demons. Every time Jack went against the demons, Tony would cringe.

"You okay?" Jack asked, as he stopped for a moment and made Tony stop too. "You look... well, you look like you may have a heart attack or something."

"I... I don't know," Tony replied.

"I don't know how to get back out and I'm not ready to try," Jack said. "Do you want to try to go back by yourself?"

Tony thought for a moment and then shrugged. "I don't know Jack. I feel... scared. Something about this place feels like it is trying to... smother me. Yeah, that's the right word. Smother."

"I know what you mean and I know why too," Jack replied. "And you do too if you think about it."

Tony thought about it for a moment. Jack thought he saw Tony's eyes clear a bit, as if understanding was coming upon him. Tony started to nod his head. "Demons," he said quietly.

"We are walking through a spiritual minefield. How do you normally face something like that?" Jack asked.

Tony looked Jack in the eyes. "Prayer!"

Jack put his hand on Tony's shoulder. "Pray for us as we walk through here and I will lead the way. Maybe you should pray for any other lost soul that might be in here too."

Tony smiled and nodded at Jack. "One other thing we need to remember Jack," Tony said.

"What's that?" Jack asked, feeling more confident in Tony being with him again.

Tony's eyes sparkled as he replied, "We already have victory over the forces of darkness, through Jesus's victory on the cross. Don't forget that!"

Jack smiled. "That's the spirit."

Jack turned and started off down the passage again. He started to pass some doors on the right wall and felt suddenly that he should go in one.

As he turned towards it, both demons dove between him and the door. They started shouting for him to go back. They threatened and swore and tried to scare him.

Jack stopped for a moment, trying to get his courage up. He heard Tony start to pray out loud.

"In the name of Jesus Christ, our Lord and Saviour, shut your mouths and stop harassing us!" Tony exclaimed.

It was like the demons were slapped in the face. Both demons fell back at the rebuke, unable to open their mouths.

Jack couldn't help but stare at them for a moment. Then he felt his courage returning and he started to walk forward again. Over his shoulder he said, "That's it! Keep it up Tony, it's working. They..." he stopped as he wondered if he should say anymore. He didn't want to give himself away, but at the same time it didn't look like it would make much difference. "...they can't stop us!"

Tony looked ahead but couldn't see what Jack was seeing. He touched Jack on the back. "They never could. Remember the story of Job?"

Jack turned slightly to hear Tony better but kept walking towards the door. "I can't right now, why don't you remind me."

Tony started to tell Jack all about the man named Job. "Permission was sought by Lucifer to be able to harass Job. It was given by God but with one condition: not a hair was to be harmed on his head. So Lucifer sent his forces and Job was harassed. Do you know what Job did? Job praised and worshipped God. Lucifer sought permission again, this time to afflict Job personally. God gave it, but with one condition: that his life was to be spared. So Lucifer struck Job with painful boils, from the souls of his feet, to the top of his head"

As Tony continued the recount of Job from the Bible, Jack opened the door and found what appeared to be an elevator. He stepped back and looked at the outside again. He saw nothing to indicate what it was inside. He looked back inside it and noticed that it did not go up, only down. Jack scratched his head and decided that, if this was where the demons didn't want them to go, it was exactly where they should go.

The demons, Jack noticed, were still trying to keep them out but without the ability to talk or touch them, they were not succeeding at all.

As Jack stepped in and Tony followed, one of the demons shot out and went looking for help. Jack pressed the button and they started to descend into the earth.

"Job was sitting in pain and scratching himself, when three friends came up and sat with him," Tony continued. "Hoping to comfort him, simply by being with him, the friends kept quiet, until Job started to complain against God."

Jack was only half listening as he stood there, waiting for the doors to open again.

"Eventually, one friend spoke up and told him he was wrong to speak this way. Job responded with more complaints. The next friend spoke up, telling Job that it was not his place to understand God. That God's wisdom was at least twice that of Job's and that God's limits are not known to us."

The elevator slowed to a halt and the doors opened. Jack indicated that Tony should stop talking for a moment. Jack stuck his head out slowly and looked around. They were in another passageway but this one appeared to be underground. The walls were dirt and every now and then there were wooden posts on the walls. It was as if they had entered an old-fashioned mine. When he looked down, Jack noticed there were even rails for a mine cart.

Jack indicated the rails to Tony so that he would not trip on them. Then they stepped out of the elevator and into the passage.

"Which way now?" Tony whispered to Jack.

Jack looked around and noticed that the remaining demon appeared to be sulking. It didn't appear that he would receive any indications from him. "Let's try this way," Jack said pointing to the left. He glanced at the demon to see how it would react and it didn't. "Or maybe this way...," he said pointing to the right this time but still got no reaction from the demon.

"Well?" Tony asked. "Which one is it going to be?"

With no indication from the demon, Jack had to make the decision himself. "Let's try... this way," Jack said, and headed off to the right.

EIGHTY EIGHT

Michael was sitting down after instructing the backups. He was a little concerned about his inaction at the moment but with so much happening in various places, there was little he could do until he heard from the messengers. Once he started to get the reports back, he would then be able to plan his next step.

Michael looked over at Saint Peter and realised that he hadn't finished the recount of his experiences in Eden. He thought that now was the perfect time to finish it off.

Saint Peter came over and sat down beside Michael. He never said anything. He did not want to increase Michael's concerns. Saint Peter hoped that Michael would continue his recount but also realised that Michael may need to sit quietly, contemplating all that was happening.

Michael smiled as he realised just how good Saint Peter was as a companion. He was thankful that this was a man that Jesus had confided in during his time on earth.

"I suppose I should continue and tell you about The Fall," Michael eventually said to Saint Peter.

Saint Peter turned and looked at Michael. "If you feel we have time," he responded.

Michael smiled again. "It could be a while before any of the messengers report back and some of them could arrive at any moment. I think it is necessary that I get this, the last part of the Eden story, told."

"Very well," Saint Peter said.

"'The Fall'", Michael started, "is the story of Adam and Eve's biggest failure. The title is really short for The Fall of Man, and is, in essence, the only reason that Mankind does not see God face to face or know Him as well as they could.

"Up until this time, God would visit with Adam and Eve in the Garden of Eden, but after it, they were expelled from the Garden and it became off limits to Mankind from that time until the Return of the Lamb.

"After the time of Adam and Eve, God would send a representative, the Angel of the Lord, whenever He needed to communicate with Mankind. On very rare occasions, He would appear too, like when He spoke with Moses through the burning bush."

"I didn't know that," Saint Peter said.

"There is a lot not mentioned in the passage in the Bible and yet it is a very accurate account of what happened. I think I will tell you this time bit by bit."

The snake was more clever than all the wild animals the Lord God had made. He asked the woman, "Did God really say, 'You must never eat the fruit of any tree in the garden'?"

The woman answered the snake, "We're allowed to eat the fruit from any tree in the garden except the tree in the middle of the garden. God said, 'You must never eat it or touch it. If you do, you will die!' "

"You certainly won't die!" the snake told the woman. "God knows that when you eat it your eyes will be opened. You'll be like God, knowing good and evil."

Genesis 3:1-5

"The Snake that is mentioned here is thought to be Satan, and quite rightly so. His appearance had become much like a snake and, because of this, he had befriended several of them. Unknown to us, the demons had been studying all of the creatures too but they did it in an entirely different way. Their twisted minds did not consider the consequences of what they were doing. They only sought to twist what God had created and try to use it against him.

"At first, several demons tried to take the same appearance as the animals. You could still tell it was a demon, as they could not imitate the character of the animal. So they tried possession instead. They found that some of the time they could succeed at this, but most of the animals resisted and grew to fear the presence of the demons, to the point that they would run if one was near. Only a few were willing to give themselves over to such an experience.

"The first recorded instance of this is right here. Satan convinced one of his 'friends' to let him 'borrow' his body. Then he could enter the Garden and seek forgiveness from the Lord. Thinking that Satan was sincere, the snake agreed. He paid for it later, but I will get to that bit in a moment.

"Instead of approaching God, Satan waited for a moment to speak to either Adam or Eve. Unfortunately, it was Eve that he spoke with first. Poor Eve did not even question why but answered the snake, thinking it was an innocent enough question. She gave the right answer and Satan knew just how to turn the words inside out and confuse her. The strangest part of this is that Satan was telling the truth... from a certain point of view.

"The death the Lord spoke of was a spiritual death; but it was also a physical death, just not an immediate one. This is what the snake meant when he said, 'You will not die.' He knew as he said it that the death mentioned was not an immediate physical one. What he did not know was exactly what sort of death it was. But even if it was an immediate physical death, then that would have been to his advantage, as he would have corrupted part of the Lord's creation already.

"Eve did not immediately go and eat the fruit. She pondered what the snake had said and wandered around some, not able to get what had been said to her out of her head. In her wanderings she passed the tree..."

The woman saw that the tree had fruit that was good to eat, nice to look at, and desirable for making someone wise. So she took some of the fruit and ate it. She also gave some to her husband, who was with her, and he ate it.

Then their eyes were opened, and they both realized that they were naked. They sewed fig leaves together and made clothes for themselves.

Genesis 3:6-7

"A while later, Eve led Adam back to the tree. She talked to him about it and what the snake had said. Adam at first refused to listen and told Eve that if the Lord did not want them eating it, then they shouldn't.

"Eventually Eve gave up and went and picked the fruit and ate it. Adam noticed a difference in her immediately and, unfortunately, felt left out. God had the knowledge and now his companion, the woman Eve, also had the knowledge. If he was to remain her companion, then he needed to be like her. So, when she offered him some, he took it.

"We had seen all this, as had the Lord. We had been told to do nothing about it. We had to let what happened happen.

"'This is the beginning of "choice" and "freewill",' the Lord told us. 'Even though you do not understand why I am allowing it, it must happen.'"

In the cool of the evening, the man and his wife heard the Lord God walking around in the garden. So they hid from the Lord God among the trees in the garden. The Lord God called to the man and asked him, "Where are you?"

He answered, "I heard you in the garden. I was afraid because I was naked, so I hid."

God asked, "Who told you that you were naked? Did you eat fruit from the tree I commanded you not to eat from?"

The man answered, "That woman, the one you gave me, gave me some fruit from the tree, and I ate it."

Then the Lord God asked the woman, "What have you done?"

"The snake deceived me, and I ate," the woman answered.

Genesis 3:8-13

"The Lord waited and watched what they were doing. At first, they appeared to be overcome with all this new 'knowledge' and they wandered around discussing differing aspects of ethics and morals. At this stage of the planet's life, there was not that much for them to consider so this didn't take too long.

"Then the Lord entered the Garden and made his presence known by walking loudly and calling out to them."

Saint Peter interrupted and asked, "How do you walk loudly?"

"By walking on sticks and other things that make noises as you step on them," Michael explained. "It helped that Jesus was there too. Together they made twice as much noise. As you know, Adam and Eve were trying to hide from the Lord God's view. As Jesus and the Lord neared where the man and woman were hiding, Jesus stopped and watched the Lord continue. He had a mournful expression on his face. I watched Jesus for a moment and I saw him look up at one of the trees and spread his arms out wide. I don't know if he knew I was there too or not, but as I watched Him, I saw a single tear slide down his cheek.

"I did not understand what I had seen or what troubled Him at the time. It would be thousands of earth years later that the significance of that moment would sink in.

"God, meanwhile, was confronting Adam and Eve and discovered the snake's role in all of this. This was something that he knew all along, of course, and had allowed to happen."

Saint Peter interrupted again, "Please wait," he said, "you are saying that God knew what would happen all along. Even with this knowledge, He created these two, knowing that they would break the only rule He gave them!"

"Precisely," Michael replied. "He is the God of all. Omnipotent. Omniscient. The All Knowing. Everywhere at once. How would He not know?"

Saint Peter thought about that for a moment. "That is something I never considered before but you are quite correct. He would have known, wouldn't He? Even before he started on day one! That would mean, He also knew what the snake would do and had planned that punishment beforehand too."

"Exactly...

So the Lord God said to the snake, "Because you have done this,
You are cursed more than all the wild or domestic animals.
You will crawl on your belly.
You will be the lowest of animals as long as you live.
I will make you and the woman hostile toward each other.

I will make your descendants
and her descendant hostile toward each other.
He will crush your head,
and you will bruise his heel."
Genesis 3:14-15

"Eve's too?" Saint Peter asked.
"Yes, and Adam's...,"

He said to the woman,
"I will increase your pain and your labor
when you give birth to children.
Yet, you will long for your husband,
and he will rule you."
Then he said to the man, "You listened to your wife and ate fruit from the tree, although I commanded you, 'You must never eat its fruit.'
The ground is cursed because of you.
Through hard work you will eat food that comes from it
every day of your life.
The ground will grow thorns and thistles for you,
and you will eat wild plants.
By the sweat of your brow, you will produce food to eat
until you return to the ground,
because you were taken from it.
You are dust, and you will return to dust."
Genesis 3:16-19

"As a simple fisherman, I would never have considered all that," Saint Peter remarked. "As a disciple of the Master, we had not time to reflect on the past teachings. He was teaching us many new things, things that upheld the laws but made it clearer and easier for us and others like us, the common folk, to understand."

"Not many do consider it," Michael said, "and for those that do, it can be a confusing issue. But as Isaiah said...

"My thoughts are not your thoughts, and my ways are not your ways," declares the Lord.
Isaiah 55:8

"So, there it is, the event that is called 'The Fall'. That is not all of it, though. It wasn't until this point, that Eve received her name...

Adam named his wife Eve (Life) because she became the mother of every living person.

The Lord God made clothes from animal skins for the man and his wife and dressed them.

Then the Lord God said, "The man has become like one of us, since he knows good and evil. He must not reach out and take the fruit from the tree of life and eat. Then he would live forever." So the Lord God sent the man out of the Garden of Eden to farm the ground from which the man had been formed. After he sent the man out, God placed Angels and a flaming sword that turned in all directions east of the Garden of Eden. He placed them there to guard the way to the tree of life.

Genesis 3:20-24

"Why did it not happen until now? I think that until this moment, they did not understand that woman was not a name. After eating the fruit, Adam realised that she needed a name. It was the right thing to do.

"Even though the transgression had occurred, the Lord still helped them. He fashioned some clothes for them and then He sent them out of the Garden. It was not right that they be rewarded with eternal life now. Especially, considering that Jesus' sacrifice on the cross would now be required to cancel the transgression.

"The other part of that, of course, is that now Adam and Eve understood right and wrong; they also understood that there had to be consequences for their wrongdoing. It wasn't enough that they be individually punished: they needed to experience a shared punishment, one that would have eternal repercussions.

"They were sent out from the Garden, beyond the hedge, which they had never passed through before. All but one entrance was sealed. The hedge grew and filled in the holes. At the one remaining entrance, He stationed the cherubim with their flaming swords. He ordered four to guard the entrance, one to face each direction. Then He ordered more to patrol the inside of the hedge.

"Over time, the cherubim have encountered a few who have stumbled upon the entrance but on every occasion they were turned away. The enemy has also searched for the entrance. We do not know why but we suspect it is for two reasons: to be closer to Heaven for an assault on the Throne and because they are now forbidden to enter it.

"That is why we fight so hard to keep Eden hidden," Michael answered. "To lose Eden would mean that Heaven and the Lord would be under threat. Something, that we are sworn to prevent."

"Thank you, Michael. You have now completed your piece of our part in preventing this threat. I will leave you now to consider all that you have told me. I will return when I have an idea on how we can prevent that from happening," Saint Peter said as he stood. He then turned and walked towards the door of the Hall.

Michael sat there and watched him leave. "Don't take too long, my friend. Don't take too long."

Eighty Nine

Cain watched as the reports were given. Lucas had everything under control now and was not calling on Cain as regularly. He was referring to the other advisors more frequently.

"I have taught him well," Cain thought to himself.

The problem was that Lucas did not like what he was hearing.

"What!?!" Lucas bellowed. "They were in our casino and they got away?"

The demon that had brought this latest bit of news was visibly trembling.

"I, um, that is, the, um, what I mean to say is…"

Lucas nodded.

Swoosh.

Bliss swung his sword and the demon's head was removed from his shoulders. The body and head dissolved in two separate swirling clouds of red.

"Yes," Cain thought to himself while smiling. "I have taught him very well. I think it is time to move onto the next stage."

He looked around at the gathering of demons and considered what the best move to make now was. Lucas was discussing something with Highrise and Goliath when Cain interrupted.

"Excuse me, my lord," Cain said.

Lucas looked over at Cain with a look that was somewhere between annoyance and anger. The look was all Cain needed to know that he had better keep talking and it had better be good. Lucas didn't like interruptions any more than he did.

"Might I make a suggestion?" Cain asked.

Lucas recognised that Cain had been very helpful to him. He decided it was better to listen to Cain and see what this suggestion might be. He could still disregard it afterward if he wished. "Go ahead," he said.

"Maybe the psychics can be of use in this matter," Cain suggested.

All of the advisors looked shocked and even Lucas looked a little surprised by the suggestion.

"I know," Cain continued, "traditionally the psychics are our best defence against the enemy. They allow us to keep hidden that which we are not ready to reveal, such as our presence here. However, the enemy only suspects we are here. If we don't capture the humans and their camera, they will definitely know we are here."

Lucas appeared deep in thought about Cain's suggestion. Cain knew he was pushing the right buttons.

Cain continued, "If we supply some item that belonged to one of the humans, then, like bloodhounds, the psychics could use it to zero in on their 'psychic presence' and therefore their whereabouts. Then all we have to do is go wherever that is and we have them."

They all remained silent. Some were thinking about Cain's suggestion; others were leaving that up to Lucas. Everyone was waiting for Lucas's response.

"What about our psychic protection in the meantime?" Lucas asked.

"Not all of them would need to be used, just the strongest," Cain replied.

"That could still leave us unprotected," Lucas pointed out.

"Yes, but it could also get us that which we seek quicker," Cain reasoned.

"What about lord Tarvyn and his security? What would his reaction be if he knew we were putting him in danger?" Lucas asked

Cain appeared to think on that for a moment. Then he answered with a question of his own, "How soon would he be leaving to move on to the conference?"

"I don't see what that has to do with this but... whenever he feels ready to go. The site is not quite ready but from what I understand, it is just as protected as we are here. He could leave tonight and..." Lucas smiled in sudden understanding. "If he were to leave today, we wouldn't have to be concerned with his safety."

Cain smiled, "Exactly."

Lucas sat back and considered what Cain had suggested. After a short while he leaned forward again and spoke, "Cain?"

"Yes, my lord," Cain replied.

"You have a better... relationship with lord Tarvyn. Perhaps you should be the one to suggest it to him. Maybe make him think that it was his idea somehow?"

Cain smiled more to himself than to Lucas. "Possibly, but I think he will need some convincing."

"What would you suggest?" Lucas asked.

"Perhaps, it is time that I moved to that project too," Cain replied, "after all, you appear to have no need of me here anymore. Perhaps...? No, he wouldn't agree with that. Or would he?"

"With what Cain?"

"Well... he may agree more easily if he knew that I was going there too. Perhaps I could even..." Cain paused for effect, "...*escort* him there."

"I value your input, Cain. Suggestions like these are worth more than gold," Lucas said. "I don't know if I am ready for you to leave here yet."

"Thank you, my Lord, but with you here now I am not really needed anymore. Besides, lord Porva was the one who suggested that I should move there once you were settled in here," Cain replied. "If you desire my presence here, then perhaps you should contact lord Porva and request –"

"No! That won't be necessary, Cain. If lord Porva wishes you to be at the conference centre, then that is where you shall go," Lucas said, interrupting Cain. "Why don't you go now and let lord Tarvyn know that you are departing this afternoon. Then suggest that he could accompany you."

"And if he disagrees?"

Lucas thought for a moment and then answered. "Tell him that with the guards required for your escort, he would have to wait until their return before he could leave too. But if he were to accompany you..."

"Then he would have his escort, along with my company and protection too?" Cain asked, trying to finish the sentence for him.

"Precisely," Lucas said with a smile.

"Good idea, my lord," Cain said with a bow of his head. "Shall I go and speak with him straight away or make my preparations first?"

"Speak with lord Tarvyn first and then attend to your preparations," Lucas replied.

"Very well. With your leave, my lord?" Cain asked with his head bowed.

"You may go now," Lucas replied, dismissing Cain.

Cain turned and left at once. "Perfect," he said to himself with a smile, "so easily led. I think I am going to miss him when he's gone."

NINETY

Kerri and Glen were sitting together, quietly watching Cairns shrink into the distance. They were starting to relax but the boat was not that far out into the bay and they still had another couple of hours until they would reach their destination.

Glen noticed that Kerri had been quiet since they had left the Casino. He nudged her with his elbow. "You okay?" he asked.

"What?" Kerri said, looking at him. "Sorry, I was miles away."

"I noticed. You have been since we left the Casino," Glen said.

Kerri nodded, "I've been thinking, that's all."

Glen nodded. "I kind of guessed that. Care to share your thoughts? I may be able to help you sort them out."

"I..." Kerri started but stopped almost as quickly. "I've been in quite a few close calls lately. There were the two today and the one yesterday. Over the last couple of weeks there have been another dozen or so. I can't explain how or why I manage to get away each time. It's like... I don't know what it's like."

Glen studied her for a moment and then spoke, "It's like someone is looking after you? Is that what you almost said?"

Kerri looked down. "Yes." Looking back up she said, "But I don't believe in that stuff."

"I see," Glen said, as he started to understand what Kerri was talking about. "Do you believe in rain?"

Kerri was surprised by the question. "Yes."

"Okay," Glen replied and then asked another strange question, "Do you believe in the wind?"

"Where are you going with this?" Kerri asked.

"Just answer the questions and you will find out," Glen replied.

"Yes, I believe in the wind," Kerri answered.

"Do you believe in the ocean?"

"Yes."

"Do you believe in the desert?"

"Yes," Kerri answered, starting to get a little impatient.

Glen picked up from Kerri's tone of voice that it was time to explain his odd questions. "A man that lives in the desert could go all his life without seeing rain or the ocean. Over time, it is possible that he may start to think they are not real. The same could be said of someone who has never been to the desert. Some people don't believe in the wind, until they feel it. In all these cases, it is simply because they haven't seen it or felt it that they question its existence. This is an easy mentality to explain and understand. But it is not correct.

"The same can be said of people believing in God and Jesus," Glen continued. "Just because they don't see them, they don't believe in them. But just because someone doesn't believe in the wind, that doesn't mean the wind doesn't exist. The bottom line appears to be, 'show me the proof' or 'seeing is believing'. People use the same saying with God, only He doesn't want us to be like that. That is why He doesn't reveal Himself physically. But that does not mean that He doesn't get involved in our lives."

Kerri was listening closely now.

"What you have been experiencing, in my opinion, is evidence of God working in your life. He has chosen to reveal Himself to you in this manner, whether you want Him there or not. The question is... what are you going to do about it?" Glen asked.

"Me?" Kerri asked in response. "But why would he choose me? Who am I that God would want me?"

"Now that is a good question, but I don't think it is the right one," Glen answered.

"What?" Kerri asked.

"It's like this. Firstly, if you believe that this is what is happening to you, then you need to follow the logical steps. Something is happening to you that you want to prescribe to 'divine intervention'. Therefore, there is something out there that is 'The Divine'. Okay?" Glen asked.

"Right so far," Kerri replied.

"Then it's a logical step to accept that God exists. If God exists, then the Bible must be true. If the Bible is true, then the events that it records are true. Still with me?" Glen asked.

"That's what I have been thinking about," replied Kerri.

"The next step is that you have to accept that even the strangest story in it is possible." Glen paused to watch Kerri's reaction to that. He continued watching her as he went on, "Jesus's birth and death. Jonah and the big fish. Noah and the ark. Moses with the plagues of Egypt and then the parting of the Red Sea. Adam and Eve. Creation."

Kerri was looking a little bit confused. "I know those stories but... I have never given any of them any credibility. Especially Creation."

"That's not surprising. In fact, a lot of 'Believers' don't believe in them as literal accounts, which is a bit sad really. Creation, for example, is discounted because of examples of evolution. But no one has ever argued that there are too many holes in the Theory of Evolution for it to be true. I mean, for example, if we evolved from apes, then why are there still apes?"

Kerri looked at Glen in shock. "I never considered that."

"My point exactly, but that's a bit off the point here. So... why would God choose you? And why is that not the right question?" Glen asked, reminding Kerri what they were talking about.

"Oh yeah," she replied.

"According to the Creation story, we were created to have a personal relationship with God," Glen started to explain. "It's right there in chapter two of Genesis. Adam and God walked through the Garden of Eden together and they were talking to each other. It doesn't say, God was walking through there and Adam was crawling after Him, just waiting to do whatever God told Him to do. Or that Adam was somewhere else doing his own thing."

A look of understanding came over Kerri's face. "You're saying that we were created to be friends with God, not some sort of servant and not separate from God."

"Correct," Glen replied with a smile. "That's the 'why', simply because He would like one of His friends back. So what is the correct question, once you understand that?"

Kerri thought for a moment. "Why would He be doing it now?" she asked after awhile.

"Another good question, but again, not exactly the right one," Glen answered.

"Would you care to explain why?" Kerri asked.

"You said it yourself yesterday," Glen answered. "You have friends that have tried to tell you about God before. This is not the first time that He has tried to get your attention. If you really want to know, He has never stopped trying since the time of your birth. The question should actually be, why are *you* listening now?"

"Oh," said Kerri. "Umm, because... Kerri said, trying to think of an answer.

"You don't have to tell me the answer to that question. You need to work it out yourself. Once you do that, you need to decide what that all means to you," Glen replied, "and what you are going to do about it."

Kerri just nodded, already lost in thought.

Glen slipped his Bible out of his bag and handed it to Kerri, "Just in case you want to look up something."

Kerri stared at the Bible in her hands. She never even noticed Glen stand up and move to sit a few seats away.

Amy, Kyle and Daniel had listened intently and had occasionally said things to help Glen and keep him on track. Amy was now watching Kerri and waiting to see what she would do next.

It was no surprise to any of them when Kerri opened the Bible and just flicked through the pages, waiting to see where it would stop this time.

Amy once again unsheathed her sword and slipped it between the pages carefully. When Kerri found the spot, Amy then covered parts of the page with her hands. Only specific verses were clearly visible to Kerri, just as before.

Peter answered them, "All of you must turn to God and change the way you think and act, and each of you must be baptized in the name of Jesus Christ so that your sins will be forgiven. Then you will receive the Holy Spirit as a gift."

Acts 2:38

Kerri's mouth dropped open slightly as she read the verse. "That's exactly what I was looking for. But how?" she thought to herself. "That is what I should do next. If I believe in God I should get baptised,"

Kerri sat back and looked out at the water again, thinking about what all this meant to her. She could see that something was happening in her life and she didn't understand it all. She also liked what she saw in Glen and knew that she wanted to be like that too. "He is confident and not guilty," she thought. "He is also self-assured. Although, that wasn't quite right, was it? It's more like he is God assured. Yes, that was more like it. It was God who gave him the assurance to live the way he did. Glen is God assured and not hiding from himself. Unlike me."

Kerri looked back at the Bible and the verse she had read. Then she did something she had never done before. Kerri closed her eyes and prayed, "I don't know why I am listening now, God, but that is not important, is it? The fact that I am listening is the important part. Please help me to understand all this. I do want to turn to you. Please help me to change the way I act and think."

Amy closed her eyes and savoured the feeling she was experiencing, the feeling of a new believer coming into the presence of God. Kerri was almost there... but not quite. Amy could feel the Holy Spirit moving her and teaching her.

Amy's eyes snapped open. She had heard something. The sound of wings, not feathered like hers, but leathery, like those of the enemy. It wasn't loud or very clear, but she knew she had heard it all the same. She stood up and looked all around. Her sharp eyes scanned the horizon, near and far. There, a small black dot was speeding away from them. It was moving too fast to be a bird... that left only one conclusion. "An enemy messenger, the kind the psychics use. It's moving too fast for us to catch before it reports our position," she thought.

Amy turned and looked down at Kerri, "She is not ready," she said to herself. Amy considered their situation for a moment. "I think we need to do this a bit quicker now," she said, and tried to place her sword into the Bible again. "Quick, look again and see what you can learn," she said, as she kept trying to insert the sword.

Kerri started to flick the pages of Glen's Bible again. A highlighted section caught her eyes as she flicked passed it. She stopped and went back, until she found the highlighted piece again. It read...

Then Jesus said to his disciples, "Those who want to come with me must say no to the things they want, pick up their crosses, and follow me. Those who want to save their lives will lose them. But those who lose their lives for me will find them.

Matthew 16:24-25

Kerri read it twice and then scratched her head. It didn't quite make sense to her. She didn't have a cross and if she lost her life, then how could she find it when she would be dead?

Glen noticed that she was looking a bit confused so he came back over and sat next to her again.

"Would you like some help understanding some of the passages in there?" he asked, indicating his Bible.

Kerri looked up at him. She almost said no, but then thought that if she was going to change the way she acted, then one of the first things she needed to do was accept help and not try to do everything by herself. "Okay," she said finally.

Glen looked down at the Bible and noticed it was a passage that he had highlighted. "Which verse are you looking at? Is it the one I have highlighted?"

Kerri nodded, "Yes, but it doesn't quite make sense. How can you lose your life but find it again?"

Glen smiled and explained the verse, "Take it from the start, here: Jesus is saying that to be one of his followers, we need to give up our essential nature – some of the other translations use the words 'deny yourself'. Essentially, it means we need to change. We need to do what Jesus did – give up our old lives when we visit the cross and leave them there. Only then, can we truly follow Jesus. By giving up that life, we will find a new one with Jesus, a richer and more fulfilling life. Not always an easy life, but, and probably most importantly, an eternal life with Him.

But if we decide that we do not want to do this and we try to keep our life for ourselves, then we will never be with Jesus... ever."

"A lot of people think that this just refers to the eternal life part of being a believer, but I think it does have an impact on our current lives too. A lot of people feel lost until they give themselves over to Jesus fully. Once they do, they never feel lost again. Does that make sense to you?" Glen asked.

Kerri nodded, "Absolutely. I was thinking that exact thing a minute ago. I can see in you an assurance, like a self-confidence in who you are, and I don't have that. I feel scared and guilty and want to hide myself away. It's like I have chosen to be lost. But you know where you are and where you are going."

"That doesn't come to me naturally," Glen said. "I went through a period of doubt a number of years ago. It wasn't until I let God have the reigns that I started to feel at peace with myself."

Kerri nodded absently, while she thought about what Glen had said. She wondered what it would be like to be at peace with herself.

Glen took the Bible from Kerri's hands and flicked over to 1 Corinthians. "Have you ever experienced true love?" he asked, as he handed the Bible back to her.

Kerri looked at Glen and then at the Bible in her hands.

"Read this whole chapter," Glen said, pointing at chapter thirteen.

I may speak in the languages of humans and of Angels. But if I don't have love, I am a loud gong or a clashing cymbal. I may have the gift to speak what God has revealed, and I may understand all mysteries and have all knowledge. I may even have enough faith to move mountains. But if I don't have love, I am nothing. I may even give away all that I have and give up my body to be burned. But if I don't have love, none of these things will help me.

Love is patient. Love is kind. Love isn't jealous. It doesn't sing its own praises. It isn't arrogant. It isn't rude. It doesn't think about itself. It isn't irritable. It doesn't keep track of wrongs. It isn't happy when injustice is done, but it is happy with the truth. Love never stops being patient, never stops believing, never stops hoping, never gives up.

Love never comes to an end. There is the gift of speaking what God has revealed, but it will no longer be used. There is the gift of speaking in other languages, but it will stop by itself. There is the gift of knowledge, but it will no longer be used. Our knowledge is incomplete and our ability to speak what God has revealed is incomplete. But when what is complete comes, then what is incomplete will no longer be used. When I was a child, I spoke like a child, thought like a child, and reasoned like a child. When I became an adult, I no longer used childish ways. Now we see a blurred image in a mirror. Then we will see very clearly. Now my knowledge is incomplete. Then I will have complete knowledge as God has complete knowledge of me.

So these three things remain: faith, hope, and love. But the best one of these is love.

1 Cor. 13:1-13

"Love is the nature of God," Glen went straight into explaining the significance of this passage. "The part in the middle about what love is and isn't. That is true love. That is God. That is what we can expect from Him when we choose to be His. This is also why He does what He does. He loves us just like that. He is always hoping, always believing in us and He never gives up on us. He keeps trying to get our attention, no matter what.

"That is also why He doesn't want to let us go once He has us. That's why He offered us eternal life, through Jesus's death. Eternal life, with God, in Heaven. Can you imagine what that would be like?" Glen asked.

"What do you mean by eternal life?" Kerri asked.

"Hang on," Glen said, as he started to turn the pages in the Bible once again.

"That's it," Amy said, looking over his shoulder, "John chapter eleven..."

"Here it is," Glen said, as he passed the Bible back to Kerri. "Read verses twenty-five and twenty-six."

Jesus said to her, "I am the one who brings people back to life, and I am life itself. Those who believe in me will live even if they die. Everyone who lives and believes in me will never die. Do you believe that?"

John 11:25-26

Kerri read it and then asked Glen, "Okay, I get that we only receive this gift of eternal life if we believe, but what does it mean by 'even if we die, we will still live'?"

"It means that we will live on, in spirit, with the Lord God and Jesus in Heaven. It does not mean that we will never truly die," explained Glen.

"Oh, thanks. That clears that up. I was beginning to think that Christians became vampires or something else supernatural," Kerri replied.

"In a way we are, but not like that. The term 'supernatural' does not just apply to the 'evil' monsters. I have seen some pretty amazing things that God has done through people and for people – healings, speaking in other languages and even superhuman feats. These are things that they did, not by themselves, but through faith in God," Glen said.

"So?" Glen asked. "Are you going to answer the question?"

"What question?" Kerri replied.

Glen pointed to the Bible. "The one in the verse you just read?"

Kerri looked back down at the Bible and read the verse again. When she was finished, she looked back up at Glen. "I..."

Glen put his hands up to stop Kerri. "I don't want to force you into this and I don't want to stop you either, but this is something that is really between you and God. I think I will go back over there and leave you alone to think about it. If you decide that the answer is yes, then you need to tell God that you believe in Him and you want to have a relationship with Him and Jesus. Then you need to tell me, for the Bible also says that if you openly profess of your friendship to Jesus, then you will be saved."

Kerri smiled at Glen. "Thanks Glen."

Glen stood up and moved away, just like he had done earlier.

Amy, Kyle and Daniel watched and waited. Kerri was sitting in deep thought – about what she had read and what Glen had told her. They could feel the Holy Spirit moving and knew that it was still trying to teach Kerri. The bottom line was that this was going to be Kerri's decision and none of them knew what decision she would make.

Suddenly, Daniel felt something that he didn't expect. He looked out at the ocean, back towards the land. He could see a dark cloud moving towards them.

Amy and Kyle looked out at what Daniel was looking at too.

"Is that what I think it is?" Kyle asked.

"I'm afraid so," Daniel answered.

They all looked back at Kerri.

"I hope she decides soon," Amy said, "or she may not get the chance."

Ninety One

Michael was sitting in the Hall while waiting for the messengers to return. He always found this part to be the hardest. He was an angel of action, always wanting to be on some mission for his Lord. Whether it is delivering important, history-changing messages or fighting the enemy, even the quiet time of solitude – when he would visit his favourite places on Earth and study the animals and plants in that part of the world – he had his purpose and he knew what to do to carry it out. Right now, he was waiting on others to deliver and gather information so that he could then formulate the next course of action.

Michael decided he would go to Uriel and see how the trap planning was coming along, when an unexpected visitor arrived.

A cherubim walked into the Hall, spotted Michael and immediately made his way to him.

"Abednego," Michael said, when the cherubim neared him, "What brings you here?"

Abednego stopped before Michael and looked down at him. "My Captain, I have been sent to you by Gabriel to advise that a portal was found that linked the city of Eden in Australia to the Garden of Eden. At this moment, my companions Shadrach and Meshach are there. The former is attempting to seal it, while the latter is guarding it, in case anyone else should try to use it."

Michael nodded at this information. "Thank you. Do you require additional guards to assist you?" he asked, indicating the group he had waiting.

Abednego shook his head. "Thank you for the offer, but I think we shall be quite capable. There are plenty of other cherubim within hailing distance, should we find ourselves unable to defend our post."

"Very well," Michael said. Was there anything else you had to pass on from Gabriel?"

"There was," Abednego replied. "He asked that I also inform you of his plan. He, along with Itzal of Eden, have arranged for the rest of his team to create localised portals to try to confuse the enemy if they are watching. He will also send a messenger to check if the portal has been sealed on our side."

"I will send the messenger on to you when they arrive, to get the answer first hand," Michael replied.

Saint Peter had seen the cherubim enter the Hall. Assuming that the cherubim may have more information, he decided to follow him into the Hall. He walked in and headed for Michael and the cherubim, to see what was going on. He heard the final part of their exchange as he neared them.

"Might I suggest something?" Saint Peter asked.

Michael and Abednego both turned to Saint Peter. "Go ahead," Michael answered, a little surprised to see him back so soon.

"I am sure that if Gabriel was sending the messenger straight away, they must be nearly here. Why not wait, Abednego, for his arrival. Then accompany him back to the portal, instead of sending the messenger on without knowing exactly where in the Garden he is to go?" Saint Peter suggested.

Michael turned to Abednego, "Sounds like a good suggestion. How do you feel about that?"

Abednego nodded his head. "It does appear to be a better idea, especially for the messenger."

"I agree," said another voice. "I think."

They turned to see Kenaniah approaching from the entrance to the Hall, with a smile on his face. "Sorry, I only caught part of it and that didn't make much sense to me. I am guessing that I am the messenger you were referring too. What is the better idea?"

Michael smiled too. "Gabriel sent you back?" he asked.

"Yes, I think my singing was getting to him," Kenaniah replied.

Michael's smile increased. Kenaniah had always liked to sing. He had been the guardian of one of the leaders of Israel a long time ago. He had helped lead Israel in song during a particular noteworthy time.

Michael explained to Kenaniah what the plan was. Then he added a little more of his own, "Once it is sealed, please return here to tell me. Then go back to Gabriel and advise him of the same."

"Before I go, I have a message from Gabriel for you," Kenaniah said. "He told me to tell you, it does appear to be connected. Itzal created the portal to help the human but he did not know where he sent him. The human never returned and Itzal was unable to follow, for fear of leading the enemy to him. I hope you understand all that because I do not."

"I do," Michael replied, "Thank you. Please go with Abednego to the Garden of Eden. If there is anything else, I will contact you there."

Saint Peter and Michael waited in silence as they left. Once they were out of earshot, Saint Peter turned to Michael and spoke, "I guess that is what started this whole thing in the first place."

"I think you may be right there," Michael replied. Looking around, he caught sight of Nicole and walked straight over to her. Saint Peter followed him.

Nicole looked up at their approach. One look at Michael's face and she knew she had more work to do. She stood up and moved to meet them.

"I need a message delivered urgently to every one of the seven groups we have sent out. You will need to get more messengers to help, one for each group," Michael said. He then outlined the exact message to her. "Then I will need to speak with Uriel. Find him and bring him back here please."

"At once, Captain," she said, then turned and left as quickly as she could.

Saint Peter looked at Michael, "Do you think that is the wisest course?"

Michael just smiled and turned to the Saint, "I didn't expect you back so soon. Do you have the answer already?"

"I have a little of it, I think. When I saw Abednego come in here, I realised that if anything new happened, I needed to be here to know of it. I can still think on this while I am here."

Ninety Two

Jack and Tony were wandering around, quite sure that they were lost. Jack would look back at the demon that was following them but was not getting any indications at all as to which direction was better for them to follow.

Tony was still praying under his breath as they walked. This did make both of them feel better. After all, it felt like they were on a mission from God, even though it was an angel that asked them to do this.

Jack leaned over to Tony as they moved down another dirt passage. "I feel like I'm one of the Blues Brothers," he said.

Tony looked sideways at Jack and replied, "Who?"

Jack was a little surprised. "Haven't you seen that movie? It's about two brothers who, well, they are in a black gospel church, where one of them has an idea and thinks that it came from God. Then every time they come up against opposition, one of them says, 'We're on a mission from God!' You don't remember that movie?"

Tony shook his head, "No, I don't. Maybe we should watch it when we get out of here. It sounds interesting."

"Maybe. It might not be your sort of movie though. It has a bit of swearing in it. It once held the record for the longest car chase with the most cars crashed," Jack said.

"That makes it a must then," Tony said rolling his eyes.

Jack smirked. "Did I mention it was a musical too?"

Tony stopped. "It's a must now!" he said in mock seriousness.

Jack stopped and looked back at Tony with his eyebrows raised.

"Black gospel church service, God inspired action, swearing, and the longest car chase with crashes... and it's a musical! Sounds like the best movie ever made!" Tony said sarcastically.

"I'm sorry I mentioned it," Jack said with a smirk. "Shall we continue on?" he said, as he started to move off again.

Tony looked around himself for a moment. "Jack?"

Jack stopped again and looked back at Tony once more. "Yeah?"

"Have you noticed that our surroundings are changing again?" Tony asked.

Jack followed Tony's gaze and looked at the walls. The passageway before the elevator had been like any other service-type passage in a building: tiled floor and plain cement walls. When they stepped out of the elevator, they noticed that the passage could have been described as a mine shaft. Every now and then the passage had improved — they had cement under their feet and wood on the walls — but it wasn't long before reverted to the mineshaft appearance of a dirt tunnel. What they were entering now appeared to be newer, freshly dug out. The walls were a darker colour so Jack reached out and touched them. They were still moist.

"This is a newer tunnel," Jack said.

Tony reached forward to touch the wall too. "What do you think they are doing down here?"

"I don't know but..." Jack looked at Tony and noticed that the demon behind him was looking very uncomfortable suddenly.

Tony turned and looked behind him at nothing. "What? What are you seeing?" he asked quietly.

"Our follower is looking... anxious about something," Jack answered just as quietly. "I think we are on the right path after all."

"Oh, right. What were you going to say?" Tony asked.

"I was thinking, this doesn't look like it is meant for the everyday person to come down here. Whatever it is for, it is something secret. We need to be extra careful from here on," Jack answered.

Tony swallowed. It was the only sign he gave of his apprehension. "Let's keep going then."

They turned and headed off quietly up the passage. The condition of the floor and walls was to their benefit as it absorbed the sound of their passing and didn't allow their footsteps to be heard by anyone ahead. Unfortunately, it worked the same way in reverse. Jack realised this, so he was moving with as much stealth and care as he could, especially every time they came to a junction or corner: he would kneel and look around the corner before proceeding.

Even so, it was a complete surprise when he spotted three other people sneaking around. It was at a junction. They had stopped so Jack could look down the cross passage and make sure that the pathway wasn't occupied. Unlike every other time he had done this in the last fifteen minutes, this one was occupied. They didn't see him as he was near the ground and they were moving slowly. It appeared to be three guards but they didn't move like guards. They moved like someone who was somewhere they shouldn't be.

Jack watched them for a moment. Something else was wrong with them, he thought. One appeared to be moving too slow and then he stopped. Almost as if he was injured. Another was staying with him and continually talking and the other appeared to be checking him over. They were not loud enough that Jack could hear their words, but the way the talking one moved made it appear as if he was trying to urge the injured one on.

Jack pulled back to look at Tony. In the quietest whisper he could manage, he spoke into Tony's ear, "There are three people down there. They appear to be guards but something tells me they aren't. Have a quick look and tell me what you think."

Tony nodded and knelt down. He slowly poked his head around the corner, only enough to allow him to see. After a short moment, he moved back and whispered into Jack's ear. "I could only see two. One of them appears to be sick."

Jack looked at him and mouthed, "Two?" with a questioning look on his face.

Tony nodded and held up his hand with only two fingers raised.

Jack had another look. There was definitely three. He pulled back and sat there for a moment. He looked at Tony and saw the demon behind him. Jack's eyes went wide and he had another look. He came back and looked Tony in his eyes. Then he whispered in Tony's ear again. "There *are* three. The third one is like our new friends."

Tony's face came around quickly. He turned Jack's head so he could whisper to him. "You sure?"

Jack nodded enthusiastically.

"Why would one of them be in here?" Tony whispered next.

Jack thought for a moment and then whispered to Tony, "They need our help to get out."

Tony looked at Jack, thinking about what he had just been told. Slowly he started to nod his head.

Both Jack and Tony started to stand up again but the demon had suddenly realised that they had stopped for longer than normal. Assuming they had stopped because someone else was down this next passage, the demon took to the air. It raced off around the corner, expecting to find at least one human with more of its own kind. But instead, found two humans with one of the enemy.

Jack saw it go and wondered why it was suddenly in a hurry to leave them.

Henry was starting to suffer. This walk was starting to take too much out of him and Alan had noticed it too.

"How are you feeling?" Alan asked.

"Tired, worn out, but otherwise alright. I just need to rest for a moment," Henry replied.

"Sit for a moment and I will give you a quick check over," said Alan.

Henry sat on the dirt floor of the tunnel, with his back against the wall, as Alan started to remove some equipment from his backpack. Alan then proceeded to check Henry's blood pressure, pulse and temperature.

There was nothing out of the ordinary with the results. The blood pressure was a little high but considering their exertions it did not concern him. It was just the healing process working the way it does.

"Well?" Henry asked, as Alan packed his equipment away again.

Alan continued to pack everything as he replied, "Nothing out of the ordinary and certainly nothing of concern. We'll just need to rest occasionally to help keep your strength up."

Gage had been standing over the two of them, talking continually to try to encourage Henry and to help keep his spirits up. He was not concerned as he could still see that Henry was healthy in a physical sense and fairly strong in spirit. He knew that his encouragement would help Henry to keep motivated.

Gage stopped. He thought he heard something. He started to move quietly down the passage, towards the noise, when he saw a smallish demon come speeding around the corner. The demon started to call out.

"Guards! Alert! They are just around..." the demon stopped talking but it was still pointing back the way it had come from. "Where are your demons?" it said and then the demon saw through Gage's disguise. "You-you-you're-a-you're..." the demon stuttered.

Gage drew his sword in a flash of blinding light. The demon panicked and turned to try to get away but it was too late. Gage was on it before it could move too far. With a quick swing of his sword, the demon was no more. Only a cloud of black, swirling mist with tinges of red remained, and it was quickly disappearing.

Gage was revealed in all his glorified splendour. The tunnel was lit up quite brightly for anyone with spiritual sight to see. This had drawn Jack around the corner and now he was standing there, with his mouth wide open. Tony was beside him, trying to get him to move back around the corner.

Gage saw Jack and was about to give him a scare, when he realised that Jack was looking at him too.

Tony was trying his hardest to convince Jack to move but Jack refused. "What are you seeing Jack?" he asked.

"It's the angel. He is... very bright and coming this way!" Jack replied.

"Quick," Tony said, dragging on Jack's arm, "on your knees."

Jack followed Tony's lead and they both went down on their knees.

Gage knelt too when he reached Jack. He wasn't as bright now as he was not in battle.

"You can see me?" Gage asked Jack.

Jack had his face down too. "Yes," he answered.

"Please," Gage said, "do not be afraid. I will not harm you."

Jack looked up slowly. Tony didn't move.

"How can you see me?" Gage asked.

"It's a long story. One which I don't think should be told here," Jack answered timidly.

Gage smiled. “You are correct, of course.”

“What happened to the demon?” Jack asked, trying to look passed the angel.

“I sent it to the Abyss,” Gage replied. “I thought it was going to give us away.”

“Demon? What demon?” Alan asked. “Who are you and what are you doing here?”

Tony looked up and saw that Alan and Henry had come down the passage to them. He looked up at Jack and saw that Jack was looking from Alan to nothing and back again.

Jack was listening to Gage. “I am an angel of the Lord God, creator of Heaven and Earth. This is my charge and his friend. We are escaping from this horrible place. Who are you and what is your purpose here?”

“Jack?” Tony asked, looking up at him.

Jack nodded. He looked at Henry and Alan and then at Tony and said, “It’s okay Tony, you can stand up now. These are friends.”

“How would you know that? We haven’t told you who we are yet!” Alan said, a bit indignantly.

“Sorry,” Jack replied. “Your angel told me. I am Jack and this is Tony.”

Alan looked at Henry with disbelief on his face. He turned back to Jack and asked, “My angel?”

Jack turned his head slightly and then nodded. “My apologies to all,” he said. “He tells me that he is God’s angel and that he is with Henry, not you.”

Henry’s jaw dropped, Alan looked dumbfounded and Tony smiled.

“Sorry,” Jack said, to no one in particular. “This is still new to me.”

“What is?” Henry asked.

“All this angels and demons stuff,” Jack answered.

“What?” Alan and Henry said together.

Tony stepped forward and took both Alan and Henry by the arm and led them away. “My friend, Jack, had an extraordinary encounter about six months ago. He has just discovered that it has left him with the ability to see the... spiritual elements that move around us. I assume that you are a Christian?” Tony asked Henry, “And that you are not?” Tony asked Alan.

He got nods from both of them. Then to Henry he said, “He is talking to your guardian angel right now. You probably didn’t realise that you had one but you do. Try not to dwell on it as it can make you feel a little uncomfortable.”

“How do you know about this stuff?” Alan said, with a voice full of disbelief.

"I'm a minister. Jack was, literally, left on my doorstep," Tony replied. "I've learnt most of this over my whole life but it wasn't until I met Jack that it started to truly become real for me. Especially the last few days, he has started to-"

"Quick," Jack said, suddenly alongside them. "There is someone coming. This is going to have to wait until we are somewhere safe. The angel says if we follow him, he will lead us to your escape route."

Alan and Henry looked at each other again. "It's hard to argue with him," Henry said. "I think we need to do it, for now. I will soon know if we are not going the right way."

Alan looked doubtful for a moment and then he caught the look in Henry's eyes. "Okay, I trust you and if you trust him, then that will have to do for me. Let's go."

"This way, quickly now!" Jack said, as he started to run down the passage.

Tony immediately took after him. Henry paused only to wait for Alan.

"You up for this?" Alan asked.

"I am, considering the alternative," Henry replied.

"Let's go, before they get too far ahead," Alan said, as he started off after the others, with Henry right on his heels.

Ninety Three

Isam looked up as two guards walked in, half leading and half carrying Bob and Rasheed. He stood up slowly, not liking what he saw before him.

"Tell me that someone is still guarding the doctor and the escapee?" Isam asked.

The guards looked at each other with a look of fear passing between them. Neither of them wanted to answer the question. They didn't need to worry, as Rasheed answered for them.

Rasheed lifted his head slightly as he spoke, "Sorry boss..." his head dropped back down as his body tried to slip back into unconsciousness. He was fighting it though. Rasheed spoke again, without lifting his head this time, and sounding rather sleepy, "they are gone."

Isam indicated a couple of chairs for the guards to put Bob and Rasheed into. Bob was still completely out of it, but Rasheed kept stirring, trying to stay awake.

The guards stepped back as Isam approached Rasheed and bent down to look him in the face. Isam tried to help Rasheed stay awake by slapping him hard across the face.

Rasheed's head did clear slightly and he looked at Isam with daggers for a moment, until he remembered who he was.

"Can you tell me what happened?" Isam asked.

Rasheed's eyes appeared to glaze over a little bit. Isam got ready to slap him again but, just as quick, his eyes became clear again. "They must have drugged us with something," he said.

Isam stood up. "I kind of worked that one out already," he replied. "How?"

Rasheed looked up and explained quickly about how they had been called into the room. The escapee had been having another fit. The next thing he knew, there was a sharp pain in his bottom and the room started to spin.

Isam stood there for a moment. He had to admit that it was clever. He walked back to his desk, hit a button on his phone and stayed standing over it.

It buzzed for a moment. Then Mr Kepler's voice came through the speaker on the phone's base, "What is it?"

"Your pet doctor and the patient have escaped," Isam replied.

There was silence from the speaker and then some choice words from Mr Kepler. "What happened?" he asked finally.

Isam reported what Rasheed had told him. "Judging by the fact that Bob is still out cold and Rasheed is not fully alert, I would say it hasn't been that long since it happened, maybe an hour. They can't have gotten far. If you wish, I will order a full lock down and start a search?"

There was only a small delay before Mr Kepler replied, "Do it."

Then it was Isam's turn to pause while he tried to think of the right words to ask his next question. Realising that there really was no good way to word it, he just asked it straight out. "Did you find out how he escaped last time?"

There was an audible sigh through the phone, "No."

It was Isam's turn to curse but he did it under his breath. "Next time we get our own doctor and not use one of the workers," he said, with a bit of venom in his voice. He hung up without waiting for an answer.

Isam sat down, looking at the guards. Rasheed had lost his battle and had slipped back into unconsciousness. He waved the other two over.

The guards stepped forward and stopped at the other side of the desk.

"Initiate lockdown protocol red six and gather a hunting party. They are to meet me in the doctor's room in ten minutes. Understand?"

"Understood, sir," the guards both replied.

"Good, get to it then," Isam said. He turned his chair around so that he was facing the wall behind his desk. There was a large map of the complex pinned on it. He sat there staring at it, listening to the guards leave as quickly as possible.

In a similar fashion, Security had spoken with the two demon guards who had come in without Rasheed and Bob's demons. The guards reported the disappearance and the smell of sulphur in the room. Both swords had been found in the room too.

Security had spoken with Wraith about the escape and the loss of two guards, because they had let the angel stay with the humans.

Then Security told the guards to gather a hunting party of their own.

NINETY FOUR

"There it is!" Deceit said to Pandora, as the boat came into view. "Let's hope the psychics are correct with this information."

Pandora turned to stare at Deceit as she flew alongside him. "If you wish to rise above your current rank, then you'd better learn to trust the psychics. They are rarely wrong. Especially Esper, who provided this location — his messengers are the most reliable. Now, rally the troops, split them into the groups we discussed and let's move in for the attack."

Deceit slowed slightly, enough that he started to drift back through the ranks. He was now among the guards and other soldiers that had been sent to assist with the search. He indicated to Rage to move off to the left and then he went off to the right.

The cloud of demons split into three, one lot moving left with Rage, the next lot moving right with Deceit and the rest continued to follow Pandora.

Below them, three speed boats did the same manoeuvre.

****

"Typical Pincer move coming up. Is everyone ready?" Daniel asked.

All around them, movement started to occur. Kyle told Glen that a storm was coming, that he should get Kerri and they should go inside. He watched as Glen stood up, pleased that his charge still responded to him so well.

"Looks like a storm coming," Kyle heard Glen tell Kerri. "Maybe we should go inside?"

Other passengers were moving too. Some were going inside and others appeared to be taking up positions just out of sight, under the cover of the roof.

****

Raphael was standing in another of Cairn's churches, listening to the prayers of the saints who met there. The angels of the church were there with their flock and the Holy Spirit was moving them all to action.

Raphael was pleased with the progress that he had made. He now had four churches and three affiliate churches, all praying for Glen and Kerri and the situation they were in.

Then he felt it. The Spirit was telling him it was time to go. He turned to thank the angels and noticed that they were looking passed him. Then he heard the sound of more angels arriving from behind him.

Raphael turned and smiled as only he could. Out of the corner of his eye, he saw a messenger standing up, looking at the gathering with awe. "You," he said pointing at the messenger. "Go and tell Michael of what you have seen here today. This gathering is no coincidence. Tell Michael it has started. He will know what I mean. Go!"

The messenger nodded and took off so fast that only his trail was seen.

Raphael turned to the gathering of angels. "You have been called here by the Holy Spirit. We are needed to fight the enemy and protect God's chosen." He raised his arm in the air, his sword in hand. "For the Glory of the Lord and His Kingdom!"

"For the Glory of the Lord and His Kingdom!" came the reply from the gathered angelic voices.

Raphael took to the air, straight up through the roof of the church. He looked down not long after clearing the roof to see at least forty angels following him. As he turned and headed towards the water, he saw more angels rising from all over the town. By the time he passed over the wharves, he had more than seventy angels following in his wake.

Raphael smiled to himself. The saints were roused and praying throughout the local churches. He knew that word would be passing to friends and relatives interstate. Raphael spun in mid-air, almost laughing now. The fire was lit. The enemy's plans would soon be undone.

NINETY FIVE

"Henry needs to stop for a moment," Alan called out to Jack, who was starting to get further and further away from them.

Jack didn't hear him but Gage did. When Gage stopped and went back to Henry, Jack stopped and turned back too.

"What is it?" Jack asked as he neared Alan and Henry. Henry was sitting on the ground, trying to catch his breath, and Alan was pulling his stethoscope out of his back pack. Tony was right behind Jack, praying for Henry's well-being and his ability to make it out of the tunnels they were in.

Jack watched as Gage bent over Henry and placed both his hands on Henry's shoulders. Gage started to glow slightly.

Jack, Tony and Alan marvelled at Henry as they visibly saw the effect of Gage's touch. Henry sat up straighter and started to breathe easier. As Alan was listening to Henry's heartbeat, he heard it start to slow back down towards the normal resting rate. Some colour even started to return to Henry's face.

Tony smiled, "I've seen prayers answered before but never that quickly."

Jack was awestruck. No one else had seen what Gage had done and this made Jack feel special, but also a little scared of what such a being could do.

Gage suddenly looked up and turned to Jack. "Quick, we need to hide somewhere. They are coming."

"Human or demon?" Jack asked.

"What?" Alan asked turning around to face Jack, who was looking slightly above Henry.

Jack looked at everyone else and relayed what Gage had told him, "We have some humans coming this way and they will more than likely have some demons with them. We have to move on now or hide somewhere until they are passed us."

"I don't think I will ever get used to this," Alan said to himself, as he looked back at Henry.

Jack ignored the comment and Tony smiled.

"Help me stand or you will not get the chance to hear it again," Henry said, as he tried to get up off the ground. He looked around and realised that he knew where they were. "I think I recognise this place. We haven't got much further to go. But I don't know if we can get to the exit before they catch up to us. Even if we do, it could be guarded on the outside now."

Jack turned his head slightly and then said, "The angel says to leave that to him. Which way do we go?"

Henry squared his shoulders. "Follow me," he said.

They set off again, a bit slower than before. Henry was checking where they were as he went along. Jack was at the back this time and he was starting to get a bit anxious.

"I don't want to hurry you but I can hear them now too," Jack said, just loud enough for the others to hear.

"Pray with me," Tony said. "Dear Heavenly Father, thank you for all that you do for us. Please deliver us from this danger that we find ourselves in right now."

Jack continued, "Lord, I know I am only a new member of your family and maybe you have only given me this special gift of sight for this exact situation. However, I don't believe that you would lead us this far only for us to be overtaken by the enemy. Deliver us from the evil one, please Lord."

Alan was a little unsure what they expected of him. He had prayed earlier with Henry but this was a bit different. Not knowing what else to say, he said, "What they said God, from me too."

Henry smiled at what was probably his new friend's very first 'out loud' prayer. Henry joined in and added his prayer too, "Thank you, Lord, for new friends. Their very presence is encouragement enough, as I know you have sent them to deliver me from this nightmare that I have found myself in. I know this is probably nothing compared with what the Jews experienced in Egypt. All the same, I think I can relate a little with what they went through and why they wanted out so badly. Please send us a modern-day pillar of smoke to help guide us safely out of this."

Tony and Jack were nodding their heads. Tony said, "In Jesus's name we pray..."

Together, Jack, Henry and Tony said, "Amen."

Alan, not recognising the lead in, added his "Amen" afterwards.

Elisha and Isabel were starting to get worried. What had they done? Their charges were in there facing unknown dangers without them. It was suddenly too much and they both felt the Holy Spirit tell them the same thing. It was time to go in and find them.

They both stood at the same time. Elisha smiled at Isabel, "You felt it too?"

Isabel nodded and smiled also.

Israfel saw them rise and understanding passed through him.

"The Spirit is leading you in there too, isn't He?" Israfel asked.

"Yes," they replied.

Israfel looked around and then pointed off to the west. "Follow that road for a short distance. You will see an exhaust vent being guarded by the enemy. That is where you need to enter. The Lord be with you both."

"And you," they replied and then moved off down the road, walking at a brisk pace.

Gage had felt the Spirit move too. He felt rejuvenated by the prayers and somehow knew help was coming.

Micah saw the angels approaching and recognised them immediately. Before he could do anything, Elisha drew his sword and took off like a rocket, straight at the demons guarding the exhaust. Isabel appeared to disappear in the cloud of dust that his swift passage had kicked up.

The demons didn't see Elisha until the last minute. All but one managed to get out of his way. The one that didn't, was now disappearing into a portal, which was linked with the Abyss. Three demons, who didn't need to move out of the way, immediately took off after Elisha.

Under the cover of the dust, Isabel snuck passed four demons that were standing there, transfixed by the crazy angel that had suddenly attacked them. She slipped inside, undetected.

All Micah and his companions could do was smile, and then they were back to waiting and watching.

Isabel immediately took to the air. She could move through the tunnels a lot faster this way. Unfortunately, by doing so, she became very bright, lit up in all her angelic glory.

It wasn't too long before Isabel found them. Jack recognised her immediately. He was suddenly afraid that if Tony could see her, he would have another funny reaction, especially since she was in her angelic glory.

Tony didn't react at all, at first, and then something like recognition crossed his face. Jack was watching his reaction closely.

They had both stopped walking and Alan and Henry noticed it almost at once.

"What's going on?" Alan asked, as he turned back to them.

Jack didn't answer but continued to watch Tony.

Tony seemed transfixed by Isabel, who was hovering before him, still lit up in her angelic glory.

Jack stepped aside with Henry and Alan but didn't take his eyes off Tony. "Tony can sometimes see his guardian angel, but for reasons that would take too long to explain now, he usually confuses her with his dead wife. She has just arrived, probably because of the prayers we just prayed, and she is unmistakably in angelic form. She is very hard to look at directly because she is so bright. Tony could react badly to this. He appears to be in some sort of denial about his wife's death."

Both Alan and Henry tried to look where Tony was staring but they couldn't see anything.

"What can we do?" Henry asked.

"We don't have time for this," Alan added. "If they are so close to finding us..."

"I know," replied Jack. "Give me a moment to see if I can snap him out of it. If I can't, then I might have to try and carry him or something."

Henry nodded, "Do what you must, we'll wait right here."

"Don't take too long!" added Alan.

Jack went back to Tony and stood between him and Isabel but Tony didn't take his eyes off of her.

"Tony?" Jack said trying to get his attention.

"What is it Jack?" Tony answered as if nothing was out of the ordinary.

"Are you alright?" Jack asked.

"I..." Tony started to answer but then changed what he was about to say. "Isabel is here."

"I know," Jack answered. He then decided to try to force Tony to see the truth. "But how could she be? We left her outside, with the angels."

Tony almost looked away but stopped himself before he did. "It isn't the same Isabel," he answered. "It's her guardian."

Jack was surprised that Tony knew this, but before he could say anything, Tony spoke again.

"Why is she here and not with Isabel?" Tony asked, looking confused.

"Tony," Jack stepped a little closer and tried to get Tony to look at him. "Tony, can you look at me for a moment?"

Tony slowly lowered his eyes and looked Jack straight in the eye.

Jack could see tears starting to form in Tony's eyes.

"I've only ever seen her like this once before," Tony said. "But she was crying then." Tony looked down and then away. He started to turn but Jack reached out and grabbed Tony's shoulders.

Isabel was still floating in mid-air, behind Jack. The look on her face was one of sadness but also relief. Jack couldn't see this because she was behind him. If he did, he might have understood more of what was happening.

Jack sensed that he needed to get Tony to follow on from what he had been saying — not because Jack needed to hear it but because Tony needed to say it. "Who was crying Tony?"

"Isabel's guardian angel," was the reply he got from Tony.

"Why would she be crying?" Jack asked.

In a very small voice Tony replied, "Something is wrong with Isabel."

Henry and Alan were watching but trying not to intrude. Alan started to get the feeling that if Jack kept Tony going down this path, he could have a break down. The resulting noise would lead their pursuers straight to them. All the same, he knew that Tony needed this. Even with his limited medical training, he understood the benefits of grief as part of a healing process. He knew that he shouldn't intrude on this but he also knew that they had to get out. He turned to Henry and indicated that they should move away and give them some privacy.

Henry nodded and followed.

"We can move on slowly, so that you are not forced to hurry, once they get this over with," Alan suggested.

Henry looked back at Jack and Tony and saw the sense in what Alan was suggesting. "Okay, let's go, but let's try to leave them some sort of path to follow."

As Henry and Alan moved away, Jack noticed their movement out the corner of his eye. He glanced quickly their way and thought he understood what they were doing. Turning back to Tony, he asked another question, "What is it, Tony? What's wrong with Isabel?"

Tony's eyes closed and tears fell silently down his cheeks. "She..." he struggled to continue as a sob started to well up within him, but continue he did, "she isn't breathing and", he struggled physically with the next words. "I can't... I don't..."

Jack cut him off with a little shake, which made Tony look up at him. "Come on Tony, don't give in to it!"

Tony glanced over Jack's shoulder at Isabel.

Then Jack saw something within Tony's eyes. It was only for an instant. Jack's eyes narrowed as he searched Tony's eyes for it again.

"What else, Tony? What else is wrong with Isabel?" Jack asked, with a small amount of force in his voice.

"There is..." Tony started to say it, but stopped again. He started to look away but Jack dropped his head so he was still looking in Tony's eyes. "I..."

Jack saw it again and he knew that what Tony was experiencing was something that he had unknowingly taken into his life.

Jack stood back up and looked over his shoulder at Isabel. Isabel had a look suddenly of a fighter. This was something he had never seen in her before. The look of steel in her eyes made him realise that she had seen it too. She looked at him and as their eyes met, Jack understood what he had to do.

"Dear Heavenly Father," Jack started, as he turned back to look at Tony. "Help this lost soul. One of your flock has been hurt and is still hurting. Your ancient foe has tried to take him from you, but we now recognise his hand in this lost soul's torment. I ask you now, in Jesus's name, to release him from his torment. Jesus, heal Tony, fill him with your love and release his soul from the grip of denial that has held him hostage for too long."

As Jack was praying, he felt a presence that he had never felt before. Another angel was with them and He was reaching out towards Tony. He removed Jack's hands and replaced them with His own. He was smiling and Tony was crying silent tears. Then He embraced Tony and spoke. It was a voice that Jack would never forget. "You are mine, Tony. Do you want release, as your friend has asked for?"

Tony nodded. He slowly sunk to his knees, head bowed and, through his tears, he managed to whisper, "Save me Lord Jesus, rescue me from this poison in my soul."

The angel put his hand on Tony's head and spoke with such an air of authority that it made the hairs on the back of Jack's neck stand up. "Denial, there is no place for you here anymore. You must leave him now."

Jack heard an unfamiliar voice come from Tony. "But he is mine," it whimpered.

"Demon, he is not yours. He is mine. With the authority that is mine, come out of him and be gone," the angel said again.

There was a wailing sound as a small and ugly little demon, fell out of Tony.

Jack noticed Isabel was now kneeling alongside Tony. As the demon struggled to its feet, Isabel's sword fell and cut it in half. Jack watched intently. The demon disappeared in on itself, as if caught in a bath as it is emptied of water, swirling around and around until there was nothing left. There was a small pop as the demon vanished completely.

Jack realised suddenly that this was no ordinary angel. This was the Lord's angel, the one the Old Testament mentions. The one that eventually took human form. Jack dropped to his knees with his head bowed.

Jesus reached out and helped Jack back to his feet. "He still needs your help, Kevin."

"What can I do, Lord?" Jack asked, trembling and still trying to avert his eyes.

"You know what to do, Kevin," Jesus answered him, smiling. "Do what I have already taught you."

Jack nodded, tears running down his face. He didn't answer — he was afraid that his voice wouldn't work. He reached out his trembling hands to Tony and helped him stand back up.

When they looked back around, Jesus was gone.

Tony looked about while wiping the tears from his eyes. "I'm sorry," Tony said to Isabel. "I have been lost for a long time, haven't I?"

Isabel lowered her head, "I am sorry too. I did not recognise his presence for a long time. Once I did, I could not do anything about it. Not until you asked for it to be removed. It is gone now and you can grieve as you should have done years ago."

Jack looked around and noticed that Alan and Henry were exactly where they were earlier when he had glanced at them. They had not taken a single step. It was as if time had been stopped and everything he had just witnessed and been involved in had happened outside of time itself. He turned to say something about it to Tony and noticed that Isabel was once again floating in mid-air, with Gage alongside her.

"It is time for you to go, quickly now," Isabel said, and she turned and sped off down the tunnel with Gage.

Jack turned to Tony and was about to mention Gage's departure, when he came flying back around the corner, to join them once again.

"Your friend's guardian told me to come back and guide you out. She said you will need me, when you reach the exit itself," Gage explained about his return.

Jack was feeling a little out of place suddenly but noticed that everyone else was moving off down the tunnel without him.

Tony stopped and smiled at him. "Come on, let's get out of here!"

Ninety Six

The messengers that Michael had sent were now arriving at their destinations.

In the Garden of Eden, Nashira and Antares spoke with the messenger. "The portal was found and is being closed. Still, be on guard, but the threat level has reduced," they were told.

One of the cherubim, Starr, overheard the message and scratched his head in response.

"Is that what this is all about?" Starr asked Nashira. "A portal?"

"Yes," replied Nashira. "Someone entered the Lord's Garden through it and the enemy heard about it. They have been searching for the portal ever since."

Starr just stood there for a moment. "I think I need to speak with the Captain," was all he said before moving away.

In Africa, Vesna and her team of warriors were watching the town called Eden and, in particular, a building site. Their messenger arrived with stealth and, once it had delivered its message, it returned to Heaven.

Vesna liked what she had been told and she readied her warriors for action. All they had to do now was to wait for the Holy Spirit to give the signal to start.

The same message was received in the Middle East by Levi and in the Aland Islands by Driscoll. Levi and Driscoll responded in much the same fashion as Vesna had.

In the Daintree Rainforest, Evangelos received a slightly different message. "Portal found. Wait for more warriors. Be patient." Evangelos looked at the den, from where he was hiding. "It had better be a lot of warriors," he said to himself.

In Kings Canyon, Israfel was standing with Nathaniel, waiting for Jack and Tony to return. They heard the messenger coming before they saw it. The demons had spotted it and were starting to cause a bit of noise over the arrival of another angel (they had been searching for Elisha since he arrived but had not found him and this had made them angry).

Nathaniel pointed at the trail coming towards them. "We need to intercept him before the enemy does."

Israfel looked around quickly and then said, "You're right. Go. Take him out passed where we saw the helicopter land. I'll grab the car and meet you out there."

Then the Holy Spirit spoke to him and Israfel knew he needed to speak with the approaching angel, immediately.

"I think I should get the car and you go," Nathaniel said, having received a similar message from the Spirit.

Israfel nodded, turned, started to run and then took off. He flew along the ground for a while and then turned upwards towards the diving angel.

Not far behind him, demons were starting to leave their concealed locations and were moving to intercept the newly arriving angel too.

The messenger saw Israfel approaching and then the demons in pursuit behind him. He turned to match Israfel's trajectory and slowed to await his arrival.

"Follow me," Israfel said as he got close to the messenger. The messenger waved to acknowledge that he had heard the instructions.

The two angels turned and dove down again, Israfel slightly ahead of the messenger. They turned again, just before they hit the ground. They were moving very fast and very close to the ground. Not one of the demons could catch them. Eventually, all their pursuers gave up and turned back.

Once Israfel noticed this, he slowed down and landed alongside the road and the messenger landed alongside him.

"Glory to the living God," Israfel said.

"And to the risen Lamb," the messenger replied.

"What is your message that required me to reveal my presence to the enemy," Israfel asked, sounding slightly annoyed.

"The portal has been found," the messenger replied, getting straight to it. "You are authorised to go 'offensive' if required. Uriel is waiting for your information, before he can complete his plan," the messenger said. "Do you have any information for me to take back to the Captain?"

Israfel stood in contemplation for a moment and then smiled. "Here is what you need to tell the Captain..." Israfel outlined what he had found out and told the messenger his part of the plan, which he had just come up with. It would be up to Uriel and the Captain to formulate what they wished to do. He then bid the messenger farewell and started to walk back to the building site. The messenger left immediately, going straight up as quick as he could.

Ninety Seven

Cain looked across at Tarvyn, who was standing nearby. There was quite a large group gathered before the main entrance of the yet-to-be-completed resort. Tarvyn had insisted upon a large guard force to escort him and his human, Luc. Luc was willingly under Tarvyn's control. Cain's human, Kane, was also there, trying to stay inconspicuous amongst so many security guards and assistants.

Luc had most of his day-to-day staff and assistants with him. If he had left them back in Europe when he came here they would have been caught by the agents of the government. Which government it was this time, he wasn't completely sure. Many of the countries within Europe contained people who wanted him now, for one reason or another. Not all of them were the authorities either. The Italian Mafioso and the Russian Mob were his biggest concerns. He had stepped on a few too many toes all around. So many, that it had become too hard to live anywhere within Europe anymore. If he was recognised, he would be imprisoned for sure. Australia, however, was a perfect hiding place for him. Lots of open places. So many, in fact, that the authorities couldn't cover it all, even if they knew he was there. It was only a week ago that he had entered the country illegally and no one knew he was even here. That, of course, was one of the reasons for building this resort away from any major city. It allowed them to sneak any of their people in undetected. That was part of the plan, once it was finished.

Luc, and his staff of twenty, had arrived in the middle of the night. None of the construction workers had seen their arrival. Now, as they prepared to leave, it was a different story. Some of the long-standing construction workers knew not to look or ask questions, but that didn't stop them from wondering where these people had come from.

Cain had noticed a few quick glances in their direction and he mentioned it to Kane, along with a suggestion for him to try to hurry this up.

Kane walked over to Luc and bowed.

Luc noticed him at once but pretended not to for a moment. "It would not do to address him too quickly – he might think he is more important than he is," he thought. After waiting almost a minute, he finally spoke to Kane, "Oui, Kane?"

"Sir, it does us no good to stand in the open for too long. There are too many eyes around us. Even though they know better than to talk openly, they may be coerced, if pressed. I would suggest that we leave for the airport as soon as we can," Kane said, as diplomatically as possible.

Luc had given Kane the same sort of offer that Tarvyn had given Cain. Part of the reason was because he had recently lost his second in charge. He needed a replacement as soon as possible. This sort of suggestion from Kane was exactly the sort of thing that Luc wanted from him. Luc smiled to himself, thinking that Kane was already serving him. Kane's decision should be delivered soon and, in all likelihood, in his favour.

"You are correct, Monsieur," he said in his French accent. He turned to his waiting staff, "Attention! We must depart now. Allez, allez! Gather your bags and get in your transport vehicles." A few of the people looked at him blankly, so he repeated his demand in French. This time he got nods of understanding from those who had not learnt enough English yet.

Luc gestured towards his limousine: "Please, ride with me, Kane." It was more of a command than a question.

Kane bowed his head as he replied, "It will be my honour, sir."

Kane waited for Luc and climbed in behind him. The driver got them a drink and then proceeded to drive them to the airport in Cairns. The rest of the staff climbed aboard a chartered bus. Once everyone was seated, it drove off after the limousine. The bus driver noticed that it was almost five minutes since the limo had left. He was not concerned about this. They would have to wait for the ferry at the river anyway.

Tarvyn and Cain were surrounded by at least twenty guards inside the limousine and upwards of fifty were flying outside, adding a second layer to their defence. Another fifty surrounded the bus, but only in one layer.

Evangelos watched them drive passed his position. He was well hidden and remained completely motionless as they went by. Once the bus was out of sight, he turned to his troops and held up his right hand with his thumb up. He got eight thumbs back.

"No wonder the Spirit warned us to be patient," Evangelos thought. "It had to be one of the seven with that much security surrounding them. How many guards are still there?" he wondered.

The same thought was going through Lucas's head as, from a window on the third floor, he watched them drive away.

"Highrise, send word to Pandora," Lucas said, as he turned from the window, "I want everyone who should be here, back here, as soon as they have possession of the humans."

Highrise stepped forward. "I will go myself, lord."

"Good," Lucas responded, "and tell her not to forget the camera."

NINETY EIGHT

Nathaniel had retrieved the hire car and was just starting to pull out of the parking lot. He was about to drive down the road to pick up Israfel, when the Spirit told him to go the other way instead.

On the other side of the building site, in Kings Canyon, Micah had seen the messenger arriving and then the Spirit spoke to him and his party too. The Spirit had told them to be ready and alert. All eyes turned to the exhaust port.

They watched as all but one of the remaining demons took off towards the incoming angel. Micah watched the demons for a moment in case it was a trick to lure them out. But the demons kept going.

Duncan touched Micah on the shoulder to draw his attention back to the exhaust port. They could see movement coming out of it.

"Quick," Micah said, "we need to get that demon away now!"

Duncan jumped up and ran towards the demon, shouting, "Battle!" while he drew his sword. The demon looked down at the approaching angel and drew his sword in his right hand, ready to meet the threat head on. At the last moment Duncan jumped to his left. He swung his sword as he flew passed the demon on its right-hand side. This caused the demon to try to defend itself in a backhanded fashion, which allowed him to block the swing but not retaliate at all.

Duncan didn't stop but continued flying away from the demon. He looked back and saw that his plan worked. The demon, which had been forced off balance when it blocked Duncan's sword, had recovered and was now flying after him.

Back at the exhaust, Gage was looking out over the edge of the pipe. He saw what Duncan had done and realised that they had plenty of help this time. He gave the all clear and Jack climbed out. Jack then reached back in and, as he helped Henry out, he noticed Gage walking across the road to Micah, who had appeared from his hiding place. Alan and Tony followed Henry out, after they had helped him from the inside. The four humans quickly walked across the road, towards Gage and Micah, who were still talking together. Gage started to signal to Jack to get over to the other side of the road as quickly as possible.

Jack and Alan were helping Henry, and Tony was following as quickly as he could, with Henry's backpack over his shoulder. Jack was directing them towards where Gage and Micah stood when Elisha landed next to him and started to help him with Henry.

Just as they got to the other side of the road and disappeared down into the bushes that Micah and his team were using, Isabel shot out of the exhaust with a group of demons chasing her. They stopped quickly once they realised that it was only one angel they were chasing. Not seeing any humans in close proximity, they decided that the angel must have tricked them. They retreated back into the exhaust, to try to find the humans who they presumed must still have been somewhere inside.

A minute later, a minivan drove past, stopped, did a three-point turn and came back. It stopped almost directly in front of where they were hiding.

Micah saw Nathaniel at the wheel and indicated that they should all get in as quickly as possible. Jack got up and headed for the van. Tony, Elisha and Isabel, who had just landed, followed but Alan and Henry hesitated, with Gage now staying with Henry. Jack stopped and looked back at them.

"Come on," Jack said. "You've trusted us this far, why not a little bit more?"

Henry got up after some encouragement from Gage but Alan still hesitated.

"Don't be afraid, Alan," a voice said from alongside him.

Alan turned and saw Micah next to him. "Where did you...?" Alan swallowed his question as he knew the answer already but hadn't been prepared to accept it before.

"You're among friends, Alan. Quickly now, get into the van and you will be safe," Micah told him, and then disappeared again.

Jack was at the door, waiting to help Henry up the steps. Everyone else was inside and seated. Alan stood up in a daze and moved forward to help Henry. The two of them climbed in and walked to the back of the van. They sat down alongside Tony and Isabel.

Once they were all inside, Nathaniel drove off. He was heading out to the other side of the resorts to pick up Israfel. He was driving fairly slowly, as he did not want to draw any unwanted attention.

Micah watched the retreating van for a moment, before he and his team made their way back to their meeting place. One by one, the rest of Nathaniel and Israfel's teams all started doing the same.

Ninety Nine

They struck with a ferocity the angels rarely experienced. The three sides were hit at the same time. The angels knew they were coming and couldn't do a thing about it. That was the worst part of being in a boat and not driving it.

The demons were rushing through the boat with their swords drawn. The group from the left passed through the boat just above the waterline and emerged out the right side. The group from the right did the same but passed just under the waterline and emerged from the left side of the boat. One group had passed through the engines and the other through the electrical systems. As a result, the engines died and the lights flashed and went out. Two crewmen, one in each of these areas, smiled, thinking they had caused the failures themselves.

The boat was disabled entirely and started to drift. The only thing that still worked was the marine radio, as it ran from a separate battery system that was kept in the radio room.

The rear attack moved slower, coming in on the passenger levels. The demons were searching the boat, with their swords drawn, expecting resistance but not finding any.

The three speedboats moved in close, one on either side of the bigger boat and one behind it. None of them docked, they just sat there alongside the ferry, waiting.

Kyle and Daniel were with Kerri and Glen. They were doing their best to try to appear to be human tourists. All around them the rest of the passengers appeared to be oblivious to the demonic attack.

The lack of lighting and engines had quite a few passengers concerned, but it had only just happened so nobody was panicking yet. To them it was all storm related. They could hear the wind rushing outside and the temperature had dropped considerably in a very short space of time. Some thought this was due to the sky having become suddenly dark, probably due to the storm clouds, but it was really all due to the presence of so many demons.

Quite a few passengers were resorting to quick prayers for help because of the fear they felt, being in an unknown situation. Most of these were only token prayers, only a few of them knew the Lord Jesus personally. All the same, God was still listening and action had already begun.

****

Michael, Saint Peter and several other angels, the back-ups, who were all in the hall, all looked up at once. They could hear a rushing of wings. They all hurried towards the door and, stepping out, they saw a large group of angels on the wing, heading for and over the edge of Heaven.

Michael held his arm out, to forestall any with him from taking flight and joining them. Looking over his shoulder at the eight angels he noticed that some of them looked confused and even a little disappointed.

"Our time will come," Michael said to them. "Right now, it is more important to wait for the call to action our plan."

They all nodded, realising the wisdom in Michael's counsel.

Turning back to stare at the retreating angels, Michael's sharp eyes picked out one that was trying to get through the departing flock as if only just arriving in Heaven.

Once it was clear of the departing group, the angel paused to wait for more of his comrades, who were heading towards him. While he was waiting, he spotted Michael.

"Captain!" the angel called out, as he approached hurriedly, ignoring the last few who were leaving.

"Yes?" Michael answered, waiting for the angel to land before him.

"I am Siri and I carry a message from Raphael," the angel stated.

"In here," Michael replied, directing Siri into the Hall they were crowded in front of. "Back inside, all of you," Michael directed to the rest of the angels, who had followed him outside.

Once inside, Michael indicated for Saint Peter and Siri to follow him over to a corner, away from the rest of the angels.

When they were out of earshot, Michael turned to the messenger and spoke, "Go ahead, deliver your message."

Siri bowed slightly, out of respect and then replied, "I have just come from a church in Cairns, in northern Queensland, Australia, where a large gathering of warriors was taking place. Raphael requested I report to you and advise you of this gathering. I have not seen such a gathering in one church, for a very long time. There were twenty-three extra angels present inside the church. On my leave, to come to present this message, I saw more angels arriving. I looked back once more, a little later, and could see Raphael and the rest heading out to sea with still more joining the group that he was leading."

Michael nodded and thought of the group that had just left. That was another fifty at least. After a moment, he asked, "Were there any other angels that Raphael was speaking with?"

"Only the church's representative," was the reply.

"What had happened just prior to all the angels arriving in your church?" Saint Peter asked.

The messenger looked from Saint Peter to Michael, not knowing if he should answer the question or not. He looked sad as he spoke, "I am sorry, sir, I have been advised not to tell of that which I have overheard Raphael explaining to my fellow church carers, except to the Captain."

"It is okay," Michael prompted, "Saint Peter has been fully briefed on the situation and it was I who told Raphael only to tell those he needed to."

"Sorry, Captain," Siri replied, "I did not know."

"Well done for sticking to your instructions. Now please, answer Saint Peter's question," Michael instructed.

"The saints were praying as Raphael had requested – for the deliverance of the Saints, and the binding of the evil one and his plan," answered Siri.

Michael smiled and then asked, "Do you know where they were going and why?"

"Not exactly," replied Siri, "But the prompting I received from the Spirit just before Raphael sent me here was to head out to sea and search for a particular boat, and then defend it."

"Thank you, Siri, you may return to your church now," Michael said, dismissing the messenger and allowing him to return to his normal duties.

Once the messenger was out the door of the Hall, Michael turned to Saint Peter. "If that many have been called to assist, Raphael's escape plan may have struck a problem," he said, feeling a little worried for the humans.

"That's what you think that is all about?" Saint Peter asked.

"I know it is," Michael replied. "But we can't do anything about that – it is in the Lord's hands now. I think we should focus on the other half of this issue. Let us gather the troops for Uriel's plan. That is, unless you have something to add?"

"Not yet," replied Saint Peter.

One Hundred

"Anything?" David asked.

"Nothing from me," Stan answered.

"As yet, I have not spotted anything that appears out of place with the rest of this debris," answered Chris.

David looked over at Troy and Rundle, who were a bit further away and had not heard him. "Let's check with those two. If they haven't found anything, then it's possible we've been wasting our time here."

As they approached them, they heard Rundle say something to Troy, who quickly moved to where Rundle was indicating. They all moved a bit quicker, hoping that something had turned up.

"I think that is the tyre track they mentioned," Troy said as the others reached him. "It is unlike the sort that is on the tyres of Phil's bike or the others'." He looked up at everyone else and there was no mistaking the excitement in his eyes.

David cautioned him, "Don't get too excited. There may have been other vehicles pass this way before the police could put up the road block."

"No. I think Troy's right," Chris said, while examining the track.

David looked at Chris, gauging his body language. He was sure that he was right. "Okay," he said, "explain why."

"Look here," Chris said, pointing at the imprint in the mud. "First of all, look at the width of the track. Much thinner than a car's track and a road bike's. Secondly, look at the outer edges of the track. It is not as clear or deep as the rest. That would indicate an older bike's tyre: they are more rounded, even more so than a normal road bike. and a car's tyre, by comparison, is flatter, to get as much contact with the road as possible."

David looked at the print and could see exactly what Chris was talking about. "Well done. Let's see if we can find more and follow them. Stan, please take to the air, about ten or fifteen feet at first. See how clear you can see this print. Then see if there are any more ahead or behind it." David turned to the others, "Let's stand back so that we don't block his vision."

"Sir?"

"Please Troy, all of you, call me David."

"David, I think it would be better to have Rundle go up instead. He spotted the print to start with," Troy suggested.

David looked at Rundle and then nodded, "Troy is correct, but not 'instead of', go *with* him. Two sets of eyes are better than one and hopefully twice as quick."

Rundle and Stan nodded and took off. David, Troy and Chris moved off to the side. Stan went one way and Rundle went the other. Every now and then, one of them would swoop down to the ground, for a closer look, shake their head and return to their previous height and continue looking.

After about fifteen minutes, Rundle called out, "I think I have something."

They all converged on the spot where he was standing.

"It's not much, what do you think Chris?" Rundle asked.

Chris bent down for a closer look. "You're right. It isn't much, but... I think it's a match. It doesn't look as deep as the previous one, though."

"Why would that be? Different soil?" David asked.

"I don't think so," Chris answered. "Most of this area is all the same type of topsoil. If it was a lot deeper, we might see a difference in soil types. No, it's something else."

After a moment Rundle asked, "What about weight?"

"What difference would that make?" Stan asked.

"Think about it," Rundle answered. "The minister is missing. His wrecked bike is there," he pointed at the debris on this side of the road, back near the first print. "How did they move him?"

"Isn't that what we are trying to find out?" Stan asked.

"Yes, but I think I know what Rundle is trying to tell us," Chris said. "Two people on a bike would make a deeper impression."

"Of course," Troy jumped in. "They would have had to carry him on one of their bikes."

"Two people on a bike would have created a deeper impression in the topsoil. The print that is deeper would have been created as they were leaving," Stan said, now on the path that Rundle was leading him to.

"Exactly," Rundle answered.

"That's great in theory, but there are a couple of problems with that assessment," David said.

"What would they be?" asked Troy.

"Firstly, you told us that there were a number of bikes, not just one. That track could be from one of the other bikes. Or even from a totally separate bike," David explained.

Troy sighed at the sobering thought and the rest of them felt a little disappointed – all, that is, except Chris, who was looking thoughtful.

"Alright, let's take what David just said and argue it out a bit," Chris said.

Rundle smiled, he liked Chris's little argument games. It usually meant he was onto something that the others had missed. "Go on," he replied.

"Your first argument, David, is that it could have been one of the other bikes in the gang," Chris said, starting off the arguments.

David didn't really know what was going on but decided to play along. "Yes," he answered.

"As a gang, one would assume that even if it was one of the other bikes that made the deeper impression, it would still be travelling with the others. Which means..." Chris stopped mid-sentence to see if someone else would fill in the rest. If they did, it would mean that they agreed with his thought process.

"They would go to the same place," Stan completed Chris's sentence.

"So, if we followed that track, it should still lead us to the gang," Rundle added.

David now understood what Chris was doing. "But what if they went somewhere different?" he asked Chris.

"It is possible, but if you think on it further, I think you will agree it is very unlikely," Chris answered.

Rundle nodded and added, "The gang has a follower mentality. They all just want to belong to something. When they meet others that feel the same way, they group together. Eventually, one steps forward and leads them. The rest just follow."

"Even if the leader said 'you go that way and I will go this way'?" David asked.

"If they did split up, then the group without the leader, would eventually give themselves away, as they don't have the leader to control them. They would come back here to gloat or they would be in a pub and say something they shouldn't," Rundle answered.

"In either case, we would probably hear about it and then be able to follow whoever it was back to wherever they were hiding," Stan added.

Troy was looking a little confused by all this, "What exactly are you saying?"

David turned to him and answered. "We are discussing the possibility of one of the other bikes making that track and not the one carrying your charge. And, if I understand what they all just said," he indicated the other three angels, "then it doesn't matter, because as long as it was still a member of the gang, we will still be able to follow the track to wherever they are hiding."

"Exactly," Chris said.

Troy nodded, a smile forming on his face, "Then what are we waiting for?"

"The second argument," David said.

"Right," Chris said, "the second argument – that it could be a separate bike entirely. What is wrong with that suggestion?"

"Why would the weight change and cause a different impression?" Stan asked.

Chris smiled. "My thoughts exactly. What would make you think it was a different bike, David?"

"Scavengers," David answered. "They were riding passed and saw the debris and stopped to take a souvenir."

"Thereby, adding more weight to the bike," Stan answered, feeling defeated.

"No," Troy answered. "It doesn't work like that."

"What do you mean?" asked Chris.

"Well," Troy answered, "to make the second track that much deeper, you would have to be carrying something almost double the weight of the rider. Apart from placing another rider on the bike who could hold onto you, you would need to hold onto whatever it is that you picked up."

"That would mean they would have to ride one handed, which can't be done," Chris added.

"Well done, Troy," David praised. "That also solves the other problem I had but creates a fourth one."

"Fourth problem?" Stan asked. "What was the third?"

"Third problem," replied David. "That track is different, thinner, and fourth, how do you move an unconscious man on a motorbike?"

There was silence for a moment while they thought about what David said.

"There is really only one possibility," Chris answered. "A sidecar."

"Sidecar?" Stan asked.

"Yes, a buggy attached to the side of a motorbike is called a sidecar," Chris stated. "They were used a lot on older bikes and because of that, had a thinner wheel. And... the passenger doesn't have to hold on to anything. They just sit in the buggy."

"So they put him in the sidecar, strapped him in and off they went," David surmised.

"Whoever made that track is carrying the minister," Rundle stated.

"Then the track will lead us to wherever they have taken him," Stan added.

"There are no other arguments or problems?" Troy asked, worried that there would be.

David smiled, "No other arguments or problems here."

"Then what are we waiting for?" Troy said in anticipation.

"Rundle and Stan, try to find more of the deeper tracks in the other direction. Clear and matching tracks that we can follow," David ordered. "The rest of us will be right behind you."

One Hundred and One

The bus was moving along at a steady rate. All the passengers were happy to just be heading away from the hotels and the construction site.

Jack looked around the bus and saw Alan and Henry sitting together. Alan was giving Henry another quick check-up. Jack looked to the rear of the bus and watched Tony and Isabel for a moment. They were talking quietly and Jack could see the tears on Tony's cheeks. He then looked over at Elisha, who was watching out the back window for any followers. Looking forward, Jack saw that Gage had moved to the front of the bus to talk with Nathaniel.

Jack thought about the group of people and angels he was suddenly in the company of. Two escapees, from what sounded like slavery, with one guardian angel, a grieving minister and his dead wife's guardian angel, his own guardian angel and another angel driving the getaway bus. Jack closed his eyes and gave a quick prayer of thanks for all that he had experienced this day and for the fact that they had escaped safely.

Jack opened his eyes again when he felt the bus start to slow down. "Amen," he thought, to conclude his prayer, and then he stood and moved to the front of the bus to find out what was happening.

Nathaniel saw Jack stand in the rear-view mirror of the bus. As he approached, Nathaniel called out so that everyone could hear him, "There is nothing to worry about, we just need to pick up someone."

Jack looked out the front window. He saw someone on the other side of the road, walking back towards where they had just come from. "Who is it?' Jack asked, as he sat behind Nathaniel.

"You'll know soon enough," Nathaniel answered, as the bus came to a stop.

Israfel crossed over the road and climbed aboard the bus. He stopped as he reached the top step. Everyone aboard was looking at him. He looked at Nathaniel and blinked but before anyone could say anything, Gage dropped to one knee.

Israfel looked down at him. "Glory to the living God!" he called out looking up again.

All the angels aboard the bus answered together, "and to the risen Lamb!"

Israfel nodded and looked at Gage once again. "Get up," he instructed him. "I am not one to be praised; I am like you."

"No, sir, you are my better, and I am only trying to show you the respect you deserve," Gage answered.

"I am still only an angel, like you," Israfel replied.

"Not like me," Gage insisted. "You are a leader amongst angels, an archangel."

"Maybe so, but I still do not deserve this kind of reaction," Israfel said. "Please, stand up."

But Gage stayed as he was.

Henry and Alan looked at each other in puzzlement, both confused by the seemingly one-sided conversation Israfel was having. Seeing the look on their faces, Isabel explained that there was another angel there.

"Guardian!" Israfel called out, as if he were the commanding officer addressing a soldier in an army. "Stand up at once! Name and Rank!"

Gage stood up at once, "Gage, guardian to Henry Guzman since conversion, sir!"

"How long?" Israfel asked, with a little less intensity.

"Twenty one years, sir!" Gage replied.

"Thank you guardian," Israfel answered, "at ease. Please sit."

Gage relaxed and sat back in his seat.

Jack had watched all this with fascination and looked back at Isabel and Elisha, to see what they were doing. Both were looking at Israfel but had not otherwise moved. He noticed also that Henry, Alan and Tony were all looking a bit confused.

"What's happened?" Israfel asked Nathaniel. "Who are all these humans?"

"This is Jack," Nathaniel said, pointing to Jack in the seat behind him, "He and Tony, the man in the back with the female guardian, are the two who went into the building. When they came out again, they had the other two with them and that is about all I know. I am sure Jack could tell you the rest."

"Okay, go outside and keep watch. Pretend that there is something wrong with the bus if anyone goes passed," Israfel instructed Nathaniel. "Take him with you," he said, pointing at Gage.

Israfel turned to Jack. "Hello Jack, I am Israfel."

"Hi." Jack noticed, as he replied, that Elisha was moving up the bus,

"Hello Elisha," Israfel greeted the other angel.

Elisha bowed his head slightly, "Welcome, archangel of the Lord God."

"I did not know you were here, old friend," Israfel said.

"I am a guardian, once again," Elisha replied smiling, gesturing towards Jack.

Israfel smiled and turned back to Jack, "Welcome to the family of God."

Jack looked from the archangel to his newly appointed guardian and back. "Thank you," he replied.

"No, it is I who should be thanking you. I understand you can see us, even when we shouldn't be seen. Because of that, you were asked to assist us in penetrating the enemies' den back there," Israfel said.

"Yes, Nathaniel asked and it felt like the right thing to do, so I did it," answered Jack.

"You are very brave, Jack," Israfel said. "Can you tell me what you saw in there?"

"I didn't go alone, Tony came with me," Jack answered, indicating Tony at the rear of the bus. "We saw some demons, and they followed us for a while. Once we went down the hidden elevator, to the subterranean levels, all but one left us. He eventually disappeared in a swirling cloud of smoke, after that angel," he indicated Gage, "cut it in half with his sword. That's when we bumped into Alan and Henry," Jack indicated the other two humans, "who were trying to escape. We helped them the rest of the way out. We were followed for a little while, until we prayed for help — and that's when Isabel showed up."

Israfel nodded. "Very good, Jack. Tell me, what was the biggest demon you saw? My size? Smaller? Bigger?"

"Just a bit smaller than you," Jack answered.

Israfel nodded again. "Anything else you can tell me?"

Jack thought for a minute before answering. "The subterranean level reminded me of an old mine shaft. Apart from that, nothing comes to mind, but maybe they could tell you more," Jack answered, and indicated Henry and Alan.

Israfel turned to look at them, "Please come with me, Jack. They may say something that reminds you of something else."

Jack stood and followed Israfel back to Henry and Alan.

Israfel sat in the seat in front of them and turned so that he was facing them.

Henry and Alan were staring at him and before he could speak Alan blurted out, "Are you really an angel?"

"An archangel?" Henry corrected.

Israfel nodded. "You have been blessed and delivered from an evil place, thanks to the help of other angels. Is meeting and talking to me so strange, after everything else that you have gone through?"

Alan had a look of awe on his face and Henry had tears running down his cheeks. He lowered his head and started to slide off the chair, but Israfel reached over and caught him.

"Do not be afraid," Israfel spoke. "But praise God for your deliverance. Do you know much about your captors?"

Henry answered first, "I was only there a short while and didn't see a lot. All I know is that they are evil men and they were forcing us to construct something under the ground. I thought they were mining at first but none of the soil was being processed like they do in mines. It was all being removed at night. That is how I escaped the first time."

Israfel turned to Alan, "What about you?"

Alan was still in awe and Henry had to nudge him to get him to speak. "I was there for longer, about three weeks I think. I started off in the tunnels too, but when they discovered that I had first-aid training, they pushed me into being the doctor to the other prisoners.

"This allowed me access to all areas, when required," Alan continued. "They are building what appeared to me to be some sort of ceremonial chamber."

"What makes you think that's what it is?" Israfel asked.

"Well, it just looked like that," Alan answered.

"When have you seen one?" Henry asked.

"I toured through the middle east with my family, when I was younger. We visited some of those ancient types of places: Babylon, Takht-I Sulaiman, Susa, and some of the surrounding ziggurats — Aqar Quf, Choga Zanbil and Ur. Their ceremonial chambers looked similar to what I saw, which is why I think that is what they are building. Or should I say, digging out. I know those places are not completely linked but there are similarities."

Israfel only nodded, he knew that those places were actually linked. That is why there are similarities. If the same sort of temple was being built here... "Did you see anything else that you think I should know?"

Henry nodded and looked at Alan, "Tell him about the body we saw?"

"While we were escaping, we hid from a group that we heard coming towards us. As they passed, I watched out of the crack in the doorway and saw some men carrying a dead body. They were taking the body to the desert to dump it. We think we recognised who it was," Alan explained. "We think it was the foreman from our worksite, north of Cairns, which is where we were before we woke up here. "

"The Daintree resort?" Israfel asked.

"You know of it?" Henry responded.

Israfel sat back in thought and then looked at Jack.

"What?" Jack asked.

"Later," Israfel answered. "I think I need to talk to Isabel now."

Isabel looked up, "Jack, can you sit with Tony?"

"Of course," Jack said, as he moved over to take Isabel's place beside Tony.

Elisha followed Isabel up the aisle, to where Israfel was leading them away from the humans.

Jack sat next to Tony, who was wiping the tears off of his face. "Are you alright?" he asked.

"Yeah," Tony answered. "I feel like I have just woken up from a bad dream, only to find that I have lost the best part of it."

"I can understand that," Jack said. "You haven't had a chance to grieve properly. Now you have that chance."

"I know. I also have the assurance that she went to Heaven," Tony replied. "It doesn't mean that I don't miss her though."

"That's only natural, Tony. Give it some time and it won't hurt so much," Jack pointed out. "I know that doesn't help right now though. Do what you have always done: turn to God and get the comfort that only He can give."

"For a new Christian, you already know the right things to say," Tony said.

"I learnt it from the best," Jack replied, smiling.

Tony was a little embarrassed by the compliment and looked away.

Jack looked back up the minibus to where Israfel was sitting with Elisha and Isabel, deep in conversation.

At that moment, Gage and Nathaniel stepped back into the minibus. "I think it's time to go," Nathaniel said, as he climbed into the driver's seat.

"Someone's coming and they have company," Gage said.

Jack turned to look out the back window. All he could see was the dust cloud that indicated someone was travelling towards them.

As Israfel stood, he looked out the back of the bus too. "I agree," he said. "My time here has been well spent but I must go now. I have a mission that I must get back to. May the Lord God bless you and keep you safe and well. Nathaniel," Israfel turned and moved to face the angel as he spoke to him, "keep driving the bus. Take them to the airport at Uluru. Go with them wherever they go. We will meet up there."

Nathaniel nodded and then Israfel turned and stepped off the minibus.

Nathaniel started the engine and drove off as quickly as he could, leaving Israfel on the side of the road in a cloud of dust.

ONE HUNDRED AND TWO

Kyle wasn't sure how much longer he could let this go on. The demons were everywhere and slowly getting closer to finding his charge. Daniel's hand was suddenly on his. He looked down at it and then at Daniel.

"Not yet," Daniel said under his breath. "We will know when but until then, you need to be patient. Until then, encourage him to pray."

Kyle nodded and lent towards Glen and spoke quietly in his ear, "Pray, Glen, pray. The enemy is near and your prayers are needed."

"How are you holding up?" Glen asked Kerri.

"I'm not sure, Glen. Something about this feels... I don't know... wrong?" Kerri answered.

"Wrong? How do you mean?" Glen asked.

Kerri thought about it for a moment before answering. "This situation, the storm, it doesn't feel... natural."

Glen looked at Kerri and then out the windows. He noticed the dark clouds and he could hear the wind rushing around the boat. He could also feel the boat rocking on the waves. He noticed the rocking of the boat wasn't as severe as the wind sounded. Then he remembered the darkness at the construction site and how unnatural that felt. Maybe Kerri was onto something.

"If this is something that is... supernatural, are you ready for it?" Glen asked.

"What do you mean?" Kerri asked.

"With God?" Glen asked. "I don't want to pressure you into this, but sometimes there are situations where you need to make a decision under pressure. I think we have entered into one of those right now. What do you think?"

Kerri looked out the window too. "I think you may be right. What should I do?"

Glen smiled a sympathetic smile. "I can't make the decision for you or tell you what to do. God would know that it wasn't really your choice and nothing would be different. I can pray with you and tell you what words to use, but it is up to you in the end. If your heart isn't in it, then it will not be real."

"That's right," Amy said from the other side of Kerri. "It *is* your decision. The Holy Spirit knows when you are on the level. If you are going to do it, then now is a good time."

"I want to, but I don't want to be pressured into this," Kerri said.

Glen sighed. "I understand," he said. He reached over and took the Bible from her hands. He opened the back cover and pointed to something that was written inside it. "See this," Glen said, as he held it towards her, "this is the prayer that you need to say, when you are ready." He handed the Bible back to her.

Kerri just stared at it. "Thanks," she said, without looking up.

"In the meantime, I think we need to pray for ourselves and this situation," Glen said. "Will you pray with me?" he asked, as he held his hand out to her.

Kerri looked at his hand and then up at him. Slowly, she put her hand in his.

"I will pray and when I have said enough, I will squeeze your hand. If you want to say something, then do it. If not, squeeze my hand back and I will pray more or say 'Amen' to finish off," Glen explained. "Does that sound alright?"

Kerri nodded meekly.

Glen smiled, closed his eyes and lowered his head. Kerri lowered her head too but didn't close her eyes.

"Dear Heavenly Father, how amazing are all your works in creation. Nothing is too big or small to escape your attention. We, your servants, have found ourselves in a situation which does not feel right to us, Lord. If we are faced with something that is of supernatural origins then, Lord, please look after us and deliver us from this evil," Glen prayed and then squeezed Kerri's hand.

Kerri hesitated. She was unsure and uncomfortable doing this, but she felt that regardless of how she felt, she needed to say something. She needed to say... "Loving God, forgive me, for I am a sinner. Thank you for sending your Son to die for me. I give you my life, Lord, and I put myself into your care."

Amy, Kyle and Daniel couldn't hold it back, but started to weep with joy for the new Christian that was sitting in their midst.

"Someone is praying..." they heard a voice hiss from nearby.

"Stop them! Stop that prayer!" they heard other voices start to call out.

Amy whispered something to Kerri, looking concerned as she did.

Kerri squeezed Glen's hand. He closed the prayer off quickly, afraid that he wouldn't be able to speak because of the lump in his throat. "Thank you, Lord, for this moment and the new believer that is with me. I ask you now to send your angels to be with us, to watch over us and to protect us, all of us that are on this boat, from the ministrations of the evil one. In the precious name of Jesus, I pray. Amen."

"Amen," Kerri said as she stood, "Thank you. Can you please excuse me for a moment. I need the ladies' room. I will be back shortly."

Amy smiled to Daniel and Kyle as she followed Kerri.

"Here! Over here! There are —" the demon's words were cut off suddenly, along with his head.

Kyle was standing there, in all God's glory. All of the demons knew he was there. It was impossible to not see the sudden light. It had sprung up in the darkness that had enveloped the boat.

Pretty quickly, the demons realised he was not alone.

Alongside of him, Daniel was standing up. As he drew his sword, the reflection of God's glory started to shine out of him too. But he wasn't the only one. All around them, everywhere on the ship, people were standing and revealing themselves as angels in disguise. They were hard to miss now that they were shining with the otherworldly light of God.

The demons started to shrink back but then jeered as they realised that they still outnumbered these few angels, by at least seventy.

Glen felt a stirring from the Holy Spirit and dropped off his chair, onto his knees and bowed his head in prayer.

"Dear Lord, watch over us, especially Kerri, a new member to your flock. Keep us safe during this time of spiritual attack," Glen prayed.

Kerri got back in time to see Glen on his knees. She rushed to his side, "Are you all right?" she asked, as she knelt beside him.

Glen looked up at her, "We need to pray! We are in danger!"

Pandora appeared with Deceit and Rage right behind her. "These are the ones we are after. Why don't you save yourselves the fight and just hand them over to us now. We have the upper hand. We have numbers that you do not. We will let everyone else on this boat go free."

Daniel stepped forward, "You know that we cannot do that, so why bother asking?"

Pandora shrugged, "Have it your way then," she said, as she prepared to strike.

Deceit lunged forward and Kyle parried the blow with ease, while Rage struck out at Kerri but found Amy's sword blocking his. Pandora and Daniel were in a similar pose, as they traded blows too.

"Danger?" Kerri asked.

"Yes," Glen responded. "Do you remember earlier when we were discussing this being supernatural? Well, I think we are in a supernatural storm and we need to pray for our safety!"

Kerri nodded, "I think you are right. Let's pray!"

They bowed their heads, holding hands as they approached the Lord God in prayer.

All around the ship, demons of various sizes struck out at the small number of angels. Surprisingly to them, the angels held their ground well. There were fifteen angels fighting against ninety demons. Kyle, Amy and Daniel stayed together in a formation that allowed them to cover each other's backs quite well. All around the ship, the angels were starting to pair up and fight back to back with the various weapons that they carried. There were swords, large and small, a spear, nunchucks, daggers and what appeared to be a two-handed broad sword. One angel even had throwing stars. She didn't manage to throw many before she had three demons attacking her with wicked looking barbed-tipped swords.

The fight was going backwards and forwards, with more losses on the demons' side than you would think possible. It was their overconfidence that was costing them. They were sloppy – they expected the angels to be scared of their superior numbers. But the angels knew something that the demons did not.

Pandora's first inkling that things were not going to go her way was when Daniel smiled and said, "I think you will find that it is us who have the upper hand and the superior numbers. Look out the window while you can."

Pandora leaned over slightly, keeping her sword pushed against Daniel's, and glanced quickly out the window. What she saw almost made her drop her sword.

Rushing towards them, from the same direction they had come, was a great gathering of angels. She could not count them. It was too hard to even look at them. There were so many that the combined brightness was starting to hurt even her demonic eyes.

Before she could react, Daniel pressed his sudden advantage on Pandora, who had become distracted by what she had seen. She reacted with startling speed and managed to block Daniel at the last moment, but not without receiving a deep cut.

Sensing that this was not going to be a fight she could win, she took off through the roof. Daniel turned to Kyle and Amy and noticed that their adversaries were looking at the spot on the roof through which Pandora had disappeared. Amy struck like lightning and Rage started to lose shape instantly. Kyle attempted the same move. Deceit, knowing that Pandora wouldn't run out on a fight they were sure to win, had taken off an instant before Kyle could hit his mark.

"I'll stay with them, you go," Amy called out to Kyle and Daniel.

"Are you ready for some serious action now Kyle?" Daniel asked.

Kyle smiled. "FOR THE LORD, GOD ALMIGHTY AND HIS KINGDOM!" he shouted, with his sword raised high in the air.

All around the ship and from outside it as well, the call to arms was heard and repeated. "For the Lord of all", and "For the risen Lamb!" were some of the shouts they heard in reply.

Together, they took off through the roof to chase after their enemy. What they found made them stop and stare for a moment.

Raphael's team was just arriving from Cairns, with a good number of angels joining in the fight – at least one hundred Kyle told Daniel later. The biggest surprise was that there were already at least fifty angels diving in and out of dogfights with the demons and Ruth was amongst them.

Pandora had shot out of the roof and seen the descending group of Heavenly Warriors. She had turned to go east and saw another group coming from out at sea. In her fright, she turned the opposite direction and flew straight into Raphael. The two of them were now rolling into and out of other fights, which were springing up all around. Pandora was trying to escape with Raphael hot on her heels, swinging his sword and barely missing her feet.

Deceit was not so lucky. He came out of the roof and right into the middle of the group that had come from Green Island. He disappeared in a puff of smoke so quickly, the warrior that had got him didn't even see it happen.

Daniel took off after Pandora and Raphael, while Kyle dove into the thick of it, hacking and slashing at any demon that got close to him.

Daniel spotted several angels he knew, fighting against their ancient enemy, but the most impressive sight was his oldest friend, Nimrod. Nimrod had a demon by the feet and was using it as a club, hitting other demons. That is until he tried to use the demon to block a sword and the demon dissolved in his hands. Nimrod laughed and dodged the strikes of the demon, until Daniel flew passed and took off the attacker's head as he went. Nimrod waved his thanks and grabbed another passing demon and used it to attack more demons.

Daniel shook his head in amazement at his friend and continued on towards where Pandora had stopped to face Raphael. Raphael was a study in concentration, blocking Pandora's strikes and pushing her back slightly each time. This caused Pandora to be continually off balance. During these moments, Raphael would stab quickly with a little dagger he had in his left hand.

Pandora was a mess of small cuts and stab wounds. Surely it wouldn't take many more before she lost enough essence to cause the rift to open and take her to the Abyss.

Just when Daniel got close enough to help, Pandora spotted him and knew she couldn't fight both of them together. She turned and flew off once more. The two angels gave chase, only to find that there was an outer ring of angelic archers destroying every demon that tried to leave the fight. Pandora saw them and turned back towards the fight, just as an arrow whizzed passed. If she had not stopped it would have hit her.

Daniel stopped and let Raphael follow Pandora back towards the thickest part of the fight. He looked all around and saw the outer ring was made up of archers. This was a new tactic that he had discussed with Jasper only recently. Not allowing any of the enemy to escape from the fight would leave their leaders wondering what had happened.

Daniel waved at the closest ones and decided to head back to the boat.

When he landed back where he had left Amy, he found Glen lying on the floor. Kyle was standing over him, with a look of anger on his face. He had a few cuts and scrapes on his arms and legs.

Kyle turned to strike at the new arrival but recognised Daniel at the last moment and lowered his sword.

"What happened?" Daniel asked.

"Some of the crewmen attacked them. I returned to see Glen knock one out but the other hit him before he could help Kerri," Kyle answered. "Then the crewman dragged Kerri away."

Daniel looked around and noticed for the first time that Kerri was missing and a crewman was lying unconscious not too far away. He looked back at Glen and bent down for a closer look. "Is he okay?" he asked.

"I don't know, I haven't had a chance to check," Kyle replied. "I was too busy fighting the demons that helped the crewmen."

Daniel spoke quietly to Kyle. "We need to see if there is a doctor on the boat, to get Glen checked out. Then we need to find Kerri."

Hesitantly, Kyle nodded his agreement.

"I will go," Daniel said, looking up at Kyle. "This is not your fault."

"We knew something was coming. But not this... not this... Kyle said, through the tears that were suddenly in his eyes.

Daniel stood up. "I will be quick. You need to be with your charge now. Do what you can for him."

In the distance, Highrise could see the fight and could just make out Pandora. She was trying to get away from a larger angel that was pursuing her.

He tried to call out a warning but knew she could not hear him from where he was, because of the distance. Then she was gone, disappearing in a swirling black vapour cloud. All that was left was the angel. Then Highrise realised it was no ordinary angel – it was one of the archangels.

As he watched, demon after demon disappeared in clouds of swirling black and red. The pops of the portals closing again faintly reached his ears. He continued to watch until there were no more demons to be seen anywhere. Not one got away.

He was about to turn away when he saw the speedboats start to retreat from the larger vessel. Almost at once, he realised they had succeeded in their goal. The spiritual attack had been used to hide the real attack.

What he couldn't see was that one demon did survive. His name was Pride and he was now in the rear speedboat. Kerri, his old host, was lying unconscious on the floor with Amy standing protectively over her. The camera was held by Kerri's attacker.

ONE HUNDRED AND THREE

Michael was standing with Saint Peter, looking at a map of Earth. They were discussing the various locations that would be involved in the plan, when Starr walked in. He had walked up behind them before either of them noticed him.

Michael turned, expecting to see Uriel and the warriors starting to come in for the briefing and was surprised to see the cherubim.

"Starr? What brings you here?" Michael asked.

"I need to see you, Captain, in regards to the portal in Eden," Starr replied.

This caught Michael and Saint Peter's attention immediately.

"What do you know of it, Starr?" Michael asked, "You may speak freely. Saint Peter has been assisting me and knows all about it."

"I was there when it opened," Starr said.

"Really?" Michael said, looking surprised for a moment. "Tell me what happened."

"Shamira and I were on duty when we heard a loud pop and the portal appeared," Starr started to explain. "A human and a demon fell through it. I dispatched the demon to the Abyss for breaking the protocols and Shamira sent the human back to Earth."

Michael pondered this for a moment and then asked, "What more can you tell me about this human?"

"Shamira saw to him, Captain," Starr answered, "I believe she did a quick mind read, just surface stuff, to find out how he got there."

Michael indicated for Starr to continue, "That's all I know. Shamira knows more. Maybe you should speak with her," Starr suggested. "I wonder if she still has the letter." Starr said to himself.

"Letter?" Michael asked.

"Yes," replied Starr, "a suicide note, I think."

Michael and Saint Peter looked at each other but before they could question Starr further, a messenger came rushing in.

"Captain, I have a message from Israfel," the messenger, Titus, called. "He wanted..."

Michael raised his hands to indicate that he wanted Titus to stop, "Just a moment, Titus." Turning back to Starr, he said, "Thank you, Starr, for your information. I think we need to talk with Shamira as you suggested. Can you find her and send her to me please? As you can see, we have some pressing matters happening here. Please excuse us. For the Lord and His kingdom."

"For the Lord and His kingdom," replied Starr.

Michael waited for Starr to get out the door before turning to Titus. "Now, what is the message please?"

Titus proceeded to pass on Israfel's message.

When he finished, Michael thanked Titus and dismissed him.

"What is it Michael? You have a strange look in your eyes," Saint Peter commented.

"I think it is all coming together," Michael replied. "Here's what we know so far... Gabriel has determined that it is a town called Eden which has the link with the Lord's Garden. Starr has told us of a human who went through that very link," Michael said, as he listed them out loud. "Starr only mentioned one demon coming through the portal. Let's assume it was a Death demon. Death rarely travels alone. Most often there will be a Despair or Loneliness demon with it. Whichever it was would have seen the portal. Imagine you are that demon. Your target and companion have both disappeared in a flash of Heavenly light. What would you do?"

"Being only a minor demon, you would have to report it," Saint Peter answered.

"The major demon wouldn't want to hear about the failure, it would strike out at the minor demon," Michael stated.

"But on later reflection, it would realise that it may have made a mistake. Maybe the little one had information that Satan would have found useful for his revenge against the Lord. A way into Eden undetected," Saint Peter added.

"But all it would have is the name of the town, 'Eden'," Michael finished. "Not which Eden it was in or the exact location of the portal."

"Wouldn't they have a general idea which one?" Saint Peter asked. "It would only be in the area that the minor demon reported in to. Why search the Edens in the other locations?"

"Good point," Michael replied.

They both stood there in silence, thinking about Saint Peter's question.

"Let's think this through out loud," Michael suggested. "They know one Earthly Eden has a portal from it, going to some unknown location. From the name of the town, it is easy to think of the other Eden, the Lord's Eden."

"Fairly easy jump of logic there but it would only be an assumption," Saint Peter pointed out.

"Even so, if they are correct in their assumption, then it is worth following up, if they can use it for quick and undetected access," Michael reasoned. "That is the perfect way to launch a surprise attack."

"But a portal only allows two or three, at the most five, to pass through at once," Saint Peter argued. "Not the large quantity you would need for such an attack. Once the attack had begun, it would be easy to send the small quantity that had got through to the Abyss and set up a defence against any others that were still coming."

A look of understanding come over Michael's face. "Not if there were more than one portal. More portals would be harder to defend than just one. If you had seven portals, for example, how many troops could you send through at once?"

"At least fourteen and up to sixty," Saint Peter answered, with realisation dawning on his face too. "The more portals you have, the more troops you could send in at once."

"That makes perfect sense then. If you want more portals, you need to find them or create them," Michael stated.

"If one Eden has one, why wouldn't another Eden have a hidden link too?" Saint Peter suggested.

Michael nodded his head. "I think that is our answer."

"So they *are* looking for a way to get into the Garden of Eden," Saint Peter said.

Michael nodded his head, "I think we need to get that portal closed, straight away!"

One Hundred and Four

The doctor straightened up, looked at the captain of the boat and the group of people that was now crowding around them. "He's going to be fine," he said.

"Thank you, Doc," the captain said, as the surrounding people gave a little cheer and clapped. "I'm sorry that I interrupted your holiday."

"It's quite alright," the doctor replied with a smile. "Even on holiday, I still have to be on call."

"All the same, I am glad I found you," the captain said, as he shook the doctor's hand.

The doctor sidled off through the crowd and left the captain there, looking down at Glen, who was trying to sit up. Glen had one hand on his head and was now leaning on the other.

The captain of the boat began to fuss around like a mother hen. He felt responsible, considering it was his staff that had perpetrated the attack. One staff member was now in custody and would be escorted by the coast guard back to shore.

At that moment, the engines rumbled to life for the first time in the last hour. The captain sent his first mate to the bridge to get the boat back under way.

"What happened?" Glen asked, as he climbed back into a chair, with the captain's help.

"I'm sorry, I don't know all the details," the captain answered.

Glen looked around for Kerri. When he couldn't find her he looked back at the captain and waited for him to continue.

The captain sat down beside him.

"Where's my friend Kerri?" Glen asked.

The captain looked him in the eye, "Are you sure you're alright?"

"You're stalling, sir," Glen replied. "Where is my friend? What happened to her?"

The captain sighed. "During the storm, at least two of my crew, or people posing as my crew, attacked you and your friend."

"What?" Glen asked, surprised.

"Well, this is going to sound crazy, but... I think they disabled our engines and power on purpose; then, using the added confusion of the storm, they attacked," the captain explained his theory.

"That doesn't explain where my friend is," Glen pointed out.

"I'm getting to that part," the captain said.

Glen sat in silence, waiting for the captain to continue.

"A few of the crew have reported different things that happened during the storm," the captain said.

"Can you tell me these things?" Glen asked, "Please?"

The captain nodded. "One said he saw another crewman who was carrying an unconscious woman. When questioned, the crewman said he was taking her to sickbay. I have checked. No unconscious woman was taken to the sickbay."

Glen sensed there was more that the captain hadn't mentioned.

After pausing, the Captain continued, "Another crewman reported that he tried to stop someone from dropping a woman over the side of the boat. He managed to grab her camera bag as she went over. It was still around her, like a sash, and it stopped her from falling. He was then attacked. He tried to defend himself with one arm and pull her up with the other, but during the struggle, the strap broke and she fell. The attacker punched him in the face and grabbed the camera bag. He then jumped over the side too. There was a boat waiting for them there. My crewman said that he saw both the attacker and your friend in it. It was headed back towards Cairns. I'm sorry that we were unable to stop this from happening," he said, sounding very sincere.

Glen was taken aback by what he had heard.

The captain stood up. "The coastguard is searching for them. They will need to speak with you later and will have someone come out to the island to pick you up."

Glen continued to sit there, staring at his hands. He didn't notice the captain walk off. He was lost in thought, thinking of Kerri. He hadn't known her that long but felt a kinship with her. The pain he felt at the loss was strong.

This was the third person he knew who had disappeared because of these people. He wondered if there were any others.

One Hundred and Five

Israfel watched as the minivan pulled away and then turned to face the oncoming vehicle and demons. He drew his sword and settled into what appeared to be a defensive pose.

He had his left foot forward and right foot back, with his left arm stretched out before him and the sword in his right hand. His left hand was in a martial-arts-type pose with his forefinger up, his thumb out and the rest of his fingers curled in towards his palm. The sword was pointing over his head towards the oncoming vehicle.

When the vehicle was about five hundred meters away, Israfel switched his grip around in his right hand so that he was holding it like a spear. Israfel targeted with his left hand and then lunged forward and threw the sword like a javelin.

The sword flew true and straight. The demons ahead of the vehicle saw it coming and dodged out of the way but the human driver could not see the oncoming sword. The sword pierced the radiator and imbedded itself into the engine.

The four-wheel drive's engine coughed and died at once and the driver took it out of gear before he lost control of it. The four-wheel drive coasted to a stop not far from where Israfel had been standing but Israfel was no longer there.

The moment the demons turned to stare at the dead four-wheel drive, Israfel took off straight up as quick as he could. He smiled to himself thinking he had stopped the enemy from pursuing the minivan.

One Hundred and Six

"What's going on?" a female voice said from somewhere to Glen's right.

Glen heard the question but ignored it for a moment. But for some reason he couldn't get that question out of his head. "What's going on?" started to repeat over and over again inside his brain.

Then it clicked... he knew the voice!

Glen glanced up to see Kerri looking down at him, a concerned look on her face and one hand on the back of her head.

Glen jumped to his feet and embraced Kerri in a tight hug. "You're alright!" he said.

"Apart from this bump on my head," she replied. "Oh, and someone stole my camera."

Glen lent back and looked at her. "How did you get away?" he asked.

"Get away?" Kerri repeated. "What are you talking about?"

Glen looked a little confused at Kerri. "A crewman saw you and your camera thrown over the side of the boat and whisked away in a speedboat."

"Really? I was in the toilet!" Kerri replied.

"No, you came back. We were praying about the supernatural storm and then we got..." Glen stopped and stood back from Kerri, "...attacked."

"Attacked?" Kerri asked. "But I was in the toilet this whole time."

A smile started to creep across Glen's face. He shook his head but couldn't stop smiling. "Tell me what happened to you."

"I went to the toilet and... I think a big wave knocked me over. I don't know. I woke up on the floor of the toilet, a big bump on my head and my camera gone," Kerri explained. "But they didn't get this," Kerri pulled something out of her pocket and handed it to Glen.

Glen couldn't believe what he had heard or what he was holding. "The film?" he asked.

Kerri nodded.

Glen was still smiling as he spoke, "Praise the Lord! Thank you Lord, you are amazing."

Kerri looked at Glen as if he had gone mad. "What's going on?!?"

Glen explained what he had experienced with the other Kerri. Kerri listened in stunned silence, disbelief etched across her face.

"It's a miracle!" Glen said finally. "You were in the toilet with the film all along!"

"Then what did... I mean who..." Kerri couldn't work out what to ask but Glen understood all the same.

"An angel," was all he said.

Kyle and Daniel nodded their agreement. So did Natasha, the angel who had watched over Kerri while she was unconscious in the toilet.

The boat lurched slightly as it got underway once again. After Glen told the captain that Kerri had been found still on the boat, Kerri and Glen settled back to enjoy the rest of the ride to the island.

One Hundred and Seven

Pride sneered at Amy as the boat rushed across the waters of the bay. "Why are you still here? You know that she is mine. I will reassert my dominance once she wakes up again."

Amy looked down at 'Kerri', lying unconscious at her feet. When she looked up again, she smiled at Pride. "I know something you don't know. Would you like to find out what it is?"

Pride was suddenly very alert.

"Well?" Amy asked.

"You have nothing!" Pride spat.

Amy stepped back as 'Kerri' sat up. "I'd listen to her if I was you," 'Kerri' said.

Pride's eyes went wide as his jawed dropped open. Then a look of absolute anger came over his face. "Who are you?" he asked.

Giving up the illusion, 'Kerri' disappeared and an angel was sitting in her place. "You can call me... Pride killer," Esther said.

Pride jumped up but it was too late. With a move like lightning, Esther produced a dagger and threw it.

It hit Pride in the head, right between the eyes, and stuck there.

As his essence oozed out through the wound, he asked, "But how? You had no... power to... do this..." he wheezed out the last words.

Amy stepped forward and leaned over to take the handle of the dagger. But before she pulled it free she whispered into Pride's ear, "Kerri became a believer right before you attacked."

A look of horror filled Pride's eyes. "Nooooooooo!" he shrieked, as Amy pulled the dagger free.

A portal opened and Pride was sucked back into the Abyss and back to Hell. He would have to fight his way out again before being able to inflict his particular brand of torment on another poor soul.

Amy handed Esther her dagger, "Thanks for your help."

"Just doing the Lord's work, same as you," Esther replied. "Let's get you back to the ship."

The two angels, resplendent in the Lord's glory, took to the air and headed towards Green Island, where the ship was headed to once more.

One Hundred and Eight

When Israfel was sure that he was not being followed he flew around and then down towards the ground, flying just a metre above it. As he neared the resort he slowed down, landed and ran the rest of the way to the meeting spot. It took him only five minutes to reach the spot at which they had met earlier.

"Glory to the living God!" Israfel called out.

"And to the risen Lamb!" came the replies and with it the rest of the group came out of their hiding places.

Micah stepped forward, "Where's Nathaniel?"

"He is driving the humans back to Uluru and then flying with them on whatever flight they take," Israfel answered. "We will catch up with him later. How did everything go here after they left?"

"It took them a little while to work out what happened and then a car took off after them," Micah answered.

"Was it a white four-wheel drive?" Israfel asked.

"Yes, did you see it?" Micah replied.

"Yes, and I took care of it too," Israfel answered. "The demons looked a bit confused but didn't leave the car. Was there any other activity?"

"Not that we saw," Micah answered.

Everyone else shook their heads too.

Israfel nodded. "Okay, it appears that we have assisted in an escape. May the Lord be with them and guide them to safety."

"Amen," the rest of the angels said in unison.

"With that taken care of," Israfel said, "it is time to move on to the next part of our mission. The messenger I spoke with told me of Uriel's plan. I told them what I found out and about Jack, and I suggested some improvements to the plan. We need to prepare for what they have in mind and await the return of the messenger to see if they have agreed."

Israfel went on to outline to each of them what the plan was and what he thought they needed to do in preparation.

One Hundred and Nine

The flight had been very uneventful, which was just as well. Cain was trying to keep away from Tarvyn for the moment so that he didn't have to give his answer. Tarvyn had made it difficult for Cain to do this, especially since there were not many places to hide on a charted plane.

Luc had reserved one of the planes for himself and his closest advisors, including Kane. This meant that Tarvyn was with Luc and Cain was expected to be with Kane. The rest of the staff were on the second plane.

It was times like this that Cain appreciated his human familiar the most. Kane had approached Luc, without his prompting, and requested to be allowed to meditate alone so that he could ponder his decision and speak with his spirit guide. Luc had agreed and dismissed Kane without a second thought.

Cain and Kane were now sitting in the back row of the plane, trying to sleep, thereby ignoring everyone else. This was interrupted by the voice-over from the captain of the plane.

"Ladies and gentlemen, we will be arriving at the Connellan Air Strip in half an hour. A connecting bus is waiting for you and will forward you on to your final destination. Your luggage will be transferred automatically to the bus and will meet you in your hotel room once you arrive in Kings Canyon."

The stewardess approached Kane and requested that he return his chair to the upright position in preparation for landing. Kane grudgingly did as he was asked.

The next half hour passed reasonably quickly as Kane was looking out the window and watching their descent. Another hour later they were all aboard the bus, heading off to their final destination.

One Hundred and Ten

Nathaniel had watched in his rear-view mirror to see what Israfel was going to do. Sitting in the back seat, Jack, Elisha, Gage and Isabel were also watching through the rear window.

Jack was amazed to see that the lone angel was not hiding from the oncoming pack of demons. When he was in the building site, just the sight of them had made him feel sick and afraid, and if Tony hadn't been there with him he may have turned and ran. Somehow he had found the resolve to keep going; maybe it was something like male bravado and not wanting to look scared before a mate. But that wasn't the case out there for Israfel.

Then Israfel threw his sword and Jack was amazed to see him wait to see it hit. Then he took off vertically and really fast, almost too fast for Jack to follow.

"What a great distraction, to stop the car like that!" Gage said.

Jack just turned and stared at Gage. Then he turned back around and faced the front again, lost in thought for a moment.

"What happened?" Tony asked from the seat in front of Jack.

Jack looked up as if coming out of a daze.

"It was amazing!" Jack said, completely awestruck. "The big angel that was just here, Israfel I think he said his name was, threw his sword at that four-wheel drive and it just stopped. He faced down all those demons and then flew away."

Tony smiled, "Wow, I would have loved to see that. What are they doing now?"

Jack turned back to look and replied, "Nothing. The demons are hanging around the car, not following us or Israfel! Hang on, they're all looking back at something... a helicopter!" Jack turned back around and shouted to Nathaniel in the driver's seat, "A helicopter is coming!"

Everyone turned to look out the back window. Alan wanted to swear but felt that he couldn't in the company he was with. Henry and Tony both started to pray under their breath and Jack went to Nathaniel.

"Is it hard to drive?" Jack asked Nathaniel.

"Same as most cars, it just handles a little differently. Why?" replied Nathaniel.

"I think I should take over from you so that you can do something with them to help us get away," answered Jack.

Nathaniel looked back at the other angels and saw them all standing with their hands on their weapons and determination in their eyes. He nodded slowly, more to himself than anyone else, and turned back to Jack.

"Okay, look here, clutch, brake, accelerator and gears. Want to know anything else?"

"That should be enough," Jack answered.

Nathaniel slipped to his right, off the seat, but he kept one foot on the accelerator and one hand on the wheel. Jack dropped into the seat and as he placed his hand on the wheel and feet on the pedals, Nathaniel passed through the back of the seat to stand behind Jack.

The bus slowed for a moment and then accelerated as Jack pushed his foot harder on the pedal. Nathaniel gave Jack a quick once over to make sure he was alright and, seeing his look of concentration, decided he was just fine.

Nathaniel joined the other angels and asked, "Is there a plan?"

"We were discussing our options," Isabel answered.

"I think we should attack as they get over us, it will surprise them to see four of us and I think we can take them all out pretty quickly," Gage suggested.

"I was thinking more of camouflage and hiding the bus somehow so that we can just slip away unseen," Isabel said.

Nathaniel looked to Elisha but Elisha didn't say anything. He had his eyes closed and was listening to the prayers being said nearby. Tony had moved over to sit with Henry and Alan and after a little convincing Alan had joined in the prayers too.

"We need to distract or disable the helicopter, without injuring the humans aboard, while defending our charges and the minibus," Elisha said opening his eyes again.

Gage and Isabel knew the wisdom of this suggestion and felt the Spirit's reassurance that this was the best option.

"They are expecting at least two of us," Nathaniel added, "but not four so we can still use the element of surprise."

Gage smiled, "Elisha, why don't you join me on the roof for defence and distraction."

"And *we* can give a surprise attack and disable the helicopter at the same time," Isabel said, indicating Nathaniel and herself.

Elisha nodded, "Let us follow where the Spirit leads us."

They could now hear the helicopter which indicated that it wasn't far behind them. Elisha and Gage climbed up onto the roof and stood there facing the demons and the helicopter, while Isabel and Nathaniel sat near the praying humans and waited for the Spirit's signal. Times like this could be nerve-wracking for the angels but they knew that the Holy Spirit was one with God and it knew things they did not. To move without the Holy Spirit's influence was to move without God's approval. To do that would mean failure in whatever they were doing and possibly worse still... they could become one of the outcasts.

As Gage and Elisha drew their weapons they started to glow brighter and brighter with the glory of God shining all around them. The demons had seen them on the roof and had grinned to themselves, but now that they were alight with God's glory they lost some of their bravado. However, it didn't slow them down at all. They kept coming with the helicopter but as they got closer to the bus they sped up flew ahead.

When they were in striking range the demons started to dive at the angels, stopping short initially but getting closer as their confidence grew.

Gage and Elisha stood their ground and started to block the blows as the demons got closer and closer, and faster and faster. Just when they didn't know if they could keep up with the pace of the blows, Isabel stood up and spread her wings, instantly bright with glory light. She took off straight up through the roof of the bus, right between Gage and Elisha.

Isabel had pierced two demons as she passed them and was now chasing a third. The demons shrank back for a moment at the sudden appearance of the third angel but then separated into two groups. One group continued to hassle the two defenders while the other started to pursue Isabel.

Then Nathaniel extended his wings and drew his sword. Instantly alight, he remained motionless and suddenly stopped, allowing the bus to pass through him. Then he launched straight at the helicopter and passed through the outer shell, stopping in the cabin with the human pilot and passengers.

Having caught up with the bus, the helicopter doors swung open and two gunmen, one on each side, lent out of the helicopter with their guns in position, ready to shoot.

Gage and Elisha immediately looked up at the helicopter and prepared themselves for this new threat. Elisha moved behind Gage as he readied himself for the oncoming bullets.

Then it started: the gunmen opened fire on the bus as the demons dove on the angels once again. Gage's arms were a blur as he blocked every bullet that came from the left gunman but the right gunman couldn't aim at all and every bullet went completely wide. Elisha was swatting the demons away as quick as he could while Isabel dove in amongst them, taking two out and then blocking six swords from connecting with her.

In the bus, Jack had joined in with the prayers from where he sat in the driver's seat. Tony, Henry and Alan moved to sit just behind him so that they could all pray together.

In the helicopter, Nathaniel had his sword extended and was lifting the gun of the right gunman up and away from the bus. When the gunman stopped to check the gun, Nathaniel swung his sword in a huge ark so that he did a complete circle. His ark had been precise; his sword had cut through part of the seatbelt of the right gunman and the left gunman's seatbelt connector, then through the pilot's seatbelt and communication cables, and then it knocked the control stick to the left and out of the pilot's hands.

The result was instant: the helicopter suddenly banked left, throwing both gunmen, the pilot and the co-pilot to the left, hard against their seatbelts. The resulting strain snapped all the seatbelts that had been cut and pulled the co-pilot's control stick away from his hands too. The right gunman dropped his gun in an effort to hold onto something and stop himself from falling out of the helicopter. His gun fell through the open doorway to the ground. The left gunman slipped backwards and collided with the right gunman, loosening his grip once again.

The pilot was not so lucky: he tried to grab at the control stick again as he slipped out of his seat but only knocked it further to the left, causing the helicopter to bank sharper to the left. He then fell free and out of the helicopter completely.

The right gunman fell out the door too but at the last moment managed to grab the communication cables that were connected to his headset. He swung under the helicopter into the landing strut and managed to take hold of that as well.

The left gunman managed to hold on to his seatbelt and not fall any further as the co-pilot struggled to grab the control stick. Eventually he managed to correct the flight of the helicopter, and just in time too. The helicopter was almost at a ninety-degree angle, from which, at this altitude, they would not have been able to pull out without hitting the ground.

As the helicopter started to veer off and level out a little, Nathaniel shot out the left side, knocking the gun out of that gunman's hands. Gage swung up to his left and took out two demons that were concentrating on Elisha from his right, allowing Elisha to drive back another two that were swooping in on his left.

Seeing the helicopter change directions, Isabel moved towards it. When she saw Nathaniel come out the side she headed straight at him. Nathaniel saw Isabel coming at him, so he moved towards her. They passed each other; Nathaniel continued straight on with a spin and took out four surprised demons as he went.

Isabel dove down, landed and caught the pilot. She dropped him on the ground from just a foot and a half. The pilot, surprised at his good fortune but still in shock from his fall, passed out. Isabel took off again at full pace back into the fight, chasing a demon that was trying to catch Nathaniel, who was also chasing a demon.

A moment later, Elisha was alone on the roof of the bus. The only evidence that he had been fighting demons was the remains of portals, sucking in the black mist that was left of the demons, and even they were getting left behind as the bus sped away.

Isabel, Nathaniel and Gage were chasing the remaining demons as they tried to return to their den. After a few minutes the angels gave up and turned back for the bus. As they went, they passed the helicopter, which had just landed on the road. Nathaniel flicked his sword at the rotor controls as he passed under it, severing the hydraulics and springing a leak. All four occupants of the helicopter had survived with only minor cuts and bruises.

The bus was already five kilometres down the road from the helicopter and getting further away by the second as it continued on to Uluru. The angels caught up fairly quickly and rejoined the humans inside the bus. After Nathaniel advised Jack to slow down a bit, as there would be no more pursuers, they settled into their seats for the rest of the ride.

A couple of hours later they were turning onto the road to the Connellan Air Strip, just out from the Yulara resort, where they had to stop to wait for a bus that was coming the other way. It was pulling out from the airstrip and heading the way they had just come, to Kings Canyon.

The angels were very interested in the quantity and size of demons that were with the bus. To them, it was obvious who was on the bus and where they were headed.

Nathaniel shook his head, "I hope Israfel is prepared for them," he said, to no one in particular.

One Hundred and Eleven

Michael and Saint Peter were barely out the door when Nicole and Uriel spotted them.

"Captain!" Uriel called out.

Michael stopped and turned to see Uriel and Nicole approaching.

Uriel asked Michael. "Captain, where are you going?"

Michael indicated the direction to Eden's gateway. "We are on our way to see if the portal has been closed and if not to assist in its closure."

Uriel was immediately lost as he did not know what Michael was talking about: "Sorry, Captain, I have no idea what you are talking about."

"Of course not, forgive me for assuming you did," Michael replied. "Gabriel was successful in finding a portal that he believes to be the one that the enemy seeks. We have since had confirmation of this from Starr, a cherubim, and another source has confirmed Starr's account. We already have angels on hand at the site in Eden and they are attempting to close off the portal for good. We are on our way to see if we can close it or find the reason for it to be still active."

Uriel looked thoughtful as he processed Michael's words. He looked at Nicole for a moment and then turned back to Michael and his companions. "I think I understand what you are talking about but can you explain part of it further for me, Michael?"

"Which part, Uriel?" Michael answered.

"How the portal is not open but still active?" Uriel asked.

"It appears to be closed but if approached from its earthly point it becomes active again," replied Michael. "The link has not been removed."

Nicole looked confused, "But that is impossible isn't it?" she asked.

"Obviously not," Michael answered.

"That could be helpful with the plan," Uriel commented.

Michael studied Uriel for a moment, "How so?" he asked.

"Before I explain it to you, where are the back-ups?" Uriel asked.

"Inside," Michael said, indicating the Hall behind them.

"I think that it might be wise to take them with you and have Nicole wait here," Uriel suggested. "That way, if we have trouble, we are ready for it and if anyone is looking for you, Nicole can direct them to where you are."

Michael thought for a moment and agreed that it made sense. He turned back to the door, stuck his head in and called the angels inside to come and follow him. Then he turned to Nicole and saw that she was already moving towards him and the doorway.

"Thank you, Nicole," Michael said. "If I need you I will send for you."

Nicole nodded as she passed him in the doorway, "Yes, Captain. I will be here if you need me, and if anyone is looking for you I will send them to you."

Michael stopped her, "No," he said. "Have them wait here and you come and get me."

"Very well," Nicole replied, as she bowed and then disappeared inside the Hall.

A moment later the angels, seven warriors and one messenger — the next group of back-ups — came out the same door. Once they were all out Michael told them to accompany him to the Garden of Eden. He then turned and all of them, including Uriel, started walking towards the gateway.

As they walked, Uriel and Michael discussed the plan and made some changes to it.

One Hundred and Twelve

The boat eased up to the jetty on Green Island and gently kissed the tyres that hung there to prevent damage to both jetty and boat. The passengers cheered upon reaching their destination at last.

The angels that had fought earlier had split into two groups straight after the fight. One group hung around to continue to guard the boat and the other accompanied the coastguard back to Cairns. The Cairns group consisted mainly of the Cairns and surrounding areas angels, while the boat group consisted of Raphael, Daniel, Kyle, Natasha, Ruth, the Green Island angels and some of the angels that had come from heaven to help.

Upon reaching shore the angels from heaven took their leave and started their return trip, the Green Island angels returned to their posts and charges, while Raphael, Daniel, Kyle, Ruth and Natasha continued to accompany and guard Glen and Kerri.

Amy and Esther were already on the island waiting for them.

Glen and Kerri left the boat and headed towards their accommodations for the night. Once they had booked in, they decided to wander the island for a little while. They were still holding hands to keep up their pretence at being on their honeymoon. In their wanders they found a photo-developing centre that promised one-hour developing.

Kerri had pointed it out to Glen and asked, "What do you think?"

Glen looked at it and scratched his chin idly. "Should be alright, I suppose," he answered. "But let's not rush into it, okay?"

Kerri looked at it wistfully for a moment.

Glen saw her desire to see what was on the photos they had taken earlier. "Before we commit to it, let's just find out what time they close, as it's almost half past five," Glen suggested.

Kerri nodded eagerly and nearly pulled Glen to the little kiosk.

"Can I help you?" the assistant asked, as they stopped at the counter.

"What time do you close?" Glen asked.

"In about five minutes," the assistant answered, checking the clock.

Kerri's face fell in disappointment.

"That answers that then," Glen said to Kerri. "Let's go back to the hotel and see what time dinner starts."

"You're staying on the island tonight?" the assistant asked.

"Yes," Kerri answered, "in the hotel."

"We have a special deal with the hotel," the sales assistant said. "We often take film from their guests, develop it out of hours and return it to the front desk for collection the following morning."

Kerri looked at Glen, "What do you think?"

"We are being picked up early, remember?" Glen answered.

"That's right. Oh well," Kerri replied.

"They would actually be at the desk later tonight," the assistant added, not wanting to miss out on another sale. It hasn't been a very busy day, especially since the last tour boat got held up out at sea.

"What time?" Glen asked.

The assistant quickly grabbed a plastic tub out from under the counter and removed a clipboard from it. There were only two other photo-processing envelopes in the tub. "As you can see I don't have many to do for the hotel tonight. I would probably have them up there by... eight o'clock."

Glen looked at Kerri who already had the film in her hand. Glen gave a little laugh and smiled at the assistant. "I think she is excited about what is on that film."

The assistant just smiled too as he passed over the clipboard to Glen, "If you could just fill out this and write your room number here."

Raphael turned to the angels who were still together, "I think we have more than enough cover now. Thank you, Esther and Natasha, for your assistance on the boat."

Esther and Natasha felt the call back to Heaven, so they said their farewells and left.

Raphael watched them for a moment as they flew away. Then he turned back to Glen and Kerri, who were still filling out the paperwork. "I will stay with the photos. Daniel, why don't you go and wait for the boat to arrive?"

Daniel agreed, turned and headed back to the jetty.

Kyle and Amy didn't need to be told that their place was with their charges. Ruth went with them to the hotel.

One Hundred and Thirteen

While Nathaniel was returning the minibus to the rental agency, Jack and Tony were at the flight desk asking if there was a flight leaving soon. Henry and Alan were just behind them, listening in, when they overheard two pilots as they walked past. They were talking about having to fly back to Cairns without any passengers.

Henry and Alan looked at each other and then turned to see the pilots and their flight crews heading towards the pilots' lounge.

"Excuse me," Alan called out, "did you say you were going to Cairns?"

The pilots had ignored Alan until he said Cairns. The whole flight crew stopped. The pilots turned to look at Alan.

Tony tapped Jack on the shoulder and nodded towards Alan and the pilots. Jack excused himself from the flight desk attendant before turning to watch.

The pilots walked back over to Alan. "We are returning to Cairns in about half an hour."

"Once we have had a quick bite and the birds are refuelled," added the other pilot.

Tony stepped forward to stand alongside Alan, looking a little confused. "But the flight desk doesn't have any passenger flights listed going out within that time."

"They wouldn't," said the first pilot. "We just landed here with a charter flight and would normally be returning empty."

"But if you wanted to tag along, for a fee of course, it could be arranged." the second pilot added. The fee would go straight into the pilots and crews pockets as the charter cost included their empty return flight.

"We left our bags at the... um... hotel," Tony said when Alan and Henry looked at him.

Jack stepped forward while reaching into his back pocket to retrieve his wallet, "Do you take Visa?" he asked.

ONE HUNDRED AND FOURTEEN

Itzal turned to Gabriel, "It shouldn't be too long now. Once the sun is fully set they will come out and test the areas where they have seen the portals."

"Are we prepared for it?" Gabriel asked.

Itzal nodded, "Yes, I have warriors all over town; the biggest force is with us here at the wharf."

"I would have thought the messenger would have been back by now," Gabriel observed.

"Kenaniah will return only when it is sealed," Itzal replied. "I picked him for that reason."

****

Meshach was watching his friends, Abednego and Shadrach, as they tried once more to place a seal on the portal. Kenaniah was watching patiently too, every now and then making suggestions.

"How have they fared?" Michael asked Kenaniah as they approached.

Kenaniah turned and bowed his head in greeting, "Not good, I am afraid."

"Just as I thought," replied Michael.

Shadrach and Abednego stopped to look at Michael.

"Why would you think that?" Shadrach asked.

"I believe it is part of the nature of this portal," Michael answered.

Everyone looked at Michael, waiting for him to give an explanation, but he didn't continue. Instead he asked, "What have you tried?"

Abednego turned to look at the portal and told Michael of the various ways they had tried to seal it: wiping his sword across it (which was the most common way of closing off a portal), trying to do the same with two swords, then three swords and finally with prayer.

"Prayer had appeared to work for a moment but suddenly stopped working and hasn't worked since," Shadrach added.

Michael just nodded. "That's okay for the moment," he said to them, "we have some other ideas that might work. But we also have a need to use the portal first."

Michael looked around and saw Starr and Shamira approaching. "Starr," Michael continued, turning to the cherubim, "can you guard the portal for a moment while I discuss with everyone else what we are planning?"

"Of course, Captain," Starr answered, and he moved forward to take Meshach's place.

Meshach made way for Starr and then joined Shadrach, Abednego and Kenaniah as they moved closer to Michael, Saint Peter and Uriel. Shamira went to Michael too – this was why Starr had brought her here after all.

****

All across Eden the demons were coming out and trying to determine which, if any, of the portals they had seen was the one they were looking for.

Itzal was pointing them out to Gabriel from their hiding place, when the portal flared before them. A small, usually insignificant demon, probably a 'little lies' or a 'biting', had snuck up the wharf, staying in the shadows caused by the setting sun, and activated it by accident, simply by being near it.

"THIS ONE!" it shrieked and then dissolved into a swirling mass with a sword sticking through it. The pop was so small from the demon's departure into the Abyss that it couldn't be heard over the sound of rushing air from the larger portal.

An angel stepped forward and tried to close the portal again, while others appeared around it, including Itzal.

"Sorry Itzal, he appeared from nowhere," the angel said, as he continued to try to close the glowing opening in time and space.

From somewhere in the darkened city they heard the demons calling each other. "Forces!"

Itzal replied quietly, "You did well to remove him as quick as you did. I should have expected a smaller demon and not one of the larger ones."

"Forces!" The call was getting louder.

"From the size of it, it must have been fairly new at its job," added Gabriel, as he appeared alongside Itzal.

"Or not very good at it yet," Itzal said in agreement.

"Forces!" a voice called out from very close.

"I think the time for hiding is past," Gabriel advised Itzal.

But before Itzal could call his troops from hiding, the demons struck. Itzal pointed at a messenger that was with him and yelled out one word: "Go!"

The messenger, Lori, had already been given her instructions and knew exactly what to do: rally the saints; get them praying; fetch the rest of the angels. She took off at once and dove under the water to get passed the demons.

Itzal had his sword, a Katana, in his hand and he was trying to use it as best he could within the tight confines in which he found himself. The demons were pressing in on every side and not enough angels were there.

The angels were all over the town, at all the places that they had tried to use as distractions. They had expected the demons to test each one and every time they got it wrong the angels were to then regroup at the next one; but because the demons had guessed the correct one so quickly it had left the angels spread too thin.

There were at least fifty demons attacking nine angels, who were trying valiantly to defend the open portal. The angels were overwhelmed and it wasn't long before a demon got through and disappeared into the portal.

****

On the other side of the portal, in the Garden of Eden, Starr suddenly called out. Michael, Saint Peter and all the angels with him turned at Starr's call.

The portal had become active.

"Kenaniah," Michael spoke quickly, "get Saint Peter away from here as quick as possible. Saint Peter, no arguments please, go with him and alert Jasper that we need reinforcements at the gateway. He will know why. Shadrach, gather the other angels and cherubim that are in the vicinity and be back here within two minutes. The rest of you, prepare yourselves!"

Saint Peter had never seen the angels actually in battle before and was suddenly awestruck as he saw them draw their weapons. All, that is, except Shadrach, who flew off so fast it seemed as if he had just disappeared. Kenaniah grabbed him and all he saw were rushing wings. Then he was back in heaven.

Saint Peter looked at Kenaniah, "Go to Zagzagel and say to him, 'They are in the Garden'."

Kenaniah looked at Saint Peter and was about to argue but then realised that something was going on about which Saint Peter knew more than he did.

"You will find him in with the messengers, in the Hall of the Word," Saint Peter called out, as he turned and started to make his way to the Hall of the Archangels as quickly as he could.

Shadrach had drawn his sword as he took flight. He flew a quick circle and called out to all he saw to follow him. The sword in his hands told them all they needed to know. The enemy had arrived!

Starr had stepped back a short distance while the rest of the angels and the cherubim had stepped forward. All they could hear was the rushing of air. Michael was wondering if he should send someone through when the demon came out.

The demon got the bigger surprise. To find he made it through only to be confronted by over a dozen angels, all with their weapons drawn, and more arriving by the second. Before it could decide what to do it had been pierced by three arrows, a dagger and a throwing star.

The weapons all fell to the ground as the demon dissolved into the Abyss.

As the angels stepped forward to retrieve their weapons Gabriel toppled through the portal with two demons in tow – one in his left hand and the other on his back.

Starr grabbed the one from Gabriel's back just as Gabriel stabbed the other in his hand. Gabriel looked up and saw Starr struggling for a moment, and then the demon started to dissolve. Meshach became visible through the dissolving demon, his sword sticking out of it. Then Gabriel saw everyone else behind them.

"The one that got through?" Gabriel asked, meaning the demon that had slipped passed him.

"Gone," replied Michael. "What's happening, Gabriel?"

"They found it quicker than we thought, Captain," Gabriel replied as he stood. "Either our ruse failed or they were very lucky in guessing which one to try first."

"Doesn't really matter now, does it?" Michael said. "Is help required out there?"

Gabriel nodded as he replied, "Definitely!"

Michael turned to Starr and the angels that were around him, at least twenty now and more coming, including four more cherubim.

"You know your duty to the Lord. Go, and protect the Throne! Glory to God on high!" Gabriel said, sending his troops into battle.

Uriel charged through the portal with the rest of the angels and cherubim right behind him.

As the cherubim reached him, Michael held out his hand for them to stop. "I need two of you to stay here and take care of any who get in," Michael said. Two of the cherubim stepped backwards. The others noticed this and nodded. "Thank you," Michael said to the two who had chosen to stay behind. "Let's go," Michael said finally and turned to pass through the portal.

The cherubim drew their flaming swords and flew through the portal behind Michael.

****

Itzal watched as Gabriel threw himself through the portal as two demons were attacking him. Before he could do anything, Itzal was set upon by three more demons. His Katana was flashing red in the eerie light that surrounded him, a combination of dissolving demons and their flashing orange eyes.

Itzal, however, was a master of this type of sword, and it was moving so fast in his hands that the enemy wasn't even getting a chance to block him. Add to that his darker clothes and it meant that they didn't always pick him for an angel either. This was just another indication to him of how dumb the enemy was. After all, even though he was dressed in black, he was still shining with God's glory.

Itzal had just fought his way back to the portal, when an angel he didn't expect, came out of it. Uriel shot out with his weapon, a great big battle axe, swinging. He was followed by another angel, this one with a longbow, and then another angel, this one with throwing stars in his hands and other martial arts weapons strapped to her body. Angel after angel appeared, warriors all, carrying their weapons of choice — swords, knives, bows, a crossbow and even a pike. Two cherubim, with their flaming swords drawn, had come through too. As Itzal smiled and turned back to the fight he saw more coming through.

It was the Captain with more cherubim. Itzal couldn't help but be in awe of his fellow heavenly warriors. He turned to block another attack and then was lost in the dance of the sword once again.

The fight went back and forth for only five minutes but it seemed like a lot longer to the combatants. Then the heavenly warriors all felt the Holy Spirit move and they fought on with a renewed sense of purpose. They knew that someone was praying nearby.

Then Lori returned with another three dozen angels from the fake portals all over town and the demons tried to flee. Only a handful succeeded and one of these was trying to hold himself together but slowly losing that battle too.

Itzal landed on the wharf and surveyed the angels and cherubim all around him. There were a few missing, some had minor injuries, cuts and bruises, and one was a lot more severe. As he watched, the angel dissolved and disappeared into a portal of his own.

Michael saw what Itzal was staring at and went over to him. "He has gone to heaven for healing. Was he a friend?"

Itzal looked at Michael and replied, "Yes, Captain, and a brave warrior too."

"How many did you lose?" Michael asked sympathetically.

"Five at least," Itzal answered. "Possibly more. I can't see them all, but at least five."

"Rest assured, they are in heaven too, being healed as we speak," Michael said to Itzal. "I can supply you with replacements right now if you like."

But as Michael turned to the rest of the warriors who were landing nearby, Itzal stopped him. "I don't want replacements, Captain. They fought bravely and should be allowed to return here to continue their duties in this community."

Michael nodded, "As you wish," he answered. "Consider these just temporary replacements then."

Itzal nodded and Michael moved away to organise the temporary replacements.

One of the angels who had been lying wounded nearby slowly rose to his feet. He was not glorified as he appeared to have been knocked out temporarily. He looked all around at the other angels nervously. No one was paying any special attention to him. He looked himself over quickly and then smiled a cunning smile. Quickly he replaced it with the look of someone who had just been injured.

Gabriel and Uriel were talking nearby and Gabriel indicated Itzal. Uriel turned to face him.

"Itzal," Uriel called to him, "Can I speak with you for a moment?"

Itzal started to move to them.

"Gabriel tells me your plans were sound and well executed. That your total preparation on this situation has been handled very well," Uriel said.

Itzal looked around and replied, "I disagree. I miscalculated and some of my troops have paid for it today."

Uriel shook his head, "On the contrary, you had every reason to expect the enemy to act one way and they didn't. I would have enacted the same plan and been caught off guard too. If we understood all there is to understand about our enemy then we would be one of them ourselves. So, do not think of this as your fault because it isn't. It was just a slight misjudgement on your part and you will do it differently next time."

Itzal thought for a moment and then nodded.

"If you are up for it," Uriel said, "I have a mission that I think you would be perfect for."

"What about my duties here?" Itzal asked.

Uriel indicated the messenger, Lori, who had rushed off to get the other angels and was now moving between everyone, checking that they were okay and helping those that were injured. "Would she be your second in command here?" he asked.

Lori approached the angel. He looked a little strange to her. She assumed that was because of the fight and that he hadn't been one of their own troops.

"Are you alright?" Lori asked the angel.

"Yes," he replied. "I think so."

"Why don't you follow the others back through the portal and rest in heaven for a while?" Lori suggested.

"Thanks," replied the angel. "That sounds perfect."

Lori moved on to another angel as Deception, disguised as an angel, moved towards the portal.

Itzal looked and saw Lori with an angel and then turned back to the archangels before him. "Yes, she is," he answered.

"Did you tell her to do what she is doing or does this come naturally to her?" Gabriel asked.

Itzal thought for a moment and then replied, "Naturally, I believe. She has a very good sense of leadership but lacks the confidence sometimes to carry out what she thinks needs to be done. However, when she acts without thought, it is always the right action. And everyone here trusts her judgement."

Gabriel looked at Uriel and Uriel nodded. Gabriel moved off towards Lori, leaving them alone.

Noting that Itzal was watching Gabriel, Uriel said, "Gabriel is going to talk to Lori and the Captain. Lori is going to be offered a promotion. She has shown she deserves it and... it will allow you to help us in our mission... if you wish to do so."

"What does it involve?" Itzal asked, starting to get interested.

"How much has Gabriel told you of this portal?" Uriel asked in reply.

"A little, but not all," Itzal answered guardedly.

"Do you know where it leads?" Uriel asked.

"Yes," Itzal answered.

"Come with me and I will tell you more about your task," Uriel said.

Itzal looked over at Lori and saw her speaking with Michael and Gabriel.

"We can wait for a moment if you like?" Uriel asked.

"Please," Itzal answered. "I would like to speak with her before we go."

"Let's join them then," Uriel said, and started to walk off with Itzal beside him.

As they approached they saw the Lamb appear.

"Lori, I think you are ready for this. Michael, Gabriel and Uriel all recommend you for this. How do you feel?" the Lamb said.

Lori bowed down before the Lamb, "I am ready, Lord."

Jesus nodded, "The Lord and I have spoken and He has told me to promote you, Lori, to guardian status and as such you will be the caretaker of this town, Eden."

The angels started to sing praises to God, giving thanks for His wisdom. Jesus helped Lori to her feet and then in a flash of light was gone once more.

Itzal stepped forward and congratulated Lori, "Congratulations, Lori. You deserve it. Many a time your wisdom has been greater than my own and your actions have preserved the Lord's kingdom in this town. Look after it and... watch out for that building committee," he said the last with a smile and a wink.

Lori looked a little embarrassed for a moment and then looked at Itzal and asked, "Are you not staying? I assumed that you would still be here too?"

"I have been asked to assist with a special mission," Itzal answered, indicating Uriel behind him.

Lori looked over at Uriel and then at the portal behind them and nodded. "It may seem too much but I am sure it is something that only you could achieve, my friend. When it is over you are welcome back here."

Itzal nodded and then noticed that the archangels and warriors were returning through the portal. Uriel was waiting for him. "Farewell and God bless," Itzal said, as he turned and headed for the portal.

"God bless," Lori replied.

One Hundred and Fifteen

Henry looked over at Alan and saw him looking out the plane's window. His body was rigid as if he was still tense about their captors. Henry stood and went and sat in the chair beside Alan.

"Hey," Henry said, as he put a hand on Alan's shoulder.

Alan jumped slightly but relaxed when he saw it was only Henry. "Hey," he replied, as he sat back in his seat.

"You can relax now, you know?" Henry said to his friend.

"Can I?" Alan asked in return. "I'm not sure that I will ever be able to relax again."

Henry looked at him for a moment and then spoke, "I may be only a builder but I think I know enough about the law to know that they have broken it. When we land, I am going straight to the cops to tell them all that has happened to me and what I saw... including George's death."

"But don't you realise that for a setup like this they probably own the cops?" Alan replied.

"Not all of them," Henry responded. "I go to one of the churches in Cairns on weekends and I have made friends with some of the locals who go too. One of them is a cop and I really believe I can trust him."

Alan looked doubtful still. "Are you sure about that?"

"It might sound naive but if someone tells me they believe in God, I believe them," Henry answered.

"Why? They could be lying just to appear good," Alan argued.

"I believe that one of the things a Christian can do is tell when someone is lying to them," Henry answered.

"You're not serious?" Alan asked.

"I sure am," Henry answered. "The Bible says that God will give us gifts of the Holy Spirit when we become one of his children and I know that 'discernment' is one of those gifts."

"You lost me there," Alan replied, looking a little confused.

"Let me see if I can help explain it better," Henry said. "When you become a Christian, a believer in God and Jesus, you accept that Jesus died for our sins. Through that act, we may get to know God in a personal relationship. As part of that relationship, God helps by giving us a part of His Holy Spirit. With me so far?"

"Yeah," Alan answered tentatively.

"Okay. Well, that gift comes with other gifts to help us. The Holy Spirit can help us in all sorts of ways and the most common is the ability to tell the difference between the truth and the lies that the devil makes up. Does that make sense?"

"Strangely it does," Alan replied.

"I believe I have that gift and so I can tell when someone is trying to pull a fast one on me," Henry stated.

"How did you end up in that building site then?" Alan asked.

"Same as you probably — I was contracted to it," Henry replied.

"Don't you disagree with building something like that?" Alan asked.

Henry thought about it for a moment before answering, "I do now but, before we started, I didn't know what we were building. I work for myself so that I can pick and choose jobs. Usually I end up with really good ones. I thought this was just going to be another hotel resort. Knowing what it is now, I think God had me there for a reason."

"Yeah, what was that?" Alan asked.

"To be able to meet and help you," Henry answered.

That left Alan speechless.

"Listen, Alan, I know you don't believe in God but I think that maybe you need to think about this," Henry said. "What we have just been through is pretty amazing and I cannot help but think that God helped us get out. Firstly, there's Jack and Tony over there — if they hadn't shown up when they did, I don't think we would have made it all the way out. Secondly, there's Jack's ability to see angels around us. Either he is on the level and we are heavenly protected or he is seriously crazy and we are all in trouble. Having said that, I feel completely safe around him, so I don't think he's crazy."

Alan looked thoughtful. "I know what you are saying and that is part of my problem I guess. You see, before I got on the bus back there, just outside the exhaust thingy we escaped out of, I think I saw one too."

Henry smiled a huge grin. "And..."

"Not only have I just made a dash for my life and my freedom but I have also had my belief system thrown into chaos," Alan replied. "I think I need a little time to digest it all."

"I understand that, completely," Henry said. "Just think on this then firstly, while you are so stressed you are not going to allow yourself to accept anything... different: if what you saw was real, then you have no reason to doubt Jack. If you have no reason to doubt Jack, then you can relax because we still have at least four angels with us."

"You know, I hadn't thought of it like that," Alan said. As he said it Henry saw a change in Alan and could tell he was starting to relax a little.

"That's it, relax. Try to enjoy the flight and once we land... then it will be payback time, God style!" Henry said, sitting back in his chair and smiling.

ONE HUNDRED AND SIXTEEN

Deception couldn't believe his luck. He had entered the portal with the rest of the angels and passed between the mighty cherubim who were guarding it on this side. He had managed to enter into the Garden of Eden as instructed. This was going better than he had expected.

"The Master will be pleased" he thought to himself.

Deception looked around and sniffed the air. It was just as he remembered it. As he moved forward with the rest of the angels he looked around and spotted his target.

One of the cherubim stopped Michael as he came through the portal. "No one got through, Captain, but something still doesn't feel right," he said.

Michael looked at the cherubim, the returning angels and then the Garden. "I don't know what it might be," he said. "Maybe it's just something in the air from our injured comrades. However, remain on alert until you find the threat or feel it has passed."

"Yes, Captain," replied the cherubim.

Deception moved away from the angels, towards his target, towards the tree. He did his best to look like he belonged here but it was difficult. His talent of deception had built a confidence in him allowing him to perfect his trickery. This, however, was the most important deception he had ever tried to pull.

He wasn't nervous about the disguise; he was confident that he could convince them of who he appeared to be – after all he had looked like this once, a very long time ago. However, having his sworn enemy all around him, in such large numbers, made it difficult to concentrate on his task and not attack them... especially when he saw Michael. Michael was the angel who had raised the alarm, who had caught Satan and uncovered his plot.

"Just think of the reward I would get if I returned and told him that I had destroyed his accuser?" he thought. "No," he reprimanded himself, "I have a more important task to carry out."

He looked up at the tree as he approached it. The Tree of Life stood tall before him, laden with its fruit.

Deception moved around it, studying it, looking for a branch that was within easy reach. A branch that had a piece of fruit on it that he could take hold of easily. It had to be smaller but still ready to be picked.

ONE HUNDRED AND SEVENTEEN

Mr Kepler was shaking in rage. A rage, he knew, that would give way to terror when he would speak to Mr Jenkins about this. There was only one consolation... Mr Jenkins was still in Sydney.

The deliverer of the bad news, one of the guards, was still standing there waiting for Mr Kepler's response. Isam walked in at that moment.

"You sent for me?" Isam asked a seated Mr Kepler.

Mr Kepler looked across his desk at Isam and then back at the guard. "Tell him what you just told me," Mr Kepler instructed.

The guard swallowed before speaking, "We think they got away in a bus. We sent a small team out in a four-wheel drive to cover the road at checkpoint alpha. But before it got to the checkpoint it just stopped dead in the middle of the road. We have a mechanic checking it now for an explanation."

"Has another team gone out in its place?" Isam asked.

"The team proceeded on foot to carry out their orders," the guard replied and then appeared to hesitate.

"Is that all?" Isam asked having noticed the hesitation. "Or is there more?"

The guard swallowed again, visibly concerned, and then went on, "They thought they saw a minibus of some sort driving away from them just as they were stopped. We sent the helicopter straight out as it would catch up quicker."

"Good thinking," Isam said, as he was turning to face Mr Kepler.

Mr Kepler spoke before he could say anything else, "Get on with it man, tell him what happened next."

Isam turned once again to the guard with his eyebrows raised, questioningly.

"The helicopter crashed," the guard said. "No one was seriously hurt."

"Hurt!" Mr Kepler erupted. "HURT! I don't *care* about that! They got away! And they had help of some sort!"

Isam was looking a bit confused and was looking from the guard to Mr Kepler and back.

"Can you tell me what happened?" Isam asked the guard quietly, gesturing to Mr Kepler to be quiet so that he could hear what the guard was saying.

The guard was starting to shake now too, visibly afraid of what Mr Kepler was going to do, but he kept his head enough to repeat what he knew to Isam. "Some sort of updraft, they reported, caused the helicopter to go out of control. They managed to regain control and get the helicopter level again, but it was too late to stop the descent. They described it as a very rough landing but some of the engine parts were damaged. This all happened after they had made visible contact with the bus and had fired some warning shots to get it to stop."

Isam stood there in thought for a moment, rubbing his chin. He stopped to ask the guard, "Anything else?"

The guard shook his head and then tried to stand to attention.

"You have done well..."

"What!" Mr Kepler exploded again.

Isam shot Mr Kepler a look that said he was to be quiet.

Mr Kepler threw his arms in the air and turned away.

Isam turned back to the guard, "You are a brave warrior to come here and report this. You should be rewarded for your bravery. Return to your post and wait for me there."

The guard bowed with a look of relief on his face and then quickly left before someone changed their minds.

Isam turned to Mr Kepler after the guard had departed and asked, "Bad luck? Or coincidence? You obviously do not think so."

Mr Kepler ignored the question and indicated the empty doorway, "What was that about?" he asked, with a bit of venom in his tone.

"He was shaking in fear, terrified, obviously from your reaction to his report," answered Isam. "Your way, the next time he would send someone else rather than face your wrath again. This way, I reinforced his ego and encouraged him. This will have a better result on his moral. He will now be thinking more about the compliment I gave him and the reward he will receive; next time he has a report to deliver it will be just as informative, maybe more so. He will make sure he has all the facts and he will probably come to me first."

"Which he should have done anyway!" Mr Kepler spat. Then he calmed down a little. "What sort of reward?"

"I'll give him a three-day leave," Isam answered, as he sat in a chair opposite Mr Kepler's. "Are you going to answer my question?"

"It's obvious, isn't it?" Mr Kepler answered. "They had help."

"But that wasn't mentioned in the guard's report," Isam replied.

"It must have been that bad spirit you felt earlier. The masters warned you of it, didn't they?" Mr Kepler asked.

Isam nodded but kept his mouth shut.

"Damn!" Mr Kepler swore. "If only I hadn't agreed with that doctor and removed the guards!"

Isam nodded again. "What are we going to do? Shut everything down and get them all out? Board up the entrances so it looks like solid walls?"

"I'll leave that decision up to Jenkins," Mr Kepler said quietly.

"He isn't going to like it," Isam pointed out.

"I know," Mr Kepler answered, as he reached for the phone. "There's no point putting it off. If we have to shut down and get out then it is better to have as much time to do it as we can."

One Hundred and Eighteen

Israfel and his team were starting to get a little restless. They had been wandering around their meeting place for too long. If any demons had been taking notice then they would surely raise the alarm about this group hanging around the sandstone domes.

Micah was about to mention this to Israfel when they heard someone approaching. Israfel indicated to everyone to follow him. He stood and turned to head up the path back to the car park.

As they turned the first bend they walked straight into Titus. Israfel recognised him immediately.

"Glory to the living God!" Titus said in greeting.

"And to the risen Lamb!" replied the group.

Titus bowed slightly and spoke as the rest of the team stoped and gathered around them, "Israfel, Michael asked me to return and advise you of the latest information."

Israfel and the team listened intently and when Titus had finished, they were all looking excited and a little renewed, eager for this plan to unfold.

"I am going to need to get my sword back," Israfel commented, to no one in particular.

Micah nodded in agreement, "I think I have an idea about that." Micah then explained his plan to retrieve Israfel's sword.

There were many nods around the group and a few smiles too.

"Bold," Israfel commented, "but simple. I like it."

There were more nods.

"Okay then, let's split into two groups and give it a go," Israfel said. "Titus, you come with me while the rest of you go with Micah."

"We'll go and get started and meet you back at the hotel," Micah said, and then turned and left, with his fellow angels following him.

Israfel and Titus waited for a few moments and then followed them. After a little while they came to a junction in the path and turned to the left. They could see the others ahead of them still, on the right-hand path.

Another ten minutes later Israfel and Titus emerged into a car park. They looked around quickly and spotted a four-wheel drive that looked similar to the one that Israfel had disabled earlier. Israfel placed his hands on it and bowed his head in prayer. After he had finished the two of them just stood there, waiting for the owners to return.

It wasn't long before the owners of the vehicle returned to it and checked it over quickly. Israfel smiled, his simple prayer had worked. This plan had God's favour.

The humans climbed into their four-wheel drive to return to their accommodations for the night. Israfel climbed into the back seat too. As the driver turned the key to start the engine, Titus drew his sword. After the engine caught he waited for the driver to place the vehicle in gear and then he plunged his sword into the engine.

The engine died immediately.

The driver, a retired accountant, turned the key again, thinking he had stalled it or something, but it wouldn't start now.

"You need to call for the tow truck," Israfel said from the back seat.

"I think we may need a tow," the female passenger said.

The driver looked at her as if she was from another planet. "I haven't even checked under the hood yet," he said in exasperation.

Titus climbed into the back seat alongside Israfel as the driver lifted the bonnet and had a poke around.

"What are you doing? You don't know anything about cars except how to drive them and fill them with petrol!" said the female passenger, the driver's wife, hanging out the window. "Can you get back in here and turn the air con back on please? I'll call the hotel to get them to send their mechanic out."

The husband nodded as he closed the bonnet again, grumbling under his breath. He climbed back in and replaced the keys in the ignition. He turned the key to allow the air conditioner to come on. The wife had her mobile phone out and was talking to the concierge from the nearby hotel.

Micah and his team had continued on the path until they came out at the resort with the unfinished hotel beside it. They then took up positions in and around it, and waited. Micah went inside and stood with the concierge. When the phone rang he made sure the concierge picked it up.

As she hung up she told her husband that the mechanic was going to be there in fifteen minutes. "Second call out today, he told me," she said to her husband.

Israfel and Titus just looked at each other and smiled. "So far so good," they thought.

Micah watched as the concierge then placed a call to the service station that was just a short way down the road. It was walking distance really, but he couldn't leave his post at the moment — everyone was returning to the hotel for dinner.

Once the concierge had finished organising with the mechanic to pick up the stranded tourists and their broken down four-wheel drive, he hung up and went back to greeting the guests as they came through the door.

Micah, however, went the other direction and walked back out the door and down the path to the outdoor café. He sat down and waited. He didn't have to wait that long: the mechanic was already driving off down the short road to the tourist car park. Ten minutes later the tow truck came back into sight with the four-wheel drive hanging off the back and four extra passengers squeezing into the truck's cabin.

As the truck reversed into the little garage, Micah watched as one of his fellow angels appeared across the road, bright as day and flying straight up into the air, sword drawn. Out of nowhere fifteen to twenty demons appeared and took off after the angel.

The truck stopped and everyone climbed out. The mechanic started to lower the four-wheel drive beside another one that had come in earlier that day.

Two more angels took off and another thirty demons followed.

The retired accountant and his wife were looking at the other four-wheel drive and asking the mechanic questions. Israfel wandered over to the other four-wheel drive too and bent over to look under the lifted bonnet. Titus was standing with the mechanic and looked to be listening intently.

Another angel took off, it was closer to Micah this time and he heard it call out "Battle" as he flew off. Micah just shook his head and smiled. He knew that it was Duncan. Years ago Duncan had seen a movie about an angel and, ever since, he always called that out when he was going into a fight or trying to distract the enemy.

Micah turned back to Israfel and saw him remove the sword from the engine he had been looking at. As he did Titus also removed his sword. They both quickly put them in their sheaths and walked away.

The demons were all looking the other way, watching to see if another angel was going to jump out and had not seen them at all.

Micah nodded. It had worked. He had been ready to fly off next but he wasn't needed. Now they only had to wait for everyone to return, but that was okay. The other plan wasn't due to be activated for a while and they needed to wait for more angels to arrive to back them up.

As Israfel and Titus sat down with him they heard the engine of the four-wheel drive start. They looked over to see the accountant and his wife smiling and the mechanic scratching his head in confusion.

One Hundred and Nineteen

Deception checked his surroundings once more. It appeared that everyone had returned through the portal and only the two cherubim were still there guarding it. No one was watching him. All he had to do was reach up, pluck one piece of fruit and get back out through the portal.

It didn't sound so hard… but there was one thing that he could not predict. What would happen to the tree? Would an alarm go off? There was no way of knowing until he did it.

Deception reached up and grabbed hold of his chosen piece of fruit. He couldn't risk being seen doing this so he moved as quickly as he could and plucked the apple-sized fruit and put it under his shirt, in his arm pit.

No alarms went off.

As quickly as he could, without raising suspicion, Deception moved away. Now all he had to do was find a way back through the portal without the cherubim stopping him.

What Deception didn't see as he moved away, was the tree did react to losing the piece of fruit. It wasn't much at first, just a single leaf dropped. Within an hour there would be many leaves and even some fruit lying on the ground under the tree.

One Hundred and Twenty

It had been hours since he had left the resort and he had been sitting here watching it for at least two hours. He had seen the humans return with the camera but he hadn't followed them. Highrise couldn't put his taloned finger on it but he knew something wasn't right. Had he been followed? Or was someone here waiting for him? Or was he being paranoid?

He couldn't help but think back to the sight of Pandora with a sword through her. Then she was gone. "Gone! What happened out there?" He wondered out loud and then got angry with himself for giving himself away to anyone who might be watching and waiting for someone like him.

Evangelos sat very still and waited. What was this demon doing? Did he know that they were there? Was he waiting for reinforcements too? It didn't matter either way. He, and his troops, had to sit and wait for the signal from Michael or the call to action from the Spirit.

Then he heard the demon speak. "Gone! What happened out there?" it said.

Evangelos looked at the angel, Dizzy, who was with him, only to see the same sort of confusion reflected back at him in Dizzy's eyes.

"What is he talking about?" Dizzy signed to Evangelos.

Evangelos shrugged; the universal symbol for 'I don't know'. "Maybe he saw the battle out there and got away from it?" Evangelos signed back. "It is handy," he thought to himself, "to be able to use sign language to communicate when they didn't want to give themselves away."

Dizzy thought back to what the demon had said. "That makes sense," he signed to Evangelos.

"So he is now paranoid? Stressed out?" Evangelos signed.

"And he doesn't want to return to his den?" Dizzy signed back.

"Let's not spook him but somehow help him on his way," signed Evangelos.

Dizzy looked towards where he knew the demon was. "How?"

But before Evangelos could suggest something the demon moved.

Highrise was suddenly satisfied that there was nothing to worry about and stood up, unfurled his leathery wings and took to the air. From below he looked like a giant bat as he passed through the rain forest.

"That was easy," Dizzy signed, "How did you do it?" he asked.

Evangelos looked at Dizzy's eyes and, seeing the humour there, he smiled.

"It's a secret," he signed back. "Seriously though, I bet he is in for a hard time when he returns alone and tells of the battle he saw."

Dizzy nodded his agreement.

Highrise was thinking the same thing too. He was ushered straight in to see Lucas.

"Highrise!" Lucas said from his makeshift throne in the ballroom of the hotel. "Where have you been?"

Highrise bowed before he answered. "I was waiting in the forest until I was completely sure I was not followed."

Lucas blinked a couple of times before he responded. "Followed? Explain!"

Highrise took a deep breath. "I went out to the boat but before I got too close I could see that the fight had begun. But it was not going the way we thought it would. From where I stopped, I saw Pandora in trouble but before I could try to assist her... she was pierced."

Lucas's left eyebrow rose, "Really?" he said.

Highrise nodded, "Our enemy used a tactic that I have not seen for a very long time and it wasn't them that used it back then. I think it was Alexander –"

"You're getting off the topic!" Lucas interrupted.

"Right," Highrise replied, "sorry."

"What did they do?" Lucas asked.

"A ring of archers cut down anyone trying to leave," Highrise answered.

Lucas's jaw dropped in shock. "Did you see anyone else get away?" he asked eventually.

"No," answered Highrise. "That is why I thought I'd better not come straight back but stop to see if I was followed."

Lucas thought for a moment before he spoke again, "Understandable and very good tactics."

Highrise bowed again thinking he had been dismissed but when he turned to go he was stopped by a sudden pain in his left shoulder. He fell to his knees as he tried to reach the dagger that was sticking out of it. He looked over his shoulder at it. Then movement caught his eye and he looked up to see Lucas standing over him with his wicked-looking scimitar in his hand.

Lucas poked Highrise with the barbed tip. He bent over and took hold of his dagger and as he pulled it out he pushed with the sword. The dagger came free easily and the sword imbedded itself slightly into

Highrise's spine. "Coward," he said and then jerked his sword to the right, the barbs grabbing Highrise's skin and clothes.

Highrise couldn't help but cry out. Then he rolled with it slightly, somersaulting and ending up on his feet with his sword in his hand. Before he could do anything else, Lucas was moving in on him, swinging his sword as he came.

The barbed tip passed across Highrise's neck. He managed to lean backwards but not far enough to avoid getting cut. The barbs connected and tore a hole in Highrise's throat.

It was not flesh as we know it that now clung to the barbs on the end of Lucas's sword, but something akin to it in the spiritual matter. Whatever you would call it, now that it was missing from Highrise, it meant that his spiritual shell had been ruptured and without the outer cover to contain it, his internal essence started to escape.

This essence cannot exist on this plane, not even in the spiritual sense, and so a portal opened. A small wormhole of sorts, that is linked with another realm, one known as the Abyss, a giant tunnel leading straight to Hell.

Hell is the place of imprisonment for those who cannot enter heaven. Those fallen angels whose deeds were so bad that they were not allowed to enter Earth and the demons, the angels that refused God's mercy after the Battle for the Throne, all end up here. If they fall in battle with an angel, then they arrive sooner, but eventually all the demons will receive their punishment and end up here. The entrance tunnel, the Abyss, is lined with fallen demons who are struggling to get back out, clawing their way slowly back to the top.

It is said that in the spiritual plane, Heaven and Hell are the only places that you can exist in. The only way into Heaven is by accepting Jesus's invitation. If you refuse him or refuse to believe in him, then the only other place you can go to is Hell. Eventually, everyone will come to this place, even human souls, and purely by the one simple choice you made in the previous existence. No matter how many times you have had it presented to you, your destination here is determined by that choice. Continually reject him and you will be rejected here; say yes, choose to live the life that Jesus shows you, and you will receive the right to enter Heaven.

This, of course, was the very dilemma that Highrise now found himself in. He dropped his sword and clung to his neck to try to stem the flow of the escaping essence. He already had a slow leak in his shoulder but that was something that could be repaired; this new hole was much larger. He sank to his knees as he was struggling to keep himself together and this sight made Lucas laugh.

Highrise looked up at Lucas laughing at him and one thought flashed through his mind, "Take him too." He looked around quickly and spotted his sword only a short way from where he was kneeling. The portal was growing around him but he wasn't ready to give in to it yet. He looked back up at Lucas and saw him watching him with a smile playing at his lips.

Highrise rolled to the side and reached for the sword. He scooped it up cleanly and rose to his feet to strike, but it was too late. He had released the wound in his neck, allowing the essence to pour out, and his roll had inadvertently caused the hole to widen. The portal grew and the sound of rushing air increased. Highrise teetered as he tried to get his arms to act.

Lucas watched as the form of Highrise lost all shape and the sword dropped to the floor. The black mist that was once Highrise spun and disappeared into the centre of the vortex and then, with a loud 'POP', it was over. The portal had closed.

Lucas turned to those present in the room, the rest of his advisors, the ones that Cain had left behind.

"That is how I deal with cowardice," Lucas said. "Learn from Highrise's lesson and do not allow it to become your own. He should have dived into the fight and tried to take as many of our enemy with him as he could. Who knows, maybe then Pandora would have survived and we would have our hands on that film too! Not just the camera."

"Now go, find them again and someone get me that FILM!" Lucas ordered, and all of the advisors turned and left as quickly as they could go.

When he was alone once more, Lucas dropped unceremoniously onto his throne. "This is not going well," he said to himself.

In fact, it was getting worse than Lucas thought. Throughout the afternoon, angels had slowly been arriving in the rainforest. First to arrive were the warriors from heaven, who had been in the battle out at sea and had veered back into Cairns, gradually making their way up the coast and into the national park. They were followed by those that had joined the battle from Cairns and other nearby towns, as well as guardians of churchgoers. Some had accompanied tour busses, some had snuck in under cars, some had crossed over the river on the ferry disguised as holidaying backpackers and some had simply walked in. However they managed it, Evangelos had counted nearly fifty more angels reporting to him as they arrived.

It wasn't only here that the build-up of angelic forces was occurring: across the globe at all the locations Michael's groups were staking out, more and more angels were arriving to assist in the big plan.

ONE HUNDRED AND TWENTY ONE

Something was happening in the Garden of Eden. Michael and his friends hadn't gotten far before being called back to the Garden. Michael was directed towards the Tree of Life and a group standing close by it. As he approached Michael looked at the group near the tree and noticed that one of the cherubim guards was amongst them.

As he got closer he could see what they were staring at. The Tree of Life looked sick. Michael had never known the tree to shed its leaves or drop its fruit but here it was, surrounded by leaves and fruit on the ground.

Michael approached the cherubim, "What is happening here?" he asked.

"We don't know. We found it like this only a moment ago and sent for you," he replied. "We also sent someone to consult the Lord."

"Good thinking," Michael replied.

They all waited there, not knowing what to do about the tree. Maybe the Lord would know what is wrong.

A short distance away, Deception approached the now lone cherubim, Noah, who was guarding the portal. "Do you know what is happening over there?" he asked.

"Something about the tree being sick," Noah replied.

"Sick? How could such a thing be?" the disguised Deception asked.

Noah turned to face the tree, "I don't know," he answered.

They stood there in silence for a moment, during which time Deception slowly walked backwards, watching Noah's head to see if he noticed his movement.

The next thing Noah knew, there was a flash of light, the sound of rushing wind. He knew it was the portal so he drew his sword as he turned to face whoever had activated it again. But there was no one there. Not even the angel he had been talking too.

On the other side of the portal, Deception was met by another angel, one of the local guards. The guard reacted when Deception came through but stopped when he saw it was another angel.

"I have an urgent message to deliver and the Captain told me to use the portal," Deception lied.

The angel nodded and Deception moved off as quickly as he could on foot.

Michael ran over to Noah, "Who activated the portal?" he asked, as he arrived with his sword drawn.

Uriel and the others followed, quickly drawing their weapons too.

"I don't know," Noah answered. "I think it was another angel. We were talking about the tree and then he was gone and the portal was open."

"I'm going through," Michael said.

"No," Itzal replied. "I will. If you go, anyone watching on the other side will know it leads to either here or Heaven itself. If I go, they will not suspect anything like that, as they have seen me before."

Michael thought about it for a moment and then nodded his agreement. "Be quick. Check with the guard on the other side whether someone came through from this side and, if so, ask where he went."

Itzal nodded once and then stepped through the portal.

Michael turned back to look at the tree and then at the portal.

Uriel followed Michael's gaze. Picking up on what Michael was thinking, he asked, "You believe they are connected?"

Michael nodded and looked momentarily sideways at Uriel. "It's too much of a coincidence," he said, and then looked back at the tree, "and I don't believe in coincidences."

"An angel did go through," Itzal said, as he reappeared next to them. "He said you sent him through with an urgent message and then he headed off into the town."

"I think our security was breached," Michael stated. He turned to Noah, "No one uses this portal unless they give the required greeting, going in or out."

Noah nodded as he replied, "Yes, my Captain."

"Captain," Gabriel interrupted, "the tree!"

Michael looked over and saw that Jasper had arrived and had started to dig the tree up.

Michael hurried up to the tree and called out, "Stop what you are doing!"

The angels who were digging stopped and looked up at Michael. Jasper waved at them to continue as he stepped over to Michael. Placing his hand on Michael's shoulder he steered him away slightly.

"Sorry I could not speak with you beforehand but you were busy," Jasper said.

"What is going on here, Jasper?" Michael asked.

"It was Saint Peter's idea," Jasper replied. "If this is what the demons are after, why leave it here? He suggested moving it to Heaven, to be closer to God, where it would have better protection. The Lord agreed and called me."

"What did the Lord tell you, exactly?" Michael asked.

"The Lord said that if it could be done, then do it," Jasper replied. "We are doing quite well so far. Some more of the fruit has fallen off, but we decided to leave it where it fell as there is plenty on the tree."

Michael was dumbfounded and couldn't speak for a moment. When he did it was to ask another question, "Saint Peter came up with this?"

"Yes," Jasper answered and, guessing what Michael would ask next, he added, "Saint Peter is still in Heaven, trying to find a suitable location to replant the tree."

"I think I shall speak with him," Michael said, and walked away.

The others rushed to catch up.

"Well?" Gabriel asked.

Michael quickly repeated his conversation with Jasper and then asked the warriors to wait as they had earlier; Meshach, Abednego and Shadrach were to remain at the portal.

"What about me?" Itzal asked.

"Come with us," Michael replied, as he reached the gate to Heaven.

This really wasn't a gate but more a gateway. That is to say, it was actually a portal and one that was semi-active all the time.

Michael sang a worship song to the Lord, and it opened for him. This was added security in case the demons made it this far. The chance of them singing a worship song to God was infinitesimal.

On passing through the gateway they came face to face with Zagzagel – an armed Zagzagel with a small contingent of warriors who were similarly armed.

"Captain!" Zagzagel cried out with joy. Then he stopped when he saw that there were only four of them, two archangels and one strangely dressed angel.

"And what are you doing here?" Michael asked, as he was surprised to see him.

"Guarding the gateway," was the reply.

"Obviously," Michael said. "But wouldn't it be better to do that from the other side?"

"No, Captain," replied Zagzagel. "We have the element of surprise on our hands here. Your faces just now showed us that we achieved our goal."

"What about the protection on the gate itself?" Michael asked.

Zagzagel stopped to consider that for a moment. Hesitatingly, he asked, "Do you mean the worship song?"

"Exactly!" Michael replied.

"I had a report that some of the preventions were down," Zagzagel replied. "Some sort of spiritual interference."

"Really?" Michael replied, thinking back to the sickness of the tree and the sudden opening of the portal. "The song worked just now. Anyway, there are so many angels in the Garden of Eden right now that I don't think you need to stay here any longer."

Zagzagel nodded and looked a little crestfallen.

Michael smiled to himself. "Why don't you come with us," he asked.

Zagzagel's eyes brightened. "Very well, Captain," he said.

Michael noticed that there were quite a few other angels starting to appear around the place, some with weapons ready and others just drawn by their curiosity. He turned back to Zagzagel and asked quietly, "How many know why you are here?"

"Just these ones with me," he said turning around and indicating the seven angels directly behind him.

Michael waved them all closer, "I need you to go into the Lord's garden and report to Jasper. Tell him I sent you to help him, even if it is only to help guard the Tree of Life."

The angels nodded and disappeared into the gateway.

Michael turned back to Zagzagel and asked him another question, "Do you know where I can find Saint Peter?"

"The last I saw him, he was with Kenaniah over near the Throne."

One Hundred and Twenty Two

As the bus neared its destination, Cain was paying more and more attention to what he saw out the window. The enemy was out there. They had to be here by now, surely. He had given them enough information to lead them here, hadn't he?

Cain sat back in his chair; he continued to look out the window but thought about all the events that he had put in motion up to now. "I hired Henry, even though I knew he had an angelic escort. That didn't go down well but he wasn't the only worker with one and the other demons managed to keep him subdued enough. Then I managed to get that *angel*," he thought, with such hatred that he couldn't help the sneer that crossed his face, "to convince Henry to call a friend; a Christian reporter friend. That wasn't easy either. I let Henry find some information that would be contrary to his beliefs. That information was not supposed to be left lying around for the construction workers to find. But it worked and he made the call.

"I knew that the phone call would be monitored and recorded, and I immediately brought it to Grom's attention. I suggested that Grom send him to the slave camp. Then, when his friend showed up and it got reported to Porva, all I had to do was blame it on Grom and suggest he be sent there too. I knew what would happen to him out there... here," he thought, as he realised they were almost there. "After that, I just left it up to the enemy to follow the tracks. They should be here by now. I will have to be very careful about where I go and how long I am here."

Cain continued to look out the window as the bus started to slow down and turn into the unfinished hotel's parking area.

The angels were, in fact, watching, just as Cain thought. But Cain didn't realise the extent of what had already happened here or what they had planned.

Israfel, Micah and Titus were watching from the other hotel's coffee shop, where they were still seated. From here they had a poor view of the other hotel but it was enough to see the quantity of demons that were with the bus. That convinced them that they were going to need more warriors to pull off what they had planned.

The other four angels thought the same thing from their various hiding places. After they had succeeded with their diversions they had returned once again by hiding amongst the non-stop stream of tourists that visited this attraction.

Unbeknown to Israfel and his team, the added warriors had already started to arrive, and this influx of tourists was a great distraction. They were coming in the tourist buses, the back seats of cars and on the back of motorbikes. Not all at once but a couple here, one there, then none for an hour, then six in that bus and another one on that motorbike. Over the next two hours, nearly two dozen would arrive like this. By then, they would have to stop arriving as the sun would be starting to set. Hardly any humans would be arriving after sunset, in fact, not again until morning.

One Hundred and Twenty Three

As Michael walked towards the Throne he realised that there were a lot of angels heading for the edge and disappearing off towards Earth. Uriel noticed Michael looking around at the activity and realised that he hadn't told Michael of this yet.

"Captain," Uriel said, stepping a little quicker to get alongside Michael, "I meant to tell you earlier that I have started to implement the plan we spoke of."

Michael looked at Uriel and asked, "Is that why there are so many warriors heading for Earth?"

Uriel nodded and answered, "Yes. Most are heading to assist with the stations we have set up and a few are heading for the location I picked for the battle. I have told them that they are to follow their instincts and the leading of the Spirit for any last-minute changes."

Michael nodded his approval, "A wise thing to do my friend. Did the Lord approve it all as well?"

"Yes," answered Uriel. "I think I even saw Him smile, but I may have imagined that. He was pleased about it and did say that we needed to watch over the human that will be there too."

"A human will be there too?" Michael asked surprised.

"Yes," Uriel answered. "I asked the Lord who he meant and he just told me to prepare someone to be there with him."

"Is that why Itzal is here?" Michael asked.

Uriel nodded. "I will fill him in shortly about it."

At that moment they came around the corner and saw Saint Peter and Kenaniah just outside the Throne. They were almost in the middle between the Hall of the Chronicles, the Hall of Worship, the Throne and the Hall of the Archangels. As they approached they could hear Kenaniah singing.

Kenaniah stopped singing, pointed at the ground and said, "Here."

Saint Peter looked down and using a small hand tool, tried to mark the place Kenaniah indicated.

"May I ask what you are doing?" Michael asked as he stopped a few feet away.

Saint Peter turned and smiled at Michael, "You're back!"

Michael smiled too. "Yes, we are. Is this where you want to replant the Tree of Life?" he asked indicating the mark on the ground that Saint Peter had made.

"It is. So you have heard about that?" Saint Peter asked.

"Yes, and I am a little surprised that the Lord has given His approval on it," Michael replied.

"To be honest, so was I," Saint Peter commented.

"Is that your answer to this threat then?" Michael asked.

"Part of it," Saint Peter answered. "When you told me about the Devil wanting to take away the need of the Saviour, by giving everyone eternal life by eating the fruit, I thought to myself, 'What if the tree wasn't there? Then he couldn't give away the fruit.' It seemed simple to me at the time."

Michael nodded in understanding. "That makes sense. But I don't think that will be enough. They can still use The Garden to try to access Heaven."

"But will your planned ambush not put an end to that?" Saint Peter asked.

"It will for the moment," Michael answered. "But I am not convinced that they will not try again."

Gabriel looked at Michael and jumped into the conversation, "Captain, we cannot plan for everything that the enemy might try."

Uriel took Gabriel's lead and added, "As a studier of the human militaries, I can tell you that almost every time one tries to predict what their enemy will do and prepare for it, the enemy ends up doing something unexpected and the preparations were all for nought. I am not saying that we shouldn't aim to keep our enemy out of the Lord's Garden, but that attempting to put some sort of eternal seal on the entrances will only convince them that they should keep trying to get in."

Michael listened intently to Uriel and Gabriel and realised the wisdom in what they were saying. "You are correct, of course, and only the Lord knows what they will do in the future. Very well, let's not dwell on that but instead concentrate on stopping them. We may even set them back a little with the ambush. Then we may have some breathing space for a little while."

"Amen to that," Kenaniah said from behind Saint Peter, "and here is the Tree of Life."

Itzal and Uriel stepped aside one way while Michael and Gabriel stepped over to stand with Saint Peter and Kenaniah.

Jasper stepped up to the mark on the ground. Bending down, he scraped his fingers across the surface so that the ground was disturbed. He then stood aside as a group of warriors stepped up with the tree between them. It was quite a sight, the warriors who had been digging up the tree were at the bottom with the trunk and roots, and the guards that Michael had sent in only a short while ago were in the air, holding on to the higher branches. Jasper directed them to the spot and as they put it down, he bent to place the roots on the disturbed ground.

The tree immediately dug its roots in and appeared to grab hold. As they watched, it started to pull itself into the ground. Bit by bit, the roots moved a little deeper and deeper. This went on for almost five minutes, until the roots were completely covered.

Saint Peter looked up, astonishment all over his face.

"That is why it took so long to get it here," Jasper said to him. "Every time we uncovered a root it buried itself again."

"Amazing," Saint Peter said.

Kenaniah started to sing and everyone there joined in a hymn of praise for the Creator. Michael then noticed that Uriel and Itzal had wandered a short distance away, probably so Uriel could tell Itzal what he was to do.

As the tree went passed them, Uriel had indicated to Itzal to follow him. They walked a short distance away from the planting area so that they could speak quietly together.

Uriel repeated to Itzal what he had told Michael.

"You want me to find this human that the Lord mentioned and try to protect him?" Itzal asked.

"Precisely," answered Uriel.

"But you don't know who he is?" Itzal asked.

Uriel shook his head as he answered, "Not exactly, but I have an idea."

"Who?"

"A human has been found who can see us. I think this is going to draw him to the fight and that will put him in danger with all of us swinging our weapons around in battle," Uriel explained.

Itzal nodded, "That does make sense. Where will I find him or would it be better to go to the proposed scene and wait there for him to show up?"

"From what I understand, he does have a guardian with him so you will not need to find him now. I think the latter is, therefore, the better option," Uriel answered.

"When do you want me to leave?" Itzal asked.

"The rest of the warriors are waiting for Michael to address them," Uriel replied. "You might as well wait for them. We will be heading over there shortly so stay with us for now."

"Ready?" Michael asked from behind them.

Uriel turned around and saw Michael, Saint Peter, Gabriel, Zagzagel, Jasper, Kenaniah and all the warriors who had carried the tree standing there. "Yes," he replied.

"Let's go then," Michael said, and started off for the Hall where the warriors and Nicole would be waiting.

One Hundred and Twenty Four

Raphael was watching the developing of the photos with little interest until the man picked up the film that Kerri had left with him. Raphael immediately moved to stand alongside the man and he drew his sword. He held the sword up in front of the man's eyes. If this had been a physical sword the man wouldn't have been able to see at all, but because it was a spiritual sword it only blocked his vision from seeing certain things. The man could see exactly what he was doing but he couldn't see the content of these photographs. To him they were all ruined, overexposed.

Raphael, however, could see exactly what the photos had captured. As the man processed them, Raphael had a quick look at them and several times his eyebrows rose in surprise.

At the same time, a boat pulled into the bay and set anchor. Two men climbed out of it and into the small dinghy. They slowly motored up to the jetty, climbed out and docked the small boat for the night.

Daniel watched all of this with interest and greeted the angels that were with him. "Hello again Jade and Pia" he said.

Pia waved and said, "Hi."

"Hi Daniel," Jade said, as she stopped before him. Then she introduced the other two angels that he hadn't met before, "This is Ishmerai and Amna. They are the guardians of these humans," she indicated Max and Tim.

"Welcome," Daniel said, as he bowed his head slightly. "They are in the hotel but we were not expecting any of you until tomorrow."

They turned and followed Tim and Max, who hadn't stopped.

"We thought we would get here early," Pia said.

"We heard there was trouble on the water today. It was a good opportunity for us to get away while there was some confusion at the wharves," Amna added.

At the mention of the 'trouble on the water' there was a brief smile on Daniel's face.

"Do you know something about that?" Jade asked, having picked up on the smile.

"Let's just say that the evil one lost quite a few of his soldiers today," Daniel answered.

"Were the humans all okay?" Ishmerai asked almost immediately.

"Yes," Daniel answered. "Kerri was injured but it was not very serious at all. As for the rest of us, there were only a couple of injuries and none of them required any heavenly visits."

"Impressive," Jade said.

"A new strategy was implemented to prevent their escape but I would suggest, from the quantity of angels that we had in the fight, that there was a lot of praying saints involved too," Daniel replied.

From there the angels fell silent as they followed the two men up to the hotel.

ONE HUNDRED AND TWENTY FIVE

The rest of their flight had been in silence. Every person on the plane had their own thoughts to contend with. Tony had spent the flight thinking, praying and grieving. Jack had been sitting with his friend and prayed with him, comforting him in his grief. His thoughts, however, were dwelling on the police and what he would tell them. Alan was throwing around this new concept of religion and angels that he had seen. This wasn't exactly like what he had been told by his friends but then again... maybe it was. Henry was resting, trying to recover from the activities of the past forty-eight or so hours.

As the plane started its descent, the pilot advised them to get ready for their arrival. They sat up and, almost as one, started to think what needed to be done next.

Twenty minutes later they were on the ground, helping each other off the plane. They were met at the bottom of the stairs by a stewardess with a wheel chair. The pilot was also there waiting for them. He quickly explained that he had noticed Alan checking Henry every now and then and thought that this might come in handy. They all thanked him, especially Henry.

Once they got through the airport, they jumped into a taxi together and then discovered that they couldn't agree on a destination. Jack and Tony were insisting that they needed to take Alan and Henry to the hospital, to get checked out properly, while Henry and Alan wanted to go to the police and contact friends and family.

In the end it was something that Tony said that decided the matter.

"Let's call the station and ask for your friend," Tony suggested. "If he is not there then we wait and try again tomorrow."

The cab driver waited while Alan went back inside with Jack and they called the police station. While they waited, the driver told Henry that he didn't look very well and should probably listen to his friends. He was not being altogether altruistic — it was further to the hospital and therefore he could get paid more. It had been a quiet night for the driver.

Moments later, Alan and Jack returned. "He's not there," Alan reported.

"Off to the hospital then?" the driver asked hopefully.

When Henry nodded his head, Tony and Jack felt a surge of relief. Tony was worried about his new friends and Jack wasn't quite ready to face the police.

One Hundred and Twenty Six

The guard could not stop smiling. Isam had just handed him his three-day pass and told him to get packing immediately if he wanted to use it now. The helicopter would be leaving for Alice Springs in half an hour if he wanted a ride. The guard saluted one more time and then ran off to start packing.

The helicopter, it turned out, only had some minor damage to the landing struts and the piece of the rotor mechanism that had broken had been replaced with a similar piece that they had in stock for just such an occasion. A proper replacement part was still required. This was in stock at the airport in Alice Springs. The struts could be repaired or replaced at the same time if necessary.

They were advised that the one-way trip should be okay. The part they had used should be good for at least a twenty-hour flight but it was best that it get replaced as soon as possible. Isam had agreed and given permission for the guard to go too, only if he was ready on time. The helicopter was not to wait for him.

The timing was perfect, as far as Isam was concerned. Mr Jenkins had given the order to shutdown the underground construction first thing in the morning. They would not need as many guards on duty for a while, for at least three days anyway.

The workers would still be there but for once they would be confined to their rooms. This would allow a lot of them to recover from sleep deprivation and overwork, a deadly combination under any circumstances.

Mr Kepler had agreed to the shutdown but inwardly he was furious, especially since one of his future guests had just arrived early. A man known only as Luc, one of the CEOs due in another week, had turned up a couple of hours ago, totally unannounced.

Isam was concerned about this too but only so far as security matters went. With the shutdown, he did have spare security that could be used for looking after, and watching, this important guest.

One Hundred and Twenty Seven

When Michael walked back into the Hall of the Lamb he saw that it was almost full. There were warriors everywhere he looked. As he stood in the doorway, Nicole suddenly appeared before him.

"They started to arrive just after you left, Captain," Nicole said. "They were not here to see you specifically so I told them to just wait until one of the archangels arrived."

Michael looked behind at the four archangels with him to see that they were as amazed as he was. He noticed Itzal, Jasper, Kenaniah and the warriors were looking around at all the other warriors too. Saint Peter was the only one who did not look surprised.

Uriel noticed Michael looking at them and said, "I told them to come here but not this many!"

Michael smiled, "I am sure we will find out shortly why they are all here," he replied.

Michael turned and headed for the area that Gabriel and David had used earlier for their research. The rest of his entourage followed him, including Nicole. The gathered warriors parted at their approach, a murmur quickly ran through the Hall and then they all fell silent.

Michael stepped up on the table so he could be seen by them all. He cleared his throat and spoke loudly and clearly, "Those of you that have been sent here please sit down."

There was a general shuffling sound and about a third of the gathered angels sat down.

Addressing the rest of the group Michael again spoke loud and clear, "Why are the rest of you here if you were not told to come here?"

One of the closer angels answered, "We saw the guards at the gateway to Eden and we saw warriors coming here. We put two and two together and are volunteering to help with the protection of Eden."

Another angel called out, "The Spirit compelled me to come."

There were quite a few calls of agreement with this.

Michael nodded. "Any other reasons? No? Very well, those of you who the Spirit sent, please sit also."

Over half of the standing angels sat down too.

"The rest of you thought you would just join in and help?" he asked.

They all nodded or answered yes.

"Do any of you know what this is really about?" Michael asked.

No one answered and quite a few were shaking their heads.

"Are you only assuming that it has something to do with the Garden of Eden?" Michael asked again.

This time he got lots of nods of agreement. Michael looked down at the other archangels. Gabriel looked thoughtful, Zagzagel shrugged and Uriel was looking a little stern and then he nodded too.

Michael turned back to the throng of angels and indicated that they should all stand again. "Thank you for coming to the aid of your Lord's Kingdom. We are under what appears to be a combined attack from The Seven. We are not sure of their ultimate aim but they are trying to enter the Garden of Eden. Saint Peter has suggested that they may be after the Tree of Life, so it has been replanted here in Heaven with the Lord's approval. Apart from that, we can only assume that they are trying to gain access to Heaven, through the Garden, and thereafter take control of The Throne."

The warriors were all listening intently. Michael got down and indicated to Gabriel that it was his turn to speak. Gabriel climbed up on the table.

"We have come up with several possible locations for their attempted entry points, one of which is definitely connected to the Garden via a portal. I have used it myself to confirm this. We believe they heard of this portal and have been trying to find it. We also believe that they think there are more of these portal links and are searching for them at this very moment. As a result we have come up with a plan that will allow us to strike first."

Gabriel climbed down and Uriel took his place.

"Where they think there is a portal, we are going to let them see a portal. In every location they are searching, we are going to open a portal. But these portals will lead to another location – one of our choice. Some of you will be at this place waiting for them to arrive."

Michael stood on the table once again and Uriel remained alongside him.

"What do you say? Are you prepared to stand and face the enemy once again? Are you ready to participate in an ambush that will set the efforts of the evil one back once more?"

Michael asked all these questions in an effort to focus the warriors on what lay ahead. The warriors were, of course, getting stirred up by this. As one, without the prompting of the Captain of the Host, they lifted their weapons in the air and shouted, "For the Glory of the Lord and His Kingdom!"

Michael turned to Uriel and smiled, "Give them their mission locations and send them on their way, some with each of us and the rest to the ambush site."

Uriel nodded and, as Michael got back down again, he went on to advise them specifically of the ambush site and plan. Itzal and the other warriors had moved around to listen to Uriel. Michael faced Zagzagel, Gabriel, Saint Peter, Kenaniah and Nicole.

"I will be heading to Daintree shortly to assist Evangelos. Zagzagel, can you go to Vesna and Gabriel can you go to Levi?"

"Of course," they both answered.

"What about Driscoll?" Gabriel asked.

"Uriel will be assisting him," Michael answered.

"What am I to do in your absence?" Saint Peter asked.

Michael smiled at him, "You, sir, are in charge of our home base. Nicole will be here with you, to help co-ordinate everything and get messages to us if needed. They will have to be sent the long way – do not use portals in case the enemy goes through the wrong one. What do you say?"

"For the Glory of the Lord and His Kingdom!" Saint Peter, Nicole and the archangels all replied.

"Excuse me?" Kenaniah interrupted, "What about me?"

Michael thought for a moment before answering, "Kenaniah, I need you to keep a watch on the tree and the existing portal. Can you do that?"

"For the Glory of the Lord and His Kingdom!" replied Kenaniah.

Michael smiled a calculating, almost cunning smile, and said, "Then let's get to it."

One Hundred and Twenty Eight

Alan walked in and sat down alongside Henry's bed, looking downcast.

"What's wrong?" Jack asked.

"I spoke with my family and they are relieved to hear from me," Alan answered. "My brother told me that a friend of mine went looking for me and hasn't been seen since. I tried to call her but there was no answer. I'm worried about her. We have experienced what happens when you don't do what these people want. What would they do to someone who was a threat?"

"I know it doesn't sound like much but we can pray for her," Tony said.

Alan smiled. He was starting to get used to Tony and his religious ideas. He nodded and said, "I'd like that."

"What about you, Henry?" Jack asked, "Is there anyone you haven't been able to get in contact with?"

Henry thought about that for only a moment before he answered, "Yeah, there is. I called a friend of mine just before I got taken away from here and I may have gotten him in a similar fix. He's a reporter and if he came out and didn't find me... well, I am afraid his journalistic instincts would have taken over and he could be in trouble too."

Tony nodded and reached out his hands from where he was sitting at the end of Henry's hospital bed. One by one they joined hands in a circle of prayer. Tony lowered his head and began to pray.

"Our Heavenly Father, we come before you at this time in a safer place, but our fears have not been put to rest. Thank you for our safe deliverance from the grip of evil. I pray for the continued recovery of our new friends and thank you for helping to get them through this with only minor injuries."

Tony squeezed Jack's hand.

"Thank you, Father, for friends," Jack prayed. "I thank you for the new friends I have made this week, human and angelic. I lift before you my new friends right now, Henry and Alan. Place a hedge of safety around them now please, Lord. For Micah, Duncan, Israfel and the rest who are back there, still in the face of the enemy, give them the wisdom to know what to do, the courage to do it and the strength to survive this battle and defeat the enemy in Your name. For Henry and Alan's friends, I pray that you have kept them safe and that you will continue to do so."

Jack squeezed Henry's hand.

Henry continued the prayer, "Mighty and gracious Lord, all powerful and all loving. Mighty are your works, both here and in Heaven. I ask for your angels to guard and protect Glen as he faces our persecutors. I pray that he is safe and whole and that you will reunite us soon."

Henry had hardly squeezed Alan's hand before he started.

"Hello God, I want to thank you too. For all these friends and the love they have shown me and each other, for not pushing this on me but for allowing me to see their relationships with you. Thank you for sending your angels to help us and allowing me, a non-believer, to see one. I pray for my friend Kerri. I pray that she is safe and that she hasn't done something stupid in her attempt to find me."

He hesitated a moment and then squeezed Tony's hand.

"Lord, we place this petition at your feet and we finish now with your prayer that Jesus taught us..."

Picking up on what he had said, Jack and Henry were ready and started to say the prayer with him. Alan only remembered bits of it, mostly from his days as a scout when he was a child, so he said the bits he remembered.

"Our Father, who art in heaven, hallowed be thy name. Thy kingdom come, thy will be done, on Earth as it is in heaven. Give us this day our daily bread and forgive us our trespasses, as we forgive those that trespass against us. Lead us not into temptation but deliver us from evil. For thine is the kingdom, the power and the glory, forever and ever, Amen."

They all felt a little better after that — as if everything would work out for the best.

Tony patted Alan on the knee, "That was good, Alan. That is exactly how to do it."

Alan looked a little embarrassed at the praise. "I'm not really a believer yet, does that make a difference?"

"Not at all, He listens to all that speak to Him, even the non-believer. Besides, God knows what is in your heart and He is ready and waiting for you. When you are ready, He will be there still," Tony replied.

Alan looked up at Henry, "What did the doctors say?"

Almost as if on cue, the doctor and a nurse entered the examining room. The doctor picked up the chart and read it quickly as the nurse fussed around Henry a moment and then proceeded to take his vitals once more. They had all turned to the doctor as he entered and they sat in silence awaiting his diagnosis. The nurse made a few notes on the chart and then handed it back to the doctor.

"You have a bit of dehydration still but the actions that your friend took probably saved your life. I'd like you to stay in overnight just to make sure there isn't something we have missed," the doctor said.

Henry nodded, "If that's what you think is best, doc."

The Doctor smiled and then left.

"He also wants to make sure you get a good rest," the nurse added.

"Fine by me," Henry said, as he slid back down in the bed.

They sat there in silence for a moment and then Tony stood and stretched.

"I'm feeling a little tired," he said, mid-stretch. "I'm not as young as you fellows, you know."

"Poor old man," Jack said with a smirk, "but he is right. We should let you rest. Do you know of a hotel close by?"

Jack had addressed his question to Alan and Henry but the nurse decided to answer it: "There is a guest room. I can check to see if it is available if you like? How many beds would you require?"

Jack looked at the nurse.

Tony looked at Alan, "Three?"

Alan nodded and answered, "Three."

The nurse left and returned a short time later, smiling. "We have a room with two beds but we can set up a fold-out bed as well if you like."

"I'll take the fold out," Jack said, and the other two nodded after the usual polite "are you sure" and "yes, I am".

Jack smiled to himself as they said goodnight to Henry and filed out of the room. Only he had heard Elisha talk to the nurse's guardian. The guardian had told the nurse to offer them a room and make sure they had enough beds. He thought that he was the only one who had seen the small gold cross pinned to the nurse's lapel.

ONE HUNDRED AND TWENTY NINE

"Hello?" Glen said, as he picked up the phone and listened for a moment.

"Okay, I'll be right there," he replied and hung up.

"Who was that?" Kerri asked.

"The front desk," Glen answered. "The photo guy is there with the photos and wants to talk to me."

"Alright, let me get a cardigan or something and I'll come too," Kerri said, as she stood up.

"I think that you should stay here actually," Glen said.

Kerri looked a little upset and was about to fire off on an argument when Glen held up his hands to indicate he didn't want to fight.

"I don't want to upset you but it isn't necessary for both of us to go; if we do, it might look a little odd," Glen said in explanation. "Please, wait here and I will return as quickly as I can."

Kerri nodded and dropped back into the seat she had been sitting on. Glen went to the door and opened it. As he slipped out he noticed that she had picked up the Bible again. He smiled and closed the door behind himself.

It was only a short walk to the front desk of the hotel and when he turned the corner he could see the photo developer waiting for him.

"Hello again," Glen said, as he entered the lobby.

"Hi," the developer replied. "I'm sorry," he said jumping right into it, "but I had some difficulties with your prints."

"Really?" asked Glen, "How many didn't turn out?"

"All of them, I'm afraid," was the reply from the developer.

Glen was a bit shocked by this, as it was unusual for no photos to come out at all. "I will tell her to get her camera checked then."

"That was going to be my suggestion too," the developer said. "Here they are and the negatives are there too. If you show all of that to the repairer they may be able to work out what is wrong quicker. And here is your money back, since I couldn't get any prints at all."

"No," Glen said, refusing the money being offered to him. "You still did the work and used the materials so you earned it."

The developer stood there for a moment, hesitating, not one hundred per cent sure what to do next.

"Thanks anyway, and thanks for waiting to explain it to me," Glen said and turned away before anyone could say anything else.

"You owe me forty dollars," a voice said from behind him.

Glen stopped, confused. "That voice... but he shouldn't be here?" he thought to himself. He turned back around slowly, only to see Max standing close by with another man alongside him.

"It is you! What are you doing here?" Glen said, as he stepped forward and embraced his friend.

"Can we talk in your room?" Max asked quietly.

"Sure," Glen answered, a little intrigued.

"This is Tim," Max said. "He's the captain of the boat."

Glen shook Tim's hand and they started to walk away, back towards the cabin-type room that Glen and Kerri were using.

"What did you mean about the forty dollars?" Glen asked. "I thought it was only twenty?"

"I bet you another twenty that you wouldn't have it ready when I saw you next," Max replied, with a smile on his lips. "Okay, I'll let you off the extra as I knew then that I would be coming up here."

"You did?" Glen asked.

"Couldn't let you have all the fun now could I?" Max said.

Glen looked serious as he replied, "This has been anything but fun."

"We heard about the boat today," Max said soberly. "That's why we came out to the island early."

Glen knocked as he unlocked and opened the door.

Kerri stood up and was almost running towards him to get the photos but stopped when she saw the other two men with him.

"Kerri," Glen said, "This is Max, my best friend who I rang last night, and this is Tim the charter-boat captain. Max, Tim, this is Kerri, the photographer I met... was it only yesterday?"

Kerri was a little shy all of a sudden. "Why are they here?" she asked.

"They heard about the boat getting stopped this afternoon and rushed out here early," Glen said.

Tim added, "We weren't sure if the ferry was going to start again so we left to see if we could help. When we heard it was underway, we sailed around for a little while, just so that we didn't show up here at the same time as you."

"So what's so important that you couldn't tell me over the phone but had to travel the thousands of kilometres from Adelaide to tell me?" Glen asked Max, as he sat down at the dinner table.

Max sat down opposite Glen, Tim sat at the end and Kerri was still standing.

"Before you start, does anyone want a coffee?" Kerri asked, as she walked into the kitchen area. As she filled the kettle, there was a chorus of "Yes please" from around the table. She proceeded to get the cups ready while the others started to talk.

"I did some checking on those company names you gave me and everyone I spoke with said the same thing," Max said, answering Glen's question. "*Stay away from them, they are trouble.* A friend in the police force even suggested that they were linked to the underworld somehow."

Glen looked at Tim for a moment and Max jumped in on Glen's thoughts. "He's okay. He's a brother in Christ. One of the families from church recommended him to me after having a holiday up here a few months back. I called him for help and explained some of it to him. The way he reacted today when he heard about the ferry attack... well, let's just say he knew it was a spiritual attack more than anything else. He told me we had to go right away. You can trust him."

Tim only nodded. Then he felt a need to explain a little bit: "A while ago I was out sailing and got stuck in a similar type of storm, only not as quick or fierce. The boat stopped and the sails filled with wind but then whipped out and filled again but from the other direction. The wind was coming from everywhere, so they wouldn't actually catch and move the boat. No matter what I did, nothing helped me. That is, until I started to pray for help. I noticed something about the storm changed straight away so I took a chance: I let go of the ropes and dropped to my knees. I had my head bowed, mostly to protect it from being knocked off by the boom. I was in the classic prayer pose, on my knees, head bowed, petitioning the Lord for protection."

Everyone was looking at him now. The sound of the kettle clicking off snapped everyone back to reality.

"What happened next?" Kerri asked, as she started to poor four cups of coffee.

"I looked up eventually, it felt like hours later. The sea was calm again and the sun was shining once more. When I looked at my watch I was surprised to see that only ten minutes had passed," Tim finished his tale. "Ever since then, I have been a prayer warrior. When I heard about the sudden and localised storm, I just knew it was a bigger version of what I went through. I started to pray and told Max he should do the same. Then we cast off and headed out as fast as we could. We were barely out of the breakwater when he got the call that the storm was over and the coast guard was on the way to help the ferry."

"We kept praying for your safety, even after we heard the boat had been started again," Max added.

"Whatever happened out there was definitely spiritual in nature," Glen said. "We guessed it was just before it hit, which was just after Kerri became one of us," Glen was smiling about this last bit.

"Welcome to the family!" Max said, and Tim congratulated her too.

Kerri looked bashful now as she handed out the coffee and sat at the other end of the table. "I don't know if this makes sense to you or not but..." Kerri said, while looking down. She paused and looked up slightly to see what their reactions were going to be, "I don't think I would be here otherwise."

Glen smiled and the other two looked intrigued.

"What happened on the boat?" Max asked.

"Kerri was attacked by someone," Glen answered, "and kidnapped."

"What?" Max and Tim asked in unison.

"How did you get away?" Max asked.

"I wasn't really kidnapped," Kerri answered.

"It was only someone that looked like her!" Glen stated.

"What? You'll have to explain that one a bit better," Max said.

Glen quickly recounted what had happened, how Kerri went off to the toilets and then the storm hit. Kerri returned and they were attacked. Glen was knocked unconscious and Kerri was taken and thrown overboard, witnessed by one of the crew. Then Glen awoke and Kerri appeared beside him, sporting a bruise where she had hit her head in the toilet.

"And I realised that it wasn't Kerri who had come from the toilet earlier but an angel in disguise," Glen said, finishing off his tale.

"Wow!" Tim exclaimed.

"You said it," Max added.

Kerri looked shy but Glen was beaming.

"Are they the photos?" Kerri asked, trying to redirect the subject away from her.

"Yeah," Glen replied, coming back down to earth. "The developer said they didn't work out." He slid the packet across the table to her.

"Wait a minute," Max interrupted. "Are you sure about that?"

"We haven't looked at them yet," Glen replied, "but I have no reason to doubt him."

"No, not that," Max said, "about the angel."

"If it wasn't an angel, who was it?" Glen asked.

Max looked around at the other two. "To be honest, I don't know. Not having had an experience like that myself, it's hard to relate to it."

"But it doesn't mean that it wasn't real," Tim said, in support of Kerri.

Kerri was surprised that it was him and not Glen that spoke up.

"But you do believe in angels, don't you?" Glen asked.

As the conversation turned in that direction, Max claiming that he wasn't sure of what he believed in that regard and both Tim and Glen trying to convince him of the spiritual forces that are at work around us, Kerri opened the photos and slipped them out to see how bad they looked.

Kerri's eyes opened wide as she flipped from photo to photo. She stood up suddenly, causing her chair to topple over backwards and the conversation to stop. She put down the photos and stepped away from the table; she stopped to pick up the chair, walked away a short distance and then just pointed at the photos lying face up on the table.

"If that doesn't convince you, I don't know what will!" Kerri said, heading for the minibar.

Glen reached for the photos and the other two stood up to move and look over his shoulder. Max took a couple from him to get a closer look.

The gathered angels had a look at them too.

Kyle turned to Daniel, "Are you sure that's you?"

"You saw me there," Daniel answered without looking at Kyle.

"I know it's you but it doesn't look like you," Kyle said.

Raphael reached forward to gather Daniel's hair in his hands and pulled it back slightly, "How about now?' he asked with a little laugh.

Max sat down in Kerri's empty chair. "I don't believe it," he kept repeating while staring at the photo.

"But the developer..." Glen said in disbelief, as he quickly flicked through the photos. "They're all okay, only these few look darker but you can still see... That's what I saw! It's an angel, it wasn't a comet. That's why it could turn as it did!" Glen looked up with shock written all over his face.

"What are you talking about?" Max asked.

"What exactly are those?" Tim asked, interrupting and pointing at the top photo in Glen's hands.

Glen looked closer and then shuddered. "If this one is an angel then I think they are demons," he answered.

"What?" Max said, reaching forward to take the photo from Glen. "Oh, my Lord," was all he could say.

Glen stood and walked around the counter to Kerri. As he took a mini bottle of scotch from Kerri's hand he said, "Are you alright?"

"That's not the sort of thing you normally see in photos," Kerri answered, "even if we can't see it clearly. What are you doing with my scotch?"

"That's not the kind of spirit you want right now," Glen said, helping Kerri stand back up and shutting the fridge behind her.

Kerri started to protest but stopped. Tim was now sitting in Glen's seat. He was flicking through the rest of the photos Kerri had dropped on the table.

"Did you see the rest of these?" he asked.

"No," Kerri replied. "Is there something else there too?" she asked, as she moved back over to him to see what he was looking at.

Glen followed her and Max also stood up to see what it was.

Kerri took a photo from Tim and stared at it for a moment.

"Do you think that is why they have been chasing us?" Kerri asked Glen, as she passed him the photo and took the next one from Tim.

"What do you think?" Glen asked Max, as he handed him the photo.

"I wouldn't want that getting out to the public if I were them," Max said. "I wonder if they have got a licence for that yet."

Glen shook his head. "No they don't. But don't look at the sign, Max, look there, in the background," he said from over his shoulder, as he pointed at the photo.

"Oooh," was all Max could say. He looked a little closer, "Is that what I think it is? Where's the next photo?"

Kerri handed him the next photo. Max and Glen looked at it and then back at the first one. Glen was thoughtful for a moment and then commented more to himself than anyone else in the room:

"That would explain the noise I heard when I first heard Kerri taking these."

"How could you not recognise the sound that would make?" Max asked.

"I heard the camera's shutter and then I heard a popping noise," Glen answered. "Not a loud crack, a quieter popping type of noise."

Max looked closer at the photo, "You might be onto something. I'm no expert but if you look closely enough, the barrel does look a bit longer than normal."

Glen took the photo and studied it. He was about to say something about it but Max spoke first.

"Definitely lucky on your timing taking these," Max commented to Kerri.

"Not for him though," Glen said. "I wonder what he did wrong."

One Hundred and Thirty

Cain was standing on the top of the construction site, surveying the land and the other hotel. He was trying to spot any sign of movement but was not succeeding. The sun was setting and the long shadows were not helping him at all.

"Cain!" he heard from below him.

Cain sighed in defeat. It was passed the time to give Tarvyn his answer and Tarvyn was getting impatient.

"There you are!" a minor demon said from below him. "The Master wants to see you in his chamber!"

"Then let's go, shall we?" Cain said, in a slightly mocking tone.

The minor demon didn't want to stir Cain up so he just nodded and disappeared back through the roof.

Cain followed slowly, dropping down and through the roof too, then through the unfinished floors and the finished ones. Down, down, down he went until he was in the tunnels underneath the building.

"This way," the minor demon said.

Cain knew the way but kept quiet and followed the demon.

After a few more moments they entered the great chamber that had been dug underneath the building site. He saw Tarvyn at once and his human host sitting on a chair below him, deep in meditation.

"You summoned me, mighty Tarvyn," Cain said, bowing.

Tarvyn opened his eyes. "Cain, you have been avoiding me," he said.

"I was not ready to give you my answer," Cain answered.

"You do not deny it then?" Tarvyn asked.

"No. There is no point," Cain answered.

Tarvyn raised one bony-looking eyebrow on his massively ugly face. "This is why I want you working for me. Your bluntness is refreshing. To try to see the hidden meanings in every word spoken gets tiring after a while. So, what is your decision?"

"I have a task from my current master that I must complete first but once that is done, I am all yours," Cain answered.

Tarvyn was happy but also concerned about this. "How long will it take?"

"Not long," Cain answered, and tried to look thoughtful, "a few days at the most."

Tarvyn smiled. "So before everyone arrives then. Very well."

"If you will excuse me now, master, I must go now and see to the other task," Cain said, so as to excuse himself from Tarvyn's presence.

"If it helps you finish it sooner, then go," Tarvyn said in dismissal.

Cain bowed and turned and left.

He travelled down a few passages, up a level, along another passage and through a door. As he entered into Wraith's office he checked his surroundings. Wraith and Security were there waiting.

"Cain," Wraith said, "you're late."

"Apologies Wraith, I was interrupted from my scrutiny of the grounds by Tarvyn," Cain answered. "I came as soon as I could get away."

"Word has it that you are about to switch camps," Security said.

"No wonder your prisoners escaped if you are too busy listening to rumour and innuendo," Cain spat back in his face.

Security was drawing his sword but Wraith stopped him.

"Enough!" Wraith said. "Is that why you were on the roof? To scrutinise the grounds?"

"Yes," Cain replied, "and I didn't like what I saw."

Security had already been angry and this comment was just fuel for the fire. "Are you insulting my security methods?" he asked.

"No. That would imply there was a method and I can't see one at all," Cain replied.

"What are you doing Cain?" Wraith asked quietly. "If you want to fight then draw your sword and attack him in the prescribed manner."

"What?!?" Security said turning to Wraith. "Do you wish him to challenge me?"

"No, but the way he is irritating you is beneath him," replied Wraith.

Cain stood there with a slight smile on his face. Not showing the slightest bit of fear or anger.

"Do you want to know why?" Cain asked.

The other two demons both looked at him. Then Wraith looked down at Security.

Security looked back at Wraith and then at Cain again. "Yes," he replied.

"Good," Cain answered. "You're not totally lost then."

Security let the comment pass and waited for what Cain wanted to tell them.

Cain waited for a reaction but not getting one decided to turn the attack back to what it really was. "The enemy is out there."

Security laughed, "Ha!" He paused for a moment and then went on, "The enemy is always out there. Why don't you tell me something I don't know?"

Cain's demeanour didn't change at all and this actually made Wraith start to worry.

"Very well," Cain answered. "You are being staked out. There is, I think, one archangel out there and at least one small squad. They are very good but I have seen a couple of them. They are preparing to launch an attack but are waiting for exactly the right moment."

Security was speechless for a moment. "Lies," he eventually said. "They couldn't be here so soon."

Cain raised his eyebrows, "Really. You are referring to your escapees from earlier today? How do you think they managed to succeed and not get recaptured?"

Wraith was still acting calm but his insides were starting to churn. "You are suggesting they had help?"

"No, not suggesting," Cain replied. "I'm telling you that they did."

Wraith looked thoughtful but Security wasn't convinced.

"You are not falling for this are you?" Security asked Wraith.

Wraith turned to Security, "As overseer for an operation like this, I have to take other circumstances into consideration. Too much has happened in the last twenty-four hours for me to ignore the possibility of what Cain is telling us."

"But —" Security started to argue but Wraith lifted one of his clawed hands and held it before his face.

"Thank you, Cain," Wraith said. "Leave us now. We need to discuss this and what we are going to do about it."

Cain bowed and then turned and left. Once outside the door, he smiled.

"Idiots," he said to himself. "They deserve what is coming to them. Can't even spell his name right. How does one go from being an anger demon to a ghostly one?"

One Hundred and Thirty One

Jack couldn't get to sleep. No matter what he did he felt restless. Eventually he sat up.

"What is it Jack?" Tony asked tiredly from nearby.

"I'm not sure," Jack answered, "but I think I have to go."

"Go where?" Tony asked, waking.

"Back," Jack replied.

Tony looked at the shape of Jack sitting up. It was all he could see of him in the dark. "Why?"

Jack sighed. "I haven't been completely truthful with you, Tony, and for that I am sorry."

"I know," Tony answered. "I also knew that when the time is right you would tell me. Is the time right... Kevin?"

Jack's head spun around quickly, "You know?"

Tony chuckled. "I suspected that *Jack Daniels* wasn't your real name. It wasn't confirmed for me until just before we left the tunnels. I heard Jesus call you by your real name, didn't I?"

Jack nodded and then thought that maybe Tony couldn't see that in the semi-darkness they were in, so he answered too. "Yes. But now is not the right time to explain everything, sorry. I'm not ready to be him again."

"I see," Tony said quietly.

"I... I will tell you, Tony. I promise. I just need to go and get my gear back from the hotel in Kings Canyon first," Jack said.

"Do you want me to come too?" Tony asked, as he got out of the bed and headed for his pile of clothes.

Jack bowed his head in thought. "No, I need to do this alone," he answered eventually.

"You will need this," Tony said, as he handed over the room key from the hotel in Kings Canyon.

Jack took it and just looked at it for a moment.

"If there is something I can do for you before you go, please tell me and I will," Tony offered, having thought his hesitation was really a call for help. "Your friendship has become very valuable to me."

Jack smiled and reached out to grab Tony's hand. "Thank you, yours is valuable to me too. More than I can ever tell you." After a moment Jack let go, stood up and started to get dressed. Once he was dressed, Jack continued. "There is something you can do for me," he said.

"Name it," Tony said.

"Can you wait here for me? In Cairns I mean."

"Alright," Tony said.

"I should only be gone a day or so. Where will I find you?" Jack asked.

Tony smiled. "At church, the one where Henry goes, I think."

"There's one more thing you can do for me please. Will you pray for me?" Jack asked quietly.

"Of course," Tony answered.

"Thank you," Jack replied.

Without another word, he turned and left.

One Hundred and Thirty Two

"What are we going to do about this?" Glen asked.

"It's obvious, isn't it?" Max said. "We need to go to the police."

Kerri flinched slightly.

"But you said the bad guys were worse than the mob," Glen argued, "if that is right then they will have people in the police. That is why we didn't go to them earlier."

They all looked thoughtful for a moment.

"I don't see how we have a choice," Max said eventually.

"I could take it to my editor in Sydney," Glen suggested.

"That would probably bring the Sydney police into it, but they have no jurisdiction here," Tim commented.

"Jimmy has contacts in the federal police. Maybe he'd pass it on to them to handle," Glen argued.

The angels were watching the course of the discussion. All except for Amy, who was kneeling with Kerri as she stood apart from everyone else.

Daniel noticed this first: "What's wrong with her?" he asked.

"What we talked about yesterday," Amy replied.

"Oooh," Daniel said.

"What?" Kyle asked.

"Kerri has a secret that she hasn't revealed yet," Amy explained. "I think that her recent decision is making it hard to keep it a secret anymore. Especially since our little companion has departed. "

"The Spirit will convict her of her sins," Raphael added. "I think you need to reassure her."

Amy nodded and spoke into Kerri's heart, "It is time, isn't it? Time to reveal what you did and face the consequences. But don't worry: God will always be with you. He knows what you did and accepted you anyway."

Kerri suddenly sobbed. The men all stopped their discussion and looked at her. They hadn't noticed her slide off the couch and onto the floor. She was hugging her knees and trying to cry quietly. Tim and Max looked at Glen as if to ask what was going on. Glen could only shrug.

"What is it Kerri?" Glen asked, as he got down on the floor next to her.

Kerri just shook her head for a moment and then continued to cry.

Not knowing what else to do, Glen tentatively put his arms around Kerri and when she leaned into him, he knew that this was the right thing to do for his friend.

Max stood up and indicated to Tim that they should go for a walk or something and pretty soon it was only the two of them in the room, both sitting on the floor.

Kerri eventually quietened down enough that Glen let her go to get a box of tissues. Kerri managed to thank him between wiping her eyes and blowing her nose.

"What is it?" Glen asked, his voice full of concern.

"I..." Kerri started and then almost burst into tears again.

Glen started to pray, "Lord, I lift this child of yours up before you. Help her, release her from this burden that lies upon her heart."

Kyle and Pia were trying to help too. They were on either side of Amy as she tried to sooth this child of God so that she could tell her story.

Kerri felt as if the weight of the secret was lifting from her. She'd had all these terrible worries — would Glen hate her if he knew her secret and would she be sent to prison. But now they were gone and she only felt at peace. As if... well, as if God had taken the punishment for her. Suddenly an image of the cross with Jesus on it came into her mind. She knew that whatever happened, God would still love her and be with her. She accepted this and surrendered to it.

"I think I killed a man," Kerri said, so suddenly that Glen almost jumped.

Glen looked into Kerri's eyes. "Do you want to tell me about it?" he asked kindly, while taking her hands in his.

Kerri felt free, really free for the first time since that fateful night. The burden she had been carrying was gone and she felt great about that. It didn't matter what Glen thought or what the police would do to her. God was still with her and had set her free.

"It was the night that I got the maps and stuff," Kerri said. "A guard had heard me and was coming into the room where I was. I tried to hide behind the door but a fire extinguisher was in the way. So I took it off its hook and held it. When he got the door open and moved in front of me I suddenly got the idea to hit him with the extinguisher." Kerri started to cry again but not like before. This was more like tears of regret, the tears of someone seeking forgiveness.

"And..." Glen prompted her after a moment.

"And I did it," Kerri continued. "He fell and... didn't get back up, he didn't even move. I was scared, so scared at what I had done that all I did was grab the papers on the bench, stuff them in my bag and get out of there as quick as I could."

Kerri's tears continued and Glen didn't really know what to say, but he had the urge to hold her again, so he did. He lent forward and placed his arms around her, just like a dad does to comfort his little girl. That's how Kerri felt suddenly. That she was in her father's arms, not her living father but her heavenly Father. He was whispering words of forgiveness, love and comfort to her.

"I kept checking the newspapers when I could but there was no mention of it anywhere, not even of the break in," Kerri said.

"Do you want to check again?" Glen asked.

"What do you mean?" Kerri asked back.

"We can check the news headlines on the internet," Glen answered. "All the major newspapers keep all the past editions archived and available on the internet. Something that big would have made its way into other newspapers too, papers like mine, and I must admit, this is the first I've heard of it."

Kerri leaned back so that she was sitting by herself and looked into Glen's face.

"Why would it not get reported?" Kerri asked.

"A number of reasons but the most likely is either that he wasn't killed or they didn't report it to the police," Glen answered. "Being a local crime, Tim might know about it. Should we call them back in and ask him?"

Kerri nodded. "While you get them, I think I will go and wash my face and clean up a bit."

Glen nodded and said, "Okay."

He then stood up and helped Kerri to stand too.

Glen returned only moments later with Tim and Max. After a quick catch up on what was bothering Kerri, they started to discuss the crime and asked Tim if he knew anything about it.

"I didn't see anything in the papers about it at all," Tim answered.

"What does that mean then?" Kerri asked, feeling confused.

"As I said before, either he isn't dead or they didn't report it," Glen said.

"There are other possibilities," Max said.

They all looked at Max and waited for him to continue. Noticing them all staring at him he continued, "Maybe they couldn't report it," he suggested.

"What do you mean?" Kerri asked.

"If he wasn't here legally..." Max answered.

"Then they would have some explaining to do," Glen added.

"Exactly," Max said.

“Thanks, guys but you’re not exactly making me feel better,” Kerri said.

“If only I hadn’t sent my laptop to Townsville too,” Glen said. “Then we would have been able to get onto the internet and check those back issues I mentioned.”

“I’ve got one on the yacht,” Tim said. “I have it hooked up with a satellite link so that I can check the weather straight from the Bureau of Meteorology.”

“Excellent,” Glen said. “Can we use it for this please?”

“Sure. Why not pack your stuff and check out?” Tim suggested. “We can all bunk down on the yacht and head back to Cairns at first light.”

“Back to Cairns?” Kerri asked.

“Yeah,” Tim answered. “I have a suggestion, but if you don’t like it we can head down the coast like you wanted to do.”

Glen was now looking a bit weary, “What’s your suggestion?”

“Well...” Tim started, “one of the members of my church is a policeman. If we head back to Cairns we can go to church and see if he is there. If so, we can approach him first and see what he says about all this.”

Max was smiling, “I like it.”

Glen looked at Kerri, “He’d be able to tell us for sure and he should be able to help us with everything else,” he said.

“I’m not fully convinced, but then again,” Kerri said, “I’m also very tired after my emotional outbreak earlier. Let’s go out to the boat. You can check the internet and I can get some sleep.”

Glen smiled reassuringly. “Sounds like we have a plan.”

ONE HUNDRED AND THIRTY THREE

All over the world the angels and archangels were arriving at their destinations. All of them were slipping in unnoticed. Some were hitchhiking while others were hiding under cars, trucks and busses.

In Daintree, the rainforest was so thick and dark in parts that all the angels had to do was enter the rainforest at any location and then fly through it until they neared their destination. Then they landed and ran the rest of the way. Evangelos was overjoyed to see Michael leading in more angels.

"Welcome, Captain!" he said in greeting.

"Thank you, Evangelos," replied Michael. "We are here to join your forces and update you on the final details of the plan."

Evangelos listened intently as Michael outlined Uriel and Israfel's plan.

"This is the location that you are to link the portal with," Michael said, as he finished.

Evangelos took the piece of paper that Michael handed him, read it and then folded it and placed it in his tunic. "I will see to it personally."

Michael nodded and turned to look out through the foliage at the den nearby. "All that is left is to wait for the signal."

****

Gabriel and his team had a harder time getting to Levi. Not that there wasn't plenty of activity in the Middle East, what with the American War on Terrorism happening nearby, but that was part of the problem too. There was plenty of traffic for them to hide in or under but there were also plenty of demons around too. They were mostly Anger and Hatred demons. This made it difficult to sneak around, but not too difficult – as it also meant that there was an increased presence of warrior angels. They were all on the move, here and there, and if any of them congregated in large numbers the demons were quick to go and see what they were up to. This meant that they had to be extra circumspect when they reached their gathering point.

Eventually, they all arrived in place and Levi was relieved to see that they had managed it undetected.

Gabriel gave out the updated orders and the portals' destination location. Levi handed that straight over to another angel who had been designated to open the portal.

****

Uriel had an easier time getting to Driscoll. The Aland Islands are not as populated as some other parts of Finland. The very small town of Eden is North of Mariehamn, the capital of the Aland Islands. The construction here had increased the population of the small town by almost double and some were coming and going on a daily basis, simply because there were a lot of local construction workers involved.

Uriel and the warriors that were with him simply hitched a ride with workers or hid under their trucks and busses as they returned to work. They found Driscoll easily through the local church's angels and, once they had made contact, they updated him on the latest additions to the plan.

Driscoll looked at the co-ordinates for the destination of the portal and smiled.

****

Vesna was slightly shocked to see Zagzagel and his warriors when they arrived.

"I wasn't expecting any assistance with this mission," Vesna said to Zagzagel after their exchange of greetings.

"Each group has an archangel appointed to it along with extra warriors," Zagzagel replied as he handed over the destination location details. "When we all meet here we are going to need them."

Vesna quickly looked over the details. "Are we expecting the Seven Deadly Sins to follow too?"

Zagzagel looked at Vesna and thought about how insightful this angel was before he replied, "Yes. We are."

Vesna looked up the road from their hiding place at the construction site and once again thought about how strange a sight it was to have that here. So far away from any tourist-type spots but almost dead centre in the continent. The amount of demons circling the structure told them that they had the right place — but were they that close to one of Satan's Generals?

"How soon?" Vesna asked Zagzagel, while still looking at the enemy's lair.

"Any time, I expect," Zagzagel answered.

"Then I'd better make sure all these troops are ready and know, at least in part, what to expect," Vesna said, turning back to the archangel.

Zagzagel nodded and followed Vesna, as she headed for the first group of warriors that were hidden here with her.

****

The other archangels were involved in separate ways with their own missions. David's was the only one not linked with this unfolding plan. He was still following tyre tracks somewhere in South Australia. Raphael was keeping a watch over his group of guardians and humans while they slept on the boat, anchored just off of Green Island, and didn't know what was happening with the rest of his fellow archangels.

Israfel, however, was in the thickest part of it and the closest to the final destination. More warriors were still arriving. One of them found Israfel and gave him an envelope, which contained updated information, before leaving to join the rest of the warriors as they staked out the den.

Micah watched intently as Israfel opened the envelope and read its contents. When he had finished and looked up again, Micah thought he looked pensive.

"What is it?" Micah asked.

"The latest word from the Captain," replied Israfel. "You may as well have a quick look," he added, as he handed over the contents of the envelope.

Micah read it quickly and then reread it. "Are they serious?" he asked, as he handed it back to Israfel.

"Very," Israfel replied.

"May I?" Titus asked, reaching towards the message.

Israfel nodded and handed him the message too.

Micah and Israfel watched Titus as he read it.

"Lord above," was all that Titus said, as he finished it. "Who will you get to —"

He never finished his sentence. The look in Israfel's face told him all he needed to know.

"Is that why you let me read it?" he asked.

Israfel nodded. "Can you do it?"

Titus looked away at the den and then at the demons that were guarding it. The demons were not bothering to conceal themselves anymore. They appeared to be trying to intimidate through their presence and number. Titus nodded as he looked back at Israfel. "For the Lord of all, I will do it."

"Good," replied Israfel as he stood. "Let's pass the word around," he said to his companions, and they all stood and went to find all the hidden warriors.

****

Saint Peter was outside the Hall of the Lamb, looking off towards the place where the tree had been planted. Nicole was watching him from the doorway.

"Wondering if you made the right choice?" Nicole asked.

Saint Peter turned to her and smiled, "No. The Lord gave His approval." He turned to look towards the gateway and thought he could see it glimmering in the distance. "I was thinking of all of our friends and the task they have ahead of them."

"They will succeed," Nicole assured him.

"Oh, I know that," Saint Peter answered, "even if it is not completely the way we expect it to be. I just wonder how much longer until the Lord signals for the end of it all and Jesus then marches out to claim his victory. How many more little battles have to be fought first?"

"It doesn't really matter does it?" Nicole asked. "The victory has been secured and as you just said, it is only waiting for the Lamb to claim it. If it is today or another hundred human years, it will still be the same."

Saint Peter nodded. "I know that, but I can't help think of all the lost souls that are down there, still waiting to be born only to be left behind in the end."

Nicole understood what Saint Peter was saying. She too had felt this way once. Now, she just did what she had to do, serve the Lord, in every way, every day.

"It is hard to accept it but the Lord gives them the choice. You made it once too and here you are. Some, a lot, possibly even all of them will make the same choice and be here one day too. Until the end has come, all we can do is hope, trust and keep spreading the good news until they have all seen the light."

Saint Peter stood there. Something that Nicole just said had unlocked an idea in his head. "That's it!" he said and turned to go but then turned back to Nicole. "I have to go to the Hall of the Chronicles, if you need me that is where I will be."

Before Nicole could answer, Saint Peter had turned and was hurrying away.

One Hundred and Thirty Four

Jack walked back into the airport, alone, except for Elisha who was by his side, wondering what was going on.

"Can you explain any of this to me, Jack?" Elisha asked. "Or am I supposed to call you Kevin now?"

Jack looked at him as he continued to walk. "Please continue to call me Jack, for the time being anyway. You will know when or if you should call me... that other name again."

Jack looked ahead to see where he had to go. "As for the rest... I left something in my bag that I can't leave there for someone else to find. I have to go back and get it."

"Can you tell me what it is?" Elisha asked.

Jack shook his head, "No. I don't actually want to talk about it. I just need to have it."

Elisha accepted this and knew that if it was something that he needed to share then the Spirit would convict him of it when the time was right. All he knew was that the Spirit was telling him not to ignore this but to seek it out too.

They approached the counter of the airline that they had flown in earlier. To Jack's surprise there was someone manning it.

"Good morning, sir," the lady said, as he stepped up to the counter. "How can I serve you today?"

"I need to get to Kings Canyon. Can I charter a flight to get there please?" Jack asked.

The lady turned towards her computer, "Just a moment please," she said, as her fingers flew over the keyboard. "You're in luck. We do have a plane leaving for that location in approximately ten minutes."

Jack was shocked. He didn't expect to be able to leave so soon and had actually been preparing for some sort of argument. He started to reach for his wallet.

"Here are your tickets," the lady said, handing the boarding passes across the counter.

"But I haven't paid yet?" Jack said with his wallet open in his hand.

"That is alright, sir," the lady replied. "You can pay the steward once you are onboard. Otherwise you may miss the plane. It is not an official passenger flight so I don't have sales information here."

Jack nodded, dumbfounded, as he took the pass.

"Quickly then," the lady said to him. "Gate seven. Have a pleasant flight!"

Jack thanked her and looked at the ticket. He had less than seven minutes now. Jack started to jog. This was too weird he thought.

Elisha was keeping pace easily alongside Jack. He slowed slightly and looked back to the counter and waved to the lady behind the desk who waved back.

They found gate seven and handed over the ticket to a door steward who then followed them onto the plane.

Once Jack was seated and the steward was sure that his seatbelt was safely on, the plane began to taxi and took off.

In the control tower, the flight controller was enjoying a non-eventful nightshift. He suddenly saw the lights on runway three light up by themselves.

He checked the radar and then the flight list. Nothing in or out for at least another four hours the list said.

The controller scratched his head in confusion and reached for the light switch. He looked at it, even more confused. It was still in the off position.

He flicked it on and then off, looked out the window and then down at his instrumentation. Nothing had happened.

Jack watched out the window as the plane took off.

The steward asked if he wanted anything to drink but Jack declined the offer and asked instead to be woken up just before they landed. Then he settled back, closed his eyes and almost instantly fell asleep.

The flight controller picked up his phone and was just dialling the number for his supervisor when the lights suddenly went out again. He put the phone back down and sat there in utter confusion. He didn't know if he had imagined it or not, no plane had come in or gone out and suddenly he thought of that movie where terrorists had taken control of the towers instruments. Bruce Willis was in it, he thought.

He made a note that something strange had occurred and what it was. Since September Eleven you had to report strange things like this. Even if it just made you look crazy.

Only two hours later, Jack was woken by the steward.

"We've landed, sir," he was told.

"Oh, thanks," he said, as he rubbed his eyes and tried to stand but remembered he was still strapped in.

Once he had undone the belt, stood and stretched, he made his way off the plane and into the terminal. He looked around. It was deserted.

Then he saw the car rental agency booth that he always used. It was empty. He checked his watch and realised that it was still on Cairns time. Once he adjusted it back to Central Australia time he realised that it would have been amazing if someone had been here at this time of day.

He turned to Elisha and said, "I wonder if I could get a ride with the pilot or one of the flight crew."

Elisha looked back towards where they had just come from. "Somehow I doubt that," he replied.

Jack looked back too and saw that the tarmac was empty. "Where'd the plane go?"

Elisha smiled and looked away so that Jack couldn't see it.

One Hundred and Thirty Five

Saint Peter was so engrossed in the scrolls and books he was looking through that he did not hear them enter the Hall of the Chronicles.

"Where is it?" Saint Peter muttered, as he put down one book and picked up another.

The Hall of the Chronicles is where everything that has happened is recorded and all information about things can be found. Just like a library, which is exactly what the large room resembled. There were scientific explanations, theological essays and lists of events all here to be found and read. That is what Saint Peter was looking for. A scientific explanation, a theological recount and a list of times all relating to a specific thing. So far, he had had no luck in finding it.

"There he is," a voice from the end of the corridor spoke. "Over here."

Saint Peter looked up to see Saint Andrew at the end of the corridor. As he watched, the rest of The Twelve appeared alongside him.

Once they were all there they came down the corridor towards him.

"Greetings Brothers," Saint Peter said, as he sat back in his chair. "What brings you here?"

"You do," Saint Jude replied.

"What are you doing?" Saint Matthew asked.

Saint Peter looked from one to another, not sure if he should share his task with them or not. Before he could decide, Saint Matthias spoke up.

"You should know that the Lamb sent us to help you," Saint Matthias said.

Saint Peter sighed in relief. He did not want to keep anything from his brothers and these eleven were the closest people he knew while on earth. Only one of them was his real brother – Andrew; the rest were his brothers in Christ.

These were the Twelve Apostles, the first Disciples of Christ whom he chose personally. All, that is, except for Matthias, who replaced the betrayer Judas Iscariot. He had been chosen by the rest of the disciples as he was one of two who fit the criteria. He had to have been a disciple during the whole time of Christ's earthly ministry, from the time of John's baptism until his crucifixion. Then his name was drawn and he became an apostle too.

"My brothers," Saint Peter said, "I am on a mission for the Lamb and I am relieved that he has sent you to assist me."

"What can we do?" Saint Bartholomew asked.

Saint Peter quickly explained what was happening and the part he had played so far. He recounted some of the highlights from Michael's Creation account and what he thought needed to be done now. The Apostles listened intently. Once Saint Peter was finished, they agreed that Saint Peter's idea had worth and so they joined him in his search of the records.

It took all of them hours to collate the information they thought they needed and as Saint Peter read over it all he couldn't help but smile.

Saint Peter looked up at the rest of the Apostles. "Thank you brothers," he said. "I think we have done it. This is what I needed to know to help the Host of Heaven. I think it will work. Even though they live in darkness, they do not like it when the light is suddenly taken from them."

"What are we going to do now?" Saint James asked.

"We?" Saint Peter asked in reply, a little confused.

"Yes, we," Saint Philip replied.

"We," Saint John continued, "were sent to help you. Not in just finding this information but to help you until your task, and I am guessing, this threat, is over."

Saint Peter looked again from face to face and saw their determination to help him. "Then *we* need to get this information to the Captain."

They all stood and headed out of the hall to deliver their part of the plan to Michael or at least to someone who could get it to Michael.

ONE HUNDRED AND THIRTY SIX

Kenaniah stopped singing for a moment as he saw The Twelve exit the Hall of the Chronicles. They all gave him a little wave as they walked past and he returned it. As they disappeared again around the corner of The Throne he turned back to the Tree of Life.

Kenaniah noticed at once that something was different but it took him a moment to realise what it was. He bent down and looked at the ground beneath the tree and then back up at the tree. Most of the fruit had fallen off. He poked at a piece that was still hanging onto the tree and it fell off too. Kenaniah was taken aback for a moment. He looked at the tree again and noticed that some of the leaves appeared to be wilting. He scratched his head and started to hum something under his breath, as he often did. He stood back up and, as he did, he noticed that the tree seemed to stand up too. The tree had been drooping but now it was reaching upwards once again.

Kenaniah stopped humming and spoke to the tree, "Something doesn't appear to be right with you."

The tree started to droop again. Kenaniah's brow furrowed in thought for a moment. Then he had an idea and he began to hum again. The tree perked up again. Kenaniah started to sing and the tree looked very healthy once more.

"I need to tell someone of this," he thought to himself, "but whom?"

Then he remembered that Jasper was still here, somewhere.

"I must find him but I dare not leave the tree for too long."

Then he had another idea and rushed off and around to the entrance to the Hall of Worship. He returned a moment later with a group of saints and told them to keep singing. The saints looked at each other and shrugged but kept singing the whole time. Kenaniah watched the tree for a moment and then turned and ran off to search for Jasper.

One Hundred and Thirty Seven

Nicole saw Saint Peter and the rest of The Twelve as they entered the hall, but it took Saint Peter a moment to see where she was.

"Nicole!" Saint Peter called out.

'Over here," Nicole replied.

Saint Peter turned and saw her, just as Simon pointed passed him towards her. They hurried over to her.

"What is it?" Nicole asked, as they approached.

"I, that is, we," Saint Peter stated, "need to get a message to Michael straight away and I think you need to take it."

Immediately, Nicole understood this to mean that Saint Peter didn't want to bring any other messengers in on this.

"What is the message," Nicole asked, a note of seriousness in her voice.

Saint Peter, with the help of the rest of The Twelve, explained what they had worked out and what they thought Michael needed to do. Nicole asked a few questions but otherwise understood exactly what The Twelve intended. She stood there for a moment in thought. The Twelve could only stand and wait for her response.

But before she said anything, Kenaniah burst in and called out, "Is Jasper in here?"

"Try the Garden," Nicole replied.

Kenaniah disappeared back out the door.

"I think I need to talk to the Lord about this first," Nicole said to Saint Peter, eventually.

The other eleven of The Twelve looked at Saint Peter, who was thinking about this. Then he nodded, "You are correct, of course; we should have done that too."

"While I do that, you need to stay here," Nicole told them. "I will go and get another messenger to come back here in case you think of something else to tell Michael."

"Good thinking," Saint Peter said.

Nicole turned and left immediately.

ONE HUNDRED AND THIRTY EIGHT

Daniel had just finished watching the sun rise on another day and was refreshed and filled with hope for what the day would bring. He was also a bit excited as this was the first sunrise he had seen at sea for a long number of years. Raphael and most of the other angels aboard didn't share his excitement (they loved the dawn but being on a boat was nothing special to them), but Ishmerai understood it.

"I have seen many from here and they always inspire me," Ishmerai told Daniel.

Daniel could only nod his head in understanding.

"Come," Raphael called to them.

Daniel and Ishmerai passed Tim as he piloted the boat away from Green Island in the early morning light. The angels all sat down or stood around the table where Glen was reading his morning devotion. He was sharing it with the rest of them and the door was open so that Tim could hear it too.

Glen was reading from the March/April 2002 edition of Every Day With Jesus. The Bible reading for 24 March was:

Brothers and sisters, if a person gets trapped by wrongdoing, those of you who are spiritual should help that person turn away from doing wrong. Do it in a gentle way. At the same time watch yourself so that you also are not tempted. Help carry each other's burdens. In this way you will follow Christ's teachings. So if any one of you thinks you're important when you're really not, you're only fooling yourself. Each of you must examine your own actions. Then you can be proud of your own accomplishments without comparing yourself to others. Assume your own responsibility.

The person who is taught God's word should share all good things with his teacher. Make no mistake about this: you can never make a fool out of God. Whatever you plant is what you'll harvest. If you plant in the soil of your corrupt nature, you will harvest destruction. But if you plant in the soil of your spiritual nature, you will harvest everlasting life. We can't allow ourselves to get tired of living the right way. Certainly, each of us will receive everlasting life at the proper time, if we don't give up. Whenever we have the opportunity, we have to do what is good for everyone, especially for the family of believers.

Galatians 6:1-10

This devotion was about being a person of good deeds. Not because we want to or for any recognition but because it is the right thing to do.

To follow the example that Jesus showed us, to do good works from an over-flowing heart of compassion and a desire to heal a sick and broken world.

They all discussed this as they sailed into the new day. Kerri couldn't help but think of the things she had done and was suddenly filled with a desire to do the right thing, no matter what.

One Hundred and Thirty Nine

In the Garden of Eden, Jasper was talking with Starr and another of the cherubim who were guarding the portal when Kenaniah found him.

"Jasper," Kenaniah said, as he approached the small group. "I must speak with you at once."

"Excuse me," Jasper said to the two cherubim, and then turned to Kenaniah. "What is it, Kenaniah?"

"I think the Tree of Life is dying!" Kenaniah replied.

Jasper was shocked at the statement, "What makes you think that?"

"I was watching it, Michael asked me to, and I turned away for a moment and when I turned back it was droopy and had dropped most of the fruit," Kenaniah said, as if that was explanation enough.

Jasper looked at Kenaniah for a moment and thought about what he had been told. "Is it possible it is going through part of its lifecycle? Like trees do on Earth during different seasons, they drop leaves and fruit."

Kenaniah hadn't thought of that. "I suppose," he replied. "But why then did it pick up again when I sang?"

"What?" Jasper asked.

"While I was thinking about what was happening to the tree I started to hum and it started to perk up again," Kenaniah explained. "The branches lifted up and it looked healthier in general. So I did a little test and found that when I didn't sing it drooped and when I did it perked up."

Jasper was a little intrigued by what Kenaniah was saying. "Really? What song was it?"

Kenaniah started to sing Amazing Grace but stopped at the third line and asked, "Do you know it?"

Jasper nodded, "Yes, it is one of my favourites, but I must admit I don't fully understand what it is about."

"I know what you mean –" Kenaniah started to reply when Starr interrupted.

"What did you just do?" Starr asked.

"Nothing," Jasper answered.

"Not you, I meant Kenaniah," Starr said, indicating Kenaniah.

Kenaniah was a little flustered by the sudden question, "Uhh, what was I doing? I was talking with Jasper and then I sang part of a song called..."

"Can you sing it again?" Starr insisted. "Please!"

Kenaniah started to sing it again but noticed Starr wasn't even looking at him so he stopped.

"If you want me to sing the least you could do is look at me!" Kenaniah said.

"I'm sorry, Kenaniah," replied Starr, "it's just that your singing is affecting the portal."

Jasper and Kenaniah looked at the portal but it didn't look any different to them and Kenaniah said so, "I don't know what you mean, it looks the same to me."

"That's because you are not singing," replied Starr.

Kenaniah sighed and started to sing again. He stopped almost at once. The portal had shrunk a little and was now returning to its original size again. He sang a little bit more and the portal shrunk again. He stopped and it grew back again.

"That's it!" he said. "That's why it did that earlier too. I was singing as the others tried to close it and that is why it appeared to work but when I stopped and watched it went back to normal."

Jasper looked at Kenaniah. "First it's the tree and now the portal too?"

"Do you think that if I kept going it would close up altogether?" Kenaniah asked.

Jasper and the cherubim thought about it and Starr started to nod his head. Jasper agreed, while the other cherubim started to nod too.

"Should I?" Kenaniah asked.

"Why not?" Jasper replied. "They wanted it closed didn't they?"

"Okay," Kenaniah answered and started to sing again. The portal started to shrink once more. Jasper joined in after a little while and so did the cherubim that were there.

"Hang on," Starr said remembering something. "We have guards on the other side too. Shouldn't we tell them what we are doing? Or at least tell them to come back first?"

Jasper shrugged. "I don't know. We need to ask the Captain."

"Why don't I do that when I go and see him?" a voice asked from behind them.

They all turned to see Nicole standing there.

"I am on my way to tell him something else and can I could ask him about that too, if you like?" Nicole asked.

Kenaniah looked to Jasper. "That would be great," Jasper said.

"But first I need to use it," Nicole said. "It will help me get where I need to go quicker."

One Hundred and Forty

Sunday, 24 March 2002
Cairns
8:30 a.m.

Henry was checking out of the hospital, with Tony and Alan helping him. The doctor had been around early that morning, given Henry a clean bill of health and told them that they could leave as soon as they were ready. Tony was outside, organising the morning's transport with a taxi driver, while Alan accompanied Henry as the nurses wheeled him to the front door. Once there, Henry stood up, thanked the nurses and walked the rest of the way to the taxi. The three of them climbed in and headed for the police station.

8:35 a.m.

While at his mooring at the marina, Tim was expertly moving the yacht into its berth. Glen and Max were ready with the lines and Tim told them exactly what to do. Once the engine was off Tim double-checked their rope work, making sure that the boat was secure.

Moving quickly the four of them busied themselves with the jobs that Tim had told them had to be done before he left the yacht and the marina. Tim, if nothing else, was very safe when it came to his profession. He made sure that before he left everything would be ready for a quick and safe launch.

9:00 a.m.

Henry, Alan and Tony walked out of the police station.

"What now?" Tony asked.

Henry's friend had not been at work that morning and they refused to tell him when he was on next. He checked his watch before answering Tony.

"Let's go to church and see if he is there. If he isn't working then he should attend the morning service today."

Alan looked a little uncomfortable with that suggestion but saw no other option, so he agreed. After waiting ten minutes for another taxi, they left for the church.

9:03 a.m.

It had taken them almost half an hour but finally Tim was happy and directed them up the ramps and into the car park. Kerri climbed into the front of Tim's car, while Max and Glen took the back seats.

"Before we go, are we going to have to do all that before you let us out of here too?" Max asked, teasingly.

It managed to get a laugh out of Glen and Kerri, but Tim just looked at him in the rear-view mirror. Tim drove them back to his house where they all grabbed a quick shower. It was going to be a fairly hot day today so they all looked for light and loose clothing to wear. Before they knew it, it was time to go and Tim was hustling everyone back out to the car.

9:45 a.m.

"I think he took the scenic route," Alan commented as the taxi pulled away, leaving them on the side of the road out the front of the church.

"That's okay," Tony said. "He must need the extra money."

Alan looked at him as if to say "you're weird".

"It's alright Alan," Tony said with a chuckle, "I don't need the money. God looks after me and He doesn't have need of it."

"I'll have to get you to explain that to me some time because that just doesn't make sense right now," Alan said, as Henry led them towards the church.

There were only a few others in the church this early and they all greeted the trio with a smile and a handshake. Henry introduced his new friends to a few people he knew and also asked if Steve Thompson had arrived. No one had seen him yet but he was expected today.

They went back outside to wait.

9:52 a.m.

Tim parked in the car park under the shade in the last space he found there. He thanked God that they had got the last one. As they climbed out, Max and Glen started to comment on the look of the church, the car park and anything else they wanted to compare with their churches.

Kerri was following along behind them quietly. She was a little awestruck by the number of cars and people who were already here. Glen noticed that she was quiet and asked if she was okay with this. Kerri smiled at Glen and was thankful that he was with her for this, her first church service in over twenty years. Practically her first service ever as she didn't think that Sunday school really counted.

"I'll be alright," she said. "I guess that if I want to stick with the decision I made yesterday then I need to come to somewhere like this."

Glen nodded and walked alongside her just to give her support.

"Kerri!"

Kerri stopped and looked around excitedly. "Alan?"

Glen turned as Kerri stopped and it took a moment for Tim and Max to realise that they were no longer behind them. They turned in time to see a man come out of nowhere and lift Kerri off the ground in a huge hug. When he set her down again it was easy to see that the two of them had tears in their eyes.

"What are you doing here?" they both said at once.

They laughed.

"You first," Alan said.

"We are here to see a man who goes here," Kerri said. "He is a police officer and we thought we could trust him to help us find you! But here you are!" and she hugged him again. "What about you? Where have you been? I've been so worried about you!"

Alan looked at her, slightly startled. "I think we are here to see the same man. As for the rest, it's a long story that will have to wait a bit longer."

As Alan was talking, Henry and Tony walked up.

"Glen?" Henry said as he spotted his friend.

"That sounded like..." Glen said, turning to see his friend, "Henry!" He stepped forward and hugged Henry. "It's good to see you, man! They told me that you had gone to Sydney."

"Really?" Henry replied. "I was nowhere near Sydney and... well, have I got a story for you!"

"Hi Henry," Max said, stepping forward and shaking Henry's hand. Max knew Henry too, though not as well as Glen did.

"Hi Max," Henry said, "What are you doing here?"

Tim and Tony looked at each other and decided they better introduce themselves, as the rest of the group seemed to be getting caught up and appeared to have forgotten about them.

It was at that moment that Tim spotted Steve arriving with his family. He excused himself and went over to intercept him.

"Steve!" Tim called to him as he approached.

"Hi Tim," replied Steve, "How goes the charter business?"

"Good," Tim answered. "Listen Steve, I hate to do this on your day off, but I need to discuss something with you. It's something that you will want to hear and I have people that you need to meet."

Steve looked at his wife who just smiled back. "I'll see you inside," she said, as she and the kids walked away.

Steve looked at Tim, slightly annoyed to have his Sunday morning suddenly hijacked. As if anything could be more important than church!

"Maybe you'd better just come over here and meet some people first," Tim suggested, after he saw the look in Steve's eyes.

As they reached the group, Henry turned and saw him.

"Steve!" Henry said, "I need to talk to you!"

"Sorry, Henry," Steve said, and pointed to Tim alongside him, "I've already been hijacked into something."

But when Tim stopped right beside Henry, Steve looked at him with surprise.

"Our stories, from what I know, are the same but from different sides," Tim said. He indicated towards Glen, Max and Kerri: "I've been helping these people. They have been looking for these guys," he said, pointing at Alan and Henry, "who mysteriously disappeared recently, only to turn up again here today."

Steve looked from person to person and stopped on Tony. "How are you connected with this?"

"I helped rescue these two men from the clutches of the evil one," Tony answered.

This surprised Steve. Never had he heard someone refer to a 'bad guy' as the evil one. "Who do you mean by 'the evil one'?" he asked, slightly intrigued.

"*THE* evil one," Tony replied. "You know the one from the Bible, Satan, the Devil."

Steve now looked sceptical. But as he looked around at everyone else, he saw that none of them were arguing with Tony.

"I think you need to tell me everything from the start," he said with a sigh.

Kerri looked at Alan and then Glen and the rest of the gathered group.

"Before we do," she said, "I need to go in there and spend some time with this God that I have come to know."

Alan was the only one that shot her a confused look. Everyone else simply smiled.

The angels that were gathered around these humans all smiled and were talking to each other about what had happened to each of them. Steve's guardian was especially interested to hear all that had happened.

Only Raphael kept quiet. He could feel something stirring. Something big was about to begin. So big, he felt, that the battle they were in yesterday would only be a small skirmish in comparison.

Raphael turned to Ruth, “We have to go,” he said, “and visit all the churches again.”

Ruth looked at him. “All of them?” she asked.

Raphael looked around, as if he was studying the very air itself. “We need prayer cover. We are going to need a lot of it and very soon.”

One Hundred and Forty One

Jack was starting to get impatient now. He had slept here in the terminal so that he could wait for the car rental agency to open, yet at almost nine thirty it was still closed. All he could do was wait and so wait he did.

At ten minutes to ten a man arrived and started to prepare for his day in the booth. Jack gave him five minutes and then approached the counter. The man looked at him and politely told him that they weren't open until ten. Jack was about to protest that he had been waiting for most of the night when he realised that another five minutes wouldn't hurt him.

It was kind of annoying to know that you had an angel with you at all times. Just the presence of Elisha had started to change Jack a little. It wasn't something he really wanted to think about, but he didn't feel he could talk to this man the way he really wanted to when Elisha was standing beside him. He wondered how other Christians managed this. Did they even know that an angel was with them at all times? Probably not. If they did, would they do things differently?

He was still thinking about this when he realised that the five minutes were up. The man looked at Jack and said, "How can I help you today, sir?"

Jack smiled at the man. Ten minutes later, Jack was in a four-wheel drive Toyota, heading back to Kings Canyon.

One Hundred and Forty Two

"You realise the seriousness of these allegations?" Steve asked them. He looked from face to face to try to gauge the responses.

They all nodded as he looked at them. It would be hard to get these people to all learn the same story. But there were patches of it that, even though it sounded farfetched, would be hard for them to keep the same. He had, after all, interviewed them separately so that they could not coach each other or "remind" each other of certain facts.

"We do," Henry answered.

Glen was nodding. "And we do have these photos to back it up," he added, while tapping the photos on the table between them. They were in the church's meeting room, which was adjacent to the minister's office.

"Kidnapping, slavery, illegal casinos, murder," Steve was mentioning the main points back to them to see if they were going to change their minds or add anything else. He referred to his notes, "Maybe two murders. This is sounding like a Hollywood mob movie or something." He paused for a moment to look at them all again.

No one moved; they all just sat there, watching him expectantly and waiting for his reaction.

"Is there anything else I should know," Steve asked. He had felt that perhaps they hadn't told him everything. "I need to know if anything has happened from your side of things... something that they could throw back at us."

Kerri's head dropped. "I..." she swallowed, as all eyes turned towards her and she suddenly felt very exposed. "I might have something else to mention." Kerri suddenly looked very small and vulnerable.

"You can do it, Kerri," Amy whispered into her ear. "It is time to release this burden. You will feel much better once you have told him everything."

The rest of the angels were all sitting or standing around their group of believers. Raphael and Ruth were waiting for the right words to be spoken and then they would be off. Daniel, Pia and Jade were standing with their backs to the group, keeping an eye out for any demons who might try to interrupt this meeting.

Glen had assumed that there was something else that she hadn't told him. She had told him as much a few days ago after he first introduced himself. He put his hand on her shoulder, reassuringly, "Whatever it is, tell him."

Kerri looked at Glen and then at Alan who was holding her hand and looked as if he wasn't going to let go. Alan nodded at her to encourage her to speak.

"After the police told me that there was nothing that they could do," Kerri started to tell her tale, "I decided that someone had to know something. I decided to do some digging on my own."

Steve started to take some more notes.

"I started to look up the company that had hired Alan. It took me three days to finally find out who it was. When I did, I looked them up on the internet. I found out that they are an international company and that they had an office in Cairns. I went to their office and demanded to speak with the manager. The man I spoke with was very rude and wouldn't answer any questions."

"Can you remember his name?" Steve asked.

Kerri thought for a moment. "I have it written down somewhere, but I think it was George... something." She shook her head, as if it would help her remember.

"Murphy?" Alan and Henry said at the same time.

"That's it!" Kerri said, surprised.

"Wait..." Steve referred to his notes a few pages back. "That's the man whose body you saw carried passed you as you were escaping," he said to Alan and Henry.

"Yes," Henry answered. "I am sure it was him."

"Okay," Steve scribbled something down, and then said to Kerri, "Go on."

"Ummm," Kerri said, as she collected her thoughts once more. "He was very dismissive and after... wait, he's dead?"

"Is that important?" Steve asked.

Kerri thought for the very smallest of moments before answering, "No."

"Can you continue then please?" Steve asked. He didn't want Kerri getting distracted from whatever she had to tell him.

"Okay, well, after talking to him for... maybe five minutes, he had me escorted out of the building. I tried again but was told that he was no longer working from that office."

"After a couple more days of getting nowhere, I decided that they were hiding something and I broke into their office after hours."

Alan's jaw dropped.

One of Steve's eyebrows went up and a thoughtful expression came over his face but he didn't say anything. When Kerri failed to continue he thought he'd better say something to get her talking again. "Why? What did you hope to find? Did you find anything?"

"Not really, I took some maps and other papers from the office. Anything I could find that mentioned Alan, and there wasn't much of that," Kerri said.

"Here it comes," Amy said to the others. "Go on, you can do it!" she said to Kerri.

Kerri paused for a moment as if she was going to say something else. But it appeared that it would not come out.

Kyle leaned over Glen and spoke quietly, "Remember Philippians 4:13."

Glen squeezed Kerri's shoulder, "In Philippians it says that we can do all things through Christ who strengthens us. If you don't feel strong enough right now then lean on Him and He will help you."

Kerri looked at him.

Ishmerai spoke to Max, "Remember Second Corinthians 4:8 and 9."

Max leaned forward from behind Kerri and, resting his hands on her shoulders too, said, "Second Corinthians Four tells us that no matter what we face, it will not overcome us... our troubles will not crush us and we are not abandoned in our persecution."

Kerri looked over her shoulder at Max, tears forming in her eyes. "How did they know this stuff?" she thought.

Steve looked at Glen and Max and at the result they were achieving in Kerri. He could see she was relaxing, that her barriers were falling down. He wondered for a moment if quoting scripture at criminals would get them to break. He dismissed the thought almost as soon as he had it. Then a scripture verse popped into his head. "So those who are believers in Christ Jesus can no longer be condemned," he said. "Romans 8:1."

Kerri looked at Steve. "I think I killed a man," she blurted out.

A few drew in a sharp breath and everyone was now looking at her.

Steve didn't react at all. It wasn't what he was expecting to hear but there was very little that people said to him these days that surprised him. He thought for a moment before he said anything. "Tell me what happened," he said.

Kerri sighed. She had felt the weight lift from her shoulders just from admitting what she had done, or thought she had done. Telling the tale now would not be as hard. "I was rifling through the office when I heard someone coming... so I hid behind the door. As they opened the door, I tried to move back into the wall but found that I couldn't. I had come in contact with the fire extinguisher. I lifted it quietly and held it in front of me so that I could get further back."

"Then the door closed. The guard was in front of me with his back to me. If he turned around, I thought to myself, he will see me for sure. I felt desperate and looked around for somewhere else to hide and looked at the fire extinguisher in my hands. I thought that if I knocked him out I could get away. I lifted it above my head and..." Kerri paused, not quite able to say it, and started to cry. Not the loud emotional sort but a quiet, sorry type of cry.

"And..." Steve prompted after a moment.

"I hit him over the head," Kerri said with the tears running down her cheeks. "He fell to the floor like a rag doll. I grabbed my stuff, then started stuffing some of the papers in my bag and then ran. I never checked to see if he was okay or anything." She looked down at her hands in her lap. "I am sorry that I did it and I am prepared to face the consequences for what I have done."

Amy was smiling and crying too. She was happy that Kerri had released her burden and admitted her sin.

Daniel nodded, understanding a bit more of what was going on now.

"Officer," Tony said, looking at Steve, "Do you mind if we stop and pray for a moment?"

Steve looked at the minister from Broken Hill questioningly.

"A sister in Christ, a believer, has just admitted to a terrible sin and released a huge burden from her shoulders. She needs to hear the healing words of the Saviour now," Tony explained.

Steve nodded in understanding and looked at Kerri. "You are very lucky to have such caring friends."

Kerri could only nod her head in reply.

"Let's pray," Tony said, and they all bowed their heads. "Heavenly Father, pour your grace and loving Spirit out on this child of yours. She has taken a big risk Lord, for a friend and now for her own self. She has dared to stand up and say, 'I have sinned', and as her friends around her have already done this day, remind her once more that, as a believer, we have no condemnation in sin because of your Son's sacrifice on the cross. Through Christ's strength in us, we are able to admit our failures and because of that same sacrifice we will not be crushed, persecuted or abandoned. You are for us Lord and not against us, you accept us in a loving embrace, no matter what we have done.

"This situation Lord has had a longer stretch than what we first thought," Tony continued, "and I think it is bigger still than what we have seen. May your angels uproot this evil from among us and bring the plans of the evil one crashing down." He paused for a moment. "Strengthen Kerri, Lord. Be with her and continue to guide her. In Jesus's precious name, we pray, Amen."

"That's the signal," Raphael said to Ruth, and they both shot off into the sky.

An angel from the church, who had been asked to stay with them, nodded and left.

"Well," Steve said, as he stood up from his place at the table. "I have some investigating to do and some calls to make. Where can I contact you all?"

"They are going to stay right here," the minister of the Cairns church, Pastor Wooden, said as he stood. He had insisted that he sit in on the meeting and had kept quiet the whole time. "We have an adjoining cottage that gets used for counselling and youth group activities. There are enough beds in there if they need to stay overnight."

"I'll give you my home number," Henry said, standing up.

"No, you will not," the minister said. "I know this isn't the Hollywood movie that Steve mentioned but all the same, I have a distinct impression that you are all in mortal danger if you leave this building. You need to stay here too."

"Thank you," Tony said, smiling and shaking the minister's hand.

The minister only smiled. "I will see to some lunch," he said, and left the room with Steve.

They sat down again and watched the door close. They looked at each other for a moment and each one was going over what they had heard and learnt from the others. It was incredible how their stories, although separate, were so closely entwined. After a short moment they started to separate and catch up in smaller groups – Henry, Glen and Max in one group and Alan and Kerri in another. This left Tony and Tim alone.

Tim wondered if he needed to stay here too as he had only been driving the boat. He hadn't had a chance to ask before Steve left, better to play it safe he thought and stay.

Tony's thoughts went straight to the one person that had been with them but had chosen to return to the 'belly of the beast'. Not knowing what else to do, he started to pray, "Dear Lord, please protect Jack, wherever he is..."

ONE HUNDRED AND FORTY THREE

Nicole's exit from the portal in Eden had shocked the cherubim on guard there but had drawn no unwanted attention, not that the cherubim had seen anyway.

From there, it had taken Nicole almost an hour to fly to the ambush site. As she landed, she called out the greeting and received the response immediately from a large warrior who seemed to appear out of nowhere.

"Is the Captain here yet?" Nicole asked.

"No, the action hasn't begun yet," replied the warrior. "I imagine he is still at his staging point."

Nicole shifted her weight from foot to foot in uncertainty. Should she go to him or wait for him here? How long would he be before he arrived here? The questions that buzzed around in her head had no correct answer. If she went to him, then she could get there too late and not even know until she reached there and found him gone. By which time it could be all over. The questions raced around her head for what seemed like an hour but only seconds had passed. Then she knew there really was only one answer.

"I will have to wait here for him," Nicole said to the warrior eventually.

"Very well," the warrior replied. "Come with me then and I will put you as close to his proposed exit point as possible."

One Hundred and Forty Four

It had taken Jack almost three hours to drive back to Kings Canyon. It was over three hundred kilometres by road from the Connellan airport just out of Yulara, the resort near Uluru, or Ayers Rock as it was more commonly known, to the resort situated at Kings Canyon.

Jack slowed as he neared the resort once again. He was looking around to see if he could notice any reaction to their escape. He was a little disappointed to see that nothing looked different. If anything, there appeared to be more demon guards than before but no other activity that would indicate something was wrong.

Jack parked the four-wheel drive and entered the hotel. He looked around and didn't notice any of the angels that he had helped earlier. He was about to comment on this to Elisha but when he turned to speak to him, Elisha motioned for him to keep quiet and keep walking.

So that's exactly what he did: he just kept walking until he reached the elevator. He pressed the button and waited for it to arrive.

Ten minutes later, Jack was in his room, grabbing the few things he and Tony had unpacked. He was shoving them back in their bags, preparing to leave again. He also took care to check that the things he hadn't removed from his bag were all still there.

Elisha was looking out the window, watching the nearby building site and the extra activity around it. To his eyes he could see differences in the enemy's movements and even how they were holding their weapons. Some appeared to be extra alert and others seemed very nervous. That combined with the extra numbers he could see told him something that Jack would never have noticed. One of the Seven was here.

"What was so important that we had to come all the way back here for it?" Elisha asked, as he turned and faced Jack.

Jack looked up at Elisha. He hesitated for a moment before opening his bag back up. He pushed a few clothes aside and revealed to Elisha what was hidden in his bag. Elisha walked over and looked in Jack's bag. He looked at Jack with a puzzled expression.

"What is the importance of that?" Elisha asked in confusion.

"It was my brother's. It's the only thing of his that I have left," Jack replied, as he rearranged his bag once more.

Elisha studied Jack for a moment.

"I assume from that, you mean he has died," he said.

Jack looked back down at the bag and he closed it again.

"Yes. That's one of the reasons I carry it with me. It wasn't very long ago and the pain is still fresh." Jack looked back up at Elisha. "There are some questions about the cause of his death and I think this will help me find the answers to those questions," he said, nudging the bag.

Elisha smiled at Jack in a comforting sort of way.

"Count me in, not that I have a choice about it," he said with a smile.

Jack nodded and his eyes suddenly took on a faraway look. He appeared to be thinking of something else, to have disappeared back into that past. He sat, absentmindedly, down on the bed. All the action of the last day and the lack of sleep from the previous night were starting to catch up with him and, before he knew it, he was laying down on the bed, fast asleep.

Elisha knew that he needed the rest so he turned back to the window and watched while Jack slept.

One Hundred and Forty Five

At exactly the same moment back in Cairns, a fairly unimportant police officer was finding out that his new friends were onto something very big.

Steve was at the station and had run a few checks. He had found out that, in every attempt to confirm the information that he had been given, they were either one hundred percent correct or there was no information at all to compare it with. He looked at the list of events that he had made earlier – a break-in, a car chase, the Green Island ferries breakdown, reports of missing persons and chartered flights from Cairns to either Alice Springs or Connellan airports. There were a few that he couldn't get confirmation on, but there was nothing to indicate that it was false either, like the murder of the guard.

The hardest part of all this was that he was trying to do it without being obvious. No one had said it but it was implied that one of his fellow officers was possibly compromised. As a result it had taken him almost two hours to get where he was now. He had made a few phone calls to some sources he had – one at the hospital, one at the airport and one at the city morgue – which meant that he hadn't done all the researching himself. It was at this moment that he found out something that really disturbed him.

Steve's phone rang and he answered it, "Officer Thompson," he said into the phone. It was his source at the airport. He listened as the source informed him of what he had found.

"Really?" he asked when the source finished. "Can you fax a few of those pages over to me?" He listened to the reply. "Email? Sure it's... oh, do you? Yeah that's it. Let me just log back into it."

Steve put the phone on hold while he got his computer out of sleep mode and entered his password again to get back into it. He opened his email and reached for the phone again.

"Thanks for waiting," he said into the phone. "Ready."

He could hear the sound of fingers on a keyboard through the phone and then his computer beeped to say an email had arrived. He checked who it was from and then said, "Got it, opening it up now."

He was looking at the electronic recordings of the flights out of Cairns for the last three months and could see several that went direct to Connellan airstrip. He started to count them but stopped at twenty-one and quickly thanked his source and hung up the phone. As he did, he clicked on the 'print' icon.

He stood and walked over to another desk, this one belonged to an associate, Bill, who worked primarily on the missing person cases. He wasn't sure how much he could trust Bill so he said a quick prayer as he walked.

"Dear Lord, please help me to make the right choices about who I speak with on this case. I do not want to put more innocent lives in danger just because I speak to a corrupt cop. Amen."

Steve's guardian angel listened to the prayer as he walked alongside Steve. As soon as he said 'Amen', the angel started to speak quietly into Steve's ear, telling him not to trust Bill but to ask to speak with his partner.

Steve stopped at Bill's desk and looked down at him.

Bill looked up and smiled, "Hey Thomo, what are you doing here today? Isn't it your Sunday off?"

Steve hesitated for a moment before he spoke. "Just catching up on some paperwork. Where's Jake?"

Bill chuckled, "Damn paperwork, we'd catch a lot more crooks if we didn't have to justify why we did it. Know what I mean?"

Steve smiled and nodded at the poor attempt to make him feel at ease.

"Sorry Bill, haven't got a lot of time today and I really need to check something with 'Action'. Do you know where he is or not?" Steve said rather flatly.

Bill looked at him and apologised. "Sorry Thomo, have a look in the break room. JJ said something about needing a coffee."

Steve thanked Bill and walked away towards the break room, hoping to find Jake 'Action' Jackson there. Steve wasn't the only one who called him 'Action' but most, including his partner Bill, preferred to call him JJ as it was quicker. Jake didn't seem to mind either way.

Steve almost ran into 'Action' as he was coming out of the break room with a coffee in his hands.

"Hey Thomo, catchin' up on some paperwork?" 'Action' asked when he saw Steve.

Steve looked around quickly and, not seeing anyone else nearby he answered, "Not exactly 'Action'. You got a minute?"

'Action' looked at the expression on Steve's face. "Do you want me to grab Bill too?"

"I don't know how to put this delicately so I will just say it straight out," Steve replied. "No. I have something that, to me, is rather sensitive and I don't think that it is for everyone's eyes, if you know what I mean."

'Action' looked back up the passage towards where he and his partner sat and could see Bill talking on the phone. "If you mean what I think you mean then, yeah, I understand. What do you need from me?"

Steve quickly filled 'Action' in on what he was thinking but didn't give him any of the background information. "Do you have a list like that?"

'Action' nodded. "Give me ten minutes and I'll bring it over to you.'

Steve replied, "I'll be at my desk."

'Action' went back to his desk and Steve went to get a coffee himself. On his way back he collected the printout from the communal printer.

When he got back to his desk, Steve picked up the photos that Kerri had taken and was studying the scene in the background. Putting the photos back down, he picked up his phone and dialled the licences authority office.

Five minutes later he hung up again. He had confirmed that there was no casino licence granted to the resort being built in the Daintree rainforest. His source had admitted that there was a rumour that it was only a formality, totally organised and accepted but not on any official paper records. Probably to stop the protestors and other concern groups from slowing the construction down.

Steve was making some more notes about this when 'Action' arrived and sat down opposite him.

"So what have you got?" Steve asked.

'Action' handed over a list he had just printed out. "Here's the list as you requested. What's it all about?"

Steve looked down the list quickly and found Alan and Henry near the bottom. "Numbers 42 and 46 have been found. I spoke with them this morning and they have quite a story to tell. I'm still trying to confirm different parts of the story but it looks like we have a kidnapping and slavery ring happening here. Fairly well funded, from what I can determine... with possibly one or two of our fellows in their back pocket."

'Action' looked back towards the other end of the building to see where Bill was sitting. "You think he is one of them?" he asked.

"Honestly, I have no idea," Steve answered.

"But you think you can trust me with this," 'Action' said, "not that I am saying you can't. What makes you think he is involved and that I am not?"

Steve paused for a moment before answering. "Do you believe in God?" Steve asked.

'Action' sat back in his chair. "I was fairly religious when I was younger but not lately. Haven't been to church for... well not since I joined the force."

"Well I am and as I headed over to speak with Bill I prayed a quick prayer," Steve explained. "I asked God to help me avoid speaking to the wrong person. As I neared Bill I felt really uncomfortable. So I asked where you were and went to the break room. When I got nearer to you, I felt relief and joy. I know it sounds weird for a cop to do that and act like that but... if you had heard what these guys went through and how they leant on God, just like that, to get through it... I reckon you'd start going to church again."

'Action' just sat there. He didn't know how to take what Steve had said, it sounded so wrong to him but then, there was that one time..."

"It isn't that unusual, really. I had a similar experience when I was younger and had forgotten all about it until you told me that just now."

There was a pause for a moment in the conversation. Both men took sips from their coffees and then 'Action' spoke again.

"Without telling me all of it, what is this list good for, other than seeing those two names and being able to remove them from it now?"

"I'm glad you asked," Steve replied. He turned and picked up another piece of paper, the printout of the email he received a short while ago. "Henry, 46 from your list, told me this morning that they had been taken to another resort, one in central Australia. The closest airport is Connellan, which is at the Yulara resort near Ayer's Rock. I spoke with a contact at the airport here and he emailed me these flight plans. Every time a plane takes off it has to have a flight plan registered to tell the tower where it is going. I thought we could cross reference the time frame of flights to Connellan with the time frame of the missing construction workers."

'Action' was intrigued, and if the time frames did coincide..."

"Let's start with Alan, Alan Bryan," Steve checked the list that 'Action' had given him and then checked the dates on the flights and found a match. "Bingo," he said.

"Really?" 'Action' asked.

"Yeah, now let's check Henry," he scanned the two lists and got, "Another match."

"Let me see that," 'Action' said, as he stood and came around the desk to look over Steve's shoulder.

"Look, another one," Steve said, pointing at the two lists.

"And this one!" 'Action' said, pointing at another one.

"This one doesn't match," Steve said.

'Action' looked at where Steve was indicating and then checked the date of the next missing person and it was the next day. He looked at the flights again and pointed out to Steve that there was a flight matching the second one. "This one matches and it is the next day. Maybe they waited and flew two at once," he suggested.

Steve looked down the list of flights. It was rare to see more than one flight in the same week but there were a few cases of disappearances being reported in the same week and then none in other weeks when there was still a flight. He pointed this out to 'Action'.

"The flights are pretty regular, like one a week, but the disappearances don't all match that. Maybe your multiple passenger theory is correct."

"Or," 'Action' replied, "the disappearances were not reported straight away. I know for a fact that they aren't all accurate. In some cases it is a friend that makes the report, someone that doesn't see them every day. They wouldn't notice it until the missing person doesn't show up for meetings or social activities. It's possible they have been missing for a week or more by the time that they report them missing."

"That makes sense, but it would make your job more difficult," Steve said.

"You can say that again," 'Action' replied. As he sat back down, he picked up the photos that Steve had been looking at earlier. Steve winced inwardly, he hadn't realised that he had left them lying out in the open.

Steve didn't say anything.

"What's the bright smudge on this photo? Sun glare? Or is it overexposed?" 'Action' asked.

"Not sure," Steve replied. Which was true, no one had told him that they thought it was an angel.

"Whoa!" 'Action' said suddenly. "Have you shown this to homicide?"

"No," Steve replied. "To be honest, I am not sure what to do with it. I'm not even sure it's a real situation and not something made up for the camera."

'Action' looked closer at the photo. "I think I know who they are," he said.

"You do?" Steve asked in amazement. "Who?"

'Action' got up and put the photo into Steve's hands. "Don't let anyone else see this, I'll be right back."

Steve watched for a moment as 'Action' headed back to his desk. When Bill looked up, Steve turned away. Like most partners, Bill's desk was opposite 'Action's'.

Steve stared at the photo for a moment and then put it face down and went back to the two lists and continued to cross check them. He almost jumped when his computer beeped to indicate another email had arrived. He opened it up and was surprised to see it was from 'Action'.

Steve quickly read it and opened the attachments. He couldn't believe it, the first attachment was a picture of one of the men in the photo. He was lying on the medical examiners table... dead. He picked up the photo again and looked at it once more. It was definitely the same guy but he was alive here. Although, judging by the gun that was pointed at him, not for much longer.

He opened up the second attachment. It was a newspaper article about the man's death. It had a photo with it asking for people to help the police with identifying the victim of the terrible murder. Steve read the rest of 'Action's' email: in it he said they still hadn't identified him but that they thought he might be an illegal immigrant due to some of the things they had found out during the post-mortem. DNA and blood tests indicated that the deceased hadn't been immunised against some of the standard things, which indicated he probably came from a poorer nation. 'Action' also said that he had been identified as working for the construction company as a security guard.

The computer beeped again to indicate that another email had arrived — it was from 'Action'. Steve opened it and read about the other mystery man in the photo. He compared the attached picture with the one in his hands and couldn't believe his eyes. It was an internationally wanted crime boss, know as Lethal Luc. That was what the press referred to him as anyway. He had somehow managed to repeatedly evade law enforcement's attempts to put him in jail. Either his lawyers were top notch and got him off on some technicality or he wasn't there when they tried to capture him.

Steve smiled. The photos of Lethal Luc murdering a man would be enough but the fact that they showed him in Australia, probably illegally, would help too.

"All we have to do now is catch him, and I know just who to ask for help with that," Steve said, as he picked up the phone and dialled.

"Federal police, Officer Ben Thompson speaking," the voice said at the other end of the line.

"Hey Ben," Steve said.

"Stevie! How are things in the local law enforcement offices of sunny Cairns?" Ben replied, with a smile in his voice.

"I have a case that I need your help with," Steve said, coming straight to the point.

Ben got all serious suddenly. It was rare that Steve asked for help with anything let alone a case. "What have you got?"

One Hundred and Forty Six

Unbeknownst to the angels, something was happening in the Garden of Eden. It was the smallest of events so it wasn't surprising that no one noticed it. When the Tree of Life had been uprooted, some of the fruit had fallen off and rolled back into the hole left in the ground. This had been noticed by Jasper but he didn't think twice about it. The disturbed dirt was thrown back in the hole and covered over the fallen fruit. Jasper had thought that this was the right thing to do. The angels had no need to eat the fruit and no one else could see it if it was underground. The result was that the first shoots of a new tree were starting to appear.

The relocated tree, however, was experiencing the opposite. It was still on the decline despite the singing. Although the singing was slowing the process it was not stopping it. The tree looked happier but that was all. The singers didn't realise this as the singing was making the tree appear okay even though it was dying on the inside and very slowly starting to droop again. Strangely enough, the rate at which it was perishing was the exact same rate at which the new tree was growing. Pretty soon both would be obvious to everyone.

The stolen fruit, however, had not changed. Deception had fled the town of Eden as quickly as he could and was now heading to his master's secret hiding place. A hiding place that only a few knew of and many were seeking.

One Hundred and Forty Seven

It had been hours since Steve had left and they had not heard a thing as yet. It was starting to get to all of them, even Tony, who had learnt as a minister that sometimes the best tool is patience. To battle this he was looking around the room at what everyone else was doing.

Max was pacing: the inaction was something that he was finding very difficult to deal with.

Glen was asking Henry and Alan all about what had happened to them while furiously taking notes. He was essentially interviewing them but was doing it in such a way as to not make them uneasy. He felt that this story had to be told. He wasn't sure it was something that would make it into a newspaper, especially with all the religious overtones. Tales about angels, answers to prayer and spiritual battles didn't usually make the grade, but being kidnapped, chased by a helicopter, attacked at sea... all this sounded like a fiction novel. Maybe that was something he could do with it... write a book.

Kerri was sitting with Alan, listening to what he had been through and marvelling at his strength of character. Tim was talking with some other members from the church who had hung around after the service and helped with their lunch.

Pastor Wooden walked back in and, as one, they all stopped to see what he had to say.

"Steve — that is, Officer Thompson — just called. He has spoken with quite a few different sources and has been able to confirm lots of different aspects of your experiences. He wanted me to tell you that as of an hour ago, he contacted the federal police and is now working in conjunction with them and Interpol."

Everyone's eyes widened with surprise.

"They are trying to coordinate a worldwide raid on all the locations marked on the maps that Kerri supplied," the minister finished.

Max gave a hoot of excitement while the others smiled and wondered at the effort that would be needed for such a thing.

"I think," Tony said, "that we should pray for the success of these raids. I think the police forces will need spiritual help. Will you join with me?"

They all agreed and bowed their heads.

"Dear heavenly Father, you are a just God," Tony started, "we know that even though there are times when people get away with the most atrocious of crimes here on this earth, they still have to face you and your judgement. It is with this knowledge that we come before you now, asking you to forgive us for our sins and to see justice done to those who seek to undermine your kingdom."

Glen joined in: "Most gracious and loving Father, I ask you now to send your armies, your warriors, the Host of Heaven, to help the law-enforcement officers, be they local police, federal police or Interpol agents. Look not at the sins they have committed but instead at the sins of those they are after."

To some surprise around the room, Alan joined in: "Lord, capture and punish those that deserve it."

Realising that his new friend didn't fully understand God just yet, Henry jumped in and added a bit to the end of Alan's prayer: "...and offer forgiveness to any who seek it. Help them to realise that although you are a just and vengeful God, you are also a loving and merciful God. We forgive them for the wrongs they have done against us."

Pastor Wooden was taken by the prayers of this small band of Christian warriors, although they probably would not call themselves that. They may not have realised it fully but they were in the middle of the spiritual battle for their souls and this small group was winning victories. He decided to wrap things up for them.

"Great God in Heaven, hallowed is your name. You bring new mercies upon us every day and your love is never ending, no matter what we do. Let us remember that as we move on through the rest of this day but mostly, we pray that your will be done on Earth as it is in Heaven. In Jesus's name we pray..."

"Amen," they all said together.

They opened their eyes collectively and looked around at each other.

"I have some more news," Pastor Wooden said, "Officer Thompson wondered if you would like to join him. He will be here in about half an hour if you do. Think about it carefully. It may not be something that you want to do but it may be something that you need to do." He turned to Tim next: "Tim, you are free to head home if you like. Steve said that as you were only the driver you didn't really need to hang around and he is sorry if he has put you out at all. He said they will fix you up for the day since you have probably lost some income due to being stuck here. He will contact you later about the specifics."

Seeing that Pastor Wooden was finished, Tim stood, said his goodbyes and left straight away. The rest of them started to discuss the offer to go along.

Unseen by everyone else, several angels had entered with the Pastor and his guardian. During the prayer their orders were confirmed and one by one they took off in different directions.

The rest of the guardians and warriors present began to prepare themselves for the battle they now knew was coming. They had discussed it between them earlier and had not expected to be part of it, but now they would be returning to Daintree... to the enemies' den.

Daniel did some fancy stretching and a spin move that looked a lot like a martial artists opening pose, like what they did in the movies just before the big fight. "Bring it on!" he said quietly, a look of confidence and steely determination on his face.

One Hundred and Forty Eight

Raphael walked into the same church as previous and looked for Sarosh. Once again they discussed the prayer needs and then went straight to the minister.

Within minutes the prayer chains were buzzing and falling to their knees in humble supplication. The prayer this time was for a victory for the Lord's Kingdom and justice to be handed out through the police against those that sought to bring it down.

Ruth had taken the same message to Sarah, the Australasia 'Pillar'. Sarah sent her prayer messengers flying as fast as they could go.

The messengers that had just left Glen and his friends all headed in various directions. One returned to the police station and told Steve's guardian what had been said and what they prayed for. The rest headed for the closest points of action, Daintree, Eden, Kings Canyon and Mount Connor.

As Steve spoke with Ben, Steve's guardian passed the message on through the phone to a messenger at the other end. As Ben spoke to his Interpol contact, his guardian passed it on in the same manner to the messengers stationed there. The word was then sent out to the European locals, Eden in the Aland Islands and to Levi in the Middle East outpost. Another call was made from Interpol to their South African contact and through it the messengers passed the word along to their counterparts there too. Pretty soon, a messenger was heading to Vesna in Eden, South Africa.

Messengers had also left to go to the local 'pillars'. Their message: "Get the saints praying."

It had only been ten minutes since Pastor Wooden had said 'Amen'.

ONE HUNDRED AND FORTY NINE

The air was charged with electricity, Cain could feel it. It made him uneasy. If he wasn't careful, his plans would fall apart. He checked his window again. He could still see him standing in the window above. He was sure it was Elisha. It had been a while but he remembered their last encounter. Elisha had come out victor, but that was a very long time ago. He wasn't sure if it was just him or if the atmosphere was getting tense too. It was time to sow a little discord and then get out of there.

Cain walked out of the room and headed for the main chamber, down in the bowels of the resort. It wasn't a long walk but far enough that some of his tension receded before he got there.

After knocking once, he walked straight in. He knew this was a risky thing to do but he also knew that it would get under their skin. Luckily for him, Tarvyn wanted his services. Tarvyn gave him an angry stare and then instantly smiled in welcome. Wraith and Security were there too. It appeared to Cain that the two leaders were grovelling just by being near Tarvyn. Apparently this was exactly what Tarvyn wanted though, as he was not unhappy about their attentions.

Once more, Cain tried to warn Tarvyn that something was about to happen:

"My lord, please listen to me, I do not believe it is safe here."

Security frowned, "You're not still going on about that are you?"

Tarvyn looked down at Security. "Maybe you should listen to him? It is what has gotten him this far, his sixth sense for heavenly presences."

"Lord, if his senses are so good, why is he not among the psychics?" Security asked. "Surely he would serve the masters better by being there?"

"Speaking of which," Wraith said, "if there is such danger, why have our psychics not picked it up?"

There was a knock at the entrance. One of Tarvyn's personal guards walked in"

"There is a psychic here to see... well, all of you."

"Speak of the demon," Cain said.

Wraith sneered at him in response. The psychic walked in timidly and bowed so low that Cain thought his nose must be touching the ground.

"Why do you disturb us?" Tarvyn asked, with an air of importance.

The psychic straightened up and then found it difficult to speak for a moment, during which time Wraith tormented him.

"Hurry up and spit it out you worm!"

The psychic glared at Wraith for the briefest of moments. Cain wasn't sure if anyone else noticed it but he did.

"We are experiencing difficulties, my lord," the psychic said.

Cain, not completely understanding what the psychic was talking about asked, "What do you mean? Difficulties in speaking to us or something else? Be specific!"

The psychic shot him a look of impatience. "I mean, that we cannot control our messengers. There is some sort of disturbance that is stopping them from returning. We have not seen a messenger for ten minutes."

Tarvyn, being one of Lucifer's generals, had learned to listen closely to the psychics. He knew by now that what the psychic was saying was that the enemy probably knew of their location and was beginning to take action against them. It had happened often enough in the past: their psychic messengers stopped returning just before an attack.

Wraith, however, had not noticed this sort of interference from the enemy before and instantly discounted what the psychic was saying.

"You are unable to control your messengers? Is that something that you warrant important enough to bother lord Tarvyn with? GET OUT OF HERE BEFORE I REMOVE YOUR HEAD!"

"Wraith," Tarvyn said quietly, "calm down. Such warnings should be heeded, especially since they back up what Cain has been telling us."

Security shook his head, "Forgive me for arguing, my lord, but our psychics have not been accurate at anything for quite some time now. Previously they were able to advise us before an escape attempt occurred, but in the last week they haven't been able to warn us about any of them."

One of Tarvyn's bony eyebrows shot up. "Escape attempts? There have been more than one? Why wasn't I told? Were they successful attempts?"

Security suddenly looked very uncomfortable and Cain noticed that this made the psychic smile. He couldn't help smiling too, despite his best efforts.

"You find this amusing?" Tarvyn asked.

Cain looked up and saw that they were all looking at him. He bowed slightly and replied, "If my expression was one of delight, my lord, it was at the plan that has just formed within my mind."

This, of course, had its desired effect and made Tarvyn curious.

"Tell me of this plan then," he said.

"Very well," Cain replied. "If the enemy is here, as I suspect and as the psychic's message indicates, then it is too dangerous to try to leave via the usual methods. I have heard of the escapes that were mentioned and I have taken steps to secure the path that was taken out of here. In doing so, I noticed that the exit point is away from the main entrance so would not be noticed by the enemy if one or two of us used it. This would work especially well if we set up a diversion at the main entrance. It amused me that we would use the same escape route that the enemy made use of when they assisted the... humans."

No one made a sound as Tarvyn pondered this. Momentarily, Tarvyn gave a quick laugh.

"It amuses me, too. There is a sense of... irony about it. Security, prepare the diversion. Wraith, prepare my transport and advise the airport that we are on our way."

"Excuse me, lord. Is that a wise choice?" Cain asked, and before Tarvyn answered he pressed on, "What I mean is, if you use the transport and have it waiting at the exit point, surely they will see through the ruse. Would it not be better to have an unmarked vehicle and only the two of us going?"

Wraith's jaw dropped open. "You need to take some of your security forces with you. I will not let you leave with only this... this... two-faced back-stabber," he said.

In a flash, Cain's sword was drawn and pointing at Wraith's throat, mere centimetres from where the Adams apple would be. "You doubt my loyalty?" he sneered, in a challenging way.

Tarvyn grinned as he watched the interaction between these two underlings. The funniest part was that neither of them was actually loyal to him. They were Porva's servants and even though he was trying to win Cain away from Porva, Wraith's attitude towards Tarvyn was one of service too, not loyalty.

"Enough of this," Tarvyn said. "Cain, put away your sword. Wraith, I have no reason not to trust Cain. He –"

"Lord," Cain quickly interrupted Tarvyn, knowing quite well what he was about to say and that if it got back to Porva then it could be him facing swords at his neck, "do you not wish me to remove this *spot* from your chamber?"

He was trying to anger Wraith, but Wraith saw through his attempt.

"Your quarrel is not with me, Cain," Wraith said, "although I admire your reflexes and quick tongue."

Cain slowly lowered his sword and then slipped it back in its scabbard.

"You would do well not to anger me," Cain said quietly.

Wraith nodded, "Thank you for the warning."

Cain turned to Tarvyn, "Think on my plan, lord. I will be in my room, away from these... these –"

Tarvyn didn't want an incident so he interrupted before Cain could think of an appropriate insult. "Very well, Cain, you are dismissed."

The psychic had watched the whole scene with interest. One of the skills a psychic develops as it grows in its power is the ability to gossip. If it wants everyone to know it can see the future it has to tell everyone about theirs first.

Cain was aware of this and had staged the whole scene just for his benefit. He had planned it for anyone that came in but for it to be a psychic was just, “Perfect,” Cain thought to himself, “the little psychic will return and tell about how the leaders are fighting amongst themselves. That should set more mistrust among them and that will help my goal along.”

One Hundred and Fifty

The journey back through the rainforest was a lot slower for Glen and Kerri this time and as they got closer to their destination, they were getting slower and slower.

Glen was sitting with Henry in the back seat of the undercover police car that Ben Thompson was driving. Another federal police officer was next to him in the front of the car. Kerri and Alan were in the car behind them with Steve and Max was in the car behind them with more federal police in each car. There was only one other normal police officer, the chief of police, and he was sitting alongside Max. In the last car, being driven by another federal police officer, were other government agents, one from the Environment Protection Agency, one from the Gaming Licences Bureau and one from the Illegal Immigration Office.

After Steve had spoken with Ben initially, he had approached his chief and explained the situation completely, including their suspicions about Bill. The chief felt that the only way to handle this was to be Steve's partner and work with the federal police. Bringing anyone else in it would alert Bill, or whoever the mole was; sending Steve alone could do the same thing. The chief often worked with his men at one time or another, to assess their performances, so it didn't appear unusual when he announced he was going to work with Steve for a few days.

The cars were nearing their destination and Glen was starting to feel a little uneasy. He was thinking that Tony's idea of staying behind might have been the better choice after all.

The quantity of demons now surrounding them was hard to count. Kyle looked around at the growing numbers and then did another quick count of the angels with them. There were the four that had been with him before the police arrived — Daniel, Amy, Gage and Ishmerai — and the police and federal police officer's guardians, who were actually warriors because of the type of work that they do, which added another nine. Thirteen angels against at least fifty, probably more like sixty, did not appear to be good odds to him. He knew, though, that there were more angels here in hiding and even more demons at the construction site ahead. Ben's warrior-guardian, Joshua, saw the look of concern on his face.

"Do not worry, Kyle, we will be triumphant here today."

Kyle looked at Joshua and thought he was the biggest angel he had ever seen. Joshua had a barrel chest, like a superhero's, and the biggest muscles.

"How can you be sure?" he asked. "We are heading into the enemies' territory and they are expecting us."

"Yes, but we have the advantage. We know what to expect of them but they do not know what to expect of us," Joshua replied.

Gage was sitting with them on the roof of the lead car, "Knowing the Captain has a plan is enough for me," he said.

Back in Cairns, Tony was talking to Pastor Wooden when they both felt the urging of the Holy Spirit to pray for their friends. Pastor Wooden turned to the assembled prayer team of his congregation and held his arms up to get their attention. The room quietened down straight away.

"Let us pray," Pastor Wooden said, and they all bowed their heads. "Heavenly Father, we come before you now to pray for our friends as they face the evil that has affected their lives. May you be with them and protect them from harm and let them not forget the victory we have already won through your Son's sacrifice for us."

Throughout the churches in Cairns and the surrounding areas similar prayers were being offered up and would continue to be offered throughout the afternoon.

The effects were immediate. Kyle, Gage, Joshua and the other angel on the roof of their car, plus the angels on the cars following felt a renewed sense of purpose and determination.

In the cars themselves, the occupants felt the flow-on from the affects of the prayers on the angels. As a result, Glen was starting to feel a little more confident. He looked at Henry and then at Ben.

"Can I ask you a personal question Ben?" Glen asked.

Ben looked at him in the rear-view mirror and answered with a question of his own: "Is now the appropriate time?"

"For this, I think so," Glen replied.

Ben shrugged, "Go ahead then," he answered.

"Do you believe in God?" Glen asked.

Ben smiled and answered, "Yes, very much so. When you see some of the stuff we have seen it makes it difficult to keep going if you don't have a belief in something bigger than yourself. Otherwise, at times it feels as if what you are doing doesn't make a difference at all."

Glen listened intently and understood a bit of what Ben meant, but that wasn't why he was asking. "What about you?" Glen said, asking Ben's partner.

"Absolutely," Ben's partner replied.

"That's great, I feel a bit better about this situation just knowing that. But I would feel better if... well, if I could pray for all of us and what we are about to encounter. Would either of you mind?" Glen asked.

Ben smiled again and his partner shot a knowing look at Ben.

"We just about always pray before a bust and this is bigger than most that we see, so go ahead and we'll join in too," Ben replied.

Henry smiled from his seat alongside Glen. "Great idea, Glen, you start us off and I will finish if that's okay."

No one objected so Glen started the prayer: "Lord God, Lord of Lords, you are gracious and just. We pray right now for your strength to be with us, for your angels to guide and protect us, for your will to be done here. Let your justice be served upon those that would seek to harm your servants."

The same was happening in each car; some prayers were out loud and others were muttered under the breath or quietly, inside the head of the believer. In each case it was a similar prayer — protection and justice were sought.

From their hiding places in the trees, Michael and Evangelos also felt the effects of the prayers. Michael smiled, and with a look of determination on his face he turned to Evangelos.

"Ready?" Michael asked through sign language.

"Ready!" Evangelos answered.

Michael turned to Dizzy and signed, "Get ready!"

Across the globe, similar things were happening. Law-enforcement officials were arriving where the angels were in hiding, ready to launch their plans. Prayers were being said and the Holy Spirit was moving. All that was left was to receive the signal.

One Hundred and Fifty One

Lucas looked out the window to see a moving wall of demons coming closer. The door opened behind him and Bull came rushing in.

"My lord, angels approach," Bull called out, as he bowed quickly.

Lucas looked back out the window and then back at Bull, "Why are we not attacking them?"

"The humans are with them," Bull answered, "the ones we were looking for and they are with the police."

"Local?" Lucas asked.

"Some," Bull answered, "but judging from the size of the lead angel, I'd say there are some national too. I think it is Joshua."

Lucas's eyes showed surprise momentarily. Then he turned and looked out the window again, trying to see for himself. He hit the window with one of his hands, "Damn it, Highrise was right," he said quietly to himself. Suddenly he realised that they had no time to waste.

Lucas turned back to Bull, "Prepare for attack immediately, get the psychics into action and draw the line. Do not let them get through the gates!"

Bull saluted, turned and left as quickly as he could.

Lucas returned to the window and watched the wall getting closer and closer. It seemed that there was a battle already raging inside of him. A choice needed to be made: face them or get out now. Joshua was with them – the mighty warrior of God. He drew his sword and studied his reflection in its red glowing blade. He smiled a wicked smile. His forces outnumbered theirs so, whatever reason they had for coming, they would not be leaving: he would make sure of that personally.

One Hundred and Fifty Two

As they turned the final corner, Glen could see the fence and gate ahead. The same guard appeared to be at the gate waiting. Unlike the last time, he was not alone. There were at least another ten guards at the gate and more were walking towards it from the main buildings.

Ben picked up his radio and called in to his central co-ordinator: "This is Falcon, come in Mother Bird, over."

They waited for a moment before a response was received: "This is Mother Bird, receiving Falcon, over."

"Falcon is ready to swoop, over," Ben said next.

"Copy Falcon. The rest of the nest is also ready to swoop, we are waiting on your go, over," came the reply.

Glen was sitting in the back seat and wondering if he had somehow fallen into a spy movie. He looked at Henry who, judging by the look on his face, must have been thinking the same thing. Ben turned to look at them and they both quickly wiped the smiles off of their faces.

"Are you ready for this, gentlemen?" he asked them seriously.

Glen nodded, afraid that he might laugh if he spoke. Henry nodded too.

Ben lifted his radio again, "Mother Bird, advise the rest of the nest that we are at a green light, over."

"Copy Falcon. This is Mother Bird. All birds to report in, over," they heard as a reply.

"Falcon reporting green, over," Ben replied.

As senior officer it was his right to call in first. Then they heard the rest.

"Eagle reporting green, over."

"That's Kings Canyon," Ben said, mentally ticking them off in his head.

"Hawk reporting green, over."

"That's the Middle East guys," Ben said.

"Osprey reporting green, over."

"That's Finland," Ben said.

"Kestrel reporting green, over."

"And that's South Africa," Ben said. "That's all of them."

"Mother Bird reports green across the board. Swoop is go; repeat, swoop is go."

"Flick the switch," Ben said to his partner, who then did as he was told and leaned over and flicked a switch. Suddenly the siren began wailing, the lights went on and all the cars raced forward just to stop again when they reached the gates, only two hundred metres away. The police, federal and local, all jumped out and raced towards the gates with hands on holsters or holding shot guns pointed in the air.

Ben walked between his fellows up to the gate. He flicked out several pieces of paper and held them in front of the guards.

"This warrant is for the arrest of several of your bosses; this one is to search your property for any illegal immigrants; this one is to check for signs of construction of illegal gaming facilities; and this one is for inspection of environmental care. Unless you want to be arrested for interfering with an investigation, you should unlock these gates and let us through," Ben spoke very loudly so that they could all hear him and there would be no misunderstanding. The other government officials lined up behind him to carry out their specific inspections.

"Let them through, they are just here to do their jobs," a voice called out from behind the guards.

Mr Fisk was walking confidently towards them.

"Be aware officers, I have already contacted the company lawyers in regards to your presence here. Those warrants had better be iron clad," he said as he approached.

Ben just smiled as he replied, "Mr Fisk, it will be my pleasure to escort you back to the city once we are finished our inspections."

The gates were opened as they spoke to each other.

"It will be my pleasure to deny you that opportunity," Mr Fisk replied, as the officials pushed through and passed the guards.

At the same time in Eden in the Aland Islands, in Eden in South Africa, in the Middle East and at Kings Canyon, the law-enforcement officers and government officials were experiencing the same thing with similar people. Each group was coming up against the same arguments, pushing passed the resistance to rush in and check things out before they could be covered up or removed.

In Kings Canyon, Jack was awakened by the arrival of the police and their sirens. Getting up to see what was going on, he saw that Elisha was at the window with his hand on the hilt of his sword, watching very intently. The pose he was in told Jack that he was ready for a fight.

"What's going on?" Jack asked.

Elisha didn't look at Jack as he answered, "The police are here. Your friends have ignited a bonfire by going to them. It was very courageous of them."

Jack came over to look out the window and he could see a whirlwind of activity. The police were there, rushing into the building, while several guards were just standing there, looking like they didn't know what to do. But that wasn't all that he could see. The demons were rushing around, making it difficult to actually see each one individually.

Jack couldn't see a reason for their unrest but something had stirred them up.

Jack didn't want to hang around and find out. He rushed into the bath room, splashed water on his face and then rushed back into the room. He scooped up his bag and Tony's and then grabbed his keys and rushed out the door. When Elisha didn't appear next to him he stuck his head back in the room to see what he was doing.

"Are you coming?" Jack asked.

Elisha turned and saw that Jack was in the doorway, wanting to leave. He nodded and moved across the room to join him. Once they reached the lobby, Jack went to the desk and checked out as quickly as possible. When he opened the door to leave he found himself in the middle of a battle.

People were rushing in off the street, scared but not knowing why. The demons were running riot, trying to intimidate the police officers and whoever else they could effect.

Jack went to leave, to make a run for his car but Elisha laid a hand on his shoulder and said one word, "Wait."

Jack looked around at him, "For?"

Elisha looked out into the street, his eyes blazing with fire. He spoke quietly and Jack had to lean in a bit closer to hear him.

"The signal," was all that Elisha said.

Jack looked down and saw that Elisha's hand was still resting on his sword hilt.

"The signal for what?"

One Hundred and Fifty Three

The disturbance was happening at all the locations and it was caused by the angels. The demons didn't react well to the presence of heavenly warriors, especially ones the size of Joshua.

For the angels' part, they hadn't done anything yet, but they were trying to get into the demons' dens and it appeared the demons couldn't stop them. The angels had to be allowed to follow their charges, so if the charges were allowed inside then the angels had to go with them. The demons were furious and as a result were flying around and around in circles, hurling insults and swinging their swords in a hopeless attempt to scare the humans enough to stop them from entering.

This was making it difficult for the hidden angels to stay hidden. All across the globe angels could feel the tension caused by this; humans everywhere were feeling the tension of the angels and, as a result, hundreds of Christians suddenly stopped what they were doing and prayed. They prayed for calm, they prayed for relief and those that were really in tune prayed for deliverance from evil for themselves and their fellow Christians, wherever they were and from whatever evil situation they were in.

Glen and Henry were feeling it too. They were still in the back seat of the police car watching Ben and his fellow officers doing their thing when they felt the need to pray again. In the middle of their prayers, Kyle whispered something into Glen's ear, who then said it aloud. It was what Michael was waiting for. It was the signal.

Glen, in the middle of his prayer, said, "In the name of Jesus Christ, my Lord and Saviour, I bind these demons."

Michael didn't hear Glen, of course, but he saw the effect that those words had on his enemy. Without warning, several demons that were flying nearby appeared to be suddenly struck by something. They lost control of their wings, dropped their swords and fell out of the sky, crashing to the ground below, unconscious.

Michael recognised what had happened immediately and said one word: "Go!"

Dizzy flew straight up into the air, a silver horn suddenly appearing in his hand and he blew one clear note with all of his might. The demons nearby were shocked to see their companions fall out of the sky for no reason. They also knew what it meant: there was someone close by praying for their downfall. They nearly fell out of the sky themselves when they saw the angel with the horn and heard the note he blew.

Michael and all the hidden angels suddenly burst forth. They were brilliantly illuminated, in all their glory, with their weapons in their hands, ready for battle for the Lord and His Kingdom.

Then they attacked. All, that is, except Evangelos. He waited a moment and then ran, still unglorified, through the undergrowth and across to a clearing. He pulled out his sword and quickly opened a portal.

Evangelos then turned and called out in a loud voice, "I found it!"

Several warriors were waiting for this and split immediately off from the skirmishes they were in and flew to Evangelos. They grouped themselves around the portal and prepared themselves to defend it.

In the Middle East, Levi and Gabriel heard the horn's note, as clearly as if it had been blown by someone standing beside them. They drew their swords and flew into action, attacking to create the diversion which would allow the appointed angel to open their portal.

In the Aland Islands, Uriel led the angels into battle while Driscoll opened the portal. In South Africa, Zagzagel was the first into battle, while Vesna opened the portal.

In Kings Canyon, Jack had heard the note too and was surprised to see Israfel rush passed, leading his gathered angels into attack.

Jack looked at Elisha with wide eyes and could see the strain on Elisha's face.

"What's wrong?" Jack asked.

"That was the signal," Elisha replied. "It was a call to arms. Only a few notes higher and it would be the announcement of the end."

Jack just stared at Elisha. "You mean that trumpet sound?"

Elisha nodded and looked at Jack.

"We should take this opportunity to go."

Jack looked back out at the street and could see the angels flying back and forth, attacking the demons. The angels with the police were standing their ground, protecting the humans from harm. Most of the demons were ignoring them now and were trying to counter the strike from Israfel and the many angels that had suddenly appeared.

There was, of course, one angel that Jack didn't see: Titus. He had gone to open the portal. Jack heard him when he called out, "The portal is here!"

He looked at Elisha again. "What is that about?"

"Don't worry about it. Let's go to the car and get out of here," Elisha replied.

Jack nodded, "You're right, of course. Let's go."

Jack pushed himself away from the door where he had been leaning and watching the confusion of the battle. He ran across the street, opened the rental car and jumped in. Elisha was right behind him the whole way and as he jumped in the car too, Jack noticed that he had his sword out.

Jack sat there for a moment. Elisha, unsure as to why they hadn't moved yet, stole a quick glance at Jack.

"What are you waiting for, we must depart!" Elisha said, with urgency in his voice.

"Right, right, sorry," Jack replied, as he snapped out of it and tried to put the key in the ignition.

Jack got the car started and reversed out of the parking space and then took off, down the road, back towards the airport and away from the battle behind them.

One Hundred and Fifty Four

Bull was locked in battle with Michael; neither seemed to be gaining or giving ground. Like most demons, Bull couldn't keep his mouth shut while he fought. He was trying to break Michael's concentration by insulting and taunting him. It wasn't working.

Michael was silent, concentrating on the fight. So much so, that he didn't see Bliss swing at him until the last moment. Bliss had been sure that he would take him by surprise but ended up more surprised himself at the speed with which Michael reacted. Michael had turned and blocked Bliss and then manoeuvred himself away from Bull so that Bliss was now between them. Bliss's attempt to corner the great Captain of the Host had failed.

"We must capture that portal at all costs!" Bull called out to his warriors.

Hammer and Goliath heard him, but they were too busy fighting to do anything about it. Then the demons seemed to get the upper hand and most of the angels drew back towards the portal.

The only angels not protecting the portal now were with the human law officials. Bull couldn't worry about them now. If he captured the portal, the reward from Lucas would be... no, not from Lucas, he thought... from lord Porva or maybe even Lucifer himself! He could see it now: Lucifer granting him the position of a Deadly Sin – whichever one he wanted. He would ask for Sloth, no – Lust!

An arrow shot passed his ear suddenly. That drew him back to the moment and he realised he had to actually capture it first.

In the loudest voice he could muster he yelled, "CAPTURE THE PORTAL! STRIKE THEM ALL DOWN!"

Unnoticed by the demons, the angels were slowly disappearing through the portal. One by one they went.

Bull smiled in delight at the thought of an easy victory.

The same was happening at the other sites too. Only a handful of angels were left in front of the portals. Some of the angels were struck down though and they immediately disappeared back to Heaven for healing.

In Kings Canyon, Jack happened to see this happen to one of the angels that he had met the day before. As he drove he noticed the portal only a hundred or so metres off the road. It was located at the National Park, away from the hotel, and he had to drive past there to leave. He thought he remembered seeing something like it before and then guessed what it was. When he saw the number of angels trying to guard it, and the quantity of demons attacking them, he knew he was right.

Jack also thought he recognised a number of the angels as they fought, but as they were moving so fast and he was driving, it was difficult to be sure. The pure spectacle of seeing the angels and demons locked in combat was enough to make him slow down and stop the car.

Elisha tried to get him moving again, "Why have you stopped here? It's not safe for you."

Jack glanced at Elisha. "Are you kidding? I bet there haven't been many humans who have ever seen this sort of thing! It's... incredible."

"And deadly to you if one of those swords goes through your heart or your head," Elisha said.

Jack swung around to look at Elisha. "They can hurt me with those swords?"

"Absolutely," Elisha replied.

Jack turned back to the fight and as he put the car in gear he saw it happen. An angel went passed the front of the car, fighting two demons at once. Jack recognised the angel from the day before but was not sure of his name. Impressed by the fighting, Jack sat there for a moment and then he watched in horror as one of the demons thrust his sword through the angel's body.

"Ivor!" Elisha cried out.

As they watched the demons moved away and Ivor sank slowly out of the sky, curled up slightly from the wound in his stomach. Jack jumped out of the car and ran towards him. It took a moment for that to register with Elisha but as soon as it did, he was out of the car and following.

Jack reached Ivor as he hit the ground. Jack had tears running down his face as he rolled him over. Ivor looked up at Jack. Jack couldn't speak. There was a lump in his throat so big that he was finding it hard to even swallow.

"Don't worry about me, my friend," Ivor said quietly. "I will return to Heaven now."

Elisha knelt beside Jack and said a quiet prayer. Ivor's wound started to glow. It got brighter and brighter until Jack couldn't look at him anymore and had to shield his eyes. At that instant, Ivor reached out and pressed something into Jack's hands. Then there was a moment of silence — everything seemed to stand still and the light went out. Ivor was gone.

Jack almost fell over, into where Ivor had been.

Jack looked up at Elisha, "Where is he? Where did he go?"

"As he said, back to Heaven," replied Elisha. "When we are injured in such a way, we are called back to heaven for healing and then reassignment."

"He's not dead?" Jack asked, as he stood up.

"No," Elisha answered. "We are not mortal so we cannot die."

There was a moment of silence as the two stood there, Jack contemplating what he had just learned and Elisha having quick thoughts about Ivor. The reverie was quickly broken as they both suddenly remembered where they were when a demon landed beside them and swung at Jack with his sword. Jack instinctively raised his arms to block the sword and was surprised to see a sword in his own hands. The swords met and the force of the blow knocked Jack over. Elisha then struck at the demon, removing its head.

They both looked away from the swirling vortex that opened to suck away the remains of the demon. Once it was gone, with the pop sound of the small vortex closing, Jack and Elisha looked at the sword in Jack's hands.

"Where did that come from?" Elisha asked.

"Ivor put something in my hands just before he disappeared," Jack replied, "I guess this was his sword."

Elisha bent over to look at the sword in Jack's hand. It was definitely an angel's weapon.

"You are special indeed," Elisha said.

Jack looked up at him. "Why do you say that?"

"Never, to my knowledge, has a human held one of our weapons," Elisha replied.

One Hundred and Fifty Five

Tarvyn was watching out the window at the battle raging outside. He wasn't sure about what was happening and thought about the suggestion that Cain had made.

He wondered what his troops would do if they saw him sneak out the back door. He was no coward but he did not invite trouble. There was an archangel out there — he had seen him. Not only that, the human law officials had arrived. They were in the building, heading in the direction of the hidden elevator that would take them to the lower levels and the slaves.

Never mind that, what if they found his human? He was here illegally. He had spent a long time getting this one to this stage and if he had to abandon him, then he would have to train a new one all over again. He would lose his title, possibly his name! Capture was not worth that. He had to get out of there now!

Tarvyn jumped when the door suddenly swung open in the middle of his thoughts. He turned and saw Cain standing there.

"What is it Cain?" Tarvyn asked, trying to look unconcerned.

"Are you aware of what is happening outside and downstairs?" Cain asked.

"Of course I am," Tarvyn replied. "I am surprised you are not out there fighting too. You are one of our best."

"Thank you," Cain said with a slight bow, "but I never participate in a losing battle if I can help it."

One of Tarvyn's bony eyebrows shot up. "You know we are going to lose?"

"Israfel is out there. So is Elisha," replied Cain. "They would not be here otherwise."

"I did see an archangel, are you sure it's Israfel?" Tarvyn asked.

"Oh yes," replied Cain, as he slowly walked into the room. "I saw him quite clearly but don't worry, he did not see me."

Tarvyn turned back to the window. "I thought Elisha was *retired*."

"Obviously not anymore," Cain answered. "He was in the other hotel, watching out a window. I don't think he is here for the fight but you never know."

Wraith and Security suddenly rushed into the room.

"They knew of the elevator!" Security exclaimed in a panicky voice.

"The secret one," Wraith added, "and they are using it right now."

"Then get down there and start killing the slaves," Tarvyn said flatly. "They must be looking for them. If you remove them, they can't testify against you."

"What about you, lord?" Wraith asked. "It is only a matter of time before they come up here too."

Tarvyn nodded. "I have considered that and as much as I hate to run from a fight, it appears that we may have already —"

Tarvyn stopped at the appearance of a psychic at the door.

"My lord, forgive this intrusion," the psychic said in a rush, "but we have found it."

"What?" Tarvyn asked.

"A portal," the psychic replied.

"Are you sure? I thought your messengers hadn't returned," Wraith asked.

"When the fighting broke out, a few started to return," the psychic answered. "When the portal was found, they returned all at once to report it."

"All at once?" Cain asked.

"Yes," the psychic replied excitedly.

Security and Wraith looked to Tarvyn in excitement while Cain stood in thought.

"Security, get the word out to the troops: concentrate on that portal. If we can capture that, then we can still win this battle," Tarvyn ordered. "Wraith, the slaves are your responsibility. Well don't just stand there, get going!"

Wraith and Security rushed from the room so fast that the psychic barely had time to get out the way.

Noticing that he was still there, Cain dismissed the psychic.

"As for us," Tarvyn said to Cain once they were alone again, "we will use your escape plan, just to be safe."

Cain smiled to himself as he bowed to Tarvyn. "A wise idea, I think," Cain said. "If you will follow me then, my lord," Cain said, as he turned and walked out of the room. His plan was going well but the fact that the psychic's messengers arrived back all at once was worrying him.

One Hundred and Fifty Six

"Defend the portal!" a voice called out from somewhere nearby.

Jack and Elisha looked around and saw Israfel standing near the portal, locked in battle with a demon. Then they noticed other angels also fighting with the demons and slowly making their way to the portal.

A demon neared the portal but stopped suddenly and started to swirl in on itself. When it disappeared, an arrow fell free to the ground and an angel arrived and picked it up again. The angel refitted the arrow and searched for another target. It didn't take him long as there were plenty to choose from.

Jack looked all around and noticed that the small band of angels, probably thirty in total, was horribly outnumbered.

Elisha was also looking around. "I think we better go before we are attacked again," he said.

Jack looked at him. "Go? We need to help them," Jack said, as he stood and pointed at Israfel and the others near the portal.

"They can handle themselves," Elisha replied.

They walked quickly back to the car.

Jack turned and looked at the angels again and then at the sword still in his hand. He turned and opened the car, grabbed his bag and opened it as quick as he could. He reached in and dug around until he was at the bottom. He grabbed out what was hidden there.

"What are you doing?" Elisha asked, as Jack put the leather jacket on.

"I'm going to join the fight," Jack replied, as he hefted the sword in his right hand.

"Jack, that is not wise. They do not die if they are hit. But you... you would be in mortal danger if —"

Elisha never got to finish the sentence. Jack called out "Duck," and swung his sword. Elisha did as he was told and ducked just in time.

Jack's sword met the sword of a demon coming the other way. Jack didn't know who was more surprised, Elisha or the demon. Probably the demon, as Elisha recovered quicker and struck at the demon. The demon reacted quickly but not quick enough. Elisha managed to cut him but not deep enough to open the vortex. Elisha swung his sword again. The demon blocked it this time. The demon was concentrating on Elisha and ignoring Jack. It was an opportunity that Jack didn't waste. He struck fast, stabbing the demon in the side.

The demon stopped and looked at the sword sticking out of him and then at Jack. "How???" it hissed as the vortex began to suck him in.

It was too late now for Jack and Elisha to leave. Their little fight was noticed and more demons came at them to replace the fallen one.

"Let's move them so that our backs are to the portal too," Jack suggested.

Elisha agreed and pretty soon they were standing with the rest of the angels, backs to the portal, fighting the oncoming wave of demons.

****

At that moment, Tarvyn and Cain exited the same exhaust that Henry had led them to the day before. As they came out they turned and looked at the fight in the distance. Their sharp eyes picked up the portal shimmering behind the angels.

"It's the portal!" Tarvyn exclaimed. "It's true!"

Cain looked on with interest and thought about it, realising that the portal didn't matter to him at all. Then he saw Jack fighting with an angelic sword in his hand. "What the...?" Cain said, when Jack performed a spin move that allowed him to see the back of the jacket for a moment.

Tarvyn started pacing. Should he fight too or should he run?

"If they could capture the portal and enter it...," he thought to himself.

Now Cain was unsure too. Why was one of his human bikers fighting with the angels? He had to find out but he couldn't tell Tarvyn the reason why.

"Cain," Tarvyn said, "we must join the fight. If we can capture that portal then we will be treated with great favour by Lucifer."

Cain looked back at the fight and nodded his agreement as he drew his sword. Tarvyn drew his and they both took off, headed straight into the thickest part of the fight.

One Hundred and Fifty Seven

The tension was still high for Ben and the rest of the police in Daintree. They were treading lightly yet with authority. They knew that these men were armed. One false step and they might draw their weapons. They had managed to get inside the fence and started to split up into different groups to check out the various charges when all hell broke loose.

It was at that moment that Dizzy had blown the horn and the angels appeared. Several guards suddenly drew their weapons and started to fire them into the air at nothing in particular. Joshua and the rest of the warrior guardians attacked the demons that were in control of the guards, while Ben and his men shouted for them to drop their weapons.

Kerri, Glen, Max, Henry and Alan had joined together between the first two cars to watch the authorities do their thing. When the shooting started they all ducked behind the car, seeking some sort of protection from the wild fire of the guards.

The guards ignored Ben's order, so the police officers started to fire their weapons in a disarming manner. They took aim at knees and legs and, once the guards fell, they rushed in to grab the weapons or kick them away.

Somehow, none of Ben's men were hurt in the shooting. Some of the guards recognised the danger; they dropped their weapons and surrendered straight away, while others ran for the cover of the trees.

Max, Henry and Alan were watching from behind the car while Glen was trying to keep Kerri calm. Henry and Alan watched the remaining guards disappear into the trees and looked at each other. Before he knew what was happening, Max was running after Alan and Henry, into the rainforest.

Mr Fisk looked like he was having some kind of fit. He was walking backwards and swinging his arms as if trying to fend off an attack of some sort. But nothing was there. Not that the humans could see, of course.

Dizzy was attacking Lucas and since Lucas was currently controlling Mr Fisk, his reactions were slow and clumsy. So he did the only thing he could do and that was to release his control over Mr Fisk. Lucas shot out of him and Dizzy went after him. Mr Fisk collapsed in a heap on the ground.

Ben ran over to him with his gun drawn but not pointing at him. He checked Mr Fisk out quickly — he was alive and breathing but had a vacant stare as if he was only just waking up. Suddenly, reality hit him and he sat up and tried to get away from Ben, hitting him in the process. "Come back," he called out. "Don't leave me alone with them!" Even though he was no longer being controlled by Lucas he still knew what he had been doing and he enjoyed the power that he held, whether his 'guide' was with him or not, but mostly when he was there. Ben and his partner grabbed Mr Fisk quickly and placed him under arrest.

Meanwhile, Lucas had stopped flying away and had turned to fight. Only it wasn't Dizzy who was following him now, it was Michael. Michael attacked as soon as he reached Lucas. Lucas used his momentum against him and batted Michael aside fairly easily. Michael spun around and blocked the next strike from Lucas. They traded blows for a while and gradually Michael got inside his arc and scratched Lucas with the tip of his sword.

Someone nearby called out, "Defend the portal!"

Michael and Lucas continued as if nothing had happened. Michael caught the next swing of Lucas's sword and pushed him backwards. Then Michael did the most unexpected thing: he turned and flew off towards the portal.

Lucas smiled, as this told him that Michael wasn't confident in facing him and winning. The fact that he hadn't actually made contact with Michael, and that he himself was pretty scratched up, meant nothing to him. He immediately took off after Michael.

The same thing was happening in the other locations too.

Someone would call out, "Defend the portal!" and all the angels fighting, except the ones with the law-enforcement officials, retreated to the portal to defend it.

One Hundred and Fifty Eight

Mr Kepler crept around the tunnels, trying to stay away from the police who were searching them. He had managed to come down the elevator unseen and only had two more bends before he would reach the room where he had ordered the slaves locked up.

Wraith was with him, doing his best to keep away from the angels. He snuck a peak around the corner and saw that the way was clear. He whispered to Mr Kepler to hurry up.

Mr Kepler got around the remaining bends to the room where the slaves were kept. The slaves looked up at him as he entered. All of them, except one, tried to retreat into the furthest corners of the room when Mr Kepler pulled the gun out of his belt. The one that didn't try to get away stood tall before the rest as he tried to protect them and talk the warden down. As Mr Kepler raised the gun, the man threw himself forward.

Wraith was surprised to see the angel in the room. As he drew his sword, the angel threw himself at Wraith.

The men struggled with the gun, locked in a tangle of arms and legs. Trying to get control of it before...

-BANG-

The gun went off. Luckily it hadn't been pointing at anyone and the bullet harmlessly embedded itself into the wall.

The man realised the danger even more when the gun went off. Keeping his left hand on Mr Kepler's outstretched wrists, he pulled his right arm back and threw the hardest punch he could into Mr Kepler's stomach. Mr Kepler doubled over immediately. The man took the risk and released Mr Kepler completely so that he could grab his head and pushed it down as he brought his knee up. Mr Kepler fell to the ground unconscious just as the door swung open again and two of the police came in with their guns out.

The angel and the demon clashed. The sounds of the swords connecting was almost deafening to them as they collided with such force. The angel blocked and then attacked quickly. Wraith blocked and then attacked and attacked and attacked. The angel backpedalled under the assault and then sidestepped suddenly. He lunged forward and down on one knee while bringing his sword through from left to right. It passed cleanly through Wraith's midsection.

Wraith staggered forward, clutching at his stomach. The vortex opened as the door did and in entered two of the biggest angels with their weapons drawn. They put them down when they saw the vortex and suddenly, with a pop, it was gone.

The slaves were overjoyed to see the police and the police quickly reported that they had found them and took Mr Kepler into custody.

When asked what had happened, the slaves reported that Mr Kepler entered, pulled the gun out and then one of them fought him. When asked which slave it was that had fought, no one was sure. They hadn't seen him before they had been locked up but he had been very caring and brave right up until the police entered. No one had seen him since.

Micah was smiling at Duncan, "Good plan, you guessed their intentions correctly."

Duncan grinned back at Micah, "And you played the caring slave well... for a messenger."

"Well, maybe it's time I rethought that," replied Micah, as the two angels walked out of the little room.

One Hundred and Fifty Nine

Max ran as fast as he could but still couldn't catch up to Henry and Alan. When they entered the rainforest he lost all sight of them. He wanted to call to them but was also aware that they were chasing people who didn't know they were being chased.

Max stopped for a moment and closed his eyes tight. He counted to sixty and listened for any noises that didn't seem natural. When he reopened his eyes he could see a lot better but he couldn't see his friends. Max was about to move forward when he heard someone behind him. He turned, ready to defend himself.

Glen appeared from between some bushes.

"Where's Kerri?" Max asked in a whisper.

Glen stopped. "Max? Is that you?" he whispered too.

"Yes. Close your eyes tight, it will take a moment for them to dispel all residual light and adjust to the darkness. When you reopen them you will be able to see a lot clearer," Max advised quietly.

"Alright," Glen replied, as he closed his eyes. "Why are we whispering?"

"Henry and Alan followed some of the thugs in here and I followed them. The thugs didn't see us chase them and I don't want to give my position away," replied Max.

"Good idea," Glen said. "I left Kerri with an officer. She didn't like the shooting but also didn't want to come in here after you."

"That should be long enough, open your eyes," Max suggested.

Glen opened his eyes, blinked them a few times and smiled at Max. "That's better. Now what?"

"Now we have to find our friends," Max answered, while turning to look further into the rainforest. "Normally I'd say we should follow the crunching sound of twigs and leaf litter, but in a rainforest everything is too wet to crunch."

As if on cue, a loud commotion came from somewhere in front of them, as if a fight had broken out. Glen and Max started to run towards the noise.

****

Alan and Henry had not stopped moving since they entered the rainforest. Alan had told Henry to blink continually until his eyes adjusted as they entered the darkened interior while doing the same himself. They slowed to a walk while they did this but kept moving all the same. They even turned when Max followed them in but when they recognised the new friend, they didn't stop and wait but continued on. It didn't take them long to catch up with the stragglers of the group of thugs who were still groping around in the half light of the rainforest.

Alan and Henry were builders, so they were quite strong and well built. Henry was a little bigger in the upper body than Alan as he was a labourer while Alan was an electrician. That didn't mean that Alan was any less imposing, as he liked to surf in his spare time. Neither man looked for fights normally but they didn't back down when they were faced with one either.

As they caught up to the guards and security workers, hired thugs really, from their previous employer, they had to decide how to tackle this situation... especially since there were seven thugs to only two of them. Luckily for them, the thugs were moving single file through the rainforest.

They decided to creep up behind them, hoping to catch the guy bringing up the rear. It didn't take long before one fell a little way behind the rest. Henry wanted to be the first to take one out so he rushed up as quietly as possible and grabbed the thug from behind. He grabbed him in a headlock with his right arm and put his left hand over his mouth. Then he dragged him back into the underbrush and held him there until Alan punched him in the mouth, knocking him unconscious.

Alan and Henry quickly took up the chase again. They soon caught up with the group. However, this time the thugs were expecting them. They had noticed that one of them was missing. When Alan grabbed the next rear thug, he called out "Now!" and the rest turned to help their fallen friend.

Alan quickly punched his captured thug, knocking him out (or so he thought), as Henry jumped forward to take on the first of the thugs to reach them. Alan returned to Henry's side as the next thug arrived. As each thug returned, they joined in the fight.

Alan and Henry were outnumbered five to two but they didn't give up, not even when the stunned guard rejoined the fight. Back and forth the fight went, neither side gaining ground until Max and Glen arrived. Glen tackled the nearest thug to the ground while Max karate kicked one in the head, knocking him out.

The new arrivals distracted the rest of the thugs enough that both Alan and Henry got in great punches and laid their combatants out cold. The remaining two turned to flee but found their path blocked by Max. Alan moved in behind them while Henry went to help Glen.

Moments later, the thugs were all unconscious. Alan, Henry and Max stayed with them while Glen went back to get Steve.

One Hundred and Sixty

The defence was holding but the numbers against them would eventually overwhelm them. Michael was locked with Lucas while the others had one or two demons attacking them at the same time.

Michael saw one angel go down on one knee and knew it was time.

"Dizzy!" Michael called out. "Sound the retreat!"

From somewhere nearby, Dizzy replied, "Yes, Captain, as soon as I can."

Evangelos finished off his demon with a quick stab of his fighting daggers and turned and threw them at the two that were attacking Dizzy. Then he jumped through the portal. Dizzy, suddenly free of his opponents, pulled out the horn and blew another note. Then he retreated through the portal too.

One by one, they all disappeared into the portal until Michael was alone, a blur of motion, holding off three demons and Lucas at the same time. He started to glow brighter and brighter until, with a sudden burst of energy, he flashed brilliantly. The demons fell away, temporarily blinded. Michael used the distraction and dove through the portal too.

****

Jack's ability with the sword was surprising the angels around him. If he'd had time to think about it, Jack would have been surprised himself. But he didn't, so he continued fighting on instinct and reactions alone.

Israfel was amazing to watch: he had three demons on the go at once and most of the rest of the group had at least two. But for some reason, it appeared that Jack was surrounded by the most vortexes. That was until a particularly nasty looking demon came in at him.

Cain was not attacking Jack with all his might — he was mostly trying to keep Jack occupied so that he could talk to him. He noticed that Tarvyn had gone straight for Elisha, so he felt confident that he would be too busy to hear his questions.

Cain managed to get Jack locked into the holding block and he took the opportunity to speak while they were close enough.

"Where did you get that jacket human?"

Jack was surprised to be asked a question. Every other demon had tried to taunt him or insult him.

"It was my brother's," he answered, pushing Cain back and then he swung at his head.

Cain, not entirely happy with the answer, blocked the swing and came at Jack again. They traded blows for a little while and just as Cain was about to ask another question they heard the second note.

"Retreat!" Israfel called out and one by one the angels disappeared into the portal.

"Come on, Jack," Israfel said from behind him, "Go through the portal."

Israfel inserted himself between Jack and Cain relatively easy. Jack staggered back, fairly tired from the fighting. He turned and saw Elisha push his opponent, the biggest demon that Jack had ever seen, away.

Elisha then started to run at him, "Go Jack, through the portal, go!"

Jack turned and saw the other angels going into the portal so he joined them and stepped through it, with Elisha right behind him.

One Hundred and Sixty One

When they heard the first note, the warrior turned to Nicole and told her that it was starting. Pretty soon the portals started to appear with the rushing noise of the wind passing through them.

Evangelos was the first one to appear through one of the portals and he came through the one closest to Nicole. He looked around and smiled and then quickly moved away from the portal.

At almost the same moment they heard the second note and all of the warriors lifted their weapons ready. The one closest to Nicole told her to be ready – they were coming.

And come they did. A steady stream of warriors started to appear from all the portals. Then came the biggest surprise – a human. But before anyone could say anything, the archangels all appeared and Michael started issuing orders straight away.

"Missile weapons get ready!" he shouted, as he moved back behind the portals. The portals had been set so that they were in a rough circle, all facing in at each other. The first row of angels behind the portals held bow and arrows, spears or some other kind of throwing weapon. Some had throwing stars, Evangelos had some throwing daggers and a couple even had blow pipes with darts in them.

As Michael moved through the front line he spotted Nicole and went straight to her.

"What are you doing here?" he asked Nicole.

"The Twelve sent me with a message and when Kenaniah and Jasper heard I was coming they sent a message too," Nicole answered.

"The Twelve?" Michael asked.

"Yes, the rest of them had heard of Saint Peter's involvement and went to him to help. They wanted me to suggest to you something about an eclipse. Saint Peter said you would understand. Something about the darkness, I think he said," Nicole replied.

Michael scratched his chin for moment. "An eclipse? That might just be the final element that we need. Okay, what did Kenaniah and Jasper say?"

"The Tree of Life is not prospering in its current location and they think they have found a way to close the portal too," Nicole answered. "They asked me to ask you if you wanted it closed yet?"

Michael looked uneasy. "The Tree is dying?" he asked.

"They have found that singing is slowing it down but wanted to know if you had any better suggestions," Nicole replied.

Michael shook his head. "Not currently but let me think on it. As for the portal, it can wait until we get back. Now please, they should be coming any moment now so get ready if you are joining in; otherwise it might be safer if you moved away. I must speak quickly with the rest of the archangels here about the eclipse."

Nicole nodded and took a step back. She pulled out two Sai knives and gave them a quick twirl.

Michael raised an eyebrow and then turned and called out to the archangels, "Council of the host, assemble in the air!"

Michael rose up above the mountain top that they had chosen for this battle. Israfel, Gabriel, Zagzagel and Uriel rose up instantly and flew to him.

"A new suggestion has been made and needs to be put into action immediately if it is to work," Michael said straight out.

The others nodded and waited for Michael to continue.

"Saint Peter has sent word: he has suggested an eclipse. Such a thing, if you remember back to the time of Creation, and almost every one that has occurred since, puts fear into our enemy's hearts," Michael said.

Gabriel looked around. "It is not the right time for one to occur here, Captain."

"I know," Michael replied, "and that is where you come in. We need to simulate one and we need to get it happening as soon as possible. That way when the zenith occurs, we will be in the middle of the fight and not already at the end of it."

"How do you suppose we go about it?" Zagzagel asked.

"I have only one idea," Michael answered, and then went on to explain it to the rest of the Council.

One Hundred and Sixty Two

In Daintree, Lucas was celebrating that they had captured the portal. Hammer was there with him and was preparing the forces to follow the angels through the portal. The angels were on the run. They had to continue to carry the fight to them.

A messenger was sent to tell Porva of their great victory and to request backups to join them inside the Garden of Eden, where they assumed the portal led.

Once that was done, Lucas decided that he couldn't wait any longer, so he gave the order and the troops started to pass through the portal as quickly as they could.

In Kings Canyon, Tarvyn and Cain looked at each other. They both knew what the other was thinking: they needed to go through the portal too. Tarvyn stepped forward but Cain reached out to stop him. Tarvyn looked down at Cain's hand.

"Why do you restrain me?" Tarvyn asked.

"It may be a trap," Cain replied, so quietly that Tarvyn on just barely heard him. "I would suggest that we send the troops through first and then follow in the midst of them. We wouldn't be such easy targets then."

Tarvyn smiled a wicked smile. "I am so glad that I have you with me," Tarvyn replied, just as quietly. Then he turned, "You there!" he called out.

Security looked up, "Yes, my lord?" he replied.

Cain had noticed Security in amongst the fighters earlier and was a little surprised to see that he had survived so far. He must have some decent fighting abilities, Cain reasoned.

"Organise your troops and prepare to follow the enemy," Tarvyn ordered.

Security smiled, "It will be a pleasure, sir," he replied.

Security was looking forward to taking the fight to the angels for once. Most of the leaders he had served under were too timid when it came to that sort of thing. He quickly organised the remaining demons and advised Tarvyn when they were ready. Tarvyn gave them the go-ahead and they immediately began to pass through the portal.

It was the same in the other locations too. The lead demons believed they had the portal to the Garden of Eden and it was best to take advantage of the open portal while they could and take the fight into the enemy's territory.

One Hundred and Sixty Three

When Jack appeared through the portal, Itzal was there waiting for him. He was surprised to see a sword in Jack's hand and when Elisha appeared behind him he was even more surprised. But Jack was the most surprised. Here he was, in the middle of a clearing on top of a mountain, surrounded by at least two hundred angels, with more coming out of other portals nearby.

"Hello Elisha," Itzal said. "Welcome human, I have been asked to help protect you during the coming skirmish. If you will follow me, we need to vacate the battle zone before the enemy appears."

"Itzal, hello to you too," Elisha answered, a little surprised.

"My name is... Jack," Jack replied. "Where are we and how did you know we were coming?"

"We are at a place called Mount Connor. My mission comes from the Lord of All," Itzal replied, as he led them out of the circle of portals and through the ranks of archers and spearmen.

Once they were a little distance away, Elisha noticed how tired Jack looked and commented on it to him. "You look worn out, Jack. Are you up to this?"

Jack sat down. "I don't know. I feel tired and worn out. Swinging a sword is not as easy as Errol Flynn made it appear."

"Who?" Elisha asked.

"He was a movie star from about sixty years ago. Famous for playing swashbuckling-type characters," Itzal said, and seeing a blank look on Elisha's face he added, "Swordfights mostly."

Itzal then looked into Jack's eyes. "I need you to sit quietly for a moment, close your eyes and receive the 'rest' of the Lord."

Jack looked a little confused but knew not to argue with an angel, so he closed his eyes. He felt Itzal's hands on him, one on his head and the other on his shoulder. Then he felt something a little strange – he was starting to feel refreshed and full of energy. He could feel it passing through him from Itzal. When Itzal removed his hands, Jack opened his eyes and stared at him.

"That was amazing!" he said. "Thank you for... whatever you just did."

"Don't thank me," Itzal replied. "It was a gift from God. Now stand up and let me see quickly how you handle that sword."

Jack stood and felt a little foolish but swung the sword around a bit as if he was fighting anyway.

"Do you feel comfortable with it?" Itzal asked. "Or is there some other sort of weapon that you would be more comfortable with?"

Jack looked at the sword in his hand. "It is a little heavy," he replied, "but other than that, it feels good in my hands."

Itzal studied Jack for a moment and then reached out for the sword. Jack handed it over and Itzal held it up in the air before him. He swung it once and then gave it a little shake.

The sword changed. The blade straightened a little and something started to fall from it. It looked like he was tipping sand out of the handle.

Itzal gave it another little shake and twist and then smiled. "I think that will be a bit better suited to you," he said, as he handed the sword back.

As Jack took the sword and hefted it, he could feel the difference immediately. He performed a few moves again and smiled when he finished. "What did you do? It feels so much better now!" he said.

Elisha smiled. "Itzal here is our sword master. He knows just about everything there is to know about swords."

Itzal smiled. "One of my gifts is the ability to discern the perfect sword for each of the warriors that choose to use one. This was Ivor's, wasn't it?"

Jack nodded.

"There is only one reason that an angel would be parted from his weapon and by the look on your face, I know that it happened," Itzal said. "Don't worry, he is not dead and will be back in action soon."

Then they heard it. It was like one big 'twang' but in fact it was around a hundred separate ones happening all at the same time. The archers had fired. That could mean only one thing: the enemy had arrived and fallen into their trap.

One Hundred and Sixty Four

Three of the portals had been used at almost the same time. There had been only microseconds between them before each one had demons coming through them.

The demons were cut down before they could realise that they were not where they expected to be. One of these was Security, who had chosen to lead his troops through the portal.

The demons seemed to continually pour out of each portal. Only seconds had passed before the next portal became active. Before the first demon had made it completely through the newly active portal, it was pierced by three arrows and a spear. It was now disappearing into a vortex, headed for the Abyss. The last inactive portal became active just as that vortex closed.

The demons started to come through each portal in groups of two. There were now more demons than the archers and other missile weapon warriors could handle.

Michael shouted, "Attack!" and rushed forward with many warriors at his side. Jack, Itzal and Elisha rushed forward too.

Gradually smaller groups formed as particular warriors singled out certain demons and vice versa. Cain and Tarvyn arrived from Kings Canyon and Lucas from Daintree. Another one of the Seven, Mephisto, came through from the Middle East along with two major-domos, like Lucas, with several lieutenants, like Bliss and Bull, from the Edens in South Africa and Finland.

Michael met Mephisto in battle and they soared back and forth over Mount Connor. Tarvyn targeted Elisha again and this time Elisha wasn't holding back. Cain came after Jack but was met by Itzal instead. Jack just stood his ground and took on anyone that came near him. Nicole joined Jack and fought at his back.

Jack, in the few moments of battle, noticed that this time he did not have the most vortexes around him. This made him realise that the earlier battle was not fought as hard as it could have been. The angels had been holding back so that they could draw the demons here for one big battle. There were many vortexes around the battle field and every now and then there would be a flare of light, indicating that an angel had fallen too.

Suddenly the noise level dropped and it took Jack a moment to work out why. The portals had been closed. There was no escape for these demons and no more backup to come to their aid. They were to stand and fight, win or lose, or, if possible, flee by flying away as fast as they could.

They had been fighting for nearly five minutes when Jack noticed the next change in battle. The demons were suddenly unsure of themselves and they started to mutter and become less attentive to the fights.

"There!" Nicole said from behind him.

Jack looked over his shoulder and saw she was pointing up. Jack's gaze followed to where Nicole was pointing and he saw it too. Something was starting to block out the Sun. He couldn't make out what it was completely but it looked like an eclipse had started.

Michael and Mephisto were in a hack and slash fight. Mephisto was one of the largest demons Michael had ever faced. He was almost as big as Baal was in Babylon all those years ago. They would exchange blows for a while and then Mephisto would try to fly away; Michael would follow and Mephisto would stop and fight again.

When the Sun started to darken, Mephisto lost his focus and Michael got in some very good stabs and cuts. Mephisto had lost one hand and part of a wing when he decided to fly away again. Michael, not content to let this leader of demons go, chased after him.

Tarvyn was attacking Elisha with a ferocity that he had never seen before. Elisha might not have been active in the last thousand years or more, but that hadn't stopped him from continuing his training. Where Tarvyn was using ferocity and anger, Elisha was using concentration and grace. Tarvyn's inability to land a hit on Elisha was adding to his anger.

They were so busy in their own battle that they never noticed the portals closure or the Sun's gradual disappearance.

Itzal and Cain were another matter entirely. Cain fought wisely, trying to wear down his opponent while Itzal also fought wisely and didn't waste any movements. He was, once again, in the dance of the blade.

Cain's large curved blade was no match for Itzal's two Katanas. So at his first opportunity he snatched a sword from a dissolving demon and tried to fight two blades with two blades. The only problem was that Cain was not accustomed to fighting like this.

For every lunge Cain made at Itzal, Itzal parried it with one blade and struck back with the second. Cain's clumsy attempts to block the second meant that his left arm was getting more cut up than his body. The more this happened the clumsier his left arm appeared as he tried to block the next lunge.

When the eclipse started, Cain actually smiled.

One Hundred and Sixty Five

Mount Connor is often confused for Uluru as it is on the left of the same road. It is only once you get closer to it that you realise your mistake as Mount Connor has what appears to be a flat top or plateau.

The action on top of Mount Connor was not going unnoticed by the nearby travellers. For years they would tell of the strange sights they saw that day. It was almost like fireworks were going off, except these fireworks were harder to see as they were only black, red and white. That was until the 'eclipse' started. Then the light show became clearer.

However, no one could not see what was causing such a phenomenon. Some thought it was otherworldly, like a UFO – or a whole bunch of them. Others thought it must be a natural occurrence, like the rays of the sun being caught in water fountains, like a rainbow. One suggested it was caused by gas from within the earth and that Mount Connor was becoming a volcano.

But no one could explain the 'eclipse'.

One Hundred and Sixty Six

Ben and Steve were not sure what had happened but something had definitely changed in the attitudes of the guards and workers at the half-constructed hotel in the Daintree Rainforest. They had suddenly lost their animosity and evasiveness, and had become slightly helpful.

One worker led the Immigration official straight to a room full of illegal immigrants. Another worker led the Gaming Licences official to a very large but incomplete room. It didn't appear to be anything out of the ordinary but could have been the proposed location for the casino. An adjacent room was of great interest to the Gaming official. It had over a hundred power points in it. This was where the electronic gaming machines were destined. This could have been explained away, as there were no machines present, but the worker said something about being sick of covering up and getting nothing in return. The worker then led them to a filing room and proceeded to pull out all sorts of documents outlining exactly what they intended to do with those rooms and many others.

The EPA official had a much easier time without any help from the workers. It was more than obvious to her that the environment was not being taken into consideration. They hadn't even stuck to the proposed boundaries and had dug and torn out trees that they were never meant to touch.

But there was no sign of their murderer or the victim... Lethal Luc was gone.

"Falcon, this is Mother Bird, over," Ben's radio suddenly squawked.

"Falcon receiving, Mother Bird, go ahead, over," Ben replied into it.

"Eagle requesting direct link, over," the radio said.

"Authorised, put Eagle through, over," Ben replied.

"Falcon, this is Eagle, copy? Over," said one of Ben's fellow Federal Officers from King's Canyon.

"Receiving Eagle, what's up? Over," Ben asked.

"Prisoners liberated, Lethal Luc in custody, and EPA guy says he is going to have a field day with the construction company, over," Eagle said.

Ben looked up and smiled, "Bingo."

"Please repeat Eagle, confirmation requested about Luc, over," Ben said into the radio.

He wanted to hear it again, just in case he had not heard it correctly.

"Lethal Luc in custody, along with all his staff, over," Eagle replied.

Ben looked at Steve, "Well done little brother, this is going to look very good on your records."

Steve smiled. "I think I will go and tell the others the good news."

Steve was heading back to the cars to let Alan, Henry and the rest of them know what was going on when Glen suddenly appeared from out of the rainforest.

"Where have you been?" Steve asked Glen, who was sporting what would become a nasty looking black eye and a few scrapes on his arms.

"There you are," Glen said, a little puffed out from his walk/run. "We followed a few of the guards into the rainforest as they tried to escape."

"You did what?" Steve asked incredulously. "Didn't I stress enough to you how dangerous these men are?"

Glen stood there, slightly bent over, looking up at Steve while trying to catch his breath. Steve couldn't believe what he had heard. He was dumbstruck that this man-

"Hang on," something just occurred to Steve, "you said we. Where are the others? Are they alright?"

"Max, Alan and Henry are fine. They are in there still, guarding our capture," Glen replied.

Steve was surprised. He re-evaluated this man who was standing before him, taking in his appearance again: scratches, black eye developing, slightly out of breath, shirt a little ripped and sweaty – whatever had happened in there, he had held his own. "Firstly, are you okay?"

"Bit banged up, nothing a few days of rest won't fix," Glen answered.

"Good," Steve said. "Where are the others exactly and are they alright?"

"They are in the rainforest. I can lead you to them. They are in better condition than I am."

Steve's eyebrows went up at that. "Why did you come back out and not one of them?"

"Simple, if the thugs wake up, they are better at knocking them back unconscious."

Steve laughed. "How many thugs are there?"

"Seven," Glen answered.

Steve stopped laughing and became all business again. "I'll round up some help. Think you can lead us back to them?"

"Easily," Glen replied.

"Wait right here then," Steve said, and turned and walked off towards a group of officers.

ONE HUNDRED AND SIXTY SEVEN

The fighting continued at Mount Connor, with the number of demons dwindling quicker than expected. The eclipse idea was definitely working. It was almost complete, at its zenith, when things suddenly changed.

Mephisto stopped running from Michael and faced him with a furious assault. Tarvyn tried to join Mephisto in his attack on Michael but found that he couldn't ignore Elisha. Michael found it difficult to manage the two but, with Elisha's help, was surviving the onslaught.

Cain gave up using the two swords and concentrated on blocking Itzal with his sword, which was in his right hand. He threw the sword in his left hand away so that he wasn't tempted to use it. He didn't lose any more of his left arm against this well-trained angel.

Lucas had been picking on smaller angels but hadn't stuck with any one single battle and now found himself facing Jack. To his surprise, Jack was holding his own.

Most of the smaller demons tried to flee while some tried to join in with their leaders. They soon found themselves with arrows or a spear sticking out of their backs.

To Cain, it appeared that the confusion and distrust he had been sowing had worked. Combined with the eclipse, they were almost in blind panics. The demons no longer listened to their leaders and just tried to flee in every direction. Even though that was part of the desired effect, now was not the time that Cain wanted it to happen. Or was it?

Suddenly Cain broke away from Itzal and dove at Jack again. Nicole saw him coming and threw one of her Sais at him. It hit Cain in the shoulder, causing him to break off his dive and head in another direction but not before he threw the ancient dagger back at Nicole. Nicole caught it without any difficulty at all.

Itzal tried to follow Cain but Cain used the confusion of the other demons, and the growing darkness, to his advantage and managed to get away. Itzal, in his chase of Cain, ended up coming face to face with Tarvyn and Elisha. Elisha had managed to draw Tarvyn, away from Michael and Mephisto. Itzal joined in, without being asked, and Elisha welcomed the assistance.

Tarvyn was no match for both of the angels. Itzal had opened so many wounds on Tarvyn, that he was becoming hard to see through the red mist oozing out of him. Uriel suddenly rushed passed, slashing Tarvyn across the back, cutting off his wings. At that exact moment, Itzal stabbed Tarvyn through the heart and Elisha stabbed him through the stomach. It was all too much for Tarvyn and a vortex opened behind him.

Moments later, with a loud pop from the closure of the vortex, he was gone.

Uriel had continued on, not looking back to see what his little bit of help had achieved. He was rushing to help the Captain. As he drew near, he sheathed his sword and pulled out a small crossbow. He fitted one of his own creations, an arrow, with two wings, in the shape of a cross, and fired it.

Michael had been ducking and weaving since Tarvyn had tried to attack him too. Mephisto was gloating, thinking that he had Michael on the ropes, when Uriel's cross shaped arrow hit him between the eyes. Mephisto toppled over backwards. Michael immediately changed his tactics and attacked. He threw his sword at the tumbling form and it passed cleanly through Mephisto's thick black hide, embedding itself in his chest. Michael then drew out two small swords, just a little bigger than a dagger, and dove at the still-tumbling demon.

Mephisto suddenly righted himself, pulling the cross out of his head and then reached for the sword in his chest. Before he could pull it out, another cross hit him, this time in his right shoulder. His right arm went numb and he lost partial use of it. Before he could think too much about it he had another three swords piercing his scaly hide. His breath chugged out in great big yellow puffs, while the red ooze seeped out of his wounds. He was in shock that this had happened to him.

Michael and Uriel reached him, Michael retrieved his swords and Uriel retrieved his cross shaped arrows. Mephisto didn't even try to fight back as Michael raised his sword and swung it at his neck. Michael had to steady himself after he had cut off Mephisto's head so that he didn't fall into the vortex by accident.

"Thank you for your help, old friend," Michael said to Uriel.

"My pleasure, Captain," Uriel replied.

They turned back to the battlefield and could barely see it. The fake eclipse had blanketed the area in almost total darkness. All that could be seen was the orange eyes of the demons and about two hundred glowing white angels.

ONE HUNDRED AND SIXTY EIGHT

Jack's fight with Lucas was fairly even, apart from the demon being so much bigger and wielding a bigger sword. This was actually to Jack's advantage as it made Lucas a little bit clumsy when fighting an earth bound and smaller opponent.

Through the fight, Jack had become separated from Nicole. He had no one watching his back or helping him. He was on his own. Lucas lunged with his left hand and Jack rolled under it and stabbed upwards quickly. That was the third time he had done that and Lucas was starting to get a sore arm. Lucas suddenly switched arms and took the sword in his right hand.

Jack ducked at the last moment from a sudden swing from the right. He realised that Lucas had been playing with him. Jack decided that he needed to end this as quickly as he could or there wouldn't be anything left of him. He attacked, he lunged, he stabbed, he swung and jumped but he couldn't get through Lucas's defence.

"Had enough puny little human?" Lucas taunted, as Jack stopped and stood still, panting for a moment.

"Why? Are you scared of me?" Jack responded between breaths. "You should be. I am going to send you back to whatever hell you came from."

Lucas just laughed.

"What's so funny?" Itzal asked from behind Lucas.

"He thinks he's going to win," Elisha answered.

Lucas looked around suddenly and realised that he was alone against his enemies. It was still dark but slowly getting brighter again. He couldn't see any other demons at all.

All he could see were Michael, Uriel, Itzal, Elisha, Nicole and then row upon row of arrows pointed at him.

Lucas swallowed hard but didn't back down. He bent his knees and stood in a ready type position with his sword held high. He knew he didn't have any chance but he wanted to try taking as many of them with him... especially the human.

He sprang at Jack with incredible speed. Before he had crossed the distance, the archers all fired. Jack anticipated the jump and rolled forward and then struck upwards. When Lucas landed, he had forty arrows in him and a huge cut running from where his navel would have been, down and around and up his back. His tail landed alongside him, separately. He swayed, unsteady on his feet, and looked down at his tail. The last thing he saw was the vortex opening to take him to the Abyss.

Elisha grabbed Jack and pulled him back from the vortex, afraid he might get sucked in too.

"Well done, Jack," Elisha said, once the vortex closed again.

"Thanks to Itzal," Jack said. "This sword was perfect."

Itzal bowed slightly, "You are more than welcome."

"Jack?" Michael said walking up to him from behind.

Jack turned around and looked up at the face of the Captain of the Host of Heaven.

"My name is Michael. How is it that you are here? Fighting with one of our swords? And please, tell me everything you can about that jacket you are wearing."

One Hundred and Sixty Nine

Kerri, Glen, Henry, Alan and Max watched as the workers were all loaded into police vans to be driven back to Cairns.

Steve walked up to them, “How are you all holding up?” he asked.

They looked at each other and answered with a chorus of, “Fine,” and “Okay.”

“What happens now?” Glen asked.

“Well,” Steve answered, “the construction will be shut down. The place will be thoroughly investigated. The bad guys will go to trial and then some of them, maybe all of them, will go off to prison – depending on how good their lawyers are.”

“And the other site?” Alan asked.

“We found an international mob-type boss hiding there and the other ‘slaves’ you told us about,” Steve answered. “That site will be shut down too, followed by investigations and trials like here. The boss, a man they call Lethal Luc, will be put away for a very long time. He will be charged with murder and illegal entry, for starters. Hiding at the location of a slavery ring, with connections to this place, means that we have a very good case against him. But the icing on the cake is your photos.”

“My photos?” asked Kerri.

“Yes,” Steve replied. “You remember the murder in the background. He is the one holding the gun and the guy he shot happens to be the same guy that you clocked with the fire extinguisher.”

“That would mean...,” Kerri started but didn’t finish.

“That you didn’t kill him,” Steve said with a smile.

“That’s great!” Glen and Alan said at the same time.

“What about the other slaves?” Henry asked. “What is happening to them now?”

“They’ll been airlifted to Alice Springs for medical checks and debriefing by the police. Once that is all over they will be flown home.”

“Excellent!” Henry said and Alan said, “That’s great,” again.

“What about the dead body we saw? George?” Henry asked.

“They are searching for it. Some of the staff became real talkative and described a spot just out in the desert where they may have dumped it,” Steve answered. “If we find it, it will be one more piece of evidence against them.”

“And what about us?” Alan asked. “Can we go home now? Is it safe for us?”

Steve smiled reassuringly. “I think that is definitely allowed. You have all been through so much and to have come through it like you have is amazing. You deserve now to go home and rest. We will, of course, be in contact in relation to the court case.”

"Fine, whatever. I just want to get to sleep in my own bed for a change," Alan replied.

"I'll second that," Henry said.

"That's understandable. I'll get someone to take you all back to Cairns. That is, if you're ready to leave?" Steve said.

Glen looked around at the group. "I can't speak for everyone but I'd like to go back to the church first."

One by one, including Alan, they all nodded their agreement.

One Hundred and Seventy

Jack looked at Michael and realised that it was time to tell the whole story to someone. “How much time do you have?” he asked.

Michael looked at him and then around at all of the angels surrounding them. “I’d better tie up some loose ends first. Will you wait and talk to me. I think I need to hear what you have to say.”

“I’ll wait,” Jack replied.

“Thank you, Jack. I won’t be long,” Michael said, and turned away.

“Jack, if it is okay with you, I am going to leave you with Itzal for a little while. There is something I need to do too,” Elisha said.

Jack looked at Itzal and nodded his head.

“Sure, go ahead. Do whatever you have to do.”

Elisha nodded and took off. As he did, the sky got brighter again. He looked up and saw in the distance, that four angels were holding up a huge rock in the air.

Elisha could see that Uriel was up there too, with the rest of the archangels, helping to take the rock back to wherever it had come from.

Michael walked over to Nicole who was talking with some of the other messengers who had been involved in the battle. They stopped talking at his approach. “I need your help one more time. Will you help me please?” he asked the group.

They all nodded and gave replies like, “Of course, Captain,” and “Whatever you need.”

“Thank you, my friends,” Michael said sincerely. “The use of portals is authorised once again. Firstly, I need someone to return to Cairns, to Raphael and Ruth, and thank them for their efforts with the prayer cover. It was perfect.”

“I will go,” Evangelos said and turned, opened a portal and left.

“Nicole, I need you to go back and check on the Tree of Life. Then report back here to me about it,” Michael said.

“At once, Captain,” Nicole replied.

She turned, opened another portal and left.

“Lastly, I need someone to go to Lori in Eden, New South Wales, and advise her that the threat is over and the portal there will be closed soon,” Michael said.

“I will take that,” Micah said.

He turned, opened another portal and disappeared through it.

With that done and organised, Michael returned to where Jack was sitting with Itzal.

“I’m ready,” Michael said, as he approached them. “We may get interrupted a few times but otherwise I am all yours.”

Michael watched as Jack looked around at all the angels still on top of Mount Connor with them. He smiled at Jack in understanding as he realised that he had one more job to do. Michael then turned, raised his arms up in the air and called out in a loud voice, "Your attention please!"

Everyone stopped what they were doing and turned to face Michael.

"Thank you all for the efforts that you have put in today and for many of you, the last couple of days," Michael began. "I know some of you are already receiving healing from others here. I thank you for enduring what we went through. I think it was a victory worth celebrating. Our ancient enemy has been dealt a harsh blow and few have escaped to be able to tell about it. Let us sing a song of praise to the Lord and then please return to Heaven, or wherever you are stationed, and continue to celebrate and worship our Lord."

Jack just sat and listened to the beautiful song they sang. Once it was finished the angels left slowly in ones and twos, and then whole flocks of ten or more. It didn't take long before Michael and Itzal were the only two left with Jack.

Michael looked at Itzal, "What about you?"

"He can stay," Jack replied.

"Alright Jack," Michael said as he sat down too. "Tell me your story."

Jack was about to start when the rest of the archangels returned.

"Jack, these are the Lord's archangels. They are my advisors. I think they should hear what you have to say too. Do you mind?" Michael asked.

Jack replied, "That's fine."

He then went on to tell Michael, Itzal and the rest of the archangels about his brother joining a motorbike gang, a particularly nasty one called Satan's Thorns. Something happened that he didn't agree with and he tried to leave. No one, however, is allowed to just leave the gang. Once you are in, it is for life. They found his brother's body a week later. Jack took the jacket and started to go from town to town, asking at the biker bars if anyone had seen the gang that wore that jacket. After two years of travelling, he had gotten sidetracked and started to get mixed up with some of the unseemly elements that he was coming into contact with. It got too much and he tried to get away and hide from it, but something was telling him that he would never escape it.

"That was when I found myself in Eden with a plan to take my own life. I tried that night but somehow I jumped through a portal that led to the Biblical Eden instead of into the stormy sea. The angels there got rid of a demon that had been following me. Then they dropped me in Broken Hill, at the foot of a minister named Tony. Tony took me in and helped me. In a way, I helped Tony too. He introduced me to his wife, who I learnt later was really his guardian angel.

"Tony decided he needed a holiday and we went away, just the three of us. During our holiday I met a bunch of angels and helped them check out a demon den."

"Just like that?" Michael asked.

"Well... no. Just after we arrived in Kings Canyon, I found out that I could see and talk to angels. While this freaked me out a little, I realised that I have been able to do it ever since I had been to Eden. The realisation that angels and demons existed brought me to the conclusion that Tony was right in his beliefs. I made the decision there on the spot to become a Christian. That's when I met Elisha. He is my guardian angel. *Then* Nathaniel asked us to go into the den.

"While inside the den, Tony and I came across two people trying to escape. We helped them and then caught a flight to Cairns, where they are now, as far as I know. I had trouble sleeping last night because of this jacket. I couldn't leave it here, so I came back for it. As Elisha and I left the resort today we saw the battle begin. As we drove past where the portal was, we saw an angel, Ivor, get taken out by a demon. I stopped the car, we ran to help him and then he disappeared. But before he did he pressed his sword into my hand.

"We ended up getting caught in the battle, mostly because I was holding the sword. From there, I went through another portal, fought some more and, well, I'm now talking to you."

Michael nodded, "Thank you, Jack," he said. "The reason I asked you that is because we have heard of that gang recently and we now have an interest in finding them too. Would you be interested in helping us with this? Before you answer, I think you need to know that I do not believe it is a coincidence that you are here talking with me now about this same group of people."

Jack sat there for a moment, thinking on what Michael had said. "The last time I was asked to help an angel it led to this battle. Do you think that is going to happen again?"

"I can't lie to you, Jack," Michael answered. "It is a possibility that it will lead to another battle. I wouldn't think it would be as big as this one though."

Jack thought about it for a moment.

"I want to go back to get Tony and ask him to come too, or at least say goodbye to him if he says no."

"It sounds like he is already involved," Michael replied, "I think that is a good idea."

"If there are going to be more battles, I think I need a sword master to train me to be a better fighter," Jack said, as he turned to look at Itzal.

Michael looked at Itzal too, "That is up to you, Itzal. You have no posting at the moment so you are free to help Jack… unless you have something else in mind?"

"I'll go with Jack," Itzal replied, without hesitation.

"Good," Michael answered. "I would suggest—"

At that moment, Nicole appeared and immediately interrupted the conversation. "Captain, you need to return to Heaven now!"

One Hundred and Seventy One

The archangels stepped out of the portal, right behind Nicole. She had returned them to the Garden of Eden.

"What's so important that we had to leave so quickly?" Michael asked.

"This," Nicole said, indicating the Tree of Life.

"What about it?" Michael said. "It's the Tree of Life."

Zagzagel stared at it. Gabriel looked towards the 'gateway' to Heaven. Israfel had no idea what was going on. Michael realised the importance of what he was seeing just as Uriel asked, "Didn't we see it get moved out there? Did someone bring it back?"

"What happened?" Gabriel asked, as Michael stepped towards the tree to study it.

"It's not the same tree," Michael stated.

"No, it's not," Jasper answered from behind them.

The archangels turned to see Jasper, Saint Peter and Kenaniah approaching. Jasper continued, "Our best guess is that the fruit that fell off when we lifted the tree out of the ground has regrown into a new tree, to replace the one that we removed."

"What about the other tree, the one that was removed?" Michael asked.

"Dead," Saint Peter said from beside Jasper. "Even though it was planted correctly in Heaven, there is something special in the soil here that it needs in order to grow."

"Once the saints stopped singing it just withered up on the spot and disappeared into the ground. Not a trace of it left," Kenaniah explained.

"In the end, moving the Tree was not the answer," Saint Peter said. "If the devil tried to control it and gave the fruit out to the human race, it would cause some issues about mortality. But as soon as they stopped eating it, they would start to grow older again and eventually die. The only true way to eternal life is through Jesus and accepting Him and His gift. He is the only Saviour."

Michael nodded his head in agreement.

"Well then, the only thing left to do is close the portal. Nicole said you know how to do it?" Michael asked Kenaniah.

Jasper and Kenaniah looked at each other.

"That's not necessary either. It closed by itself about an hour ago."

"Just all of a sudden, pop, closed," Jasper added.

Michael smiled to himself. That was about the same time that the other portals had all closed. He had wondered who could have done that. Now he knew. It could only have been the Lord.

Epilogue

Four hours later, Jack was back in Cairns.

Elisha knew that Jack would want to return to Cairns. When he left Jack on the mountain top with Itzal, he went first to Connellan Airport and arranged a flight to Cairns. Then he went back to Kings Canyon to get the car. Elisha then carried the car back to Mount Connor as he hadn't attempted to drive one of these machines yet. Once there, he collected Jack and Itzal, and the three of them drove the remaining distance back to the airport. They found their plane waiting for them — another charter plane — and it flew them non-stop back to Cairns. Jack then took a taxi to the church that Tony had mentioned and found Tony, Henry and Alan still there.

After an hour of swapping stories, Henry, Alan and Kerri excused themselves and left for the night. Glen had managed to get his rental car back from where it had been left the day before and had offered to give them a ride. Max left with Glen.

Once they were gone, Jack told Tony about the mission that Michael had given him and asked Tony if he wanted to join him. Tony didn't answer but instead informed Jack about Alan having become a Christian too.

"In the end the evidence was too much for him and he couldn't deny it any longer. Kind of like what happened to you, Kevin," Tony said.

Jack hesitated for a moment, he felt like the proverbial deer caught in the headlights. "About that," he said, "my name is really Kevin, Kevin Daniels to be precise. In my university days I picked up the nickname of Jack, as in Jack Daniels the drink, and it kind of stuck with me through uni. When I left uni I dropped it and went back to being Kevin. When I started out searching for my brother, I thought it would be safer not to use my real name. I started to use Jack again. I'm sorry for misleading you."

"That's okay," Tony replied with a smile. "I'm glad you feel comfortable enough to tell me now. However, I am getting on in life and trying to remember which name to call you is going to be hard. How about we just leave it as Jack for now?"

Jack smiled at his friend.

"When do we leave to go searching for this bike gang?" Tony asked.

"Michael told me to start the search in Port Lincoln. That was where they had been seen last," Jack replied. "I guess it would be as soon as we can catch a flight to Adelaide. We can catch a smaller plane to Port Lincoln from there."

****

Later that night, Glen was going over his notes once more and he came to a sudden realisation. He hadn't heard back at all from his friend, Pastor Phillip Hunter.

He grabbed the phone and started to make some calls, if only to see if he was alright. No one answered his cell phone. He tried the church office again and got the answering machine. It told him that the pastor was away preaching in Ceduna and would be back early the following week. Glen decided to leave a message so he waited for the beeps and then spoke:

"Hi Phil, it's Glen. Just wanted to let you know that I am alright and I am sorry if I alarmed you at all with my call the other night. I have an amazing story to tell you when you have the time. I am thinking of turning it into a book... anyway, if you call my office when you get in, they can call me and—"

"Glen!" a teary voice suddenly said on the other end of the line.

"Hi, who's this?" Glen asked, as he didn't recognise the voice.

"It's me, Sally," Sally, Phillip's wife, answered.

"Hi Sal, I didn't recognise your voice. Have you been crying?"

"Phil's missing Glen. I don't know what to do," Sally replied.

"What do you mean he's missing?" Glen asked concerned.

"He never turned up at the church, they weren't even expecting him! The police said that there was some evidence that he may have been in an accident. They found his bike all beat up but he wasn't there," Sally explained. "Someone has taken him, I just know it!"

"Calm down. Have they checked the hospitals then?" Glen asked.

"Yes. They say it is only a matter of time before he turns up but I don't know. Glen, I'm scared for him," Sally said.

"Where did this happen, Sal?" Glen asked.

"Between Port Lincoln and Ceduna," Sally answered. "Police in both towns are involved in the search."

"Okay, listen to me Sal: I'm going to get on the first flight out of here to Adelaide and from there I'll fly to Ceduna. I'll find him, Sally, I promise you, I'll find him," Glen said.

"Thank you, Glen," Sally said. "You are a great friend."

"I'll let you know what I find and I'll keep you in the loop at all times, okay?" Glen asked.

"That would be great, Glen. I better go now," Sally said.

"I'll call you tomorrow from Adelaide or Ceduna, depending on the flights," Glen promised, and then they both hung up.

"That sounded intense," Max said from the doorway.

"Phil's missing somewhere near Ceduna," Glen said.

"Count me in, then. I know that area pretty well," Max said.

"I was hoping you'd say that," Glen replied. "I'll call the airport and see when the next flight is and if we can get on it."

****

Cain landed on the outside of the building and checked all around before he entered. He was injured but not too badly. He hoped he would have another chance to battle Itzal again one day. The next time he wouldn't run. But with everything he had planned he couldn't afford to mess it all up now by getting sent to the Abyss. He would have to bide his time for now; heal up and then move to the next phase of the plan.

"Halt!" a voice called out of the darkness ahead.

"I thought I told you to attack first and not to speak," Cain challenged the speaker.

"Master Cain, I didn't expect you. I mean, I will do what you ask, master," the hidden guard said.

"Let me through you imbecile," Cain called to him.

"Sorry, master," the guard replied, as he stepped aside.

Cain walked through the secret entrance to their lair without looking back at the guard. He continued on through a doorway and into another hallway. The hallway was longer than it needed to be as it was a secondary safety precaution. Halfway along was another secret entrance on the left. If you didn't know that and you kept walking you would fall through a trap door and land in the guard dogs' pens.

Cain went through the secret entrance on the left and kept striding right passed his troops and their human familiars and on to the viewing room.

"You have returned, master," Deception said. "I was successful in my mission." Deception indicated the fruit in the next room.

"We succeeded too," another demon said from nearby.

Cain looked through the glass window which separated him from his trophies: a minister, a captive angel and a piece of fruit.

To be continued...

APPENDICES

Appendix 1 - General Information

I found that there was a lot of information about angels and Heaven. The only way I could decide what I thought was good enough to use or not was to weigh it up against the Bible. Bottom line, if the Bible didn't back it then I didn't believe it or use it. However, I have embellished some things, which you will not find in the Bible. What you will find is that the Bible does not contradict it either.

Some ground rules for the story were:

God is the most important entity in the book. The angels need to seek his advice and do not do anything that He tells them not to do.

The angels never do anything that is against God's teachings as found in the Bible

Angels do not try to teach; that is the job of the Holy Spirit. Angels will lead you to the information but leave it up to you to pay attention to it. The Holy Spirit will then help impart the knowledge you need.

Angels are neither omnipresent nor omniscient. God is. Angels require information to be given to them and spread throughout their ranks by word of mouth or by the Holy Spirit.

Humans generally do not know that angels or demons are there, unless the angel or demon (or God) wishes them too.

Angels and demons can change form to appear however they like but their natural form will always return and cannot be hidden, if discovered.

Angels should not be worshiped; God is the only one who deserves that kind of attention. (If an angel asks you to worship it, then it is not an angel of light, no matter how it appears to you.)

Angels have no agenda of their own; they simply wish to do God's bidding, which is usually to help further his Kingdom on Earth. (Again, if an angel asks you to do something other than God's will, then it is not an angel of light.)

A few times I refer to the saints as in "the saints are praying". This is a reference to Human Christians. They are the present-day saints.

If information I found contradicted any of this, I chose not to use it.

Appendix 2 - Map of Heaven

This is only for the purpose of this book, I have never seen Heaven or had anyone else tell me what it looked like.

This is all for the purpose of position. None of the buildings actually have dimensions; they are as big as they need to be.

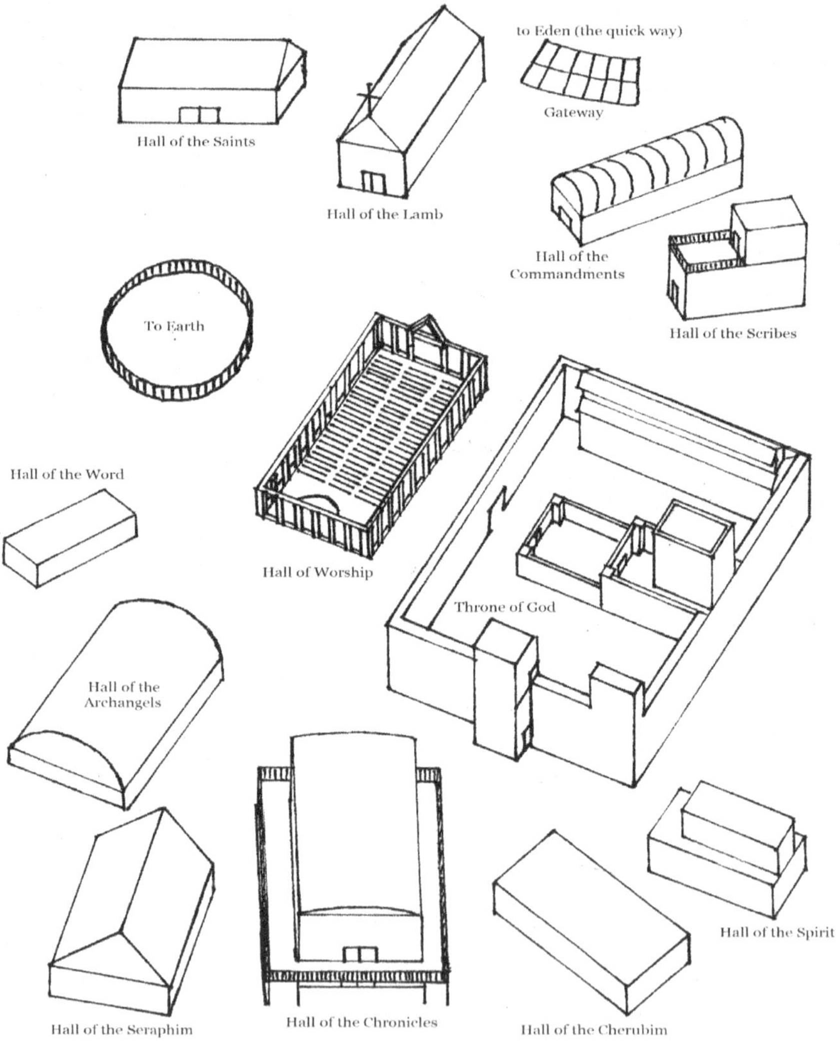

Appendix 3 - Types, Ranks and Duties of the Host of Heaven

There are lots of opinions on this one, but this is the structure I chose and worked with.

There is only one type of angel within this book and six ranks. The Bible only mentions two types and these are Angels and Archangels. The Cherubim and Seraphim are thought to be types of angels but this is not confirmed anywhere. I have chosen to refer to them as a form of rank within the angel type. The ranks are Angels, Cherubim, Seraphim and Archangel.

How many are in each group?

No one knows for sure, I think that the Seraphim, which are the closest to God, would be, therefore, the most powerful and also the smallest in number. The angels are the most numerous as they are the ones who are on Earth carrying out God's will. Generally it is agreed, that the total number of angels is innumerable. For the purpose of this story, I chose to have the numbers like this: Archangels: 7; Seraphim: 20+; cherubim: 50+; Angels: innumerable.

These ranks do not have static figures and they can fluctuate as needed. Angels may change ranks because of several reasons but the most common would be when recuperating from injuries (see "Can they change ranks?" below).

What do they do? Or what are their duties?

For the purpose of this story, the duties are as follows;

- Archangels: stand before the Throne on our behalf, intercede with God, usually are the ones who "show" themselves to humans, the leaders of all the other angels.
- Seraphim: ministering to God, proclaims His Glory, His Overseers.
- Cherubim: guarding important items like the Ark of the Covenant, the Garden of Eden and God Himself, they go where God sends them, His personal guards.
- Angels can be:
  - Guardians – Guard/Help the humans
  - Messengers – Pass messages between all the angels
  - Warriors – fighters against the demons
  - Veritas – keepers of Truth
  - Worship – praising God

- Commandos – an elite group of warriors
- Sentries – guards
- Scribes – recorders of History
- Case workers – specific interaction with humans when necessary
- Coaches – train other angels in specific tasks or duties.

(Not all of these were mentioned in this story.)

Can they change ranks or duties?

Within the story, I state that when any warrior has doubts or is injured they can return to a safer duty, such as either a guardian or messenger, to recuperate and/or build up their confidence in themselves again. Some never tire of this change in duty or rank and remain doing this for very long periods of time. Eventually, they can be promoted up the ranks again, but each promotion comes from God and only He knows when they are ready.

Sometimes, they do not get promoted up one rank, but many. An angel can become an archangel, if God decrees it. This happened to Michael and David at the end of the "Battle for the Throne". For Michael to be captain, he had to be a Seraph and the same with David, being a watchtower. Both angels showed incredible courage and loyalty to God during this troubling period. Lucifer, who was the captain until he turned, convinced many of the angels to join him. Those that didn't were the first that were attacked. No one suspected an attack was coming, let alone from within. Those that were injured were demoted to different levels, depending on how badly hurt they were. Raphael and Gabriel dropped back to being cherubim for a short time. Uriel only dropped back to being a seraph and quickly returned to being an archangel. There was a short period of time, where the cherubims acted as seraphs, until the seraphs recovered. Others found themselves promoted up permanently; Israfel is one who was a cherubim, prior to the war, but an archangel after. These are but a few examples.

What ranks do the characters mentioned hold and what duties do they perform?

Most of that is evident, as their rank is mentioned in the story, but there are other specialties within the archangels that don't really class as ranks but do give them specific areas of authority.

Top of this list would have to be Michael. He is the Captain of the Heavenly Host, he watches over everyone, commands a special commando group and watches over reptiles too. David is the watchtower, which means he watches over all the gates or connections to other realms; he also commands the sentries, flowering plants and prisons. He was known as Raguel in some ancient texts, but was renamed after he assisted a farm boy who fought against a giant. Gabriel is the head messenger; he watches over land animals and has contact with the prophets. Raphael is the healer and the head guardian and watches over the aquatic plants. Uriel is the head warrior. He is known as the Fire of God and he watches over the aquatic animals and the poets. Israfel has a talent for music and worship; he always meets new angels and helps to get their instruction started; he also cares for the trees. Zagzagel is known as the wise one, therefore truth or veritas is important to him too; he deals with the scribes and looks after ecology in general.

Other angels can have interests that they pursue too, for example Kenaniah loves music and singing, while Itzal loves the art of sword play.

The Twelve (Apostles) look after the twelve tribes along with their namesakes, for example Saint Peter and Judah together look after the tribe of Judah.

Appendix 4 - Demons

Some explanation has to be given here as to the rank, names etc. of the demons. What I have done is partly based on other authors' works, as well as some ideas of my own. Where and how the other authors got their information and what it is based upon, I do not know. I believe it is a simple and easy way to look at them.

Starting from the bottom, the lowest ranks have no names, just a job description, for example Persuasion, who we meet in Chapter Four. Other examples are Malice, Theft, Confusion, Rage and Drugs.

If they are good enough at what they do they can earn a name, which they will pick for themselves – not always a good thing, take Grom, for example: he must have spent long hours working out that one.

If one of the demons is good at his job (of being bad) and lasts long enough, he may be promoted to a leadership role, in which case he will give himself some grand name, such as "Commander" or simply "Leader", if it is not too bright. Some try for lofty names, such as "President" or even "Prince", but they generally get cut down by those higher up, because this shows some desire to be better than they are, putting the superior demon in danger from the newly promoted one. It isn't always better to be an over-achiever among this lot.

The next step is to become one of the Seven Deadly Sins. This is what they call their top leader, the generals, sometimes referred to as the Kings of this Age. They are, in reverse order of importance, Pride, Envy, Wrath, Sloth, Avarice, Gluttony and Lust. Pride is the first level so to speak, going all the way up to Lust. It has been thought that if you were to grade the sins committed, the ones that would be worst in this group would be those of Lust.

There is only one who is higher than the Seven and that is Satan, Lucifer himself. No demon has ever overthrown him or ever will, although some do see themselves as having a chance of doing so, like "Satan's Thorns". The title Satan means "the accuser" in Hebrew. Some texts define it as "the destroyer".

Appendix 5 - Hell

Throughout the Bible, Hell is spoken of many times and in many different ways, with many different meanings. Typically Hell is thought of as "the place of disembodied spirits" and more specifically "the abode of the wicked" and "a place of torment". I referred to it in a few different languages throughout the book and specifically used all of these in Chapter Forty-Four. These are the translations I found.

Sheol is Hebrew and can mean "the unseen state", "grave" or "pit" and has been described as deep, dark, with bars and the dead "go down" to it. In most passages it is referred to as the abode of the wicked but this has been used to describe the abode of the good too. It is mainly used in the Old Testament.

Hades is Greek and is described fairly similarly to Sheol but only in the New Testament. (This indicates a difference in the world around the writers; the Old Testament was a wild world where the people were trying to be a nation of their own with their own language – Hebrew. The New Testament is set in a newer world where the lands have been taken over by the Romans and Greek is recognised as a uniform language.).

Hades has been described as the unseen world, as a prison with gates, bars and locks. It is downward. Similar to Sheol, it refers to the righteous and the wicked being there. It says that they are separated and that the blessed are in the part referred to as Paradise; the blessed are also said to be in Abraham's bosom.

Gehenna is also Greek and signifies the place of torment. It only appears in the Greek New Testament to designate the place of the lost. The fearful nature of their condition is described with expressions like...

"the furnace of fire; in that place there shall be weeping and gnashing of teeth"

Matthew 13:42.

Tartarus is also Greek and signifies the infernal region.

Not mentioned in this book is Hinnom. I thought I would include that here as it is thought to give a historical background as to where the Jews idea of what Hell would be like came from.

Hinnom was a valley alongside a town. It is mentioned within the Bible as a place where children were burned alive as a sacrifice to other gods. After the Exile, the Jews took over the town and used this valley to dispose of the offal. The offal was essentially part of the Jewish sacrifices to God and needed to be burned to ashes. Part of the rules concerning this practice, stated that this fire was not allowed to go out.

The Jews then associated this valley with the sufferings of the victims (that had been sacrificed) and of filth and corruption (the items left over from their sacrifices). Over time it developed into a symbol of "the abode of the wicked hereafter" or, in other words, Hell.

Easton's 1897 Bible Dictionary states this about Hinnom: "It might be shown by infinite examples that the Jews expressed hell, or the place of the damned, by this word. The word Gehenna [the Greek contraction of Hinnom] was never used in the time of Christ in any other sense than to denote 'the place of future punishment.' About this fact there can be no question."

Jesus and His Death

It is written in the Bible that when Jesus died on the cross he took our sins upon himself, not only the sins of those living and to come, but also the sins of the saints already departed.

They receive God's approval freely by an act of his kindness through the price Christ Jesus paid to set us free from sin. God showed that Christ is the throne of mercy where God's approval is given through faith in Christ's blood. In his patience God waited to deal with sins committed in the past.

Romans 3:24-25

With all these sins placed upon Jesus, he had to go to Hell to receive the punishment due. While there, he collected the past Saints from "Abraham's bosom" (as mentioned above), because their sins were now paid for, and took them to Heaven.

We believe that Jesus died and came back to life. We also believe that, through Jesus, God will bring back those who have died. They will come back with Jesus.

1 Thes. 4:14

Recently, I read a book about a man who spent twenty-three minutes in Hell. He tells how one night, he awoke in a "cell" with bars on it. How demons were there and how they delighted in torturing him. He had a glimpse of the fiery pits and he could hear and see others being tormented in them.

Then Jesus came and lifted him up, out of his torment, up through a deep, dark tunnel (the Abyss) and upwards until they were out of the Earth and in the clouds above.

He was given a glimpse of the eternal suffering that awaits those that do not know Jesus as saviour. Jesus told him to tell of his experience. Why? So that others would not experience that fate and go to Heaven instead.

I believe his experience is true. There are many verses in the Bible that back up his story, his experience, and describe the same things (just like the descriptions of Hell above). Whether you call it Hell, Sheol, Hades or some other name, it's the same place and it exists.

Save others by snatching them from the fire of hell. Show mercy to others, even though you are afraid that you might be stained by their sinful lives.

Jude 1:23

About The Author

Peter Way lives in South Australia and has a wife and two daughters. Peter became a home dad in July 2006. Prior to that, he was working for a major telecommunications carrier in Australia as a mobile phone technician.

Peter's main interests are basketball, computers and reading. One of his favourite books is *This Present Darkness* by Frank E. Perretti, which has been a source of inspiration for his series *God's Warriors*.

Peter has been a Christian since the age of eleven and was baptised at thirteen. He has attended many churches and denominations but his current spiritual home is Seeds (previously Aberfoyle Park) Uniting in the southern suburbs of Adelaide.

Mid-2010, Peter was diagnosed with an internal form of skin cancer (an inwards form of melanoma) which is currently incurable and was unremoveable but in mid-2011 the doctors discovered they had misdiagnosed the cancer. It was in fact a curable form of lymphoma. Through the grace of God he overcame this attack on his health. While the doctors say they made a mistake, he believes it was the miracle that he (and his friends and family) prayed for.

Christ carried our sins in his body on the cross so that freed from our sins, we could live a life that has God's approval. His wounds have healed you.

Peter 2:24